D0369595

Mountain Lake,

MINNESOTA TRILOGY

KIM VOGEL SAWYER

Mountain Lake,
MINNESOTA TRILOGY

KIM VOGEL SAWYER

HENDRICKSON
PUBLISHERS

Mountain Lake, Minnesota Trilogy

Hendrickson Publishers Marketing, LLC
P. O. Box 3473
Peabody, Massachusetts 01961-3473
www.hendrickson.com

ISBN 978-1-61970-157-1

A *Seeking Heart* © 2002 Kim Vogel Sawyer.

A *Heart Surrenders* © 2004 Kim Vogel Sawyer.

When a Heart Cries © 2005 Kim Vogel Sawyer.

This edition by arrangement with the copyright holder.

All rights reserved. No part of this book may be reproduced or transmitted in any form or by any means, electronic or mechanical, including photocopying, recording, or by any information storage and retrieval system, without permission in writing from the publisher.

Third Hendrickson Edition Printing — January 2019

A Note to Readers

Thank you for choosing to spend time with Samantha and Adam and the residents of Mountain Lake. This story is particularly dear to me because it is loosely based on my family history. I still remember with deep appreciation my visit to the Mountain Lake community years ago.

The Mennonite Brethren referenced in the Mountain Lake, Minnesota Trilogy originally resided in Germany. Persecuted for their faith, which included resistance to taking human lives even in times of war, they accepted the invitation of Catherine the Great to settle on the *steppes*, those grassy plains of Russia, and live their beliefs without government interference. They built colonies and settled the untamed land, living peacefully for a century before new political leaders once again demanded their sons serve in the military and otherwise intruded upon their peaceful village life. Consequently, a number of the families chose to leave Russia and immigrate to the United States of America, where they could practice their religion freely, without fear of those terrifying knocks on the door from soldiers with official documents and weapons.

My great-grandparents, Bernard and Maria Klaassen, were part of a large number of German Mennonites who left Russia in the 1870s to start a new life in America. They established a farmstead near Mountain Lake where they raised their nine children, including my grandmother, Elizabeth. My grandmother's caring, giving spirit is captured here in the character of Laura, and it gives me great pleasure to honor her tender heart and deep faith.

May God bless you richly as you journey with Him,

Kim Vogel Sawyer

A Seeking Heart

Dedicated lovingly to Mom and Daddy—
thank you for making sure
my heart never felt the need to go seeking
for love and acceptance.

Contents

Klaassen Family Tree

Simon James Klaassen (1873) m. Laura Doerksen (1877), 1893
   Daniel Simon (1894) m. Rose Willems (1892), 1913
     Christina Rose (1915)
     Katrina Marie (1916)
   Hannah Joy (1895–1895)
   Franklin Thomas (1896)
   Elizabeth Laurene (1898) m. Jacob Aaron Stoesz (1897), 1915
   Adam Earnest (1899)
   Josephine Ellen (1900)
   Arnold Hiram (1903)
   Rebecca Arlene (1906)
   Theodore Henry (1909)
   Sarah Louise (1911)
Hiram Klaassen (1872) m. Hulda Schmidt (1872), 1898

O'Brien Family Tree

Burton O'Brien (1870) m. Olivia Ruth Stanton (1873–1900),
   1891
   David Burton (1894)
   Samantha Olivia (1900)

Chapter One

August 1917

O n the outskirts of Mountain Lake, Minnesota, a young girl was seated beneath a gnarled, century-old cottonwood. It was one of the few trees left standing when the farmers cleared the land to plant their Turkey Red wheat some seventy-five years past. But she didn't know that, not yet. She rested her back against the bark, the tree's shade a welcome respite from the stifling August heat. The gentle whisper of the wind through the leaves was as pleasing as a lullaby to the weary traveler.

She *was* tired. *Bone-tired*, her Gran would have said. She had come a long distance, sometimes hitching rides in the backs of rattling wagons and once having the luxury of a leather seat in a Model T. But mostly she walked. Her feet carried blisters and calluses representing the many miles covered, and now she pushed them into the soft soil beneath the tree to cool them. Her inner thighs were sore, chafed by the four-sizes-too-large overalls she had donned for her journey, and her wrists were grubby and dirt streaked from constantly rolling up the sleeves of the loose flannel shirt. Her attire was most inappropriate for the heat of the summer, yet she had carefully chosen each item before setting out. Her attempt was to pass as a young farm boy rather than the seventeen-year-old young lady she was. She had her reasons.

The abominable itching of her scalp bothered her more than anything else. She'd tucked her nearly waist-length hair up into a worn brown suede hat discarded by her father years ago. She longed to pull it off, shake out her hair, and scratch her skull until it tingled, but she didn't dare. She might not be able to cram it all back. So she satisfied herself by shifting the hat around on her head. It offered some relief.

Moving her position against the tree, she closed her eyes and released a deep sigh. Her belly rumbled, and she rubbed at her empty midsection. "I know, I know," she mumbled, "I should find something to eat. Soon." She grimaced as her stomach cramped painfully.

It was noon yesterday when she had eaten last, and then only a handful of soda crackers and a wormy apple she'd snitched from the Blue Earth Mercantile's apple barrel when no one was looking. The problem was that her meager cash supply was fearfully low, with her hunger immeasurably high. She crossed her arms over her belly and pressed in, hoping to still the hunger pangs and wondering what she should do.

Truth of the matter was she'd been formulating a plan under her battered suede hat ever since she'd passed a neat farm house about a mile and a half back. The white-washed two-story, its big wrap-around porch and bright marigolds lining the pathways from the house to the dirt road, bespoke of no little wealth. And judging from the number of dungarees, work shirts, and stockings hanging on lines between the barn and outhouse, it also indicated a whole passel of youngsters— too many for one rural farmer in Mountain Lake, Minnesota, to keep track of, the girl reasoned.

Luckily the owner had painted his name on the road side of the barn in neat block letters for all to see: KLAASSEN FARM. It seemed to her as though the man was offering to become her benefactor. She stayed seated, though, pushing the plan back and forth in her mind. Hungry as she was, the thought of stealing rankled. Oh, she'd done her fair share of pilfering, like the crackers and apple, and if you came right down to it, she'd actually stolen the clothes she was wearing from the trunk in the cellar back home. But thievery still didn't set easily on her shoulders. A necessity rather than a choice, she concluded with a sigh.

Another rumbling, this time not from her stomach, brought her bolt upright, prepared for flight. From around the bend came a boxy wagon, its high sides painted celery green and pulled by two large, well-muscled horses, though they also looked like they might be well along in years. Atop the wagon seat, holding loosely onto the reins with elbows resting lazily on his knees, was a figure in a gray plaid shirt, its sleeves rolled above the elbows, faded blue britches, and a fringe of brown hair below the straw hat.

He must have spotted her and nodded a greeting. "Howdy, boy." His smile seemed relaxed, unthreatening.

She gave a barely perceptible nod in return and turned away, heart pounding. The young man clucked to the horses and continued on. She watched around the tree, her heart bumping its apprehension inside her chest, until the wagon disappeared over a gentle rise in the road, headed back the way she had come. When only a cloud of dust remained, she collapsed against the tree trunk.

He thinks I'm a boy. . . . Knowing her disguise was working gave her the confidence she needed to go ahead with her plan. She waited a few minutes to be certain the wagon and its driver were well ahead of her, then pushed to her feet. She reached for her boots, but couldn't bear the thought of confining her poor feet inside those instruments of torture again. She tied the rawhide laces together and slung them over her shoulder. With a sigh—and another loud growl from her middle—she began following the wagon tracks back toward the town.

⤳

"Whoa, there, Bet, Tick," Adam Klaassen called as he pulled the team up in front of Tucker's Lumber and Hardware Store. With practiced motions he wrapped the reins around the brake and leaped off the wagon, his landing a soft *fump* in the dirt street. He whipped the straw hat from his head and banged it against his pant leg a time or two to loosen the dust, ran his fingers through his hair, then slapped the hat back on his head.

Three long strides put him on the stoop to Tucker's store, and he squeaked the screen door open. He stood in the doorway a moment, allowing his sight to adjust from the bright sunshine to the gloom of the store's interior. Although the building boasted two large windows, one on either side of the wooden entry door, the owner didn't seem to find time or impetus to clean them. The accumulated dust and grime, whirled up from the street by the near-constant wind, adequately blocked the light from the shop.

Adam stepped a few feet into the building. "Mr. Tucker?" He glanced around at the wild disarray that made up Nip Tucker's stock. Barrels of nails, makeshift shelves holding a variety of tools, and stacks of lumber in various lengths created a mind-boggling maze of disorganization. Adam moved closer to the tall, dusty counter at the rear of the store and called the owner's name again.

Adam cocked an ear at rustling from behind the counter, followed by the squeak of tin upon tin, and finally a resounding burp. He held back a grin as Nip's huge frame straightened from his attempt at concealment. Nip slipped a slim tin canister into the hip pocket of his enormous overalls before leaning beefy hands on the counter. He greeted Adam with a face-splitting smile, revealing a gap from a missing tooth.

No one knew Nip's real name, but his nickname came from his habit of partaking frequently of the tin canister he tried to conceal in his ample pocket. Despite Nip's obvious weakness for the tobacco chew he kept in his mouth, he was an honest businessman and well liked in the community by townspeople and farmers alike.

"Well, howdy-do, Adam." Nip's broad face remained locked in a cheerful grin. The man had more smile lines than anyone else Adam knew. His fuzzy white hair stood in tufts around an oversized head, and with his round belly and red-veined nose, he resembled a jolly, giant carved elf from the Old Country.

"Howdy to you, Mr. Tucker." Adam smiled back and leaned his elbows on the unkempt counter. "Pa sent me in for some two-penny nails and a leather piece, say"—he gestured—"so big."

"That I c'n do, I shorely c'n do it." Nip stuck out his lower lip and scratched at raspy chin whiskers. "Let's see now . . . two-penny nails." He ambled around the counter and waddled between aisles of barrels, giving each an inquisitive peek. The man could have done with more room between them, but the store's size and the quantity of stock were realities he couldn't change.

Adam knew the minute Nip found what he was looking for by a happy hiccup. As Nip made his way back to the counter for a paper sack, Adam wondered at the near-miraculous ability of Nip to find anything he wanted. Adam had never been able to spot any kind of organizational system in the cluttered shop. Yet, to his knowledge, Nip had never disappointed a customer.

Nip dropped two huge handfuls of nails in the sack, then carefully weighed them, squinting at the rusty scale with great concentration. "Pound an' a quarter." He peered at Adam over his shoulder. "That enough?"

"Ought 'a be."

"An' a strip o' leather, so big?" Nip held out those large hands.

Adam nodded. "Yep. It's for a hinge on the chicken coop. Pa says the busy rooster just plum wore out the other one."

The men shared a snort of laughter. Nip located a pocket-knife in the depths of his overalls and whacked off a four-inch piece of leather from a much longer strip. He dropped it in the sack with the nails and handed the bag to Adam.

"Can you add this to our tab?" Adam rolled down the bag's opening. "Pa will be in at the end of the month to settle with you."

Nip flapped a big paw in agreement. "No problem, Adam. Your pa's always good for it."

"Thanks a lot." Adam headed for the door with his purchase. He pushed at the door, but before he could step outside Nip called to him.

"Adam, hold up a minute, would'ja? Wonder if you'd mind playin' delivery boy for me." He huffed his way around the counter, waving a thick roll of gray mesh with one hand and toting a clanking burlap bag in the other. "Lank Schroeder ordered up a passel o' drawer pulls for them bureaus he's always building, and I got this here screen to replace that what's tore on the back door of your uncle's store. Could'ja run these things over to the furniture place an' the mercantile fer me?"

Adam noted the time and effort it took Nip to pull his big frame around the counter and through the shop to the doorway. It would take the man most of the morning to make the two deliveries. Adam wasn't in a big hurry to return home. He could do this favor. "Don't mind a bit, Nip."

"Thank ya much." Nip gave Adam's shoulder a friendly slap on the back that sent him through the doorway and out into the August heat. Nip followed with the two items, his heaving breaths providing further warmth on the back of Adam's neck. He dropped his little bag over the edge of the wagon bed, then took the two deliveries from Nip's big hands.

"Thanks again, boy," Nip said.

"Sure thing. Have a good day, Mr. Tucker."

It would take more time to get Bet and Tick moving again than to simply hoof it. Adam tossed the burlap bag over his shoulder, tucked the roll of screen beneath his arm, and aimed his feet toward the furniture shop.

⌒⊙

The small figure stood at the north edge of Tenth Street beside a Baptist church and surveyed the area with practiced nonchalance. Her pa had been in the habit of calling her dim-witted, but her brother David said she was as bright as a new penny.

One thing she knew is that she must be very careful, miss nothing of importance to her plan. But there wasn't much to see as she looked around. Mountain Lake was hardly a town at all compared to where she had been born and raised.

While this town was small, she had to admit the businesses appeared to be well-kept and the houses showed neat yards and recent paint jobs. The people living here apparently took pride in their town. For some reason she couldn't understand, it rankled her a bit.

Meandering on still-bare feet past a pool hall, she headed for the small business district. Across the street, the green wagon and horses she'd seen earlier on the road hunkered down in the shade of a large, gray-sided building with "Tucker's Lumber & Hardware" painted on the side in childish letters. The rather shabby store stood in contrast to the neat park with its mowed grass and tall trees on the next block.

She stepped from the dirt road onto a raised walkway, the boards warm and smooth beneath her feet. A cozy little house sat on the corner of Tenth Street and Fourth Avenue, nestled next to a series of businesses from shoe repair to implement sales to a tall bank building made of stone. Her lower lip pulled between her teeth, her gaze whisked over the signs. *Where was a mercantile?* On the opposite side of the street and down the block, a huge building sported a sign which read "Hiebert & Balzer Store" in fancy painted letters. Hope ignited in her breast.

After a glance right and left, she scurried kitty-corner across Third Avenue and stepped onto another boardwalk running the length of the second block of buildings. She pressed her palm to her rumbling belly as she peeked through the shiny glass window of Hiebert & Balzer's, the words restated in a gold, swirly typeface on the pane. A quick look confirmed it had what she needed. But several wagons waited outside the large store, which meant a number of shoppers would be milling inside. Lots of eyes watching. She held back the impulse to enter the store, do what she'd come to do, and get on her way. Eagerness might lead to carelessness. With a sigh, she moved on.

Scuffing past a drugstore and another general merchandise store which she chose to bypass for the same reasons as the previous, she stopped to scope out the opposite side of the street, scanning the names of the businesses. A hardware store, a tailor shop, a house, another drugstore, and—she let out a little gasp of delight. Between John Schroeder Drug Store and First State Bank stood the Family Mercantile of Mountain Lake.

A narrow, two-story wooden structure with a square, false front painted white and sporting dark green window trim, it took up merely a quarter of the space of the intimidating Hiebert & Balzer Store and was also smaller than A. A. Woodruff's. It displayed the only porch along the length of the boardwalk. Spooled posts decorated with bands of green and yellow held up each corner of the porch roof, giving the mercantile a pleasant, homey appearance. The girl smiled as she examined the shop. *Small. Welcoming to families. Not likely to be filled with people.*

She trotted across the street and leaned against one of four limestone posts, iron rings embedded in their tops, standing in a precise row in front of the bank. One lazy-looking horse hitched to a fancy, two-seater buggy stood dozing in front of the second post, his tail swishing in slow motion.

Relying on the horse to partially hide her from view, the girl licked her dry lips, her thoughts scrambling. South of the mercantile, Tenth Street intersected with railroad tracks angling their way out of town. She curled her arm around the warm limestone post, planning her best course afterward. Straight south through the stockyard—no one would want to follow her there—then west along the railroad tracks until she'd hit the edge of town.

The escape route chosen, she sucked in a big breath for fortification, pushed off the post, and moved purposefully toward the Family Mercantile of Mountain Lake.

*T*he girl paused briefly outside the scrolled screen door to dampen her dirty palms with her tongue and swipe them roughly against the seat of her equally filthy overalls. She peered at her hands in vexation. Still streaked with dirt. But they'd have to do. One last tug on her hat brim brought it comfortingly low around her ears. She assumed a casual pose, hooking her thumbs in the rear pockets of her britches.

Her boots still swung over one shoulder, thumping her chest and back as she moved. With the other shoulder she bumped the door open. A cowbell hanging above the screen door clanged a noisy greeting, startling her out of her attempt at nonchalance. She regained her composure quickly, though, as the shopkeeper lifted his bald head from measuring flour for a young woman with a shopping basket in hand and a straw bonnet on her head. Looking at the woman's flower-sprigged dress and cheerful bonnet, the girl felt more dowdy and disheveled than ever. The desire to turn tail and run smacked her hard.

"Be with you in a minute, son," the shopkeeper called out. *Whew!* Dirt or not, she was safe for the moment. He was a man small of stature, and he possessed a surprisingly deep voice. Another urge to hightail it out of there pricked hard, but running would look plenty suspicious, so she nodded a silent reply and ambled between two aisles.

The store was as tidy as Gran's pantry at home, the girl noted, and it smelled wonderful. Tangy pickles, malty yeast, and pungent apples combined to create a heady aroma that sent her nostrils twitching, her saliva spurting, and her stomach into spasms of desire. She turned a slow circle, examining, sniffing, enjoying. Canned goods lined up with military precision on homemade pine shelves. Household items stood arranged for easy contemplation and selection. The store epitomized order and cleanliness, as well as a true pride of ownership. Guilt niggled. Could she really steal from this obviously honest merchant? But another sharp pain of emptiness shot through her belly and overrode feelings of remorse.

She shuffled forward, swallowing. A wondrous selection of fabrics and sewing notions beckoned from the northeast corner of the store, stirring a feminine rush of pleasure. But wouldn't she look silly examining the array, all decked out in her overalls and lumpy hat? Besides, she was *hungry*. She moved resolutely to the west side where the canned goods beckoned to her.

The cowbell clanged, announcing the exit of the woman customer, and the shopkeeper began dusting small bottles of medicinal cures lined neatly along a narrow shelf behind the counter. But the girl sensed his watchful eyes following her, measuring her as carefully as he probably measured his dry goods. She tried to appear as if she was checking off a mental list as she made her selections. Bending her arm into a makeshift sling, she loaded herself down with a large tin of Edgemont crackers, two cans of spiced peaches—even though she wasn't sure she'd be able to pry anything in cans open—along with several cans of Van Camps beans. With a burst of extravagance, she added an egg-shaped tin of ham on top of the awkward armful.

While she shopped, she reviewed the simple plan. The mercantile owner would keep an account book for customers to charge their purchases, with balances due at the end of the month. It worked that way at home, but she and Pa were never allowed to charge since Pa couldn't be trusted to pay up. She'd just tell the owner to charge her selections to the Klaassen account, he would do it, the Klaassens would probably never even notice the small discrepancy on their account—from the looks of that fine farmhouse, they sure could afford it—and she'd have food for a couple of days till she hit the next town. It was a good plan, and no one would be the wiser.

Balancing her armload, she leaned back and shuffled her way over to the counter where she dropped it all in a series of resounding thuds. The shopkeeper placed his feather duster beneath the counter, smoothed a pink palm across his equally pink dome, and sent a glance over the accumulated items.

"Is that all?" His tone was pleasant enough.

The girl's eyes settled on the large glass jars displayed prominently on the countertop. Each wide-mouth jar contained a different treat to satisfy the most discerning sweet tooth. From peppermint sticks to sour balls, licorice whips to brightly colored gumdrops and jelly beans, her gaze roved, mouth watering.

The shopkeeper smiled his understanding. He popped the cork on the closest jar and fished out a walnut-sized sugar-coated red gumdrop. He extended it on an open palm almost beneath the girl's nose. Uncertain, she looked up at him, and he bobbed the candy in invitation. "Take it. No charge."

The girl licked her lips in anticipation and reached out for the proffered indulgence. Suddenly a voice in her head snapped, "Never take charity, girlie!" She drew back her hand as if slapped.

The shopkeeper thrust the candy forward. "Go ahead, it's yours."

She reached again, her hand slowly moving toward his. She fought the urge to peek over her shoulder to be sure Pa wasn't watching. Dummy, Pa's not here. She snatched the candy from the man's hand before she could change her mind again. It was settled in a bulky wad inside her mouth before she remembered her manners and muttered around the candy, "F'ank 'oo."

The shopkeeper swished his palms together to disperse the leftover sugar. "Now then, let's tally this up, shall we?"

He produced the stub of a pencil from behind his ear, licked the point, and began figuring on a pad of paper resting near a hinged tin box, which presumably held his cash supply. After scratching out several numbers, he pushed the pad aside and announced the total. He aimed his eyebrows high and peered down at her. "Will that be cash or charge, mi'—I mean, son?"

The girl had chewed down the gumdrop considerably. She swallowed the remaining lump and cleared her throat before managing a low, "Charge, please."

The shopkeeper reached below the counter to bring up a leather-bound book which he plopped on the countertop and opened to the first page. She gazed at the book, her hands clutching the edge of the wooden counter, elbows splayed outward, trying to look calm and matter-of-fact. When he made no move to record her purchase, she glanced up to find him staring at her. Her heart skipped a beat.

He cocked his head. "Account name?"

Mentally kicking herself for being so dense, she drew herself upright. "Klaassen." She blew out a breath and dropped her gaze back to the book. His hands didn't move. She looked up again. The man's stare was accompanied by a frown that brought his bushy eyebrows downward and created a series of deep furrows across his pink forehead. "Klaassen, did you say?" His voice came out low and rather steely.

She gulped, her pretend bravado fading fast.

She lowered her hands to her sides. "Y-yessir."

He leaned forward, his gaze narrowing. "*Simon* Klaassen?"

She couldn't be certain it was Simon Klaassen's house she'd seen, but she felt agreeing was the safest bet. So she nodded, her heart pounding in her throat.

The man snapped the book shut, and for a fleeting moment the girl wondered if Mr. Klaassen hadn't paid his account regularly. The shopkeeper's eyes pinned her in place as effectively as a nail holds a shingle. "And just which of the Klaassen boys are you?"

She felt like she had a hairball stuck in her craw, but she choked out a reply. "Uh . . . S-Sam."

The man lowered his chin and scowled at her through the curly hairs of his eyebrows as he slowly rounded the counter. The girl backed up a step as he neared. Her muscles tensed, poised to run.

"Sam . . . hmmm." He crossed his arms. His forehead puckered so tightly it looked painful. "Funny. My brother Simon has five sons, but I don't recollect a one of them's named Sam."

His brother. The shopkeeper was kin *to those Klaassens*!

The girl's chest clenched in panic, and as the man reached for her, she reacted instinctively. She kicked him as hard as she could in the shin, which no doubt hurt her bare toes as much as it did his leg, grabbed up the tin of crackers, and careened out the screen door, sending the cowbell clanging angrily behind her. Risking a glance back over her shoulder at the no-doubt furious shopkeeper, she missed seeing the tall, straw-hat-topped young man stepping up on the planked walkway. She ran full-tilt into his solid chest. He lost a roll of screen he was carrying, and her tin of crackers fell to the boardwalk with a clunk.

He caught her by the shoulders, chuckling. "Whoa there, what's your hurry?"

Frantic, she pushed on his chest with both hands. The shove off-balanced him, dislodged his hat, and nearly threw him on his backside. His hands flew from her shoulders, and she leaped from the boardwalk. Her original plan in tatters, panic racing through her veins, she ran a zigzagged pattern up the center of the dusty main street of town.

*A*dam shook his head, watching the kid go, and leaned down to scoop up his hat and the roll of screen lodged against the side of the building. The cowbell above his uncle's shop door clanged, and his uncle stood in the doorway, shaking his finger and pointing after the fleeing youth.

"Get 'im! Catch 'im! A thief!"

"Uncle Hiram, what—?"

But after a quick glance at his uncle's expression, Adam thrust the roll of screen into his uncle's midsection and took off down the street. The thief had gotten a good head start, but Adam's stride was twice the length of the fleeing figure, and his feet were protected by sturdy work boots. It wasn't hard to overtake him. Adam reached out a long arm and caught an overall strap, swinging the lad around.

The stubborn kid spun in circles, trying to free himself. Suddenly he swung his boots by the laces. The heels smacked Adam hard on the shoulder and bounced off the side of his head. He released his hold, his ear ringing from the blow, and stumbled sideways a few steps. Before he could regain his balance, the boy charged at him, burying his head in Adam's stomach.

The motion carried them both several feet back before Adam fell, snatching an overall strap once more as he went. He landed flat on his back with the kid sprawled across his chest. Now instinct took over, and with a simple maneuver Adam rolled over, pinning the scrappy youngster neatly beneath him. He panted with exertion from the brief chase and subsequent scuffle, but he managed to hold the boy, who bucked and bellowed, by the shoulders against the ground.

"Get off me, you stupid honyocker!"

Adam didn't know whether to chuckle or give the kid a sharp clop for using the insulting label for farmers. "Not till you promise to behave yourself." He sat a little harder on the boy's stomach, and the wild kicking calmed. But the youth's pale, frightened face stirred Adam's sympathy. He said in a soothing tone, "That's better. Now, if you'll be still, I'll—"

Adam stopped and stared, astonished. His assailant's battered hat flipped off, revealing a mane of tangled auburn curls. Eyes as blue as cornflowers stared back at him. Slender arms flailed to reach the hat,but Adam still held the boy's—the girl's—shoulders against the ground, and she couldn't reach it.

"Sure enough, it's a girl." Uncle Hiram's voice blasted out from behind Adam. "I had an inkling something like that might be going on."

Adam heard an amused guffaw, and he looked beyond his uncle at spectators—overall-clad men, women in go-to-town dresses and bonnets, and a cluster of snickering youngsters with cane poles propped on their shoulders—gathering on the boardwalk. Even the banker stood in his doorway, watching with an amused look on his mustached face.

Adam leaped up, never having been as embarrassed as he was at that moment. Why, he'd never tackled a girl before. Not even his sisters. And he'd done this in the middle of main street while townspeople lined the boardwalks. Heat rose from his neck to his hairline.

The girl rolled over and pushed herself to her feet, and Hiram grabbed an overall strap. She tried once to pull away, but he gave her a firm shake. "You're coming with me, missy." He began herding her back toward his store.

Shame faced with the public humiliation, Adam grabbed up the ugly brown hat and followed. Uncle Hiram's feet sent up angry puffs of dust with each step. The girl walked stiffly with her chin held at a defiant angle, but she seemed to have lost her fire. Back in the store, Hiram gave her a shove toward the apple barrel. "You sit right there, young lady."

She did so without a fuss and held her knees together with her palms pressed between them, back ramrod straight and head tipped downward. Adam held out her hat, but she didn't even glance up, simply snatching it with a dirty hand and throwing it to the floor by her feet.

Uncle Hiram paced the floor, his bald head glowing bright red. Adam had never seen him so upset. Adam adopted a calm voice. "Uncle Hiram, what's she done?"

"Done?" He whirled toward Adam, his arm gesturing vigorously toward the girl. "What's she *done*? Why, she tried to make out with half the store and put it on your father's account, no less. Stood right there at my counter and claimed to be Sam Klaassen. That's what she's done."

Adam raised an eyebrow and looked over the girl, sitting stiff as a board and poker faced as a judge, not even flinching. If she was scared or nervous, she hid it well.

"I knew something was amiss the minute I laid eyes on him—her." Uncle Hiram aimed himself for the door. "I'm going for Sheriff Barnes. I can't believe how she tried to hornswoggle me, and after I'd given her something. For free." Over his shoulder he said, "Adam, you stay here and see she stays put." At the girl he waggled a finger. "Don't you move an inch, missy, you hear?"

If the girl heard, she gave no indication of it. She didn't even blink. Hiram snorted and shoved his way out, sending the cowbell into frantic clamor once more. Adam reached up and caught it, stilling the sound. He stayed by the doorway, arms crossed over his chest, and watched the girl as Hiram stomped away. Adam speculated that his uncle didn't really want to file formal charges but wanted to scare the young thief—wanted her to sweat a bit. The girl sat still, staring at her hands in her lap, a sullen expression on her face. If Adam hadn't known better, he might have thought she was carved of stone. He'd never seen anyone who could sit without even a muscle twitching.

After a few more tense minutes, the silence began to grate on Adam's nerves. He cleared his throat, and the girl's jaw tightened, but she didn't look up. Adam dropped his arms and sauntered across the floor, seating himself on a keg nearby. She shifted slightly to increase the gap between them. Adam swallowed a grin. *Sure is a belligerent little thing.*

"What's your name?" He used his friendliest voice, but she gave no response. "Who're your folks?"

The girl shook back her hair, aimed her gaze to the side, and set her lips in an even more grim line.

Adam tried another tack. "You do realize stealing is a crime, don't you?"

The girl angled her face to give him a narrow-eyed look that demanded his silence. Their eyes locked—Adam's amused, hers stony—and both seemed stubborn enough to hold that gaze for an eternity.

Uncle Hiram shoved his way back into the store, and Adam stood to meet his uncle halfway across the floor. The girl went back into her head-down pose.

"What'd the sheriff say?"

Uncle Hiram threw his arms around in agitation. "Wasn't even there. Old Hilarius Schwartz's cow wandered away again, and Sheriff was out helping hunt her down. Honestly, if Hilarius would put a bell on that animal, it would make for a lot less fussin' and bother."

Adam hid his smile. Uncle Hiram had to be mighty upset to complain about ninety-year-old Mr. Schwartz and his beloved bovine. Everyone knew Rosalee was Hilarius's best friend, and Hiram himself had helped bring the wandering cow back in the past. Whenever the cow took a mind to meander, finding her was a challenge without the telltale clang of a bell to guide the posse. Hilarius believed a cowbell would make Rosalee nervous and refused to hang one around her neck. Any other day, Hiram would have laughed it all off. But not today.

Adam leaned against the counter, watching his uncle pace. "So what are you going to do with her?" He kept his voice just above a whisper.

Hiram stopped pacing to fire an angry glare at the still-silent girl. "I guess just send her home." He marched across the room to stand in front of her, hands on his hips. "Okay, young lady, what's your name?"

The girl didn't give him any more attention than she had paid Adam.

"You've got a name besides 'Sam Klaassen,'" Uncle Hiram spat. "So what is it?"

When the girl did not so much as move a muscle, Hiram let out a mighty snort and shook his head at Adam. "I guess I'll just have to keep her here till Hank comes back, then hand her over to him. Maybe a night in the hoosegow will loosen up that tongue."

"Jail?" Adam straightened quickly. "Do you really think that's necessary?"

"The last I knew, stealing was still a crime." His uncle's eyes narrowed. "Besides, there's also the matter of assault, and—"

"Assault?"

Uncle Hiram glared at Adam, his expression daring his nephew to argue. "Yes, assault. She kicked me hard enough in the shin to raise a welt, not to mention how she barreled into you."

Heat filled Adam's face. "Well, I'd as soon forget—"

"Besides," Hiram continued, "you know as well as I do there'd be nobody at the jail except old Fitz sleeping off his weekday drunk. She'd be out of harm's way until her family could come and get her." He shot the girl a meaningful look. "Assuming, of course, we can figure out who she is."

Adam leaned in close to his uncle and spoke softly, but loud enough for the girl to hear if she wanted to. "Uncle Hiram, I'm not sure jail is the answer here."

"What then?" Hiram lowered his voice to match Adam's.

"Look at her." Adam waited until his uncle's face turned toward the scrawny girl so bent on ignoring them. "She's just a kid, probably no older than Arn." His fourteen-year-old brother had always been Uncle Hiram's favorite. "And look how thin she is. Stealing isn't right, but doesn't she look hungry? Seems to me what she needs is a bath, a good meal, and a warm bed, in that order."

The lines around Uncle Hiram's eyes softened.

Adam plunged on. "Since she tried to charge the food on Pa's tab, maybe I ought to go ahead and take responsibility."

"I'll take her home, let Mother see to her needs, and you can get hold of Sheriff Barnes and have him get word to her family. I reckon her own pa will have a dose of medicine waiting for her when he hears of her mischief, so let's let him handle it."

A slight movement captured Adam's attention, and he glanced over at the girl. Her face had gone white, and she clenched her fists in tight balls. Suspecting she might bolt, Adam shifted his body to block the door.

"What do you think, Uncle Hiram? Should I take her home?"

Hiram shrugged and shook his head. "All right, Adam. I'll walk over to the post office and leave a message for the sheriff that we've got a runaway on our hands. I imagine he'll come to your place and get her name out of her." He pointed a finger at his nephew. "But you watch her. Don't let her rob you blind."

Adam crossed his finger across his chest, tongue in cheek.

Uncle Hiram snorted. "You and your strays." He shook his head again, but his eyes now had a twinkle in them. "Never could stand to let so much as an abandoned kitten starve in an alleyway, could you?"

Adam lifted his shoulders and quoted, " 'Whatsoever you do for the least of these . . .' " He let the words drift away.

Hiram gestured toward the girl. "Get her out of here before I change my mind." He headed to the counter and began to gather up a variety of cans scattered across the wooden top.

"Ain't going."

The low voice from the thus silent girl startled both men.

She lifted her head and fixed Adam with an icy glare. "I'm no stray."

So she had been listening. Adam examined the stubborn jut of her chin. She tried to look tough, but with all that wild hair falling around her face, she just looked ridiculous. And vulnerable.

Uncle Hiram took a step in her direction. "Listen here, young lady, I don't recall you being given any choice in the matter."

The girl went back to folded arms across her chest. "Ain't going."

Uncle Hiram opened his mouth, but Adam held up a hand and sent the girl a steady look. "You can come home with me to a good meal and a warm bed. . . ." He paused for effect. "Or you can spend the night in the city jail. Actually, it's just the cellar under the post office, so it's not so bad except for the mice and spiders. And Fitz is harmless. Just snores and spits a lot."

The girl winced at the mention of spiders, but then she shook her hair back and thrust out her chin. "I don't cotton to no charity."

She had spunk—Adam would give her that.

"You sassy, ungrateful little wretch!" Uncle Hiram threw his arms wide. "You'll try to steal me blind, but you won't take what's offered? Why, I ought to—"

Adam put a restraining hand on his uncle's arm. "Home with me, or the jail. It's your choice. What'll it be?"

Her chin quivered, and for a moment Adam thought she might cry, but a fierce pride must have kept the tears at bay. She sat in silence for several long seconds before heaving a mighty sigh. "All right. I reckon I'll come with you." She stood and bounced a glare between Uncle Hiram and Adam. "But I'm leaving at first light tomorrow. And all I want is the meal and bed—no bath."

he ride to the farm from Mountain View was totally silent. Adam had tried to help the girl up on the buckboard seat beside him, but she had shrugged him off and climbed over the sides into the back. Once home, Adam handed a stiff, sullen girl over to his mother's capable hands. Ma's eyes softened with genuine care as she looked at the skinny, filthy waif before her, and pride swelled in Adam's chest at his mother's innate compassion for those in need.

"I don't know her name," he admitted.

"That's all right." Ma placed her hand on the girl's flannel-covered arm, and she jerked away as if struck. Ma's brows came together in momentary concern, then smoothed out. She spoke gently to her new guest. "We can get acquainted when you're cleaned up. Come with me, and we'll get a bath drawn for you right away." She placed an arm around the girl's stiff shoulders to guide her.

Adam watched the pair enter the house, one smiling and one scowling in what was an already familiar look of defiance. Turning away with a shake of his head, he sought out his father. He found Pa in the tool shack where he was braiding several thin strands of leather together to repair a broken harness.

Adam leaned against the door frame. "Hey, Pa. I'm back."

Simon Klaassen looked up and shot his son a lopsided grin. "I thought maybe you'd decided to spend the night with Nip." His comment was as close as he would come to commenting on Adam's late return.

Adam chuckled. "Not this time. But I did bring someone to spend the night here."

Pa grinned. "Nip?"

Adam gave an amused snort. "No, not him." Briefly he explained his encounter with the young lady he'd left at the house, being careful to leave out the part about tackling her in the street. Just thinking of it made the blood rush to his face—the fewer who knew, the better. Although with half the town watching the incident . . . .

"You did the right thing, son," Pa said at the end of Adam's report. He released a throaty chuckle. "I sure would've liked to have seen Hiram's face when he knew his thief was a girl."

Adam smiled in spite of his own embarrassment at the revelation, recalling his uncle's expression. "I left her at the house with Mother. She had sworn off a bath, but, knowing Ma, I expect she'll be convinced of the benefits one way or another."

"Reckon so." Pa raised one eyebrow. "Now, about the chicken coop . . . ."

"First thing in the morning, sir," Adam promised with another chuckle and a crisp military salute. He headed back to the wagon to unhitch the horses and give them their supper and a good brushing.

As he loosened the animals from their riggings, he saw his younger brother and sister, Teddy and Becky, filling buckets at the iron pump. The youngest Klaassen, Sarah, waited by the back door, ready to open it for their return. He grinned to himself as he led the horses to the barn. It looked as if there'd be a clean young lady at the supper table after all. His mother was gentle and strong, all at the same time.

He came in from putting up the horses and crossed straight to the wash basin tucked below the stairs next to the pantry. He dropped his suspenders from his shoulders and let them dangle at his knees. After pushing his shirtsleeves well above his elbows, he leaned over the basin to splash water on his face once, then again. He lathered his hands with his mother's homemade lavender-scented soap, scrubbed his face, washed clear to his forearms, then rinsed. Only when he had dried himself with the rough towel hanging conveniently on a nail hammered into the pantry doorjamb did he realize he was being watched. As he pulled his suspenders back in place, he looked over his shoulder to find himself under the careful scrutiny of a young girl.

She sat on a chair in the corner of the kitchen. A light spattering of freckles danced across her cheeks and the bridge of her nose. Her hair, damp, hung in shining curls well below her shoulders. In the yellow lamplight of the kitchen it held a reddish cast. Had it not been for the unwavering stare from her unusual eyes of cornflower blue, he might not have realized it was the same girl he'd tussled with in the street only a short hour or so ago.

Gone were the grimy overalls and the man's hat. In their place she wore a lightweight calico dress that Adam recognized as having belonged to his sister Liz. The transformation amazed him. She looked small and vulnerable . . . and painfully young. Adam felt a swell of sympathy. He sent her a smiling nod, but she responded by turning her head toward the commotion in the kitchen. And there was quite a commotion.

At mealtime, Laura Klaassen was fond of saying, the children melted out of the wallpaper. It must have appeared that way to the Klaassen's dinner guest. She tucked her bare feet under the straight-backed chair on which she perched, left foot over right. Occasionally she rubbed her left foot up and down the top of her right one in apparent nervousness. The only other movement she made was the widening of her eyes as the number of people in the kitchen multiplied with the slam of the back door or a clatter of feet on the stairs.

As for the Klaassen children, they eyed their guest with friendly interest, some smiling and others speaking a polite greeting. The girl remained still and silent on the chair, watching with wariness the bustle of activity. Each Klaassen had a job to do, and they accomplished the tasks amongst teasing comments and much laughter. Seeing to his own responsibilities, Adam caught himself wondering what thoughts lurked behind the girl's watchful gaze.

Pa entered the house, and Sarah clattered her handful of silverware onto the tabletop and raced to him. Pa swung her into his arms, making her squeal. She rode his hip as he crossed the floor to deliver a kiss on Ma's upturned cheek. Adam had witnessed this ritual for as long as he could remember, but tonight he viewed it through fresh eyes. Although the girl angled her face toward the corner, he noted her eyes shifting to take in every bit of the bustling scene. And he was certain he glimpsed jealousy pinching her lips into a scowl.

Pa lowered Sarah to the floor and whispered something in her ear. The child scampered off with a cheerful giggle, and Pa moved to take his turn at the washbasin.

Adam crossed the kitchen and lifted the lid on a heavy black skillet resting on the stove.

"Here, now, no sampling." His mother took the wooden spoon he'd picked up for that purpose and replaced the lid on the pot. When he made as if to reach around her, she gave his wrist a playful pat. "You can wait a few more minutes."

Adam rolled his eyes, feigning frustration. Then he grinned and planted a kiss on his mother's cheek. It never ceased to amaze him that his tiny mother had brought ten children into the world and still had the energy to keep up with all of them. He respected his father, he loved his sisters and brothers, but he adored his mother. It was on her lap that he'd snuggled to hear his first Bible story, and it was beside her he'd knelt in the chicken coop—of all places—when he was only five years old to ask Jesus into his heart. Yes, his mother was special.

Pa joined the pair at the stove and reached past Ma to sneak one of the pickled eggs she'd arranged on an oval platter. Adam noticed Ma didn't slap Pa's hands.

"So what's the story on our little beggar?" Pa asked quietly behind Ma's ear.

Ma shot the girl a quick look. Adam listened in when Ma replied. "She says her name is Frances Welch. She claims she's nineteen years old"—Pa's eyebrows raised to his hairline and Ma nodded in understanding—"and on her own."

Adam repeated what he'd shared earlier with his father about the attempted grocery theft.

Ma shook her head sadly. "Poor thing. She must have been awfully hungry to try something like that."

They all looked over to observe the girl. Little Sarah animatedly entertained their guest with a picture book. Frances Welch wore the closest thing to a smile as one can get without actually smiling.

Pa exchanged a look of indulgence with his wife, then brought his palms together in a brisk clap. "Come, family. Let's eat."

With much foot stomping and careful shoves, the siblings slid into place on long benches that lined both sides of the plank table that took up much of the center of the kitchen. Ma carried the platter of pickled eggs to one end of the table, and Si moved to the opposite end. Ma set down the platter and held out a hand to the girl who remained in the corner.

Her shoulders hunched in a self-conscious gesture, the girl rose and crossed to Ma. Ma slipped her arm around the girl's shoulders and sent a beaming smile down the length of the table.

"Children, this is Frances Welch. She is going to be staying with us for a few days."

The girl shot Ma a startled look. Her jaw dropped open, but before she could speak Ma went on.

"You won't be able to remember all these names right at first, but . . ." She introduced each member of the family in turn. "This is our youngest, Sarah." Sarah beamed a bright toothless smile. "Then there's Teddy, Becky, and Arn." Teddy, nine years old and scared of girls, ducked his head and blushed when his name was mentioned. Becky, eleven years old and fearless, nudged him and snickered. Arn's freckles seemed to glow like copper pennies in his friendly face.

"On the end is Mr. Klaassen," Ma continued. "You met Adam in town"—Adam waved a hand in casual response—"then there's Frank, and Josie."

Frank bobbed his chin, and Josie offered a soft smile which Frances did not return.

Ma finished, "We have two more children, Liz and Daniel, but they're married and living on their own now. You might meet them later."

The girl cast a doubtful look in Ma's direction.

Ma gestured to the spot on the bench next to Josie. "You slide in here next to Josie now."

Josie smiled and patted the seat next to her. The girl's muscles tensed, and Adam braced his hands on the bench, ready to bounce up and take pursuit if she chose escape. But after a moment's hesitation, her shoulders wilted and she slid into the bench. Adam released a sigh of relief, and his father clasped his hands in front of him.

❧

Miss Samantha O'Brien, masquerading as Frances Welch, watched beneath eyebrows drawn into a frown as everyone around the table followed the father's example. They all folded their hands in front of them, then bowed heads in unison. All but Samantha.

While the Klaassen family listened to the head of the household deliver thanks for the evening meal, the girl silently filled her pockets with two pickled eggs, a funny little double-decker roll, and a chunky piece of sausage, all the while carefully observing the bowed heads to be sure she wasn't caught.

At the other end of the table, Mr. Klaassen concluded his prayer with a reverent "Amen" that all family members, large and small, echoed. Then bowls and platters of food started around the table, everyone spooning healthy servings onto the well-used Blue Willow plates.

Samantha's empty stomach growled in anticipation as she helped herself to crisply fried potatoes, garden-fresh tomatoes and green beans, puffy browned rolls—funny-looking buns with a top that was smaller than the bottom—sausage links, and a host of relishes. She thickly spread the buns with butter and sweet-smelling preserves. It took every bit of self-control she possessed to avoid sneaking bites between the passing bowls.

At last each plate held all it could hold, and the eating commenced. Samantha attacked her plate with the single-minded purpose of filling herself to the limit. Her nose hovered mere inches above her plate, the fork moving steadily between plate and mouth. Conversation buzzed around her, accompanied by the clink of silver utensils against china plates, but she ignored it all and didn't lift her head until every bite was gone and she'd sopped up the remnants of grease from the sausage and potatoes with a last one of those funny-looking but delicious two-level rolls.

When she finished, Samantha sat up and wiped her mouth with the cloth napkin resting beside her plate. She suffered a moment of embarrassment when she realized none of the others were even close to finishing, but no one seemed to take notice.

Mrs. Klaassen turned toward Samantha. Her smile brought out gentle lines around her eyes and mouth. "Frances, would you care for anything else?"

Samantha offered a silent shake of her head.

"Would you like to be excused? Maybe look around a bit?"

Without replying, Samantha slipped off the bench and headed for the back door.

"Frances?"

She froze, her hand curled around the porcelain doorknob, at the sound of Adam's voice.

"Don't wander too far away. It'll be dark soon."

Resentment prickled. *What makes him think he's my keeper?* She sent as withering a glance as she could muster over her shoulder. "Seein' as how your ma took my shoes, don't know how I can go far. So don't be frettin' over me." She witnessed expressions of shock and dismay coloring the faces around the table. She expected anger to flicker over Adam's, but only a slight amusement lingered there.

She swung around and marched out the door, though the boots sure would have helped make her point more firmly.

*S*amantha located the porch swing by accident, but once she was settled in the shadowy corner set off by lilac bushes she felt more secure than she had for a long time. She needed a quiet spot to think—not only about her plans to move on, but also about the funny feeling inside.

She furrowed her brow, perplexed and unsettled, pressing her arms across her midsection, and tried her best to figure out the strange feeling. Not the fearful churning produced by her father's drunken rages. Not hunger pangs, for sure. She'd not only eaten a plateful of food in the house, she'd already consumed everything stashed in her pockets. Had she made herself sick by eating too much? But no, it wasn't a sick feeling, either. More a hollowness—an emptiness that eating couldn't fill.

She'd watched the family inside the house preparing for their supper, working side by side with smiles and laughter. She'd seen their genuine enjoyment of being together, and it touched something deep inside of her. When the father swung his little girl high in his arms for a hug, she had wondered what it felt like to be lifted high in a father's strong, capable arms and held there. Even the praying part had stirred a reaction, a yearning. All those heads bowed together, sharing something they all believed and respected . . . She started the swing in motion with one bare foot, restless, wanting to escape. But how could she escape these feelings? Wouldn't they go with her?

When she was riding with Adam in the wagon—after deciding it would be easier to slip away from a bunch of honyockers than from a lawman—she'd concocted the name Frances

Welch. If they didn't know her name, they couldn't send her home. That mother—Laura—had accepted her words as fact without a question. It should have pleased her, knowing she'd fooled them. But instead it left her with a scorching remorse. They were obviously good people, and they deserved better than a thief and a liar in their midst.

And that's what she was—nothing but a sneaky, lying criminal. Samantha hugged herself fiercely, anger binding her in knots. A bunch of farmers shouldn't have such an effect on her.

But her thoughts pressed onward in spite of her attempts to put them aside. Samantha remembered a time when she'd been loved, when she'd been taught to kneel beside her bed and recite her "God blesses" at the close of a day. There was a time when grace had been spoken before meals, too, but it was a long time ago. When Gran was alive. Even now, after more than ten years, the lonely ache of Gran's death was still there.

Samantha wrapped her arms more tightly across her tummy and spoke softly into the slight breeze whispering through the thick leaves of the huge bushes. "Oh, Gran, I miss you so much. Why'd you have to go? Why'd you have to leave me? And David . . . gone, too. Everybody I've loved, gone. Why? Why . . . ?"

No answer came. Not that she expected one. She'd asked the questions before. Her father had caught her talking to the wind one day and had called her foolish. "*Real smart*," he had sneered, "*yappin' at the breeze. All it does is grab your words and carry 'em away.*" And he'd made her come in the house. Even so, foolish or not, she still talked to the wind. It was comforting somehow, talking to something more powerful than herself. Only she was careful about staying far away from her father when she did it.

Lifting her face to the graying sky, she spoke proudly. "It's not foolish, Gran. 'Cause maybe, just maybe, someday those words will be swept up to heaven and you'll hear me. And you'll send me somebody who will listen when I talk, like you used to, and maybe even care about what I say. And then I'll feel good again. Can you do that, Gran?"

She paused, face turned to capture the faint breeze, breathing in the sweet scents of nature and the leftover aromas from supper. Eyes lifted heavenward, she held her breath as her heart begged for a response. Then she heard a twig snap and went cold all over.

She clutched the swing seat, her feet planted and ready for flight. "Who's there?"

"Just me—Adam." He stepped up on the porch, stopping a few feet away from her and leaning against the railing that separated the slender posts. He gave her a brief glance over his shoulder. "Nice night, isn't it?"

She looked at him sideways, her heart pounding. Had he heard her? She searched his face, looking for signs of the amusement she'd glimpsed earlier. If he laughed at her, she'd tackle him again. And she'd come out the winner this time. No humor sparked in his eyes, and gradually her racing pulse calmed. She sank back into the seat, making the chains squeak. "Yeah. It's nice enough."

He turned, face up to the sky where the first stars were beginning to appear. He seemed completely at ease with himself. Almost unaware of her presence. Apparently he hadn't heard her babbling. This time. But she'd have to be careful until she left. There were too many pairs of ears around this place.

Adam asked, "Are you tired? Mother sent me out to find you and offer a bed."

Samantha fought back a yawn at the idea of bed—a real place to sleep after all those nights in barns, sheds, and even a mossy place in the woods. "I guess." Then she bolted upright.

"But just for one night. What your ma said at supper, 'bout me being here a few days? That's not right. I'll be on my way tomorrow."

"Well, I haven't got a problem with that, but I imagine the sheriff will want to talk to you first." Adam shifted his weight on the railing and crossed his arms. After a while he turned his head to look directly at her. "I tell you what, come on in now and let Mother show you your place for the night, then we can worry about arranging your travel plans in the morning."

Samantha stared outward, trying to decide how to respond. At last she sighed and pushed to her feet. "All right. I'll talk to your sheriff. But after that, I'm leaving." She pressed her lips together, thrust out her jaw, and glared at Adam to emphasize her words.

Adam raised his hands, palms up, and she marched past him and headed for the back door. She heard a soft snort behind her, but she decided to ignore it.

◦───◦

Laura Klaassen tucked the younger children into bed, checked on each of the older ones—their guest lay stiffly next to Josie in her big feather bed—then paused at the head of the stairs to call her customary blessing brought over from the Old Country, "*Schlop Die gesunt*," before returning to the kitchen.

Adam leaned in the kitchen doorway, but he shifted to let her pass, nodding a silent communication as his head tilted toward the kitchen. She turned the corner and found the swarthy sheriff seated at the plank table with Simon, enjoying a cup of coffee. Laura smiled and crossed to the man, holding out her hand.

"Good evening, Sheriff. I imagine Hiram sent you out?"

Sheriff Barnes chuckled. "He sure did. He's got a head full of steam, too. Si and Adam here filled me in on what you folks know about the girl." He shook his head, his lips pursing. "Didn't take 'em long. You don't seem to have been able to find out much."

Laura sighed in acknowledgment of the sheriff's comment. She sensed there was a story hidden beneath the girl's sullen exterior, but it would take a great deal of time to extract it. The young woman carried a stiff shield of defensiveness. "Would you like a piece of pie to go with your coffee? I have a big slice of rhubarb in the icebox."

The sheriff declined with a humorous pat on his extended belly, so Laura poured herself a cup of coffee and sat down with the men. Si slipped his arm around her, connecting them. She always found security in her husband's presence.

"Our young guest feels compelled to leave first thing in the morning," Laura informed the sheriff, one hand curled around her coffee mug and the other reaching up to grasp Si's draped over her shoulder. "Although I think she's very good at hiding her feelings, she still seems frightened of something." She turned to her husband, worried. "You don't think she's running from the law, do you?"

Si squeezed Laura's shoulder. "I realize she was trying to steal from Hiram," he said, "but she hardly seems old enough to have gotten into too much trouble yet." He quirked his lips into a grin. "She might have told you she's nineteen, but I have my doubts."

Sheriff Barnes stroked his bushy mustache thoughtfully with a forefinger. "My guess is she's a runaway—wants to be on her own. I suspect a mighty big hunger led her to attempt the food robbery. She didn't threaten Hiram in any way." He grinned. "Although she did give him a pretty good bruise on the shin. And barefoot too. She's probably got a very worried mama sitting at home, waiting for her return."

When Laura and Simon exchanged glances, Adam caught her eye. Concern pinched her son's brow, and Laura's heart turned over. Of all her children, Adam possessed the biggest dose of compassion. He already cared about Frances Welch's well-being. And he would be most bothered if they were unable to help the girl.

She turned to the sheriff again. "What do we do in the morning when she tries to leave?"

Sheriff Barnes snorted. "Whatever her reasons for being here, her family will have to be contacted. Despite her claims to the contrary, it's obvious she isn't old enough to be on her own. She'll have to be sent home."

Behind the sheriff, Laura could see Adam's flinch.

The sheriff continued, "If we find she doesn't have a family . . . Well, we'll cross that bridge if we come to it. To keep her here, threaten her with criminal prosecution for attempted theft. For good measure, throw in assault and battery for that kick Hiram got. I'll do some checking—her family will have gone to the authorities about their missing daughter, so someone will know something."

The sheriff stood to leave. He thanked Laura for the coffee, took a big breath that expanded his middle, then rolled back on his heels and gave Si and Laura a stern look. "Si, Laura, you're good people. You mean well, and I know I'm leaving that girl in good hands. But I feel I should offer a word of warning. Be *careful*. No telling where she comes from or what she's learned. I'd hate to see you taken in by a little con artist. Or worse."

"We'll be careful, Hank." Si rose and shook the sheriff's hand. "Thanks for coming out."

"Just doin' my job." Sheriff Barnes grinned, plopped his hat back on his head, and left.

Laura lifted her cup for another sip as Si locked the door behind their visitor. When Si returned to the table, Adam moved forward and slid into the space the sheriff had vacated. "Pa, Ma, I know what Frances did was wrong, but deep down, I don't think she's *bad*."

Laura searched her son's face. Adam met her gaze, his cheeks flooding with color. She stretched out her hand and placed it over her son's wrist. "What are you thinking, Adam?"

Adam drew a deep breath. "I think she's scared, and I think she was really hungry and desperate. I don't think stealing is something she does as a habit." He paused, lowering his head. "When . . . when I went out after supper to find her, I . . . I heard her talking."

Laura offered a gentle squeeze, encouraging Adam to continue.

He lifted his face. True concern shimmered in his gold-flecked brown eyes. "At first I thought she might be talking to someone else—maybe a partner in crime, so to speak, but then I understood what she said." His brow furrowed. "I won't repeat it. I think it's private. But after hearing it, I just know she isn't bad. She's . . . *sad*. And very lonely."

Adam heaved a sigh, slipping his hand away from Laura's touch. "I don't know how long she'll be here, but I think what she needs from us is someone to be her friend, her listener." He flicked a glance at Si, then turned back to Laura. "I intend to be her friend, Ma. And maybe, with someone around who cares, we'll see a change for the better in her life."

Laura offered her son a smile she hoped communicated her approval of his tender heart. "I think you're right, Adam. I think beneath that defensive frown is a hurting little girl in need of a friend." And Laura knew exactly what Friend would offer the very best help to their small guest.

Adam rose. "Well, I guess I'll turn in. I've got a chicken coop to work on tomorrow in addition to my other chores. 'Night, Ma, Pa." He gave his mother a kiss on the cheek and squeezed his father's shoulder as he headed for the stairs.

Si watched Adam go, then looked again into Laura's face. His brow etched into lines of worry. "You don't think he's smitten with the girl, do you?"

Laura laughed softly, rising and carrying their coffee cups to the sink. "Si, you know as well as I do, Adam has always been our champion of the underdog. He sees a person in need, and he can't stop himself from reaching out. He isn't smitten. But he does care." She smiled over her shoulder. "We raised him right."

Si nodded, but she noted his forehead remained creased.

Laura turned to the sink and began washing the cups. Her thoughts turned inward, Adam's concerned face playing in her mind's eye. Yes, her son had a gift for compassion. *Which means he could be easily hurt, Lord.*

Laura stacked the clean cups on their shelf while her silent prayers whispered through her heart. *Let us minister to this stranger in our midst, Father, but guard our hearts from stepping beyond Your will. For her. For our family.*

amantha slowly drifted awake to the soft patter of raindrops against cedar shingles. She stretched beneath the warm covering, eyes closed, savoring the comfortable feather bed and sweet-smelling sheets. She brought her fists up and rubbed her eyes, yawning as she did so, then opened her eyes slowly to squint around the dusky room.

She jerked upward and leaned back on her elbows, disoriented. Remembering, she fell against the thick pillow while it all came tumbling back. Her long sigh captured all the swirl of emotions she was feeling.

She pushed back the colorful patchwork quilt and padded on bare feet to the window. She drew the green gingham curtains aside and peered out at the late-summer rain and groaned her frustration.

"Oh. You're up."

The little voice from behind startled her, and she quickly spun around.

"I'm thorry." The smallest Klaassen peered up at Samantha with large blue eyes. "I didn't mean ta thcare you."

"Y-you didn't," Samantha lied, entranced in spite of herself by the child's china-doll features and endearing lisp. "I just didn't hear you come in, that's all."

Sarah laughed, a tinkling sound that reminded Samantha of sleigh bells. "I can be quiet ath a cat when I want. Frank thinkth I try to be thneaky, but I don't. I'm jutht not big enough to make a lot of noithe yet."

With effort, Samantha stifled a chuckle. The child was animated and lively. Completely irresistible.

"Sarah Louise . . ." Mrs. Klaassen stepped through the doorway and gave the little girl a stern look. "Did you wake up poor Frances? She needs her sleep—."

"She wath awake already," Sarah explained quickly as she wrapped her arms around her mother's waist and turned an innocent face upward. "I jutht came in to talk to her."

The woman's eyes crinkled over a smile. "Well, I can't say I'm surprised, my little chatterbox." Mrs. Klaassen lifted her head to smile at Samantha. She said to Sarah, "Why don't you go downstairs and tell Josie that Frances is awake and will be needing some breakfast, hmm?"

Sarah skipped to the door, then paused to wave to Samantha. "Thee you later, Frantheth." She disappeared around the corner.

Samantha fixed her face in a frown and took a step forward. "Thanks for the bed an' all, but I don't have time for any breakfast. I need to get my hands on my own set of clothes. Then I'll be on my way."

Mrs. Klaassen's brows rose. "On your way? But, my dear, it's raining. You surely don't expect us to allow you to run off in the rain, do you?" She moved into the room and scooped up the dress Samantha had worn after her bath yesterday afternoon. "No, you'll stay until the weather clears," she said, her tone matter of fact. "Why, you'd catch your death out there."

The woman pressed the dress into Samantha's unresisting hands. "I doubt this got soiled at supper last night, so just slip it back on after you wash up. Your other clothes are in need of washing, and we do the wash on Friday. By then the rain will have let up, and you'll be able to be on your way. Oh, and I brought you a pair of shoes—too small for Josie and too big for Becky." She set them down by Samantha's feet and headed toward the doorway, gesturing toward the washstand with its full pitcher of water. "Wash the sleep from your eyes, my dear, dress, and come on down. You know where the necessary is. One egg or two?"

Samantha's mouth dropped.

Mrs. Klaassen paused in the doorway, her expectant face aimed in Samantha's direction.

Samantha gulped. "Uh, one'll be fine."

"Very well." Laura smiled. "Now don't dally. The water's still warm for you." She left, closing the door firmly behind her.

Samantha plunked her hands on her hips and glared at the door, then at the dress and shoes. That woman sure took a lot for granted! After a moment's worth of stewing, she sighed, shrugged her shoulders in defeat, and moved to the washstand.

⤜◯

Samantha finished her breakfast—two eggs along with three more of the rolls she'd enjoyed at supper the night before. Becky called them *zwieback*, which she said meant "two buns." Samantha had never heard of such a thing, but the bread had a soft texture and delicate flavor that pleased her taste buds. She drank two cups of coffee and a big glass of milk, then moved over to the sink to wash her dishes. And the entire process took only thirty minutes. The day ahead stretched out endlessly before her. Samantha's stomach jumped with nervousness and questions. How would she fill the long hours? What was going to happen to her?

Sarah and Becky tried to engage her in conversation. Samantha's short responses stilled their questions. They brought

out puzzles and asked Samantha to help them put the pieces together, but she shook her head. After an hour of being rebuffed, the pair scampered up to the attic to play with their rag dolls. Samantha sighed with relief at their departure. Time with people led to attachments. She had no desire to form anything of that sort here.

The men, from Mr. Klaassen on down to Teddy, must have been outside somewhere. There wasn't a male in the house, at least. That suited her fine too. Samantha wasn't much on the company of males—whatever their ages. In her experience, men were demanding and temperamental—not the type of company one sought out for any length of time. Samantha's experience with females wasn't much better. Where she came from, girls her age were catty and condescending, seeming to take great pleasure in making one feel foolish and gauche.

Trust in humankind had definitely not had any chance for development in Samantha. She basically had been on her own since she was six years old, and she didn't see that changing in the near future. Nor did she see any need for it to change. *I'm doing fine*, she told herself firmly as she wandered hesitantly into the parlor.

She moved carefully to the middle of the room and looked around. The plain whitewashed walls, lacy curtains, and fine furnishings looked so beautiful and welcoming. She thought about the three-room cracker-box of a house that she called home back in Wisconsin. The Klaassen's home was as clean as rain-washed flowers. The room smelled good, too—herbal and fresh. A little snooping uncovered a tiny mesh bag filled with dried flowers hanging on the wall near the corner woodstove. She sniffed the contents of the bag, absorbing the delicious aroma, then tucked the bag into the pocket of her dress to carry the good smell around with her. But after a moment, she returned it to its place on the wall. It might only be a tiny bag of dried petals, but it wasn't hers.

She seated herself on the edge of the camelback sofa, taking care not to touch the highly polished wood-trimmed armrest to avoid smudging its surface. She rubbed her hands over the dark-brown upholstery, noting that it was smooth when she moved her hand one way, rough when she slid it back. She gazed at the window, where rain continued to fall. Her thoughts ran faster than the raindrops racing down the long, narrow panes.

Despite her uncertainties about it all last night, she felt pretty clever now, having come up with a false identity. If she was stuck here, being known as Frances Welch would make it nigh on impossible for them to trace her back to Pa. A small-town sheriff wouldn't be terribly bright, she was sure, so no doubt he'd only look into the name she'd told them, not her description.

She gave a little sniff, imagining how Pa would have described her when alerting the authorities that she'd run off again. *"Jest a sawed-off runt, spindly, with a long ol' rat's nest o' red hair on 'er head . . . an' dumber'n a rock, that'd be my girl,"* she'd heard Pa say about her to one of his cronies. At the time she'd trembled with rage and had wished him dead for the hundredth time.

Pa was right about one thing. She wasn't so awful big. But dumb? Not hardly. She'd managed to get away, and he hadn't found her, not yet. She fully intended to stay away this time. Never, never would she go back to that house and her drunk of a father.

Anxiety twisted its way through her chest like an undergrowth of creeping charley. If only the rain would stop so she could get moving! The longer she stayed in one spot, the more likely it was that somehow, someway, Pa would catch up to her. He seemed to possess some sort of sixth sense peculiar to drinking men; he always found her. And she was determined to escape the prison that had been home, just as Davey had escaped.

As always, thoughts of her brother brought a lump to her throat. She swallowed hard, trying to force it down. That deep longing also made the tears come, and Samantha didn't cry—not anymore. Tears were for weaklings, and Samantha was no weakling. She'd kept any weeping at bay since she was six years old, and she wasn't about to let down her guard now. She was going to prove to Pa and to anyone else who cared to look on that she was strong enough to stand on her own, just like Davey was. He had proved it when he'd run off almost seven years ago. He'd promised to come back for her, but she figured that once he'd gotten settled, he'd decided it was easier not to have to worry about a kid sister. She had waited and watched for him, but he hadn't come back. And after all this time, Samantha had determined she couldn't rest her hopes on Davey; she'd have to depend on herself.

From the kitchen came the murmur of voices. Josie and her mother must have finished their upstairs housekeeping chores, for she had heard them come down the stairs, chuckling together at something or other. From their voices and the occasional burst of laughter, Samantha could tell their conversation was lighthearted. She felt a pang of desire to join them, to feel just once what it was like to be part of a family such as this one. But she quickly squelched the yearning. *Not for the likes of me*, she told herself as she stood up.

She marched over to the kitchen doorway and interrupted. "Can I go out and sit on the porch swing?" If she was outside, she wouldn't be tempted to pretend she belonged.

"Certainly, Frances." Mrs. Klaassen offered one of her a crinkling smiles. "I enjoy that swing too. Perhaps I'll join you when Josie and I have finished mixing the bread dough."

Samantha shrugged. "Suit yourself." She slipped out through the parlor door which led directly to the swing area of the large, covered porch. She sat in the center of the swing and pushed her feet against the wooden porch floor, setting the creaking swing in motion. The scent of rain filled her nostrils and suddenly, unbidden, a memory surfaced, no doubt aided by the quiet patter of rain and the fresh smell.

She was a little girl again, standing in the rain at a gravesite, holding a large cluster of wildflowers beneath her chin, listening to the droning voice of a minister give the words of the final farewell. Samantha squeezed her eyes tight, trying to shut down the replay in her mind, but behind her closed lids she could see clearly the plain pine box which held the body of her dear Gran. She could see her pa, too, standing sullenly beside her, chin thrust out, hands behind his back, his hat firmly on his head to shield himself from the falling rain. And Davey was there too, hat in hand, his tears mixing with the raindrops that ran in rivulets down his thin cheeks.

She stood abruptly, sending the swing banging against the wall, and moved to the porch railing. She dug her fingers into the painted wood as pain and fury mingled in her chest. Had Pa been sad that day? Had he cried on the inside only, as she had, afraid that if the tears began they would never end? Gran was his own grandmother. Did he miss her at all? Somehow, Samantha doubted it. Someone as self-centered as Burt O'Brien had thoughts for no one but himself.

In all likelihood, any of Pa's contemplations that day had been on who would do the cooking and cleaning with Gran gone. How he'd ranted that night, complaining about the scanty meal six-year-old Samantha had done her best to put together for them. David had eaten silently, not a word of complaint, but Pa . . . but then Pa always bellyached about everything.

Samantha scowled, despair filling her once more as she remembered helping Davey pack. He whispered in the dark so Pa wouldn't hear. *"Soon as I'm settled, Sammy, I'll send for ya. Just wait for me, okay, Sammy?"* And Samantha, trusting, had waited. Waited seven long years. Years of Pa's drunken rages, years of lying awake in the dark, thinking, This is the night Davey'll be comin'. Well, she wasn't waiting anymore.

She pushed herself away from the porch railing and stood as straight as she could, arms folded across her chest. From now on, Samantha O'Brien was responsible for Samantha O'Brien, and the fewer people she trusted, the better.

Across the wide yard, young Teddy caught her attention as he splashed through a mud puddle, a huge grin splitting his face. The boy was soaked, his pants muddy to the knees. Samantha stiffened, imagining the trouble he'd be in when his pa caught him fooling around so. Mr. Klaassen stepped into the doorway of the barn, and she held her breath.

Although Samantha couldn't make out Mr. Klaassen's features from this distance since he stood in the shadow in the barn doorway, his stance seemed relaxed, not angry. Feet planted wide, torso leaning back, hands resting loosely in his overall pockets. Then, much to her surprise, he bent down and yanked off his boots and socks. With a gallop he crossed the ground to join his son. The man and boy hooted with laughter together as they splashed around in the muddy water. "Feels good on my hot feet, Teddy boy! Great idea . . ."

And something thick and stifling rose within Samantha. She turned away only to catch a glimpse of Laura's laughing face in the parlor window, watching their antics with obvious pleasure. She spun away, her heart pounding.

As a child, if Samantha had come home dirty, she got a good licking for soiling her clothes. She had learned early to sidestep mud puddles and to hold her skirt high to avoid being splashed by others sloshing through them. But here was a grown man, playing like a child, and his wife laughing about it.

Samantha stared from Si to Teddy to Laura, then back again. Had she ever witnessed such strange behavior? *What's wrong with these people?* She turned her face to the rain and sent a silent wish for sunshine so she could be on her way before she was totally undone by this family and their cheerful manner of living.

*T*he rain lasted three of the longest days of Samantha's not-so-long life. During that time she watched and listened, expending a great deal of energy trying to look as if she *wasn't* watching and listening. By the end of the third day in the Klaassen household, Samantha convinced herself there had to be something seriously wrong with the whole family.

For one thing, Mr. Klaassen didn't go into town to be with the men and didn't seem to require whiskey to keep him happy. Samantha couldn't get over how hard he worked. Had she ever seen such an industrious man? Yet he was lighthearted, too. She'd seen it the day he'd pranced in the mud puddle with their youngest son, Teddy.

The children all minded him, but Samantha never once heard him raise his voice, and certainly never saw him raise his hand to any of them. Samantha couldn't figure out for the life of her how he and Laura Klaassen managed to keep everybody doing what they were supposed to be doing. Oh, she'd seen an occasional friendly tussle between Arn and Ted turn into something else, with their father or mother having to intervene—making them stop and shake hands. But any argument that might look like it was getting out of hand was nipped in the bud.

And Mrs. Klaassen was even more of a puzzle. Her face always held a hint of a smile. More in her eyes than on her lips. Samantha thought people who grinned all the time seemed feeble-minded, but she'd never be able to accuse Mrs.

Klaassen of lacking intelligence. The woman had tons of work to do, too—chickens to look after, wash for her large family as well as meals three times a day and all the baking that went with it, a garden to care for, a house to keep clean. . . . The tasks seemed overwhelming to Samantha, who was accustomed to a very small home and very few people around to look after. Yet Mrs. Klaassen never complained. She smiled and teased her way through the days, completing her tasks in a cheerful manner. One afternoon Samantha had even found the woman sitting in a rocker in the parlor with a book in her lap! Of course there was Josie to help, but still. . . .

Samantha had always been a hard worker herself—more by necessity than design—but she couldn't claim to be cheerful about it. At home, she'd no more than get things straightened around when Pa, alone or with some of his cronies, would come through with dirty feet and lips full of snuff and muck things up again. With so many Klaassens coming and going, every day contained its share of messes. How could Mrs. Klaassen maintain a happy attitude with so much to do?

And what about the Klaassen kids? Consider Frank, nearly as big as a barn himself, still living at home and minding his Pa. Samantha figured once kids grew to be big enough to take care of themselves, out they'd go in a flash. But Frank—and Adam, too—were more men than boys, still following their father's lead and seeming to not mind it a bit.

Josie, and Becky, too, had lots to do, helping their mother keep things in order. Arn was always out with the men— every time Samantha looked at him he'd go red in the face, which made his freckles glow—and didn't seem to mind the work either.

Teddy and Sarah didn't have as many responsibilities as the others, being the youngest, but they had their own chores.

Only once had Samantha seen any of them shirk their duties, and that was Sarah, whom Samantha had decided was just a wee bit spoiled. But she was sure the family couldn't help themselves—even Samantha found her own heartstrings pulled by the loving little "Tharah."

When those occasional scuffles between siblings arose, they ended quickly with apologies and forgiveness. And at times with no interference at all from the Klaassen parents. Apparently the family didn't know about carrying grudges. Yes, something was definitely not right here.

But if this was "not right," it wasn't exactly wrong, either. It sure wasn't normal—not from Samantha's standpoint—but it was . . . well, peaceful, a feeling Samantha hadn't known heretofore. And she wondered if, when she left, she'd be able to find it somewhere else on her own.

❧

Adam spent time in deep thought during the rainy days that kept him and the other Klaassen men holed up in the barn. There was always busy work to fill their days, but they wished they could be in the fields. The vow he had made to himself to be a friend to Frances Welch turned out to be a pie-crust promise—easier made than kept. The girl eluded him at every turn. Any attempt at conversation was met with an even stare that seemed to look through or past a person. If any response came at all, it was in monosyllables at best.

Adam scrubbed at the old paint on the hay wagon, thinking of the way Frances's big eyes watched all of them. Usually you could look into someone's eyes and tell what that person was thinking, but not this Frances. She could hold a blank face better than anyone he'd ever met. Often he'd covertly watch her watch them and wish he knew what she was thinking. It was obvious she was uncomfortable—she was restless, almost like a caged animal, pacing from place to place in the house and avoiding all of them whenever possible. Had she been mistreated at some point in her life? She was so distrustful of everyone, particularly older male family members. He'd also noticed that whenever his mother tried to touch her—Ma was a very demonstrative person, and touching and hugs came naturally to her—she would pull away.

His hands stilled momentarily as he tried to pinpoint what it was that made her so different. Then it came to him. There were no emotions. She didn't smile, didn't laugh, didn't cry. . . . Her face wore a mask of indifference to everyone and everything around her. What kind of life had she led that would bring about such a closed, empty shell of a person? Such an impenetrable barrier she'd built around herself. But why? Whatever the answer was, he was sure he wouldn't hear it from Frances's lips.

He set to work again as his thoughts tumbled onward. He hadn't known such close-mouthed females existed. All the ones around this house were chattering all the time. Had the situation been less serious, he might've had some fun with that little characteristic of hers. The only person able to put her at ease was Sarah. The six-year-old, with her bright smile and endless babble about this and that, seemed to be winning Frances over from sheer innocence.

Adam frowned, his hands slowing. There had to be a way to gain Frances's trust and let her know that someone cared about her. Especially the One he'd come to know when he was a very small boy out in the chicken coop. If only he could tell Frances about the loving God in whom Adam and his family placed their trust, she would have a permanent friend—a "listener," as she had put it that night he'd heard her on the swing—to be with her no matter where she went.

Adam ceased his scraping and paused to look out the open barn door. Becky and Josie bent over the washtubs, scrubbing bedsheets. He sighed. With all of them busy with chores, there wasn't much time to talk to Frances about God's unwavering love for her. But even if they didn't find time to speak of God, they could show Frances through their actions the importance He held in their lives. Everyone down to Sarah could help with that.

Adam returned to his task, determined to somehow break through the barrier his family's guest had built around herself. He decided to talk it over with his pa as soon as he could find him.

Arn came bursting into the barn. "Pa says come quick and help. Hilarius's Rosalee is loose again."

Adam dropped his scrub brush over the edge of the wagon. "I'm a-comin', Arn." He would watch for a chance to talk with Pa.

～の

"Frantheth, gueth what?"

Samantha stood at the parlor window, inwardly rejoicing that the rain was letting up. Freedom was near! She shifted her gaze to Sarah, who peered up at her with those blue, blue eyes that always seemed to catch Samantha off guard with their depth and expressiveness. "What it is, Sarah?"

"Day after tomorrow is Thunday, and Liz an' Jake are going to come here for dinner. Mama'th gonna make a thcripture cake, too. Won't that be good?"

Samantha nodded dumbly, wondering what in the world a "thcripture cake" was. By now she knew what Scriptures were, that's for sure. After three days of being stuck in this house with the Klaassens, she'd been introduced to a fair amount of it. Mrs. Klaassen had a verse for every occasion, and her children often winked at one another when their mother got to quoting. Plus the day got started with everyone sitting around the table, listening to Mr. Klaassen read a little something from the Bible then all holding hands for the prayer. Samantha had been invited to join them, but she'd felt foolish sitting there holding hands with Becky and Josie, so after the first time, she'd stayed out of the kitchen till all that stuff was done. Though she'd caught herself listening to a story that had somehow gotten her attention from her perch in the parlor, something about Jesus and His "disciples"—whatever they were—on a little boat in a storm. Her imagination had captured that image in her mind, and it stayed with her through the rest of the day.

Sarah now caught Samantha's hand and drew her into the kitchen. "An Liz ith going to have a baby, too," the little girl was saying. "It'll be jutht a while now an' that baby'll be here. I'm gonna be an aunt again."

Samantha's eyes grew wide. "You're an—an *ahnt*?" She pronounced the word the same way Sarah had. "But you're just a little kid."

Sarah laughed. "I'm little, but Liz ithn't. She'th real big an' fat now." She held out her arms in front of her tummy to illustrate. She pushed Samantha onto the nearest kitchen bench, then straddled the wide plank seat and swung her feet as she continued. "After Liz hath her baby, there'll be three babieth in the family. My brother Daniel got married to Rothe, and they have two babieth already—Chrithtina and Katrina. They're real cute. They live way away in Minneapolith, but Liz an' Jake live in Mountain Lake. Not far. I'll get to thee Liz an' Jake'th baby a lot more than Chrithtina and Katrina, for sure."

Sarah finally stopped talking long enough for Samantha to absorb it all. If Sarah was an aunt already, then Mrs. Klaassen was a grandmother. Samantha turned her gaze to watch the woman at the dry sink, rolling out dough to cut noodles. She looked nothing like the grandmother Samantha remembered. Mrs. Klaassen was tiny—eleven-year-old Becky was only a little bit shorter than her mother—and the coil of her nut-brown hair sported fewer than a dozen white hairs. Her brown eyes sparkled with vitality. She looked far too young to be a grandmother.

Mrs. Klaassen looked over at Sarah, eyebrows pulled down a bit. "Sarah, aren't you supposed to be helping Josie and Becky with the wash? If everything is to be dry by evening, they'll need your help."

Sarah gave her mother a pleading look. "I wanna thtay here and talk to Frantheth. It'th hot outthide. Why do I have to hang wash?"

"Because when everyone does his or her share, the work gets done much faster." Mrs. Klaassen's tone brooked no nonsense. "Now scoot along with you."

Sarah's lips pulled down for a moment, then she sighed and swung her leg over the bench. As she stood, she looked at Samantha, hope dancing in her wide eyes. "Want to come, too?"

Samantha hesitated.

Mrs. Klaassen sent a smile across the kitchen. "Go ahead, both of you. Just don't let Sarah try to talk you into doing her share of the hanging."

"Come." Sarah captured Samantha's hand and pulled her out the back door.

Samantha hop-skipped after Sarah, who refused to relinquish her hand until they had reached the other two girls. They were wringing out the wet wash and hanging it over the lines to dry. Becky turned, spotted Sarah, and made a sour face.

"Where have you been? We're practically done."

"Now, Becky," Josie said, "you weren't much better about your chores when you were Sarah's age." Becky opened her mouth in protest, but Josie shook her head. "Let's not spend time fussing, or we'll be out here all afternoon."

Sarah stuck out her tongue at Becky, grinned at Josie, then giggled and ran to the basket. She wrestled out a towel and twisted it, but her small hands proved inept at wringing out the water.

Samantha moved over to help. She showed Sarah how to hold tightly to one end of the towel while Samantha twisted it. As she hung the heavy towel on the line next to similar items, she noticed her own overalls and flannel shirt hanging amongst the men's things closer to the barn. Her heart did a happy flip-flop. With her clothes clean and dry, she could be on her way. Maybe even by this evening.

Josie started singing a nonsense song about little children eating oatmeal, and Becky joined in. Sarah lisped her way on the words she could remember, just singing "La, la, la" in place of the ones she couldn't. Samantha listened to it all while moving between the baskets of wet laundry and the clotheslines, her hands busy and her heart lighter than it had been for quite a while.

Before she knew it, the baskets were empty and three long lines of wet clothing, sheets, and towels flapped in the warm, end-of-summer breeze.

Becky stood back, hands on her hips, and surveyed the rows of clean items with satisfaction. "Sure feels good to have that done."

"Sure does." Josie stacked the empty baskets together and scooped them up. "It'll be nice to sleep on those sun-dried sheets tonight, too."

Sarah skipped along beside her older sister as the four girls headed toward the house. "I love the thmell of fresh sheetth."

Josie reached out a hand to rustle Sarah's soft blonde curls. "Me, too, *liebchen.*"

Samantha had heard Mr. and Mrs. Klaassen use the nickname when addressing Sarah. She wondered what it meant, and she started to ask Josie. But a shout stopped her words.

"Hey! Girls!"

All four twirled to see Arn coming from behind the barn at a trot. He panted to a stop in front of them, his face beet red. "Guess what we found?"

Becky huffed, impatience crinkling her nose. "Just tell us."

A huge grin split Arn's freckled face. "Mushrooms! Pa says if we get 'em picked now, Ma'll have time to fix 'em with our gravy. Want to help?"

The younger two girls squealed and dashed to Arn's side. Samantha shrugged and moved a step toward the boy.

Josie said, "Let me put these baskets on the back porch and check with Mother to make sure she's done with us for now."

Arn gave a teasing snort. "Well, hurry up, grandma!"

Josie made a face at him and hurried to the back door.

Becky pulled at Samantha's hand. "Have you ever hunted mushrooms, Frances?"

Samantha tugged her hand free of Becky's grasp. These were the touchiest people she'd ever met. "No. I never ate one neither."

Arn, Becky, and Sarah stared in amazement. Becky shook her head, her brown braids flopping. "You've never eaten a mushroom? Didn't they have 'em where you used to live?"

For reasons she couldn't explain, Samantha experienced a rush of irritation. She answered sharply. "I don't know. I never asked."

Becky ducked her head, her cheeks splashed with pink. Samantha considered apologizing for her brusque tone, but Josie raced out the back door, letting it slam behind her.

"We can go as long as we're back in time to make the beds before supper. Come on."

"Great!" Arn's voice cracked on the single word. He was at the awkward age between boyhood and manhood, and his voice tended to run the scales like an inept piano tuner.

His sisters giggled and poked at him as they dashed off at a pace that wasn't sensible considering the August heat. Samantha followed automatically, curiosity about mushrooms propelling her along behind the others. Between these mushrooms and the promised "scripture" cake—whatever that was—meals around here were getting to be quite an adventure.

The girls followed Arn past the grazing area behind the barn clear out to the stand of maples, apple, and mulberry trees that bordered the Klaassen property. Sarah shivered and reached to grab Samantha's hand. "Oooh! We're goin' in the woodth!"

Becky rolled her eyes. "This isn't the *woods*, silly."

"I can call it the woodth if I want to," Sarah argued.

Josie slowed her pace to fall in with Samantha and Sarah. "Woods or not, isn't it a pleasant place to be? I love to come out to the trees. Especially in the spring and summer. It's so nice and cool, and the breeze stirs the scents of ripened fruit, damp earth, and decaying leaves—."

"Stop talking like a teacher, Josie." Becky shot a wrinkle-nosed look over her shoulder.

Josie laughed. "But I want to be one! Why shouldn't I practice?" She aimed a quick smile at Samantha. "I also like all the wildflowers that grow here in the protection of the trees. God did an amazing job, making the world so beautiful."

Samantha considered Josie's comment. Caught up in mere survival from day to day, she'd never taken the time to examine the world's beauty. But now she looked around at the delicate white angel's breath and chubby lavender bluebells. Fallen mulberries lay like a purple and magenta carpet beneath her feet. She felt her heart expanding inside her chest. Loveliness did exist here. But was it to be found in other places too?

Arn came to a halt, his head swinging back and forth. Then he yelped, "This is the spot." He dashed ahead to a row of spine-covered bushes, one of which sported a red bandanna tied to a spindly branch. He pushed aside the branches so the girls could pass. "Look out for prickles. The mushrooms are under the trees there."

As she came through the bushes, Samantha stopped short at the sight of Adam on his knees, plucking squatty, round-topped plants from the soft ground and dropping them into a burlap sack.

Sarah ran to him, obviously delighted. "Adam, how come you're not in the fieldth?"

Adam poked a finger into her round middle, making her laugh. "Because the 'fieldths,' as you say, are too wet to be worked. We'll get out there Monday if the sun holds through the weekend. So today I hunt mushrooms."

Samantha swallowed a rush of apprehension. Being with the girls and even Arn was one thing, but being in the vicinity of Adam was another. He was as tall as her father—a boyish face but he looked big enough to be a man. Every time she found herself within Adam's range, she remembered the humiliation of him sitting on her, holding her down, in the middle of the street.

Of course, he'd done nothing remotely close to that to her since. He'd been kind and considerate. But his kindness only added to her shame as she recalled calling him "a honyocker." She wasn't exactly sure of the meaning, but she knew the term to be uncomplimentary. Adam hadn't deserved to be called that awful name, and she wished she had the nerve to apologize. But to apologize, she would have to engage him in conversation, and that was far more difficult than bearing her guilt.

She now turned her flustered gaze away from him and became overly interested in a dry piece of skin on the cuticle of her left thumb.

Adam grinned around at his family. "Pick away. That rain probably brought them out. There must be a hundred."

Josie and Becky knelt and began picking the smooth, brown-capped mushrooms. Sarah danced around excitedly, stubbing her toe at one point and howling in indignation. Adam spared a moment to give her a consoling hug, then went back to collecting. Samantha, thinking the mushrooms looked like ugly toadstools, sat off to the side and watched.

Arn squatted close to her, apparently feeling his job had been to fetch more pickers, not pick the mushrooms himself. "Ma will cook those in butter, then mix 'em in with some gravy to pour over potatoes or cornbread stuffing." Arn's cheeks blotched pink, and he whisked a sideways glance at Samantha. "They're really good."

Samantha hadn't spent any time near Arn. He seemed gangly and awkward to her with his long limbs that hadn't yet filled out and a wide face full of freckles. If she was going to choose the company of any of the Klaassen males, she'd probably pick Teddy since he was small and unassuming—and if she had to, she could beat him up. But Arn sat looking at her expectantly, as if a reply would be a gift. So she gathered her courage and ventured to ask, "Do you eat them a lot?"

Arn shook his head, making his cowlick bounce above his forehead. "No, they're pretty hard to spot. We look at 'em as pretty much of a treat."

That explained why they'd all come running. "How'd you find them this time?"

Arn chuckled low in his throat. "I didn't. It was Rosalee."

Josie quickly looked over at them. "Rosalee?"

"Yep." Arn turned to Samantha. "Hilarius Schwartz is our nearest neighbor, and Rosalee is his old milk cow." He shifted to address his siblings. "She wandered clear over here this morning, and Pa asked me to herd her back before Hilarius called out the sheriff. When I was taking her home, I spotted the mushrooms."

Becky wiped at a trail of sweat running from her temple. "Maybe we should take a few to Hilarius as a thank you. Or maybe Rosalee too."

Josie and Arn exchanged glances. They chorused, "Or maybe not." All of the Klaassens laughed together.

Josie said, "We'll think of another way to thank them," and this brought another shared chuckle.

Samantha watched Adam tie a knot in the top of the burlap sack, now full of the funny-looking plants, and toss it over his shoulder. Those mushrooms must be pretty special. The Klaassens had decided they wanted to keep the mushrooms all to themselves.

As she followed the others back to the farm, trailing well behind Adam, she decided maybe she'd stick around just one more night. She could start out fresh after a good night's rest. Besides, she had a sudden hankering to sample some of those mushrooms.

*T*he mushrooms proved to be sumptuous fare indeed. By the end of the meal, Samantha's stomach was aching. They'd feasted on fried pork, stewed tomatoes, fresh ears of corn, and cornbread stuffing which they doused with the delicious brown mushroom gravy. Samantha could hardly believe that the Klaassens had produced every last bit of food on the table themselves.

She had discovered they raised and butchered their own hogs and chickens, kept a massive garden, canning enough vegetables to last the winter, had their own wheat ground into flour, and cared for three cows that provided milk and butter for their own needs as well as for Simon's brother Hiram and his wife in town. All this, plus raising a money crop of corn along with the wheat. And of course the work of keeping up a house—one with a couple of additions jutting out as their family grew—and caring for horses besides. If she hadn't seen with her own eyes how much Mr. and Mrs. Klaassen genuinely loved their children, she'd suspect they'd had a big family just for the help in keeping the farm running smoothly.

After supper Samantha joined the female family members in clearing the dishes and preparing for the washing up. The idea of accepting charity still stuck in her craw, so helping out with the chores, she figured, took care of their providing her with meals. Besides, it helped pass the time.

Before the meal Arn had brought in a big kettle of water to heat, so hot water was all ready for the task. "Josie, you and Becky bring in the wash from the lines," Mrs. Klaassen told

the two. "Since the sheets weren't dry before supper, you two now can get the beds made while Frances, Sarah, and I do the dishes."

Josie dropped the dishrag in the sink and moved toward the door. "Sure. I'd rather make beds and fold laundry than wash dishes any day." She and Becky headed outside.

Sarah cast a hopeful look in her mother's direction. "Can I make bedth, too, Mama?"

Mrs. Klaassen smiled at the cherub. "Why, certainly, *liebchen*." She tapped the end of Sarah's nose with a finger. "You can make your own bed *after* the dishes are done."

Sarah stuck out her lip in a pout, but when no one paid any attention to her, she trotted over to the dry sink and began stacking dirty plates together.

Mrs. Klaassen scraped bits off a bar of lye soap into the enamel wash pan and swished her hand through the water to make some suds. She turned her head toward Samantha. "What are your plans now, dear?"

Samantha blinked. "Well, ma'am, I reckon since my clothes are clean again, I'll just be on my way. I reckon I've eaten up enough of your food by now."

Mrs. Klaassen set the bar of soap aside. "Oh, no, that's not what I'm worried about at all. I'm thinking about you, dear, and how you'll manage. I'm assuming you don't have a definite destination in mind?"

Samantha bit down on her lower lip. Sometimes when Laura talked, she sounded like a fancy lady, and the words didn't match the picture of a farmer's wife. She couldn't decide how to respond.

Mrs. Klaassen's face softened. "Have you thought about where you'll settle?"

Samantha's cheeks heated. "No, ma'am. Not exactly yet."

Lifting the steaming kettle from the stove, Mrs. Klaassen sloshed more water into the waiting wash pan. "I've been thinking. You'll need money for the journey, and money to pay for lodging once you've decided where to stay. I can imagine you're a little low on cash. Am I right?" She sent a sideways look at Samantha, her eyebrows high.

The heat in Samantha's face increased. She offered a hesitant nod.

"It seems to me that before you leave, you will need some money."

Suspicion rose in Samantha's mind. She backed up two steps. "I know I've been eating an' sleeping here, but I won't take money from you too. Don't ask me to do that, ma'am, because I won't."

Mrs. Klaassen reached for a dishtowel and dried her hands. Then she caught Samantha by the shoulders and looked her straight in the eyes. "Frances, I wouldn't shame you by offering you money."

Samantha stiffened beneath the woman's hands, but Mrs. Klaassen held firmly.

"I was going to offer you a chance to *earn* some traveling money."

Samantha gulped. "Earn it?"

Mrs. Klaassen turned back to the wash pan. After instructing Sarah to be careful with the glasses, she said, "You see, as Sarah told you, our daughter Liz is expecting her first child. Now, I would dearly love to go and spend a few days with her after the baby is born. But this is such a busy time of year I can't afford to be gone. Too many vegetables are awaiting canning, and school will start soon so I must get clothes ready for the children. Then there's all the work that goes with harvest. . . . There are too many needs here to be met for me to be somewhere else right now."

Samantha lifted the glasses Sarah had dried and stacked them in their places on the cupboard shelves. "Can't—can't Josie stay with Liz?"

"She could, if she weren't going to be in school." Mrs. Klaassen pulled a soapy plate from the pan and set it aside. "This will be Josie's last year of schooling, and then she'd like to test for a teaching certificate. It's important for her not to miss any of the school year if she plans to teach. Besides, I depend on Josie for help with canning and sewing. She can't be spared either. I'm thinking Liz could use your very capable hands, Frances."

Samantha couldn't help a quick glance at her hands. She'd never thought of herself in the same sentence with a fancy word like *capable*. She moved on about her task, thinking. She paused in front of the possum-belly cabinet that housed the larger bowls, chewing on the inside of her lip. It would be nice to have some traveling money, to be able to buy food instead of steal it. But by taking the job, she'd be stuck here in Mountain Lake for a while longer—maybe a *long* while longer.

Samantha turned back to Laura. "I'd like to dwell on it some, if I could. Maybe meet Liz and see how we'd get on and such . . ."

Mrs. Klaassen reached out a damp hand to Samantha's cheek. "That sounds very sensible, a practical approach to your decision. You sleep on it, and I'll pray about it. The Lord will let you know the best thing to do."

The older two girls trooped through the back door, full baskets in hand. Mrs. Klaassen reached toward Sarah, trailing behind. "Come along now, *liebchen*. We'll make your bed."

Samantha watched the mother and daughters turn the corner of the stairs. Her cheek still tingled from the whisper-touch of Laura's hand. There hadn't been time to back up and avoid it, and emotion built in her chest at the longing the touch inspired. She put the last of the dishes in the cupboard and headed out to her favorite spot—the porch swing behind the lilac bushes—to give this job idea some serious thought.

❧

Saturday began with an announcement from Si that they'd all pitch in to get usual chores done as quickly as possible, then everyone out to the fields to make up time for the days they'd lost to rain. Rather than whining, the children all brightened and flew around getting things in order. Mrs. Klaassen supervised the preparation of a picnic lunch, and finally they climbed into the green-sided wagon for the trip out to work on the harvest.

Samantha stuck close to Josie, following her lead on what needed to be done and how to do it—mostly gathering wheat stalks for the boys to fasten into bundles and stack for drying. She was as glad as anyone when it was time to stop for their lunch.

By the time the little team of harvesters had returned to the farmhouse and eaten a quick meal of leftovers, Samantha could hardly climb the stairs, she was so tired. She discovered, though, that Saturday night was bath night in preparation for Sunday, so she reluctantly joined in the ritual. Actually, it felt kind of good to be clean from head to toe once again.

The next morning, Samantha awoke to a whirlwind of activity. Everyone flew around, readying themselves for church. The night before, Mrs. Klaassen had given everyone's shoes a going-over with a cold biscuit so they'd be shiny for the service. Talking all the while, she'd also found a fresh, clean "dress of Liz's that doesn't fit her anymore and would fit you just perfectly, Frances. . . ." and she couldn't get a word in edgewise about not accepting any more "charity."

Now Sarah was in a tizzy because she couldn't find her good hair ribbons, and Teddy had pulled a button from his pants. There was some discussion about whether a button could be reattached on the Lord's Day, but they soon decided "yes" when Adam reminded them of the scripture about a cow being pulled out of a hole on the Sabbath, ". . . and we sure wouldn't want his britches to fall down in church," Adam finished to gales of laughter.

"Josie, grab a needle and thread and help Teddy with his button." Mrs. Klaassen swept a wet rag over the crumb-spattered table top. "Sarah, stop sniffling and go look under your bed. That's where we found your ribbons the last time. All right, Teddy, no need to remove your trousers, just hold still. Josie won't stick you." Samantha would have yanked out her hair in frustration had she been in charge, but Mrs. Klaassen seemed to take it all in stride.

Samantha had found a pair of black lace-up shoes to wear over borrowed stockings at the end of the bed that morning. Josie offered to braid her hair, but since her hair was clean and extra curly, Samantha simply brushed the front of it back from her face and tied the rest of it with a ribbon loaned by Becky. She felt fresh and ready to face the day. Of course, if she'd had a choice, she'd be wearing her own overalls and shirt and wouldn't be going to church at all. But everyone seemed to expect it of her, and she decided it was best to go along with the tide rather than create more conflict for Mrs. Klaassen.

After a cold breakfast of biscuits and jam, everyone climbed into the back of the clean hay wagon and settled in amongst the piles of straw Adam had thrown in for the occasion. The Klaassens sang all the way to church, rivaling the goldfinches that sang from the fence lines as they rattled by. Everywhere Samantha looked, fields of golden wheat stretched toward the horizon. The wind passed across the prickly tops of the shafts, creating a soothing waving motion she found pleasing.

Josie had told Samantha that with harvest here, all the men in the community pitched in to help in their neighbors' fields. According to Josie, this was an exciting time for the community, and when it was complete, there would be a big party at the schoolhouse to celebrate. Josie seemed to assume that Samantha would still be here by then, but Samantha wasn't so sure. *All depends on how well Liz and me get along*, she told herself.

At the south edge of town, they drove up to a simple white clapboard building with a door on each side of the front. Mr. Klaassen drew the wagon alongside many others lined up in the grassy area at the side of the building. It seemed as if the whole town turned out for services.

Samantha wasn't much of a churchgoer. As a small child she had gone with her gran, but Pa hadn't shown any interest in taking her or David after Gran died, so Samantha had stayed home. Everyone here looked as spit-shined as the Klaassens, and Samantha surmised they'd all turned out in their best clothes. Ladies wore straw bonnets with little flowers, and most men had on black coats over their white shirts even though the late August heat was stifling. Men and women were separating as they walked toward the building, the men entering the door on the right, the women and young children on the left. Samantha turned to Josie to ask about the practice, but the bell in the tower began ringing loudly, making conversation impossible.

Adam helped Sarah and Becky over the edge of the wagon, then reached a hand to Samantha, but she braced herself on the edge and leaped out without his assistance. The dreadful memory of their Main Street tussle filled her mind, and she couldn't meet Adam's gaze. Would any of these churchgoers recognize her as the same girl who'd been rolling in the dirt with Adam just a few days ago?

The Klaassen family took up quite a bit of space as they entered from the assigned doors and met in the aisles. The two parents ushered their offspring toward what must have been familiar benches. Samantha followed blindly, eager to find an inconspicuous spot to sit. Hovering between Josie and Becky, Samantha watched Laura move into the center aisle to greet with a hug a pretty young woman. As the pair pulled apart, she realized the young woman had Laura's soft brown eyes and long, thin nose—plus a popping belly. This must be Liz, and the good-looking tall man her husband, Jake. Samantha examined them through squinted eyes. They were a nice-looking couple, and they held hands even in the church. Embarrassed, Samantha turned away.

"Let's sit," Becky said, pushing Samantha with her elbow.

She plopped herself onto a backless bench between Sarah and Becky, with Laura, Josie, and Liz taking up the rest of the bench to Sarah's left. Samantha peeked back over her shoulder and realized with a start that the whole left section of the church was filled with women, and the right was all men. What an odd setup. But there wasn't time for further wondering, for things were starting.

She did her best to pay attention, but Sarah and Becky kept leaning across her lap to whisper. Each time Laura would look over and frown. The unpadded benches were not comfortable, and she was relieved when they stood up for hymn singing. She couldn't join in the songs, however, because they sang in some foreign language—German, she surmised, from having heard Mr. and Mrs. Klaassen converse in similar words at their home. So she stood silently, listening to the others.

Mrs. Klaassen's pure soprano carried above the others, accompanied by Josie's pleasant alto. Adam and Frank's resonant voices drifted from across the aisle. Samantha experienced a tingle of pleasure. Obviously they all enjoyed singing, and even though there wasn't a hymnbook in sight, not a one of them seemed to miss a note or a word. They looked as familiar with church and its goings-on as they were with their own backyards. Her brow puckered as she considered if attending these services made them so different from people she knew back home, most of whom weren't churchgoers by any means.

Afterward, no one rushed to leave. They all milled around outside, gathering in small groups to visit. Samantha found herself corralled with Josie and a small cluster of giggling girls who peeked over their shoulders at a larger group of young men in which Adam seemed to be the center.

A husky youth with a shock of red hair poked Adam in the chest, said something behind his hand the girls couldn't hear, then threw back his head and laughed. The other boys joined in, and Adam shrugged, pushing the toe of his boot into the loose dirt.

Someone tapped Samantha on the shoulder, and she turned to face a petite young woman with sparkling blue eyes, a tiny upturned nose, and full rosy lips. A wondrous mass of glossy black curls framed her face, contrasting shockingly with her bright eyes. She was by far the prettiest girl Samantha had ever seen, but the prettiness was spoiled by a haughty angle to her head, the hint of a superior glint in her eye, and a snooty twist to her lips. Samantha was immediately on guard.

"Aren't you the girl who tried to steal from the mercantile last week?" the girl asked.

Anger flashed inside Samantha's chest and created a rush of fire in her face.

Josie stepped forward. "Priscilla, this is Frances Welch, and she's staying with us." Josie's tone said far more than her words.

Priscilla tossed back her curls. "So nice to meet you, Frances." Her tone dripped vinegar. She held her chin at a pert angle, fixing Samantha with narrowed eyes. "But you didn't answer me. Was that you?"

Samantha clenched her fists. "It was me. But I don't see how it's any of your business."

Priscilla held up her hands in a mock show of apology. "Oh, dear, I didn't mean to offend you." A sly grin flickered over her face. "I heard Adam carted home another stray—this time one caught stealing. I just wondered if it might be you. I meant no harm."

Josie put her arm around Samantha's shoulders and tried to pull her away, but Samantha shrugged it off. "He didn't *cart* me home; he invited me. I'm not a stray. And I'm smart enough to know you *do* mean harm, all right. But you don't bother me any. I'm used to your ilk and worse. So you can just keep your wonderings to yourself."

Priscilla gave a little giggle and turned to the other girls who had the grace to duck their heads in embarrassment. "I seem to have offended poor Frances here. Actually, I envy her. Wouldn't I love to be chased down the street by Adam Klaassen and then be taken home by him. Oh, my." She fanned herself with both hands.

"Come on." Josie steered Samantha toward their wagon. "Don't pay any attention to Priscilla Koehn. She's nothing but trouble. She's had her eye on Adam since we were in pinafores, but if Adam ever so much as *looks* at Priscilla, I declare I'll never speak to him again."

Becky clomped along beside them. "Give Adam credit for some sense. He knows Priscilla's nothing but a fickle flirt."

Samantha sent a withering glance over her shoulder. Priscilla stood within the circle of girls, jabbering away. "Makes me no never-mind," Samantha spat out. "But *she* better stay outta my way."

Samantha seethed all the way back to the farm, and not until the dinner dishes were cleared and the scripture cake served did she relax her tense jaw. By then her teeth ached from being tightly clenched, and she wished she'd never stepped foot in that church. Her speculations that churchgoing was what made this family unique were completely wrong. That awful Priscilla attended church, but she didn't possess the sweet spirit that marked the Klaassens. *It has to be something else, but what?*

The family retired to the parlor after dessert to relax and enjoy the one day of the week that wasn't filled with endless chores. Mr. and Mrs. Klaassen sat together on the camelback sofa with Sarah snug between them, drowsing against her father's chest. Teddy and Arn sat on the floor near the bay window, each with a leaflet in hand, reading. Josie ran an embroidery needle through a piece of muslin in a wooden hoop, creating a circle of flowers, and Becky leaned over her shoulder, providing unasked-for advice.

Frank disappeared upstairs for a nap after stating his plans to use the buckboard later to visit his girlfriend, Anna Harms. Adam perched on the seat of the bay window, trying to read over Arn's shoulder. Jake and Liz had joined the family for Sunday dinner and now shared the narrow courting bench across from the sofa. With Liz's extra girth, it was a tight fit, but neither of them seemed to mind.

Samantha sneaked upstairs and changed into her own set of clothes—clean, but still as oversized as ever and of course nothing like the frock she wore to church. She returned and stood in the parlor doorway, unwilling to intrude upon the family scene but also reluctant to stay away.

Laura motioned for her to come in. She gently pushed Sarah onto Si's lap and scooted over to create a slice of space. "Here, Frances, sit down. Liz and I were just talking about you."

Samantha prickled. Had they heard what Priscilla said after church?

"We wondered if you'd decided yet whether to stay and work for Liz," Laura began.

Samantha released a sigh of relief. She slid into the edge of the sofa, her hands in her lap. "I'm not sure. . . ."

Liz sent a beseeching look in Samantha's direction. "I'd love it if you could, Frances. Truthfully, even though the baby isn't here yet, I could use your help now. I'm so big, it's hard just to pull myself around. Jake has had to take on many of my chores—"

"And he's not complaining." Jake placed a kiss on his young wife's temple.

Liz smiled at him and patted his hand. "Which he's done cheerfully, but it makes for an awful lot of work for one person." She shifted her gaze to Samantha again. "He has his own work to do, and he really doesn't have the time to spare for mine."

Jake linked his fingers through Liz's. "She's right, Frances. I've kept up so far, but mostly because of the rain we've had. Now that things are drying out and we'll be starting harvest, Liz needs someone close at hand. We'd both appreciate it—a lot—if you could help us out."

Samantha hesitated, looking from Liz to Mrs. Klaassen. As much as she needed the money, should she stay in one spot for so long? She didn't know how to ask how long she'd be needed without having to explain her reasons.

Jake said, "As for wages, I was thinking four dollars a week. We can raise that after the baby's born, as I'm sure your workload will increase then."

Samantha gawked at Jake. "Oh, no. That's more'n enough. That's plenty, even *after* the baby's born. I just—well, I don't know how long I can stay around here. How long do you reckon you'll need my help?"

Liz and Jake looked at each other. Liz shook her head and shrugged. "I'm really not sure. I've never had a baby before. Mother was up and around in three weeks or so after her children were born. Could you stay that long?"

Samantha chewed her lip. Three weeks . . . Pa could cover a lot of territory in three weeks. And that baby wasn't even here yet. But if she had three weeks' worth of wages in her pocket, maybe she could buy a train ticket and get clear across country. Pa'd *never* find her then.

"I'll hire on," Samantha blurted. "I'll just go with you folks when you go home tonight and stay till the baby's born and Liz's back on her feet."

"Wonderful!" Liz broke into a relieved smile and leaned against Jake, who squeezed her shoulders and beamed down at her.

Laura Klaassen patted Samantha's knee. "Thank you, Frances. You're an answer to prayer."

Those words wove a web of pleasure around Samantha's heart. Heat rose from her chest to her face, and she ducked her head, too embarrassed to meet anyone's gaze. Had anyone ever said something as kind to her before? Face aimed downward, she made a silent vow to prove the woman's confidence in her was well placed for the time she remained here. She'd leave them with no regrets for having placed such trust in her.

amantha easily settled in with Liz and Jake. Neither of them was much older than she—Liz only twenty and Jake one year older than that—but they seemed eons older in life experience.

They lived in a small, square house with a room that served as both kitchen and parlor, a back bedroom, and a small pantry lean-to on the ground floor. A narrow stairway split the little house down the middle and led to two small attic rooms. Since the upstairs rooms were tucked in under the rafters, the ceiling slanted on either side of the door, ending with a four-foot-high wall. Across from the door was one small four-pane window, the frame of which was painted white and covered with a bleached muslin curtain.

The walls and ceiling had been plastered by Jake and his father, and wide pine planks formed the floor over which Liz had thrown several small rag rugs for color and warmth. Next to the door in the room Samantha used was a narrow bachelor's chest that held her meager belongings—Laura had insisted she bring along the borrowed clothing from her time at the Klaassens—and a white iron single bed pressed beneath the eave. Beside the bed was a small washstand with a china pitcher and bowl, both of which carried chips but were more than serviceable. The room, though unpretentious and without unnecessary trappings of any kind, was paradise to Samantha.

Samantha's room was to the left of the stairs, and Liz had been fixing up the other one for the baby. But poor Liz was so awkward and heavy now, it was too hard for her to get up there.

So it became Samantha's job to finish the curtain hanging and furniture placement. Liz had already painted the walls a pale yellow, and Jake had moved a handmade cradle that had been used by several Klaassens, a dresser, and an oak rocker into the room. Samantha hung the curtains of goldenrod calico and arranged the furniture, delighting in her part to ready the room for the new little one.

Liz spent most of her time in the kitchen rocker, stitching sheets and tiny gowns and flannel diapers. The pile of baby things grew in the basket beside Liz's feet over the course of the day, and in the evenings Samantha carried everything upstairs, cradling it in her arms with great care, to put it all away.

Samantha's days, though quite full of duties, were pleasant. Some of the work was hard; she was responsible for all the housecleaning, the gardening chores, washing clothes, feeding the chickens, and milking the cow. Since she had been largely responsible for her own little house back in Wisconsin since she was quite young, she found no difficulty in meeting the demands of her new job, but she'd never realized how pleasant tasks could become when performed for people who appreciated your efforts and weren't adverse to saying so. At night she fell into bed blissfully exhausted with words of thanks echoing in her ears. She'd never been happier.

"Frances," Liz said on the fourth morning of Samantha's employment, "how would you like to make blueberry preserves today?"

Samantha hunched up one shoulder. "I never done—did— that before. I don't reckon I could do it on my own. Might mix something up."

Liz heaved herself with difficulty from her rocker and swayed across the floor. She placed her hand on Samantha's shoulder. "I realize I've been more than just a wee bit lazy lately, but I would not expect you to do something as time consuming as making blueberry preserves on your own."

Samantha's lips twitched into a small smile. "Well, if you're helping, I reckon I can do it. Should I pick the berries now?"

Liz nodded. "Yes. It's been wonderful to eat fresh berries this summer, but they won't keep through the winter unless they're made into preserves, so we better hop to it. I'd pick with you, but I just can't take the heat these days—makes me so dizzy. Besides, bending over . . ." They looked at each other and laughed.

Samantha had never considered the miseries that went along with carrying a child. She glanced at Liz's swollen belly, hoping it was all worth the trouble. "You just sit and stitch on some of your baby things. I'll fetch a basket from the cellar and get to pickin'. It won't be so bad in the morning—sun's not so high and hot yet."

The humidity was certainly high, though, Samantha realized, and by nine o'clock her clothes bore damp patches from perspiration, and sweat ran down her forehead in rivulets that stung her eyes and tickled her temples. Strands of hair worked loose from her braid and fell across her damp cheeks. She longed to stop and fetch a cool drink, but determination kept her hunched over the plants, pulling ripe berries from their hiding spots among thick green leaves, stopping occasionally to swat a mosquito.

She'd filled one basket, and was well on her way to filling a second, when a shadow crossed her path. She shielded her eyes with one hand and looked up, expecting Liz had come out to check how things were going. But Adam stood over her wearing his familiar straw hat and easy grin. "Well, you're certainly hard at it," he commented, leaning over to pick a handful of berries and bring them to his mouth.

Samantha shoved back the errant wisps of hair flying around her face. What a sight she must be, her hands as dirty as her overalls, and and hair standing on end. But if Adam thought she looked a mess, he gave no indication.

"Use a little help?"

Samantha watched his teeth bite through the fruit. A tiny spurt of juice came out the side of his mouth and ran down his chin. He brought the back of his hand up to catch it, grinning all the while. Samantha surprised herself by asking, "With picking or eating?"

Adam's eyebrows rose toward the sky, and after a moment of dead silence, he snatched the hat from his head, banged it against his knee twice, and let out a whoop that startled Samantha as much as her teasing must have surprised him.

"Maybe a little of both." He lifted out another plump blueberry, but this time he offered it to her.

She looked at the berry held with the tips of his fingers, then up into his smiling face. His brown eyes sparkled at her in a friendly manner. Hesitantly she gave a quick flash of a smile in return, took the blueberry, and popped it into her mouth. The warm sweetness exploded against her tongue, and she closed her eyes. "Mmmm."

When she opened her eyes again, Adam was still beside her, his eyes glued to her face, his hat back in place on his head.

"So, Frances . . ." His unwavering gaze warmed her more than the sun beaming overhead. "Do you want my help?"

Her heart pounded hard beneath the bib of her overalls. "Uh, are you sure you can spare the time?"

"Wouldn't be here if I couldn't."

Samantha let her gaze sweep across the remainder of the berry bushes. "There is a heap of picking to be done."

With a nod, Adam scooped up a basket and headed to the opposite side of the patch. Samantha watched him go, flustered yet pleased that he had come. She gave herself a little shake. *Quit thinking that way about him. If he knew how your thoughts were flying, he'd turn tail and run. Now get to work.*

Reluctantly, she turned back to her task, allowing herself only an occasional peek at her helper.

～◯

Adam stood side by side with Frances at Liz's sink. He sorted and removed any stems from the berries then dropped them into the sink basin for Frances to wash. Her hands moved steadily between the sink and a large kettle, her lips tipped into a slight curve that might be contentment. Adam had a hard time keeping his focus on the berries. What a change her days with Liz and Jake had already brought to the girl's demeanor.

Although Frances was still wearing those overalls and ungainly shirt, she'd pulled her hair back into a sweet, feminine braid tied with a bit of yellow yarn. Her lips, which she'd usually kept set in a grim line, formed a gentle curve that softened her entire face. Steam from the kettle raised a sheen of perspiration, highlighting the pale freckles dancing across the bridge of her nose. Sunlight slanted through the window above the sink and brought out the golden shimmers in her red-brown hair. Curling dark lashes threw a soft shadow on high cheekbones, and her blue eyes were almost luminous in the bright light. What a pretty girl she was.

Adam smiled to himself. He'd known Liz would be a good influence on Frances. Only thirteen months separated him from Liz in age, so he was closer to her than his other brothers and sisters—agewise and otherwise. The two favored one another in looks, with their brown eyes and sandy hair that insisted on curling. Both were good-natured as well as deep thinkers, and sometimes found they knew what the other was pondering without saying a word.

Adam glanced quickly again at Frances. Being with Liz had erased the deep furrow of distrust from her brow. Twice he had heard soft chuckles as she and Liz exchanged idle chitchat and Liz offered instructions on the task at hand. The sullen exterior had all but disappeared, and while Adam couldn't say she seemed cheerful, she did appear to be peaceful. Frances had needed gentling as well as encouragement, and clearly Liz had offered both. He intended to give his sister a very long, very grateful hug for working this small miracle in his small foundling's attitude. Of course he would never say "his foundling" out loud.

Adam handed the last of the berries to Frances, then turned to Liz. "They're all ready for the pot. Finally!" He swiped his hand across his brow. "Should we cook them now?" He liked the sound of that "we."

Liz stopped the clack-clack of her knitting needles. "Yes, but mash them a bit first so they'll cook faster. Measure equal parts of berries and sugar, then boil them until the sugar is dissolved and the juice looks clear and shiny." She gestured to the tiny lean-to off the kitchen. "I have a second boiler pot out there. Would you get it, Adam, please? You'll be able to go twice as fast with two kettles. And, Frances, you know where the sugar is. I hope there'll be enough left in the barrel to finish the preserves today. Jake and his sweet tooth . . ." She shook her head, smiling indulgently. "I go through more sugar for the two of us than Mother did with all of us underfoot."

Adam and Frances moved to obey. Adam nearly tripped over her, and he caught her shoulders to keep himself from stumbling. Her face lifted and their gazes collided. His heart gave an odd hiccup. Something flickered in her eyes—apprehension? Awareness? He stepped aside quickly, his face flaming. She scuttled toward the pantry, and he ducked into the lean-to. He swept a shaky hand through his hair, giving himself a mental kick. He needed to be careful. *No sense giving her ideas* . . . or himself, for that matter.

Pot in hand, he returned to the kitchen, determined to help with the preserves and then go home before he made a *complete* fool of himself. He stood by while Frances scooped rinsed blueberries into the pots cup by cup, counting out loud along with her. He measured out a matching number of the sugar, then lifted both pots onto the stove. The heat of the stove combined with the heat of the day made the room nearly unbearable. Adam went around propping open the front door, the lean-to door, and all the windows in the house as well.

Liz watched him over the snarl of yellow yarn filling her lap. "I realize we need the breeze, dear brother, but now the dust will come through here and ruin the cleaning job Frances completed yesterday afternoon."

"Then I'll shut it back up." Adam reached for the window above the dry sink.

Frances grabbed his sleeve. He shot her a startled look, and she pulled back quickly. Clasping her hands against the bibbed front of her overalls, she licked her lips. "C-can you just leave it open? The breeze feels good, an' I can always dust again. I'd rather feel cooler. The air an' all . . ."

Liz cleared her throat. Adam flicked a glance in her direction and caught a worried pinch in her brow. Heat rose in his cheeks that had nothing to do with the temperature in the room. Turning away from his sister's questioning look, he saw Frances pull the collar of her flannel shirt away from her neck as she stirred the cooking preserves with a long-handled wooden spoon.

Sympathy replaced the awkwardness of the previous moment. "I bet you're really warm in that getup. Wouldn't you rather change into something else?"

"Don't have anything else. Your ma tried to get me to bring the two nice dresses she borrowed to me. . . . Not so good for workin' in, I told her."

Adam turned to Liz. "Don't you have an old summer dress Frances could wear for these chores? She's cooking faster than the berries are."

But now Liz wasn't paying any attention to him. She drew in a breath and clutched at her distended belly with two hands, dropping the half-finished baby afghan to the floor.

"Liz!" Adam darted across the kitchen and knelt beside her chair. He took her hand, and she clung hard, her eyes closed and lips forming a thin line. It seemed a lifetime passed before his sister relaxed her hold on his fingers. Little beads of sweat had popped out across her forehead, and a weak smile creased her face.

"Oh, my, that one was a whopper."

Adam frowned. "Whaddaya mean, *that* one?" Realization dawned. He scrambled to his feet. "You're having pains?" At Liz's nod, he stepped back, his fists on his hips. "How long has this been going on, missy?"

"Awhile."

"*Awhile*?" Adam threw his hands wide, fear and irritation fighting inside his chest. "Why, tell me, have you been messing around here, preserving berries and who knows what else, for Pete's sake? You should be in bed—"

"Adam, you sound like a mother hen." Liz shook her head, her expression calm. "I hope you're ready to calm down now and quit your scolding, because you're about to become an uncle."

Adam gulped. Cold sweat broke out over his body. "You mean . . . it's *time*?"

She laughed, increasing his ire. "Yes, it's time, and don't look like that, Adam. You didn't think I was going to carry this baby forever, did you?"

"Well . . . well . . ." Adam's anger dissolved, but he couldn't gather his thoughts.

At the stove, Frances had swung around, spoon in hand, with berry juice dripping onto the kitchen floor.

"Watch out, Frances—the spoon is making a mess on the floor," Liz said. She gave Adam a pointed look. "Help me into bed, then get Jake for me. I want him here. After that, run for Mother. I'm not having this baby without her."

Adam remained rooted in place, muscles too stiff with shock to move.

Liz pushed herself out of the rocker and slugged Adam on the arm. "Adam! For goodness' sake, stop acting like a ninny. You've been around at enough birthings to keep your wits about you this time."

Adam grabbed a deep breath. "Oh! Yes. Of course." He placed a shaky arm across her back and guided her to the bedroom. She sat on the edge of the bed, and he lifted her feet as carefully as if they were formed of spun glass, settling them on the mattress.

She nestled against the pillows. "Thank you, Adam."

"Now I'll get Jake." He moved to the door. "And then Mother." He returned to the side of the bed. He didn't know what to do with his hands, so he stuffed them into his trouser pockets.

Liz sighed. "Adam, Jake is in the east field, and Mother is probably at home in her kitchen. Do you think you can find them?"

Adam darted to the door again. "Yes, sure, I'll get them. I won't be long." Then he stomped back and delivered a kiss to his sister's forehead. "Take it easy, Sis."

Liz touched his cheek, a smile on her face. "*You* take it easy—I'm fine, really. And Frances is here with me, you know."

Samantha stepped into the doorway, the wooden spoon clutched in both hands. "What—what can I do for you?"

Liz smiled. "Stir the blueberries, Frances. I can't abide burnt preserves."

*I*f anyone had stopped to think about it, they might have found it amusing that the only calm person in the little house was Liz, who had the best reason for being distressed. Samantha knew by the low moans escaping Liz's throat that having a baby wasn't easy, but so far Liz seemed to take the whole thing in stride. Between those labor pains, as Liz called them, she smiled at her husband, squeezed his hand, and assured him that she was fine. Whenever another one hit, Jake leaned over his wife, his face contorted, seemingly in pain himself.

When Adam had returned, he'd brought not only Laura, but Si and Josie as well. Samantha watched Adam pause just long enough to peek in at Liz, with Jake now by her side, then rush off again to fetch Dr. Newton. Liz had told him to slow down or he'd give himself heat stroke, adding with a teasing smile that she wanted the doctor focused on her and the baby, not her brother. Adam had quipped back, "You always did have to be the center of attention," and Liz had laughed, then grabbed her midsection, face contorted again.

Samantha was relieved of her berry stirring by Josie, who said she absolutely *had* to have something to do, so Samantha busied herself hauling in water, heating some on the stove, and bringing extra sheets down from the *Schrank*, the shelved wardrobe that sat on the small landing at the top of the stairs. Mrs. Klaassen had indicated these items would be helpful, but no one else seemed to have the ability to go beyond planning to doing.

Josie stirred berries. Mr. Klaassen paced back and forth in the kitchen, hands behind his back, his brow furrowed. Mrs. Klaassen hovered beside Liz's bed, wiping her daughter's face with a cool cloth and murmuring to her in German, words Liz seemed to understand.

Jake kept a grip on his wife's hand, and his face grew more pale with each pain. He asked repeatedly, "When will Doc Newton get here?" No one had an answer.

Samantha, her tasks completed, stood at the window and watched for Adam to return. When she finally spotted him on horseback, followed closely by the doctor's little black buggy, she turned around excitedly. "Adam's here. The doctor, too."

Mr. Klaassen gave a huge sigh and went to the bedroom doorway to relay the news.

Although Adam pulled up first, the doctor beat him to the door. He was a small man with a narrow pencil line of a mustache, green eyes, snub nose, and short-cropped hair that stuck up in the back. His suit was rumpled as if slept in, and his wire-rimmed glasses sat on the tip of his nose in a way that made him appear absent-minded.

He acknowledged the people waiting in the main room of the house with a single nod but didn't slow down for pleasantries. He passed straight to the bedroom. "Jake, kiss your wife, then kindly leave. We'll all do better without you." As Jake reluctantly rose to obey, the doctor said, "Laura, please stay. I'm sure you'll be a comfort to Elizabeth here. And a help to me."

Jake paused in the doorway, and the doctor promptly shut the door in his face. Mr. Klaassen put his arm around his son-in-law's shoulder. "Come sit down, son. Liz is in good hands, and fretting and stewing won't speed things up any."

Samantha hid a smile. Mr. Klaassen was better at giving advice than he was at taking it; as soon as he got Jake settled at the table with a cup of buttermilk from the icebox, he took up his pacing again.

Adam entered the house, sweaty and breathless and smelling of horses. He went to his father. "Is Liz all right?"

Mr. Klaassen barely paused in his back-and-forth trek across the narrow floor. "The doc is in there, and your ma. Liz'll be fine." He paused to squeeze Jake's shoulder on the way by.

Josie turned from the stove. "Frances, where are Liz's canning jars? These preserves are ready to pour."

"In the cellar," Samantha said. She hated the underground cellar with its cobwebs and damp smell. With a little shudder, she reached for the cellar door at her feet.

Adam hurried over. "Let me do that."

Samantha nearly sagged in relief. "Thank you."

As soon as Adam retrieved the wooden box full of canning jars, Samantha slipped them into a large pot of boiling water along with their lids. After the jars were sterilized, Josie filled them and Adam sealed them tight. No banter accompanied their task. All ears were tilted toward the bedroom door, listening for any sound that would give a clue as to what was taking place behind that closed door.

The sparkling jars of preserves marched across the wooden work table like jewels. Lunchtime came and went without anyone even asking about eating. To Samantha, it felt like the whole house was laying in wait.

Late afternoon Mr. Klaassen and Adam headed out to take care of the milking and feeding the chickens and geese. Jake insisted on following them, though Samantha could tell the poor father-to-be was torn. Josie promised to fetch them immediately if anything happened. Josie and Samantha put together ham sandwiches and cut up radishes and carrots to go along with them.

"I'm not hungry," Josie admitted, piling vegetables into one of Liz's serving bowls, "but no one's had a bite since breakfast. We'll not be good for much if we don't eat."

The men returned and ate the simple meal. Samantha nibbled at half of a sandwich. She might have been eating saw-dust for all she noticed it, but she did feel better after having a little something in her stomach.

Mr. Klaassen leaned back in his chair to let Josie reach his empty plate and glanced at the ticking clock on the wall. "After five . . . I guess I'd better run home and check on the children, then—"

A sound cut through the quiet kitchen. Every head turned toward the closed bedroom door. Jake jumped up and placed both hands flat against the paneled door, his face nearly pressed against the wood. Adam half stood, hands tensely pressing the tabletop. Mr. Klaassen covered his mouth with a shaky hand, and Josie reached blindly for Samantha who clutched at her, thankful to have something to hold onto.

Samantha had never heard a noise like that before. Low, guttural—a harsh, anguished sound that cut through the hearts of everyone in the room.

The doctor's voice, tense and authoritative, carried from behind the door. "Come on, Liz, bear down. Push, girl! I need your help."

Jake pressed his forehead to the door. His hands curled into tight fists and thumped at the wood softly. Si went over and placed a hand on the younger man's taut back. Adam crossed to stand between Josie and Samantha, and Josie turned into his chest, leaning against him. Samantha, so caught up in dismay of what could be happening to Liz, unthinkingly moved into his embrace. His arm coiled around her, holding her snug against his side. They stood thus, silent and straining for any further sound that could reassure them.

Then it came—a new, soft, mewling sound that brought joyous smiles to the faces of the listeners. Josie hugged Adam, crying against his neck.

Adam chuckled shakily. "It's all right now. No need to cry." But tears glinted in his brown eyes. A lump filled Samantha's throat. She swallowed hard, trying to dislodge it.

She suddenly became aware of Adam's arm around her waist and stepped quickly away.

The bedroom door opened, and Mrs. Klaassen stepped out. She moved directly into her husband's arms, a weary smile on her face. With her cheek pressed to Mr. Klaassen's chest, she held out her hand to Jake. "Congratulations, Papa, you've got a fine-looking son."

Jake took a deep breath and then smiled so wide the room seemed lit by his happiness. "Can I see him—and my wife?" He turned toward the bedroom door.

"The doctor will call you in just a moment." Mrs. Klaassen stepped away from Mr. Klaassen and wrapped Jake in a hug.

Samantha stood to the side while the others buzzed happily, congratulating Jake and asking Mrs. Klaassen how things had gone. Their happy news sharing ended abruptly, however, when the doctor's voice called out. "Mrs. Klaassen, come here—quickly! I need you."

She shot a panicked look at Mr. Klaassen before disappearing once more into the bedroom and closing the door firmly behind her. Everyone froze in place, not daring to look at one another. Liz's moaning, a baby's weak cry, and the doctor's and Laura's hushed, frantic voices carried from the other room.

Samantha thought her heart might burst, it banged so hard against her ribs. What was happening in there?

Mr. Klaassen stretched his arms wide. "Jake, Adam . . ." His voice, gravelly with emotion, held authority. "Come. Josie, Frances—you, too. Come close. We will pray."

Samantha skittered to the circle and took hold of Josie and Adam's hands. They bowed, their heads almost touching, hands squeezing tightly. Samantha, unfamiliar with praying, wasn't sure what to do, but she found her thoughts begging someone, someplace. *Oh, please, please, let Liz be okay. And the little baby, too. Keep them both safe for Jake—he loves them and needs them so much.*

It seemed hours passed before a creak announced the opening of the bedroom door. Samantha spun toward the opening with the rest of them. The doctor stepped out and released a heavy sigh. He pulled a wrinkled handkerchief out of his pocket and wiped his face.

Jake crossed to him, his fingers woven together. "Dr. Newton, Liz—is she . . . ?"

Dr. Newton reached out and put a hand on Jake's shoulder. "Liz is fine, Jake. She's had a rough time of it. The baby was breech. She'll be down for a while, but she'll be fine."

Jake blew out a relieved breath, then looked straight into the doctor's face. "The baby . . . my son—?"

"That wife of yours is sure one for surprises," the doctor responded with a shake of his head. He expelled a huff of laughter. "Go on in. I think she should be the one to share the news." He headed for the door, still shaking his head and chuckling softly.

Jake frowned in confusion. He stepped into the bedroom and crossed quickly to the bed. Samantha trailed behind the others, straining to peek over their shoulders. Jake sat on the edge of the bed, his broad back blocking Liz from view, but his shout nearly raised the rafters. "Why, Liz Stoesz! No *wonder* you were as big as a house."

A tinkling laugh—Liz's—rang out. "No shouting. You'll wake them."

Samantha's gasp was echoed around the circle crowding against the doorway. *Them?*

The group surged forward. Mr. Klaassen rushed to his wife's side, and Adam and Josie followed, stopping at the foot of the bed. Samantha came more slowly, afraid of intruding but unable to resist. She stood close to Josie and gaped at the extraordinary scene.

Two tiny bundles snuggled securely in Liz's arms. Liz looked pale and weak but undeniably happy. "Can you believe it, Mother? Twins."

Jake beamed. "Two sons, Simon. Liz has given me *two sons*."

Mr. Klaassen leaned in and deposited a kiss on Liz's sweaty forehead. "They're just beautiful, Liz."

Liz smiled. "Yes, they are, Papa. The most beautiful babies ever."

Samantha thought they were about as attractive as newborn baby birds, but she kept the comment to herself. Besides, it didn't seem to matter much what they looked like. They were fine, and Liz was fine. Her heart bumped in her chest. Someone had heard their prayers.

Liz adjusted the blanket more snugly around the baby boy on her right. "We do have a small problem, though."

Jake's eyebrows raised. "How on earth can we have a problem?"

She touched the fuzzy dark hair on the head of the baby on her left. "This one is Jacob Andrew. He was born first, so he should be given the name we chose. But we can't name his brother Amanda Joy, now can we?" A hint of teasing had entered Liz's otherwise frail voice.

Jake laughed and stroked the cheek of the unnamed baby. "No, I suppose we can't." The baby puckered up a tiny mouth and twisted his head within the confines of the blanket.

"So we have a problem," Liz said.

"Not much of one." Jake turned to Adam. "Uncle Adam, how would you feel about having a little namesake?"

Adam looked dumbstruck. "A—a namesake? Why, I—I—."

Liz touched Jake's hand. "Perhaps Adam would like to save that for his own little boy someday, Jake."

Adam shook his head. "No, Liz. I mean, yes, maybe someday I'll have a son, but I never considered naming him after myself. I'd be honored to have the baby given my name."

Jake turned back to Liz. "Little Jacob Andrew was named for my pa and me. How about we name his brother for Adam and your pa's middle name? Adam James?"

Mr. Klaassen nodded sagely. "I like that idea."

"That sounds fine." Liz yawned behind her hand.

Mrs. Klaassen waved her hands at those gathered around the bed. "Come now, everyone out. Liz has labored harder today than any of you, and she needs her rest." She leaned over the bed to kiss first Liz, then the heads of each of her new grandsons. "*Schlop Die gesunt, kleine mudder,*" Mrs. Klaassen whispered.

Josie whispered to Samantha, "She means 'sleep well, little mother.'"

Liz's eyelids drifted closed.

Everyone quietly left the room, Samantha once again trailing behind. When Adam reached the door, he paused and looked back. A smile lifted the corners of his lips, and somehow Samantha knew he was looking at his little namesake.

He turned to her. "It's something, Frances, having a baby named in your honor," he said, his voice low. He placed a palm on his chest. "I feel so proud. And responsible." Sucking in a breath, he lifted his chin. "I want to always be the kind of example little Adam can look up to."

Samantha, observing the determination in Adam's eyes, experienced a funny swelling in her chest. Adam was so unlike the men she'd known before. He could be moved by the coming of a baby, and he wasn't ashamed to show it. He seemed more manly than any of the tough, hard-nosed men in her past.

She closed the bedroom door behind the little group, sealing the new mother and babies away together. Mr. and Mrs. Klaassen each gave Jake a hug, and then Mr. Klaassen asked Adam to hitch the horses back up to the wagon. "We need to head home and share the good news with the others."

Josie caught her mother's hand. "Ma, can I stay here tonight? I can help Frances, and I'd like to hold one of the babies yet before I go home."

Mrs. Klaassen looked at Jake. "Is it all right with you?"

Jake nodded. He stood so tall and proud. "That's fine. She can bunk with Frances, and——." He slapped a palm to his forehead. "Oh, no!"

Everyone started, and Mr. Klaassen bolted forward and grasped Jake's arm. "What's wrong?"

Jake blinked twice, his jaw hanging open. "I just realized— I'm going to need another cradle."

*S*amantha settled into a routine as comfortably as a pair of old slippers. Her days were filled with household chores and garden work that she found to be mostly enjoyable. Her nights were sometimes disturbed by the sound of a tiny cry from downstairs, then another one, but she just put her pillow over her head and went back to sleep.

Liz devoted her time to caring for the two small boys who grew more plump and attractive each day. Samantha loved those times when Liz called to her to hold one of them while she nursed the other. They looked so much alike that most couldn't decide which was Andy and which was A.J., as Jake called them. Liz, however, could determine which one was fussing when a pathetic, hiccupping wail trailed to her ears. These first weeks of their life, they shared the bedroom with their parents, tucked side by side in a dresser drawer set securely on a small table. And Jake was busy fashioning another cradle for when the two would move to the bedroom across from Samantha.

She grew, too, during the last days of summer, in contentment and self-confidence as she successfully handled the responsibilities bestowed upon her. And she did earn that four dollars a week. She'd never canned vegetables before, but with Liz in her rocker, handing out instructions in her patient voice that reminded Samantha so much of Mrs. Klaassen, Samantha put up quart jars of green beans, tomatoes, carrots, and corn. She even pickled beets. She made herself overcome her fears about the cellar, and she couldn't help but smile when she had all those winter provisions lined up on the wooden shelves down below.

She baked bread for the family's consumption, washed loads and loads of tiny flannel diapers and gowns, gathered eggs, kept the house clean. . . . The workload was never-ending, but not once did she complain. When she dropped into bed at night, exhausted, it was a happy exhaustion that she'd not known a person could feel. It was so wonderful to be needed, and to be appreciated, to maybe even be loved. . . .

One thing bothered her, though—living a lie all this time. Samantha admired Liz and Jake and the whole Klaassen family so much, and she wanted to be honest with them and confess she wasn't Frances Welch. At first it had seemed clever to fool them, but as she'd gotten to know them and be accepted into their loving family unit, her conscience pricked each time one of them called her Frances. She longed to tell them who she really was, but one fear always stopped her. Her pa. If they knew her real name, then the sheriff would send her name down the line, and sooner or later Pa would arrive to take her back home.

Home. Already this place, Mountain Lake, Minnesota, was far more home than the house where she grew up had ever been. Even when Gran was alive it hadn't truly been the kind of home where the people within its walls loved and respected one another. Samantha hadn't even known that kind of family was possible until coming to the Klaassens. Gran's loving presence had made those early years bearable, but Samantha knew now all that she had missed.

Whenever her conscience started bothering her again, she got busy with something else and sent those uncomfortable thoughts far away. She wasn't willing to give up what she had now—not just yet.

Harvest was well under way by the second week of September along with the beginning of the school year. Samantha watched children walking along the road early in the morn-

ing, swinging their tin lunch pails and carrying books and tab-
lets. Deep inside she couldn't help but envy them. When Josie
stopped by on the way home in the afternoon for a visit with
her nephews, she reported anecdotes from the school day, and
Samantha secretly wondered what it would be like to go, too.

She'd been a better-than-average student at the school in
Milwaukee. But with the kind of life she lived, she was always a
misfit. School was a lonely place. Samantha wondered if things
would be different here, going with Josie, Arn, and the others.
Then she remembered Priscilla Koehn and decided it was best
to stay away. Besides, once harvest ended, Liz wouldn't need
her any longer. Another four weeks or so, and she'd need to
move on.

But where?

⁓

Adam loved harvest time. Being outside in the fields,
smelling the scent of fresh-cut grain, bantering with the men
with spirits as high as his, working hard and sweating much.
. . . He couldn't help himself. Farming was in his blood, and
he'd been quite young when he knew he would be staying near
the family homestead and farming with his father, taking over
when Pa decided he was too old to continue. Adam had helped
with harvests since his thirteenth birthday, delaying school the
first weeks until the work was done. It had never bothered him
to work rather than be there at the start of school. He always
caught up and never felt at a disadvantage; his education was
in the fields too.

Arn, now fifteen, didn't share Adam's enthusiasm for
farming, however. Adam occasionally caught the younger boy
looking off toward the schoolhouse during those days when

harvesting and school overlapped. He was expected to help with harvest, but he wasn't required to enjoy it. Although Arn was fast developing the husky build of his farm-loving brothers, he didn't possess the farmer's heart. Adam figured when Arn was grown, his vocation would be closer to Daniel's than Pa's. Another man might feel threatened by the realization that his son didn't want to follow in his footsteps, but Adam knew Pa would support Arn's decision in whatever job choice he made, as long as he was satisfied with it.

Adam scraped fallen stalks of wheat together with a long, wooden rake, his thoughts wandering to Liz and Jake's house. He remembered holding little Adam James for the first time. The baby had fit snugly in the crook of his arm, a warm and soft bundle with a certain smell better than his mother's best meal. When he had touched a finger to the baby's palm, A.J. had curled his tiny hand around Adam's work-roughened finger. Liz explained it was a reflex reaction, but Adam preferred to think the little boy was accepting him as his uncle, the one for whom he'd been named.

He remembered something else: when he'd looked up right then, he'd caught Frances watching him with an expression on her face he couldn't quite read. Gentle, tender, and maybe a little sad. When their eyes met, she'd colored prettily and looked away, fussing with her braid in a peculiar way. Had he embarrassed her somehow? The girl remained a puzzle in many ways.

The sullen, defensive girl he'd tackled in the street seemed to be long gone. This new one—although never overtly outgoing—now could offer a warm smile and engage in conversation. He reflected on the morning in the blueberry patch when she'd teased him a little bit. She was uncommonly pretty with that wild mane of hair and unusual pale blue eyes. If the new, warmer, more open side of her was for real, he could imagine being attracted to her. . . .

The thought brought Adam up short. He stopped raking. *Attracted*? Yes, she was appealing, both in looks and personality. That spunk was still there, and from someone so small it was both cute and endearing.

But could he think of her *that way*? An image—the shy way she behaved when he spotted her observing him with the baby—filled his mind. He swallowed. Could it be possible that *she* was thinking of *him* that way . . . ?

"Adam?" His father's voice cut into his thoughts. He turned his head to locate Pa.

"It's not lunchtime yet, son. Keep 'er moving."

Adam nodded and began raking in earnest. He'd have to give his feelings for Frances Welch some serious consideration. *When the work is done.*

∿Ↄ

Wednesday evening at supper time, Jake paused with fork in hand and sent a serious look across the table to Samantha. "Frances, starting tomorrow, I'm afraid you're in for it."

Samantha's stomach turned a flip. She looked up from cutting a bite of her chicken. "What do you mean?"

Jake chuckled. "Don't look so worried, goofy. I'm not planning to string you up by your fingernails. But after the next few days, that might look pretty good, just to get out of the work. Next Monday the harvest crew will begin in my fields. That means you and Liz will be responsible for fixing them breakfast, lunch, and two snacks during the day. It's a heap of cooking, and Liz is still pretty tied down with Andy and A.J. So the majority of the work will fall to you."

Samantha breathed easier, then swallowed. "I'm okay at cooking for *us*, I guess." She glanced across the bowls and serving plates filling the center of the table. The fried chicken was crisp and tasty, the boiled potatoes and gravy passable, and she'd flavored the green beans with some chopped onion. Even her bread was getting to be as good as Liz's had ever been. "But I've never cooked for that many people before. . . ."

Liz reached across little Andy, who nearly dozed at her breast, and patted Samantha's arm. "Now, Frances, one thing you need to keep in mind; when those men come in, they're so hungry you could feed them boot leather. They wouldn't complain as long as you provided salt and pepper to season it. You're a fine cook, and I'll help you judge amounts so we're sure to have enough. I cooked for the last two harvest crews, and I wasn't any older than you the first time. You'll do fine."

Samantha nibbled her lower lip, still uncertain. "Well, if you can supervise, I guess I can do it." Andy had fallen asleep, his little mouth drooping open as he relaxed. She reached for the baby. "Give Andy to me. I'll carry him up to bed so you can eat your supper without droppin' anything on him."

Liz laughed softly and relinquished her bundle. "Thank you. It would be nice to finish my supper without having to lean over a little body."

Samantha cuddled Andy close as she mounted the stairs. It felt good, holding him. At first she'd been nervous to even touch the babies, but Liz had assured her they wouldn't break, and soon she learned the enjoyment of doing things for them. Of course Liz took care of most of their needs, but there were times, like now, when an extra pair of hands was very useful.

Useful. Samantha savored the word. Before coming here, she'd felt more useless than anything. As she tucked Andy into his cradle, Samantha hummed softly. She rubbed Andy's tiny back until she was sure he was sound asleep. Smiling, she leaned down and placed a kiss on the slumbering infant's moist neck, then turned to the other cradle.

Baby A.J. lay on his side, his nearly transparent eyelids quivering. As Samantha watched, he stretched one arm upward toward his nose, curled his hand into a tiny fist, then let it relax again, bringing the arm back down. His rosebud mouth puckered, and he made a soft sucking sound. He was waking, and no doubt would soon squall to be fed.

To be sure he wouldn't disturb his sleeping brother, Samantha scooped him up and tiptoed out of the room. She paused at the top of the stairs, holding the baby nearly beneath her chin, breathing in his scent. Andy and A.J. looked alike—two peas in a pod, Mr. Klaassen laughingly called them—but over the weeks Samantha had learned which was which by observing their distinctive personalities.

A.J. wasn't quite as demanding as his brother—when Andy wanted something, you'd better get it quick or prepare for a storm! A.J. seemed to enjoy snuggling more than Andy, and he was more relaxed—easier to placate. Although she felt stirrings of love for both little boys—in their helplessness, their darling little faces, how could she not?—she admitted to herself that she found herself favoring little Adam.

She walked slowly downstairs with the now-awake baby, who peered up at her curiously. His tiny dimpled hand grazed her cheek, and she tipped her face—better to feel the softness of his palm. Jake certainly had named this baby aptly. He seemed to have inherited his uncle's mild disposition and loving spirit.

Samantha sat back down at the table, A.J. cradled in her arm.

Liz looked over. "Is he ready to eat now?"

"He was waking up, so I brought him down in case he decided to howl." Samantha pressed her cheek to the baby's downy hair. He wriggled, nestling closer, and she smiled. She was learning the joy of touching and being touched by the tiniest of teachers. "I'll hold him while you finish up, long as he stays quiet."

Jake held out his arms. "Here, let me have him, Frances. I've not been around enough during the day lately to really enjoy my boys. I'll hold him while you get the clean-up started."

"Well, I guess his papa can have him," Samantha quipped as she slowly rose and handed little A.J. to Jake.

As she started to pick up the dishes from the table, Jake added, "You'll probably want to turn in early tonight. We're working you extra hard these days until harvest is done."

Samantha nodded. That's why she was here. But *when the crops are in, what then?*

*S*amantha woke promptly at five o'clock Monday morning, the crowing of the rooster signaling the sun's arrival and the dawn of another day helping Liz. She yawned, snuggling into her pillow for an extra few minutes of rest. Then she remembered today was the start of the harvest crew coming to work in Jake's fields. Throwing the covers aside, she hooked her heels over the edge of the mattress and pulled herself out of bed. An all-over stretch completed, she squinted into the early morning gloom.

Her fuzzy gaze located a shadow . . . of something . . . next to the door that hadn't been there the night before. She rubbed her eyes and looked again. A dress. Curious, Samantha lightly ran across the floor and pulled the frock from a nail next to the doorjamb. Holding it toward the little bit of light flowing through her window, she checked it over. Pink-and-white-checked fabric proved faded at the elbows, and the skirt bore a short, stitched-closed tear. So it wasn't new. *Must be a hand-me-down from* Liz.

She fingered the collar, trying to decide what to do. She glanced to the overalls and flannel shirt draped over the small chair in the corner. The bulky clothes were so hot and uncomfortable. And they needed washing—again. It was hard to get the heavy materials dry enough to wear the next morning. She held the dress against herself, imagining how much cooler it would be than the britches and shirt.

The decision made, she slipped out of her nightgown and into the dress. As she fastened the buttons up the front, she

noted it was a bit loose, but she could easily take it in if Liz
loaned her a needle and thread. She pulled on stockings and
boots, then tiptoed down the stairs, wincing at the one that
squeaked. Liz was already at the stove, measuring coffee into
the blue enamel pot. She turned when Samantha entered, and
a smile lit her face.

"You found the dress. Does it fit?"

Samantha smoothed the skirt. "Pretty much."

Liz crossed to Samantha and pinched the fabric, pulling
it away from Samantha's waist. She chuckled. "'Pretty much,'
she says. At least two sizes too big!" She placed her hands on
her hips and shook her head. "You're much smaller than I ever
remember being, even before the twins added to my girth. But
it'll do, I suppose, in a pinch. I can take it in for you when I get
a minute."

Samantha toyed with the buttons, a question hovering in
the back of her mind. She'd been here for several weeks already,
shuffling around in her makeshift clothing. Why was Liz giving
this to her now? Before Samantha lost her nerve, she blurted a
simple question. "Why'd you give it me?"

Liz's cheeks blazed pink. She said, "I should have done it
much sooner, Frances, but, well, Ma said you seemed really determined to wear . . . your own clothing, so I was a little shy
about bringing it up." She turned back to the stove to move the
boiling coffee off the burner.

"So why now?" Samantha pressed.

"Frances, I need to tell you something, but—but I don't
want to hurt your feelings."

Samantha shrugged.

Liz lifted a skillet onto the stove's top and fidgeted with
the handle, her lips pursed in an embarrassed grimace. "Jake
is rather old-fashioned, and while he likes you very much,

he—well, he's a little uncomfortable with you wearing boys' clothes," she finished in a rush.

Samantha felt herself bristling, her defenses rising. "Well, those are all the clothes I've got. I've been so busy, I haven't had time for dress sewing."

Liz stepped toward Samantha, her hands reaching without touching her. "Oh, Frances, I know we've kept you awfully busy, and neither of us is faulting you for the clothes you wear. It's more my fault than anyone's. It's just that—well, with the harvest crew here and all, Jake was hoping I might be able to persuade you to wear one of my dresses." Liz blew out a breath and lifted her hands, palms up. "Some of the men might snicker and poke fun, and we'd feel terrible if you were . . ." She started over. "We'd feel a lot better if you were in a dress. There."

Samantha stared at Liz in amazement. Not once had she imagined that Jake didn't approve of her overalls. They were hot and uncomfortable, but they were the only clothing that was hers. Well, actually, they were "borrowed" too. And while she'd been wishing she had something else to wear, Jake and Liz had been secretly wishing the same thing. Amusement chased her defensiveness away, and she released a bubble of laughter.

Liz offered a lopsided grin. "You aren't upset with me?"

Samantha shook her head. "No, I'm relieved I won't have to drag myself around in those durn overalls one more day."

Liz laughed too and threw an arm around Samantha's shoulders for a quick squeeze. "I'm glad, too." And they shared a smile.

Samantha stepped away from Liz's embrace. "I'll get to the milking now." She scooped up the bucket beside the kitchen stove and headed outside. The sun formed a bold white arc on the horizon, flooding the fields with a shimmer of gold. Samantha paused to admire the sight. A smile tugged at her lips. It'd be a golden day for sure. And she sure would be cooler.

~⊙

Samantha lugged back a pail of milk, and promptly at six o'clock, as Liz had predicted, stomping feet on the front stoop alerted Samantha to the harvesters' arrival. She poured batter into the sizzling pan as Jake threw open the door and shushed the men's greetings with a finger against his lips. "The babies are still sleeping." The men nodded their understanding, walking in as if on eggshells.

Samantha hid an amused grin. Grown men tiptoeing with hunched shoulders and tightly pursed lips looked rather funny. But they wasted no time seating themselves. Normally there were only four chairs at the round table, but Jake had hauled in some old nail kegs and wooden boxes from the barn to create makeshift seating. Eight of the men crowded around the table, their elbows pressed together. The rest caught a seat wherever they could and balanced plates on their laps.

Liz and Samantha served up fried eggs, fried potatoes, pancakes, *zwieback*, and coffee. Samantha stayed beside the stove, frying more pancakes as needed, while Liz made her rounds refilling coffee cups, holding out a jar of preserves for sweetening the *zwieback*, and carrying plates back and forth between the stove and the men needing "just a couple more o' those pancakes" or "a good-size spoon a' them potatoes, please."

Samantha glanced over at the table to see Adam watching her, but he looked away. She would have liked to ask after Mrs. Klaassen, Josie, Becky, and the little kids—but there wasn't the time between the requests for refills.

As Liz prepared to fork the last pancake onto her father's plate, one of the babies upstairs began to tune up. She flicked a glance at Samantha. "Uh-oh . . ."

Samantha took over Liz's tasks, and Liz darted toward the stairs, wiping her hands on her apron as she went.

Mr. Klaassen ignored the pancake on his plate, grinning from ear to ear. "I was hoping they'd wake up before we headed out. Haven't seen those little guys in over a week."

Since it was now unnecessary to be quiet, a big-boned man named Elmer Harms laughed heartily. "I betcha they're growin' like weeds, huh, Jake?"

"Oh, sure," Jake said. "We'll have them out milking cows in another week or so."

The men laughed, then all eyes turned toward the stairway as Liz descended, a baby on each arm.

Samantha moved out of the way as several of them forged forward to take a look at the twins, reaching out thick fingers to poke at tiny tummies or ruffle their downy hair. Andy and A.J. seemed to take it all in with big, curious eyes for about two minutes before deciding being wet and hungry outweighed being cute and entertaining. First Andy opened his mouth to yell, and A.J.—no doubt startled by his brother—joined in. The men backed off, and Liz shut herself in the bedroom with the babies to change their diapers and give them breakfast.

The group began filing out the door, placing empty plates on the dry sink as they went. Adam was last in line. He paused, offering Samantha an apologetic look. "I guess you're the whole cleanup crew, huh?"

"I guess so." Samantha surveyed the pile of dishes, forks, cups, and skillets. She hoped there'd be time to get everything washed before she had to make lunch.

"I'd stay and give you a hand, but . . ." He gestured toward the open door. Out in the yard, men were clambering into a waiting wagon.

Samantha gave a little sniff and waved both hands at him in dismissal. "Oh, go on, do your work and let me do mine." She softened the command with a teasing grin.

He bowed at the waist, his eyes showing a mischievous sparkle. "Yes, Your Highness." He headed for the doorway, but before stepping through he paused and glanced over his shoulder. "By the way, you look right nice this morning, Miss Frances."

Fire ignited in Samantha's face. Overwhelmed by the emotions his simple comment raised, she spun, presenting her back to him. She held her breath, willing her galloping pulse to calm. When she felt she could speak, she turned to thank him for his kindness. An empty doorway greeted her eyes.

She dashed to the door and peered out in time to see the wagon roll out of the yard, a puff of dust rising from its wheels. She couldn't distinguish Adam from the other workers. Crestfallen, she shuffled back into the kitchen. Then she squared her shoulders. Liz had said Samantha would need to take a snack to the fields midmorning. She'd make sure to thank Adam then.

Cheerfulness restored, she set to work washing up, humming a little tune she sang to the babies when she was sure no one could hear her.

❀

Despite the hearty breakfast, Adam's stomach was growling well before noon. Pa had assigned him the task of following the reaper and forking cut stalks into the hay wagon. His arms ached, straw and dust clung to his clothes, and the sun baked his head. He wished he knew how long it would be till their morning break when he could rest in the shade of the hedge apple windbreak, enjoy a drink of water, and eat a sandwich

. . . or whatever Liz might send out. And eagerness to see Frances again nibbled at the corners of his mind. Well, more than nibbled—it was taking over.

An image of her at Liz's stove, the rosy flush in her cheeks matching the pale pink checks of the dress, filled his mind's eye. She'd looked so pretty, thick hair pulled back into a wavy tail, neat apron tied around her narrow waist. Her weeks in Mountain Lake had put a little weight on her reed-thin frame, and although she was still slender, she now looked healthy rather than half starved.

But more than her physical changes held Adam captive. The relaxed curve of her lips and the spark of teasing in her eyes made his pulse stutter. What would she look like—and how would he react—if she ever completely released her guard and returned a full-fledged smile? He tried to imagine it, but a picture wouldn't form. How he wanted to coax a real smile to her lovely face.

A shrill whistle cut through Adam's reflections, and just ahead Ed drew the team pulling the reaper to a halt. Adam saw Jake at the edge of the field, waving his hands. "Come on in! Snack's here!"

Adam squinted against the sun and then frowned. Frances—astride Liz's sorrel mare—had brought out the promised snack, but she was wearing her old overalls and shirt again. He leaned the hay fork on the reaper and trudged in, apprehension swirling through his gut. Had his compliment embarrassed her enough to return to those clumsy britches and plaid shirt?

She unhooked a burlap bag from the saddle horn and handed it to Jake, then slid down unassisted. Strands of hair had pulled loose from the piece of yarn and blew around her cheeks. She stayed near the horse, placing paper-wrapped sandwiches into the men's hands as they filed by, her gaze low.

At each man's thank you, she offered a brief nod. Adam received his sandwich and paused, hoping she might look up, but she shifted her gaze behind him as if looking for the next worker to be fed. Disappointed, he moved out of the way so Lucas, Jake's youngest brother, could step up.

To further Adam's frustration, Lucas opened his sandwich right there in the sun next to Frances, one arm draped over the saddle's smooth seat and the other gesturing with the sandwich. Adam sat in the shade with the other men, his gaze pinned on Lucas talking so easily and friendly-like with Frances. She lifted her chin, crinkling her nose when the sun hit her full-face, and Adam watched her lips move as she answered Lucas. Lucas laughed hard at whatever she'd said, and jealousy smacked Adam with such force he couldn't finish his sandwich.

He leaped up, determined to figure out how to send Lucas away from Frances, but before he made it halfway to them, Jake sidelined him with a smack on the shoulder. "All right, everyone, let's get back to it!" he called.

With a small groan, Adam turned his steps toward the field. But he angled his gaze over his shoulder, keeping watch on Lucas. He clenched his teeth together when he saw how Lucas linked his hands, offering Frances a leg up into the saddle, and she accepted. Astride the horse again, the empty bag curled in her fist, she gave a little wave—to Lucas!—and pulled the reins so the horse aimed for the road.

Adam watched until the horse disappeared in a puff of dust, but Frances never looked back.

s Samantha rode back down the road toward Liz and Jake's place, she reflected on the brief conversation with Jake's brother, Lucas. She'd never engaged in idle chitchat with a young man before, and even though she'd had trouble thinking of responses to what she recognized as his flirting, she'd found their little exchange enjoyable. His attention had given her a lighthearted, pleasantly female feeling that was new and exciting.

The moment she returned, Liz called over her shoulder, "I put the pies you fixed up this morning in the oven, but there's much to do to be ready for lunch. And I've soon got to feed. . . ."

Samantha heard the rest of the sentence as she headed for the stairs. She'd asked Liz earlier if it would be okay to change into her overalls so she could ride astride Liz's horse, and Liz quickly agreed. She was sure Jake wouldn't mind when he realized her reason. But the flannel shirt and heavy overalls felt even heavier and more cloying than ever, and the pink-checked dress beckoned to her.

"Where are you going?" Liz called to her.

"I'm gonna change—"

"There's not time for anything but cooking, Frances." Liz's voice and face held an uncharacteristic note of impatience. "Those men'll be hungry and won't want to waste daylight hours waiting for us to put lunch on the table. Let's get busy."

With a sigh, Samantha changed direction and got to work readying the two fresh-killed chickens for the stew pot. While the chickens simmered, Samantha set up a makeshift table in the side yard, placing several long planks over a pair of wooden sawhorses. Perspiration rolled down her forehead as she surrounded the table with the chairs, boxes, and kegs the men had used at breakfast time. Oh, how she missed the coolness of that loose-fitting dress! On the other hand, dragging planks and sawhorses around seemed to call for overalls.

The wagonload of men rumbled onto the yard promptly at noon, and, after washing up at the pump, they gathered around the improvised picnic table for their lunch of the stewed chicken, corn on the cob, sliced tomatoes, pickles, mashed potatoes, *zwieback*, coffee, and apple pie. Samantha tripped around the table in her ungainly overalls, making certain the cups stayed filled and the men's needs were met.

Unlike breakfast's low murmurs, the men now chatted and laughed boisterously, telling wild stories about hunting trips and other harvest experiences, and ribbing Frank Klaassen about having to spend so much time away from courting his Anna. Frank took it well, though his ears glowed red. Samantha had determined his temperament wasn't as even as Adam's, and it looked like the men were having a good time trying to get him riled.

"Yeah, yeah, Frank," one of the men—Samantha thought his name was Girard—hollered from his end of the table, "ya' can't be away from 'em too long, or they lose interest. Gotta keep plyin' 'em with sweet talk and posies. Can't do much o' that when you're workin' mornin', noon, and night." The man slapped his knee and guffawed.

Frank gave the older man a quick frown. "Reckon not."

The man across the table from Frank pointed with his fork. "'Course that Anna, she's still a schoolgirl. Got her days pretty well filled up with book learnin'. The mornin's shouldn't be much of a problem—ya' just needs to worry 'bout the evenin's."

"Uh-huh, you got that right." Girard apparently enjoyed being in the middle of things, as he jumped in again, twinkling eyes pinned on Frank. "I heard the new school teacher, man named Reimer, is not too bad to look at, an' not a whole lot older'n Frank here. Anna bein' free these days might look a mighty good prospect. . . ." Another loud laugh.

Frank's lips formed a tight line, his shoulders bunching.

Adam cut in, his voice calm. "I'm sure Frank and Anna have things pretty well arranged between them."

Samantha nearly heaved a sigh of relief when Girard shrugged and turned his attention to his plate.

The man named Ed poked Adam with his elbow. "How 'bout you, Adam? You got things 'arranged' with some special young lady?"

Samantha paused, coffeepot clutched in her hands as an odd feeling tiptoed through her middle. She held her breath, awaiting Adam's response. But instead it was Lucas who called an answer from across the table.

"Adam may not have much to do with it, but that pretty little Priscilla Koehn seems to be workin' on arrangin' some-thin' with him. She sure was eyeballin' you at church a Sun-day or two ago, Adam." He spun, fixing his smile on Samantha. "You were talkin' to her, Frances. Did she say happen to say anything to you about likin' Adam?"

Samantha gave Adam a quick glance. To be a part of the group, she would have liked to join in the teasing—but the strange feeling that filled her at the idea of Adam with some special gal held her tongue. She finally said, "Maybe she did, and maybe she didn't. A lady wouldn't be tellin' secrets, so keep me out of it."

The men laughed loudly, and one of them elbowed Lucas. "Not many females around who won't spread a good piece of gossip. Reckon we got ourselves a real special one here. 'Course, it's hard to tell if she's a lady or not, since she's covered head to toe in a pair of men's pants."

The men roared again. Samantha scowled, wishing she could whack the man over the head with the coffeepot. He should leave her and her britches alone!

Ed's neighbor whistled and leaned toward Adam. "You could do a lot worse than Priscilla Koehn, Adam, boy. Priscilla's a mighty lovely little lady. She'd look right smart on your arm."

Samantha stifled a snort. Adam had more sense than to get himself involved with a shallow little flirt like Priscilla. She cocked an ear to catch his reply.

"You fellows might oughtta concentrate a little harder on your plates before those of us more interested in eating than yapping finish it all and you end up without second helpings." While the rest seemed to consider that prospect, Adam motioned to Samantha. "Frances, I sure would appreciate another piece of pie. Did you bake them?"

Samantha nodded, heart pounding.

"They're every bit as good as Mother's."

Pleasure raised gooseflesh across her arms. She retrieved the pie pan and hurried to his side. As she scooped a sizable wedge onto his plate, he said in a near-whisper, "I liked the dress, but I suppose it would be hard to ride Tess in it."

Suddenly she got a mental picture of the dainty Priscilla with her perfect curls and impeccable clothing. Priscilla wouldn't be caught dead wearing a pair of men's oversized overalls. That same feeling—which she now recognized as jealousy—flooded her as she imagined Adam and Priscilla walking arm in arm.

The feeling welled up and spilled out in a tart hiss. "My britches are better suited to a lot of things, horse riding included." She stuck her nose in the air, turned on a bare heel, and thumped back into the kitchen. Once inside, her anger deflated. She placed her hands on her warm cheeks and berated herself. Why had she responded like that? He'd complimented her on how she looked in the dress, then complimented her pies. And she'd returned the favor by being peevish.

Samantha sighed. What an addlepated fool she was, repaying a kindness with a fit of impatience. But maybe she could fix it. Quickly, before she could change her mind, she dashed up to her room and changed back into the dress. She took an additional few minutes to brush her willful hair into a neat braid and formed a bow of yarn at the curling end. Back down she ran, only to step out into an empty yard, save Liz who was cleaning up.

Samantha's heart sagged. She had wanted Adam to see that she could be a lady. It was as close to an apology as she could make herself give. But she was too late. He, along with the others, had already headed back to the fields. A lump filled her throat as she considered how her golden day had ended.

With a sigh, she moved to the table and began to stack dirty dishes. And if she carried Adam's plate a little tighter than the others, it was no one's business but her own.

∽◌

The harvest crew spent five days in Jake's fields before all the wheat was cut, raked, threshed, and scooped into baskets to be transported to the railroad. The days passed in a blur for Samantha, who kept so busy she almost felt as if she walked in her sleep at times. She'd worn Liz's dress continually after the first day, sitting sidesaddle for the trips out with snacks, but Adam hadn't made any further comment, and she found herself growing irritated with him for not noticing and with herself for worrying so much about it.

When the next Sunday arrived, Liz, Jake, the twins, and Samantha were invited to have dinner with Laura and Si. Samantha started in about wanting to stay at the house rather than go to church, but Liz took her aside. "I could really use you there, Frances. It's Jake's turn to lead the singing, so I'll be left holding both babies. Please, won't you come along and help me with the boys?"

Samantha grudgingly agreed and sat on the bench beside Liz, cuddling little A.J., who slept contentedly through the whole service. Not until midservice did she realize Liz's mother would have gladly held one of her grandsons while Jake was at the front of the church. Apparently church attendance was important enough to Liz for her to use some wiles to get Samantha there. She shot a glance at Liz and caught her employer's attentive expression as she listened to the minister. Samantha turned her focus to the front.

Her earliest church experiences had taken place when she was quite young, so she didn't have many memories from that time. But she did seem to recall the preacher at Gran's place of worship doing a lot of Bible thumping and thundering at his congregation. This minister, Reverend Goertzen, was so soft-spoken, one had to strain to catch his words.

Samantha found her attention captured when the man started reading from the book of John. "'Greater love hath no man than this, that he lay down his life for his friends.'" He paused to look around at the little congregation. "This, then, is what our Lord and Savior did for us: He gave up His own life, that we might have redemption for our sins. He claimed us as His friends, even before He knew us. How humbling to think that this perfect person, God's holy Son, could love us enough to die for us."

Samantha shifted in her seat. Humbling, the minister said, and he was right. But the preacher couldn't possibly mean her when he said "us." After all her wrongs, she surely didn't deserve the love of God.

The minister continued. "We wonder, how can we deserve that kind of love?"

Samantha nearly gasped. Had he read her thoughts? She leaned forward, eager to hear what he'd say next.

"And, people, I can tell you, none of us deserves it. We can't earn it by doing kind deeds or dropping hundreds of dollars into the offering plate on Sunday morning. No matter how we try, we can't live a perfect life and work our way into God's favor. We're sinners; we were born sinful, and we do many wrong things. . . . But yet He loves us. He loves us enough to die for us."

Samantha shook her head, disbelief clouding her mind. Why would the perfect Son of God go to all that bother? And certainly not for her.

Reverend Goertzen smiled, lines crinkling around his gentle eyes. "He loved us because He created us. He saw in each one of us the potential to be like Him. But He knew that sin would drag us down, keep us from being what we could be. So how do we get past that sin? How can He look past it?"

The minister's gaze roved over the congregation, and Samantha ducked her head, fearful he could see inside to the sins hiding there.

"Remember what the Scripture said," he went on. " 'Greater love hath no man than this . . .' I wonder how many of us would be willing to bear the punishment for our brother's sin. Or our neighbor's wrongdoing. Yet we claim to love our brothers and our neighbors. But we don't love them with the kind of love God has for us. Not until we invite the Lord Jesus Christ to be the king of our hearts can we love one another with that kind of love."

Samantha frowned. *What on earth does he mean?*

"Brothers and sisters . . ." Reverend Goertzen placed his palms on the homemade wooden podium and leaned forward, his expression fervent. "We can go to church, we can tithe our income, we can help our neighbors, but until we accept Christ's gift of love and receive Him into our lives and hearts, all that goodness is ashes in the wind. Until Christ's love is inside of you, you remain apart from Him. And His death was in vain."

Samantha braved a glance at Mrs. Klaassen, seated on the other side of Liz. She carried the love of which the minister spoke in her heart. And so did Liz and Jake and Adam and Josie. . . . They all had Christ's love. Samantha was sure of it. And that was what made them different from most other folks. That's what made them reach out to her in kindness even when she'd tried to steal from them. When she was living a lie.

Her heart thumped wildly in her chest as a strong desire caught her. *I wish I could be like them. . . .*

*S*amantha hardly noticed when Jake lifted A.J. into his own arms. She blindly followed Liz through the narrow aisle, nodding when spoken to but her thoughts fixed elsewhere. The preacher's final words were whirling through her mind. "Jesus loves you—every one of you, and He is holding out that love to you this morning," he said, his voice low but clear. "Take His love, His forgiveness, with you as you leave here this morning."

Out in the sunshine, Josie skipped over and linked arms with Samantha. "Want to ride home in the wagon with us instead of going with Liz, Frances? I haven't talked to you in ages."

Samantha moved along in silence.

Josie tugged at her arm. "Frances? Are you sleepwalking?"

Samantha gave herself a shake and forced her attention to Josie. "I guess I was daydreaming. What did you say?"

Josie laughed. "I asked if you want to ride home with us. It'll give us a chance to catch up on things. You won't *believe* what happened at school this last week."

Liz smiled and waved her on when Samantha told her about Josie's invitation, and she climbed into the wagon with the Klaassen family. Once they were bouncing along toward their farm, Josie poked Becky. "Tell Frances what Priscilla did last Thursday." She leaned over to Samantha and said, shaking her head, "Wait till you hear this."

Becky scooted closer and cupped her hand over her mouth with a giggle. "That Priscilla!" She kept her voice low. "She was in such trouble with our teacher, Mr. Reimer. He made her stand with her nose in the corner for fifteen minutes. At lunchtime she was so mad she was almost spitting."

"Never mind that." Josie glanced around the wagon and whispered, "Tell Frances why she was in trouble."

Becky's dark eyes sparkled as she related the tale. "Last Thursday Mr. Reimer gave us an assignment to write an essay about the future, what we were planning for our lives. We each had to read ours aloud to the class. So Priscilla writes this lovey-dovey poem about how she was"—Becky's eyes fluttered upward, and she clasped folded hands beneath her chin— "going to be a farmer's wife and 'live with the most handsome farmer around all my life.' "

Becky dropped her simpering pose. "It went on and on, and she even drew pictures to go along with it of a man and woman in wedding finery, with the words 'I do, forever and ever' written underneath the picture. And in a half circle over the man's head, she wrote Adam's name, and her own name over the woman's."

Josie cut in. "Mr. Reimer was really angry. He said school assignments weren't to be wasted on such foolishness. He gave her a failing grade and made her stand in the corner like a six-year-old. It was so funny."

Samantha forced herself to join in the laughter with Josie and Becky, although thinking about Priscilla and Adam in the same breath gave her a stomachache. Priscilla was so sure of herself. What if the self-confident girl convinced Adam he should give her a further look? Samantha shifted to peek at Adam, who sat at the back of the wagon with Sarah snug at his side, reading a Sunday school paper to her. He glanced up and caught her eye. He smiled. She looked away, flustered and confused.

She hadn't spoken to him after that encounter over her clothing. He'd been at Jake and Liz's house every day of that harvest week, but she'd kept her distance, too embarrassed to face him. And he hadn't sought her out either, which had gotten her dander up. If he felt bad about being hissed at, he sure didn't act like it. Maybe she shouldn't feel guilty about it, either. She had enough other things to feel guilty about without worrying about stepping on Adam Klaassen's toes.

As the wagon pulled into the yard, she remembered how the minister had said if people refused to accept Jesus' love, it was as if they were saying Jesus had died in vain. If it was true that Jesus had died for everyone, then that included Samantha O'Brien, and she was guilty of more than just fibbing about her name or trying to steal some groceries—or filling her pockets with the Klaassens's food while they were saying grace, no less!—she was guilty of letting Jesus die for a person who wouldn't repent. Although the concept of someone loving her enough to die for her was new, something about it sent down roots deep into Samantha's heart. Observing the Klaassens, how they lived and loved each other—and even her—Samantha had seen firsthand the difference Jesus could make in someone's life.

Then Priscilla's smirking grin flashed into her memory. From the way Priscilla behaved, Samantha presumed Jesus died in vain for that young woman. She gulped. She wanted to be like the Klaassens, not like Priscilla, but how could she change things? Her thoughts came to an abrupt stop when someone tapped her on the shoulder.

Adam stood outside the wagon bed, his hand extended to her. "Want a help down?"

To her surprise, the others had all left the wagon and were halfway across the yard. Her heart fluttering, Samantha nodded.

She placed her hand gingerly in his much larger one, inwardly hoping he didn't notice how it trembled. With her other hand, she braced herself on the wooden side of the wagon bed and hopped down, stumbling just a bit on the landing. Adam held her arm till she had her footing.

She tried to step away from Adam's grasp, but he closed his fingers around her arm and gave her a serious look. "Frances, I feel I owe you an apology."

Samantha wanted to pull free and run, but the fervent look in his eyes kept her rooted to the ground. "W-why?"

"I'm afraid I hurt your feelings when I commented on—well, on your overalls."

His sincere expression pierced Samantha through the center of her heart. She looked down, unable to look into his caring face.

"I didn't mean to make you uncomfortable," he said quietly, "but I think that's what I did, and I'm sorry."

Samantha fidgeted. She owed him a bigger apology, but her tongue felt swollen. She couldn't form the words to get started.

Adam ducked down to look eye to eye with her. "Will you please forgive me? So we can be friends again?"

Heat flooded Samantha's face. He'd said they were friends. She had to say something! Gathering her courage, she peeked at him through her eyelashes. The hint of a smile showed on his lips. The sun had already put little crinkles around his eyes from squinting. He was so handsome, and it was so hard to talk to him. But his sincerity tore at her heart. She had to put him at ease.

"There ain't—there isn't anything to forgive." Her words escaped in a raspy whisper. She swallowed, and when she spoke again the rasp had disappeared. "You didn't say anything wrong. But I did." Ducking her head again, she admitted, "I'm sorry I yelled in your ear. I was feeling, well, unladylike, wearing my overalls, so I acted unladylike. I'm sorry too."

Adam released a big breath. "Whew!"

She looked up at him, startled.

He grinned. "Well, I feel better." He sandwiched her hand between his palms. "Do you?"

She bit the insides of her cheeks to keep from smiling. She nodded.

"Good." He abruptly released her and took a little step backward. "I'd better get these horses taken care of, and you'd better catch up with the others or there won't be any dinner left for either of us."

With another nod, she turned to go. But she took only three steps before stopping and turning back. "Adam?"

He paused, one hand on the harness. "Yes?"

She took a deep breath and finally managed to say the words she'd wanted to say for weeks. "That day I was trying to steal from your uncle's store—and we . . . tussled. . . ." Her glance skittered away briefly and heat nearly scorched her cheeks. She turned her eyes back to his and continued bravely, "I called you a honyocker. You're not a honyocker. You're a really nice person, and I shouldn't have said it."

Adam's ears turned red. "Aw, I would've expected to be called something worse than that for sitting on you like I did. Let's just call it even, okay?"

Happiness exploded through her and found its way to her face. She beamed at him. "Thank you."

He stared at her, amazement dropping his jaw. "I was right. . . ." He swallowed, making his Adam's apple bob. "A smile truly can transform a person."

Samantha stared back, uncertain.

He gulped again. "You're beautiful, Frances."

Delight nearly lifted her feet from the ground. He'd said she was beautiful!

But then shame sent the rapture into hiding. He'd called her Frances. . . . There was more she had to confess.

Picking up her skirts, she turned and raced for the house.

*A*s Samantha had learned was customary on Sundays among the Mennonite Brethren, they enjoyed a cold lunch of *zwieback*, sausage, cheeses, and pie. A simple meal allowed the women more time to get to church and to rest afterward, and Samantha found she appreciated the extra time it left for visiting.

Several times during the meal, she looked up from talking with Josie or the younger girls to find Adam watching her. Each time he would smile briefly then turn his attention elsewhere. But then when she'd look, his gaze would be on her again. It gave her a funny feeling—a light, quivery lifting up inside that pushed at her heart. A not unpleasant, feminine feeling. And at the same time, it frightened her in ways she didn't understand.

When they'd finished eating and everyone had stacked their plates for washing later in the day, the women congregated in the parlor, cooing over the babies and chatting about their harvesting activities and the like, while the men congregated at one end of the porch to talk more harvest along with the war in Europe. Samantha eventually wandered outside and headed to her favorite spot, the porch swing on the other end near the lilac bushes. Adam and Teddy stumbled upon her a few minutes later. Teddy was cuddling a yellow and white fur ball.

Samantha exclaimed, "Oh! A kitten . . . he's so sweet."

Teddy dropped the kitten into Samantha's lap. "Wanna keep that one?"

She stroked the tiny head, and the kitten set up a loud purring response. "Are you sure . . . ? Is it all right?"

The boy shrugged. "He's my favorite, but there's four more I can go play with, so it's fine."

Samantha flashed a grateful smile. "Thank you."

Teddy trotted off toward the barn, but to Samantha's discomfort—and mixed in, a feeling of gladness—Adam didn't follow. Instead, he settled into the opposite end of the swing.

The fluttery feeling returned with Adam so near, rendering her tongue-tied. She had never experienced such a response to anyone before, and her confusion grew. Instead of looking at him, she turned the baby kitty onto its back and teased it with one finger.

Adam planted one foot on the porch floor and set the glider into gentle motion, rocking the swing slowly up and back, up and back. He reached out to poke at the kitten too, and it squirmed around, curling tiny paws around Adam's forefinger and biting down on the tip.

"Ouch!" He jerked his hand back and put the finger in his mouth.

Samantha laughed, then quickly covered her mouth. She rubbed her hand against the kitten's tummy. "Shame on you, baby, attacking poor Adam that way. Why don't you find someone your own size to pester?"

Adam snorted. "Size has nothing to do with it when you've got teeth like razors." He examined his finger. "I was just trying to play, and he goes for blood."

Samantha swallowed another giggle. The kitten yawned, showing off a little pink tongue and minuscule teeth, before curling himself into a ball on her lap and drifting off. While the kitten drowsed, Adam's foot kept the swing moving in a rhythmic squeak. Through the window came the muffled sound of voices; from the other end of the porch the men were talking about whether America would get into the war; from the barn drifted the occasional snort of a horse and boys laughing. From the distance, whip-poor-wills called and mockingbirds answered. The scents of cut wheat, marigolds, and grass mingled, creating a heady perfume. The September sun sent golden shafts of light through the porch railings, creating a series of shadows marching across the porch floor and across Samantha's lap, where a little yellow and white kitten continued to nap.

Adam released a contented sigh, and Samantha sneaked a peek at him. He sat with his eyes half closed and his lips tipped into the hint of a smile. Another pang of remorse shot through her for misleading him into believing she was someone she was not. How quickly would his contented expression change if she opened her mouth to admit her name was really Samantha O'Brien and not Frances Welch, as he believed?

Focusing her attention on the kitten, she bit down on her lower lip to hold the confession inside. Living a lie wasn't easy—for one thing, it was hard remembering to keep the lie straight, but further, it pricked her conscience sorely, especially now that she had grown to love this wonderful family. But would it be better to spill the truth, even if it meant she'd be sent back to Pa? Having gotten a taste of happiness, she was more than reluctant to lose it. Besides, soon harvest would end. Jake would be around home most days, and Samantha's help wouldn't be needed any longer. She'd be free to head on down the road, and the Klaassens would never know they'd been deceived.

The thought provided no comfort. She realized moving on would be even harder than keeping her secret had been.

Adam gave a huge yawn and raised his arms to stretch, his hands balled into fists. He swiveled his gaze and grinned at Samantha. "Think maybe I'll go in and help myself to another piece of rhubarb pie. Want to have one too?"

Oh, how Samantha wanted to accept his invitation. But time with Adam would only lead to greater heartbreak in the future. She pointed to the kitten sleeping peacefully in her lap. "I'll just stay put till this little one wakes up."

Adam rose, and the swing jerked sideways. The kitten's eyes popped open, and it flexed its little paws. Adam grimaced an apology. "I guess I disturbed your guest. Since he's awake, why don't we walk him back to the barn to his mama? You can come have a piece of pie after all."

Samantha had no more excuses. She scooped the little kitty against her chest as she stood. "All right, but instead of rhubarb, I'd like the apple pie. I've never cared for rhubarb."

Adam held his hands wide, palms up, and shook his head in mock dismay. "Don't care for rhubarb? How'd you manage to get this far through life without developing a taste for rhubarb?"

Samantha stepped off the porch. "I'd rather eat hay than eat rhubarb."

Adam laughed as he caught up with her. "Well, then, you're in luck, because right this way is a very large supply of hay. You can just eat all you want. Just like our cows."

Samantha couldn't help but chuckle at that mental image. Despite her intention to stay at a distance from Adam, she grinned at him and shook her head.

He grinned in return, looking warm and approving.

A wistful thought drifted from Samantha's heart. *I wish harvest could last forever, so I could stay on working here forever. . . .*

✑

After a supper of leftovers from the noon meal, Liz, Jake, and Samantha placed Andy and A.J. into baskets softened with quilts and climbed into the buckboard to head back. As the wagon rattled along, Liz sent her husband an inquisitive look. "What were you and Frank discussing so seriously in the corner of the kitchen before we left?"

"Thomas—Henry Enns's oldest boy."

Samantha looked up from tucking A.J.'s blanket a little more securely around his chin. The concern in Jake's voice made her concerned, too.

"He ran off and joined the army. With the United States coming in to the war last April, he thinks he should go over there and help out."

Liz drew in a quick breath and curled her arm through Jake's, leaning against him.

Jake went on grimly. "Henry's pretty well beside himself. Thomas is nineteen, though, and doesn't need permission to go."

Samantha didn't know much about the war in Europe. She'd picked up bits and pieces of conversations here and there. She knew the wheat prices were higher than they'd ever been and that farmers were exempt from the draft since they were needed to produce wheat. But hearing of someone she knew, although only slightly, going off to fight made her chest go tight. She patted A.J.'s tummy absently as she listened.

She heard Liz murmur, "Has Henry spoken with Reverend Goertzen? Maybe he could help."

"In what way?" Jake's tone took on a hard edge Samantha had never heard from him before. "Talking to the minister won't change anything. The boy's gone. He'll be holding a gun—and somebody will be shooting back. Henry's worried sick, and no amount of talking—even to the pastor—will eliminate the worry."

Samantha noticed Liz squeeze Jake's arm, and he released a heavy sigh. "I can't imagine having a child fighting somewhere.

Before we had the twins, I never gave much thought to such things. Being a father myself makes me understand Henry's anguish. I never want to experience the pain of seeing one of our boys march off to war."

Liz, silent, laid her forehead against his shoulder. He placed his free hand on her knee and left it there. Her hand covered his, and their fingers interlaced.

As Samantha observed the pair, a lump rose in her throat. How must it feel to love and be loved by someone? Even though Liz and Jake were sharing feelings of sorrow for a friend, Samantha found it beautiful to behold. Would she ever know such beauty for herself?

Her thoughts skittered back to the minutes she and Adam had shared, side by side on the porch swing in the quiet afternoon. Other images flashed through her mind: Adam ardently arguing with his uncle on her behalf; holding tiny A.J., a soft expression on his face; teasingly offering a blueberry, then laughing with his head thrown back; comforting Sarah when she stubbed a toe; redirecting the conversation of those farmers when they were trying to rile his brother. . . .

She held her lips tightly together, battling tears. How she wished her situation were different—that she belonged here, that she wasn't living a lie, that she was worthy of the love of someone as special as the Klaassens . . . as Adam. She gave a quick shake of her head. She might as well wish to be the queen of England. Samantha came from a world where wishes never came true.

he reminders of summer drifted away like the clouds in an azure sky, replaced by a lovely, mellow fall that pulled at Samantha's heartstrings with its earthen colors of mahogany red, pumpkin orange, and golden yellow. Many times she stopped on the narrow stoop at Jake and Liz's front door, arms often full of clean, dry clothing from the line, and drank in the pleasant changes in nature. She'd never seen so many colors before. Fall arrived in Milwaukee too, but in the city it was different from out here in the country with all the open spaces and towering trees and wild breezes carrying wondrous scents Samantha couldn't even name.

Although harvest on the Stoesz farm had already ended, Samantha stayed on. When Samantha tentatively brought up the subject, Liz begged Samantha to stay until Jake had finished his part harvesting the neighbors' farms and was home again. Liz insisted she simply couldn't do without her, it was so exhausting trying to keep up with the needs of two babies at once. Samantha agreed to stay. Truthfully, she didn't need an excuse to stay. She'd been in Mountain Lake for several months now with no sign of Pa. She was finally allowing herself to relax and bask in this new sense of security. And the longer she stayed, she told herself, the more money she could put aside for traveling later on.

One sunny Saturday afternoon in late September, the rumble of a wagon's wheels on hard-packed ground carried through the open front door. Liz set down her mending and crossed to the door. She flashed a smile to Samantha, who stood at the table kneading bread dough.

"It's Ma and the youngsters."

Samantha quickly cleaned her hands on her apron and ran to the doorway. She watched Adam help his mother to the ground. Teddy, Sarah, Becky, and Josie leaped out the back and charged toward the house. Sarah waved a brown paper-wrapped package, and the others were clamoring so that Samantha couldn't distinguish one voice from another.

The ruckus awakened the twins, who joined their indignant cries to the merry exclamations of the Klaassen siblings. By the time Mrs. Klaassen and Adam stepped through the door, Samantha wanted to clap her hands over her ears. Adam glanced over the fray with a frown, then placed two fingers in his mouth and blew. The piercing whistle stopped the commotion instantly, even stilling the babies for one startled second. All gawked at him, open mouthed.

"That's better." He strode across the room and took little A.J. from Samantha's arms, turning the baby against his shoulder. "It sounded like a gaggle of hungry geese in here." He patted the baby. "No wonder you were bawling, isn't that right, A. J.?"

Liz handed Andy to her mother, shaking her head. "What on earth was all that racket about, pray tell?"

"This! This!" Sarah waved the package over her head.

Teddy added, "It's a present for Frances."

Samantha's eyes grew wide and fastened on the slightly lumpy package wrapped in brown paper and string. "For *me*?" She pressed her hand to her chest.

"Yes." Becky gave Sarah a little nudge. "Hand it over, Sarah."

Sarah thrust the package into Samantha's arms, then danced up and down in excitement. "Open it! Open it quick, Frances!"

Samantha held it gingerly, unsure of how to behave. She couldn't remember the last time she'd been given a present. "But . . . but . . ." She shook her head, confusion making her tongue stumble. "It's not my birthday or Christmas or anything. W-what's it for? Why'd you all—?"

"It's a thank-you present," Josie put in, slipping her arm around Samantha's shoulders and beaming.

Samantha stared at her friend, then let her gaze travel over the circle of smiling faces, finally settling on Mrs. Klaassen's. " 'Thank you?' For what?"

Mrs. Klaassen's warm smile flooded over Samantha like warm honey. "For all the help you've given Liz. She tells us you've worked as much as two people these past weeks, and we're so grateful you are here for her and for the twins. The gift is a little something to show our gratitude. From all the Klaassens."

Samantha blinked quickly against the tears gathering in her eyes. She swallowed the lump in her throat and looked down at the crumpled brown paper, squeezing it with both hands. It was soft, with a funny little bump in the middle. A *thank-you present to show their appreciation*. She swallowed again, harder this time. They didn't understand. Instead of them thanking her, *she* should be thanking *them*.

They'd given her a place in their family, made her feel wanted and needed, had shown her more kindness than she'd ever known in her entire life. And now they were *thanking her*? Overwhelmed by emotions she couldn't put into words, she clung to the package while her heart thudded hard in her chest.

Sarah had taken to jumping up and down once more. "Open it, Frances!"

"Yes, do," Josie said, giving Samantha's shoulder a squeeze.

Adam's low voice reached Samantha's ears. "Give Frances a minute, girls. I think we've taken her by surprise."

Samantha lifted her eyes to his, and the gentle smile above A.J.'s downy head seemed to say, *It's okay. Just relax and enjoy this.*

"Well . . . Well . . ." She directed her words at Adam. Slowly, her pulse ceased its reckless pace. "Let me sit down first."

Teddy jerked out a straight-back chair from the table for her, and Samantha sank into it before her quivering knees gave way. The youngest two Klaassens crowded close, getting in the way while Samantha tugged the string loose. She placed it on the table, taking care to form a coil. Then she carefully pulled the brown paper aside slowly, savoring the anticipation.

As she pulled the paper back, she had a glimpse of roses and vines on a pale yellow background. She took a deep breath, then held it. Opening the wrapping completely, she discovered two neatly folded lengths of fabric—rose-print calico on top, and a piece of sky blue gingham on the bottom. Sandwiched between them, two spools of thread and a small wooden tube of sewing needles created the bulge.

"Oh, my . . ." Samantha's breath eased out slowly. With one finger, she traced a vine weaving between the calico blooms. "It's beautiful. They both are."

Mrs. Klaassen said, "I hope you don't mind that we picked out the fabric for you. We thought about taking you into town and letting you choose your own, but that would have spoiled the surprise. If you don't care for either of them, we can certainly exchange them for something else."

"Oh, no!" Samantha couldn't take her eyes off the fabrics in her lap. "These are just perfect. But—" At last she looked up, fixing an uncertain gaze on Mrs. Klaassen. "I've been paid for my work here. I don't understand. . . ."

Josie shrugged, a grin bringing out her dimples. "It's a bonus. One which you have richly earned, dear Frances." She laughed. "Besides, we figured you might be tired of wearing

Liz's old too-big hand-me-overs." Josie grinned at Liz, who returned the favor with a mock glare. "Now you'll have a Sunday dress *and* a work dress all of your own."

Samantha pressed both palms onto the soft cotton fabrics, reveling in the crisp newness. *Two dresses. One for Sunday and one for everyday.* She couldn't wait to start cutting out pieces and threading the needle and turning these wonderful fabrics into clothes. She wanted this more than she'd ever wanted anything.

But a heavy weight bore down on her, forcing her brows into a frown. She looked into the happy faces surrounding her. "This is—this is so wonderful. But I just don't know. . . ."

Mrs. Klaassen curled her hand over Samantha's shoulder, the touch warm and tender. "What's troubling you, dear?"

Samantha swallowed and gave her head a brief shake. How could she tell them that they'd already given her much more than she ever expected to receive in life? And then there was the secret lie she was living. . . . She didn't know how to respond. Ducking her head, she finally said, "I don't want to take more'n I deserve."

Mrs. Klaassen's hand slipped around her shoulder and tightened briefly. "There's about as much chance of that happening as—as Sarah here suddenly sprouting a mustache."

Samantha lifted her face and caught the teasing glint in the woman's eyes. Humor had diffused the emotionally charged moment. She managed a nod, a quick little grin in Sarah's direction, then met Mrs. Klaassen's gaze squarely. With all the sincerity she could muster, she said, "Thank you very much."

The woman's face lit up in a smile, and she leaned down to deliver a two-armed hug. Samantha didn't pull away. She didn't return the embrace, but she leaned into it, savoring it.

"Now . . ." At Liz's admonishing voice, Mrs. Klaassen released Samantha and stood back, giving her a chance to regain her composure.

"If you all will clear out of here," Liz said, "Frances and I can restore some semblance of order. We'll dish up gingerbread and whipped cream for anyone who wants some. Shoo now, kids—out of here till we call."

With a whoop, the three youngest dashed outside. "Let's play tag," Teddy shouted. "I'm it!" Mrs. Klaassen carried the babies up to their bedroom to finish their naps. Adam announced he was going to go say hello to Jake in the barn. Liz scurried to the icebox for the cream.

And Samantha remained in her chair, emotions reeling. She scooped up the folds of fabric and lifted them to her nose. A delightful aroma—clean and fresh and *new*—filled her senses. Pressing the bundle close to her heart, she finally rose and carried the gift up to her room. Still hugging the package, she peered out her little window and caught a glimpse of Adam striding toward the barn. As she watched, he paused and turned his face upward, almost as if he knew she was there. . . .

Her breath caught when he saw her. A smile brightened his face, and he lifted his hand in a wave. After a moment's hesitation, she waved in return. Then, her heart light, she laid the fabrics on the end of her bed and hurried back down to join the family.

Every spare minute of the following two weeks, Samantha holed up in her under-the-eaves bedroom, stitching feverishly. Gran had started her on sewing when Samantha was just a little girl, and then she continued making her own clothing while she was growing up, though never with brand-new fabric. When a neighbor took pity on her and gave her some cast off, she had remade it into a dress for herself.

Now she created a pattern by tearing apart one of Liz's threadbare dresses and modifying some pieces to fit her slimmer frame. Finally she attached the final button and donned her favorite—the morning-sunshine yellow covered with delicate pink roses and trailing deep, green vines.

She turned this way and that in front of the little mirror on her dresser, trying to get a glimpse of the whole thing. She blew out an exasperated breath. The mirror was just too small. She reached out to shift its position, angling it sharply downward, then looked again.

Someone knocked at the door, and Josie stuck her face around the opening without waiting for an invitation. Her eyes widened as she stepped fully into the room. "Oh, Frances, you did such a good job. It's beautiful—*you* are beautiful."

Samantha, embarrassed yet pleased at Josie's praise, fingered the tiny stand-up collar she'd embellished with a bit of white lace purchased with her very own money. "Does it look all right? I can't see the whole thing at once."

"Yes, it fits just right." Josie handled Samantha like a large doll, turning her in circles. "Even the buttonholes are perfect, and the gathers on the skirt are nice and even," she exclaimed. "And look at the lovely puff at the shoulder of the sleeves. You look like an angel, Frances."

Samantha wasn't accustomed to such compliments, but pleasure flooded through her. She toyed with the skirt, her head bent.

Josie tugged at her wrist. "Come downstairs. *Tante* Hulda is here with Mother and Liz, putting her stamp of approval on the twins. You remember, Uncle Hiram's wife. Come show off your creation."

Samantha drew back. "I don't want to show off, Josie."

Josie laughed at her. "I don't mean you will really be show-ing off, silly. Mother will adore this dress, and even *Tante* Hulda will be impressed."

So Samantha allowed herself to be led down to the kitchen, where she blushed self-consciously under Mrs. Klaassen's along with the girls' and Aunt Hulda's exclamations of admira-tion. "That's a lovely dress, Frances," Aunt Hulda said in her thick, husky voice. "The colors make you look healthy." Aside, to Mrs. Klaassen, she whispered too loudly, "That girl is too thin." Then she waved a pudgy hand at Samantha. "Come closer, child. Let me check the stitching."

Reluctantly Samantha obeyed the somewhat intimidat-ing woman, allowing her to scrutinize Samantha's handiwork. Hulda muttered, "Mm-hm," and "Ah," under her breath as she tugged at the skirt and sleeves and turned Samantha this way and that. At last she settled back in the rocking chair, crossing heavy arms across her ample bosom. She peered up at Saman-tha from over round lenses sitting precariously on the end of her nose. "Well, Miss Frances, you've done a commendable job. You've obviously sewn before."

Samantha moved away now that the inspection was over. "Yes, ma'am. I was taught to sew a long time ago, by my great-grandmother."

"She taught you well." Hulda pursed her her lips and squinted at Samantha. "I don't suppose you would be inter-ested in sewing for profit?"

Confused, Samantha turned to Mrs. Klaassen for help. "She means, would you be interested in sewing for other people, who would pay you?" Mrs. Klaassen explained.

"Pay me to sew?" Samantha thought the idea ludicrous. Who would pay her to do something they could easily do themselves?

Hulda said, "Many of the women in town do not enjoy sewing or feel inadequate in their ability, so they either buy from a catalog already made"—she snorted, waving her dimpled hand in a gesture of derision—"or hire someone to sew for them."

Samantha gaped at her. "Of course—of course I'd be willing." The idea of earning money appealed to her. "But I don't know if I'm good enough to sew for others."

Hulda gave another short laugh. "There's no doubt you are good enough, dear. I could put a sign up at our store by the dress goods, offering your services. We would capture customers quickly if we hung a sample garment. . . ."

Without thinking, Samantha placed her hands protectively against the skirt of her dress.

An understanding smile creased the older woman's face. "But I suppose we could do without. Just wear this dress to church on Sunday, and we shall have business. Mark my words."

Samantha looked from Josie to Mrs. Klaassen to Hulda. Worry scurried around in the back of her mind. "I'm not sure Mr. Klaassen or—or the sheriff would approve of me working out of your store. After all—" She ducked her head in embarrassment. "I did try to steal from there. . . ."

"Nonsense." Hulda shrugged. "Water under the bridge. Hiram wouldn't hold a grudge, especially when the venture will prove profitable to him as well." Her eyes sparkled with mischief. "We do have the fabrics available for sale, and even after the ladies pay you to sew, they will spend less than they would on a ready-made dress. Anyone can see the advantages there. No, Hiram won't argue. I'll bank on it . . . and he'll take it to the bank." She laughed at her own cleverness.

Samantha thought about having access to the many fabrics and laces at the store, cutting and stitching until a finished dress emerged from only assorted shapes of material. She thought of earning extra money that would keep her far away from her pa. She thought of being able to stay in Mountain Lake, close to the Klaassens. *Close to Adam* . . .

She smiled at Hulda. "If you think it will be all right, I'll try it."

"This is just wonderful!" Josie scurried over to wrap Samantha in an impulsive hug.

"Now sit down here by me," Hulda ordered, "and have some applesauce cake to celebrate our new business venture."

Still basking in the warmth of their confidence in her, Samantha eagerly joined the others for cake and chatter. As she daintily smoothed the skirt of her fine new dress across her knees, she wondered with a spark of unfamiliar vanity, *What will Adam think when he sees me in this?*

*A*dam couldn't stop a rush of jealousy as he watched Lucas Stoesz hotfoot it across the churchyard at the approach of his older brother's buckboard. Lucas hurried around to the back and helped Frances down. Adam caught his breath at the sight of her in the trim-fitting dress she had made from the rose-covered fabric Ma and Josie had chosen. The perky flowered bonnet added an appeal and a maturity to her appearance that made Adam feel as if someone had socked him hard in the midsection. The feeling was all mixed up with another much less brotherly, and he carefully guarded his expression as he followed his family into the church and settled himself on the familiar bench.

Out of the corner of his eye, Adam saw Lucas steer Frances in next to Liz, then lean down to whisper something in her ear before straightening. Frances, pink-cheeked, lifted a bashful face to Lucas's and nodded slightly. A huge grin split the young man's face, and he unabashedly winked at Frances before moving down the aisle to sit with his father.

Adam's brows pinched together. *That Lucas is just a little too sure of himself.* Samantha didn't have a father or other family member around to look out for her. It was Adam's duty as her benefactor, so to speak, to provide protection when needed. He was uncomfortable with the idea that protection from his brother-in-law's sibling would be necessary, but he knew Lucas well enough to be concerned. Lucas had always been more reckless than wise.

Rev. Goertzen stepped up to the pulpit, and Adam turned to the front of the church. The minister's somber expression—so different from his usual Sunday morning smile—caught Adam's full attention. Apparently he wasn't alone, because the sound of stirring and soft murmurs drifted across the congregation.

"Brothers and sisters . . ." Tears glittered in Reverend Goertzen's eyes. "I must begin our time together this morning with some distressing news. I have just come from the Enns farm. Henry and Marta received a telegram yesterday, informing them that their son, Thomas, was killed in a training accident."

Shocked gasps came from every corner of the church. Adam clutched the edge of the bench, almost dizzy at the terrible news. *Thomas . . . gone?* The sound of a woman sobbing quietly came from behind him.

The pastor continued, "This morning, I ask that we unite our hearts in prayer for the Enns family. They are much in need of comfort. Shall we pray?"

After the service, which was more brief than usual, Pa and Ma asked Adam to take the children home in their wagon, and they rode with several other couples to the Enns farm to spend the afternoon with Henry and Marta. Jake and Liz decided to go over to the Klaassen farm rather than heading to their own little house alone. At this time of sorrow, they needed one another.

Liz, Josie, and Frances set out lunch, but no one ate much. Sarah and Teddy couldn't really understand the impact of what had happened, but they must have absorbed the tense currents because they reflected the somber moods of the older ones around them. After pushing their food around on the enamel plates for a while, Liz sent the two youngsters out to the barn to entertain themselves with the kittens, and she supervised the little cleanup that was needed. The afternoon stretched before them, with very little conversation to fill the sorrowful hours.

Adam joined Frank, Arn, and Jake on the porch, as was their custom on nice Sunday afternoons, but restlessness drove him to the yard. He needed to think. He needed to do something. He decided to take a walk to clear his head. But he really didn't want to be alone. Frances and Josie were on the porch swing, and he crossed the yard with long strides and paused at the foot of the steps.

"I'm going for a walk. Anyone want to come along?"

Josie shook her head. "I'll stay around in case Liz needs help with the twins. Why don't you go ahead, Frances? You've been doing a lot of extra duties lately. A walk would do you good."

Frances looked from Josie to Adam, indecision in her face.

"I'd like the company," Adam said, trying to keep his voice matter of fact.

"I suppose I'll go then." Samantha pushed out of the swing. "It's awfully warm for fall, isn't it? Must be Indian summer."

"Nah, can't be Indian summer until after the first hard frost."

"Well, how about a walk to the lake? Is it very far? We could dip our feet in the water and—."

"Lake?" Adam frowned.

"There must be a lake. The town's named—"

"Oh!" Adam released a short huff of laughter, but he quickly stifled it when she drew back, her brows drawn together. "There isn't a lake," he said. "Then why—?"

"There was a lake here when the town was founded," Adam explained, motioning for her to join him, "but since most of the people who chose to make Mountain Lake their home wanted to farm, the town leaders drained the lake. In 1905 or 1906, I think. So it's all farmland now."

"Hmmm," was all she said, but she looked disappointed as they started to move away from the porch.

"But with the north pasture cut now," Adam offered, "it'll be easier to walk there. Shall we go that way?"

She clasped her hands behind her back with a shrug. "That's fine."

So Adam set off, Frances moving quietly at his side. Neither spoke, and Adam discovered he didn't mind walking along with Frances in silence. A light breeze whirled leaves across their path and gently rubbed the tips of empty branches together. The fall sun beamed down, and Adam could see it bouncing off the glossy strands of her hair and bringing out reddish glints.

Such a beautiful day . . . and such heavy thoughts. A sigh shoved up through his chest.

Frances flicked a glance at him. "You're thinking about your friend, aren't you?"

A lump filled Adam's throat. "Yes." He couldn't say anything more.

She sighed too. "I didn't know Thomas—I'd only seen him in the churchyard with you and the other young men. But he'd looked young and healthy and full of life, and now he's gone." Her voice cracked. "It doesn't seem fair."

No, it wasn't fair, but lots of things weren't fair. It seemed especially wrong when Thomas hadn't even been in combat. Uncertain how to respond, Adam remained silent. Samantha set her lips in a grim line and continued to trudge along beside him. Their shoulders bumped occasionally as they moved across the uneven ground, and he considered putting more distance between them but decided against it. He found a level of comfort having her near enough to touch, even if the contact was brief and impersonal.

The wind picked up, and she nearly tripped when her skirt tangled about her ankles, but Adam reached out and caught her arm, keeping her from a likely tumble. She gave a small smile of thanks, stepping back to smooth her dress. He glanced over his shoulder, stunned by how much distance they'd covered. They should turn around and go back.

He gestured toward the house. "Should we—?"

"What is that?" she interrupted, pointing in the opposite direction.

He followed the line of her finger. "What?"

"Over there." She squinted. "It looks like the front of a shack getting swallowed up by the hill."

Adam shaded his eyes for a moment, then dropped his hand and grinned at her. "That's Grandpa Klaassen's dugout."

She sent him a curious look. "Dugout?"

"It's the first house built on our land. When Grandpa and Grandma settled here, he didn't have time to build a proper house before winter hit, so he just dug into the side of a hill, stacked some logs for a wall, and made a house out of the hole. I haven't been out there for years. Want to take a peek?"

She gave an eager nod, so Adam caught her elbow and steered her toward the small dwelling. As they drew near, a smile of wonder grew on her face. "Oh, my. It *is* a house dug right into the side of a hill! I've never heard of such a thing."

Adam planted his shoulder on the warped door and pushed hard. A discordant creak sounded as he forced it open. The smell of earth and neglect greeted his nose. Frances leaned forward, peeking into the dark, musty space, and then jerked back. Her expression turned dubious.

"Will there be . . . are there critters . . . in there?"

Adam shrugged, hiding a grin. "Maybe."

She inched backward, nervously twining her fingers together. Adam was sure she had no idea how cute she looked with her nose all wrinkled up with worry. Stifling a chuckle, he stepped into the dugout. He waved his arms around, breaking down cobwebs and scattering dust everywhere. A glance around the room confirmed no dangerous animals had taken up residence. He turned to the open doorway with a smile.

"It's safe. C'mon in."

Hesitantly, Frances stepped over the dirt threshold. She immediately sneezed.

Adam pursed his lips in sympathy. "Not too clean, though, is it? Dark, too. Maybe I can open the shutters."

The oiled paper windows had long since rotted away, but sturdy wooden shutters still protected the openings. Adam forced them outward, and a negligible amount of light made its way into the room, followed by the sweet fall breeze. He stood in the shaft of light from the window, looking around the small room. An old table still remained along one wall, and a pile of old clothing, mouse eaten and filthy, lay discarded in a corner. Frances kicked at it, sending up a puff of dust. She covered her nose and moved nearer the door where the air was fresher.

"Josie and Liz used to play house out here." Adam wandered the small space, remembering. "I came out here a lot, too, as a kid. I thought it was a neat hideout. It doesn't look like anyone's been around for a long time, though."

He stood back and watched Frances ease farther into the room. She slid her fingers along the smooth dirt wall, raising her face to examine the sturdy overhead beams of the ceiling. Lowering her gaze, she moved over to the shelves wedged into the back wall of the dugout. A row of grimy glass jars still rested there. She lifted one down and cradled it in her palms.

"The place is not large, as you see," he told her, "but there's ample room for a bed, table, and a couple of chairs."

She gave an approving nod. "A fine little house," she said. Her gaze drifted in a circle, her lips turned up in a smile. Returning the jar to the shelf, she moved across the floor to the fireplace centering the side wall. She squatted down, peering into the dark shaft. Then she fingered the outer structure of the fireplace.

She sent a glance over her shoulder to Adam. "What are these?"

Adam walked over and hunkered down beside her. "Mud bricks. Formed of mud, grass, and cow manure."

She jerked her hand back and brushed her palms together.

He bit down on the inside of his cheeks to keep from laughing. "The Mennonites formed bricks of those materials in Russia, so of course Grandpa would do the same thing here. The bricks are amazingly strong. They built entire structures of these mud bricks."

Keeping her hands in her lap, she examined the fireplace again. "Clever . . . but, well, a little unusual."

Adam nodded.

Slowly she turned her head and looked into his face. Sunshine slanted across the floor, painting the two with its yellow glow. Only inches apart, he glimpsed his own reflection in her irises. Tiny particles of dust danced around them like glittering bits of sunshine.

Emotion glimmered in her eyes—an emotion he couldn't define—and suddenly she sucked in a sharp breath. Averting her eyes, she jolted upright and swished dust from her skirts. Adam rose, too, both disappointed by her abrupt withdrawal and relieved. What had he been thinking?

She began a casual stroll around the room, her hands linked at her waist. "So . . . this was your grandparents' home?"

Adam chuckled, "Grandma called it her badger's den. She joked that when she'd married Grandpa, back in Russia before they immigrated here, he had been worried about his penniless state, but she had assured him she could be happy living in a hole in the ground as long as he was in it with her. So Grandpa put her word to the test."

Frances laughed, the sound giving Adam's heart a lift. "Your grandma must be fun."

He bobbed his head in agreement. "Both of my grandparents are wonderful. I miss them."

"Are they . . . ?"

Adam understood the abbreviated question. "Both are well and living in Minneapolis. My oldest brother, Daniel, lives near them in the city. He keeps an eye on them. They always visit at Christmastime. Maybe you'll meet them then."

Her brows puckered briefly, and she again took up her slow perusal of the space. "Did your parents live here, too?"

"Nope." Adam leaned on the wall, observing her. "Grandpa built the house we live in before Pa and Uncle Hiram were born. Then, when Grandpa had a stroke and couldn't farm anymore, he split the land between Pa and Uncle Hiram and took Grandma to the city. Uncle Hiram found out he wasn't that interested in farming, so he sold Pa his half of the farm and opened up his mercantile."

Frances paused, sending him an interested look. "Your family's been on the land for quite a long time. . . ." She tipped her head, one strand of hair curling around her cheek. "Will you stay on the farm, like your pa has done?"

Adam answered promptly. "Sure will. Pa's already told me this north pasture and the east field will be mine, and the other side will go to Frank. There's enough land to support more than one family here, and I have no desire for city—or even town— life. Daniel and Arn are welcome to it."

Samantha nodded, a lilting smile lifting the corners of her lips. "Farming takes strength of body and spirit—being at one with the land. It seems to me you have all the requirements to be a farmer." She turned her head away as if embarrassed, but her words pleased him more than he could really understand.

He finally said, "I know what I want—what God wants for me. And I'm not afraid to work for it." Satisfaction welled in his chest. "When I inherit this land, I'll also inherit the knowledge and commitment of the people who've gone before me. They've given me a good, solid base on which to build, both physically and spiritually."

She sighed. "I envy you, Adam. What a wonderful family history you have." Her eyebrows scrunched together. "I hope you know how lucky you are."

Adam knew well how lucky he was. How blessed. Being in the dugout again brought back many memories of childhood, listening to his grandparents' stories. He came from a God-fearing family, and he was proud to be a part of it. Watching Samantha move around the small space, poking her nose into corners and swiping at the dust motes in the air, he had to wonder about her background—who her people were, where she'd come from. Time had passed, but none of them were any more enlightened than they had been the first day she arrived and tried to withhold her name.

Curiosity got the best of him. "Frances, do you have grandparents?"

She stiffened and froze in place, her gaze aimed at the shelves on the wall. Then slowly she turned, her face down. "No, not anymore."

"Parents, then?"

"I'll wait for you outside." Without looking at him, she skittered out the door.

Remorse tangled Adam's insides into knots. She'd been enjoying herself. He'd been enjoying her enjoyment. And then he'd chosen to pry, ending their time of easy camaraderie. He sighed and closed the shutters, reminding him of how Frances sealed herself away from all of them. What deep pain held her captive? Would she ever trust them enough to let someone in?

As he stepped into the sunshine again, a prayer winged from his heart. *Lord, shine the light of Your love and healing into Frances's soul. Replace her pain with joy.* He couldn't help his young friend, but he knew who could. He'd trust God to meet Frances where she was and to give her what she needed.

*O*nce again, Samantha fell in step with Adam. Her heart ached. This day had started out with such promise. With only a little prompting from Hulda Klaassen, her new dress had gotten just the reaction at church they had hoped for; she'd noticed Adam watching her with an expression of interest; and Lucas Stoesz, who was admittedly handsome, had openly flirted with her and asked to walk her home after the service. Even though she had no intention of taking Lucas up on his offer, she'd settled onto the church bench feeling happy and accepted. But now the day seemed tarnished, battered, and scarred.

Although she kept her face aimed toward the farmhouse in the distance, images from her visit with Adam in the dugout played across her mind's eye. When they had knelt side by side in front of the fireplace, the sunlight streaming through the door had turned his hair to burnished gold, and green flecks appeared in his brown eyes. Looking into his face, a feeling as real as the ground now beneath her feet had coursed through her, catching her breath and causing her heart to flutter. Through her mind had flashed a mental image of her tending a fire and Adam returning home to her, belonging to her in the way that Jake belonged to Liz or Si belonged to Laura. It lasted only a moment—a wonderful, heartfelt moment—and then it was replaced by the realization that it was only a dream. A fantasy that couldn't—*couldn't*—come true. Because she wasn't who he believed her to be.

The weight of the secret seemed to fall on her with new force. She stumbled but caught herself before Adam came to her aid as he had before. Oh, if only she could be as open with him as he had been with her. But surely he'd turn away in disgust if he knew the legacy of her family—Pa's drunkenness, Davey's abandonment, the lie of her assumed name. She had nothing to offer Adam. As much as it pained her to continue living the falsehood, it was better for everyone if she continued to be Frances Welch, homeless and alone.

As she'd watched Adam secure the shutters of the little dugout, she had reached a sad realization. She did not belong here. She was not like the Klaassen family, not Adam's kind, and she never could be. Her foolish heart had been planting ideas in her head that could never come true. Adam's questions today proved the Klaassens would one day demand answers, and it would break her heart to confess how she'd misled them. She must move on—now, before her heart was so firmly planted that it could not be uprooted. She would talk to Liz. Soon.

They reached the house, and Adam lightly touched her back. "Go on in. I'm going to feed the horses." He trudged toward the barn without a backward glance.

Stung by his distance and abrupt departure, Samantha slowly entered the house. Mr. and Mrs. Klaassen sat at the table with Liz and Jake, and all four glanced up as she stepped into the kitchen.

"There you are, Frances," Liz said.

Samantha winced, the false name stinging like the lash of a whip.

"We're ready to go home now. We were just waiting for you."

Samantha nodded wordlessly and reversed her steps. Liz and Jake followed, each carrying a twin. They settled the boys in their baskets in the back with Samantha and then climbed onto the wagon's seat. Side by side. Shoulders touching. Samantha angled her gaze low to avoid witnessing the sweetness of their love for each other.

When they were back, Samantha prepared a simple supper of cold sausage, *zwieback*, and cheese. She began to clean up while Liz tucked Andy and A.J. into their cradles. When Jake went out to see to the evening chores, Liz sank into the kitchen rocker with a pair of Jake's socks and her darning needles in hand.

Now, Samantha told herself. She pulled out a chair from the table and sat. Hands clutched tightly in her lap, she took a breath, trying to gather her courage.

Liz glanced up from her mending and offered a tired smile. "It's been a long day, hasn't it?"

Samantha nodded. "Yep, and not an easy one for you folks." And she was about to make it more difficult. Guilt smote her, but she pushed the feeling aside. This had to be done. "I sure am sorry about Thomas Enns."

Liz sighed. Tears in her eyes caught the light. *Brown eyes, like Adam's.* "It's going to be terribly hard for Henry and Marta. Thomas was their oldest, and his signing up and leaving without their permission was awful enough without having to face the fact that he's never coming home again."

Never coming home again . . . Samantha understood the feeling all too well. A lump filled her throat. But she swallowed resolutely and forced the words she had to say from her stiff lips. "Liz, it's time I be on my way."

Liz's head came up sharply, her hands stilling. "Oh, Frances, no! You've become part of the family. And what on earth will I do without you?"

How good it felt to be needed. Samantha smiled sadly. "You'll do just fine, and you know it. The twins are sleeping through the night now, and there's just the Voths's wheat to be finished harvesting, so Jake will be here days again. I appreciate the job you've given me, but it's time for me to go."

Liz stared, eyes wide and distressed. It was hard for Samantha to meet her gaze. "Have I done something to offend you, Frances?"

"No, nothing like that!" Her guilt rose by the minute. "But when I took this job, it was for harvest. Well . . . harvest is over."

"But what about the deal you made with *Tante* Hulda? I thought she'd already gotten interest from two ladies for dresses. You'll sew those, won't you?"

In all honesty, Samantha had forgotten. "I—I don't know. I'll have to talk to Mrs. Klaassen about that. I just wanted to let you know what—what I am thinking."

Liz rocked, a speculative gaze pinned on Samantha. "You've been happy here, haven't you?"

Samantha wouldn't lie. She gave a miserable nod.

"Then what happened?" Liz frowned. "Did you and Adam have a spat this afternoon? If so, I'll—"

"No!" Samantha jumped from the chair. "Nothing happened. Nobody did anything to me." Her heart pounded so hard she wondered if Liz could hear it. "It's just like I said. The job is done. I need to move on."

Liz stared at her in silence for several tense minutes. Then she blew out a little breath and returned to her mending. "When do you want to leave?" She sounded terse. The tone bruised Samantha's heart. "Now. Before the cold weather hits. I need to be settled somewhere before the snow flies."

Once again, Liz dropped her hands to her lap. Her voice gentled. "Where will you go, Frances?"

Samantha bit her lower lip. "I'm not sure yet. The city, probably. Maybe Minneapolis. I can get work there." *And Adam's grandparents and brother live there, so maybe I'd run into him someday. . . .*

Liz lifted the sock. "All right,. I won't try to stand in your way. But will you at least wait until the Voths's wheat is in? It would help me a lot."

An agonizing war took place in Samantha's soul. Desire to stay battled with the need to escape. How she wanted to please Liz, who'd been so kind to her. But how even more she needed to get away before she and the others learned how they'd been duped.

"I . . ." Her dry mouth made her voice sound strangled. "I don't know." She turned and raced up the stairs before Liz could offer another argument.

√❨

As Adam hitched the team to the wagon Monday morning for the trip with Pa, Frank, and Arn over to the Voth farm, the clatter of hoof beats reached his ears. He turned to see Liz rein in her horse next to the corral. *What is she doing out so early?*

He met her halfway across the yard. "Liz, is something wrong? What—?"

"Frances is leaving."

He felt as though a lightning bolt had shot from the sky and seared his insides. "But—but she *can't* go!"

Liz stared at Adam's face, her expression apprehensive. "I don't want her to leave either, Adam, for strictly selfish reasons—she's such a help." She rested her fingertips on his forearm. "What are your reasons for keeping her here?"

Adam swallowed. How should he answer? What *were* his feelings for Frances Welch? Sympathy for her aloneness? Brotherly caring? Simple Christian concern for a fellow human being? Or did it go beyond any of those? Was it possible he actually *loved* the girl? The thought brought him up short. Had he ever really defined his feelings for Frances?

"Liz, I . . ." Adam stared helplessly at his sister.

Liz's eyes filled with compassion, as if she already knew the answer and understood the conflict involved. Adam, as a Christian man, would not become seriously involved with a non-Christian no matter how much his heart might wish him to. With a sad smile, she opened her arms, and he moved into her embrace. After a long hug, he pulled back and took Liz's hands.

"Sis, I don't want her to go. If she has no family, she needs us more than you've needed her. I can't let her know how I feel—and we can't pressure her. She'll run like a scared rabbit." Adam dropped her hands and turned away, running his fingers through his hair. "I know why she wants to go. She's scared. I scared her."

"How?"

Adam shook his head, anger with himself putting a bite in his tone. "Yesterday Frances and I went walking, and ended up at the dugout. We started talking about Grandpa and Grandma, and I asked her about her own grandparents."

Liz shook her head. "I can imagine her reaction, knowing how she's responded to questions about herself in the past."

Adam gave a terse nod. "She closed her mouth and wouldn't even look at me." He slammed his hands over the top rail of the corral. "After all my intentions to go easy with her, to let her open up to me on her own terms, in her own time. I wanted her to trust me. And then I had to go and open my big mouth."

Liz curled her hand over Adam's. "One simple question, and in the context of your discussion, could hardly be considered applying pressure. It sounds like the conversation moved naturally in that direction. We have a right to ask questions occasionally. If that makes her lack faith in you, then I think the problem lies with her, not you."

Adam appreciated his sister's attempt to absolve him of blame, but he couldn't accept it. "No, I frightened her, and I need to set it right. I'll talk to her."

"Do you think you should?" Worry creased Liz's brow. "Maybe it would be better to——."

"To let her go?" Adam frowned at his sister, then his shoulders slumped forward. He hung his head. "No, Liz, right or wrong, we can't just let her go. I've got to try."

The day crept so slowly at the Voth farm that Adam wondered if the sun stood still. But at last evening fell, the men returned to their own homes, and Adam was free to go speak with Frances.

The horseback ride over to Liz and Jake's proved chilly, a huge change from yesterday. Rain scented the air, and clouds sent a gloomy cast across the sky. Adam pulled the collar of his jacket tighter around his jaw and wished he'd grabbed gloves too. By the time he arrived on Jake's property, the clouds had parted to reveal the moon and a dusting of stars high in the sky.

Liz answered Adam's brief knock, gesturing him in with a wave of her hand. Jake looked up from the table where he was working some figures on a lined pad of paper. A grin broke across his face. "Hey, Adam. What brings you here at this hour? I hope it's a game of checkers."

Adam smiled but shook his head. "Not tonight, Jake. I came to see Frances."

Jake's eyebrows shot up. His gaze went to Liz, who'd moved to the stove and was fingering the lid on the coffeepot. Adam imagined him thinking, *So that's how it is.* Embarrassment gripped Adam, but he wouldn't back out now. He asked, "Is she in?"

"Up in her room. I'll give her a holler." Jake moved to the bottom of the staircase. "Frances? Company."

Adam stayed beside the door, watching as Frances descended. When she saw who was there, her steps slowed and a look of surprise—and maybe a bit of pleasure?—crossed her face. Then she settled her face in neutral expression and came the rest of the way down.

"Hi, Frances," Adam said quietly.

Looking wary, she avoided letting her eyes meet his. "Adam." She nodded but stayed a good five feet away from him, twisting a strand of hair that fell across her shoulder. She wore her blue gingham dress and looked very young, very uncertain—and oh so appealing.

Adam cleared his throat, painfully aware of his audience. "I wondered if you'd like to take a little walk to the corral. The night sky's real pretty. Get a breath of fresh air. . . ." He hoped the clouds hadn't clustered in again, or she might think he'd told a fib.

Frances looked at Liz. Liz shrugged with a little smile and pointed toward the hooks on the wall near the door. "If you go out, take a shawl. It's chilly tonight."

Adam lifted down a woolen shawl and draped it across Frances's shoulders, taking care not to touch her. He opened the door, and with a final solemn glance at Liz, followed Frances outside. They walked silently across the yard, their feet making crunching sounds in the dry grass. The air was crisp, the sky bright, as he'd promised. He wished they could relax and enjoy it. He wished he knew exactly what to say . . . how to say it.

They stopped by the corral fence. Frances clutched the shawl tightly with two fists and leaned her elbows on the top rail. Adam turned to lean against the fence backward, one foot propped up on a low rail. Both examined the sky for a few moments.

Adam broke the silence. "Liz tells me you're planning to leave, Frances."

She shot him a quick look. "Yes."

He could hardly hear her, but the single-word answer rankled. It reminded him of the days when she had first arrived, tight lipped and sullen. He thought she had progressed beyond that, and he expected more from her now. But if she wanted to be difficult, two could play that game. "Why?" His tone sounded stiff to his own ears.

She had turned her gaze back to the stars. "I really don't understand why it concerns you, but if you must know, I feel it's time. Liz doesn't need me like she did at first, and I need to find a job. My own place . . ."

Adam chose to ignore her assumption that it didn't concern him. "You have a job here in Mountain Lake—sewing for the mercantile customers."

Frances huffed, the sound fraught with frustration. "I need a job where I can support myself. I can't make enough sewing dresses now and then to pay for lodging and food and all of my other needs. So I need to move on."

"You *need* to, or you *want* to? There's a difference, Frances." He paused, but she remained stubbornly silent, refusing to look at him. He went on. "I suspect your leaving has less to do with needing a job than with simply running away."

She dropped her arms and gaped at him. "Running away? Running away from what?"

Adam let his foot fall, and he shifted to face her. They were less than two feet apart, and their breath hung heavy between them in the cool night air. "That's what I would like to know." His eyes locked on hers. He gentled his voice, genuine desire to understand writhing through his chest. "What are you trying to escape, Frances?"

She set her jaw and glared at him. "What are you saying, Adam?"

He met her anger with his own steady look. "I'm saying something happened to frighten you into leaving. I'm saying you're running like a scared rabbit instead of sticking things out."

Brown eyes met blue, and sparks flew from both.

She dropped her gaze first. "I'm not running away."

"Then why this talk of leaving when I know you've been perfectly happy here." Adam longed to pull her against his chest, to hold her tight and protect her. He clamped his arms against his sides and continued. "You have a place to stay, a job, people who care about you. Two little babies I know you love. Why not stay?"

Defiance flared in her eyes. "Just because you helped me out when I needed it doesn't give you the right to question me and tell me what to do."

Her obstinate attitude brought a rush of temper. It was on the tip of Adam's tongue to holler that loving her gave him every right to question her and expect a straight answer. But he couldn't shout out something like that in anger. And now wasn't the time, anyway, to be admitting he loved her. He released a huff of aggravation. "Well, *someone* needs to tell you what to do. You're not thinking straight, girl."

Her gaze narrowed. Her jaw clamped so tightly he heard her teeth grind together. "Nobody tells me I'm dumb anymore. Nobody!" She pushed off from the railing with a shove of her palms. "I've already overstayed my welcome here. I'm thankful for all your family's done for me, but the job is finished, and it's time to move on."

Adam forcibly calmed himself, remembering her reaction to his questions about her family. His voice took on a pleading quality as he attempted another tack, trying to placate her. "Frances, the other day at the dugout—"

She cut him off with a shrill snort of forced laughter. "You think *you're* responsible for my leave taking? You think *you* said something yesterday that makes me want to leave?" Her lips twisted into a cynical smirk. "You think too highly of yourself, Adam. This decision is my own, and no one else helped it along." She yanked the shawl tight across her chest and turned toward the house. "Good night, Adam."

"You sure are a stubborn little thing," Adam muttered under his breath. As she took a step toward the house, he reached out to catch her arm, intending to make her stay and talk this thing out. The moment his hand closed on her forearm, she released a panicked cry. Her arms flew upward, curling around her head, and she dropped into a crouch, pressing her face against her knees.

Adam stared in shocked silence. For a moment he couldn't move, just stood motionless, his eyes riveted as she crouched, arms protectively over her head. Moonlight bathed her, making her fingers glow white as she clutched the back of her neck. The incongruity of the moment—the beautiful, starlit night and her frozen, fear-filled reaction—struck hard. Compassion filled him, his anger dissolving as quickly as it had flared.

He dropped to his knees beside her, reaching out a tentative hand to gently stroke her tense back—once, then again. Her muscles quivered beneath his touch. He swallowed hard. "Frances? Hey, Frances, look at me."

Instead of raising her face, she pulled tighter into her cocoon, as if folding into herself both physically and emotionally. Adam stroked her back again, his fingers brushing as softly as a butterfly's wings. He moved gently. Persuasively. His touch heartbreakingly light. He kept his voice whisper-soft, tender as his touch.

"Frances, please listen to me. I wasn't going to hurt you. This is Adam, remember? I'd *never* hurt you, Frances." *Oh, Lord, what have I done to her?* "I was upset, yes, but I wouldn't hurt you. You believe me, don't you, Frances?"

Ever so slowly she brought down her arms, and she peered at him sideways through a veil of hair. The emptiness in her eyes pierced Adam more deeply than fury could have. "Come on now, Frances, stand up. It's okay now." His hands trembled as he held them out to her.

She jerked back from his offered hand, standing quickly and stiffly. She moved several feet away, still watching him with a stoic yet wary expression. Her hands grasped convulsively at the shawl. "I want to go in now." As if it took great concentration, she began walking toward the house, her steps measured and stilted.

Adam stood in place, watching her go. As she entered the house, closing the door without a backward glance, Adam felt his throat constrict. Now he understood her reluctance to talk about her past, to share anything of her upbringing. Horror seized his gut as he pictured her, hunkering into that pose that said clearly what she expected to happen next. He forced his fingers through his hair, squeezing the strands with his fists, frustrated and more angry with himself than ever. He spun, dug his fingers into the wooden rail of the corral fence, and raised his face to the heavens. *What a horrible life she must have led. And I reminded her of it. I made her think I would hurt her, that I could treat her like that. That I would ever harm a hair of her head.*

In time he calmed, but he couldn't face Liz or Jake. He crossed with heavy steps to his horse, leaped on, and grabbed the reins. He jabbed his heels into the horse's side. "Gee-up!" His voice was hoarse, tear choked. He whispered, "Good-bye, Frances." For he was sure that he had lost her now.

By the time Samantha had hurried across the kitchen to the stairs and reached her room, humiliation had replaced the numbing shock. She sank onto her bed, burying her face in her hands. When Adam grabbed her arm, there hadn't been room for reasoning. Her reaction had been pure instinct, her body acting without a thought. Her brain screamed for her to protect herself, and her body obeyed.

What must Adam think of me now? She curled into a ball on the straw-filled mattress. Now he knew. . . . His gentle hand on her back, the shimmer of sympathetic tears in his eyes spoke the truth. He knew what her pa had done to her. Her chest convulsed with shame. How could she ever face kind, tender-hearted Adam again?

Her throat ached with the need to cry, but her eyes remained dry. Samantha didn't cry. Her thoughts begged, *Oh, Gran, please help me now. Give me the courage to do what I must do. Give me the courage to leave this place and this man. Please, please.*

She lay in her bed, dry eyed and hurting, her arms wrapped tight around herself, wishing . . . wishing . . . wishing for what could never be.

amantha sat shivering on the hard wooden bench at the Mountain Lake train depot, shivering. Was it cold or fear that made her tremble? She tugged the woolen shawl more snugly around her shoulders, trying to hunch down inside of it as best she could. She would purchase a ticket for Minneapolis as soon as the depot opened. She held her money in her fist beneath the shawl, waiting for the train to come and carry her away from the community and the family who had come to mean as much to her as her Gran had.

Guilt niggled at her as she considered how she'd sneaked out before the break of dawn. But if she'd waited to say good-byes, there would have been an argument or at least a series of questions she couldn't answer. So she'd lain in her bed to be certain both Liz and Jake were still asleep before creeping down the stairs, avoiding the ones that she knew creaked. She needed some kind of wrap, so she'd left $2.50 of her hard-earned money on top of the hook before pulling the shawl around her and beginning the long walk into town. In the moments when she had hovered over little A.J. and Andy's cradles to bestow a farewell kiss, she'd almost changed her mind. The little boys smelled so sweet and tugged at her heartstrings in a peculiar way. It was *so* hard to leave. . . .

But she surely had to go. She knew that. Particularly after her disagreement with Adam. She closed her eyes, picturing his stricken face, his eyes sorrowful and sympathetic. She could only imagine what he'd been thinking as she'd cowered on the ground before him. Well, before any more of her secrets were revealed and Adam realized how he'd been fooled, she'd be off. She couldn't bear to look into Adam's eyes and see that expression of pain again.

Shivering, she shifted on the bench, feeling the consequences of the long walk on top of very little sleep. She checked the clock hanging above the ticket window. The train wasn't due for another hour or so. Maybe she'd lean her head back against the station wall, close her eyes for just a bit. . . .

⚬⚬

"Jake! Jake!" Liz ran across the hard ground, apron flying and money clutched in her hand. Jake met her in the doorway of the barn. She fell into his waiting arms. "She's gone. She didn't come down this morning, so I went to her room to check, and she's gone."

"Now, settle down, honey." Jake rubbed her shoulders, his voice calm. "I'm sure she can't have gone far. We'll find her, don't worry. I'll head out—."

"No, she won't let you find her." Liz shook her head, tears springing into her eyes. "Look—she left this money on top of the hook where the shawls are—she took one of them with her." Liz began to sob. "She was so upset last night when she came in. I could see it. I should have gone up and talked to her. I should have—."

"Liz, don't you start blaming yourself." Jake gave her a little shake. "She's made it clear she was ready to go, and she went. I'm willing to look for her if that's what you want, but not if it's only because of some sense of guilt, because you have no reason for it."

Liz shook her head, swiping at her tears with shaking fingers. "It's not guilt, honest. I just can't let things go like this.

She was upset. . . ." Liz clutched her husband's hands, drawing strength from his firm grasp. She had someone on whom to depend; Frances had no one. The girl needed them. "Go get Adam. Adam will know what to do."

Jake delivered a quick kiss on Liz's forehead, then released Samson from his stall. "Don't worry, honey, we'll find her, and everything will be just fine."

Liz watched Samson gallop down the lane, Jake hunched over the horse's broad back. *Everything will be fine*, he'd said. How she hoped and prayed her husband was right.

She walked back to the house, praying as she went.

∾⊙

Adam dug his heels into Bet's side, encouraging her to move faster. He should have guessed Frances would do something like this after the way he'd left her. What else could she do but run? She was no doubt scared to death of him now. He should never have grabbed her like that. It wasn't like him to lose his temper, but when faced with losing her. . . .

He had to find her. He had to set things right. He needed to assure her that he was nothing like whomever it was who had mistreated her so terribly in the past. As he moved at a fast trot toward town, the horse's hide warm against his legs, his thoughts drifted backward over the past months. Frances's odd behavior finally made sense. Having been mistreated, of course she would be leery and insecure. Of course she would be reluctant to talk about her past. What they had seen as sullenness had really been protective walls she'd built around herself—a necessary way to cope with the unthinkable.

He clenched his fists around the reins, resisting the urge to press Bet into a full-out gallop. *Lord, please let me find her, and*

help her understand that she doesn't need to be afraid anymore. Give me a
chance to show her how much I care.

◦──◦

The shrill blast jolted Samantha out of a sound sleep. She jerked upright, wincing as her cold, stiff muscles strained against her abrupt movements. Smoke smudged the sky above the trees; the train would be here soon. In a few minutes she'd be off to a new city and a new life.

But only dread filled her stomach. She knew she'd made the right choice, though. The Klaassens—especially Adam—would be better off with her gone. She could start over again, free from Pa and free from the guilty feelings from pretending to be someone else.

The ground vibrated as the train chugged into the depot. As the huge black engine screeched to a noisy stop, Samantha stood, scooping up her bundle of clothing. She had convinced herself that the two dresses she'd made were hers, since the fabric was a gift. Her reasoning hadn't made her feel much better, though.

She scurried to the ticket window, her bag clutched in her fist, and glanced at the signboard on the wall. She drew in a deep breath. "Ticket to Minneapolis, please."

The smiling stationmaster stamped a cardboard ticket. "That'll be three dollars."

Samantha slipped her hand into her pocket, and panic gripped her. Where was her money? She checked her other pocket, then rifled through her bag, her alarm mounting. "I—I seem to have misplaced my . . ."

The stationmaster's smile faded. "Miss, there are others waiting. Will you hurry, please?"

Samantha whisked a glance at a trio of impatient faces behind her. "I'm sorry. My money—it's . . ." She dug through the bag again, but no bills appeared. Her shoulders sagging, she stepped aside and allowed the others to press forward. She found her way back to the bench and sank down. When she'd fallen asleep, she'd been gripping the money in her fist. It must have blown away while she slept. Perhaps she could still find it. She searched underneath the bench and along the platform, but she found nothing except some old newspapers flapping in the breeze.

Discouragement overwhelmed her. Burying her face in her hands, she battled wailing in fury. Why must everything go wrong? The train would leave soon. A conductor walked up and down the track, checking cars, but maybe she could sneak onto a later one. Snatching up her small parcel, she tossed the bundle over her shoulder and moved off the platform. She'd rest on the other side of the depot—soak up the morning sun's warmth, and wait for the next train. . . . If she were lucky, she'd be able to climb into one of the boxcars without being seen.

Adam reined Bet in hard next to the depot and swung down. His heart beat in hopeful double beats. He let his gaze move across the people milling on the wooden platform. Where was she? It made sense she'd take a train out of town. But was he too late?

Flinging Bet's reins around a hitching post, he stepped onto the platform, nearly colliding with a scruffy-looking man with several days' growth of gray whiskers dotting his cheeks. The man's tobacco-stained teeth showed behind his sneer. A foul odor rose from his dirty, wrinkled clothing.

"Excuse me, sir." Adam shifted aside so the man could pass. The man grabbed his arm. "Where's sheriff's office?"

Adam pointed to the right. "Three blocks that way. Sign above the door."

With a bob of his shaggy head, the man turned and shuffled off. Adam resumed his search, trotting from one end of the platform to the other, searching the faces of every person on the wooden walkway and peering from the windows of the passenger cars. But Frances was nowhere to be seen. Frustration and fear fought against hope, and he turned back toward Bet. Then a flash of blue on the other side of the depot caught his eye. He moved quietly sideways, peeking around the wall, and there she sat huddled against the side of the building.

The relief nearly buckled his knees. He stumbled toward her. "Frances!"

Her entire body jolted, her wide-eyed gaze spinning to meet his. She pressed one fist to her mouth and held herself tightly against the lapped siding.

Adam thought his heart would burst from sorrow. He approached slowly, fearful of sending her into panicked flight. "Frances . . ."

Leaping to her feet, she grabbed her bundle and darted around him into the depot. He followed her to the ticket window where she slapped the counter and cried out, her voice desperately shrill, "I need a ticket. Please, I *must have* a ticket."

Adam, his chest tight and aching, stretched out his hand but stopped short of touching her. "Frances, please, I must to talk with you."

She shot him a glance so full of pain he felt it like a blow to his heart. She twisted back to the agent. "A ticket. Hurry, please. I'll—I'll pay you when—"

"Frances?" Adam inched closer.

She froze, her fingers digging into the wooden counter. A low moan escaped her quivering lips. She spun away and marched back out to the edge of the boardwalk, her back stiff. "Why . . . ?" Her voice trembled. "Why'd you have to come now? I was so close."

Her words pierced him. He eased up behind her, hands pressed once again tightly against his sides. "Liz sent me to find you. She was worried." He didn't add how much he'd been worried. "Why did you take off that way, Frances?"

Her shoulders rose and fell in shuddering heaves, but she didn't speak.

He leaned closer, his breath stirring the little coils of hair trailing beside her ear. "Frances, can we go somewhere and talk . . . please?"

She drew in a deep breath, tension emanating from every part of her body. Then her tight fist released, her bundle falling from her hand with a soft thud against the wooden walkway. Her shoulders slumped, her hands lifted to cover her face, and a heart-wrenching cry burst from her lips.

Once started, the sobs and tears struck like a gale force. Her shoulders shook, and tears rained down between her fingers.

A murmur of voices sounded from behind him, and Adam glanced back at a small gathering of curious onlookers. Frances was a private person; this public breakdown would humiliate her. Grabbing up her bag with one hand and slipping his other around her waist, Adam guided her behind the depot building to a small storage shed.

dam yanked the door open and guided Frances into the dark shed. It took only a few moments for his eyes to adjust to the dimness, but it seemed a lifetime passed as he stood listening to Frances's painful sobs. Hands on her shoulders, he eased her onto a closed keg and helped her sit. She doubled up and buried her face in her lap as she cried. Adam found another keg and pulled it close to her, seating himself with his knees nearly touching hers.

Years of comforting crying little brothers and sisters made Adam long to reach out and hold this distraught child-woman, to somehow end her suffering. But he sensed these tears were needed to cleanse her of too-long-held sorrows, deeper than he could fathom. So he cupped his hands over his knees and sat, silent and still, breathing the musty odors of grease, dirt, and mold, listening, praying, his heart aching for the pain being so wrenchingly expressed.

Gradually the wild crying began to quiet, changing from harsh to quiet sobs. Eventually, after what seemed an eternity, it faded to weak hiccups. And, with a series of shuddering sighs, the sobs died out.

Slowly Frances sat up, taking in one long, ragged breath. Adam reached into his back pocket for a handkerchief which he laid in her lap. She mopped at her face, then blew her nose noisily. With shaking fingers she explored her swollen eyelids. Lowering her hands, she sighed. "I haven't cried like that since I was six years old." Her voice sounded hollow and raw.

Adam dared give her knee a gentle squeeze. "Then I think it was about time."

She twisted the soggy handkerchief in her hands, staring downward. She went on as if he hadn't spoken. "Yes, the last time I cried like that was when I was six. When Gran died." Lifting her face, she said, "Have I ever told you about Gran?"

Adam shook his head, afraid to speak. She'd never told him about anything, as she well knew.

She gave a nod, her lips trembling, then began speaking in an emotionless, even tone that somehow was more chilling than her wild weeping had been. "You see, my mama died birthing me. Pa wanted to take me out and drown me like some unwanted kitten, but Gran wouldn't let him. She moved in with us and took over. She cared for me and Pa and my brother just like it was nothing. It was really something, though. She was past seventy when I was born, but she ran that household as well as any woman half her age. Wasn't easy, either, with Pa . . ." She paused, seemingly lost in thought.

Adam held his breath, wanting to ask questions but afraid of frightening her again, maybe into permanent silence.

In time she continued. "Gran was . . . Gran was a lot like your mother. Always smiling and kind, never finding fault or fractious. She had this soft lap just right for snuggling up in. She used to hold me after Pa would—after he'd. . . ." She swallowed.

The image of her huddled in a ball in the moonlight flashed through Adam's mind. He leaned forward and pressed his hands around hers, telling her without words he understood. She needn't say anything more.

She pulled in another shuddering breath. "Afterward, she'd hold me and comfort me, and tell me not to believe the things he said, that I *was* special, that I *was* good. When Gran told me that, I could almost believe it." Her tone turned wistful.

Still holding her hands, Adam prompted quietly, "Your Gran died when you were six?"

Frances nodded, her head bent. "Yes. She was Pa's grand-mother. You'd think he'd have been sad, but I think he was angry, because then there wasn't anybody to wait on him, ex-cept me and my older brother, Davey, and we couldn't do it good enough." Her face turned up toward his, and she looked earnestly into his eyes. "We tried, though. We really did." Another deep sigh sagged her shoulders. "But it was never good enough."

She pulled her hands loose from his grasp, leaning against the shed wall. "Davey stuck around for a while—about three years, I guess, after Gran died. But then he said he had to git. Told me to wait for him, told me he'd be back for me. He *promised*." She bit her lip, blinking back more tears. "That promise wasn't worth much. I haven't seen him since."

Adam battled a wave of sorrow. She'd lost so much.

"A person shouldn't make a promise he might not be able to keep." The hurt in her tone sent another shaft of pain through Adam's middle. "I waited every night for seven years, hoping he'd come back and rescue me. Took me a long time to figure out no one was going to rescue me but *me*. So I made my own plans to leave. I ran off, but I didn't get far. Pa always caught up with me. . . ."

So she was a runaway, just as the sheriff surmised.

"Till this last time. I decided if I was going to get away, I'd have to be somebody else. So I stole some clothes out of a trunk in the cellar to make me look like a boy, and when Pa was sleeping off a drunk, I lit out. I just wanted to get away from Pa, like Davey had—as far away from Milwaukee as I could. I just wanted to escape. I didn't mean—" Her chin shot upward. Her throat convulsed.

"Frances, what is it?" He used his gentlest tone. "You didn't mean what?"

Tears flooded her eyes as she began babbling, almost hysterical. "Oh, Adam, I'm so sorry. At first I thought it was smart and funny, fooling you into thinking I was somebody else. But then I got to know all of you. I knew it was wrong, and I wanted to tell you. Honest, I wanted to. I didn't mean to lie to you. But I had to or you would send me home. Back to Pa. That's why I *had* to lie. Oh, please, can't you understand?"

Adam stared at her confusion. It had been obvious early on that she wasn't a boy. "I *don't* understand, Frances. What—?"

"I'm not Frances." She shook her head wildly, impatience pursing her lips. "I'm Samantha."

Adam sat back as if he'd been pole-axed. Samantha? Her name was *Samantha*?

More tears rolled down her cheeks. She leaned forward and clutched his hands, her cold fingers digging into his palms. "At first I was Frances to fool you and keep me from having to go back. But the longer I was Frances, the easier it was to *be* Frances, and after a while, I almost believed it myself. I hated it, lying to you—you all were so nice to me. But if I told you the truth, you and the sheriff could find out where I came from. And . . . and I'd have to leave. I'd have to go back." Desperation tinged her tone. "I didn't want to go back."

Adam's world spun. Not Frances, but Samantha. All this time . . . and she *had* been running—from her own family, though, not him.

Tears rolled endlessly down her cheeks as she pleaded with him, one hand wrapped around his wrist with a strength he wouldn't have thought possible from such a small person. "I don't expect you to forgive me, Adam. I couldn't expect that. But can't you please try to understand? You and your folks were nicer to me than anybody ever was—except for Gran, and maybe Davey. I couldn't tell you the truth. Not without you being able to send me home. And I couldn't go home. I just couldn't."

In flashes of thought Adam silently compared her childhood to his, balancing his secure home against her unstable one, his knowledge of being loved against her feelings of unworthiness. He possessed so many warm, wonderful memories of family and home and acceptance. He almost felt guilty for having been born into his family when Samantha had been thrust into such an abusive, angry environment.

He *could* understand. And he could comfort her now. He reached a hand to smooth the tangled hair from her tear-stained face. He ran his thumbs beneath her eyes, whisking away the tears, and spoke her name—her true name—for the first time. "Samantha, it's all right. I understand." Then he stated the words he knew she needed to hear. "And I forgive you."

Her face crumpled, but she held the tears at bay, looking at him for a long moment, an expression of gratitude shining in her swollen eyes. Then she threw herself at him, wrapping her arms around his neck and clinging hard. He returned the embrace, cupping the back of her head closely against his shoulder.

He closed his eyes and tilted his head to feel her warm hair firm against his cheek. As he held her, offering the comfort of his embrace, he prayed, *Help her, Lord. Heal her, please . . . and help me to know just what she needs.*

In time she pulled away, flicking a self-conscious smile in his direction before letting her gaze skitter elsewhere. She lifted his handkerchief and wiped her face once again. Crushing the sodden wad of cloth in her fist, she offered a wobbly smile. "Want to hear something funny?"

Smiling, Adam gave a nod.

"Gran believed like you do—that there's a God who loves us and watches out for us. I used to say my bedtime prayers when I was little: God bless everybody. Gran would listen to my prayers then tuck me in. Like your ma does with Teddy and Sarah."

Adam was grateful she had this small memory. At least there was something pleasant in her fractured past.

Her voice lost its blithe undertone as she continued. "When Gran left the room, I'd tell God I really didn't mean God bless Pa. I'd ask would God please make Pa go away. But instead of taking Pa away, He took Gran, and then Davey. . . ." She swallowed, pain again creasing her face. "Adam, do you think God took Gran and David away to punish me for those prayers?"

Adam captured her hands once more. "God loves you. You were only a little girl. He would never hold you responsible for those prayers."

"Then why did Gran die? And Davey never come back for me? I loved them both so much, and they left me."

Her voice, so full of wounded bitterness, shattered Adam's heart. He prayed for the right words to ease her pain. "Listen to me, Samantha. Your Gran was old. She was doing much more than she had the strength for, but she wanted to do it, because she loved you. You weren't responsible for her death. And David had reasons of his own for leaving. He wasn't leaving to get away from you, but from his own unhappy circumstances. I don't know why he didn't come back for you as he promised, but there probably is a good reason. Either way, you can't blame yourself."

"But Pa said—."

Adam squeezed her hands. "Your pa is a bitter, unhappy man. Maybe your mother dying so early made him bitter, maybe he was always that way. Some people seem to enjoy being un-happy. The only way they can make themselves feel better is to make everyone around them feel bad too. Instead of hating him, we should feel sorry for him. He must be very miserable to act the way he has. And by his actions he lost a son . . . and a very special daughter."

Samantha looked at him doubtfully. "Me? Special?"

"Yes, you." Adam stroked the backs of her hands with his thumbs, determined to help her understand. "Why, with all the people in my family, you'd think we'd never need anyone else. But we did, Samantha"—he let his voice linger on her name—"and there you were. You came into our lives just when we needed you. And you've been such a wonderful help to Liz and Jake and the twins. You're a good friend to Josie, and Sarah adores you." He raised her hands to his lips, pressing a kiss on her knuckles. "Samantha, you are loved by every member of my family." *Especially me.* But he held the words inside. The time wasn't right. She needed time for healing—from the inside out. "And as much as *we* love you, *God* loves you even more."

Samantha's chin quivered. "I want to believe I'm somebody special, and worthy of love but . . ."

"What's keeping you from it, Fran—Samantha?"

Tears swam in her red-rimmed eyes. "I lied to you. I pre-tended to be somebody I wasn't. And before that, I tried to—"

Adam gently placed two fingers over her lips. "And you think that makes you unworthy?" Her face told him clearly that yes, that's exactly what she thought. "Samantha, God sent his Son, Jesus, when we all were still sinners. You can't have any greater love than that. He didn't wait around for us to become perfect, then love us. He loves us just where we are—imperfect and floundering and needy. All we have to do is accept that love, and the whole world changes."

"You believe in that love, don't you?" Wonder bloomed on her face. "I can tell by the way you are with other people. All of you—kind and giving. I've never heard your mother or father say hateful things. They act the way I think God must be."

"That's because we've accepted the love of Jesus and asked Him to live with us, inside." Adam touched his hand to his chest, and he could feel his heart beating hard against his shirt front. "When Christ's Spirit is a part of you, you begin to be bent to His nature. 'Old things are passed away; behold, all things are made new.' And here's a promise you can hang on to forever—'I will never leave you nor forsake you.' Christ will be with you every day, helping you become the person you want to be—ought to be."

Samantha sat in silence for several long minutes. Adam waited patiently, praying quietly for the truth to become real to her. From her brief sketch of her childhood, he couldn't help but marvel at her resilience and courage.

The years of suffering had damaged her emotionally, but he knew her feelings of worthlessness could be changed with God's help. He prayed that he could get through to her, to help her realize that what he had, what the Klaassens and so many others had, could be hers only for the asking.

∽◯

Samantha recalled words she'd heard the minister speak in church. She remembered signs of God's power she'd seen in the lives of the people around her. More than she'd ever wanted anything, she wanted the peace and happiness that Adam and his family had. And according to Adam, all she had to do was *ask*. It seemed almost too simple to be true. But Adam had said if she'd just believe, it could be hers, too.

I believe. I do believe.

"Adam?" She drew in a breath, pushing aside doubt or fear. "Will you please pray with me?"

Without hesitation, Adam dropped onto his knees beside the nail keg. Samantha joined him and, right there in the musty storage shed beside the train depot, Samantha asked Jesus to come into her life.

When she'd finished, Adam rose, holding out a hand. She took it, and he drew her to her feet. She gazed into his face. Did the warmth beneath her skin show? Could he see the joy blossoming through her heart? Looking into his compassionate eyes, she believed he could. Without even trying, a smile burst across her face. "Thank you, Adam."

Unshed tears brightened his eyes. "Thank You, Jesus." He gave her a quick hug. "Come on, Samantha. Let's go home."

Home . . .

*A*dam swung himself onto Bet's broad back, then reached a hand down for Samantha. She hesitated only a moment before placing her hand in his and allowing him to pull her up behind him. With her little bundle fastened in front of Adam, she leaned against him, relaxed and trusting, her arms holding lightly to his waist.

As the horse moved slowly along the leaf-strewn road, the gentle swaying motion must have lulled her to sleep. Her head tipped forward against his back, and a quick look over his shoulder showed her thick lashes throwing a shadow across her cheek. Gazing into her peaceful face, he smiled. *Samantha.* The name suited her far better than Frances. *Samantha of the russet hair and cornflower eyes.*

The significance of what had occurred in the storage shed behind the depot brought a lift of joy to his heart he wasn't able to describe. Samantha now knew the Lord too. The barrier that had kept him from truly acknowledging his love for her was removed. His heart thrummed happily. Now he could—with a jolt he realized he didn't even know how old she was. Was she old enough to be betrothed?

He mentally scrolled backward in time. Her great-grandmother died when she was six, her brother had been gone for seven or eight years after staying home for—what? Three years after Gran's death? That would make her seventeen or so. Josie's age. . . . Taking another look at her relaxed face, he decided she seemed younger—especially in sleep. But her age mattered not a whit. If she was too young now, he'd just wait. He certainly wasn't so old he had to be married right away. And she was worth waiting for.

He experienced a rush of feeling for the young woman who lay so trustingly with her cheek pressed to his shoulder blade. She was a beautiful person with well-placed features. And that hair. It waved around her face in wild disarray, but he loved it. It was perfect for her—free and flowing and uninhibited. But more than her physical beauty, there was her inner beauty. Oh, she could be stubborn at times, but he'd seen her sweet, giving spirit. The stubbornness, he was convinced now, was just a cover for the insecurity she felt.

Compassion filled him—what an unhappy life she'd had before coming here. Somehow he would make it up to her. He would spend the rest of his life showering her with tenderness, giving her every happiness, if only she would accept him. If only she returned his feelings. . . .

The farm waited around the next bend. He should wake Samantha before entering the yard. He drew back on the reins, bringing Bet to a snorting halt. "Samantha?" He turned as best he could, giving her a gentle shake. "Samantha, you need to wake up."

She smiled sleepily, her eyelids fluttered, and then she straightened to meet Adam's gaze. A blush stole across her cheeks. "Not much company, was I?"

"Nope." Adam grinned, the temptation to tease too strong to resist. "And did you know you snore?"

Samantha jerked upright, her eyes round. "I do?"

Adam laughed. "Of course not."

She giggled, shaking her head in mock dismay.

Adam bobbed his head toward the house. "What say we get down and walk the rest of the way?"

She yawned and nodded agreement. "That would be best." He helped her slide off before hopping down beside her. They shared one last lingering look before Adam tugged at Bet's harness and they headed for the house. As they entered the yard, Samantha pointed to a buggy beside the barn. "Looks like you've got a visitor."

"Reckon so." Adam recognized the rig as John Jenkins', the town blacksmith who also rented it out. And wasn't that the sheriff's horse tethered next to it? "Go on up to the house while I take care of Bet. I'll be there in a few minutes."

Samantha sucked in her lips, her steps faltering. "They— they probably all know how I took off in the night, don't they?"

Sympathy welled in Adam's chest. "I'm sure they do, but they won't hold it against you."

She dipped her head and dug into the ground with the toe of her shoe. "Can—can I stay with you? Then we can go in together. . . ."

How could Adam refuse such a sweet request? "Come with me then." Her smile rewarded him. He enjoyed her company while he brushed Bet with a wide, short bristled brush, speaking his usual words of small talk to the horse as he worked. A barn cat rubbed against Samantha's leg, and she scooped it up, scratching its chin and making it purr.

She murmured silly things to the cat, and when she looked up and caught Adam watching her, her cheeks turned rosy. "Guess it's kind of silly, talking to a cat." She put the animal on the floor.

Adam shrugged. "No sillier than talking to a horse."

She gave a soft chuckle. "Then we're both silly."

Placing the brush on its shelf, Adam swished his hands together. "Two of a kind, that's us," he agreed, his throat tight as he considered the deeper meaning behind his simple statement.

They stood silently in the barn, oblivious to the purring cat and Bet's snorts of contentment. Nothing existed in those moments but Adam and Samantha. A question crossed his mind: *Should I?* In silent answer, he very slowly moved toward her, scuffing up bits of hay as he came.

He could see her draw in her breath and hold it as he approached, her eyes locked on his. He saw the question in her eyes: *Would he? Would he really?* . . . When he stood mere inches in front of her, he stopped, bringing up his hands to cup her upper arms. Her gaze flittered from his eyes to his lips, then to his eyes again. He watched the course of her blue eyes, and one side of his mouth quirked into a smile before he bent forward. "I love you, Samantha." He didn't wait but placed his lips softly—ever so softly—on hers.

When he straightened, she released in one *whoosh* the breath she'd been holding. Adam dropped his hands and stepped back. Bold crimson painted her cheeks, but she didn't avert her gaze. He had told her how he felt about her, he had kissed her, and she wasn't running scared. His heart turned over in his chest. He held out his hand. "Let's go see the folks."

She slipped her hand into his. "I'm ready."

⌒◯

They ambled toward the big house hand in hand. Adam opened the screened door into the kitchen and held it while Samantha entered. With a sharp intake of breath she stopped immediately inside the doorway. Adam peered over her shoulder.

Sheriff Barnes and the scruffy looking man Adam had encountered at the depot was sitting at the kitchen table with his ma and pa, sipping coffee. As the door slammed back into its frame, all four looked toward them.

The disheveled man grinned, showing his crooked yellow teeth. "Well, hello, girlie. Betcha yore surprised ta' see me here, huh?"

Samantha stood as still as if she were made of stone. Adam slipped a hand under hers and squeezed gently, a fearful understanding forming in his mind.

Ma stood slowly and moved toward them. Sympathy was clear in her eyes. "Adam, this is Burt O'Brien, from Milwaukee, Wisconsin. He's come to pick up his daughter."

Adam looked into Samantha's stricken face. His legs went weak. Why did her father have to come now? *I should have let her board that train.*

Sheriff Barnes pushed to his feet and crossed the room to stand beside Samantha. "Is this your father, young lady?" His tone was gruff, but his eyes looked sad.

When Samantha nodded woodenly, Adam put his arm around her stiff shoulders, hoping to comfort her with his presence. "Ma, Pa, I found Samantha at the train station. She agreed to come back home with me. We—."

Samantha's father blasted a snort. "*Home?* I hate to tell ya, sonny, but this ain't her home. She'll be a'certain to go home, though. Right now. With me." He lurched around the table and grasped Samantha's arm just above her elbow with grime-encrusted fingers and pushed her toward the door.

"Wait!" Adam leaped into their way.

"Wait fer what?" Burt O'Brien's harsh, grating voice scraped across Adam's ears. "S'pose yo're wantin' me to thank ya fer keepin' track o' my gal. Wal, fine. Thank ya. 'Preciate your hospitality." He spat the words, his taunting grin making a mockery of them. "Now lemme pass. I'm takin' my girlie home."

Ma and Pa followed as Burt pushed Samantha out the door. He stomped in a blundering gait across the yard, Samantha stumbling along as if in shock. Adam trotted beside them, wanting to stop the man but afraid to intervene. Burt O'Brien was a violent man. If Adam created a scene, Samantha could be hurt.

With a mighty shove, Burt forced Samantha into the buggy and climbed up awkwardly beside her. Adam ran around to the opposite side of the rig, reaching up to clasp Samantha's icy hand. "Samantha, I—" But what could he say? *I'll come for you.* Only an hour ago she had tearfully told him that people shouldn't make promises they couldn't keep. He wouldn't add another broken promise to all those made before. So he squeezed her cold hand and tried to tell her with his eyes what was on his heart.

Her lips wavered into the saddest smile he'd ever seen. "Adam, don't worry. I'll be all right." Then a smile reached her eyes, igniting an inner fire. "I have Someone stronger than me with me now."

Her bravery tugged painfully at his heart. Despite her determined expression, he sensed the fear in her stiffly upright position. *Oh, Lord, how can I help her now?* His Bible . . . he'd give Samantha his Bible. He waved both hands, inching sideways. "Wait, please, just wait a minute. Don't leave. I've got something—." He spun and took off at a run for the house.

He clattered up the stairs, his heart pounding so hard it hurt to breathe. He snatched the Bible from its spot on the bedside table and raced back out. The buggy waited, both passengers on the seat, with Pa and Ma at its side. Ma was telling Samantha's father about her good job working for Liz.

"That so?" O'Brien shot his daughter a speculative glance.

"Yes. She's done such a fine job," Ma continued, her eyes hopeful, "that we'd like her to stay and—."

"No." The man spat over the edge of the buggy, his brown-tinged spittle landing near Pa's booted foot. "She ain't stayin' here. She's got her own house to tend, an' she's gonna tend it. Now you folks jus' step back so we can git to the train station afore the next train goes without us." He raised his hands as if to slap the reins down against the horse's back.

Adam reached across Samantha to capture the man's grubby wrist. "Mr. O'Brien, please—just one more minute." The man scowled, but he held his hands still. Adam pressed the Bible into Samantha's lap. "Here are promises you can count on, Samantha." *They will keep you until I can make my own promises to you*, he tried to tell her with his eyes.

She looked down, and tears swam in her eyes. She clutched the book to her breast and nodded, smiling weakly through her tears.

"Hi-yup!" O'Brien brought the reins down on the horse's back, sending the startled animal into a trot.

Samantha turned backward in her seat, her face pinched and pale. But she offered a brave, tremulous smile, lifting her hand to wave. Adam took two steps forward, ready to chase down the buggy and bring her back.

Ma placed a hand on his arm. "Let her go, son. We have to let her go."

"But, Ma, that man—" Adam's voice broke. "He'll hurt her. I know he will."

Ma squeezed Adam's arm, the touch wrought with sympathetic understanding. "We have to let her go, Adam, and trust the Lord to watch out for her."

Adam looked to Sheriff Barnes for help, but the big man simply shook his head, an expression of regret in his face. "I'm sorry, Adam. She's underage—not old enough to be on her own. If her pa wants her home, I had to send her."

The buggy rounded the bend, carrying Samantha away. Adam pressed his hands hard into his jacket pockets, his jaw clenched. He'd only just gotten her—she'd only just become his. And now she was gone. It wasn't fair. *Oh, God, it isn't fair.* He looked down into his mother's empathetic face. "Ma," he choked out, but he could say no more. Lowering his head, he turned away and wept.

*O*ctober passed, bleak and dismal with overcast skies and biting winds that matched Adam's somber mood. The first snowfall, usually an event of celebration, cheered Adam not in the least. Samantha's abrupt departure from his life—as sudden and unexpected as her entrance had been—left a hollow void he found impossible to fill. His days were full and busy, yet empty. The joy was gone. And he didn't know how to recapture it.

He haunted the post office, hoping and praying for some word from Samantha that would let him know how she fared. But nothing came, and gradually he came to accept that she wouldn't—or couldn't—write to him. The memories of their brief time together were no doubt as painful for her as they were for him. It was better to let go.

The day he overhead Sarah ask, "Mama, will Adam ever smile again?" he realized he must somehow regain his old, cheerful spirit. But how? He agonized, the image of Samantha cowering in fright after their brief argument haunting his dreams and creeping into his mind at odd times during the day. There were so many other images he could conjure—Samantha in her overalls picking berries with her hair wild around her piquant face; Samantha smiling blissfully as she cradled little A.J.; Samantha happily exploring the dugout; Samantha rising from her knees in a storage shed, her face shining. . . . Yet that horrible picture overwhelmed him.

Was she being abused now? Was she lying somewhere, bruised and broken, waiting for a rescuer? Those images tortured him until he wanted to scream at the heavens.

Adam needed a change. He needed a task so mind consuming that all thoughts of Samantha would be erased. He thought of his friend Thomas Enns and where he had gone. The idea of going off to fight, as Thomas had, filled him with dread, yet if he went, he felt certain he could rid his thoughts of Samantha. There were great risks involved, and his family would be in opposition to such a plan. Yet in his despondent state, the idea held merit.

He could enlist in the army. Frank and Arn, with Teddy's help, could handle the farm work so he didn't need to feel guilty about leaving his father short-handed. The plans fell into place in his mind. He would wait until after Thanksgiving. One last holiday with his family, and then he would go. The course of action decided, Adam made a determined effort to at least pretend to be his old, jocular self again. He wanted to leave his family with pleasant memories to recall while he was away. He didn't allow himself to dwell on the reason, but he knew it was just in case he didn't return. . . .

⁓⊙

Back in Milwaukee, Samantha settled into her familiar routine. Household chores, caring for Pa's needs . . . The days were as she remembered—strained and bleak and joyless. She printed up a little sign and hung it in the post office, advertising that she would mend or construct garments for people. Before long, she had a steady business going, and she carefully hoarded away half of the money she earned. Pa took control of the other half, and most of it he squandered on drink. She read Adam's Bible daily, taking comfort in the words she found there. And as time passed, she discovered a peace of spirit within herself despite the outer turmoil in her life.

As she learned more about Jesus and His love for her, she began seeing her father in a different light. She understood that Jesus loved her pa, too, and if she wanted to be like Him, she must try to see her father through Christ's eyes. Instead of viewing him as hateful, she looked deep inside to a man so full of unhappiness that only hate could come out. Instead of reviling him, she began pitying him, and she prayed for him daily that he might come to know the peace she now held in her heart.

On Sundays she walked to the little church she had attended with Gran all those years ago. A new, young minister was serving there now, and his teachings were as gentle and mind soothing as Reverend Goertzen's. Samantha drank in the words spoken by the light-haired man behind the pulpit, reflecting on those words through the week. The more she listened and learned, the easier it was for her to bear Pa's ranting and raving. She was maturing into a spiritual young woman, and the changes did not go unnoticed by the young minister. However, as attentive as Samantha was to his teaching, she remained aloof to any other attentions. Her heart still remained in Mountain Lake.

Her mind carried her back to Mountain Lake often. She wondered how big the twins were, how Liz was feeling, if Sarah's front teeth were clear in and how that might have changed her looks, whether Hulda Klaassen had found someone else to sew up those dresses she was supposed to have made. . . .

But most often she thought of Adam, although she tried not to. She loved him more than she had ever thought possible, but the realization only brought heartache instead of the carefree joy she'd always imagined loving someone would bring. Some days she hoped she would find a letter from him, other days she was glad she didn't. This was her life now, and dreaming of other times and places served no useful purpose. So she immersed herself in her work, in her Bible reading, and her attempts to change her father.

One day as Samantha sat in a rocker near the small four-pane kitchen window, putting the hem in a petticoat, David weighed on her mind. He would be twenty-four years old now. Old enough to be married, maybe even have children. What was David like now?

She remembered him as a thin, pale youth, taller than Pa already at fifteen, with a headful of russet curls that refused to be tamed and her own pale blue eyes. Always somber, rarely smiling. Her brother . . . did David ever think of her? Ever wonder how she was doing? Ever think of returning for her?

She nipped the thread with her teeth and let the white cloth drop into her lap. It seemed sometimes that she had lost every person she'd loved. First Gran, then David. And Adam. It hurt most, losing Adam, because she'd had him for such a short time. Being yanked from him was like being wakened rudely from a happy dream.

The old Samantha would have engrossed herself in self-pity, but the new Samantha saw each loss as a means to strengthen her. She reminded herself that her Book of promises gave the assurance that all things work together for good. Adam had told her she could count on those promises.

She held to God's promises. Her life held meaning now, and purpose. It was only a matter of time before all things became good.

~⊙

The week before Thanksgiving Adam broke the news to his father about enlisting in the army. They were in the tack shed, rubbing soap into two new saddles, when Adam interrupted the comfortable silence to announce his intentions.

Pa glowered. "You will do no such thing."

Adam put the soap aside and leaned forward, resting his elbows on his knees. "Pa, please, can't we talk about this?"

"Absolutely not." Normally mellow, Pa's voice took on a hard edge. "I forbid you to do such a thing."

Adam hung his head. He spoke to the spot of ground between his boots. "I'm not asking for your permission. I'm just telling you what I intend to do." He'd never defied his father before. His chest felt tight, but he wouldn't back down now.

Pa bolted to his feet, pacing back and forth twice in the small space. His breath came out in white puffs, his face set angrily, resembling a disgruntled dragon. "Don't think I can't figure out why you think you need to go. It's the girl, isn't it? It's because of Samantha."

Adam kept his head down, closing his eyes momentarily to mask the stab of pain the mention of Samantha had brought.

Pausing in his clomping progress across the floor, Pa clamped his hand over Adam's shoulder and shook it. "Answer me. Isn't it?"

Adam pushed aside Pa's hand and rose. "Yes. She's in my heart, Pa, and I can't get her out. I need to get away from here. I need to get my mind so wrapped up in something else that no thought of Samantha can intrude. I can't go on like this anymore."

"And you think taking up a weapon and facing an enemy bigger than your own mind will chase her out again?"

"Yes!" Angry tears threatened, and he set his jaw firmly to keep them at bay. He would not humiliate himself by breaking down now.

Pa huffed out a derisive snort. "I would've expected such rash behavior from Frank. He's been our impulsive one—acting first and thinking later. But you? You've always been reasonable and logical." Shaking his head, Pa scuffed his hand across the work table in the corner, seeming to forget Adam was in the room. "Fool boy. Foolish, heartbroken boy. Would never have imagined him threatening to march off to war. If it weren't for that girl . . ."

Adam's defenses rose. "Don't blame Samantha."

Pa released a mirthless laugh and turned to face Adam. "Oh, I'm not. I'm leaving the blame fully at your feet, son. She's not the problem. *You* are the problem. You're your own worst enemy right now." He tapped his graying temple. "Instead of using your head you're letting your heart misguide you. But I know you well enough to know eventually your head will convince your heart to do the right thing."

Adam thrust out his jaw. "I've been thinking. I've thought of nothing else since she left. And I don't know what else to do."

Pa pulled up a sawhorse and seated himself close to his son. "Listen to me, boy." He placed his thick, leathery palm on Adam's knee. "It's one thing to mope, but it's another to throw your life away. You have feelings for the girl. You're worried about her. I understand that. Even respect it. But how can making a foolhardy move like joining the army fix anything?"

Adam didn't have an answer, so he sat in stony silence.

Pa sighed and wiped a hand across his face tiredly, drawing his skin downward. He suddenly looked old to Adam, and it scared him. Pa slapped his hands down on his thighs. "You're twenty years old now, and if you mean to go, I reckon I can't stand in your way. But I can tell you to use the brain God gave you and think. Think long and hard on this before you go traipsing off. You accused Samantha of running away." He paused for a moment, his gaze boring into Adam's. "Just what do you call what you're doing?"

Adam didn't answer. There wasn't much to say when he knew, deep down, that his father was right. But he also knew, right or wrong, that he would go. Because he could think of no other way to rid his mind—and heart—of Samantha O'Brien.

With a heavy sigh, Pa pushed himself upright. He clapped one hand on Adam's shoulder. "I'm gonna go talk to your ma now. Tell her what you're planning. Ask her to pray." He chuckled, the sound sad. "I can tell you what she'll ask the Lord—to change your mind."

Adam whisked a hard glance upward. "About Samantha?"

Pa shook his head. "That'd be foolhardy on our parts. A person doesn't choose to love—it happens. And you can no more choose to turn off your love for Samantha than you chose to have it grow. But our understanding is one thing—giving our blessing to you drowning your sorrows in the horror of battle is quite another." Once again, Pa seemed to drift away. "No one said raising children was easy—and it sure doesn't improve with age."

With another squeeze on Adam's shoulder, Pa pulled his hand away. "Your ma and me are going to put you and your heartache in the Lord's hands, son. Just do one thing for me, will you?"

Adam kept his lips pressed tightly together, but he looked into his father's lined face.

"Heed His voice. Open your heart and your head, and *listen* for His leading."

*T*he day after Thanksgiving, Adam stood on the wooden platform in front of the tiny depot building. His family gathered close, bestowing their good-byes in voices loud enough to be heard over the raucous rumbling of the engine waiting to depart. He was leaving, but not to Europe. Ma had suggested if he needed to get away, a visit to his brother and grandparents in Minneapolis would be much less drastic than enlisting to fight. Although initially resistant, he'd finally conceded that going to Minneapolis might be a good idea. Spending a few weeks keeping up with Grandpa and Grandma Klaassen might be just what he needed to clear his Samantha-filled head. And if not, the army would still be there when he returned.

"Give Daniel and Rose our love," Ma hollered next to Adam's ear, "and kiss little Christina and Katrina for me."

"I will."

Josie grabbed his arm, her mouth opened to speak. He turned to her with a smirk and cut her off, "And I'll give them the doll clothes you made the minute I arrive." She'd only reminded him seven times already. How could he forget?

With a playful grin, Josie punched him on the arm his arm. Then she hugged him hard, her arms curled around his neck. "Take care, Adam."

He planted a quick kiss on her cheek. "You, too—and stay away from Stephen Koehn until I get back." Adam laughed as she blushed and turned away. It hardly seemed that Josie could be old enough for young men to come courting, but she must be, for it was happening. But then, she was the same age as Samantha, and she—. He cut those thoughts off quickly. The purpose of this trip was to forget about Samantha.

Sarah tugged at Adam's coat sleeve, demanding to be lifted up for a hug. She gave him a noisy smack on the cheek. He lowered her to the ground and reached for Teddy, rubbing his little hat over his head affectionately. "Be good," Adam told the two youngest.

Next came Becky, then Arn who stood as tall as Adam now and insisted on simply shaking hands. His hug from Liz was longer and harder than the others, and he returned it with equal pressure. She pressed her nose against his, smiling into his eyes. "Come back happy," she said. He nodded.

Frank stood close, an arm curved around Anna. Yesterday at the height of celebration, they'd announced their intention to marry in February. Adam placed a gloved hand on Frank's shoulder, giving him a warm squeeze. "Take care of each other. I'll see you soon."

Last, Adam turned to Pa. Father and son clasped gloved hands, snowflakes flying wildly around their heads and cold air lifting their hair. They stood, a mere twelve inches separating them, for several long seconds before Adam lurched forward and found himself held firmly in his father's strong embrace. Pa bellowed in Adam's ear, "Be back in time for Christmas." Adam understood Pa meant for him to be back to himself again by Christmas. Without Samantha, would he ever be whole again?

The men pulled apart as the conductor bawled, "Bo-o-oard."

Arn grabbed up Adam's carpetbag and the whole family accompanied Adam to the steps that led to the railroad car. One more hug from little Sarah, and Adam hopped up into the car. He turned back for a last smile and wave before stepping inside the long box. He chose a seat then used his sleeve to clear a good-sized spot on the frosted glass. Pressing his nose to the open spot, he waved.

As the train started its chugging motion, Teddy ran down the boardwalk beside it, leaping off the end and continuing until Pa waved him back. Just before the train turned the bend, Adam glimpsed Pa slip his arm around Ma's waist and pull her snug to his side. Even from this distance, he recognized the shiny paths on Ma's face as tears. Pressure built in Adam's chest. *I don't want to hurt them, Lord,* he prayed as he settled into his seat for the journey. *But I don't want to hurt anymore, either. Help me, Lord. Please, help me.*

❧

Thanksgiving had been just as Samantha expected. She had hoped that maybe—*maybe*—this year would be different. But she should have known better, she decided with a flash of cynicism.

She'd prepared a fine meal, using some of her saved sewing money to purchase a goose and stuffing it with a savory sage dressing. She'd prepared three different vegetables and baked bread, even stirred up a sweet potato pie in a flaky crust. But by the time Pa had staggered in, reeking of whiskey and mumbling belligerently, the food was cold. Some Thanksgiving it had been. . . . Although two days had passed, the sting of regret still clung to her heart. Samantha could not remember a holiday, ever, that had not been spoiled by her father's drinking.

She put a few dishes back on the warped shelving above the dry sink, and couldn't help but sigh. She had so hoped this Thanksgiving would be different. All the prayers, all the changes she'd made within herself, came for nothing. She rested her hands on the sharp edge of the dry sink and let her head drop low. Pa would never change. What was the use?

Suddenly an image of a family seated around a long trestle table popped into her mind. She could see their smiling faces, hear their laughing voices, and she was hit with a wave of melancholy so powerful tears spurted into her eyes. Oh, she missed the Klaassens and Mountain Lake. She missed them *so much*. . . .

She crossed the dim room to light an oil lamp and curl up in her familiar rocker, the old rocker in which Gran used to sit. She remembered well the security of cuddling up in Gran's soft lap and being rocked. She remembered, too, being cradled in Adam's arms that one time as they had ridden back to his house on Bet's strong back. What she wouldn't give to have one of them here to hold her now.

The front door rattled, startling Samantha out of her reverie. She heard a grumbled curse, and the sounds of the doorknob being violently twisted broke through the room. Pa was home. Samantha rose and hurried to the door to open it for him.

As he lurched through the open doorway, the stench of stale whiskey and cigar smoke drifted past Samantha's nose causing her to wince. He gave her a bleary glare. "Whatsamatter, girlie? Ain'tcha glad to see yore ol' man? Huh?" He laughed horribly, his breath making Samantha take a backward step.

"Come, Pa. Sit down and I'll get you some coffee." She guided him to the small table and helped him into a chair. He slouched drunkenly, watching Samantha through watery, red-rimmed eyes as she poured a cup of coffee and ladled out a bowl of vegetable soup. When Samantha placed the cup and bowl in front of him, he reached out with strength belying his drunkenness to grasp her wrist. A strange light shone in his blood-shot eyes, and his grin seemed somehow evil. Alarm bells rang in Samantha's mind. "W-what is it, Pa?"

Pa tightened his grip on her wrist and lifted his other hand to pinch a strand of her hair between two dirty fingers. "Jus' quite the li'l homemaker, ain'tcha? All growed up an' knowin' how to take keer of a man . . ."

An unnamed fear claimed Samantha. She twisted her arm, trying to pull away. "Pa . . . ?"

As suddenly as it had begun, his strangeness ended. Throwing her wrist away, he ordered thickly, "Oh, git away from me, girl. Git me some o' that bread to sop up this soup. Y'know I can't eat soup without bread."

Her heart thudding, she skittered to obey.

◦⌒◦

Adam stood outside a large store in downtown Minneapolis, admiring the variety of toys in the window. Wouldn't his little nieces, Katrina and Christina, love those golden-haired dolls dressed in satins and lace?

During his three weeks in Minneapolis, he'd thoroughly enjoyed the time spent with Daniel and Rose and getting acquainted with his two small nieces. The girls were sweet and loving, dimpled and curly haired, and Adam found them irresistible. His grandparents were as pert and lively as ever, and many pleasant evenings were spent in their company. He'd even gone with Daniel to his law office several times and developed a respect for Daniel and his work.

But as much as he enjoyed his visit, he hadn't accomplished what he had come for—he hadn't managed to forget Samantha. The idea was ludicrous. How could he forget? But although she still hovered on the fringes of his mind, he no longer felt the stabbing pain of remembrance. Time in prayer with his wise, loving grandparents and with his older brother had soothed the edges of his tattered heart. Thanks to God's healing touch, thoughts of Samantha brought a gratefulness that she had entered his life and that they had been able to touch one another in a special way. Daily, he prayed for the Lord to keep her in His capable care, and he trusted that wherever Samantha was, she was at peace with herself.

Now he turned his attention back to the store window display. In the center of the toys, a tin train circled a metal track. Andy and A.J. would coo with delight if the train ran around their Christmas tree. He pulled out a folded wad of bills from his pocket. Counting it, he decided there was enough for two of the big, golden-haired dolls and the train. Maybe he could even get a doll for Sarah and a painted top for Teddy, as well as gifts for his other family members.

He stepped inside the warm store, glad to be out of the biting December wind. Minnesota wasn't known for its mild winters. He purchased the toys, asking the gray-haired man behind the wooden counter to wrap each gift. Smilingly the man began pulling out patterned paper and bright colored ribbons from beneath the counter.

"I'm going to look around a bit while you wrap those," Adam told the clerk.

The man gave a genial nod. "Certainly, sir, go right ahead. Take your time."

Adam browsed the store, picking up a round polished rock paperweight. He bounced it in his hand, envisioning it on Daniel's work desk. He found a kaleidoscope for Becky and spent a few cheerful minutes peeking into the brass tube, enjoying the varying designs that appeared as he turned the end.

On another table woolen scarves of every imaginable color caught his attention. He chose a blue one for Arn and a green one for Frank. For Pa he selected thick, wool-lined gloves of brown suede. Turning from the scarves, he spotted a glass-covered jewelry case. Broaches and necklaces, earrings and bracelets each set with colored rhinestones stretched across a background of black velvet. He selected a heart-shaped pin with a red center stone for Ma and dainty necklaces of crystal teardrops on gold-plated chains for Josie, Anna, and Rose. Moving on, he came to a large display of music boxes. He lifted the lid on the one closest to him, smiling as a tinkling melody spilled forth.

A saleslady came up behind him. "May I help you?"

Adam gestured to the boxes. "These are sure pretty."

"Yes, sir, they are." She fluttered her eyelashes, her smile flirtatious. "Any young lady would be pleased to receive one. Do you have a special young lady in mind?"

Samantha's face appeared before Adam's eyes. Yes, he had a special young lady in mind. But how would he get it to her? Buying one would be foolhardy, almost tempting fate. It was illogical, unreasonable, and probably even a waste of his hard-earned money. Adam said, "Yes, I do."

The saleslady seemed to deflate momentarily, but then she straightened and inquired brightly, "Which one do you think she would prefer?"

Adam's eyes drifted across the selections. There were at least fifteen music boxes, each with a different picture inlaid on the tops with what appeared to be bits of shell. His eyes roved, and one jumped out at him. It had a gold filigreed edge, with a cream-colored pearlized cover. A perfect opened rose, each petal set individually in varying shades of palest pink to deep burgundy, filled the center. It brought to mind Samantha's dress of roses and trailing vines.

He pointed. "I'll take that one."

The saleslady scooped it up and carried it to the counter.

Adam leaned against the wooden counter as the woman poked around somewhere below it, scouting for something. She finally stood, a scowl on her face. "I'd like to wrap it in paper and put it in a box, but I can't find a box." She headed for a door at the back of the store. "Stay here. I'll have our stockman look in the storage room. Surely there's something there that will hold your music box." Her pointed-toed shoes clicked purposefully on the tiled floor as she disappeared from view.

Adam gazed at the rose, a bubble of happiness pressing against his heart as he thought of Samantha's hands holding the music box. She would love it; he knew she would.

"We found one, sir." The saleslady approached, followed by a tall, slender young man. The young man held a stack of boxes in his freckled arms. "Just put those under the counter, David," the saleslady instructed the stockman.

She reached for Adam's music box, flashing a smile. "We'll get you fixed up in no time, sir." She set to work wrapping the box in a cloud of white tissue paper.

Adam watched the stockman bend to place the supply of empty boxes below the counter. There was something vaguely familiar about him. David, the woman had called him. Adam stared, trying to remember where he'd seen the man before. He was tall, his face freckled slightly, his head covered with auburn curls that seemed unable to behave. And his eyes were pale cornflower blue, just like—

Adam's jaw dropped. *David.* Could this be Samantha's brother who had run away? The stockman, his task completed, headed for the back of the store. Adam offered a quick apology to the saleslady then scurried after the stockman. "David?"

The man turned around, his thin face attentive. "Yes? May I help you?"

Now that he had the man's attention, Adam found himself tongue-tied. He couldn't very well accuse him of running away as a boy and leaving his sister behind. "I wondered . . ." The man waited, his expression wary. Adam released a nervous laugh. "Do you have a sister? A sister named Samantha?"

David's cornflower eyes narrowed, and his glance darted around the store as if seeking someone out. His eyes came back to Adam. "Why do you want to know?"

Adam recognized in the tall young man the same defensiveness that Samantha possessed. He found the physical resemblance and the familiar mannerisms uncanny. "I'm a friend of Samantha's. She told me about a brother named David, whom she hasn't seen in several years. I thought . . . well, I wondered if you might be him."

David stood still, staring off somewhere behind Adam, his face expressionless. For Adam it was eerie. It was as if seeing Samantha again, only not Samantha. But he couldn't squelch a bubble of hope. How excited she'd be if this was her brother.

The man finally shifted his gaze to look at Adam. "I'm sure there are dozens of Davids in the city." His voice sounded empty. Hollow. "I'm sorry, but I'm not the right one." He turned and hurried away, disappearing through a swinging wooden door.

Adam watched him go, frowning. He couldn't be certain the man was Samantha's brother—it could be wishful thinking on Adam's part that made him see the similarities between the two—but he got the impression that David *was* Samantha's brother and was unwilling to admit it for some unknown reason. Adam wouldn't press the issue now. He knew the name of the store, and he could come back. With that thought in mind, he gathered up his purchases and left.

avid emerged from the back area of the store and rushed to the front windows, watching as the man headed down the snow-covered walkway with his arms laden with packages. David sighed, pressing his forehead against the cold glass. He thought back to that night seven years ago, when he had kissed his little sister good-bye and sneaked away, promising to come back for her. She'd been only ten or so then, a skinny little waif with too much hair for her slender neck.

Seven years . . . Samantha would be grown now, a woman. The man had said he was a friend. The man was well-dressed, polite, obviously from a good family. How would Samantha have met someone like him, coming from their part of town? What was she like now? Was she still with Pa? So many questions . . . And that man could have answered them, had David summoned the courage to ask.

He pushed away from the window, heading back to his work area. He thought of Pa. Had Pa changed at all? For Samantha's sake, he hoped so. Life with him had been unbearable. David carried the emotional scars of his childhood yet.

There had been no choice about leaving. He couldn't take it a day longer, he'd told himself over and over. But guilt overwhelmed him once more as he remembered leaving Sammy behind. He'd wanted to bring her with him when he stole away, but how could he? She was just a kid. She would've needed the kind of care he couldn't give, not on the run like he was. Did she understand how hard it had been for him to go without her?

David worried so often over the years, wondering if Pa had taken out his anger at his son's escape on the unwitting Samantha. The guilt had been horrible. Almost as bad as his pa's beatings. He'd promised to go back for her, though, and he had—three years later, after he'd established himself in the city. Pa had answered his knock at the door, and when David demanded to see Samantha, Pa only laughed. His father's voice echoed in his memory. "*She ain't here no more. Run off, just like you done. You ain't gonna find her here.*" David's body jerked as he relived the slam of the door in his face.

His heart ached anew, wondering—just as he had then—where had she gone? How was she taking care of herself? That man who knew her could have answered David's questions, if only he'd asked. But after being David Bryant for so many years, he didn't know how to be—or if he even wanted to be—David O'Brien again. And why would Samantha want anything to do with him after he'd abandoned her?

Turning back to his work, David assured himself that his sister must be doing fine if she had a friend in that well-dressed, polite man. He didn't need to worry about her anymore. Still, it was hard not to be curious. His little sister . . .

∝◯

Adam deposited his purchases at the stately two-story home his brother and sister-in-law occupied. He spent a few moments fending off questions from Christina about the many ribboned packages before telling Rose he was going out again. He bundled up once more and caught a horse-drawn cab to ride to Daniel's law office.

"Daniel, I need your help," he blurted the moment he stepped through the door.

Daniel's eyebrows rose, but he set aside the papers he had been examining. "Professional or brotherly?"

Adam grinned. "Both, I guess. I was just at Smothers' Department Store, and I met a man . . ." Adam filled Daniel in, on how the man's name was David and how he resembled Samantha physically right down to the spattering of freckles across the bridge of his nose. "I'm certain the man is Samantha's brother, but he denies it."

Daniel leaned back and rested his elbows on the armrests of his chair, making a steeple of his hands in front of his chest. "So what do you want me to do?"

"I want you to find out if he *is* who I think he is—if he is Samantha's brother, David. Can you imagine what it would mean to Samantha, to have him back in her life? Why, she'd be beside herself with joy."

Daniel rocked his chair a couple times, his head cocked. "Adam, it would be a simple matter to check at the store, find out this David's full name. If his last name is O'Brien, I think that would prove to be too much of a coincidence to overlook. Then I would say he is Samantha's missing brother. But proving who is he and reuniting him with Samantha are two different things. Have you considered why he might have told you he wasn't the man you were looking for? Have you considered that perhaps he has no interest in being reunited with Samantha?"

Adam shook his head, baffled. Would a brother refuse to reunite with a sister? "I just figured maybe I caught him by surprise. I tried to be discreet, but to have Samantha mentioned after being separated for all these years . . . No, I'm sure if he really is Samantha's David, he'll want to see her."

"Well, then . . ." Daniel drummed his fingers on the desk, his tone less like a lawyer and more like a brother. "I think you need to consider something else. Samantha lost her brother a long time ago. From what you've said in the past, she feels abandoned by him. What will she think if she finds out he has been as near as a two-hour train ride all these years and never made the effort to come for her? Are you sure that wouldn't be more hurtful to her?"

Adam considered Daniel's question. The old Samantha—the sullen, withdrawn girl who had arrived at the Klaassen farm—would certainly be angry and bitter at the knowledge that her brother had been this close yet stayed away. But he couldn't help but believe the new Samantha would be willing to forgive. The new Samantha would make an effort to understand.

Adam blew out a noisy breath. "We have to take that chance, Daniel. Her brother is all she has in the world. She needs him in her life."

Daniel grimaced. "I hope you're right, little brother, because if I go poking my professional nose into this man's business and he is who you think he is, I am going to be opening one big can of worms."

Adam threw his arms wide. "Big brother, open away."

*S*amantha draped evergreen boughs and tiny red holly berries along windowsills and shelf edges. She had no tree, but this bit of greenery was almost as nice, she decided as she stepped back to survey her work. She placed two thick candles on the windowsill and swished a match along the underside of the sill, cupping the flame as she raised it to light the candles. She smiled at the result. Festive and warm.

Christmas Eve. Soon she'd leave to go to the service at church. She'd received a special invitation from the young minister, Reverend Johansen. It had taken her by surprise, but she'd recovered quickly, managing to smile in a friendly manner and thanking him without conveying any additional meaning. The blond, blue-eyed man had acted a bit disappointed by her casual response, but he hadn't pressed the issue. For Samantha, no one—not even a handsome, well-stationed man such as Reverend Johansen—could measure up to Adam Klaassen.

Her pa slept in his small bedroom. He'd staggered home almost two hours ago, having spent most of the afternoon at his favorite tavern. Samantha had helped him into bed, relieved when he'd immediately fallen asleep. His rumbling snore drifted through the closed door. He'd probably sleep the rest of the night.

She checked the small wind-up clock on the table. Almost seven. If she didn't leave now, she'd be late. She tiptoed across the wooden floor and tapped lightly on Pa's door. No answer—

just a snuffle and the squeak of the mattress as he apparently rolled over in his sleep.

Samantha cracked the door. "Pa? I'm going to the church now."

Burt made a growling sound as he came awake. He sat up groggily and turned his bleary gaze on Samantha, blinking as if to clear his vision. "Wha—whaddaya wan'?"

Samantha bit her lower lip. He was still pretty drunk. The nap hadn't done him much good. She stepped a bit farther into the room. "I'm going to the church now." She kept her voice low. Pa couldn't abide loud noises when he was coming down off of a drunk. "Can I get something for you before I go?"

Her final word must have penetrated the fog of Pa's alcohol-laden brain. He swung his feet over the edge of the bed, swaying and grabbing at his bedside table as he struggled to find his balance. "Go? You ain't goin' no place, girlie."

Samantha took a hesitant step backward. "But, Pa, it's just to church. I'll be home in an hour, and we can have some cider together."

"I said *no!*" He swung his arm, knocking the china bowl and pitcher from the table beside his bed. The subsequent crash made him clutch his ears in agony. "Oooh, my head. My head."

Samantha rushed to his side. "Are you all right, Pa? Here, let me help you." She reached for him, but he slapped her hands away.

"No!" His bellow echoed more loudly than the breaking china had. "Git away from me. Jus' leave—go on, git. Jus' go."

Samantha hovered, uncertain and scared. He was so unpredictable. "I—I'll clean up this mess." She gestured to the broken pieces of china scattered across the floor. "I don't want you to cut yourself." She knelt, beginning to stack the larger pieces together.

Pa stared at her glassy-eyed, mumbling. "Uh-huh, yup, you clean it up. Allus so worried 'bout 'er pa. Allus takin' keer o' 'er Pa. But she don' really keer. Not really. She don' really keer—nobody does, nobody . . ."

An ominous tone crept into her father's voice. Samantha stiffened. She understood what was happening, having lived it hundreds of times before. *Oh, God, please, not again . . .*

Pa lurched to his feet. "You don' really keer." He roared, his face near hers, his breath hot and foul smelling. His hand snaked out, and he caught her by the arm, drawing her to her feet and shaking her violently. "Ya left me. Jus' like yore ma, ya left me. Took off—you, an' Davey an' 'Livia. Ya don' keer. Yo're nothin' but a liar, S'mantha. A liar."

Samantha screamed as he released her to swing his arm. The back of his hand struck her hard across the cheek. She tasted blood, and she tried desperately to duck away. He raised his hand again, continuing his verbal barrage with loud curses. The second blow caught her on the side of the head, making her ears ring. In defense, Samantha brought up her arms to protect her face. Her elbow caught him under the chin and he stumbled. He fell forward, hitting the table as he fell and taking it with him.

Samantha scrambled sideways, crawling across the pile of the shattered china. Sharp pieces cut into her knees and the palms of her hands, but she paid no attention to the pain. She had to escape.

Out of her father's reach, she untangled her skirts from around her knees and rose clumsily to her feet. She looked back at her father. He'd passed out and remained on the floor as he'd fallen. The table lay beside him, one leg broken and hanging crazily. She slumped against the doorway in relief. She was safe. For now.

Samantha remained in the doorway, breathing heavily. The inside of her mouth was cut, and the sickening taste of blood filled her mouth. She touched her cheek. It felt swollen, and her fingers encountered a small amount of blood where he'd broken the skin on her cheekbone. Snow. That would bring the swelling down.

She staggered to the door, swinging it wide and breathing in the cold, clean air. She shivered but stayed where she was, letting the cold air wash her clean of the horror of the last few moments. It had happened so quickly. Finally she scooped up a handful of snow and placed it gingerly against her cheek. It stung, but she knew it would keep the swelling down.

Stepping back inside, she closed the door and leaned against it. The clump of snow began to melt in the warm room, and a trickle of wetness ran down her arm. Her palms and knees stung, her head ached, and she trembled weakly. She stumbled across the floor to wilt into her rocking chair. She set the chair into gentle motion. She would not be attending church this evening.

~⚬

Adam sat on the window seat, bouncing little A.J. in his lap. "Giddyap, horsie, go to town. . . ." The chubby infant chortled as Adam chanted.

His family gathered in the parlor, wrapping paper scattered across the floor, happy smiles and cheerful conversation winging from every corner. Observing the scene, he sighed in contentment. What joy he'd discovered in releasing Samantha into the Lord's keeping. He'd also released Samantha's brother.

Daniel had checked into the background of the man named David who worked at Smothers' Department Store. The man, who called himself David Bryant, clung to his story that he had no knowledge of a woman named Samantha O'Brien. Adam still didn't believe him, but as Daniel had pointed out, it wasn't against the law to change your name or disown your relatives, so they had no way to force him into admitting the truth. Adam had left David Bryant his name and address in case he changed his mind, and all he could do now was hope for the best.

Coming home, he discovered, was bittersweet. Sweet to be among his dear family again, bitter because Samantha wasn't here to share in the homecoming. He hadn't placed the music box beneath the tree. It was hidden in his bedroom, under the bed behind the chamber pot. No one would look under there, he was sure. That gift was his promise to himself, to some-day find Samantha. And when he placed it in her hands, he wouldn't let anyone carry her away from him again.

"Adam, thank you." Sarah hugged the beautiful doll he had purchased in the city. "It's the prettiest one I've ever seen."

Adam teased, "Are you sure you're not too big to play with dollies?"

"Huh-uh." Sarah stared in wonder at the china face complete with two tiny teeth, the perfectly curled ringlets, and deep purple velvet dress.

"I'd rather have my kaleidoscope," announced tomboy Becky.

Adam grinned as, one by one, his family acknowledged the gifts he'd chosen for them. It was a good feeling, making them happy. Regret smacked as he realized how much his unhappiness had affected them. He made a silent vow to never again allow himself to become as despondent as he had been over Samantha's departure. No problem was worth distressing the people he loved. He needed to remember all of the lessons of his childhood—the most important one being that God is in control, and "all things work together for good."

At the Klaassen farm, Christmas day was bright with snow outside, and bright with happiness inside.

◦◦◦

In Minneapolis, in cramped quarters above the department store where he was employed, David O'Brien—known to his fellow employees as David Bryant—sat on a worn sofa and sipped a cup of weak tea. He stared out the curtainless window at the falling snow. It seemed the whole world was white. White—colorless—matching David's mood.

On the battered table beside the sofa rested a folded piece of yellow paper. He reached out a slender hand and fingered it for the hundredth time. All it would take was a telegram to this Adam Klaassen and all of his soul searching would end. Should he? Should he open himself up to this stranger—this man who claimed to be a friend?

He dropped the paper and sighed. A tired sigh. He was so lonely. It seemed he'd been lonely his whole life long. As a child he didn't have friends—not the way other children were friends, visiting one another's homes and playing after school. He'd held himself away from the other children, ashamed of his tattered clothes—although Gran had made sure they were clean tatters—and ramshackle house. And his alcoholic father.

Especially his alcoholic father.

He'd tried to hide the fact that his father was a drunk, but everyone had known. He'd heard the titters of his classmates when his back was turned, calling his father Ol' Burpy Burt. A stupid name—should have even been funny. But it wasn't. It had hurt. It still hurt.

At least he'd had Gran, and there'd been his little sister. He closed his eyes, sliding downward on the threadbare cushions and holding the now-cold mug two-handed against his stomach. How well he remembered the night Samantha was born. He'd been quite young—only seven—but he remembered.

The events of the night rolled in his mind. Mama crying out. Pa stomping around the room with a white face, cursing in fear. A doctor emerging from the bedroom and announcing somberly, "I'm sorry. There was nothing I could do. She hemorrhaged. She's gone." David hadn't known what hemorrhage meant, but he knew what the doctor meant when he'd said his mama was gone. Sorrow swept over him anew as he recalled throwing himself into the corner, weeping inconsolably at the loss of his mother. Gran came in and showed him a tiny, red-faced bundle. "This is your sister, Davey," she'd said. He'd only wanted his mama back.

His opinion had changed in a hurry though. Oh, he'd still missed and wanted his mama. But that Samantha. He smiled, remembering. She'd been such a happy baby. Pretty, too. She'd wrapped him around her little finger the first time she'd given him her spitty, toothless smile. As she'd gotten bigger, he'd thought of her as a friend. She'd followed him around endlessly, getting her nose in the way of everything he did and asking enough questions to drive a fellow to drink.

That expression sobered him in a hurry. He drew a hand through his hair. What kind of a life might they have had if Burt O'Brien hadn't been driven to drink? Try as he might, he couldn't remember a time when his father hadn't turned to drink to drown his sorrows. Gran had told him that Burt had once been a fine man, a good worker and provider for his wife and baby son. But he couldn't remember. Other memories crowded it out.

David scowled, his memories holding him trapped in another time. The night his mother had labored to deliver Samantha, Gran had begged Burt to fetch the doctor. Olivia was in trouble. But his Pa had complained that they couldn't afford a doctor. Gran had secretly sent little David after the old doctor against Burt's wishes. But it had been too late. By the time the doctor had arrived, Olivia had begun to hemorrhage—to bleed, David knew now—and there wasn't anything he could do.

Is that why Burt had started drinking? Did he keep himself in a drunken stupor to forget his guilt over his wife's premature death? He'd always blamed his children, but maybe . . .

David shook his head, sending the memories to the dark corners of his mind. Dwelling on the past accomplished nothing. Could he change any of it now? He pushed off the sofa and crossed to his dry sink, dropping the mug into a pan of oily water. He stood there, staring into the pan of unwashed dishes.

This, now, was his life. No better than the life he'd had before—alone and lonely. Did he really want to drag Samantha down with him a second time? His head shot up, his mouth dry, as another question wiggled through his heart. Would he be dragging her down? Maybe she was as lonely, too. Maybe . . .

A smile tugged at his lips as he pictured a tousle-haired little girl with adoring eyes turned in his direction. Oh, how he'd loved her. She'd been the best thing in his life. And he'd walked away from her. Would she be able to forgive him for that? Would she be able to understand why he hadn't returned?

David stamped across the quiet room to grab up the slip of paper bearing Adam Klaassen's address. Crumpling it tightly in his fist, he turned to stare again at the falling snow: great, fluffy flakes that coated everything, making the world clean and bright. Not colorless, as he'd thought before, but new and full of promise.

All right, then. He relaxed his fist, then smoothed the paper flat against his palm. He'd do it. He'd find out. If she wouldn't accept him, he'd be no worse off than he was right now. But he'd never know until he tried.

*T*wo days after Christmas, Uncle Hiram's young assistant, Will Boehr, delivered a telegram to Adam. He read the stilted message—"Am Sam's brother. Would like contact. Please reply. David O'Brien"—and let out a whoop that startled the chickens into nervous flapping.

It took Adam a month's worth of telegrams and a trip to the city to finalize his plans to reunite David and Samantha, but it was well worth the time and expense. He and David dined together at a Minneapolis restaurant, and the two men talked for hours. David had been shocked to learn Samantha was still living with their father and was very eager to see her safely removed from their childhood home. By the time they parted, Adam felt as though he'd known David for years. And he was certain of David's love for Samantha.

He'd encouraged David to go with him to Milwaukee, but Samantha's brother feared his appearance would stir his father's wrath, and Samantha could get caught in a skirmish. Adam agreed it would be best for him to go after Samantha himself and bring her to Mountain Lake, where David would join them.

The last day of January 1918, Adam rattled across the country in a smoky train car, heading for Milwaukee. In his pocket he had the address provided by David to locate Samantha's home—or at least the home she'd lived in as a child. If she was no longer there, it would give him a starting point to begin his search.

He also had the Christmas gift he had purchased for her, the rose-topped music box. And a heart that beat out a message in time with the rocking rhythm of the train: I'm *coming, I'm coming. Wait for me, wait for me.*

David, he presumed, was on another train, traveling to Mountain Lake. The two men had decided it would be best for Adam to bring Samantha back to his own home for the reunion—a neutral territory, so to speak. David would stay in a room at the Commercial Hotel, and Frank would bring him to the farm when Adam returned with Samantha.

Only a few more hours and he'd hold Samantha close again. And this time, Adam had no intention of ever letting her go. Closing his eyes, he willed the train to move quickly.

When he disembarked at the Milwaukee station, a lineup of cab drivers waited along the curb to transport travelers. He approached a short, white-haired man who tipped his felt hat.

"Need a ride, sir?"

"Yes, I do." Adam jiggled the paper holding Samantha's address. "To Front Street."

The man rubbed his raspy chin with glove-covered fingers. "I reckon I c'n getcha there. Got any bags I c'n holp ya with?"

Adam indicated his single travel pouch. "Just this."

With a bright grin, the man snatched it up. "Wal, then, let's go."

Soon Adam was bouncing through busy city streets, peering out anxiously as the horse skittered around new-fangled automobiles.

"Here, now, Tootsie . . ." The driver used a soothing tone when addressing the horse. "Y' keep yer attention where it belongs."

Adam smiled. It sure was different in the city—noisier, busier. . . . The sky was tinged with a gray smoke, no doubt from the factories that dotted the outskirts of the city. There were more buildings than trees, more people than cows, and more automobiles than he'd care to deal with on a daily basis.

The driver of one auto turned a corner sharply, the nose of the vehicle dangerously close to Tootsie's nose. He grabbed the edge of the conveyance and let out a yelp of surprise.

"Crazy fool nincompoop!" The cab driver shook his fist at the vehicle driver. Then he turned an apologetic smile on Adam. "Pardon me, sir, but those young people and their autos. Nothin' but a menace, an' a waste o' road space, if ya ask me."

Adam nodded in agreement. Daniel and Rose were considering purchasing an automobile, but Adam felt more comfortable with a horse. A horse was safer, softer, and more companionable.

It took almost a quarter of an hour to reach the area of town where David had said his old home was located. Adam hopped out of the open-topped cab and held out a coin to the driver. "Thanks for the ride."

The man pocketed the money. "An' thank you, sir."

Adam stayed beside the curb as the horse named Tootsie carried its driver away. Alone now, he perused the area. Hardly a fancy neighborhood—most of the houses looked more like shacks—but somewhere Samantha was waiting. He began to walk.

He searched the street for someone who might be able to direct him, but no people loitered outside today—too cold. The wind bit his nose with its frosty breath. Adam turned up his collar and tugged the flaps of his hat low over his ears, but the chill wind still crept beneath the layers of clothing and made him shiver. He walked briskly, stamping his feet down firmly against the ground to warm them. He counted the houses on Front Street as he walked—two, four, six. . . . There—number nine. That's where David said he'd lived as a youngster with his sister and father. Adam's heart hammered in anticipation.

The house was much like the others on the street—small, squat, weatherworn. A stovepipe jutted from the narrowly sloped roof, emitting a steady series of coal-colored puffs. The windows bore faded calico curtains pulled to the side and tied with yellow ribbon. The ribbons—the bright splash of color—gave him hope he'd reached the right place. His heart caroming wildly in his chest, he stepped to the warped, planked door and knocked.

After only a few moments, the door squeaked open, and there she stood. Samantha. Warmth flooded his frame, joy exploding through his middle. The inside of the house was dark, shielding her in shadows, but he could make out her expression of happy surprise as her eyes widened.

"Adam!" Her voice expressed the joy coursing through his soul. "What—?" Then as suddenly as she'd brightened, her expression turned wary. She peered beyond him, her gaze bouncing around nervously. "W-what are you doing here?"

Adam's elation plummeted to concern when he got a good look at her in the sunlight. A sickly yellowish-green smudge marked her cheekbone, and blood-stained strips of cloth wrapped both hands. He caught her chin between his fingers and lifted her face, examining the ugly mar. "Samantha, what happened to you?"

She pulled away. "Nothing. Just a little accident." She wove her fingers together, he wide eyes holding a note of alarm. "Adam, as wonderful as it is for me to see you, you can't stay. Pa will be home soon, and—"

Adam gazed at her, dismay tangling his emotions in knots. Where was the happy reunion he'd envisioned? "But I've come all this way to see you, and to tell you—"

"Wal, wal, wal . . ." A third voice—harsh and grating—cut from behind Adam. "What've we got here? Comp'ny, huh? S'mantha, girl, why di'n't ya tell me you was 'spectin' comp'ny?"

Adam turned to face the same man who had carted Samantha away from him only two short months ago. By the drawl in the voice and his defensive stance—arms slightly akimbo, neck angled forward, and jaw jutting—Adam knew Burt O'Brien was in an ornery mood. He kept his own body angled to protect Samantha. Her shallow, frightened breaths filled his ears.

"Mr. O'Brien," Adam said, holding his tone steady yet firm, "my visit is a surprise. Samantha did not know I was coming."

O'Brien dismissed Adam's words with a wave of an ungloved, dirty hand. The man's coat hung open, revealing his grime-covered shirt. He wore no hat to fend away the cold, and his lank, gray hair stood up in the wind. His voice bore a menacing undertone as he snorted. "I ain't s'prised to see ya, boy. Knew that girl'd have comp'ny when I was out. When the cat's away . . ." And he laughed, baring his tobacco-stained teeth. He pointed past Adam's shoulder to his daughter, who cowered there, her eyes wide with fright. "You entertainin', girl? You looking' to treat this feller like yore man?"

Sickened by the man's implication, Adam stepped off the cracked concrete slab that served as a porch. "Now wait just a minute. You have no right—"

O'Brien charged forward and jammed one short, stubby finger into Adam's chest. "I got all the rights!" Adam winced. Up close, the man's stench was overpowering. O'Brien's watery eyes narrowed. "I got all the rights 'cause I'm her pa. Don't be tellin' *me* I got no rights."

Adam held up his hands as a sign of surrender. The man was completely unreasonable—no doubt hurting from a lack of alcohol in his system which made him worse than rip-roarin' drunk. Best to try and calm him. "I'm sorry, Mr. O'Brien. I just want you to understand that Samantha has done nothing wrong. I came here to bring her some news, and to deliver a Christmas gift." The mention of the Christmas gift reminded Adam that when he'd been delivered to Front Street, he'd been so anxious to get to Samantha, he'd mistakenly left his bag on the cab. *The music box.*

He turned to Samantha. "I brought you a gift, but I accidentally left it—"

A hand clamped on Adam's shoulder and spun him around. O'Brien glared at him, one fist balled and waving beneath Adam's nose. "Don't you go turnin' your back on me—treatin' me like I ain't even here. I'll teach you manners, boy!"

Before Adam could apologize, the older man planted his fist into Adam's midsection with an amazing amount of strength considering his age and obvious poor health. Adam doubled over, his breath escaping in a loud whoosh.

Samantha danced forward, trying to come between them. "Pa, don't!"

Adam threw out his arm to keep her back. "Go back in the house, Samantha."

O'Brien laughed and waved at Samantha. "Yeah, girlie, go in the house. Let us men handle this'un."

Samantha skittered backward but remained in the doorway, watching with wide, fear-filled eyes. Assured she was safe, Adam turned his attention to her father. "Mr. O'Brien, I don't want to fight you."

The man's face twisted in an ugly scowl. "No, you jus' wanna see my girl. Wal, ya can't, so jus' git on outta here. Git."

Adam held his ground, unwilling to leave Samantha alone with a man so clearly out of control. His hesitation must have stirred O'Brien's fury, because the man cursed and charged, fists flying. Adam fended off the older man's blows. Although unsteady on his feet, weakened from the cold and the alcohol that had damaged his system, O'Brien possessed the tenacity of a fire ant. They tussled, O'Brien pursuing and Adam deflecting blows rather than delivering any of his own. With conscious thought, Adam worked his way toward the street, well away from the house and Samantha. Near the curb, he caught the older man in a bear hug, intending to bring him under control, and the man's wild struggles toppled them both to the ground. They rolled several times and came back up again, their clothing coated with snow.

"Pa, stop it! Please!" Samantha danced on the porch, her face pleading. "Let him go!"

Burt pulled away from Adam, his heaving breaths sending heavy white puffs into the cold air, and glared at his daughter. He jammed his finger at her. "*You.* You brung this on! You wan'ed 'im to come, din'cha?"

Samantha covered her mouth with both hands and shook her head. Her huge blue eyes shimmered with unshed tears.

"Liar!" O'Brien sneered. "Yo're nothin' but a *liar.* Girl, I'm gonna—" He started for the house in his uneven gait.

Adam bolted forward. He couldn't let the man hurt Samantha again. Grabbing O'Brien by the arm, he swung him away from the house and toward the street.

O'Brien stumbled but caught himself before falling. He turned on Adam and doubled up his fist. "Why, you—"

The clatter of horse hooves on cobblestone intruded. Tootsie rounded the corner, her driver waving from the seat. "You there, sir, you left a package on board!"

To Adam, watching from the curb, the world suddenly took on an aura of unreality. O'Brien whirled toward the approaching buggy and stepped off the curb with one foot. Unbalanced, he fell heavily into the street. O'Brien's hands flew upward—a useless attempt to protect himself as Tootsie reared, confused and frightened by the strange lump at her feet. Samantha's scream ringing in his ears, Adam reached frantically for the horse's bridle, pulling her head down to keep her from stamping again.

The driver leaped out of the cab, crying out, "Oh, good lord in heaven, what've I done?" He managed to back Tootsie away from O'Brien, but the damage was done. The man's neck cocked at on odd angle as he lay in the snow. His out-flung arms, the palms facing up, lay unmoving in the dirty snow. A thin trickle of blood ran from his ear. Adam knew he was dead.

Samantha's sobs cut through the air. She dashed toward the street, her arms stretching toward her pa. Adam caught her and pulled her tight against his chest. She clung, crying, repeating in a pathetic voice, "Oh, Pa . . . Pa . . ."

Adam's heart ached at her obvious distress. He stroked her hair and pressed his lips against her temple. "Shhh, honey. He's not hurting. And he can't hurt you now." He was holding her—not the way he'd intended, but he had her in his arms. And as he'd promised himself, he wouldn't let go.

Her warm tears soaked into his collar, her shoulders shaking convulsively. "He's dead, Adam. He's dead."

Adam could only hold her, rock her, comfort her. He placed a kiss on the top of her head, on her russet waves that were as untamable as the wind, letting his lips rest there as she sobbed against his neck.

Neighbors came from their houses. Two men lifted O'Brien's lifeless body and placed it in the back of the cab, which still stood near the curb. The driver approached, twisting his hat in his hands. "I'm so sorry." He touched Samantha's shoulder. "If I can do anything . . . ?"

Adam spoke over Samantha's head. "Could you take the body to the undertaker's? I'll make arrangements for burial later."

"Surely, sir, surely." His gaze drifted to Samantha, who burrowed against Adam's chest. "Will the little lady be all right?"

Samantha's sobs had quieted, but she clung tenaciously to Adam's coat front. He nodded, swallowing the lump in his throat. "Yes. I'll see to her. Thank you."

The man nodded, placed his hat on his head, and left. Adam guided Samantha into the house, shutting the door against the curious neighbors. A rocking chair sat near the stove, and he eased her into its smooth seat. Kneeling in front of her, he kept a grip on her icy hands. She kept her head down, refusing to meet his eyes.

A cold shaft of fear whizzed through Adam's middle. Did she blame him for her father's death? His heart pounding, he gave her hands a gentle squeeze. "Samantha, I'm so sorry about your pa. I didn't want to hurt him." He gulped, fear making his throat dry. "You know that, don't you?"

Her face lifted. Fresh tears spurted into her eyes. "Yes, I know." Her chin quivered, her face crumpling. "Pa, he . . . he's always . . ." One harsh sob escaped. "It was just so awful. . . ."

"I know, honey, I know." Adam smoothed the tangled hair away from her tear-stained face and stood. "Let me get you something hot to drink. And a blanket." His gaze searched the small space.

She reached out and grasped his hand. "No, I don't need anything but . . ." Tears rolled down her pale cheeks, her luminous eyes beseeching. "Please, Adam, just hold me?"

Without a moment's hesitation Adam scooped her into his arms. He slid into the rocker, cradling her in his lap. She nestled against him, and his arms curved around her to provide warmth and comfort. They remained in the rocker until the coals in the stove burned themselves out and the sun slipped over the horizon.

*F*our days later Adam assisted Samantha from the train at the Mountain Lake depot. Arms outstretched, she moved directly into Ma's waiting embrace. She clung, the tears that had plagued her constantly since her father's death flowing again, but she smiled through her tears as she said, "It's so good to be here."

Adam stood back, observing as Samantha moved from Ma to Pa and then down the row of assembled brothers and sisters assembled, hugging each in turn. Would he have ever imagined her entering willingly into an embrace? She'd changed so much.

He hadn't mentioned locating David. She'd been so distraught about her father, and then her focus shifted to the memorial service, which was attended sparsely by neighbors, mostly out of compassion for the daughter left behind. Wishing to spare her, he'd made all of the arrangements for burial and care-taking of the grave.

Adam had telegraphed his parents to inform them of Burt O'Brien's accident, so David was aware of his father's death. If David had come to the funeral, the separation would have reached a natural conclusion. But he'd remained in Mountain Lake, waiting for Adam to bring Samantha. She'd have to be told about her brother soon.

Liz kept her arm around Samantha's shoulders. "Do you want to come to our home or go on and stay with Mother?"

Samantha looked from Liz to Laura, then back again. "I— I'm not sure." She shook her head and released a rueful chuckle. "The simplest decisions just seem beyond me these days."

Ma reached over to cup Samantha's wind-reddened cheeks in her hands. "That's fine, Samantha. Why don't we all come to the farm for our evening meal, and then you can decide where to go from there."

Liz offered another quick hug. "You are welcome at either place."

Adam caught Samantha's elbow, steering her toward Pa's wagon. No matter where she was welcome, she'd be staying close to him if he had anything to say about it.

⌒〇

Samantha allowed Adam to lift her into the wagon. She flashed a smile of thanks before settling into the mound of soft hay meant to protect the riders from the January cold. Josie and Becky wriggled in on either side of her, forcing Adam to the opposite side of the wagon. Although only a few feet separated them, she missed his presence. He'd been such a comfort in the past difficult days.

The girls chattered cheerfully all the way home, and Samantha found herself joining in despite herself. How wonderful to be carefree and laughing again. A twinge of guilt stilled her laughter. Shouldn't she be despondent? Pa lay dead. Sorrow pressed on her—she couldn't deny it—but most of her unhappiness was regret for what could have been, but wasn't. She'd prayed so hard for Pa to change—for him to become the loving father she'd always longed for him to be. Now he was gone, and with his death the chance for a loving relationship was forever gone. That was her deepest sorrow.

As they gathered around the table for the evening meal, Samantha looked around at her surrogate family. Her heart swelled. What a gift she'd received when she'd met the Klaassen family. She had so many people to love now—people who loved her in return. Tears stung the back of her nose as she thought of everything they'd given her.

Her gaze traveled to Adam, seated on her right in Josie's usual place. He'd traded spots with his sister, as if afraid to let Samantha out of his sight. His nearness made her feel protected and secure and—her heart pattered wildly—even loved. What would she have done these past days without him?

The Klaassen family held hands around the table to pray, and Samantha placed her hand in Adam's firm, warm grasp. When Mr. Klaassen said, "And thank You, Lord, for bringing our Samantha safely here again," Adam's fingers tightened on hers. Samantha peeked at him. He peeked back. They both smiled.

Ah, it was good to be home.

***

Adam paced in the parlor, his ear tuned to the kitchen where Samantha helped Ma with the breakfast cleanup. The younger children had trooped off for school in a thunder of footsteps, so other than Ma and Samantha's soft chatter, the house was quiet. A perfect setting for a serious talk.

His mouth went dry. He'd gone over in his mind a dozen different ways to tell Samantha he'd found her brother, but he still wasn't sure how to approach the subject. She still possessed hurt bitterness about the broken promise he'd made to return for her. Could she move past the bitterness and on to acceptance?

Impatience to finally let his secret loose propelled him across the kitchen floor. Samantha was laughing with Ma over something Sarah had said at the breakfast table, and he interrupted by touching her lightly on the shoulder. She turned, and the happy look of contentment on her face took his breath away.

She tipped her head in query. "Yes, Adam?"

"C-could we go into the parlor and . . . talk?" He fiddled with the buttons on his flannel shirt, unable to stand still. "There's something I need to discuss with you."

Samantha flashed a puzzled look at Ma.

Ma smiled. "Go ahead, Samantha. We're nearly finished here." She returned to sorting the silverware in its drawer.

She shrugged, her shoulders hunching in a jerk. "All right then."

Adam guided her with a hand on the small of her back, gesturing for her to sit in the upholstered settee. Once she'd settled herself, he pulled a small parlor chair forward and sat, carefully to keep his trouser-covered knees from brushing her rose-scattered skirts. He ran a nervous hand through his hair, leaned forward, and rested his elbows on his knees. Head low, he stared at his clasped hands and gathered his courage.

"Adam?"

Her confused single-word question made Adam jolt. He peeked at her. She nibbled her lower lip, her brows pinching. "Is something wrong?"

He gulped. In his mind, everything was right. "No. No, not at all."

"Are you sending me away?"

His jaw dropped. He sprang upright, shooting out one hand toward her. "No! Why would you think such a thing?"

She offered a slow shrug, her gaze flitting to the side. "You've seen where I come from—my pa, my neighborhood. Everything." She swallowed, her pale blue eyes shifting to meet his. "Maybe now that you know, you don't want me here anymore."

Adam's heart ached. How could she ever think he'd hold something outside of her control against her? He grasped her hand. "Samantha, none of that matters. You're *you*, and I—" He bit down on the tip of his tongue, holding his profession inside.

"Then what is it?" Her voice held an undercurrent of fear. "Something is bothering you."

He gave her hand a squeeze then released it. "Nothing's wrong. I just need to tell you something, and it's hard to know how to get started."

A soft chuckle escaped her lips—a nervous sound. "You've never had any trouble talking to me before. Why not just say it?"

She was right. He should just spit it out. Clamping his fingers over his knees, he drew in a deep breath, and finally divulged the secret. "I've located David."

Samantha gasped. She clapped both palms to her chest. Her mouth dropped open and her eyes grew as wide as a pair of full moons. She looked like she might suffer apoplexy. "W-what did you say?"

Adam bounced from his seat and dropped down beside her, slipping one arm around her shoulders. He fanned her with his free hand, willing her white face to gain some color. "I'm so sorry. I shouldn't have blurted it out that way. But I know even though you miss him, you're still angry with him, and I wasn't sure the best way to say it, so I just *said* it." He fanned with one hand, patted her back with the other, and inwardly prayed for understanding. "I wanted you to know right away because he's here in Mountain Lake. He's eager to see you—and I'm sure you'll want to see him once you're over the shock, and—"

Pink crept back into Samantha's face. She caught his flapping hand and lowered it to his knee then placed her fingers over his mouth. "Adam? Please stop talking and take me to my brother."

❧

David held his sister at arm's length and shook his head. Astonishment and joy mingled in his chest. "Sam . . . Sam . . . You're all grown up. And you're so pretty. All these years I've pictured you as the little girl I left behind. . . ." A lump filled his throat. He held her face with his long, narrow hands, regret for the lost years nearly strangling him. "Sammy, I'm so sorry I left you. I came back for you, just like I said I would, but Pa—he said you'd run off. I should've known he was lying. This happened a few years before you'd actually left. I should've stuck around, kept looking for you. I'm so, so sorry. . . . Can you ever forgive me?"

A tender smile curved her lips. She curled her hands around his wrist, looking directly into his eyes which matched her own. "There's nothing to forgive, Davey. I have you back again, and that's all that matters."

David pulled her tight against his chest. His sister—his sweet little sister—snug in his arms. Had he ever believed this day would come? He flicked a glance at Adam, who sat on the sofa in the corner of the tiny apartment. What a debt of gratitude he owed the man. He planted a kiss on the top of Samantha's head, battling joyful tears.

Samantha's muffled voice came from somewhere in David's shirt front. "Davey? I love you, but I can't breathe in here."

David released her with a loud burst of laughter. The sound startled him. When had he last laughed out loud? He couldn't remember. But only five minutes of having his sister back, and he'd regained the ability.

Adam rose and crossed to the pair and put his hand on Samantha's shoulder. "How about we go out to the house? Mother and Father are eager to see you two together. When the kids come home from school, there'll be no peace. If we want a quiet conversation, we'd better go now."

As much as David wanted to keep Samantha to himself for a while longer, he also wanted to thank Adam's family for rescuing her. "I would like to get to know the family who befriended Sam." He linked fingers with his sister, smiling down at her. "Let's go."

The evening that followed was one of the happiest in Adam's memory. David and Samantha's joy at being together once again was beautifully heart wrenching. The pair couldn't be separated—they stuck as close together as two kernels on a corncob. Ma prepared a homecoming feast fit for royalty, and afterward the entire family, which included Frank's betrothed, Anna, gathered in the parlor to light a fire in the fireplace, pop popcorn, and drink hot homemade apple cider spiced with cinnamon and cloves. David contributed little to the conversation, as reticent as Samantha had been upon her arrival in Mountain Lake, but Samantha joined in as easily as if she'd always been a part of the Klaassen family.

As much as Adam gloried in Samantha's delight at having her brother so near, he experienced a slight twinge of envy. He tried to squelch it—he shouldn't begrudge the too-long-separated brother and sister time together—but he'd also suffered separation from Samantha. He longed to slide in next to her on the settee, to see her sweet face tipped to him and only him in attentiveness, to experience a oneness with her.

A little after eight, Frank caught Anna's hand and drew her from the window seat. "We need to head back. I promised Anna's pa I'd have her home by eight thirty." He turned to David. "I'll drop you off at the boarding room on the way."

David heaved a sigh heavy with reluctance, but he rose and bestowed a shy good-bye on everyone. Samantha curved herself against his side and walked him to the back door. Adam trailed behind, watching as the pair paused in the doorway to exchange a lengthy hug.

David pressed his lips to the top of Samantha's head—he bent his tall, lanky frame like an apostrophe to reach her. "No more unfulfilled promises for either of us now, Sammy. This time, I'm in your life to stay."

Adam's heart caught as Samantha lifted her beaming smile to her brother. Tears shimmered on her thick lashes. "That's the only way I'll have it."

David placed a quick kiss on Samantha's cheek and then hopped off the step and ran to climb into the wagon. Samantha remained in the doorway, arms wrapped around her middle, gazing after him. Adam hesitated, wanting to draw her back inside yet unwilling to intrude.

"So when are you going to propose?"

Adam spun around, surprised when Liz whispered in his ear. He shot a frantic glance at Samantha, but she remained looking outward, seemingly unaware. He caught Liz's arm and tugged her to the opposite side of the kitchen. "You hush that kind of talk!"

Liz laughed. "Oh, nobody's listening—they're all having too much fun." A burst of laughter carried from the parlor, proving her words. She looked past Adam, her eyebrows high, as Samantha scuffed her way toward the parlor. When she'd disappeared through the doorway, Liz shifted her attention to Adam. "So . . . when?"

Adam played dumb. "When, what?"

She punched him on the shoulder. "You know what. It's as plain as the nose on your face. You love her. You're glowing, just having her back here. So when are you going to let her know?"

Adam scratched his chin. He tipped sideways, peering through the wide doorway to Samantha, who sat on the settee again, now with Sarah and Josie—surrounded by his family and obviously at home in their midst. A smile tugged at his lips. He sighed. "Soon, I hope. But her life has been full of half promises and uncertainties. I need to make sure that when I propose, I have more than just my name to offer her. When I promise to care for her, I need to have a home ready, I need—"

Liz shook her head in amused exasperation. "Adam, Adam, Adam . . ."

He didn't need to play dumb now. "What?"

"Samantha is so head over heels in love with you, she needs nothing more than *you*." Liz bumped him lightly with her shoulder as if to say, *silly man.*

Adam cocked his left eyebrow. "That's all?"

Liz laughed. "That's what I like about you, Adam. You really don't have a conceited bone in your body." She socked him again in sisterly fashion. "Yes, you silly goose. If it will make you feel better, ready your home and do whatever else you think needs doing. But I'm telling you right now, all that will be more for your benefit than Samantha's. The offer of your name is all she needs." With a grin, Liz scurried to join the other.

Adam remained in the kitchen, lost in thought. He appreciated Liz's advice, but Liz didn't understand everything. He'd listened to Samantha pour out her hurts in the old shed behind the depot. She needed security and promises that would be kept. He shook his head, discounting his sister's opinion. Liz might be right in some things, but this time she was most certainly wrong. He had a lot of things to work out before he could officially ask Samantha to be his wife.

And he knew just where to get started.

*T*he next three weeks, Adam was rarely at the house. The winter months were the slow months on a farm. Not having crops to attend, the men had a few hours of precious free time. So once morning chores were completed, Adam disappeared, returning briefly for his noon meal, then taking off again until it was time for milking in the evening. Although his family questioned him—Sarah nearly pestered the patience out of him—he refused to tell anyone where he spent his time or what he was doing.

The rest of the family had no secrets, though. Si and Frank spent most of their day in the barn, working on furniture for the small frame house that had been erected in a tree-laden area near the soybean fields to the west of the Klaassen's homestead. The date of Frank and Anna's wedding crept over closer, and Frank readied the house like a mother robin readies her nest. Laura stayed busy finishing a lovely Double Wedding Ring quilt, the rings of which she'd formed from pieces of Frank's and Anna's old clothing. It was a beautiful quilt, the colorful patchwork rings showing crisply against the bleached muslin. But more beautiful than the pattern was the thought behind it. Bits and pieces of each of the couple's past, sewn together into a circle—a never-ending symbol of love. Samantha longed for the time when she, too, would make preparations for a home and family. And those longings always centered around Adam.

Samantha had taken several dress orders and kept her hands busy stitching, but her mind was restless, wondering where Adam was, what he was doing, who he was with. . . . The beautifully feminine Priscilla Koehn niggled at the back of her memory. Could he be spending his time wooing her? Priscilla would certainly welcome the attention. The green-eyed monster, jealousy, visited her often.

She sat in the parlor, sewing the hem on a new dress for a friend of Laura's, trying to reassure herself that certainly Adam wouldn't have come clear to Milwaukee for her if he didn't care for her. But on the other hand, Adam was such a caring person, he probably would have done it for just about anyone he thought was in trouble. Still, she had gotten that one kiss from him, and he had held her so tenderly after Pa died. . . . But she'd been horribly upset that day. Maybe he was just comforting her the way he'd comfort Sarah if she was hurting.

Her trembling fingers skipped a stitch, and with a huff of frustration she set the dress aside. Crossing to the window, she hugged herself and stared across the brown yard. If only she knew how she stood with Adam! He'd been wonderfully kind to her, had treated her as if she mattered deeply, but he'd never come right out and said how he felt. Was it simply brotherly affection, special friendship, or did he love her? She longed for the courage to simply ask him. That is, if she could pin the man down long enough for a conversation these days.

She searched the yard, seeking a glimpse of his familiar blue plaid shirt and thick brown hair. Where was he keeping himself lately? What could he be doing that would consume so much time? Christmas was over; it couldn't be Christmas secrets. But a secret it was. One of the best-kept secrets ever. It drove her to distraction, trying to discern what his disappearances, smug grin, and boyish winks could mean.

With a sigh, she returned to the settee to continue sewing. But her tangled emotions held her captive. She couldn't focus on stitching. David had started working at the Family Mercantile with Hiram Klaassen. Maybe she could ride in and visit with him. Folding the dress neatly, she placed it on the window seat and went to the kitchen where Laura kneaded a huge ball of bread dough. Samantha paused beside the flour-strewn table. "May I take Bet to town?"

Laura glanced up, her brows puckering. "You have an important errand?"

She needed her brother to help her sort her thoughts. "Yes, ma'am."

Laura examined Samantha for a few moments, as if waiting for a further explanation. Samantha remained quiet. Finally Laura offered a nod. "I suppose it's fine. But bundle up in my wool coat and a knitted scarf. There's the scent of snow in the air. And try to be back well before dark. I don't want you caught out in the cold."

Laura's motherly caring warmed Samantha more than the coat ever could. She gave the dear woman a brief hug. "Yes, ma'am. I won't be long. And thank you."

Soon she was on Bet's back, snug in Laura's wool coat with a thick scarf draped over her hair and around her neck. The extra layers made her feel bulky, but she appreciated the protection from the chill air. While she rode, she admired the beautiful landscape. Yesterday's snowfall coated the ground like frosting on one of Laura's scripture cakes. Fence posts wore little pointed hats of snow, and leafless tree branches were dressed up with a fine lining. A pair of cardinals flitted through the trees above her head, their brilliant red a beautiful contrast in the world of white.

"You sure created a wonderful world, God." Samantha spoke aloud into the quiet beauty, startling a small white rabbit into zigzagged escape. She laughed at the rabbit's frantic course then prodded Bet with a few bumps of her heels. "Come on, old girl. Let's hurry a bit."

Samantha hitched Bet to the wooden rail outside Klaassen's Family Mercantile and gave her nose a brief rub of thanks before entering the store. The doorbell clanged, and David looked up from a stack of cans on the counter.

His eyes widened. "Sam! Did you ride in?" He crossed the floor toward her, hands outstretched.

Samantha moved into his embrace. "Yes, I did."

"Brr, you're cold." David shivered and turned her in the direction of the potbellied stove that filled the corner of the store. "Come warm yourself."

Samantha offered no argument. She hunkered near the stove, rubbing her hands together and allowing the heat to steep into her bones. She glanced around the quiet shop. "Where's Mr. Klaassen?"

David's chest puffed. "Gone for the afternoon. He left me in charge—books and all." David squatted down next to Samantha, a look of wonder on his face. "Can you imagine someone trusting the son of Burt O'Brien to care for his property?"

Samantha patted his knee. "Davey, you are much more than just Burt O'Brien's son. The Klaassens know that, and so do you, I think."

David nodded, his expression pensive. "Still, it's hard to imagine. . . ." He brightened and asked, "So what brings you into town on this nippy day?"

"You." Warm again, she moved to perch on the cracker barrel. David seated himself on the apple barrel nearby. She fixed her gaze on her brother's serious face and confided, "I was feeling restless and decided I needed a chat with my big brother."

David's narrow face creased with a tender smile. "Got a case of cabin fever?"

Samantha shook her head. "Not that kind of restlessness. I need to . . . make sense of confusion."

David closed his long-fingered hand over hers. "What's the problem, Sammy?"

Frowning, Samantha shrugged. "I'm not sure there is a *problem*. It's more an unanswered question." She paused, chewing on her lower lip, her brows pulled into a puzzled frown. Drawing in a deep breath, she forced herself to ask the question that plagued her mind. "Davey, do you think I'm good enough for Adam?"

David reared back. His frown turned stern. "What kind of a question is that?"

"He's seen where I come from, and he knows how Pa liked to drink more than he liked anything else. If you put our family up against his, look at the differences! Sometimes I think he cares for me, but other times . . ." She bit her lip again, lowering her gaze to her lap. "I don't know what to think."

"Well, I do." David gave her hand a shake. "Look at me."

She did, seeing his face blurred by the tears flooding her eyes.

David swept the moisture away with his thumbs. "None of the Klaassens look down their noses at you—and that goes doubly for Adam. What did you say to me a little bit ago? There's a heap-sight more to you than just being Burt O'Brien's daughter. Adam sees that."

Samantha sighed. "I want to think so, David, really I do. But since I've come back here he's been so odd. He spends all his time away from the house—away from me—and he won't say where he is or what he's doing. It's as if he's avoiding me for some unknown reason." Tipping her head, she fixed David with a worried look. "Do you think he knows how I feel about him, and he's staying away as a means of telling me he doesn't feel the same?"

David sucked in a slow breath. "How *do* you feel about him?"

Samantha answered promptly. "I love him. I love him *so much*. . . . When I was away from him, I felt incomplete. When I'm with him, I feel like I'm a better, bigger person than I was before. Somehow he makes me *more* than I've ever been." She lowered her head, laughing self-consciously. "I suppose that sounds funny."

David cupped her chin, lifting her face. "No, Sammy, it isn't funny. It's wonderful, and I'm so happy you've found someone like Adam. If I could have handpicked someone for you, I would have chosen him. He's a good man."

"Yes, he is." She threw her hands wide. "I just wish I knew if he cared at all for me, too."

David grinned. "Stop wishing. Adam's got feelings for you, have no doubt. Now, I don't know what he's doing off by himself, but I can almost guarantee it's not to avoid spending time with you. That wouldn't be Adam's way of handling things. He'd come right out and tell you if he thought there was a problem between you."

Samantha considered David's words. She knew Adam to be open and honest. He wouldn't run from a conflict. The knowledge only confused her further. "Then what—?"

"Has it crossed your mind, little sister, that he's planning a surprise for Frank and Anna? Their wedding is when—next Saturday?"

She nodded.

David gave a knowing wink. "Well, my guess is he's off doing some special fixings for his brother and future sister-in-law."

"That would make sense." Samantha worried her lower lip for a moment, contemplating. "If I only knew for sure . . ."

David stood, holding out his hand to Samantha. She took it and allowed him to tug her to her feet. He slung his arm around her shoulder and walked her toward the door. "Well, don't stew about it. The wedding is only a week away. I'll wager you'll know soon enough what Adam's up to. In the meantime, try not to turn those puppy dog eyes on him at every turn, or he may end up spilling the beans and spoil a good surprise."

She laughed. "David, it's so good to have you back. It's wonderful to have my big brother to talk sense into me." Then she hung her head as another thought struck. Didn't the Bible Adam had given her assure her the heavenly Father had good plans for her? Why was she wasting so much time worrying instead of trusting His leading? *I'm sorry, God, for not asking You what I should do concerning my feelings for Adam.*

"Sam?"

She looked at David, who watched her with lines of concern marring his brow.

"Are you all right?"

"I'm fine. I won't worry anymore. I promise."

"Good." He pulled her close, resting his chin on her hair. "Then can I give you one more piece of big brotherly advice?"

"What's that?"

He bounced her against him once and ordered with mock sternness, "Get on your horse and go home before the sun drops any further. And when you get there, drink a cup of hot tea to warm up your innards."

Samantha giggled. "Yes, sir."

David followed her outside and helped her into Bet's saddle. Placing the reins in her hands, he offered a tender smile. "See you later, baby sister."

She smiled her reply and headed for home.

The evening before the big wedding day, Grandpa and Grandma Klaassen, Daniel and Rose, and little Christina and Katrina arrived by train. The house overflowed with people, chatter, and laughter. While happy chaos, it was chaos just the same, and midevening Adam observed Samantha drawing a shawl around her shoulders and slipping out onto the railed porch. The idea of a few quiet moments alone with Samantha appealed, so he tugged a jacket into place and followed.

She held to the porch railing, her face aimed upward. Stargazing, seemingly lost in thought. If she sensed his presence, she gave no indication of it. Her eyes remained riveted on the black velvet sky which wore a spattering of sparkling diamonds. Adam perched on the porch railing and watched her admire the sky. He'd been so busy lately, gone so much, that her beauty took him by surprise. Hers was a simple beauty enhanced by her modest nature and caring spirit. In his eyes, she was a perfect gemstone set in a moonlit mounting of gold. His heart swelled in anticipation as he thought of the preparations he'd been making. The time neared to tell her his plans. But for now he simply enjoyed watching her as she gazed heavenward.

At last she turned to meet his gaze. Her lips tipped into a self-conscious smile. "Did you think you were being ignored?"

He shifted his weight to lean more comfortably on a post as she turned to perch gracefully on the railing. "Maybe. Just a little."

"Probably the way all of us have felt here lately, by you."

He caught the hint but he smiled, refusing to rise to the bait.

After a few moments she turned her attention to the sky again. She released an airy sigh. "The night never fails to move me."

His gaze pinned on her sweet profile. Lit by the soft glow flowing from the parlor window, her hair became burnished copper, her thick lashes casting small shadows on her cheeks. He swallowed, nearly undone by her beauty. "How, Samantha?"

She searched the sky, her eyes roving over the millions of stars winking on their carpet of ebony. "The sky is so soft and black—like fine velvet—and the stars blink and shimmer. . . . Sometimes I pretend they're looking at me, sending me a message from heaven—maybe from Gran. And I feel so close to them, I could just reach out and put one in my pocket to save for a sad day when I need some beauty." She raised her hand, the fingers reaching skyward. Then she peeked at him, color flooding her cheeks, and she pulled her hand back to the railing. "I must sound awful foolish."

"For wanting to put a star in your pocket?"

Her head low, she nodded.

Adam chuckled. "Not at all. That's like carrying around a special wish and being able to take it out and hold it now and then, knowing that it's yours to keep forever."

Samantha's chin bobbed up, her eyes widening in surprise. "You *do* understand."

"Well, sure." Adam angled his body to face her. "I have wishes, too, Samantha. We all do. They might be different desires, but no one *never* makes a wish on a star." He tipped his face upward. "If I could put one in my pocket, I'd choose that one." He pointed to an exceptionally bright star that blinked almost blue.

Samantha followed his gaze. "Yes, that's a nice one, but I'd choose"—she pointed, too—"that one, because it's smaller and off by itself, and it looks as if it could use someone to love it." *Just like me.* The words, unspoken, hovered in the air between them.

Adam stared at the star for several silent seconds before he found the courage to ask softly, "Do you feel like that star, Samantha?"

The rosy color in her cheeks deepened. Hugging her arms around herself, she swallowed twice. When she spoke, the quaver brought the sting of tears to Adam's eyes. "Sometimes. I used to feel very alone. But now . . ." Abruptly, she turned to look him full in the face. "Now, I know God loves me. I've found people who care about me. So . . . now . . . I can dare to believe that my wishes could come true."

Their eyes locked. They leaned close. So close her warm breath brushed his cheek as she exhaled in tiny puffs. So close, he could see the reflection of the stars in her cornflower blue eyes. Adam's heart thrummed. *Yes, Samantha, I will make all your wishes come true. Just be patient with me. Let me make things perfect for you.*

Her eyes beseeched. Her breath coiled around him in a wisp of white. Her lips parted, as if ready to ask a question, and he held his breath, waiting. Then the parlor door swung open, sending a shaft of golden light across their feet and surrounding them with the laughing voices of his family.

Sarah called, "Mama says come in. We're gonna make taffy." The door slammed, sealing them once again in peaceful darkness.

The intimate moment had passed. Reluctantly Adam slid from the rail, his feet echoing against the floorboards. "Come, Samantha." He held out his hand, and she placed her palm on his. He curled her fingers around her small hand. It fit, just right, in his grip. Just as she fit, just right, in his heart. He'd tell her soon, but for now he led her back inside to join his family.

Frank and Anna's wedding day dawned bright and clear, a crisp windless winter day with bright sun bouncing off the snow and sending millions of shimmering diamonds into the air. Samantha pulled aside the lace curtains that shrouded the parlor window and looked out at the perfect day. A hint of melancholy tugged. If only this could be her wedding day. Hers and Adam's . . .

"Samantha! Samantha!" Sarah's voice intruded.

Samantha turned in time to catch Sarah, who threw herself against Samantha's middle in a boisterous hug.

"See my pretty wedding dress?" The little girl spun an impromptu pirouette in the shaft of sunlight that streamed through the bayed windows. The confection pink dress with miles of lace trim was an ideal wrapping for Sarah's china doll prettiness.

"It's lovely, Sarah. You'll make the prettiest flower girl ever."

Giggling, Sarah dashed away. Samantha's thoughts drifted to the previous evening, when Laura read the list of wedding plans, ascertaining all was ready. Sarah would be the flower girl, with Anna's youngest brother, Benji, as ring bearer. Anna's sister, Katherine, and Josie were serving as attendants to the bride. Daniel and Adam were standing up for Frank. Arn and Becky would light the candles that lined each window sill and the edge of the altar at the front of the church. Anna's brothers, Mort and Matthew, were singing two songs, and Teddy had responsibility for carrying all the gifts that arrived to a decorated table.

When Laura had finished, Frank exclaimed in exasperation, "If we'd had one more brother or sister to find a wedding assignment for, I would have insisted we elope."

Anna had leaned close and gently chided, "Would you rather have no family at all?" They'd both looked at Samantha, and Frank had ceased his grumbling, but the funny feeling that filled her stomach at their words remained like a lump of dread in her belly. Now that David was here in Mountain Lake, she had someone. One someone. Was it wrong to want more?

After breakfast, everyone climbed into the buckboard, which the Klaassen siblings had decorated with huge tissue paper flowers and crepe paper streamers in pink, yellow, and blue. Even Bet and Tick wore paper flowers on their ears, and they stamped their feet, blowing billows of steam from their noses as if to say they understood the importance of the day.

The ride to the church was raucous. Joyous jabber and playful ribbing rang from every corner. Frank sat nervous and twitchy, fiddling constantly with the perfect black bow tie resting below his chin. Samantha thought he looked particularly fine in his wedding suit of black broadcloth and crisp white cambric shirt. But not as handsome as Adam would be in such finery. She imagined Adam standing at an altar, his head held high, his brown eyes shining with love as she walked down the aisle toward him.

Sadness threatened to grip her. She must stop indulging such fanciful imaginings! She turned to Josie and joined in the conversation, determined to enjoy Frank and Anna's special day.

When they reached the churchyard, everyone spilled out of the wagon. Other wagons and buggies were already there, with people milling around outside, enjoying the sunshine. Laura herded the younger children inside. Si, Arn, and Frank unloaded the food and gifts the family had brought. Adam helped Grandpa and Grandma Klaassen down from the high wagon seat and escorted them into the church. Daniel and Rose each took a small daughter by the hand and headed inside behind them. Samantha lagged behind, feeling out of place and sorry for herself.

The service was brief considering the amount of time spent in preparation for it. Anna's mother cried through most of the ceremony, dabbing at her eyes with a lace handkerchief. What were her tears all about? Was the woman overwhelmed with happiness or filled with regret over her daughter's choice? If it were Samantha's wedding day, would her mother-in-law-to-be shed tears of regret or joy over the wife her son had chosen?

She looked at Laura who was seated next to Si—no man and woman separation on this day. Her gently lined face tipped upward, her ever-present smile soft and accepting. Would she be wearing that same expression of contented happiness if Adam and Samantha stood at the altar?

Her eyes moved to Adam, so straight and tall, flanked by his brothers. He stood with his hands clasped at his spine, his gaze on the minister as the man advised the young couple on the seriousness of their commitment. Tears stung her eyes. He was so handsome. *Oh, Adam, can't you see me as I see you?*

As if he sensed her yearnings, he turned his face slightly, his eyes seeking. When his gaze found her, his expression softened. His lips tipped into the sweetest smile she'd ever seen— a full-of-promise smile that lit him from within. Her breath caught. She sent him a timorous smile, tears filling her eyes as emotions too heady to contain swept through her. For only a few seconds, they gazed into one another's eyes, and then Adam turned his attention back to the minister.

Samantha crossed her hands over her pounding heart. Her thoughts raced. *Dear Lord, I saw something in Adam's eyes. Something different, something special. I saw . . .* She hardly dared to believe it. *I saw love.*

Adam forced his gaze forward but everything within him strained toward the lovely young woman sitting only a few yards away. His thoughts tumbled, making his pulse gallop. *It will be our turn soon, Samantha. Soon it will be you and me standing here before our family and friends, exchanging vows that will bind us together for the rest of our lives. Believe it, Samantha. It will happen. Soon . . .*

Reverend Goertzen turned the couple to face the congregation and announced, "I present to you Mr. and Mrs. Frank Klaassen. Frank, you may kiss your bride."

Frank's face flooded with color as he leaned toward Anna and she lifted her face for his kiss. Their lips touched briefly, and as they separated, a whoop resounded. The people filling the pews came in a rush, flooding the newly joined couple with well-wishes.

Adam stood to the side, watching the throng swarm his brother and sister-in-law. He needed to get out of the way, and he sidestepped, placing the heel of his boot on someone's foot. He spun around, an apology forming on his tongue, to find himself face-to-face with Samantha. The secret he carried trembled in his throat, and a smile broke across his face without effort.

People continued to mill around them, causing them to shift and move with the tide of bodies. But her eyes remained locked on his, as if unable to look away. He caught her arm, drawing her from the throng. Once safely in the corner, he brushed her arm with his thumb. "I'm sorry I stepped on you."

"It's all right." Her words came out with little huffs, as if she'd just run a footrace. Her cheeks bore bright streaks of pink, and her eyes shimmered. "You didn't hurt me."

"I'm glad. That's the last thing I'd want to do." Remembering the evening in Liz's yard when he'd frightened her so, pain pinched Adam's heart. He leaned close, hoping she'd read the sincerity in his eyes. "You believe me, don't you?"

She nodded slowly. "Yes, Adam, I believe you. More than I've ever known anything, I know you wouldn't hurt me."

At her reply, his heart lurched and fluttered, rising up into his throat. He wanted to say more—to offer other assurances—but the wedding party was moving toward the double doors, Frank and Anna in the lead. He'd have to wait. With a gentle nudge, Adam turned Samantha toward the others.

She remained close to his side as they stepped out into the churchyard. Together, they cheered when the others cheered, threw wheat kernels when the others tossed handfuls into the air, and even chased the buggy that bore the newlyweds toward their new home until it rounded the corner and headed out of town. But when their steps slowed, and the merrymakers had turned back to the church for the after-wedding celebration, he caught her arm and held her back, and within minutes they were alone, side by side, in the middle of Main Street.

Adam grinned and couldn't help teasing, "Remember the last time we ran down Main Street?"

She blushed prettily, but she laughed. "Yes. You tackled me."

"You deserved it."

"I did." Her eyes sparkled with laughter.

But something other than humor simmered beneath the lapels of his jacket. "Samantha, I'd like to show you something. Would you mind skipping the party at the church and going for a ride with me instead?"

She shook her head, the movement barely discernible. "I'd love to go for a ride with you." The simple reply seemed laden with meaning. She leaned toward him—so without guile or coquettishness he believed the gesture was done unconsciously. Her face lifted, her blue eyes speaking volumes without words.

Adam's heart read the unspoken message shining from her face. And he responded in kind. He leaned forward, his movements slow and deliberate. He watched her draw in a breath, her eyes slipping closed as his face came nearer, nearer. Their noses bumped lightly, and hers was cold. But her lips were warm. Their mouths brushed once, twice, then they pulled back slightly, foreheads pressed together lightly, and he sensed her smile even without looking.

They opened their eyes at the same moment. Brown eyes met blue, and he discovered he'd been right. Her face was nearly split by her happy smile. He brought up his gloved hands and closed them on her shoulders. Her hands came up to grasp his forearms, gripping hard through the layers of clothing. They stood thus, sunlight reflecting off the crystal snow and surrounding them with thousands of tiny prisms.

Adam couldn't keep the smile from his face. In minutes— mere minutes—his secrets would be revealed. He would be free to make promises that he intended to spend a lifetime keeping. It was time. Their time.

Unable to hold back any longer, he said, "Let's go."

and in hand, they laughingly ran to the waiting wagon. Samantha started to climb aboard, but Adam grabbed her around the waist and boosted her onto the seat. He jumped up beside her and placed one quick, impetuous smack on her lips.

"Adam!" She glanced around, seeking prying eyes. "What if someone sees you?"

He shrugged, his grin so boyish it stole her breath. "Then they'll say, look at that lucky guy, stealing a kiss from the prettiest girl in town."

"Oh, Adam . . ." Her face flooded with heat, and she ducked her head. But she couldn't stop smiling.

He laughed aloud as he raised the reins and flicked them downward. "Let's get movin'." And they were off.

The air was crisp, clear. It stung her lungs as she inhaled, but she wouldn't complain. She was with Adam, in a world of their own—a shining, shimmering, brighter-than-sunshine world of happy abandon. Never had the sky seemed bluer, the clouds fluffier, the birds as full of cheerful chatter as they were on this day. Hoarfrost coated everything from the tiniest tree branches to the barbed wire that ran from fence post to fence post, catching the sun and bouncing it back into millions of tiny rainbows.

She turned toward Adam and caught him staring, smiling, admiring. She smiled and admired right back. She asked, "Where are we going?"

He waggled his brows. "You'll see."

She pretended to pout. "You won't tell me?"

"Not a chance."

She tipped her head and batted her eyelashes. Had she ever openly flirted with anyone before? No, but with Adam she felt at ease and truly beautiful for the first time in her life. "Pleeeease?" She drew out the word, giving him her best pleading look.

He laughed. "Don't even try it." With a grin, he advised, "Just settle back and enjoy the ride. We'll be there soon. Why don't you tell me what you thought of the wedding?"

So Samantha and Adam chatted away as the sun shone down and the clouds floated lazily in the clear blue sky and cardinals scolded the squirrels that danced in the treetops. In time, Adam pulled back on the reins and called in a deep voice, "Whoa now, Bet and Tick." When the horses came obediently to a stop, Adam tied the reins around the brake handle and leaped off the wagon. "We'll walk from here." He reached for her, and she placed her hands on his shoulders as he lifted her down. Her feet touched the ground, but Adam kept his hands on her waist, hers remaining lightly on his shoulders.

A smile—tender, yet containing a controlled excitement—lit his eyes. "I have a surprise for you."

Her pulse began tripping in erratic double-beats. What was he up to? "For me?"

"Yes. I wanted to get it ready for you as quickly as I could, and it took longer than I'd expected. So I haven't spent much time with you since you've been back. I hope you aren't angry with me."

Angry? How could she be angry when he looked at her with his warm, brown-eyed gaze? Her heart felt light and fluttery, and her stomach leaped in happy flip-flops of anticipation. A giggle spilled from her throat. "Well, what is it?"

He smiled a reply, took her by the hand, and led her through a small wind block of scrub maples. Samantha recognized the area—the north wheat field. Puzzled, she scanned the snow-dusted landscape, seeking her surprise. Adam led her straight toward the hill where his grandfather had constructed the dugout. She sent a curious glance at him then looked ahead. She let out a little gasp that created a small cloud in the chill air.

The old dugout had undergone a transformation. A new door, painted a green as deep as the pine needles on a Christmas tree, stood in place of the old warped plank door. The shutters had been repaired and painted the same dark green. Bright curtains hung behind—was she imagining things?—real glass windows. Samantha's feet stumbled to a halt. "Adam . . . ?"

Beside her, Adam fairly twitched with excitement. He urged her forward with a tug on her hand. "Come inside, Samantha."

She allowed herself to be pulled along. Her mind raced with a dozen questions, but her tongue felt thick and dry. She couldn't speak a word. Adam turned the bright white enamel door knob and swung the door wide. When Samantha got a look at the spanking clean, whitewashed interior, she clapped her hands to her cheeks. Her startled gaze swung to Adam, her mouth hanging open.

Chuckling, he reached out with one finger to close it for her. "I could see your tonsils." How could his teasing sound so sweet?

Samantha gulped, staring around the room in amazement. Wide pine planking covered the dirt floor. Muslin stiffened with whitewash hid the crumbling dirt walls. A round claw-footed table stood in the middle of the room, flanked by two pressed-back chairs and topped with a red-and-white checked oilcloth. A rocking chair sat invitingly in front of the stone fireplace. Samantha, frowning, crossed to it and stroked it with her fingers. Why, it was Gran's old rocker!

She spun to face Adam, her heart pounding and her hands trembling. He remained planted next to the door, hands thrust deep into his pockets, a knowing smile lighting his handsome face. His eyes seemed to tell her to go ahead—explore, examine, enjoy. So she continued her perusal of the room.

In the far corner, a green enamel kerosene stove took up residence, and on new shelves mounted on the wall beside it sat a selection of turquoise graniteware pots and pans, plates, bowls and cups. Samantha moved along the shelves, fingering each item, a lump in her throat.

A blue calico curtain split the room slightly off-center. Samantha pulled it aside and peeked behind it. A bed with a tall, carved maple headboard and footboard filled the space. Her breath coming in little spurts of uncertainty, Samantha stepped over to it and pressed both hands down on the Trip-Around-the-World quilt covering the straw mattress. All these new, bright, wonderful things. What did they mean?

Adam appeared at the curtain. Dimples winked on his tanned cheeks. "Well, what do you think?"

Samantha straightened and turned an amazed circle. "It's wonderful, Adam. Why, it's like new in here. And Gran's rocking chair—how did it get here?"

"David arranged to have it shipped. He knew you would want it."

She shook her head, awed. "And this—" She gestured to the curtain, the new shelves, the floor. "You did all of this?"

Adam shrugged in feigned nonchalance, a secretive smile playing on the corners of his lips. "Liz helped a bit with the curtains and tablecloth and quilt."

Smiling but still puzzled, she repeated, "It's wonderful—a snug, perfect little home. But—" She bit her lower lip. Who was it for? For her to live there on her own? For her to share with David? Or . . . She wouldn't allow herself to consider her deepest hope.

Adam pointed to the other side of the curtain with his thumb. "There's something for you on the mantel."

Samantha sent him another seeking look, which he returned with a smile of encouragement, as she passed him to cross back to the fireplace. Next to the glowing lantern she found an enameled box with a beautiful rose on its top. Her fingers quivering, she lifted the lid. A tinkling melody poured forth. She recognized the tune—"Lohengrin," the traditional wedding song. Her heart leaped into her throat.

Adam crossed to her slowly, his steps measured and purposeful. He stopped inches in front of her. Taking her by the shoulders, he turned her and gently eased her into the smooth seat of Gran's rocker. He bent down on one knee, sliding his palms down her arms until he reached her hands and linked fingers with her. The tune continued to play as he began to speak.

"Samantha, this little dugout was prepared over fifty years ago by my grandfather as a first home for himself and his new bride. It was simple, but it was built by loving hands and was offered with a loving heart. Grandpa told me that he and Grandma were as happy as could be in this little dugout, because it was their *home*. They didn't have much in the way of material possessions. They'd just arrived from Germany—two young people far away from their family and friends. They were scared and probably lonely, but they had each other. They had a common faith, as well as a lot of love. So when Grandpa dug out the side of this hill and made a house around it, he was building on the promise of love and of better things ahead."

Love and better things . . . Yes, that's what Samantha had discovered since arriving in Mountain Lake. She held her breath, her gaze pinned on Adam's sincere, fervent face, her senses so alive the air seemed to crackle.

"It took a lot of faith in one another to make their new start a bright one, but they did it. And when the dugout was complete, he painted a plaque for Grandma which they hung beside the door." Adam released one of her hands to reach beneath his jacket. He withdrew a small, flat package wrapped in tissue and placed it in Samantha's lap.

She stared at the package nestled in the folds of her dress, afraid to touch it, afraid to speak. She dared not break the spell his words spun around them.

"Samantha . . ." He paused, and she lifted her gaze from the package to look back on his. "I've dreamed of the day when I would embark on the same journey my grandparents made—a journey of living and loving and becoming one with a special woman."

The breath she'd been holding released in little puffs of delighted disbelief. Was this moment true? Was this man— this wonderful, tender, open, loving man—truly speaking such words to her? Her—Samantha O'Brien, a nobody. She felt at once undeserving of it and full of longing to hear him continue his soliloquy.

"I'm ready for that journey." His brown eyes glowed, capturing her with their intensity. "I've met that special woman, and I know that God will bless the union." He took in a deep, shuddering breath before continuing. "Samantha, I want nothing more than to begin a new life with you, here, in this little dugout that I've made ready for you much the same way Grandpa made it ready for Grandma all those years ago."

Tears sprang into the corners of his eyes, emphasizing the flecks of green that rested in the velvet brown of his irises. He squeezed her hands. "Samantha, I love you. I am asking you to marry me."

*S*he inhaled sharply, taking in a great, choking breath of joyous disbelief. He'd said it. He'd said he loved her. He *loved her.* "Oh, Adam . . ." Too overcome for words, she covered her lips with her trembling fingers as the room began swimming through a spurt of happy tears.

He dipped his head to peek at her impishly. "*Oh, Adam . . . ?* Does that mean yes or no?"

Samantha lowered her hands. Tears overflowed to stream in warm rivulets down her cheeks. "Yes, Adam—oh, yes!" With a joyful burst of laughter, she threw herself into his embrace. "I love you so much, Adam. I can't believe it—your wife. Your *wife.* Oh, I'm so happy I can't bear it."

Her chest would surely burst from happiness. She clung to his neck as he rocked her in his arms. He buried his face in her tumbling curls, and she heard him murmur, "How I love your wild, untamed hair . . ." Her heart caught. He even loved her hair? What a gift God had bestowed when he brought Adam into her life.

Finally he set her aside and picked up the paper-wrapped package, which had fallen to the floor beside their knees. "Here . . . open your present."

She took it, her smile so wide her cheeks ached. With shaking fingers, she pulled the string that held the paper closed. A giggle rose from her chest. She felt giddy with excitement. She peeled the paper wrapping aside and revealed a nine-inch square of cedar, sanded smooth and bearing a painted image of a small yellow frame house at the top, a crude red heart at the bottom. Some sort of writing filled the center.

She frowned, staring at the lines of print. "What does it say?"

Adam cleared his throat."*Ein Haus wird gebout von Holz und stein; Aber ein Heim bout mon von Liebe alein.*" The unfamiliar words sounded melodious when uttered in his even, baritone voice.

"Is it German?" she asked.

"Yes. Low German, the language of my heritage."

She wished she knew the language of his heritage. "What does it mean?"

Without looking at the plaque, Adam recited, " 'Houses are built of wood and stone; Homes are built of love alone.' "

She retrieved the plaque and ran a finger across the painted words, leaving it to rest on the last two words. " 'Love alone' . . ." Her voice drifted as soft as a feather floating downward. Her gaze lifted to meet Adam's again. "Our home was built with love, and it will always be filled with love, Adam." She knew the pain of broken promises. She didn't make promises lightly. Her chest swelled with conviction as she stated firmly, "I promise you that."

Tears glittered in Adam's eyes. "I make that same promise to you, my Samantha. Forever, and ever."

"I believe you." A weight seemed to fall from Samantha's shoulders as she spoke her assurance to Adam. Such healing God had brought, that she could accept his words as truth and not doubt.

Fresh tears crept down Samantha's cheeks. Adam used his thumbs to whisk them away then cupped her face with his palms, his fingers woven through her hair. "Miss Samantha O'Brien, you have made me the happiest man in the world today. I'm so blessed to have you in my life."

Samantha caught his hands and drew them downward. "Adam, the blessing is mine. You'll never know what it means to me to be loved by someone like you."

He opened his mouth to speak, but she shook her head to silence him. "Please, let me finish. I need to tell you this."

He settled back on his haunches, fixing his attentive gaze on her face. "I'm listening."

Completely confident in his love for her, she opened her heart to him. "When I came to Mountain Lake, I was frightened and filled with angry bitterness. I didn't—couldn't—trust anyone. I didn't know how. Where I came from, if you trusted, you got hurt. So I'd closed myself off. But a person all shut away inside himself is a lonely person." She swallowed, experiencing a sting of pain as she relived the past. "I was so very lonely, Adam . . ."

He took her hands, offering a gentle squeeze.

Encouraged by his understanding, she continued. "You asked me once what I was running away from, and I told you I wasn't running away. You didn't believe me, but it was true. I wasn't running *from* something, I was trying to run *to* something. But I didn't know what. I've been seeking that illusive something since I was six years old and they covered my gran with dirt."

Tears clouded her vision, but she smiled, her lips quivering tremulously. She clasped his hands between hers and lifted them, creating a steeple of their joined hands. "My searching neared its end the day you came dashing down the street after me—when instead of treating me with anger, you reached out to me with kindness. Me, some dirty little thief from the wrong side of the city. I never could have imagined being loved by someone like you—someone good and kind and virtuous. I never could have imagined deserving the love of someone like you. But because of you, I don't see myself in the same old way anymore. I'm not that same frightened, lonely, seeking person anymore."

She gulped, gratitude and love filling her so fully her throat went tight. "Adam, you've given me everything my heart ever longed for. You introduced me, through example and word, to a Savior who will ever be with me. You found my brother and brought him back to me. You gave me love and self-respect and helped me open up to trusting again. You gave my seeking heart a place to call home. I've never done anything to deserve you, but you're mine anyway, and because of the things you've taught me, I can accept you as my own without feelings of guilt or unworthiness. You've even given me *me*. I am so thankful for you."

"Ah, Samantha . . ." He withdrew his hands from her grasp and pulled her close. He lowered his head and pressed his lips to hers. Their kiss was salty and wet with tears. But only happy tears. His hand on the back of her head, he drew her into his embrace then rocked her gently, slowly, contentedly. She relaxed against him. She could remain here forever.

Suddenly he stiffened, and a huff of laughter blasted in Samantha's ear. She pulled back, startled. Adam threw back his head and laughed again, uproariously, uninhibited. She pressed her palms to his jacket front, confused. "What's so funny?"

Adam's eyes crinkled merrily. "You."

She shook her head as if to clear it. "Me?"

"Yes, you, Miss Samantha O'Brien." His voice warbled with suppressed laughter. "When you came to town, you were trying to pass yourself off as Sam Klaassen." He leaned down and kissed the end of her nose. His face close to hers, he finished with a impish smirk. "Well, now I intend to make an honest woman out of you."

She burst into happy laughter as well. He opened his arms, and she fitted herself against Adam's chest. When his arms closed around her, Samantha's seeking heart beat a happy message—*I'm home.*

LAURA KLAASSEN'S SCRIPTURE CAKE

(Use King James Version for references)

1½ cups Judges 5:25
3 cups Jeremiah 6:20
6 Jeremiah 17:11
3½ cups Exodus 29:2
2 tsp. Amos 4:5
2 Chronicles 9:9 to taste
A pinch of Mark 9:50
1 cup Genesis 24:17
1 tblsp. 1 Samuel 14:25
2 cups 1 Samuel 30:12
2 cups chopped dried Song of Solomon 2:13
2 cups slivered or chopped Numbers 17:8

Preheat oven to 325 degrees. Cream together butter and sugar; beat in eggs one at a time. Sift together flour, baking powder, salt, and spices. Add alternately with water to creamed mixture. Stir in honey, fold in raisins, figs, and almonds. Mix well. Turn into two well-greased 9x5x3" loaf pans. Bake about 60 minutes, making sure not to over bake, until loaves test done by the toothpick test. Let cool for 30 minutes in pans before turning out onto rack. Cool completely before slicing. Serve with whipped cream or ice cream, if desired.

Acknowledgments

Mom and Daddy, whose encouragement propelled me down this road to writing. And Mom, thank you for sharing your German-Mennonite heritage with me. I pray I bestow the best parts of it to the next generations.

Hulda Just, who translated the poem from English to Plautdietsch for me.

Jill Stengl and Beverly Olojan-Sticken, my first critique partners, whose patient tutelage gave more than they'll ever know.

My agent, Tamela Hancock Murray, for her endless efforts on my behalf.

Carol Lehman, librarian of the Plum Creek Library in Mountain Lake, for her assistance in research.

Carol Johnson, who gave me a second chance to spend time with the Klaassen family.

And most important, God, who answers the call of every seeking heart. May any praise or glory be reflected directly back to Him.

A Heart Surrenders

Dedicated to Sabra Henson and Philip Zielke—
two lifelong friends who encouraged me
to never lose sight of my dreams.

Contents

Klaassen Family Tree

Simon James Klaassen (1873) m. Laura Doerksen (1877), 1893
- Daniel Simon (1894) m. Rose Willems (1892), 1913
  - Christina Rose (1915)
  - Katrina Marie (1916)
- Hannah Joy (1895–1895)
- Franklin Thomas (1896) m. Anna Harms (1900), 1918
- Elizabeth Laurene (1898) m. Jacob Aaron Stoesz (1897), 1915
  - Andrew Jacob and Adam James (A.J.), 1917
- Adam Earnest (1899) m. Samantha Olivia O'Brien (1900), 1918
- Josephine Ellen (1900)
- Arnold Hiram (1903)
- Rebecca Arlene (1906)
- Theodore Henry (1909)
- Sarah Louise (1911)
Hiram Klaassen (1872) m. Hulda Schmidt (1872), 1898

O' Brien Family Tree

Burton O'Brien (1870) m. Olivia Ruth Stanton (1873–1900), 1891
- David Burton (1894)
- Samantha Olivia (1900) m. Adam Earnest Klaassen (1899), 1918

*D*avid O'Brien stood stiffly at the back of the Mountain Lake Congregational Church, his chin angled upward and his blue eyes holding a telltale sheen. His beloved sister, Samantha, stood beside him, hand resting in the crook of his arm. He wasn't sure if the quivering he felt was caused by his nervousness or her excitement.

He sneaked a glance at the young woman at his side. She was so beautiful. He felt his chest expand with pride. The gown, a shade of cream, was a soft material and perfect with her russet hair, similar in color to his own. David thought her hair usually fell free in unruly curls around her face or was pulled back in a bow, but today it was twisted up in the back. He'd describe it as resembling an egg in a nest. A few tendrils had pulled away into curls on her slender neck. She turned her face up to his, and the joyous expression in her eyes, the same blue as his own— cornflower blue, he'd heard it said—brought a lump to his throat.

At the front of the church, the organist ended the hymn with a mighty thrust of the pedals, and the final note echoed through the small sanctuary. A pause, and then the woman reached up to open the cover of a small enameled music box resting on the top of the organ. The tinkling notes of the traditional wedding march, *Lohengrin*, sounded through the church. David pressed her arm against his rib cage and squeezed Samantha's hand reassuringly. He paused long enough to whisper, "Are you ready?"

She nodded, her lips curving into a smile of readiness and her eyes shining with anticipation. Those eyes were aimed straight ahead toward the black-suited young man waiting at the head of the center aisle.

They began their slow walk in time to the music. David's gaze ranged from side to side as they moved up the aisle, watching as the people seated on the backless benches turned their heads to follow their passage. Happy expressions all, with the exception of one. A young woman with dark hair seemed to glare at Samantha as they moved slowly by. David's eyebrows drew together in a frown. A quick glance at Samantha confirmed that she hadn't noticed the other woman's sour expression. He wanted nothing to spoil this day for his sister. She deserved this happiness after all she had been through.

They reached the front of the church just as the final notes of *Lohengrin* rang out. The organist gently closed the lid on the music box before moving to one of the front benches.

The black-suited minister smiled at the pair from behind the pulpit. "Who gives this woman?"

David cleared his throat and answered, "I, her brother, do." He started to turn toward his place, but Samantha tightened her grip on his arm, holding him.

She lifted her face to him, and he stooped downward for the fleeting yet heartfelt kiss she planted on his cheek. When he straightened, he returned her loving smile with one of his own and made his way to his seat.

He sat straight on the bench, pressing his knees together and holding his hands in his lap, his gaze resting on Samantha. As happy as he was for his sister and as much as he admired and respected her Adam, this day was proving more difficult for him than he had imagined it would.

David and Samantha had been separated for seven years—seven lonely, difficult years for both of them. Four months ago they'd been reunited, thanks to Adam and the Klaassen family, and for David they had been the happiest four months of his life. He knew Samantha was marrying a fine man with a fine family—there were no regrets concerning her choice—but it was hard to see her become a wife and belong to another so soon after they had rediscovered each other.

The young woman seated at his right quietly reached over to give his hand a brief squeeze. He glanced at her, and her reassuring smile brought a lift to his heart. David was glad for the presence of Adam's sister beside him. Josie was Samantha's age and had become a dear friend to Samantha. Although David didn't know her well, Samantha often talked of Josie's sensitive, caring spirit. He managed to give her a grateful look before both of them turned their attention back to the front of the church.

The minister challenged Adam and Samantha on the seriousness of the commitment they were making to one another, read some Scripture passages of instruction on holy matrimony, and now the two were ready to speak their vows.

David watched Adam's sincere and caring expression as he spoke directly to Samantha, "I, Adam, take thee, Samantha, to be my wedded wife, to have and to hold, from this day forward; to love, honor, and cherish. . . ." The words seemed to float around David's head, and he fought the urge to weep.

Samantha's face glowed with intense happiness, and David felt a lump in his throat. She'd known way too little of joy before Adam came into her life. David was so thankful for the course that had finally brought his little sister to Mountain Lake, and so sorry for his own inability to find and rescue her himself. His emotions nearly strangled him as the two of them faced each other.

David took a deep breath and listened to Samantha's voice, soft and expressive, as she delivered the vows that would bind her to Adam forever. "I, Samantha, take thee, Adam, to be my wedded husband. . . ."

Samantha hadn't even let him bring up those awful years in Wisconsin with their drunkard father. "He's gone now, David," she had told him, "and we don't need to concern ourselves with the past any longer. Seeing you again, being with you here in Minnesota, has healed those memories, and you should not concern yourself any longer with what you might or might not have been able to do."

David noticed the expression in Adam's eyes as he held Samantha's hands and gazed at her while she recited her vows. David had no doubt that Samantha was loved by Adam and would be tenderly cared for by him. Tenderness is what Samantha needed. If he'd made the choice, he couldn't have found a more perfect mate for her. The thoughts were reassuring, and the smile he gave his sister as she turned with her husband to face the congregation was nearly as joyful as theirs.

After the announcement of "Mr. and Mrs. Adam Klaassen" to the congregation and their first public kiss, the newlyweds shared a hug, with Adam laughingly sweeping Samantha clear off her feet. But after he set her back down on the wooden floor, Samantha ran straight to David, throwing her arms around his neck to hug him.

David felt warm tears against his neck, and he pulled away to look into her face. "Hey, what's with the waterworks?"

Samantha laughed through her tears, wiping at them with shaking fingers. "They're happy tears, David, every one of them. My heart's just so full I can't contain all of it!"

David held her against his chest, fighting tears himself. He rocked his sister back and forth, pressing his cheek against her hair. "Always be this happy, Sammy. For me?"

Samantha leaned back to smile up at him. "For us both."

David nodded and released her to join her husband and greet the waiting crowd. Adam's family, by turn, embraced her, welcoming her officially into their fold. David stood off to the side, watching, battling his own mixed emotions. A hand tugged at his sleeve. He looked down to find Josie at his side.

"Adam will take good care of her for you, David." Josie's brown eyes held understanding and sympathy.

David swallowed and gained control before answering. "I know, Josie. I know Adam loves her—and she loves him. I know she'll be fine. It's just . . ."

Josie patted his arm, then clasped her hands together. "You feel as if you're losing her."

David nodded.

"But you know," she continued, "you're not letting her go forever. She and Adam will be right here in Mountain Lake, and so will you. You'll see her often, still be involved in her life. Samantha wouldn't have it any other way. She's worried about losing you, afraid you'll go back to Minneapolis now that she's married, instead of staying on with Uncle Hiram at the mercantile."

"She is?" David was rather startled at this news.

"Mm-hm." Josie went on in an earnest tone, "David, don't feel abandoned. Samantha will always have room in her life for you."

How on earth could such a young woman, barely more than a girl, possess such insight? That's exactly how he was feeling—abandoned. Foolish? Yes, but the truth. He stared at Josie in amazement. "Thank you, Josie. I needed to hear that," he finally managed.

"Come on," she said. "Let's chase the buggy, and shower them with good turkey red wheat kernels!"

David joined the other happy celebrants in sending the wedding couple away on the road to their new life together.

When Adam and Samantha disappeared around the bend in the road, everyone returned to the church to continue the celebration. Women had brought double-decker rolls called *zwieback*, preserves, cold meats, pickles, and assorted baked sweets for a light supper.

David filled his plate like everyone else and seated himself at a makeshift table in the sunny church yard. Weddings were cause for merry making, and the whole town had turned out to wish Adam and Samantha well. Adam's extended family—his parents, uncle and aunt, grandparents, all eight brothers and sisters, as well as the siblings' spouses and children—were all in attendance. They filled one plank table, plus most of another.

Although Josie had invited him to sit with the Klaassens, he got separated in the confusion and sat instead with a group of chatting townsfolk. Across and slightly kitty-corner from him was the dark-haired girl he'd noticed earlier in the church. What was her name? He frowned and tried shake it loose from his memory. Oh, yes, Priscilla, Priscilla Koehn, the only daughter of John and Millie Koehn. He'd heard rumors that Samantha had suffered some intimidation from that spoiled young lady.

David watched Priscilla out of the corner of his eye as he ate his meal. She was undeniably one of the most attractive women he had ever seen. Long, curling black lashes surrounded bright blue eyes, topped by arched brows that made a perfect frame. Her bowed lips were soft rose with a full lower lip, and her complexion retained its milky white color thanks to a wide-brimmed straw hat trailing an abundance of pink satin ribbon. Her glossy black hair fell in lovely waves down her slender back. Yes, she was definitely pretty.

Too bad she knows it so well. David watched her flirt expertly with a handsome young man on her left, who responded with equal proficiency. David knew who he was—Lucas Stoesz, the younger brother of Jake Stoesz who'd married Adam's sister Liz. Jake was a good, solid man. David had found little of the wholesomeness Jake possessed in young Lucas, who struck David as cocky and full of himself. No doubt a good match for the haughty Miss Koehn. He went back to eating.

"Mr. O'Brien?" he heard a feminine voice call from the other end of the table.

David lifted his head to see a coquettish smirk from none other than the subject of his observations. "Yes? Miss Koehn, isn't it?" He couldn't help but be pleased with his dispassionate tone and mock uncertainty.

The girl batted her eyelashes with practiced ease. "I wanted to say I thought it was a lovely service. Samantha was so pretty. And I'm sure you're just thrilled that she's managed to land the most handsome—as well as one of the wealthiest—bachelors in town!"

The hairs on the back of David's neck prickled. How dare she insinuate his sister was a gold-digger? "I can't be more delighted that Samantha is happy and married to the man she loves. That's all I could want for her."

Priscilla laughed—a laughter that held little gaiety—then pulled her face into a little pout. "Oh, my, I've managed to put my foot in it again." She rested her forearms on the edge of the white tablecloth and crossed her wrists. "Mr. O'Brien, I meant no offense. Now, it's no secret that I did fancy Adam. He is, as I said, quite a catch! But I wish Adam and Samantha nothing but the best." Tipping her head, she fluttered those long eyelashes again, the bright blue eyes wide and teasing.

David resisted rolling his eyes. "I'm sure you do, Miss Koehn."

"Oh, please, call me Priscilla." Her lips curled into a beguiling smile. "'Miss Koehn' sounds so stilted and formal."

David glanced down at his now-empty plate. He stood, nodding in Priscilla's direction. "Please excuse me, Miss Koehn. I'll be joining the Klaassens now. Have a good day. Good-bye, Lucas."

❧

Priscilla watched in disbelief and annoyance as David O'Brien turned his back and walked over to seat himself beside Liz and Jake. He'd dismissed her! Just who did he think he was, marching off as if she was a nobody? Narrowing her eyes, she jerked around, quivering with indignation.

Lucas bumped her arm with his elbow. "Well, well, whaddaya know," he said with a smirk. "There's one man immune to your fatal charms."

"Oh, shut up!" Priscilla muttered and jumped up from the table. She stormed away, leaving her half-filled plate behind for someone else to carry to the washtub. Sending a murderous glare in David's direction, she silently vowed to get even. Priscilla would not be one-upped by anybody. Even someone as good looking as David O'Brien!

*M*ama, will you please hurry?" Priscilla shot a glance over her shoulder. "The store will close before we get there at this rate!"

Mama puffed along behind, her heels tap-tapping on the boardwalk. "I don't know why we can't just go to Hiebert & Balzer's, Priscilla. It's closer to home, and they have ready-made. No waiting for an order from the catalog."

Priscilla whirled around and stopped in the middle of the walkway. "I already told you," she said, gesturing with her hands. "I've seen their ready-mades, and I don't like any of them as much as the one in the catalog."

Mama's shoulders heaved with her sigh, and she pressed one palm to her breast and fanned herself with the other. "Why in the name of all things sainted do you need a new dress anyway? You've got three new dresses from last spring hanging in your wardrobe, and they're all perfectly fine."

Priscilla let out a little grumble of annoyance. *Why must Mama be so stubborn?* Hadn't Daddy already told them both that Priscilla could order a new dress? Whatever Daddy said was the order of the day, and that was that. Mama knew that as well as Priscilla. Tossing her curls over her shoulder, Priscilla spun back and hurried on, determined to complete her errand.

Mama followed, murmuring under her breath, but Priscilla ignored the disgruntled complaints. Mama's opinion didn't matter. Priscilla couldn't help her smirk, remembering Daddy's response to Mama's claims about a new dress. His chiding voice echoed in her mind. "Now, Millie, I see nothing wrong

with Prissy picking out a new dress. After all, it is spring! A new season, a new wardrobe . . . Plus her graduation is coming. Take her down and let her choose a pretty dress from the Sears, Roebuck catalog."

Priscilla had wrapped her arms around her father's neck and squealed, "Oh, thank you, Daddy! You're the sweetest, most wonderful daddy in the whole wide world!" And he'd responded with a fond chuckle and a teasing, "Oh, get on with you, you little imp."

As the only daughter following the four Koehn sons, Priscilla had been pampered and cosseted by her father since birth. Although stern with her brothers, Daddy never used any kind of discipline on her. She supposed there were many who considered her a spoiled brat, but what did she care? As long as she got what she wanted, nothing else mattered.

Priscilla stepped daintily over the threshold of the Family Mercantile. She had given the screen door an extra hard push so the little bell hanging above the door jangled wildly. Mama stepped in behind her and moved directly to the counter, but Priscilla paused in the middle of the floor and glanced around the store. Where was David? Ah, there in the corner, stacking work boots on shelves. She stared at his back, willing him to turn around and look at her. But he kept working. With a little toss of her head, she joined Mama at the counter.

The proprietor's buxom wife, Hulda Klaassen, bustled from a door at the back, tugging at her apron. "Why, good morning, Millie! What can I help you with today?"

Mama released a tired sigh. "Priscilla would like to see the catalog. She's ordering another dress."

Priscilla laughed—deliberately high and tinkling, she hoped. But David still didn't turn around. "Now, Mother, you know perfectly well I have Daddy's permission. Don't sound so gloomy."

Priscilla ignored Mrs. Klaassen and Mama exchanging a meaningful look. Turning, Mrs. Klaassen called, "David, would you please bring out the new Sears, Roebuck catalog? Priscilla here would like to look at it."

"Certainly, Mrs. Klaassen." David disappeared behind a checkered curtain into the storage area.

Mama leaned forward and whispered to Mrs. Klaassen, "Is the young man here to stay?"

Priscilla toyed with the lace at her collar, pretending not to listen.

Mrs. Klaassen nodded, her extra chins quivering. "Yes." She whispered too. "Hiram has hired him as his assistant, and the young man plans to stay on. You see—"

The sound of a clearing throat brought both women up short, their lips pursed. David was standing at the end of the counter, and he held out the catalog. "Here you are, ma'am."

"Thank you," Mrs. Klaassen said, her cheeks pink. "Here, Priscilla, come take a look."

Priscilla made a deliberate circle around Mama so she could sashay past David, her nose in the air. She sneaked a peek in his direction, but he'd gone back to his boot stacking, seemingly unmindful of her presence. She seethed. Fat lot of good it was going to do to ignore him if he didn't notice her, one way or the other! Her mind raced, sorting through some means of capturing his attention. Mama always said one caught more flies with honey than with vinegar. Maybe Mama was right this time.

She swung her hair over her shoulder, angling a glance at the back corner of the store. "Oh, Mr. O'Brien, would you come here for a moment, please?"

Mama's eyebrows rose in an unspoken question. Priscilla tossed a scowl in her mother's direction, and Mama backed up a step. Priscilla pointed to one of the dresses as she turned a pretty expression of indecision in David's direction. "I just can't seem to make up my mind between this one"—she flipped two pages to point at another dress—"or this one." She paused, peeking out from beneath her lashes. "Which do you like best?"

"Priscilla!" Mama nearly sputtered. "How presumptuous, taking Mr. O'Brien away from his work to make a decision for you."

Priscilla raised her eyebrows innocently. "Well, a single lady must consider what a gentleman will find appealing. I'm simply requesting his opinion. There's nothing presumptuous about that at all, Mother."

Mama crossed her arms and frowned, her discomfort evident. Priscilla turned to David. "Well . . . ?"

David flipped the pages of the catalog back and forth, examining first one and then the other. Finally he pointed to a third dress—the simplest dress on either of the pages. Solid pale green with a plain rounded neckline—no collar or embellishments of any kind—and straight long sleeves. Ivory buttons fastened it from neck to waist. "This one is nice."

"That one?" The words came out in an unbecoming squeak. "Why, that's the ugliest dress I've ever seen!" Priscilla stared at the gown, then back at him.

David looked over at her. "Really?" He paused. "I thought it suited you."

Fire ignited in Priscilla's cheeks. She forgot about the vinegar-and-honey theory. Arching her neck, she planted her fists on her hips and glowered at David. "You are insufferably rude!"

David looked a bit startled, then arched a brow. "You asked for my opinion, and I gave it. If it doesn't please you," he said with a shrug, "you're free to choose something else." He looked briefly at Mrs. Klaassen. "Now if you'll excuse me, I have more boots to put away." He turned and moved back to his corner.

Priscilla sucked in a sharp gasp. He'd done it again! Stomping toward the door, she shot over her shoulder, "I do not wish to order a dress today. I'm going home."

Mrs. Klaassen let out a low chuckle, which further incited Priscilla's ire.

"Mama! Let's go!"

"Yes, dear." Mama scurried after her.

❧

David bit the inside of his cheek to hold back his smile as Priscilla darted out of the store. He supposed he shouldn't needle the girl. She was, after all, a customer, and his handling of the situation might convince her to shop elsewhere. And the Klaassens might wonder if he was good for business. But Mrs. Klaassen didn't seem at all upset with him. In fact, she winked and smiled. Grinning, he returned to boot stacking. Then the cowbell clanged again, announcing the arrival of another customer.

Josie Klaassen entered the store, but her gaze was aimed out through the screen door at the boardwalk. She gestured and asked, "What has Priscilla in such a dither?"

Chortling, Mrs. Klaassen came around the counter and embraced her niece. "Oh, you know Priscilla. When she doesn't get her way, she can get herself—and everybody else—all in a tailspin faster than a spring tornado." Holding on to Josie's hands, she said, "What brings you to town this morning?"

"Several things." Josie swung her aunt's hands from side to side, her smile bright. "Mother needs some baking powder, and Becky needs another writing tablet. This close to the end of the term, it seems a shame to buy another one, but she has to write on something."

David found himself sending surreptitious glances in Josie's direction. After the encounter with Priscilla, Josie's sweetness felt like a soothing balm. A grin tugged at his cheeks, and he gave a little wave when she looked in his direction. "Good morning, Josie. How are you today?"

A smile broke across her face, and she moved toward him. "David! I was just about to ask where you were."

Pleasure bloomed in his chest. He worked his way out from behind a stack of boxes. "Oh, and why is that?" For the first time he noticed that Josie had a spattering of pale freckles, and her clean, open face seemed refreshing and appealing.

"Mother would like for you to have supper with us Saturday. Samantha and Adam will be there, and she thought you might like to come, too."

David definitely wanted to come. Having grown up in their Wisconsin home with a widowed, abusive, alcoholic father, he and Samantha had both responded to the warmth and happiness and, yes, the faith exuded by the Klaassens. Even though he didn't really understand the faith part of it, when he and his sister had finally been reunited, he determined that she had been transformed from a timid little waif to a young woman who was lovely from the inside out—one most certain to capture the eye and the heart of someone like Adam Klaassen.

He followed Josie back to the counter while she waited for Mrs. Klaassen to get the items the needed. He couldn't help but note how different she was from Priscilla. Josie was too honest and sensible to engage in idle flirtation. He found Josie's simple, unassuming ways preferable to the beguiling Priscilla.

A blush warmed Josie's cheeks as she took a quick glance at David. She brushed a hand across her mouth. "Do I have some breakfast on my face?"

"No, not that I can see."

She gave a little chuckle at his confused tone. "Well, did you hear what I asked? About Saturday?"

David felt his ears grow hot. "Of course—you invited me to supper. Or rather," he corrected, "your mother did. And you can tell her, yes, I'd love to be there, especially since my sister is invited." But he wasn't sure if it was Samantha or Josie he wanted to see.

"Josie, here's your baking powder and a tablet for Becky." Hulda Klaassen pushed the items toward Josie's waiting hands. "Have you made arrangements to take the teaching exam yet?"

Josie nodded, her brown braid bouncing against her spine. "Yes. The day after graduation. Only three more weeks! I admit, I'm rather nervous about it—I want this so badly."

Samantha had told David that Josie was planning to be a teacher after she graduated from the community school. He thought she had the right personality to be a teacher—steady, even-tempered, unflappable. . . . But cute as a button, unlike some schoolmarms he'd sat under. No doubt the boys of all ages would have crushes on her.

"Will you teach here in Mountain Lake?" he asked.

Josie crinkled up her nose. "Probably not. The teacher who's been here for the past three years, Mr. Reimer, has given no indications of leaving. He's getting married this summer to a local girl, so I'm sure he's here to stay. He's very good at what he does, and we're glad to have him. I'll submit applications to all the area schools and wait to see what happens. I'm praying the right door will open up for me."

David had no response for that. He wasn't a praying person himself, although he knew the Klaassens and his sister believed prayers were important—that they actually were heard and answered. "Well, good luck to you. And I'll see you Saturday."

"Yes, Saturday," Josie said. She turned her smile on her aunt. "Good-bye, Tante Hulda. Have a nice day." She left to the clanging cowbell.

David glanced out the window as he headed back to his assignment, then paused a moment to watch Josie crossing the street to a waiting buckboard. A young man approached and took the purchases from her. Josie smiled at the dark-haired young man, who helped her up into the buckboard. The man stayed close to the wagon, his elbow draped over the edge of the seat. The two engaged in conversation.

David began his work and kept his tone conversational. "Mrs. Klaassen, I haven't met the man out there with Josie. Do you know who he is?"

The older woman walked to the window and glanced out. "Oh, that's Stephen Koehn." She paused, her brow furrowed in thought. "Hmm, I thought he was still in Blue Earth, helping his grandfather. Must be home again." She glanced over at David. "Stephen is Josie's beau—since Thanksgiving of last year. But he's been gone for a while. When his grandfather took ill, he had to go help mind the farm. Things must be better there."

"Stephen Koehn . . . Any relation to Priscilla Koehn?" he asked.

"Brother and sister," Mrs. Klaassen replied, shaking her head, "but as different as air and smoke. There are four Koehn boys, all older than Priscilla, which I suppose is why John Koehn has spoiled the girl. Why, she—"

"So Stephen Koehn is a decent fellow?" David cut in. He wasn't interested in hearing any more about Priscilla.

"My, yes. One of the most decent young men in town."

David's heart dropped with disappointment. He put the last pair of boots on the shelf. "Well, I've got that shipment of dried beans to inventory. Guess I'd better get to it."

Mrs. Klaassen clicked her tongue against her teeth and followed David into the storeroom. "Now, young man, I have a question for you." David turned to face Mrs. Klaassen as she folded her arms over her ample chest. "I'm going to ask you straight out. Do you have a shine for our Josie?"

Had he been so obvious? Heat filled David's face.

The woman tsk-tsked. "Now, David, I'm going to be very honest with you because I like you. You're a good worker, and both Hiram and I have found you to be an honest young man. But Josie is a Christian, and—"

"It's all right, Mrs. Klaassen." He shouldn't interrupt, but he couldn't bear to listen to all the reasons why he wasn't good enough for Josie. He knew more than anyone just how unworthy he was. "I'd better get to those beans before lunch. Excuse me please."

He moved quickly to the twenty-pound bags of beans, tossing them into a crate. It was just as well Josie had a beau, he decided as the last bag landed in its place. She deserved a steady, dependable man like Stephen Koehn instead of an unpolished fly-by-nighter like him.

aturday morning, while Hiram Klaassen readied the cash box, David opened the mercantile's front door and propped it open with an iron doorstop shaped like a sleeping cat. He paused for a moment on the front stoop, breathing in the fresh scent of a new spring. A sense of belonging filled him.

He loved his work, his place of residence, and the people of Mountain Lake. The Klaassens had accepted him as readily as they had Sam, and this evening he'd be enjoying supper with their family. Had he ever experienced such a feeling of "home" before? No. He could cheerfully live here forever.

"Good morning, Mr. O'Brien."

The voice, with its slight note of challenge, sent a prickle of awareness across his scalp. He turned to find Priscilla Koehn and a heavy-set, gray-haired man approaching on the boardwalk. David nodded his head in greeting.

"This is my daddy, John Koehn." Priscilla's blue eyes flashed, daring David to parry with her when her father was in attendance. "He came to order my dress."

"Well . . ." David cleared his throat. "Welcome." He nodded to Mr. Koehn as he held the door open. "You can ask Mr. Klaassen for the catalog." He went inside behind the two and quickly found something to keep him occupied in the storeroom. Just seeing the girl gave him the urge to throttle her. Her father certainly wouldn't stand for that. David would keep his distance.

His back to the curtained doorway, he bent over a recently arrived crate from Chicago and examined the contents. He felt a tap on his back. He jolted upright and spun around. Priscilla!

Irritation clenched David's chest. "Miss Koehn, customers are not allowed in this room." He kept his voice even and low so as not to attract attention, but his face burned. He couldn't believe this woman! He gestured toward the curtain. "You'll need to get yourself out there. Please."

Priscilla locked her hands behind her back and cocked her head. "I just wanted to let you know that I ordered a dress— the pink and white striped one I showed you the other day. My daddy says it will make me look as sweet as a candy peppermint stick. Mr. Klaassen told me the dress will be here in three weeks, and I'll want it delivered immediately. Please make note of it, as I assume you're the delivery boy in addition to your other duties here."

The way she said "boy" rankled. He spoke through clenched teeth. "Miss Koehn, that message could have been left with Mr. Klaassen. I can only presume, then, that your intentions are to insult me, get me riled."

"And have I succeeded?"

Her too-perfect face was set in a knowing smirk. What a shame all that beauty was wasted on someone so shallow. David balled his hands into fists and pushed them deep into his pockets. He'd never laid a hand on a woman, but at that moment he would like to have turned her over his knee for a sound paddling.

"It's not something of which to be proud, Priscilla," he finally said. "For the life of me, I can't figure out why you take such pleasure in aggravating people."

Priscilla laughed. "Oh, not just anybody, David." She emphasized his name, causing heat to flood his ears as he realized he'd called her by her Christian name. "You make it so easy for me. But really, now, you must learn not to be so suspicious. And you think so ill of me. What can I do to change your opinion?"

David drew in a deep breath, ready to let her have it with more than she'd wish to hear. Before he could speak, however, the curtain parted, and Priscilla's father stuck his head in.

"There you are, Prissy. Did you get the delivery for your dress worked out?"

"Yes, I did, Daddy." Priscilla answered sweetly, still holding David with those blue eyes of hers. "David says he'll be delighted to deliver my dress as soon as it arrives. Isn't that right, David?"

Apparently Mr. Koehn wasn't interested in David's response, because he didn't give him time to answer. "Well, come on then. I can't remain here all day."

"Of course, Daddy." Priscilla turned toward the door obediently. But before she stepped through the curtains, she sent one last look over her shoulder at David and waved two fingers.

David sat on the edge of the crate and ran a hand down his face. Mercy, that girl was a problem. Was she like this with every young man she encountered, or did she save it all up just for his benefit? Hard as he tried, he couldn't imagine what he'd done to earn this treatment. He pictured her as she'd stood in the storeroom, her hands locked primly behind her back, her lustrous hair trailing over her shoulders, eyes sparkling. She was an incredibly beautiful girl.

"An incredibly beautiful, obnoxious girl," he said as he stood up. He shook his head. That girl was trouble with a capital T. The less he saw of Priscilla Koehn, the better off he would be. Determinedly, he put Priscilla from his mind and got back to work.

David sipped a final cup of coffee while cheerful chatter swirled around either side of him. Samantha had once laughingly told him that mealtimes at the Klaassen home were always an adventure. With people everywhere, including unexpected guests at times, all kinds of subjects came up in conversation, and one never knew what new delight Laura Klaassen would prepare.

Tonight they'd feasted on *verenike*—cottage-cheese-filled dough pockets which were boiled and then smothered with ham gravy. Thick slices of ham straight from the Klaassen smokehouse, *zweiback*—which was delicious spread with Laura's strawberry-mulberry preserves—fried potatoes, and a sweet soup called cherry moos rounded out dinner. David concluded his sister was right: meals here were definitely an adventure and a most pleasant one, at that.

The part of the meal he enjoyed the most wasn't the food, though, but the company. To David's delight, he'd been seated next to Josie. The girl was intelligent and even opinionated, David discovered, but not off-putting at all. Her brown eyes sparkled as she joined in the conversation that flew around the table, asking David's input from time to time and making him feel included. He appreciated it, and he found himself admiring her more and more as the evening progressed. He fleetingly wondered where "Josie's beau" was tonight but not enough to ask.

When everyone had finished eating, Adam invited David to walk around the barn for some exercise. Although David hated to leave Josie's company, he wouldn't refuse time with Adam. This man had befriended Samantha—yes, rescued her—at a time when she was at her most vulnerable, and David felt a deep debt of gratitude. But he also admired Adam's level-headedness and strength of character—attributes he believed were sorely lacking in his own life.

"Sounds good," David said over a chuckle. "I could use some exercise after that wonderful meal." He rubbed his belly, his eyes following Josie as she moved around the table, clearing dishes. He added, "If I ate like this every day, I'd be as big as your barn. Thank you for the invitation, Mrs. Klaassen," he called over to her as she stacked plates in the sink.

Laura Klaassen lit up, the corners of her eyes crinkling into her smile. "You're quite welcome, David. You feel free to come by here anytime."

"Thank you, ma'am, I just might take you up on that." He sent a quick glance at Josie, but she didn't look his way.

Adam said, "Sammy, honey, David and I are going to stretch our legs a bit." The two men turned toward the back door.

Samantha dashed across the kitchen, a dishtowel flapping from her shoulder. "Wait just a minute there, mister!" She turned her face upward for a kiss, and Adam grinned and placed his arms around her waist, dropping a light kiss on her mouth.

"Check on the sow, too, while you're out there," Adam's father, Simon—often called Si—called to them from the parlor. "She's due to farrow soon," he said, now standing in the kitchen doorway. He peered at them over his reading glasses and his *Farmer's Almanac*. "Remember, you and Samantha will be raising a piglet or two from this litter."

Adam saluted in response, then sent Samantha back to his mother with a teasing, "Now head over there and do your duty, missus." Samantha laughed and went back to his mother to help with cleanup.

As the men sauntered toward the barn, David commented, "Sam seems really happy."

Adam nodded. "There's no 'seems' about it. She is happy. And so am I."

"I'm so glad for you both." David put a hand on Adam's shoulder. "It means a lot to me, seeing her like this. Happiness was a pretty scarce commodity when we were growing up."

"Samantha's told a lot of it to me." Genuine sympathy colored Adam's voice. "I'm sure, though, there's a lot she hasn't shared yet. The memories are painful, as you know, David. But I'm doing my best to replace the unhappy ones with good ones. I hope you know that."

"I do." David gave Adam's shoulder a squeeze and dropped his hand.

"Keeping Samantha happy gives me the greatest joy." Adam's boots scuffed up dust as the men moved across the farmyard. "I plan to spoil your little sister rotten."

David laughed along with Adam. But then he slowed his step, turning toward his new brother-in-law. "Speaking of spoiled . . . I have a little problem."

Adam stopped in an attentive pose—feet widespread, arms crossed, face creased in concern. "What is it?"

David stroked his chin. "Well, it's a who rather than an it." He drew in a deep breath. "Priscilla Koehn."

"Ah." Adam grimaced. "What's she up to this time?"

David drew back. "This time? You mean she's generally stirring things up?"

Adam laughed. "You haven't been around long enough, my friend. Yep, our Miss Priscilla Koehn lives to get things into a turmoil of some kind. She's been a troublemaker since she was in pinafores, and none of us can figure out why John Koehn allows it. He's always been firm with his boys, keeping them in line. But Priscilla walks all over him." He snorted. "Let's face it—Priscilla walks all over everyone."

David fell back into step with Adam as the two ambled on in the direction of the barn.

"I guess it's because she's the only daughter," Adam continued. "Maybe I'd do the same with a little girl. I suppose even Ma and Pa have spoiled our Sarah, since she's the baby. Not to the extent of Priscilla, though. All I know is John has never enforced any kind of behavior standards with Priscilla, and the result is one spoiled, selfish young woman." He leaned against the corral fence, the hint of a grin on his face. "What's she done now?"

David ducked his head, embarrassed to admit he couldn't manage a girl seven years his junior. He cleared his throat. "Oh, I guess she's just managed to get my dander up by acting coy and then arrogant. And I've heard she's been spiteful toward Sammy." A rush of protectiveness washed over him.

Adam worked the toe of his boot against the ground. "My advice to you is to make sure she never knows she's getting to you. As I said, she loves to stir things up. If she thinks she's annoying you, she'll keep it up till you're ready to smack her one."

Remembering the urge he'd had earlier in the day, David gave a brusque nod.

"Keep a handle on your reactions to her needling," Adam advised, "and she'll soon tire of the game."

David sent Adam a sidelong glance. "I'll tell you something if you won't get big headed about it."

Adam shrugged.

"After your wedding, Priscilla mentioned she'd always had eyes for you—that she considered you 'quite a catch,' I think she put it."

Adam threw back his head and laughed. "I hate to say it, but that isn't news to me. Priscilla has chased me around for years. But I was always very careful not to be caught. Can you imagine?" He stopped his amused chuckle as realization seemed to dawn. He pointed a finger at David. "You know, that could be why she's giving you a hard time. She's jealous of Samantha because Samantha got something—or rather, someone—she wanted. Priscilla isn't used to not getting what she wants. I'm sure she knows how protective you and Sam are of one another. By trying to get under your skin about Samantha, she's upsetting you. Which invariably will upset Samantha. And me . . . well, you get the picture."

David considered Adam's comments. "That makes sense. Also makes me want to pound the dickens out of her."

Adam chuckled. "Get in line." Then he added more seriously, "But really, David, you can't let her know she's aggravating you. That will only add fuel to the fire. As much as is possible, ignore the girl. In time, if she can't rile you, she'll back off."

David blew out a big huff of breath. "I hope so. She's one persistent little female."

"That she is." Adam slapped David's shoulder and pushed off from the fence. "C'mon now, let's go check on that sow for Pa. Get our minds off of Miss Priss."

David grinned broadly. "That sounds good to me." As he followed Adam into the barn, he admitted to himself there was another young lady in Mountain Lake he'd rather think about. If only Stephen Koehn hadn't already staked a claim on her . . .

*W*hen Adam and David returned to the house, David pointed to a buckboard hitched in front of the smokehouse. "You've got company."

Adam nodded. "Looks like the Koehn buckboard."

An uneasy prickle climbed the back of David's neck. Could it be Priscilla? The men entered the house, and David was relieved to see Stephen Koehn seated at the Klaassen's plank kitchen table. But his relief was quickly replaced by a stab of jealousy. The fellow looked as if he belonged there.

Samantha, Josie, Liz, Jake, and Laura also sat around the table, each enjoying a glass of cold milk and homemade oatmeal cookies. Samantha made room for Adam and David to sit beside her. Adam gave his young wife a kiss, then reached across the table to offer Stephen a firm handshake. "Have you met Samantha's brother, David?" he asked. After the introductions, Adam asked, "When did you get back, Stephen?"

The man grinned, showing one dimple. His face was square, with a prominent chin and broad forehead. His hair, as shiny as a raven's wing, brushed back from his forehead in thick waves curling up at the collar of his plaid shirt. He had an earthy kind of wholesomeness about him that David couldn't help comparing to Priscilla's undisciplined flightiness. He also found himself comparing his own ordinary features and tall, lean frame to Stephen's undeniably handsome face and muscular build. Small wonder Josie found Stephen attractive.

"I got back day before yesterday." Stephen's deep voice registered his pleasure at being home. "Grandpa's doing fine, and

I'm not needed anymore. So home I came." He reached for another cookie, then quickly looked at Laura Klaassen. They all laughed at his expression—like a boy caught with his hand in the cookie jar. Laura handed him one, her eyes twinkling.

"Well, it's good to see you," Adam said.

Josie nodded agreement, David noticed.

"Glad to hear that." Stephen shot Josie a quick smile before turning back to Adam. "I intend to make a regular nuisance of myself around here."

The Klaassens all laughed again, and Laura said, "Now, Stephen, you know you are never a nuisance! You're always welcome here."

Apparently the open invitation applied to every person who walked by out here. How deflating, realizing Laura's statement to him earlier was being echoed already to another young man who obviously held the same intentions David had been considering. He bit into one of Laura's oatmeal cookies, hardly tasting it.

Samantha reached across Adam to tap David's arm. "David, Adam and I will stop by the boardinghouse and pick you up for church tomorrow."

David raised one eyebrow. "Yes, ma'am, I'd be delighted to accept your gracious invitation."

Samantha's expression turned sheepish.

David offered a grin. "Does lunch figure into that invitation as well?"

"Of course!"

He'd never pass up the chance for lunch with his sister, even if meant sitting through church first. "I'll be ready." He stood. "Mrs. Klaassen, thank you once more for your kind hospitality. I think I'd better be heading home now."

Laura rose, too, reaching out to clasp David's hand. "You're very welcome, David, and please consider yourself one of the family. Come by anytime."

David got in a quick glance at Stephen. The man was studying him. "Yes, ma'am, that I will." Was Stephen as unflappable as he appeared? Some sort of deviltry made him want to find out. He turned to Josie. "Josie, it was wonderful visiting with you this evening. You are a pleasant dinner companion."

Josie's faint freckles disappeared beneath a flood of pink. "Now, David, you're embarrassing me." She covered her face with both hands. "Go on, now!"

David laughed. "Yes, ma'am," he drawled, smiling to himself at the look on Stephen's face. It gave him pleasure to rattle the other man a bit.

They all called their good-byes, and David received a tight hug from Samantha before he headed out to begin the ride back to his quarters on his borrowed horse. Not until he was half a mile down the lane did it strike him. By intentionally trying to nettle Stephen, he'd behaved in the same way he found so annoying in Priscilla.

What on earth had come over him to conduct himself in such a manner? Not too difficult to figure—the old green-eyed monster, jealousy. He was jealous of Stephen Koehn—of Stephen's handsomeness and position in the community as well as his familiarity with Josie. The realization gave David a bit of understanding about Priscilla's motives. Although he still couldn't abide her blatantly self-centered behavior, he could at least imagine how jealousy could make a person act in an undesirable manner.

And now that he'd recognized it in himself, he could do something about it. The next time he saw Stephen, he would apologize for his behavior at the Klaassen home. He could do something about Priscilla, too, he decided. The next time she pulled one of her attention-getting schemes, he'd let her know he understood by refusing to rise to the bait. Maybe a little consideration was in order there too.

Maybe . . .

⌒〇

A tapping on David's door at nine-thirty Sunday morning announced the arrival of his ride to church. David swung it open to find his sister dressed in an attractive rose-print calico dress and a charming little straw bonnet perched atop her bountiful russet hair.

"Well, aren't you as pretty as a picture." He grabbed his brown bowler from the hook on the wall and placed it over his own unruly hair.

"You're very handsome yourself, David," Samantha returned, smiling up at him.

David snorted. "Handsome? Yeah, right."

Samantha touched his arm. "Yes. You're very handsome. The most handsome man in town!" Her expression turned impish. "Next to Adam, of course."

David laughed.

She tipped her head, giving him a speculative look. "Are you intending to turn the head of some special young lady this morning?"

An image popped into David's mind, but he pushed it aside. "In church? I think not."

Samantha teasingly knocked her shoulder against his as they made their way to the waiting wagon. "But there are lots of girls in church. That's where to find the nice ones."

David offered Samantha a hand up next to Adam. "That's the trouble, Sammy. Too many nice girls—but no girl for a not-so-nice man like me."

As soon as David settled himself next to her on the seat, she placed her hand over his knee and peered up at him with tears shining in the corners of her eyes. "Davey, please don't talk that way about yourself. I know Pa always told us we were worthless, but he was wrong. None of us are worthless. We're loved by God, and He has wonderful plans for us. Don't let Pa's senseless rambling hold you captive any longer."

David swallowed the bitter taste of that memory. He wouldn't argue with his sister. He loved her too much to hurt her. But he couldn't accept her statements about God. If God existed, He must not have much use for David O'Brien or He'd have made Himself known a long time ago. "We better get moving, or we'll be late," he said.

Adam flicked the reins, and the horses jolted forward. Samantha kept her hand pressed over David's knee, her eyes closed, on the way to church. David suspected she was praying. Praying for him. The thought put a lump in his throat. He set his jaw and tried to ignore the uncomfortable feeling.

David paid attention to little of what went on in the church service. He had to admit, Adam and Samantha, as well as most of the congregation, seemed to find it all interesting, judging by their rapt attention to the minister's words. But how did church—or God—benefit anyone? Pa had always said a man was responsible for himself. If people weren't able to be responsible for their own lives, then maybe believing Someone bigger and stronger had control would make them feel better. But David had a stomach full of his pa ordering him about. He didn't need anyone else—particularly God or even his beloved sister—telling him what to do.

He sat on the hard bench trying not to fidget, and he sneaked a surreptitious peek in Josie's direction. She sure had a pleasing profile. She kept her eyes on the minister, Reverend Goertzen, looking like she was completely caught up in what he was saying. Something about a man named Lazarus. David didn't know who that was. He gazed at Josie for a long time, hoping for her to return his look, but she remained focused on the front of the church.

Stifling a sigh and shifting his position, he glanced over his shoulder. He felt a jolt go through him when he realized Priscilla Koehn's dark blue eyes were pinned on him. She sat primly beside her mother, her hands resting palms up in her lap—the picture of piety and attentiveness. When his glance met hers, she turned her perfectly shaped nose in the air and pinched her lips together.

The same irritation shot through him again. Last night he'd resolved to offer understanding. But looking at her arrogant expression, he decided the resolution would be much easier made than kept. However, he did owe Stephen an apology, and he would do that just as soon as this service was complete.

After the closing hymn, David skirted past the parishioners pausing in the aisles to chat and trailed after Stephen. The other man was already halfway across the church yard. David cupped his hands around his mouth and called, "Stephen, hold up there a minute, would you?"

Stephen stopped and turned around. When he saw who had called him, he looked surprised but held out a hand. "Hello. It's David, right?"

"Yes." David gave his hand a shake then shoved his hands into his jacket pockets. "I need to talk to you, if you have a little time to spare."

Stephen shrugged, glancing around. "Sure."

David cleared his throat. He wished he'd planned his apology in advance. He now found himself searching for appropriate words. "Um . . . the other night at the Klaassens, I think I left you with the wrong impression . . . about Josie. About Josie and me."

Stephen pulled his mouth sideways. "Yes . . . ?"

David scraped the toe of his boot in the dirt. "I shouldn't have tried to mislead you. You see, I do find Josie interesting, and I guess I wished she would pay attention to me like she was paying you. So I intentionally made it sound like—well, like something it was not. I'm sorry."

A grin slowly curved Stephen's lips. "Wow, that's most interesting, David. And I can't say I'm not relieved."

David shook his head regretfully. "She's a sister to my brother-in-law, so I'm bound to see her now and then, but not the way you might have thought."

Stephen wiped a hand across his forehead and blew out his breath. "You had me worried, old man. After all, I was gone for almost four months. Josie and I hadn't made any promises, and a lot can happen in that amount of time. I thought maybe . . ."

David forced an answering grin. "No, nothing like that. I was just feeling a bit of the old Nick, I guess. I'm sorry."

Stephen clapped David on the shoulder. "No hard feelings at all, David. And thanks for letting me know."

"Letting you know what?" A female voice sounded from behind David.

He looked over his shoulder, then sighed. Priscilla. He exchanged a look with Stephen, noting the other man's lips pressed together in what looked like irritation.

"Well, aren't you going to tell me?" She placed her hands on her hips, glancing perkily between the pair of men. "What are you two whispering about over here?"

David started to answer, but Stephen moved a step forward and poked his finger against her shoulder. "You. We were trying to decide whether to tie you to that tree"—he pointed to the elm at the corner of the church—"or the tall oak next to the schoolhouse. Maybe keep you from sticking your nose in other people's business."

She slapped his hand away. "You are such an idiot. You know very well that's not what you were talking about."

"No, it's not, but it's all I'm going to tell you. What David and I were discussing is none of your concern. And your name did not come up. Not even once." Her brother seemed to take some delight in letting her know that.

Priscilla crossed her arms and leaned back at the waist, a too-familiar look of disdain on her face. "We'll just see about that, Stephen Koehn." She whirled away, her long hair swinging in a curtain behind her.

David watched her go and shook his head once. Understanding? Who could understand that girl. Certainly not him.

Stephen released a sigh. "Now it's my turn to apologize to you . . . for my sister. I'd like to say she isn't normally like that, but my mother taught me not to tell lies."

David chuckled. "Don't worry about it. I've had a couple of toe-to-toes with her, and I imagine she's just letting me know I'm not going to get away without a fight."

Stephen gave David a pensive look. "You've bumped heads with Prissy?"

David nodded, embarrassed. "I'm afraid so."

"And who came out the victor?"

David pulled at his cheek with a finger. "Well . . ."

Stephen chuckled low in his throat. "Don't answer, I can guess. I was hoping maybe she's finally met the man who can subdue her."

"Subdue Priscilla?" David held up his hands in defeat. "Don't look at me."

Stephen laughed loudly, then sobered. "What did she do to ruffle your feathers?"

David offered a shrug. "I guess maybe I ruffled her feathers, and she wasn't used to that. Then she came back at me, and I—."

"I'm not surprised." Stephen dropped his gaze for a moment. "My sister has a way of rubbing everyone the wrong way. She seems to think it's her God-given right." He met David's gaze once more. "I hope you won't judge all of us by Priscilla's actions."

David would be the last one to judge someone based on their relatives. He'd been on the receiving end of that treatment more than once in his life, with people shying away from him because of his father. "Don't worry about it. I admit, I might envy your friendship with Josie, but I sure wouldn't trade my sister for yours."

Stephen laughed good-naturedly, impressing David further with his even temperament. "I won't hold that against you." He paused. "You know, David, I'd like to get to know you better. Would you be able to come home with me, for *faspa*?"

David drew back a little, uncertain how to respond. He wasn't accustomed to friendly overtures—particularly when he'd set out to mislead the man just the evening before. Pleased yet puzzled by Stephen's invitation to the family's Sunday-noon meal, he recognized the beginnings of a friendship forming. But he had to decline this time. "Thank you for asking, but I've already got plans to go out to Adam and Sammy's and eat with them."

Stephen shrugged. "Maybe another time?"

David nodded. "Yes, I'd like that—especially if your sister has another event to attend." He grinned to take any sting out of the remark, and Stephen laughed too.

"All right then." He stuck out his hand, and David shook it. "I'll talk to you later."

David trotted over to Adam and Samantha in their wagon. Samantha greeted him with a little huff. "Finally! What were you two yammering on about over there? I didn't know you were friends with Stephen Koehn."

David climbed up beside her on the buckboard's front seat. "I'm not friends with Stephen Koehn—yet. But I think I will be. And as for what we were talking about—mind your own business. You're as snoopy as Priscilla."

Samantha gasped then gaped at him. "Well!"

Adam whistled. "Oooh, brother, them's fightin' words."

David laughed and threw an arm around Samantha's shoulders, pulling her against him in an affectionate hug. "Sammy, you are about as much like Priscilla as I am like Adam's Tante Hulda."

Imagining tall, slender David standing next to short, rotund Hulda sent all three into gales of laughter.

"All right, you're forgiven." Samantha relaxed against his shoulder. "Maybe I'll feed you after all."

"And there are at least two of us who are grateful." David bestowed a kiss on his sister's cheek as the wagon rolled out of the church yard. He kept his arm around her shoulders, grateful that she was nothing like Priscilla Koehn. What kind of life would it be with someone like that living under your roof, interfering in your every move? David shuddered. Lucky for him, he'd never have to find out.

*P*riscilla sat at the table, pushing the food around on the china plate but carrying none of it to her mouth.

"Priscilla, what's the matter? Finish your food," Mama scolded.

Priscilla rolled her eyes. "I'm not hungry." She inserted the hint of a whine into her voice, hoping Daddy would notice. He did.

Leaning across the table, Daddy cupped her hand. "What's the matter, Prissy?"

Priscilla shot a look of pure venom at Stephen, who sat on Mama's right, then hung her head, affecting a persecuted air for her father's benefit. "It's nothing, Daddy. I'm just a little upset, that's all. I'll be fine." She peeked up at her father, biting the insides of her cheeks to hold back a satisfied smile.

Daddy's gaze went from Priscilla to Stephen and to Priscilla again. His eyebrows pulled down sharply. "Has Stephen done something to upset you?"

"Oh, John," Mama interceded, "why must you assume . . . ?"

A stern look silenced her, and she turned her face to her plate, her lips set in a grim line. Stephen slumped down in his chair, glaring at his sister. Daddy patted Priscilla's hand. "Come now, Prissy. Let's have it. Tell me what's wrong."

Priscilla sighed. "Oh, Daddy, I don't want to cause problems. Really, it's not important. But Stephen and that awful David O'Brien were talking about me after church today, and . . . well, it's gotten me upset, that's all."

Daddy turned his frown on Stephen. "What's this all about?"

Stephen slapped his fork onto to the table. "Pa, David and I were talking after church. It had nothing to do with Priscilla. She came up behind us and demanded to know what we were discussing. I told her it wasn't her business." He sat up straight. "And it wasn't. I should be able to have a conversation without her sticking her nose in it."

Daddy turned to Priscilla. "Is that what happened, Prissy?"

Priscilla brought up her head and pointed accusingly at Stephen. "He said he was going to tie me to the old oak tree by the school!" She quivered her chin and blinked rapidly, willing the presence of indignant tears.

Daddy reared back. "Stephen!"

Priscilla ducked her head to hide her smirk.

Stephen blew out a noisy breath. "Of course I wouldn't do such a thing. I was aggravated and merely wanted to put her in her place."

Mama held out a hand in entreaty. "Yes, John, I'm sure Stephen—"

"Stephen, you will apologize to your sister. And then I think it would be best if you did not spend time with this David O'Brien. He upset your sister yesterday at the mercantile with his impudence. He doesn't seem to be the kind of person with whom we need to associate."

"Oh, but, Pa—" Stephen tried.

"Apologize to your sister," Daddy commanded in a thunderous tone.

Stephen's face glowed red. Priscilla pushed two peas back and forth with her fork, waiting for her brother to follow their father's directive, the way he always did. Finally Stephen muttered, "Sorry, Pris."

His words emerged through gritted teeth, but Priscilla tossed her head and offered her brother a sweet smile.

Daddy squeezed her hand. "There. He's apologized." He released her hand and pointed to her plate. "Now sit up there like a good girl and finish your food. Go ahead."

Priscilla picked up her fork and carried a bite to her mouth. Daddy beamed. "That's my girl."

Priscilla beamed back.

❧

Stephen smoldered, watching his sister out of the corner of his eye. So smug, her eyes sparkling with success. Why did his father cosset her so? He wasn't doing her any favors. Priscilla was the most self-centered, unfeeling person he knew. And others knew it too.

And how humiliating to be reprimanded like this at his age. Twenty-three years old and treated like a child. It was time to get away from his father's house. Suddenly he had the need to see Josie and bask in her goodness. Josie would restore his feelings of control.

He dropped his napkin onto the table. "Ma, will you excuse me, please? I'll be out for a while." Although he tried to be polite, he knew his voice sounded strained.

Pa shrugged when Ma looked to him. "Yes, Stephen, go ahead." Her eyes offered Stephen a silent apology.

Stephen leaned over and gave his mother a kiss on the cheek before leaving the room. He made a promise to himself to never treat his own wife in the demeaning manner Pa used with Ma. His wife would be a partner.

He took deep breaths to help calm his churning insides as he went out to the barn for the horse and wagon. During his ride across the countryside, the final tensions of his latest family argument faded away. He even found himself whistling a cheerful tune as he bounced along on the wagon's high seat. Spring was here, and with it the promise of new growth, new beginnings.

Stephen mulled over the possibility of his own new beginnings. The sun beamed down warmly in the west, baby birds poked their little noses out of nests and demanded their dinner, and wildflowers sprang from dried brown stalks, bringing a welcome splash of color. Stephen flicked the reins, clicking his tongue to hurry the horses. He could hardly wait to see Josie and find out if maybe spring was touching her the same way.

He parked the wagon in front of the Klaassen farmhouse, then trotted around to the back door, eagerness lightening his steps. Becky answered his knock and called out in a sing-song, "Oh, Jo-o-o-sie, it's your knight in shining ar-r-mo-o-or!"

Mrs. Klaassen scolded, "Becky, it's not polite to embarrass our guest." She held out a hand of welcome to Stephen. "Come right on in, Stephen. We've finished the kitchen cleanup, and Josie ran up to change her clothes. You can sit in the parlor with Mr. Klaassen until she comes down."

"Thank you, ma'am." Stephen removed his hat and hung it on a hook by the back door. "I bet you didn't know that when you offered to let me come anytime that I'd take you up on it quite so soon."

Mrs. Klaassen laughed and waved him through the kitchen. "I never say something I don't mean, and I did mean 'anytime.' Now go on in and visit with Mr. Klaassen. The boys went out right after eating."

Stephen passed through the kitchen and stepped into the parlor, greeting Mr. Klaassen with a handshake and smile. He felt better already, just being here.

"Sit down, Stephen, sit down." Josie's father motioned to the upholstered sofa. "What brings you out here this Sunday afternoon, as if I don't know?" His eyes twinkled with fun.

Stephen grinned, grateful for Mr. Klaassen's welcome and seeming acceptance of the friendship with Josie. "Well, I was hoping to take Josie for a walk, if that's all right with you."

Mr. Klaassen nodded his graying head. "Perfectly all right with me, but you might want to ask her. You might have already discovered she does have a mind of her own."

The two men chuckled together, and Stephen said, "That she does." She was no empty-headed, simple-minded, and overly agreeable "pretty face." Josie was unique, someone whose attractiveness was matched by her lovely nature. And Stephen couldn't help but be hopeful.

The men discussed the recent headlines—the end of the war, which pleased everyone; the outbreak of the Spanish influenza, which concerned everyone; and local news, which certainly would never make the headlines but affected everyone in the community. Stephen was leaning forward, making a case for the importance of changing to motorized farm implements, when Josie appeared in the doorway.

Stephen quickly finished his sentence and stood up. "Hello, Josie. I hope I'm not disturbing . . ." He paused and started over. "Well, I'm wondering if you'd like to take a walk."

Josie moved across the room at the same time he did. As they met in the middle, she said, "It's nice to see you, Stephen. And yes, I would like a walk."

After the dreadful scene at his home table, Josie seemed like a breath of fresh air.

Ever respectful, Josie looked past him to her father. "Is that all right with you, Papa?"

Mr. Klaassen waved a hand at them. "Certainly, long as you're home before suppertime so you can help your mother."

Stephen assured him, "I'll have her home well before then, sir. Thank you."

Stephen held the door, and as Josie slipped by him he caught a clean, attractive scent. Halfway across the yard, he reached for her hand. When his fingers closed around hers, she drew to a halt, peering up at him inquisitively. He suspected he knew what had brought her up short. He lifted her hand between them. "Do you mind?"

Josie pursed her lips, looking thoughtfully at the clasped hands. "I'm not sure, Stephen. It seems a bit . . . well, too friendly—"

"Aren't we friends?" Stephen asked in mock hurt.

She laughed. "Of course we are, but I'm friends with lots of fellows. I wonder how you would feel if I allowed one of them to hold my hand."

David O'Brien immediately surfaced in his mind. The idea of David holding Josie's hand did not sit well, no matter how much he appreciated the man's honesty and apology. Yet Stephen hadn't staked his claim, so to speak, where Josie was concerned. She had every right to be friendly with other young men if she desired. His heart pounded with his frustration and uncertainty. He had been gone for four months, and maybe his expectations were not the same as hers.

Still holding her hand, he led her to the wooden swing beneath the crabapple tree in the middle of the Klaassens' yard. He guided her into it, then sat on the tender shoots of grass near her feet. He pulled one tiny blade of grass free from the earth and watched it as he twirled in his fingers.

When he looked up he saw the new green leaves above Josie like a canopy, and the spring flowers around them created a heady backdrop of scent and color. Josie was dressed simply in a dress of blue cotton, only a small ruffle at the neck and sleeves. Her sandy brown hair, pulled into its usual single braid, swung across one shoulder. The light spattering of freckles across her nose gave her an innocent, fresh appearance that Stephen found most alluring. And there was much more to Josie than her pleasing appearance. She was intelligent, caring, and moral—the perfect choice for a lifelong mate.

He stared into her face. Was this the time to let her know? Had her question about whether he wanted her holding hands with another man been some kind of a hint? Females could be so confusing. . . .

"Stephen, what are you thinking about?" Josie's voice cut into his thoughts. "You have the oddest expression on your face."

He squinted into the setting sun between the branches of the tree. "I'm sorry. I didn't ask you to come out here so I could stare at you." He grinned and added, "Not that staring at you isn't a pleasant pastime." Her blush pleased him. She was so open and innocent.

"Now don't start that, Stephen Koehn," she said and chuckled, "or I'll get up and go back in the house." Then she sobered, an earnest look crossing her face. "Really, I do want to know what you're thinking. Please tell me, Stephen. Something is on your mind."

Stephen rested his elbows on his knees and tossed aside the little blade of grass. "Did you miss me while I was in Blue Earth, Josie?"

"Well, of course I did. I've known you forever. Why wouldn't I miss such a good friend?"

"That's all?" he asked, his heart sinking. "You missed me as a friend?"

Josie frowned. "Well, shouldn't I think of you as a friend, Stephen?"

Stephen shifted his position. "Well, yes, I hope you think of me as a friend." His voice came out sharper than he intended. He softened his tone. "But isn't there—well, something more?"

"Like what?"

Frustration pressed at Stephen's chest. Was Josie purposely making this difficult? Why did he have to spell it all out for her? "I'd been calling on you for two months before I left for Blue Earth. I wasn't calling on anyone else, and I haven't called on anyone else since. I thought we might have . . . well, an understanding."

"No one else has called on me, Stephen."

A wave of relief washed over him. Stephen scrambled to his feet and pulled Josie out of the swing. "Come on, let's walk."

But Josie stood in front of him without moving a step. "I'd rather finish this conversation before moving on to something else. You definitely have something on your mind, Stephen, and I hope you trust me enough to tell me about it. If you don't, then I think there's something important lacking in our relationship."

He clung to that last word. "Do we have a relationship, Josie?"

"I thought we did." Impatience colored her tone. "But I'm starting to wonder what your intentions are. If you can't even express them, then—"

He halted her words by grasping her shoulders and placing his lips against hers. When he pulled back, she was staring at him with wide eyes. "Why, Stephen!"

He couldn't help his amusement at her reaction. "Do you know what my intentions are now, Josie?"

She took a big breath and let it out. "Does this mean it would bother you if I held hands with some other man?"

He growled menacingly. "Just let someone try it, and see how the fur flies."

She giggled. "I've been warned." Then she sobered. "But, Stephen, we still need to talk. Just kissing me doesn't tell me what I need to know."

Stephen cupped her shoulders with his hands. "What do you want me to say, Josie? When I was in Blue Earth, I missed you desperately and couldn't wait to return to Mountain Lake. To you. When I think of starting a family of my own, you are always at the center of those thoughts. Last night when David O'Brien thanked you for your attention during supper, I was shocked and near green with envy." He paused, his hands tightening on her shoulders. His voice dropped to a near whisper. "Josie, I want to marry you. I want you to be my wife."

Josie took in a sharp breath. "M-marry me?"

Stephen chuckled, then stopped when she did not join in. "Well, yes, you silly girl. You didn't think that kiss was for nothing, did you?"

"No, and I don't take kisses lightly either, but . . ."

"But . . . ?" He ducked down and peered into her face.

Josie turned her head away, sucking on her lower lip. "But I'm not sure . . . I'm not sure we're ready to think about getting married."

Stephen's hands dropped slowly from her shoulders, and he took a step backward, his gaze still fastened on her face. His arms hung limply at his side. "Why not?"

Josie twisted her hands together, a pleading expression on her face. "Stephen, you kissed me and told me you want to marry me, but there's something you haven't said."

Her tone was kind, but Stephen caught the undercurrent of disappointment in her eyes. He lowered his head. "What do you want to know?"

"You said you think of me when planning to start your own family, you missed me when you were away, you were envious of the attention I paid to David. . . . But you didn't tell me you loved me. Shouldn't that be said before a marriage proposal is made?"

Stephen lifted his head. "I'm sorry, Josie. You're right. I should have said that first." But he fell silent.

Josie tipped her head and looked him straight in the eyes. "Do you love me?"

"I care for you deeply, Josie, you know that." He glanced down again.

"Yes, I do know that, but that isn't what I asked." She stepped forward, reaching out to place a tentative hand on his forearm. She repeated very softly, "Stephen, do you love me?"

Stephen swallowed. Hard. "I think I do." He met her gaze, both anguished and bewildered. "I've never felt about anyone the way I feel about you. I want to be with you every day, every hour. Does that mean I love you?"

Josie turned away slightly, giving him a view of her profile. "I don't know. Only you can answer that."

Stephen held out a hand toward her. "Josie, are you saying you won't marry me?"

Josie sighed. "No, Stephen, I'm not saying I won't marry you; someday, maybe we will be married. But I think some misplaced sense of jealousy or spring fever or seeing me again after your time away—or something has caused you to step over an important part of getting to truly know each other. Of knowing your heart—and mine . . . Unless you are sure you love me, we shouldn't even be discussing this."

She was right, but he wasn't willing to admit it. His ego felt bruised. He turned away in frustrated silence.

"I think we need some time, Stephen," she went on in a calm, sensible tone. "I would like to continue seeing you, but I don't think either of us is ready to make plans for a future together. After all, I plan to take the teacher's examination, and you aren't sure. . . . Maybe we both need to rethink where we're going with this."

Stephen stared at her, dumbstruck. He'd come out here intending to sweep her off her feet—maybe even ask permission of her parents to make their engagement official before he left—and here she was, sweetly as you please, telling him that he should think about it more and that she was still planning to go off somewhere and teach.

"Well, all right then," he blustered, his chest tight, "if you want to think, then fine. Take all the time you need to think. And when you're done thinking, you know where to find me." He whirled away.

Josie's hand shot out, catching his arm and holding him in place. He glowered at her, and she frowned. "I'm only trying to be sensible, Stephen. One doesn't make an important decision like getting married without giving it serious thought. There's no reason to be angry."

He jerked his arm free. "I'm not angry."

"You must be angry, because you're yelling."

"I'm not yelling!" he yelled. Then he fell silent. His head drooped, his chin nearly touching his chest. It was springtime, and he'd been all ready to take the young lady of his choice to be his wife. It wasn't supposed to be this difficult.

Josie stepped close to him again, and he raised his head to meet her gaze. A shimmer of tears brightened her brown eyes. He hadn't meant to make her cry. He swallowed his anger and reached out to brush her cheek with one finger. "Maybe you're right. Maybe we should take a little more time and . . . and think this through before making a commitment."

She nodded. The crestfallen expression on her face tore at Stephen's heart. "I still want to see you, Stephen." She sounded sad yet hopeful.

He managed a reassuring smile. "I want to see you, too. Shall we plan on meeting next Saturday? Maybe go on a picnic?"

A slight smile appeared. "I'd like that. Should I pack a lunch?"

"No, this time it's my treat. I'll have Ma throw some sandwiches together."

Teasing glinted in her eyes. "Sounds as if it's your mother's treat."

He gave the expected chuckle. "Yeah, well, I don't cook so good. . . ."

Josie looked toward the house. "I'd better go in now, Stephen. I'll be praying about what you asked me. I want to do what's right. What's right for both of us."

He nodded. "Me, too."

She paused. "I'll see you Saturday."

"Yes, Saturday." Stephen slipped his hands into his pockets. "I'll pick you up before noon, and we can drive over to Goose Pond."

She began backing away, her hands clasped behind her back, the braid still over her shoulder the way Stephen liked. She smiled tremulously. "Saturday . . ." At Stephen's nod, she spun and ran to the house, disappearing inside.

Stephen stood in the yard, staring after her. *Well, Lord, I sure messed that up.* The brightness was suddenly missing from spring.

*G*raduation Day for the Mountain Lake Community School senior class of 1918 took place on a golden afternoon in late May, right outside in the school yard. Josie sat with the other graduates on the raised platform built for this occasion, facing the audience. As her gaze roved across the sea of familiar faces, it wasn't hard to imagine that at least half of the people on hard benches beneath the bright May sun were there just to see her receive her hard-earned diploma.

Josie's grandparents and oldest brother, Daniel, had traveled with his family clear from Minneapolis for her big day. The biggest surprise of the day was what had carried Daniel, Rose, and their two little girls to town—a brand-new, black shiny Model T Ford. It was the first automobile to chug down the cobblestone streets of Mountain Lake, and it caused quite a commotion. Josie smiled to herself as she recalled some of the stunned expressions when Daniel chugged to a stop beside the horse-drawn buggies and wagons that had brought the others to the graduation.

Her smile faded, though, when she confirmed one important face was missing from her group of supporters this morning—Stephen's. Ever since their talk when she had gently declined his marriage proposal, he had been cool and distant. Although they had gone on the picnic that Saturday a few weeks ago and had gone walking together after church on Sundays since, the old ease of being together had slipped away.

Could he be holding himself aloof to punish her, to force her into bending to his will?

Irritation mounted as she mulled it over. He knew she had her own goals—mainly, of teaching. Why should she have to give up her dream simply because he decided he was ready to settle down with someone? Especially when he couldn't even say the words I *love you* to her. Josie realized she should wait until her own head and heart were in agreement before making a life-changing decision like getting married. One would think an intelligent man like Stephen would be that sensible, too.

But she was going to ruin this day for herself if she didn't think of something positive. Determinedly, she turned her attention elsewhere. A baby gurgled somewhere in the throng, and Josie twisted in her chair and spotted one of Liz and Jake's twins, little A.J., with a grip on his Uncle Adam's nose. She covered a smile with her hand when she saw that the tyke wouldn't let go. Beside Adam, Samantha shook with silent laughter as she tried to wrestle the baby's chubby hand downward, but A.J. chortled loudly and flapped his dimpled hands at his Auntie Sam. David sat next to Samantha, smiling at the little boy's antics. The Klaassens considered David an honorary member of the family, but until recently he'd kept himself a bit at arm's length. Josie had made sure her parents invited him to the graduation, but she hadn't expected to see him. He sat grinning at Adam and Samantha as they tussled with A.J. Then he turned his head and caught her watching.

He smiled, lifting a hand to wave briefly. Her cheeks went hot. She nodded, flustered. Would he think she'd been staring at him? She didn't have much time to worry about it because the ceremony began.

Reverend Goertzen stepped onto the platform and asked the congregation to rise for an opening prayer. Josie stood nervously and squeezed the hand of Tessie Jost, seated on her left. It gave her some assurance that Tessie seemed to be just as nervous as she was, considering the girl's moist hand.

The graduating class of 1918 had only five members—four girls: Josie, Tessie, Mary Wiens, and Priscilla Koehn; and a lone male, Joseph Enns. Their teacher, Mr. Reimer, gave a brief address, instructing the graduates to fulfill their dreams and look above for guidance in the pathways their lives followed.

The school board president, Mr. Arthur Neufeldt, solemnly shook the hand of each graduate as he handed them the rolled piece of parchment that signified their successful completion of school requirements. Josie had to hide another grin as she took hers; sweat poured from the poor man's bald head like water from a sieve. Josie turned toward her family and flashed a beaming smile. Each member returned it a hundredfold from across the audience.

The rest of the school's students gathered in a group at the front and sang the hymn "Jesus, Gentle Shepherd." Then Reverend Goertzen prayed once more, bestowing a final blessing on the young people, and it was over.

Josie hugged each of her classmates in turn, even briefly embracing Priscilla who offered her cheek with her usual condescension. Then Jodie stepped off the platform and bounded over to her family in an unladylike manner, waving her diploma over her head. "Now to take the teachers' exam, and I'm all set!"

Congratulations floated around her as she moved from one person to another, receiving enthusiastic hugs and kisses. She turned from Adam's hug to find herself face to face with David. The warmth ignited in her cheeks again.

"Congratulations, Josie." David held out his hand rather than opening his arms. Self-consciously, she took his hand and felt his long, hard fingers close tightly around her own. "I have a gift for you." And he held out a small square package bound in brown paper and tied with string. "I couldn't find a better wrapping . . ." He seemed embarrassed by its plain appearance.

Josie beamed at him, trying to put them both at ease. "Why, thank you, David." She took the package and held it against her graduation dress of mint faille. "You didn't need to do that. Just coming today is all the gift I need."

David shrugged and ran a hand over his unruly hair. "Well, it's not much. But graduations are special, and I was grateful to be invited. I'm proud of your accomplishment."

Josie's eyes widened in surprise. She'd never have imagined him saying something like that. And he was pink around the ears himself.

"Josie, come on." Sarah tugged at Josie's sleeve. "Mama baked a big ol' white cake with strawberry icing! Let's go eat it!"

Josie laughed at her youngest sister's eager face. "All right, I'm coming." She paused, looking back at David. "Are you . . . coming too?"

Ma stepped up and slipped her arm around Josie's waist. "Why, yes, David, do come out. The party wouldn't be complete without you."

A smile crept over David's narrow face, lighting his pale blue eyes. "Thank you, I will." He fell into step behind them, his long shadow falling across Josie's frame. She hurried her steps, suddenly uncomfortable but uncertain why.

⌒⌒

Josie's graduation party turned out to be a raucous affair. The children dashed between the legs of the adults, earning reprimands but slowing not a whit. Laura Klaassen provided enough food to keep a whole army fat and happy. The womenfolk carried things from the kitchen into the yard for a good fifteen minutes. The men gathered in clusters to discuss the things males liked to discuss, and frequent bursts of laughter resounded from their ranks. David mingled in their midst, treated as if he belonged. It warmed him. How wonderful to fit in somewhere after all those lonely years.

When bowls of food filled the plank-and-sawhorse tables, Si Klaassen gave a whistle and motioned everyone to gather around. "Children, it's time to settle down," he admonished. When they had finally done so, he looked around the table at the sea of faces. A smile crossed his face when his eyes found Josie, and he held out his hand to her. "Come here, Josephine."

Josie tucked herself beneath her father's arm, grinning up at him.

"Josie—" Si lifted his voice for all to hear—"we're all very proud of you, and we want to wish you God's richest blessings for what lies ahead. Graduation is the finish of school, but it's just the beginning of everything else to come. And I know great things are in store for you." A hint of moisture brightened Si's eyes, and his arm tightened around her.

Josie blushed, laughing as Si put his other arm around her in a tight embrace. "Thank you, Papa."

"Let's pray," Si said, and all around the long table bowed their heads. "Lord, we're together as a family to celebrate Josie's graduation from high school. You know her heart and the hopes she has to become a teacher. We ask that you bless her desires and open the doors to let her fulfill those dreams. Be with all of us as well. Now bless this food and the hands that prepared it. Amen."

"Amen!" echoed more than a dozen voices, and Liz and Jake's nine-month-old twins hollered in unison, "Amaah!" Laughter erupted, and the eating commenced amidst much talking and more joyful merrymaking.

David found himself sandwiched between Frank and Arn in the middle of the table. Josie sat at the head, Si having given her the seat of honor with a dramatic wave of his arm to more laughter.

David thought back to Si's prayer, specifically the words "We're together as a family," and his heart expanded at the feeling those words evoked.

Samantha sat next to Adam, helping Liz with one of her twins, laughing over her shoulder at something Adam whispered in her ear. She looked as if she were born to this world, as if she'd never known anything else. David envied her the ability to let go of the past. How had she managed to do it? In all likelihood, Adam's love had brought her around. The love of someone as special as Adam would be enough to change anyone.

His heart hammered at the next thought. Could someone special possibly fall in love with him and bring the same change in his life? His eyes wandered to Josie. She was definitely her brother's sister. Both were self-assured but not overbearing, each in possession of a contentedness that David couldn't imagine ever experiencing. His heart lifted as he watched her, the center of attention and thoroughly enjoying every minute of it, but still managing to allow everyone to share in her happiness. Yes, Josie was definitely a very special person.

All the Klaassens had those qualities, and David marveled at the legacy the Klaassen grandparents had handed to their offspring. Quite different from the self-loathing and uncertainty that David and Samantha's alcoholic father had bestowed on his children. Samantha had broken those chains, thanks to Adam. Would it be possible for David to throw off his cloak of despair with the help of a special woman?

He rested an elbow on the edge of the table, his chin on his fist, and gazed in Josie's direction while questions filled his mind. Why wasn't Stephen here? He'd noticed the man at the graduation ceremony standing at the back of the school yard, gazing at Josie, but he hadn't approached her. Did it mean they were no longer seeing each other? Was she free to accept the attentions of someone else? Maybe his attentions . . . ?

"Hey, brother," Adam called, interrupting David's thought. "Are you going to sleep over there?"

David sat up, his face heating. He quipped, "Not a chance with all this racket."

"Well, I'm glad," Laura joined in, "because it's time to watch Josie open her graduation gifts. You won't want to miss out on that."

David smiled and nodded. He most definitely would not want to miss watching Josie, no matter what she was doing.

The two youngest Klaassen offspring, Sarah and Teddy, brought Josie her gifts. First she opened a fabric-backed journal and pen from Daniel and Rose. Josie grinned appreciatively at her oldest brother and his wife in a silent expression of thanks. When she opened a box holding lace-edged handkerchiefs and a small glass decanter of perfume from Frank and Anna, she immediately touched the stopper to her wrist, sniffed, and proclaimed, "Mm! Delightful!"

Similar expressions of gratitude accompanied each package, and David's admiration of the young woman grew with each happy exclamation. His ears went hot when little Teddy laid the next gift into Josie's lap. He sat in anxious silence, his heart pounding, as she pulled off the plain brown paper and opened David's gift. She ran her fingers over the pale-pink stationery and matching envelopes, fastened together with a ribbon. "Oh, thank you, David! This is wonderful. Now I'll have nice paper to write letters home on when I go away to teach."

David didn't dare ask whether she would write to him too. "You're welcome," he managed, and everyone's attention went to the next package.

Grandmother Klaassen had crocheted a beautiful shawl in shades of burgundy, wheat, and palest pink. Josie buried her face in its softness. When she emerged, tears were flowing. "Oh, Grandma, it's just beautiful! And you did this with your poor fingers."

Grandmother Klaassen pooh-poohed Josie's exclamation with a dismissive wave of an arthritic hand. "You surely do not think I would reward an occasion as important as this with some store-bought trifle! As long as I am still breathing, I will continue my needlework."

Josie darted around the table to give her grandmother a long, heartfelt hug.

From her seat next to Grandmother Klaassen, Hulda Klaassen called, "Now open ours."

Josie eagerly reached for the next package, a small one, and lifted a beautiful cameo pin from its velvet-lined box. "Oh, this is too much!"

"Not at all." Hulda pulled her face down until her extra chins formed a perfect double-U beneath her chin bone. "Graduations come once in a lifetime. We want you to remember this one."

"Oh, I will," Josie breathed, awe in her eyes. "Thank you so much."

David, observing the bright eyes and love glowing on the women's faces around the circle, felt a lump in his throat. He'd never forget this day, either.

Teddy thumped the next package onto the table. Josie peeled back the paper and squealed. "A dictionary! My first teacher's book! Thank you, Liz. You too, Jake!"

Little Andy banged a spoon on his high-chair tray, and Josie added seriously, "Oh, you, too, Andy and A.J. I'm sure you helped your mama and daddy pick this out." Everyone laughed, and both babies cooed and slapped their hands against their trays as if they knew they were being included.

Only two more packages remained—one round hatbox, and one rectangular box of substantial size. Josie rested her hands on the top of the second one, glancing impishly at her mother out of the corner of her eye. "Given Mother's penchant for practicality, I hope this isn't underwear."

Laura jumped up, laughing. "It would serve you right if it was!" She rounded the table and rubbed noses with her daughter. Then Laura ordered, brows furrowed into a mock scowl, "Open it up, you ungrateful child."

Josie tugged the top off the big box, then paused, her mouth hanging open. Slowly she reached in and lifted out a beautiful dress of deep garnet organdy. She stood and held it against herself and stared down its length. Although David didn't consider himself a fashion connoisseur, he recognized the sophisticated cut of the dress. The frock gave Josie a maturity that he found most fitting—and irresistible.

Frank joked, "Somebody reach over and close my sister's mouth for her before she starts drawing flies."

The whole group burst out into more laughter, and Josie twirled in a circle with the beautiful garnet dress held in place at her shoulders. "Oh, Mother, Papa, this is the most wonderful, unexpected present. Oh, it's just perfect! However did you manage it?"

Samantha leaned forward, her eyes twinkling. "It wasn't easy. Mother Klaassen and I have been working on it at our place so you wouldn't find out about it. Adam says you are the worst snoop."

"Oh, I know I am," Josie cheerfully admitted. "But this is a wonderful surprise. I'm so glad it isn't underwear!" she said to more chuckles.

Her father shoved the hatbox under Josie's nose. "See what's in here now."

Josie carefully placed the dress in its wrappings, touching it briefly with a trembling hand before turning to the hatbox. When she lifted the lid, she squealed once more. A beautiful store-bought hat—the exact shade of garnet as the dress—appeared, and Josie perched it on her head, beaming at them all from beneath the dipped brim. A tiny cluster of satin ecru ribbon and pearl buttons attached an ostrich feather fit snugly into the dip. Josie placed both hands on the edges of the hat to hold it in place and swung around once more. "I'll be the best-dressed teacher in Minnesota!"

Teddy pulled a slender box from beneath his jacket and thrust it at his sister. "This goes with it. It's from me, Arn, Becky, and Sarah."

Sarah bounced in her seat. "Open it fast, Josie. I can't wait!"

The ostrich feather bobbing, Josie grasped the box in both hands and slid the lid up with her thumbs. She let out a squeal and held a hatpin aloft. A good twelve inches in length, the gold shaft was tipped with a deep-red center stone the size of a man's fingertip. Josie went over to the line of siblings, hugging each. She finally returned to her place at the head of the table, glowing with brightness and joy. Her ostrich-feather hat was still on her head with the hatpin angled artfully across it. Happy tears shimmered on her eyelashes. "This has been the most wonderful day. Thank you, all of you, for your gifts and sharing this day with me. I'm so glad you all belong to me." And then she covered her face with both hands and burst into tears.

The women surrounded her, patting and laughing and crying a little themselves. Even the men looked misty eyed. And David experienced a deep desire to be a permanent part of this happy circle. He wanted what his sister had found with Adam— love and acceptance and peace. And, he decided with sudden resolve, Josie was the key. *Somehow, Josie must be mine.*

*J*osie passed the teachers' exam a week after graduation and received her teaching certificate bearing the seal of the state examiner. She floated for days on a cloud of anticipation as she sent out letters of application to every school within a hundred miles of Mountain Lake. Pa and Ma suggested she was pushing herself out a little farther than was necessary, but when Josie assured them she'd prayerfully consider any offer before accepting it, they gave her their blessing.

Stephen continued to sulk. At least, that's how Josie saw it. He made no effort to seek her out, and it wasn't her place to go chasing after him. Josie missed his company—although Stephen seemed uncertain of his feelings for her, she knew that she did love him. She had since she was just a little girl in pigtails. But she couldn't tell him so—not when he was uncertain about his feelings for her. So she busied herself at home, helping her mother put in their huge garden, sewing two more dresses appropriate for a teacher to wear—praying as she stitched that they would be put to good use, and hand feeding a little calf that had been rejected by its mother. Although her days were full, she thought of Stephen often and wondered if she might get a note or if he'd show up and surprise her.

Samantha came over the day they planted corn. She and Adam lived in a dugout that had been built by Adam's grandparents when they immigrated to America almost fifty years before. The little dwelling was near the fields Adam's family planted with wheat, but there wasn't a plot for a garden. So Samantha helped with the large garden at Si and Laura's home in return for some of the harvest. Josie and Samantha worked side by side in the sun, dropping the seed corn into furrows and tamping the dirt down. Planting was a long, tedious chore, and by midafternoon both needed a break.

They collapsed in the shade of Josie's favorite crab apple tree. Becky brought out glasses of lemonade, cooled with ice from the Klaassens' own icehouse. After taking a long swallow, Samantha placed the sweaty glass against her equally sweaty forehead and sighed. "Ah, that feels good."

Josie planted her palms in the grass behind her and let her head hang back, gazing at the bright leaves overhead. "If it's this muggy already, what will it be like in July?"

"Unbearable," Samantha predicted. She drained her glass dry, then rattled the ice chips in the glass. "Josie?"

Too tired to even respond, Josie sat in silence.

A bare toe poked at Josie's leg.

Josie sighed and looked at Samantha. "What?"

Samantha grinned. "Can I be nosy?"

Josie released a soft chortle. "Yes, to my experience, you can be very nosy."

Samantha grimaced. "Spoken like a true teacher. *May* I be nosy?"

Josie crossed her legs and leaned her elbows on her knees. "You've never bothered to ask permission before. Go ahead—but I reserve the right to refuse answering."

"Fair enough." Samantha set the glass aside, wiped her forehead with a grimy hand, and asked, "What's happened between you and Stephen?"

Josie groaned and buried her face in her hands. "Oh, I don't want to answer that."

Samantha reached over and clasped Josie's hand, her expression sympathetic. "Adam and I have been worried about you. Did he stop seeing you because you want to teach?"

Josie looked up. "I'm not sure he's stopped seeing me—for good, I mean. He's a little upset with me right now." She cocked an eyebrow. "He asked me to marry him, and I said not now."

Samantha sighed her understanding. "I see."

Josie pulled free from her friend's touch and shook her head. "No, I don't think you do. I love Stephen, and I want to marry him. But when he asked me, he couldn't even tell me if he loved me. Why would a man propose marriage to someone he's not sure he loves? And how could I say yes to a man who isn't sure he loves me?" She took a deep breath, raising her eyes to the tree branches overhead for a moment, then looked back at Samantha. "And then there's my wanting to teach. Stephen knows I've wanted to teach since—well, since I was a little girl. I see no reason why I can't teach for a year or two, then get married. I know by my age lots of girls get married and start a family, but I'm not ready for that. I don't think that means there's something wrong with me. Do you?"

"Of course not!" Samantha squirmed around to face Josie. "Does Stephen think there's something wrong with you?"

"I don't know." Josie forced out a frustrated breath. "Maybe not wrong, exactly, but he's not sure what he wants. When I told him I thought we needed to think some more about getting married before we became engaged, he got angry and stomped around. I'd never seen him act so high-handed. I didn't like it. Things haven't been the same between us since."

Samantha scooted close and put her arm around Josie's shoulders. "I'm sorry. Can I do anything to help?"

Josie smiled sadly. "It's helped some to get it off my chest. Thanks for sticking your nose in. This time, at least."

They both giggled and shared a quick hug. Then Samantha looked over at the garden plot. "Well, should we finish up the corn? We could probably get the cabbages in, too, if we hurried."

Josie stretched her arms over her head with a groan. "Why not? If my hands are busy, my mind doesn't run so much."

Samantha stood and held out her hand. "Come on." Josie allowed herself to be pulled to her feet. But then Samantha just stood still for a moment, holding Josie's hand, her head tipped and brows pulled low. "You say you know you love Stephen?"

"Yes, I do." Longing washed through Josie's middle. "He's the only one I've ever even considered spending my life with. Why?"

Samantha dropped Josie's hand. "No reason." Yet Josie suspected something else was on Samantha's mind. Before she could ask, however, Samantha brushed the back of her skirt and headed for the garden plot. "Come on, let's go get our hands busy."

The pink and white striped dress arrived at the mercantile the last week of May. When Hiram pulled it from its shipping box, he turned to David and raised bushy eyebrows. "Well, Mr. Delivery Man, are you ready for this?" By now it was no secret that David and Priscilla got along about as well as two tomcats in an alley.

David shook his head and blew his breath out. "I really do not want to see that girl, Mr. Klaassen. She gets my goat worse than any female I've ever met."

"I've noticed," Hiram said wryly. He folded the dress neatly and put it back in its box, then shoved it down the counter close to David. "But I can't afford to lose any customers, so I'd appreciate it if you would try to keep a handle on your tongue when you make this delivery."

The two men—one tall and lean, one short and wiry—faced off. David did not want to do it, but delivering was part of the job he was hired to do, and Hiram would never give in. David reached for the box.

"I'll make a deal with you." Hiram placed a bony hand on David's shoulder. "You make this delivery to the unpleasant Miss Koehn without causing a ruckus, and when you return, I'll send you out to Si and Laura's with that old trunk of mine Josie asked to use."

David perked up. "Trunk? Did she get a teaching position somewhere?"

Hiram snorted. "Nah, not that I've heard—yet. But that girl has got to be organized. She wants to be packed and ready when the call comes."

David smiled. That sounded like Josie, all right. He grabbed up Priscilla's dress. "Mr. Klaassen, you have yourself a deal. I promise—no trouble this time."

His resolve faded fast when Miss Koehn herself answered his knock and her lips turned immediately into a familiar, arrogant smirk. "Well, well, well . . . If it isn't the Klaassens' dependable delivery boy."

David held out the box. "Your dress arrived this morning, Miss Koehn."

Priscilla feigned a pout and twisted a silky black lock of hair around her finger. "Now we're back to 'Miss Koehn,' are we? I thought we'd gone beyond that . . . , David."

David formed a sharp retort, but he'd promised not to rise to her bait. He cleared his throat. "Do you want me to leave the package here, or shall I bring it in for you?"

Priscilla pushed the door open, inviting him in with a flamboyant swing of her arm. "By all means, bring it right in."

David stepped into the Koehns' parlor and couldn't help but gawk. He'd been in several homes in Mountain Lake, but this was much more ornate than any other he'd seen. The windows were dressed with tasseled curtains of heavy peach jacquard, and each piece of furniture held a patterned throw or was stacked high with fringed pillows. Every bit of wall space held framed photographs or actual oil paintings of flower arrangements or landscapes. A heavy carpet covered the wood floor, and bric-a-brac of every variety covered any available surface. David stood with box in hand, his gaze moving from one cluttered area to another. Where should he lay the box?

Priscilla swished past him, motioning for him to follow. He trailed behind her down a darkened hallway with doors opening off in both directions. At the end of the hall, she stopped and pointed into the last room. "Put it in there." She didn't even pretend to be courteous.

A four-poster rice bed, bearing a flowered appliqué quilt, filled the center of the room. A delicate china doll dressed in satin and lace leaned against the ruffled pillows. A maple dresser and washstand of the finest quality stood against the wall. The woodwork was white, and the walls were covered with a vines-and-flowers wallpaper in soft pastels. A large cheval mirror stood prominently in one corner. He nearly snorted at the sight of the mirror.

Suddenly it struck him that the house was awfully quiet. "Miss Koehn, is your mother here?"

She crossed her arms with a meaningful grin. "What's the matter? Do you feel the need for protection? A big, brave man like you?"

Anger smoldered beneath the surface, and he wished he could drop the box. Forcefully. On her head! But that wouldn't do. He stepped into the room and placed the box on top of the appliquéd quilt and turned to leave. But Priscilla stood in the doorway, blocking his exit.

He stopped three feet away from her. "Excuse me, Miss Koehn."

Priscilla locked her hands behind her back and tipped her head in a cocky manner. "I prefer to be called Priscilla."

David bit down—literally—on his tongue. For ten interminable seconds he held it tightly, painfully, between his teeth. Then he relaxed his jaw and spoke carefully. "Miss Koehn, I have other deliveries to make. Now if you will kindly step aside—"

"Oh, gracious sakes, go!" Priscilla stepped back and gestured as she had before, with dramatic flair. "Run along, Mr. O'Brien, and make your deliveries. Don't let me stand in the way of your very important business."

David shouldered his way past her and back up the long hallway to the front door. Just before his hand closed around the cut-crystal doorknob, Priscilla darted in front of him, placing her back against the door and holding up her hand, nearly putting it against his chest.

"Miss Koehn, I need to be leaving." Only the promise he'd made to Hiram kept him from moving her bodily out of his way.

Priscilla held her head high, glaring at him with narrowed eyes. "But I haven't tipped you." Her condescending tone made the blood rush to David's face.

He gritted his teeth. "I do not require a tip, Miss Koehn. Delivery of purchased goods is part of the service the mercantile provides."

Her face twisted in an odd expression, her eyes flickering with some emotion he couldn't read. She lifted the heavy strand of hair that fell across her shoulder and swished it back and forth. "Did you read that in a book somewhere?"

Impatience got the best of him. "Miss Koehn, you are by far the most irritating young woman I've ever encountered. You are spoiled and willful and so full of yourself there isn't any room for anyone else." Suddenly he remembered his vow to be agreeable, and he shut his jaw so forcefully his teeth clacked together.

Priscilla's expression hardened, but she spoke very sweetly. "I simply offered to tip you. I fail to see why that should make me irritating and spoiled and willful and full of myself." She extended a finger for each description David had mentioned. "It seems to me that it makes me generous."

She flounced from the door, her head high. When she was several feet away from him, she spun around and gestured to the now unblocked doorway. "Well, go ahead—leave. But don't expect me to give a glowing report on your far-from-cheerful service."

What he wouldn't give to reach out and shake the arrogance out of her. David grabbed the doorknob and wrenched it open, nearly throwing the door against the parlor wall. As he stepped out into the May sunshine, he felt a light tap on his shoulder. He looked back to see Priscilla stepping back safely behind the screened door.

"I've decided to excuse your impertinence this time, given your rather unpleasant upbringing. I suppose instead of being insulted, I should feel sorry for you. So I forgive you for your unwarranted attack on my honorable intentions."

The impudent little upstart! To save face, he said, "That's very mature of you, Priscilla." But she'd won. She'd managed to make him drop his guard and call her Priscilla. He could have kicked himself.

"Good-bye, David." She shut the door but not before sending him off with a satisfied grin.

David stood a few seconds on the Koehns' front porch, stifling the urge to pound on the door and . . . and what? That girl was some piece of work. He stormed toward the mercantile, dirt rising with every step, his mind trying to comprehend the reason behind Priscilla's terrible behavior. He had suspected jealousy was what motivated her, but now he wasn't so sure.

His steps slowed as he pictured her as she had looked just minutes before, standing in her bedroom doorway, her long dark hair falling in beguiling waves across her shoulders, her huge blue eyes sparkling with some emotion he couldn't recognize. She had a face that could stop men in their tracks, a beauty that would evoke admiration or jealousy from other women. Now that he'd seen her home, he knew she had all that money could provide. Of what could she be jealous? She seemed to have everything, didn't she?

Except happiness.

He stopped short right in the middle of the street, reminded of his father. Burton O'Brien had been filled with bitterness and anger. With all that unhappiness inside, what could come out but hatefulness and spite? Could it be that Priscilla was reacting to her own inner unhappiness?

But why should she be unhappy?

He shook his head. Why bother trying to figure out Priscilla Koehn? In all likelihood, the only thing wrong with Priscilla was a father who had spoiled her shamelessly instead of teaching her proper behavior or any manners.

He set his feet in motion again. He'd get that trunk and take it out to Josie. Time with her held a lot more anticipation than thinking about Miss Priscilla Koehn's problems. But for some odd reason he didn't pretend to understand, he had a hard time shaking from his mind the image of Priscilla and her unreadable, incredibly intriguing, bright blue eyes.

avid gave the reins a gentle tug to the right, and the horse pulled Hiram's wagon onto the Klaassens' yard. Squinting against the sun, David spotted three gardeners busy in the large plot east of the house, all wearing skirts and shirtwaists along with floppy straw hats on their heads. As the wagon lumbered on toward the barn, the trio turned in his direction, and the middle one—Samantha—pulled off her hat and waved it over her head.

"David!" Samantha tossed the hat aside and hop-stepped out of the garden area as David pulled it to a stop next to the barn. She lifted her arms for a hug the minute David leaped down.

David pulled away and held his nose, wrinkling up his face. "Phew! I hate to mention it—"

"It's just good honest sweat!" Samantha pushed at him, laughing. "What could smell better than that?"

"I can think of lots of things," David retorted, but he left his arm draped around his sister's shoulders as they walked around to the back of the wagon. Josie and Becky, carrying Samantha's discarded hat, joined them.

"Hello, David." Josie approached slowly, her lips curved into a hesitant smile. "What brings you out this afternoon?"

David's stomach did a funny somersault at her unusual reserve. Coming up with a cheerful smile himself to make up for the one she lacked, he flapped his hand at the wagon's bed. "Take a peek."

All three women stepped forward and peered over the high side. Josie's reticence disappeared in an instant. She clapped her hands and let out a squeal of delight. "Oh, my trunk!"

David swung it out, grunting a bit with the effort of clearing the side of the wagon. "Yep, it's all yours." The trunk against his thighs gave him an awkward gait as he headed toward the house. "Where shall I put it?"

Becky opened the back door for them, and Samantha and Josie followed David in, Josie sticking particularly close in her excitement. She clasped her hands together. "Could you please take it up to my room? I'm afraid there are no other men around here right now."

David looked down into her face. Strands of hair, pulled loose from her simple braid, clung to her sweaty cheeks and neck. Her nose was sunburned, her freckles stood out boldly, and a smudge of dirt decorated her right cheek. David grinned. She sure was cute.

"I think I can handle that." He pushed the trunk a little higher with one knee. "But everybody get out of the way in case I fall—or drop it. I don't want to hurt anyone."

The girls obediently cleared a path, dashing upstairs to the far edge of the landing. They watched, wide-eyed, as David made his way to the top of the stairs. He couldn't see his feet, and once he almost missed a step, causing the girls to gasp, but he quickly regained his balance and arrived with his burden.

"Whew!" Josie offered a broad smile, which gave David's heart a lift. "You made it."

"Which room?" His arms were starting to ache.

Josie pointed to a door on his left, and he turned sideways to get through it. He set the trunk down carefully at the foot of the bed, careful to keep from scratching the hardwood floor. He straightened and pushed a hand against the small of his back with a little groan.

"Heavy?" Samantha asked.

"Nah." David shook his head. "But I'm not offering to carry it down when you've got it all filled up with your female frippery."

"Female frippery, huh?" Josie, hands on her hips, grinned and then shrugged. "Very well. I guess you've done your part." She turned to her younger sister. "Is there any of that lemonade left?"

Becky nodded. "Sure, at least one glassful."

Josie sent a look in David's direction. "Does that sound like a fair reward?"

David gave a quick nod. "That sounds wonderful." Becky hurried downstairs.

He turned in a circle, taking in the simple furnishings of the room—the green-painted iron bed with its homey patchwork quilt, the tall, unadorned *schrank* that probably held Josie's entire wardrobe, and the washstand with its plain white pitcher and bowl beside the door. The walls were plastered and painted but unpapered, and the single nine-over-nine pane window bore simple homemade curtains of yellow gingham.

On the floor beside the bed rested a bright rag rug, obviously handmade. The only unnecessary fixture in the room was an oval photograph with a domed piece of glass protecting the picture beneath. David bent closer to see it more clearly. No doubt a wedding picture, the man and woman standing side by side in their best suits of clothing, somber expressions on their faces. David smiled to himself. From the looks of them, marriage wasn't such a pleasant undertaking.

He tapped the glass. "Who's this?"

Josie inched up behind him and touched the picture with a finger still holding dirt from the garden. "My grandmother and grandfather Klaassen, on their wedding day."

He glanced down at her, grinning again as he spotted the unbecoming smudge on the glass. "They look pretty serious."

Josie shrugged, her forehead wrinkling briefly. "I suppose. But, then, marriage is a pretty serious business."

David turned from the photograph and let his gaze rove over the room once more. He mused aloud, "This is the second young lady's bedroom I've seen today."

"Where else have you been today?" Samantha demanded. Even Josie looked up at him expectantly.

David wished he'd kept his mouth shut. "I made a delivery to the Koehn house with a package for Priscilla. She wanted it in . . . in the bedroom." Heat blazed his ears when he recalled the visit. He'd spare the girls the details. "Her room is sure different from this one."

Josie nodded her agreement. "Oh, I know it. I've been in Priscilla's house." She headed for the stairs, and David and Samantha followed. "Millie Koehn has the best of everything. They were the first family in town to get indoor plumbing, and John Koehn spares no expense on decorating."

When they reached the kitchen, David accepted the iced lemonade from Becky with thanks.

Josie went on, "But I'd rather have my house. It might not be fancy, but it's homey. The Koehn home is—" She frowned, as if seeking the right words. Then she lifted her shoulders in a sheepish shrug. "Well, it's kind of cold, impersonal. Of course, I might be a little biased."

David chuckled. "You might be biased, but I think you're right. This home is definitely warmer and more inviting." He took another sip of his lemonade, then decided to add, "You're also marked."

She drew back, startled.

David reached over and touched Josie's cheek with the tip of one finger. "Right here. You have a dirt smudge."

Flushing, she spun around, her hand rubbing at the spot he'd touched. "Sam, why didn't you tell me?"

"I'm sorry, I didn't notice." Samantha burst out laughing. "Josie, you aren't helping it a bit. Look at your hands."

Josie held her dirt-coated hands in front of her and groaned. She'd masked her freckles under a smear of dirt. She headed for the stairs, calling back over her shoulder, "Please excuse me. I'm going to wash up."

Becky followed, and Josie's indignant voice trailed behind them down the stairs. "Why couldn't someone tell me my face was dirty?" David and Samantha shared a grin at her expense.

Samantha examined her hands and grimaced. "Oh, my. I need to do the same." She pumped water from the kitchen sink into a pan.

David leaned against the work table and finished his lemonade, watching Samantha. "Did you get the garden all in?"

Samantha turned, rubbing her hands dry with a towel. "Gracious, no. We've still got beans, carrots, tomatoes, okra, turnips—"

"You needn't say more." David held up his hands. "A farmer's wife's work is never done, right?"

Samantha nodded, looking content. "But I wouldn't have it any other way." She hung up the towel and turned back to David. "The potatoes have been in for a couple weeks, and we got the corn and cabbage done today. We're well on the way."

David nodded, and glanced around. "Where are Laura and the youngest two?" The house was uncharacteristically quiet without Sarah and Teddy running around.

Samantha linked arms with David and guided him toward the porch. "Mother Laura took the youngsters into town to visit some friends who had a baby last week. They should be back before supper time." The two settled themselves on the porch swing, and Samantha set it into motion.

David rested his arm across the back of the swing, shifting sideways so he could look at Samantha while they talked. "I imagine you and Adam will be having callers for the same reason before too long."

Samantha's cheeks grew pink. "Oh, I'd like that. I wouldn't mind having a baby right away, and neither would Adam. He's used to a big family, and we both want lots of babies. But Mother says we're young, and there's plenty of time, that we should enjoy each other for now. She's probably right."

David peered over at her, pleased by the relaxed expression on her face. "It sounds funny, hearing you call someone Mother."

Samantha's brow puckered. "I've never used the title before since our mother died when I was born. I like having someone I can call 'mother.' But . . . does it bother you?"

"Not at all," David assured her, "it just seems a bit odd. I'm happy you feel so close to Laura Klaassen. But since I remember our mother, I can't imagine calling someone else that name."

Samantha leaned against him lightly. "You remember our mother well?"

"I do." David's heart caught. "I still see her often." Samantha drew back with a puzzled look. David settled her against him. "In you, Sammy. I see her in you. Your hair, your eyes, the way you hold your mouth when you're thinking hard about something. You even have her ears." And he flicked one small ear-lobe with a finger.

She covered it with her hand and laughed softly. "Oh, you're teasing—you don't remember her ears."

David nodded, serious. "Yes, I do, Sam. She had small ears, with small lobes, just like yours. And she wore her hair up in a tight coil during the day, but at night she'd take it down and brush it out, and it glittered red in the lantern light. Even then, I thought she was beautiful with her hair down." He broke off, staring ahead.

Samantha placed her hand on his knee. "David? She was a good person, right?"

David nodded, his gaze still aimed into the distance. "She was a wonderful person. We had a very kind, very special mother." Against his will, other thoughts clouded his mind. Of their father, who could never be described as kind or special. And there were so many more memories of him. Of his drunkenness, his wild ravings, his punishing fists . . . Pa had controlled David completely with the man's fearful, incomprehensible anger.

"David?" Samantha's worried voice cut through David's recollections.

"W-what?"

"You don't have to think about him." Her voice was gentle, understanding.

How could she have known? But of course she'd know. She'd suffered at Pa's hands too. He hung his head, shamed that he'd damaged their time together.

Samantha's hand tightened on his knee. "He's gone, David, and he has no hold on either of us anymore. Not unless we let him. You have to let go of the unpleasant memories and put your trust in a heavenly Father who loves you and wants you to be His own. With Him, you'll find all the love and acceptance you need."

Despite his sister's kind tone and sweetly beseeching expression, David experienced a rush of anger. After escaping Pa, he had no desire to call anyone else father. He started to tell her so, but before he could speak Josie stuck her head out of the parlor door, her face clean and shiny and her hair neatly combed.

"Sammy, I'm going to start supper now. Are you two planning to stay?"

Samantha rose from the swing. "I can't. I promised Adam I'd be home before then. If it's time to fix supper, I'd better get going."

David wanted to stay, but responsibility called. "I still have some work to do at the mercantile, and I've frittered away enough of the afternoon." He looked at Samantha. "Do you need a ride home?"

Samantha shook her head. "I rode Pepper over here. He'll get me home again."

David gave her a hug and took a step toward the porch stairs.

Josie dashed over and gave David a brief, impetuous embrace that set his heart thumping. Before he could wrap his arms around her, she shifted backward with a pink-cheeked grin. "Thank you for bringing my trunk, David. I'll need it when I get my teaching job. And now I can have it all ready to go."

David forced his shoulders into a nonchalant shrug. "It was no problem. I—I hope you get to use it." His conscience panged. He'd just told a fib.

Josie beamed, swinging her arms. "Oh, I do too! I've been praying about it, so now I just have to be patient and wait."

Praying again . . . David set his lips in a firm line and stepped aside as Samantha and Josie shared good-bye hugs and their next gardening plans before disappearing into the house.

David reached for Samantha's arm, and they walked around the house to the barn where he had hitched the wagon. The horses nodded lazily in the late afternoon sun. He saddled Samantha's horse and hooked his fingers together to give her a leg up. "Good luck with the garden, Sammy," he told her with a pat on her leg.

She waved and laughed. "You'd better wish me more than luck, brother. I reckon you'll be eating some of the fruits of my labor too."

He grinned and patted his belly. As he turned toward the wagon, Samantha called to him. "David, will you think about what I said . . . about Pa?" She peered down into his face, tears winking in her eyes. "God can wash the hurt away, and when you're empty of the pain, you'll be open to new loves, just like me with Adam. That's what I want for you, Davey."

Something tight wrapped itself around David's chest. "I'm glad you've found happiness believing in God, Sam. But I don't need Him. I don't want Him. And the sooner you accept that, the better off I'll be." Steeling himself against her stricken expression, he strode toward the wagon, climbed in, and aimed the horse toward town.

*O*ne mid-June morning, Josie met Arn in the yard, and he handed off the family's mail before trotting on toward the fields. She flipped through the few envelopes—and discovered one addressed to her from the Winston School superintendent. Closing her eyes for a moment, she prayed for the strength to face yet another rejection. "You know I want Your will, Lord," she finished as she often did.

Three other letters had arrived, each one a thank-you-but-we-are-not-in-need-of-teachers-for-this-term variety. Polite, but disappointing. So she had little hope as she peeled back the flap and removed the letter typed on official stationery. But when she read the opening lines—"Dear Miss Klaassen, We have received your letter of application, as well as a high recommendation from Mr. Joel Reimer, so it is with pleasure that we ask you to consider the position of teacher for the first-, second-, and third-grade students of Winston School . . ."—she gave a shriek of delight.

Letting the screen door slam behind her, she raced for the stairs. "Ma! Ma!" Josie took the steps two at a time, tangling herself in her skirts and tripping on a step. She rubbed at her shins and scrambled the rest of the way upward, calling, "Ma! Mama, come quick!"

Laura emerged from Teddy and Arn's room, her arms full of sheets and her face pale. "Josie, what on earth—?"

"I got a letter! From Winston!" Josie wrapped her arms around her mother, sheets and all, and spun them both in a circle. She laughed and tried to talk at the same time. "They want me to teach first through third grades!"

She paused in her ecstatic dance to hold the letter in front of her nose, her hands shaking so badly the words bounced on the page. She read it again, interpreting for Ma. "They got my letter, then contacted Mr. Reimer to ask about me, and they were impressed with his recommendation, and they want me!" She hugged the letter to her chest, her heart pounding so fiercely her ribs ached.

Ma dropped the sheets and embraced Josie, her eyes shining with pride. "Oh, Josie, I'm so happy for you." After a brief laugh, she said, "I can't help but be happy for Pa and me, too. Winston is close enough that we can go get you for weekends. I didn't want you very far from home, especially for your first year."

Josie paced back and forth, unable to stand still. "I'm supposed to be there by the second week of August, he says, and I'll be staying in a rooming house where the other single teachers stay, and school will start the third week of August, and—oh, Ma! This is so wonderful."

Laura caught Josie around the waist, forcing her to stand quietly for a moment. "Is some kind of reply in order?"

"Reply? For what?"

"To the superintendent. What was his name?" She pointed at the return address. "Benjamin Kleinsasser. Are you supposed to let him know you accept?"

Josie slapped a hand to her forehead. "Oh, my goodness!" She laughed. "Of course I need to reply." She headed for her bedroom. "I'll just ride into town right now and wire a telegram." She grabbed a comb and smoothed errant wisps of hair into place as she continued her planning. "And while I'm there, I'll stop by the mercantile to tell Uncle Hiram and Tante Hulda and check to see if any new fabrics are in, because I really should have one more dress and I might as well wire the boardinghouse, too—the name of the owner is in my letter—and let her know I'll be taking the room that's available. . . ."

She had run out of breath and returned to the landing, where Ma waited, a smile on her face. Tipping her head to the side, Josie said, "What else should I do, Mother?"

Ma picked up Josie's braid and flicked her chin with the curled tip. "Do you think maybe Stephen might want to know?"

Josie's excitement flickered. She bit her lower lip for a moment, then offered a slow nod. "Yes, I suppose I should tell him too. I just hope he'll be nice about it. He's been so unpredictable lately."

Ma gave Josie's cheek a soft pat before scooping up the sheets. "I imagine he's concerned about being separated. You can't blame him for that."

Josie sighed. "I suppose not. But he's known forever that I planned to be a teacher. Why does he have to make it so hard on me?"

Ma headed for the stairs with Josie following. "Because men like to be first in a woman's life," Ma said over her shoulder. "Oh, they might act tough and self-reliant, but underneath they all want to be needed. I'm guessing that Stephen feels threatened by your desire to teach and be on your own for a while. He probably thinks it means you don't need him or that he's not as important to you as teaching is."

"But that's silly," Josie countered. "He has other interests— his job at the mill, hunting, even playing checkers at the mercantile on Saturdays. I've never felt threatened by any of those things."

Ma dumped the sheets on the table in the kitchen and turned to face her daughter. "No, I'm sure you haven't. But as I said before, men like to be first. Before children or hobbies—or the desire to teach." Ma's soft smile helped soothe the edges of Josie's frustration. "That doesn't make you wrong or him wrong, it just means you have different opinions on this. It will be a challenge for both of you to respect one another's viewpoints. But if you plan to spend a lifetime together, it's very important to begin building the groundwork of respect now. And respect goes two ways."

Josie considered Ma's comments. Stephen was so head-strong! Would he be able to respect her decision to accept this position? Or would there be another display of temper? She loved Stephen and wanted to be with him, but there were other desires in her heart requiring attention also. The desire and ability to teach were God-given gifts and shouldn't be ignored. Could Stephen accept her desire to use those gifts without feeling he was less important? Somehow, she'd have to make him understand.

Josie leaned forward and kissed Ma's cheek. "Thank you. I'll see Stephen after I send my wire."

"Good girl."

Josie crossed to the door and then paused, sending her mother a thoughtful look. "Ma, did you have to give up any dreams to marry Papa?"

Ma gathered the sheets to her chest, a contented smile creasing her gently lined face. "Your papa is my dream, Josie. Being his wife and the mother to his children was all I ever needed."

Josie frowned, biting the inside of her cheek.

Ma added, "But that was me, Josie. You are you, and you must do what you feel is the right course for your life. You're an intelligent, rational young woman, and I know you've prayer-fully considered becoming a teacher. Teaching is right for you, and your father and I support that decision. We wouldn't try to change you, Josie—for you are you, not me."

Josie dashed across the room to throw her arms around Ma with the bundle of sheets getting most of the hug. She gave her mother a boisterous kiss on the cheek before pulling back and winking through grateful tears. "Thank you, Mama."

"You're welcome, sweetheart." Ma gave her a gentle push. "Now go send your wire and see your young man."

Josie laughed, waved over her shoulder, and headed for the door.

✎

The cowbell above the mercantile door clanged wildly, and David turned from organizing bolts of fabric. When he saw Josie skipping over the threshold, her face ringed with joy, his heart gave a happy flip. He hadn't seen her since delivering the trunk to her home, trying to keep his distance in an attempt to forget his attraction to her. But his reaction to the sight of her smiling, freckled face told him his plan hadn't worked.

"Good afternoon," Hulda Klaassen greeted her niece, delivering a kiss on Josie's flushed cheek. "Look at your eyes all sparkling. You look sea *schaftijch*."

Josie hunched her shoulders and giggled. "I am very happy, Tante Hulda. I came in to buy fabric for a dress, because I just sent a letter to Benjamin Kleinsasser in Winston accepting the position of first-, second-, and third-grade teacher for next term!" With each syllable, her voice rose in volume and pitch—and speed as the words tumbled over each other. As her excitement built, David's diminished.

Hiram bustled around the counter and stood beaming at his wife and niece as Hulda threw her arms around Josie. Hulda crowed, "Your first teaching job! What a joy!" The two rocked back in forth in a lengthy hug, both laughing, and then Hiram extracted Josie from Hulda's embrace and aimed Josie toward the fabric display. "Come right over here now. We've got in a new shipment of fabric only yesterday, and there are some very nice choices."

David dropped the bolt of cloth he'd been holding and backed away as Hiram and Hulda propelled Josie across the floor.

"But don't choose for just one dress, Josie," Hulda said. "You choose for two! Then go to the millinery shop and have another hat made to match as a congratulations present from your uncle and me." The pair smiled at Josie as if they were second parents.

"Oh, but you just bought me a graduation gift, and—"

"And that was for graduating. This is something entirely different." Hulda shook her finger at Josie. "And if you argue with me, I will consider you to be impertinent and disrespect-ful." Her extra chins quivered in mock indignation.

Josie glanced at David helplessly, and when he had nothing to contribute to the discussion, turned to her aunt and uncle and shook her head, another smile lighting her face. "All right, you've won—and thank you. It would be nice to extend my wardrobe a little bit."

David rounded the display, hand outstretched, battling the desire to hold tight when Josie placed hers in his. "This is what you wanted, isn't it?" He shook her hand and hoped the sad-ness filling his chest didn't reflect in his eyes.

"Yes, it is." She giggled, the sound melodious. "I'm so ex-cited I was dancing jigs at home."

"When do you leave?"

"In two months—mid-August."

David sucked in a breath. So soon . . .

Josie turned to Hulda. "Do you think there will be time to get two more dresses made, and a hat, too?"

"Ask Sammy to help you," David suggested. "You know how she enjoys sewing, and I'm sure she'd be delighted to give you a hand."

Hulda bobbed her head in agreement. "My, yes, and she does such a nice job. As for the hat, just take a snippet of fabric over for Emma to use for matching ribbons and such. She won't need a finished garment."

"You're right." Josie sighed her relief. "Here I am planning to teach, and I can't even think straight."

"Oh, you're just excited." Hulda wrapped her heavy arms around Josie's slight frame and squeezed. "And you have every right to be." She pulled back. "Have you told Stephen yet?"

David took quick breath and waited for her answer.

Josie shook her head. "No, not yet. I'm going over to the mill next. I'm not sure how he'll take it."

So Stephen didn't want her to teach. David busied his hands smoothing a rumpled bolt of cloth, keenly attune to the women's continued conversation.

Hulda gave Josie's shoulder a consoling pat. "Now you listen here, young lady. Don't let that stubborn young man talk you out of doing what you know is best for you. The good Lord opened that door for you, so you need to walk right on through it."

"Your aunt is right," Hiram added. "If Stephen is too hard headed to see that, then you just tell me, and I'll thump him over the head with one of his own flour sacks!"

Josie laughed, and David swallowed a grin at the thought of wiry, gray-haired Hiram tussling with young, stocky Stephen.

"You are a woman worth waiting for, Josie," Hiram added, "and don't you forget it."

Josie's brown eyes misted over with tears. "I won't forget it, Uncle Hiram." She gave the older man a quick hug then made her fabric selections. Only minutes later, she left the store, her steps light and her face glowing with excitement.

David watched her go, a confusion of emotions tangling him in knots. He didn't want to see her happy mood disintegrate. Yet if Stephen reacted negatively she might end the relationship with him. She might turn to another man. Maybe even . . . him. His heart skipped a beat at the thought, and he tried to squelch it. Still, it niggled in the back of his mind as he returned to work. Sometimes all a man had to cling to was a dream.

*A*t a tap on his shoulder, Stephen glanced up at his brother Matt, who pointed toward the mill door. Stephen's pulse tripped into double beats, competing with the noise of the flour mill. Josie . . . Was he dreaming? No, there she stood, hands clasped behind her back, braid falling sweetly over her shoulder, her face holding a pensive expression.

His heart leaped. Certainly she'd come to tell him that she'd changed her mind—that she'd given up this silly idea of teaching somewhere and would marry him now, before the summer was over. He slapped Matt on the shoulder and bellowed over the noise of the grinder, "Gonna take a break."

Matt nodded and grinned, and Stephen loped across the flour-spattered floor. The sound of the gears and steam engine would make conversation impossible, so he guided Josie through the mill with a hand on her back, opened the wooden rear door for her, then sealed the noise behind them. They stood under the summer sun with only the breeze to keep them company. He took hold of her shoulders and released a heavy breath. "Josie, I've been hoping you'd come."

"I've missed you, Stephen." Josie brought up her hands to hold on to his forearms. "It's been very lonely without you."

He tipped his head forward to kiss her, but she turned her face slightly. He frowned. "What's the matter?"

"I came to talk, not spoon."

"Can't we do both?" He smiled, moving his hands to her upper arms and squeezing gently.

"Stephen, please." She took a backward step, ducking from his grasp. "This is important."

He pushed his hands into his overall pockets. Maybe she wasn't here for the reason he'd thought. "What's so important?"

She removed a folded square of paper from her pocket and held it out to him. "This."

After a moment of hesitation, he took it and unfolded it, his eyes on her. She angled her head to the side, biting on her lower lip. Trepidation made his mouth go dry. He read the letter once, then again. A weight settled in his middle. He slapped the letter against his pant leg, drawing her attention.

"I bet you're happy." He refolded the missive and thrust it at her. "It's what you wanted."

She tucked the folded square into her dress pocket. An apology glimmered in her eyes. "It's not what you wanted, is it?"

"No, it's not." He honestly tried not to sound curt, but his tone came out sharply anyway.

Palms pressed to her bodice, she implored him, "Can't you be at least a little bit happy? For me?"

He faced the hedgerow that separated the yard of the mill from the yards of the houses behind it. He searched his heart for a hint of happiness, but only disappointment swirled through his chest.

Josie stepped closer to him, one hand extended but not touching him. "Stephen, I'm going away to teach because it's what I've always dreamed of doing. I'm not going to get away from you."

Stephen spun toward her, anger rising. "What about my dreams, Josie? My dream is to get married and start a family. I can't do that all by myself. What am I supposed to do while you're off fulfilling your dream?"

"I'll be back. I'm not leaving forever."

He snorted. Her reasonable tone did little to placate him.

Josie folded her arms over her chest, eyes now snapping. "And to be quite honest, Stephen, I couldn't marry you right now even if I wasn't planning to take this job. You said you thought you loved me—not that you knew you loved me. Even as much as I love you, I can't marry you when you aren't sure."

She loved him! He'd heard her admit it. He turned to her, hope rising in his chest. "You love me, Josie?" She couldn't leave him. Not if she loved him.

Josie hung her head, her shoulders slumping. "Yes, Stephen, I do love you. I've known that for some time now. But I can't marry you until you can honestly tell me you love me and mean it with all your heart."

"So you're going."

She nodded.

Frustration again boiled in Stephen's gut. He muttered, "I don't see how you can say you love me, then say you're going to leave. I don't understand that at all."

"You left me for four months to go to Blue Earth after claiming to care for me."

He sputtered, "I went because I was needed. My grandfather was ill. And it wasn't for a year—only a few months."

"Well, the truth is I'm going where I'm needed, too. And it's not a whole year—just nine months. Besides that, I'll only be gone a week at a time. I'll be home every weekend. We'll be able to see each other almost as often as if I was home."

Her calm reasoning only served to incense Stephen further. "Someone else could certainly teach at that school." He pointed a finger at her. "You aren't the only one who could do the job, but I was." He shoved his thumb against his own chest for emphasis.

Josie sighed, shaking her head. "Stephen, I can see you aren't going to give an inch, so there's no point in continuing this conversation." She blinked quickly. "My mother told me two people have to respect one another's opinions if they are to have a good relationship, and obviously that's something we can't do. Not on this, anyway." She squared her shoulders. "In two months I will be leaving to teach. I would rather go with your support, but if you can't give your blessing, I'll simply have to go without it." Her voice got a little wobbly, and she stopped and took a deep breath. "In the meantime, I'm going to pray you will come to understand this is what's right for me now, and that doing what's right for me doesn't take anything away from you." She turned and walked away, her back straight and shoulders stiff.

Stephen, watching her go, could tell she battled tears. His heart demanded him to go after her and set things to right, but stubborn pride held him in place. He was the man. He shouldn't be the one to give in. Giving in would be exhibiting weakness, and a man couldn't be weak. He'd learned that much from his father. John Koehn never backed down from his convictions just because a female had other ideas.

Turning his back on Josie, he stared at the hedgerow, his thoughts tumbling. He was twenty-three years old, and he wanted to move out of his father's house to start a family of his own. What was wrong with that? Absolutely nothing! It was perfectly natural at his age. These crazy ideas Josie had about needing to be more than a wife and a mother were the unnatural ones.

Why did she have to be so set in her ways? He'd invested the better part of a year in courting Josie, and now she was leaving after refusing his marriage proposal. He kicked at a clump of new grass, sending the bright green blades scattering in an arc across the ground. He didn't want to start over with another girl—besides, there hadn't been any other girl but Josie since he was twelve years old. He only wanted her. And she was leaving for a whole year.

His stiff shoulders slumped. His dreams were turning to dust.

☙

David stepped out of the post office just as Josie came charging into the doorway. With her head low she plowed directly into him, her toe catching against his foot, and with a squeal of surprise she fell forward. David dropped the mail and caught her around the waist, setting her back on her feet. She looked up at him, her eyes wide.

"Are you all right?" David asked. "I'm sorry—you could've taken a tumble."

Josie wiped at her eyes with trembling fingers and smoothed her blue cambric skirt. In the white blouse and plain skirt, she looked every bit the schoolmarm. "I'm fine. Just clumsy. Thank you. You saved me from adding some extra bruises to my shins."

"Extra bruises?" David frowned and reached out to raise her chin, looking directly into her eyes. Her red eyes and blotchy face told him she'd been crying.

She forced a chuckle. "Yes. I bruised my shins this morning when I stumbled on the stairs." She looked away and sighed. "This just hasn't been my day. . . ."

After the undeniable cheerfulness she'd exhibited earlier, her sorrow pained him. Things must not have gone well with Stephen. Although David had other errands to run for Hiram, he decided taking care of Josie was more important. Hiram would understand. In a deliberately playful tone, he asked, "Not your day, huh? I seem to recall you thinking otherwise just a little while ago. Let's go for a walk, and you can tell your ol' uncle David what happened to spoil it for you."

Tears shimmered in her brown eyes, but Josie held her chin erect. They took a few steps, and then she flapped her hands in aggravation. "It's men. Why must men be so *stekjsennijch*?"

David couldn't help but laugh. He knew she wasn't trying to be funny, but she looked so endearing standing there with her arms crossed, her lower lip in a pout, and those cute freckles dancing across her nose—complaining about men. She looked no more than twelve years old. "So what does that mean? You know, *steksenick*, or whatever you said."

Josie glared. "Hardheaded—you know, stubborn. Men are so stubborn."

"Men?" He raised one eyebrow. "Or one particular man?"

Josie's anger faded, and she pursed her lips, clearly uncertain. Before she might choose to dart away, he caught her elbow and guided her to a bench on the boardwalk in front of the jewelry store. He nudged her onto it, then seated himself next to her. He would like to have laid his arm across the back of the bench, but he decided that would not be wise. Not in her current emotional turmoil.

He smiled encouragingly. "Now, tell me what's wrong, and maybe I can help. Sometimes it takes a man to make another man's viewpoint understandable."

Josie took in a deep breath, then released it, ruffling her fine, airy bangs. She looked at him out of the corner of her eyes. "You're right. It is just one man. It's . . . Stephen."

"Ah." David injected great meaning into the simple word. "He didn't take your news well?"

"I should say not!" Josie grimaced. "He doesn't want me to teach." She paused. "Well," she said, her tone softening, "I guess that's not entirely true. It isn't the teaching he opposes so much as my going away for the next school year." She looked at him sideways again, pink stealing up her cheeks. "I hope you don't mind my telling you this. You see, a few weeks ago, he asked me to marry him, but I want to wait. I think he's still a little mad at me about that."

David narrowed his gaze, thinking. "Stephen is older than you, isn't he?"

"Five years. He's ready to settle down. But . . ."

"But you're not?"

She shook her head, then turned to him once more. "It's not that I don't want to marry him. I love Stephen—I really do. But our desires right now are different. He wants to get married and start a family, and I want to be able to spend some time as a teacher before settling down. He knew when he started seeing me that my plans were to teach, but I guess he figured I'd change my mind once he proposed marriage."

She averted her gaze and went on almost as if to herself. "If only he'd been able to tell me that he loved me, maybe I would have changed my mind. But I can't change courses based on a maybe."

David sat quietly and sorted through what he'd just heard. So there was some question in Josie's mind about Stephen's true feelings for her. But why would the man propose if he wasn't sure he loved the girl? That didn't make sense. Unless he simply wanted to settle down, and Josie was available. David studied Josie's profile—the high forehead, the brown eyes that usually sparkled with openness, the pert chin now angled downward as she struggled with hurt feelings. She deserved a man who was willing to give her his whole self, not just a halfhearted proposal based on his own selfish needs.

David's ire rose as he considered Stephen's bullheadedness. The fellow meant to intimidate Josie into bending to his will. If Stephen knew upfront what Josie's intentions were, he shouldn't act put-out now when she was seeing those plans through. On the other hand, he could understand how Stephen felt. If Josie was his girl, he'd have a hard time letting her trot off on her own for any length of time.

He swallowed and carefully chose words he hoped would offer her some comfort. "Have you heard the old adage, 'Absence makes the heart grow fonder'?" He waited until she nodded, then said, "I'll bet when you've left for Winston, Stephen will come to his senses and realize what your Uncle Hiram told you is true: you are a woman worth waiting for. Wait and see. Things will work out for you."

"Do you really think so, David?" Her brown eyes begged him to be right.

David reached over for her hand and squeezed it. "Yes, I do. Don't let his fear of letting you go put a damper on your happiness or make you let go of your dream. If you do, you'll regret it, and you'll resent Stephen. We men can be *sheck . . . schteksennyick . . .* you know, that." He smiled at her chuckle. "But somehow you women always manage to turn us around."

Josie's smile lit her face. "Thank you, David. I'll try to be happy. And as I told Stephen, I'll keep praying that he'll come to understand I had to do this, for me." Then, unexpectedly, she leaned forward and delivered a little kiss on David's cheek.

The moment her lips touched his skin, David went stockstill as if he were cut from stone. She jerked away, color flooding her face. Before he could say a word, she bolted to her feet, ran down the boardwalk, and disappeared around the corner.

David remained on the bench for several long minutes, his errands forgotten. He sat, the spot on his cheek burning as if lit from within by the gentle touch of her lips. His heart pounding fearfully in his chest. Feeling things he had no business feeling for a girl who had just admitted that she loved another man. But feeling them just the same . . .

ednesday evening while his sister and brother-in-law attended services in the little church in the valley outside of town, David pulled the straight-back chair in his room to the open window. He sat, then propped his feet on the windowsill and leaned the chair back on two legs. Hands locked behind his head, he rocked. And thought.

Although his eyes were aimed at the line of sparrows fluttering along the top of the false-front of Koehn's & Sons Milling across the street, his mind's eye held an image of Josie as she sat next to him on the bench in front of Nickel Jewelry. He smiled, remembering how her brown eyes flashed when she had announced that men were hardheaded. But then when she'd confessed that she loved Stephen, the look in her eyes had been soft and forthright. David didn't doubt her sincerity. But then . . .then she had kissed him. Confessed that she loved Stephen, but kissed him—David.

He dropped his feet from the windowsill and the chair come down with a bang against the wooden floor. The sparrows scattered. He squeezed his fingers together at the back of his neck, frowning. From the way she'd turned bright pink and escaped, he was sure she hadn't planned to give him that kiss. He was equally certain that she rued her impulsiveness before she'd even stood up to flee. But her moment of recklessness had been his moment of reckoning.

David was hopelessly attracted to Josie. He was, he admitted, falling in love. He sighed, stood, and moved to the oval mirror above the washstand. He had to lean down a bit to see himself, and grimaced at the image of his round-shouldered reflection. He wished for the hundredth time that he was a handsome man. He was too tall, too lanky, with a face that was too narrow and too freckled—and his hair. What woman could possibly look twice at a man who had a mop of waves that refused to lie down and couldn't even be described with one color?

When he pictured Stephen Koehn—wide-shouldered, ravenhaired, chisel-featured—he gave a snort of disgust and spun away from the mirror. Comparing a scarecrow to Adonis. When up against someone like Stephen, he didn't stand a chance. And it wasn't just in physical appearance that he lost out.

David threw himself down on the bed hard enough to make the springs twang. He recalled Adam telling him about the turmoil he'd gone through when he'd realized he was falling in love with an "unbeliever," as he'd put it. Samantha's conversion to Christianity had allowed Adam to confess his love for her openly. No doubt Josie too placed importance on a man believing as she did. And Stephen was a churchgoer. Probably a Christian, too, or Josie wouldn't have been seeing him.

David's heart sank. He lost in every category—looks, personality, religion. No matter how much he might care for Josie, she wouldn't reciprocate those feelings because he was an unbeliever. Church and her faith were important to her.

So now what? He was falling in love with a Bible believer who might be available but who loved someone else. He groaned. What a mess. He never did anything right. He buried his face in his hands, battling self-recrimination. Just as Pa always said, he was a complete failure. The way he had it figured, he had two choices: he could give up on Josie, or he could start going to church regularly and try to understand and accept what was taught there.

He sat up on the edge of the bed, pressing his palms hard against the mattress. The first choice was out of the question. His heart wouldn't allow him to give up on her. But the second choice wasn't easy, either. He wasn't interested in religion. But he was interested in Josie, and her religion was a big part of her. Should he go—for her? It seemed deceitful, attending church to impress a girl. Church was considered of great importance to many people who mattered to him, and he felt guilty for even considering going there simply to win Josie's favor.

There was something else to think about, too. He'd been awfully adamant when turning down invitations to church in the past. What would Sammy think if he suddenly showed up on a regular basis? She'd probably think her prayers had been answered. And—the thought hit with physical force—maybe his ponderings right now were the result of Sammy's prayers.

He shook his head and crossed to the window. Although he couldn't see the church from this distance, he imagined the clapboard building with its bell tower. Inside, Samantha and Adam—and Josie—gathered with others in the congregation. Were they praying for him right now? Praying that he'd come . . .?

With a snort, he spun from the window. What a silly notion. This was his own idea, not some subconscious thought planted in his mind by a Superior Being. Still, regardless of the origin, becoming a churchgoer was the best way he knew to win Josie's trust—and maybe her heart.

Starting Sunday, he'd go. He'd listen and try to understand. But he would do it for Josie, not for himself.

~~~

David sighed as he dusted the narrow shelves behind the counter at the mercantile. Each slim bottle of medicinal cures had to be picked up and placed on the counter. Using the feather duster, he'd sweep clean the empty shelf area and, finally, wipe each bottle neck and top with a soft cloth before returning them to the shelf. Such a tedious task.

The simple repetition left plenty of time for contemplation of other subjects. David's favorite thoughts were, of course, of the young woman whose heart he was trying to win. He smiled to himself, thinking how pleased Josie had been when he'd started attending church. He whistled softly between his teeth as he worked, picturing her straight back and interested expression, her face properly aimed toward the front. He went early so he could sit on the bench right across the aisle from her familiar spot. He would have preferred sitting beside her on the same bench, but for some reason he didn't understand, the women all sat on one side and the men on the other. There were a lot of things he didn't understand about church yet, but one thing was clear: his attendance pleased Josie—and Sammy.

Why, Samantha had almost shouted her joy the first time he had shown up without an invitation. She all but glowed during services, she was so happy to have him there. She had assumed he'd come because of his interest in the teachings rather than his interest in Josie. Guilt pricked. But, he assured himself, Sammy wouldn't mind what brought him, as long as he was there.

So he would sit across the aisle from Josie and Samantha— his two favorite ladies, he called them, making them giggle— and assume an attentive pose. Oddly enough, the longer he sat there trying to appear to be listening, the more he actually heard. And he even caught himself reflecting on some of it afterward. Samantha had told him his reflecting was the Holy Spirit knocking at his heart's door. He thought it was probably idle curiosity.

There was one other young lady—the one David thought of as the thorn in his side—who also took notice of his attendance. More than once, he'd sensed someone watching him, only to turn and find Priscilla Koehn fixing him with a pensive look that sent prickles of awareness up his spine. How on earth could that girl have attended church for her entire life and not taken any of the lessons to heart? The minister spoke of kindness, of treating others the way one would like to be treated, of emulating God's love through word and deed. . . . Hadn't Priscilla been listening at all? David was relatively new at all this being-like-God business, and already he possessed—without effort, he thought smugly—more Christian qualities than Priscilla Koehn.

As usual, thoughts of Priscilla created a tumult of aggravation within him, and he slammed the last bottle down on the shelf a little more firmly than was warranted.

"Be careful, David," came a female voice from behind him, "or those glass bottles might break."

He whirled around to find the object of his annoyance standing primly on the other side of the counter, a small beaded purse held against her ribcage with two white-gloved hands. He nearly groaned. Why hadn't he heard the cowbell? And why couldn't she have come at a time when David wasn't minding the shop on his own? Hiram had run to the bank, and Hulda had gone home complaining of "the vapors," leaving him alone. He couldn't escape and let someone else see to Priscilla's needs.

Stifling a sigh, he placed the feather duster beneath the counter. "What can I do for you today, Miss Koehn?"

"I've come to buy a birthday present for my daddy." She held up the little purse. "This is not to go on his account; this will be my own purchase."

She'd been there two minutes and hadn't said or done anything to rile him yet. Surely a record. He could be polite for as
long as it lasted. David offered a tentative smile. "Did you have
something in mind?"

Priscilla nodded. "I would like a pair of suspenders, and a
bottle of shaving cologne. He prefers the kind that smells like
sandalwood—the shaving cologne, not the suspenders." She
smiled at her own little joke.

My, wasn't she in a good mood today? David couldn't decide what to make of her unusual affability. With some apprehension, he moved toward the flat, glass-covered display case
at the end of the counter. "The suspenders are over here, and
the shaving lotions and colognes are behind the counter. I'll
see if I can locate the type you requested while you choose a
pair of suspenders." He lifted the glass cover for her, then returned to the safety of the high wooden counter.

As he searched through the selection of bottled shaving
colognes, he kept a covert eye on Priscilla. She lifted each elas-
tic suspender in turn, giving each a thorough examination before laying them gently back in their wooden display box. A
slight smile graced her face, and she hummed softly, seemingly
enjoying the prospect of choosing something special for her
"daddy." To his surprise, he discovered when she wasn't sniping
at him she was almost pleasant to have around.

At last she returned to the counter, a pair of blue and
brown striped suspenders in hand. "I like these. I think Daddy
will too." She placed the suspenders on the countertop with a
delicate flourish. "The blue is for his eyes, and the brown for his
hair." She laughed, a tinkling sound, and covered her mouth.
"At least, the color his hair used to be. It's not brown anymore."

David considered telling her the gray hair probably came in
after her birth. But somehow it didn't seem appropriate, given

her thus-far amiable treatment of him. Instead, he held out for her approval of the bottle of shaving cologne he'd selected. "I think this is what you want. Take a sniff of it and see."

Priscilla took the bottle, uncorked it, and sniffed deeply, her face a study in concentration. A smile broke across her face, stunning in its sincerity. "Oh, yes, that smells just like my daddy." She pressed the cork back down firmly and set the bottle on the counter next to the suspenders. Her bright eyes met David's with happy expectancy. "Can these be wrapped?"

"Certainly." David reached beneath the counter for paper and string. "One package or two?"

Her expression changed to puzzlement. She tipped her head. "Why are you being so nice today?"

Startled, David shook his head. He hadn't treated her any differently than he would any customer and started to say so. But then he realized, much to his embarrassment, he'd never before carried on a civilized conversation with the girl. Heat blazed his face. "Well, um, that's my job, isn't it?"

Priscilla continued looking at him with that same questioning look in her eyes, her head angled to the side. And then, abruptly, she said, "Two. That way, he'll have more things to open."

It took David a moment to realize what she was talking about. He wished he could ask her the same question. This genial behavior was certainly out of character for her. Maybe the act of giving was bringing out a positive change in her attitude. Or maybe she'd discovered a new way to rattle him. More than likely it was the latter. Whatever the reason, he'd be wise to keep quiet and pretend this was normal between the two of them.

He put her purchases in two conveniently sized boxes, wrapped them with plain brown paper, and tied them with pink ribbon in place of the string. Somehow, pink suited the prissy young woman on the other side of the counter. As he tied the bow on the first package, he realized she was wearing the pink and white striped dress he'd delivered to her house. And she did looked as sweet as a peppermint candy stick in it.

Much to his chagrin, his hands began to tremble. He pushed aside remembrances of previous encounters and concentrated on the task at hand. When he'd finished wrapping, he slid them across the counter, figured the total on a notepad next to the tin cash box, and announced the amount due.

"Let's see . . ." She dug through her ridiculously small purse. At last she extracted several coins and placed them in his extended palm. Her gloved fingers rested against his palm momentarily.

A fresh rush of heat ignited David's face. He rattled the coins into the money box. "Y-your change." He slid a nickel and two pennies across the wooden counter. "Thank you," he said as he did to all the customers, "and come again."

A sweet smile graced her face. She glided toward the door, her gaze aimed at him over her shoulder. When she reached the doorway, she paused, and her long eyelashes dipped against her cheek. "Good day, David."

David's head bounced in a jerky nod. "Good day, Miss Koehn."

The cowbell clanged as she left—he heard it clearly this time—and he broke out in a sweat. The pleasant Priscilla was almost more difficult to deal with than the patronizing, haughty one had been. He pondered the reason, then decided one couldn't be certain of her motives. Without doubt, that young woman had something up her pink and white striped sleeve. And he was sure it was only a matter of time before she lowered the boom.

But she was gone now. Heaving a sigh of relief, he returned to dusting.

*P*riscilla made her way toward home, maintaining her graceful carriage—chin up, shoulders back, tummy in. She smiled and nodded to those she passed on the street, completely aware of—and at ease with—the lingering looks from the men and the raised eyebrows on the women. She was accustomed to attracting attention with her natural beauty, and she relished it. Was there any better place to be than the center of attention? Of course not.

She smiled to herself, thinking of the clerk at the mercantile—poor David. She didn't quite know what to do with him, which was certainly an unusual state of affairs. Her usual feminine wiles seem to be wasted on him—or worse, had sent him the other way.

Goose bumps rose on her arms, and she released a dreamy sigh. David O'Brien . . . Images filled her mind's eye. So tall—a good two inches taller than any other man in town. And his hair! The color of maple leaves in late September—not red, not gold, but a gentle blending of the two. A lustrous color. Oh, how she'd like to stick her finger in one of those curls and discover if they were as soft as they looked. She even found his freckles attractive, scattered as they were across his narrow, serious face.

But serious—what a sourpuss! She wrinkled her nose, envisioning his somber expression. Today he'd come close to smiling, though. How his mind must be churning, wondering about her recent placid demeanor. Well, drastic measures were needed; he seemed absolutely immune to her charms. If employing a spoonful of sweetness would turn his head, she'd give it a whirl.

If it hadn't been for the kind of attention she'd received from other men, she might wonder if there might be something wrong with her. But, no, it had to be him. Oddly, the more he resisted her, the more she wanted to win his favor. So far she'd managed to keep him off-kilter by being flirty, then strident. But that had only turned him away. It was the positive variety of attention she wanted from him now.

She swung her little purse by its gold chain, shaking her head. Seeing him in church had certainly been a shock. But his attendance there would make him more acceptable to Daddy, and she did so want to please Daddy. After all, she needed her father to keep her in clothes and baubles, defend her from those false accusations of selfishness—and on center stage.

A satisfied smile crossed her face. If there was one man she could manage without even trying, it was her daddy. It seemed she'd spent her whole life controlling him and consequently the rest of the household. And what did that say about her family, that a mere girl ran roughshod over all of them? She gave a little snort of derision, then shrugged. She wouldn't complain. She always succeeded in getting her way, and that was what she liked, wasn't it?

A sudden picture of David, his nose only inches from hers, his pale blue eyes snapping, flashed through her mind, and a chill of delight raced up and down her spine. Now there was a man she wouldn't be able to control easily. And for some reason even she couldn't grasp, that made him all the more appealing.

When she reached the corner of her street, she saw Mama on the front porch, hanging paper streamers from porch post to post. Priscilla gave a little hop-skip to speed herself along and bounced up the steps. Priscilla took in the red streamers that looped across the porch and waved in the gentle breeze, making soft crinkling noises. "What are these? What are you doing, Mother?"

The woman stepped back to survey her work. "I'm decorating for your father's birthday. This is his sixtieth, you know. That's quite a milestone. I think it deserves some extra attention, don't you think?"

Priscilla wrinkled her nose. "Daddy doesn't seem the paper-streamer type to me."

Mama's brows dipped together. "I only want to please him." She clasped her hands together nervously. "He is a bit hard to second-guess, but surely he'll see this as a sign of how much I want to make his day special."

"Well, maybe . . ." Priscilla swished by her mother into the house. Inside more streamers swung from the brass chandelier outward to window casings. Mama had cleared the low, claw-footed table in the center of the parlor of its usual collection—an urn of peacock feathers, a stereoscope with a selection of photographs, and the clutter of small porcelain birds, china bowls, and tatted doilies. Now the table wore a Battenberg lace tablecloth, linen napkins of deep green, Mama's finest china dessert plates, silver forks, and the biggest cake Priscilla had ever seen. She peered at the cake in wide-eyed wonder.

Four layers high, covered with creamy white frosting, and decorated with painstakingly shaped roses. What a cake! Mama surely must have spent half the day baking and decorating it. Priscilla placed her gifts on the corner of the table with two other wrapped packages.

Suddenly Mama hurried through the front door. "Your father is coming—I saw him. Oh, I told Stephen to keep him at the mill until four o'clock, and it's only three-forty! I'm not ready for him yet!"

Priscilla hid a smile at Mama's nervous twittering. She couldn't recall ever seeing Mama so excited. She walked over to her mother and offered several consoling pats on her shoulder. "Calm yourself, Mama."

"But I wanted to change my clothes yet, and my hair—"

"Your hair is fine." Priscilla rolled her eyes as her mother worriedly inspected herself in the hall mirror. "Besides, when Daddy gets a look at all this, he'll understand why you're still in your everyday clothes." She suddenly grinned as a devilish thought struck. "Let's peek out the window and watch his reaction to your streamers." Priscilla could pretty well guess what his reaction was going to be—if she was right, the fur was going to fly.

Priscilla followed her mother who crept on tiptoe to the bowed parlor window. The woman peered furtively between the lace panels. Stephen and Daddy were striding up the cobblestone street side by side, apparently deep in conversation. Daddy was gesturing broadly about something when he suddenly stopped in his tracks, his arms locked in a widespread position. Priscilla had no doubt he'd spotted the streamers. Even from this distance, she knew he wasn't smiling.

"Oh, dear," Mama murmured, touching trembling fingers to her lower lip. She dashed for the door, Priscilla trailing.

∽⚬

Stephen looked into his father's dumbstruck face, then ahead. Bold red strips of crepe paper created a spider's web of color on the front porch, matching the angry slashes on Pa's whiskered cheeks. Stephen cringed.

Boots clomping, Pa stormed toward the house. Stephen trotted alongside him, scrambling for words that would pacify his father's temper. "Pa, don't—"

"Help me get these things down!" Pa yanked at the streamers, filling his arms with snarls of the red paper. Ma and Priscilla darted onto the porch. Pris took one look at Pa's stormy face and headed back inside, but Ma rushed to his side and caught his arm.

"John, I—"

"Good heavens, woman, what are you trying to do? Make me the laughingstock of the neighborhood?" Pa reached for a streamer dangling over his head. "I'm a grown man, not a child."

Ma wrung her hands. "I'm sorry, John. I just wanted to make your birthday a bit more festive. I didn't think—"

Pa thrust the tangled wad of torn paper into her hands. "You didn't think, all right." He pointed to the house. "Get that nonsense inside before anyone else sees it."

Trembling, Ma skittered for the door. Pa thumped in behind her, and Stephen followed Pa, his chest tight. Why must Pa overreact to everything? Ma's gaze circled quickly around the parlor, and her shoulders seemed to sag with relief. Stephen caught a glimpse of Priscilla darting down the hallway, one strip of red paper stuck on a heel. Apparently Ma had decorated inside too. Stephen sent a silent thank-you to Pris for saving Ma another tongue lashing.

Ma offered a penitent look in Pa's direction. "I'll dispose of this." She bobbed her chin toward the paper in her hands. "Sit down, and we'll have some cake when I get back. I'll only be a minute." She disappeared down the hallway to the kitchen.

Stephen stepped fully into the parlor, and Pa passed him to glare down at the monstrous cake. Hands on his hips, Pa snorted, "Good heavens."

Stephen couldn't stay silent, even if it did mean risking Pa's ire. "Ma was only trying to make your day special, Pa. You shouldn't be angry. She's gone to a lot of work . . ."

Stephen didn't continue as Pa blustered under his breath, but his face slowly faded to its normal shade. He shot a sour look at Stephen "She should have more sense. Streamers and cake . . . parties are for children."

Ma returned on the last comment, and Stephen's heart lurched when he saw her blanch. She moved hesitantly toward her husband and touched his sleeve. "I'm sorry, John. I thought you would appreciate the festiveness, considering that this birthday is such an important one. I didn't mean to offend you. Will you forgive me?"

Pa pushed out his lower lip, leaving his wife to suffer for several pained seconds. Finally he blew out his breath. "Yes, of course I forgive you. Just try to remember that I am a respected member of this community. I will not abide being made to look the fool."

Ma nodded meekly.

Pa waved his hands at the cake. "But would you remove those garish roses? It looks like a wedding cake, for good-ness' sake."

Ma wilted. "But it took me so long to—"

Pa glared.

Ma sighed. "Of course, John." She carefully lifted the dozen roses from the cake and placed them on a linen napkin. Her steps plodding, she carried them out to the kitchen.

Pa looked down at the cake, nodding in satisfaction. "That's better—except for those gaping holes. Looks as if it's been overrun by mealy worms." He laughed at his own joke.

Stephen bit down on his tongue lest he be disrespectful. When Stephen's brothers and their wives arrived a few minutes later—at the time Ma had specified, four o'clock—Pa told them about the paper streamers that he had mutilated and the silly, girlish roses that had circled his massive cake.

Matt's wife, Sadie, said, "I think Mother Koehn had a lovely idea, trying to make your birthday special."

Matt shook his head at his wife. "You'd do well to listen and learn. You women and your female notions are a tremendous bother to us men. I would react in exactly the same way if I came home to find paper streamers and sugary roses waiting for me. It's an embarrassment, Sadie. And men do not respond well to embarrassment. I hope you'll remember that."

Sadie blushed, lowering her gaze.

During the afternoon, Stephen sat back and observed Ma and his sisters-in-law waiting on their husbands like servants to their masters. The women seemed to anticipate every need of their men and jumped up to fetch and serve before a request was even made. None of the males had to refill a coffee cup, carry a plate to the kitchen, or even wipe up a crumb. The women were there, waiting and ready to take care of everything. Although the attitudes of the men were overbearing at times, Stephen had to admit the women were eager to please.

Unlike a certain young woman . . .

When Pa had finished his cake and coffee, he sat back in his overstuffed chair, and Priscilla handed him his presents one at a time. Stephen noticed that, ironically enough, Priscilla's gifts to her father were tied with pink ribbon—not a masculine color choice at all. But the man didn't rant and rave at his daughter. He laughingly said, "Why, these ribbons match your dress, Prissy. What a clever idea."

Priscilla beamed. "That nice clerk at the mercantile—David—helped me."

Pa gave Pris a speculative glance but didn't comment. He held the suspenders at arm's length. "Well, now, that's a good-looking pair of braces. And I'll need them after today." He patted his belly, chuckling. "After all that cake, I'll require some help keeping my britches up." It was the closest he would come to complimenting his wife.

He opened his other gifts, gave cursory thank-yous, and set them aside. Then he stood and stretched. "Well, I've had a birthday worth remembering. And since Stephen is going to go back and close down the mill for me, I believe I'll retire to my bedroom and take a little predinner nap. Millie, try to not clink dishes together too much so I won't be disturbed."

"Of course, John," Ma agreed.

Mitchell turned to his wife. "Mary, give Ma a hand here. I'm sure Sadie, Lillian, and Priscilla will help, too."

Stephen's sisters-in-law followed Ma to the kitchen without a word, but Priscilla crossed her arms over her chest. "I already did my part by pulling down Mama's ridiculous streamers in here before Daddy could raise the roof. I intend to go to my room and read."

Mitchell glared at his sister, but he waved his hand. "All right, then, Miss Pris, go read. But be quiet." Priscilla stuck her nose in the air and flounced away to her bedroom. Mitchell looked at Stephen. "She'll never change, will she?"

Stephen shrugged. "Why should she? She's got Pa wrapped around her little finger, and she knows it."

Stanley shook his head. "I pity the poor sap that ends up married to her. Can you imagine?"

Matthew shuddered. "It would be a life sentence of misery." The brothers shared a laugh, then Matthew turned to Stephen. "So when will you be tying the knot, little brother? Heaven knows you're old enough. I'd already been married three years by the time I was your age."

Stephen ducked his head as frustration rolled through his gut. "I reckon I've got time yet."

Mitchell said, "Ma said you were seeing one of the Klaassen girls—Josie, I think. How old is she by now?"

"Eighteen." Stephen set his jaw. Old enough to be married, that was for sure. . . .

"Good age," Stanley mused, smoothing his mustache hairs with thumb and forefinger. "Old enough to know how to take care of things, young enough to be trained."

Stephen shot his brother a startled look, but before he could question Stanley's meaning, Mitchell cut it with a hard laugh.

"You're forgetting that Priscilla is also eighteen, but she's way beyond training."

Stanley rested his elbows on his knees. "But Pris is a special case. You can bet the Klaassen girls were never pampered the way Priscilla has been. Surely that girl—Josie, you said?—is ready for marriage." He turned back to Stephen. "Isn't she?"

Stephen crossed his leg, resting his ankle on his knee and patting the shank of his boot. "So tell me about that horse you bought last week, Stan. Still happy with it?"

Matt shouted out a guffaw. "What's the matter, little brother? Did the girl turn you down?"

Stephen bristled. His brothers could be as annoying as Priscilla when they wanted to be. "Maybe she did. How does that concern you?"

Matt held up his hands in mock surrender, while Stanley and Mitchell chuckled. Mitchell said, "Now, don't get mad, Stephen. Each of us has a good marriage. We want the same for our brother."

"That's right." Stanley nodded. "Come on, talk to us. If there's a problem, maybe we can help."

Stephen looked at the three with narrowed eyes. They were older, and each certainly seemed to be content with the relationship he had with his wife. If they'd set aside their teasing, maybe they could offer some advice on how to deal with Josie's independence. He wasn't sure he wanted to admit that his marriage proposal had been declined, but he could benefit from their experience.

He sighed. "Well, there is a problem." He sent a hesitant glance across their curious faces. "Josie wants to be a teacher instead of getting married right away."

"A teacher?" Stanley gawked at Stephen. "Teaching is for men and old maids. What's a young girl like Josie want with something like that?"

Stephen shrugged. "She's wanted to teach since she was little. Now that she's old enough, she's planning to go to Winston and teach."

Matt asked, "Have you tried to change her mind?"

"Sure I have." Frustration welled again as Stephen remembered his conversations with Josie on the subject. "I asked her to marry me, but she said no, she wants to teach for at least a year first."

Matt shook his head. "That's rough, brother."

Mitchell frowned. "I hope you didn't just give in to her."

Stephen frowned. "What do you mean?"

Mitchell blew out a breath. "I hope you made it clear what you want her to do," he said sarcastically. "Women get funny ideas sometimes, but if the man is firm with his expectations, they always come around. After all, the man is supposed to be the head of the house. Surely Josie knows that."

Stephen swallowed a grim chortle. If Josie knew, she sure didn't indicate it to him. He said, "Josie knows what I want. But she's still going to teach."

Matt slapped his thigh. "Then cut her loose. You don't want to be married to a demanding woman. You'd be battling her all the time. Since you've given in on this point, she'll expect you to give in on the next conflict, and the next, and the next. Pretty soon she'll be running over you just as badly as Pris overruns Pa. Is that what you want?"

Like Pris and Pa? Stephen shuddered. "No, but—"

"No buts," Matt said. "Find yourself a girl who's willing to let you be the man. You'll be better off all the way around."

Stephen sank back on the sofa. In his mind, he reflected on the subservient attitudes shown among his brothers' wives and his mother. Is that how he wanted Josie to be? He didn't think so. But these men had the experience. . . . He sighed. "Maybe you're right."

"Sure he's right." Stanley leaned forward, his expression earnest. "You've never seen Pa kowtowing to Ma, have you? Or us to our wives? Absolutely not. And that's the way it should be. God named woman to be man's helpmeet, and Scripture clearly says she is to respect and honor her husband. It sounds to me like Josie wants to be the one in charge. I say, if that's what she wants, then good riddance. You're better off without her."

Mitchell added, "That's right, Stephen. Remember what Pa always says—living with a rattlesnake is easier than living with a bossy woman."

Stephen weighed his brother's comments against his own conscience. Something didn't set quite right, but he couldn't figure out the source of his unease. With another sigh, he pressed his hands to his thighs and rose. "Well, thanks, brothers." But as he stepped through the kitchen to see his mother and sisters-in-law tiptoeing around in their carefully silent cleanup duties, he wondered whether their mindless submission was preferable to Josie's self-assuredness. His brothers seemed pleased with their situations, but why wouldn't they be? What did the womenfolk think about it? He couldn't imagine expecting such servitude from Josie.

But wouldn't it be easier for both of them if she wasn't so set in her ways?

Confusion sent him out the back door and across the yard, taking a familiar shortcut to the mill. His thoughts continued to roll, snippets of his brothers' advice colliding with the images of the women in his mind. The Bible taught that the man should be the head of his household, but the way his brothers and father ruled their wives . . . An uncomfortable feeling nibbled at him. Was their way the way God intended? Still, he wanted to be the leader in his own home, as Scripture instructed. If Josie was going to be a part of that home, then she was going to have to make some changes—the main one being putting Stephen first.

Stephen stepped into the mill and went through his normal closing-down routine. As he turned the last crank, he made a decision: he'd give Josie the rest of the summer to stew and wonder if she'd managed to lose him, then he'd offer one more chance to give up this silly notion of teaching and become his wife instead. If she still saw teaching as more important than being with him, so be it. He'd let her go.

He squared his shoulders and headed back toward home, his jaw thrust forward. But halfway there, his determination sagged. Can I really let Josie go? The day she'd shown him the letter from the school in Winston, she'd indicated she would pray for him to understand that what was best for her took nothing away from him.

Stephen's steps slowed, his heart heavy. *Lord, I don't know how to pray except to ask . . . don't let her leave me. What would I do without her?*

*J*une and July melted away beneath the punishing summer sun. Minnesota lakes were a source of great pleasure and beauty, but during the hottest months, they were a source of high humidity and contributed to an onslaught of mosquitoes. Josie battled both as she stooped over time and again, plucking gritty green beans from their hiding places within the leafy plants. She stood, swishing her hands around her head in aggravation at the swarm of whining insects that tormented her, then placed a hand on her back and stretched. Mercy, it was hot.

Across the patch, Becky stood straight as well and swept her hand across her forehead and its shimmer of perspiration. "Can we take a break? I'm miserable, Josie."

Josie shot back, "Well, so am I, but standing around bellyaching won't get the beans in. Let's just get it done."

Becky's lower lip poked out. She bent to her task, mumbling, "Don't know why we bother. We'll just have to start all over again tomorrow. Dumb beans multiply like bunnies."

"Don't be so crude, sister. You know better."

Becky glared across the garden, mimicking Josie's grouchy attitude. "And I don't know why Sarah can't be out here helping. I picked plenty of beans when I was her age."

Josie huffed an impatient sigh. "You know she's helping mother wash and peel tomatoes. Those've got to be canned, too."

"I know, I know." Becky grabbed beans off the vines with rising fervor. "But it seems like she always gets the easy jobs."

Josie didn't respond further to Becky's complaints. What could she say? They all had jobs to do, and one was as unpalatable as another as far as she was concerned. All of the family was short-tempered from the hot, humid, long days of work. Well, everyone except her mother.

Josie's head ached from the blast of the sun's heat and the constant stooping. She reminded herself how good the beans would taste boiled with new potatoes, and how welcome they would be during the long winter months when fresh vegetables were unavailable—thoughts that had always managed to change her negative attitude in the past. But this time nothing helped. Josie's positive outlook on life seemed to have disappeared with spring's departure into summer.

If only the summer hadn't proved so disappointing. She'd imagined her last summer at home would be filled with social gatherings and long visits with the people she'd soon leave behind. But Stephen stubbornly avoided her, even at church, and there hadn't been time to get together with schoolmates. Summer was a time for work. So, mostly, she worked.

Foolish, she admitted, to have expected a carefree summer. If anything, her plans to teach had created more tasks to be accomplished—extra clothes to sew, purchases to make and box away for her trip, countless details requiring attention. In only two more weeks, she'd leave for Winston, and she hadn't enjoyed one single evening of fun just for fun's sake. Sweat dribbled into her eyes, stinging as fiercely as the disappointment that stung her heart. She sighed. Becky was right: she needed a break. But a much bigger one than simply a respite from picking beans.

Dropping her basket between rows, she knelt in front of it. Maybe kneeling for a while would relieve her aching back. Her hands were buried deep in the prickly leaves of a bean plant when a shadow fell across her pathway. She looked up, shielding the sunlight with one grubby arm angled above her eyebrows. Slowly her squinting eyes managed to focus. To her surprise, Stephen was looking down at her. She settled back on her heels and gawked at him, her arm still blocking the sun.

"Hello, Josie." The sun sent bluish glints off of his dark, dark hair and lit his deep blue eyes. He'd left the top two buttons of his cotton shirt unfastened, and his tan extended to the exposed wedge of skin. His sleeves were rolled up, revealing muscular forearms and their covering of dark hair. A sheen of perspiration made him glow as the sun beat down. Despite the casual appearance, Josie found him undeniably attractive. But she stayed on her knees. She didn't have the energy to greet him enthusiastically. Once bitten, twice shy . . .

"Hello, Stephen." Her dry throat made her voice sound raspy. She swallowed. "I wasn't expecting to see you."

Stephen shrugged sheepishly and lifted his chin, as if studying the clouds, before looking back at her. "Yeah, well, I guess I've been missing you."

The heat and sweat and her pounding headache combined to result in her sharp retort. "You guess you missed me. . . . You tend to guess about everything, don't you, Stephen?"

Stephen shook his head, pursing his lips. "At it already . . ." He squatted down next to her, picking up a plump green bean from her basket and twirling it between thumb and forefinger.

She dropped her arm. "What brings you here, Stephen?" The question came out on a disinterested sigh.

He bit the inside of his cheek, then said to the bean, "You. I need to talk to you one more time, try to make you understand."

Josie released a great huff of breath. "I don't mean to be rude, but I think I do understand. I understand that what you want right now and what I want right now are two entirely different things. Unless one of us has changed his stance, I don't see any point in dredging it all up again."

It looked like he clenched his jaw so tight the muscles bulged. "I notice you said 'his stance.' You still think I'm in the wrong, don't you?"

Josie met his gaze steadily, brown eyes boring into blue. "Yes, I do."

Stephen lurched to his feet, flinging the green bean back into her basket. He balled his fists and blew out a noisy breath. "Honestly, Josie, I sometimes wonder why I bother. You are by far the most stubborn female I've ever encountered. You just will not give in, will you?"

Josie was on her feet in an instant. "First of all, I am not stubborn. I simply know what is right for me, in here." She thumped her chest with a fist. "And why do I have to be the one to give in? I needed more than that halfhearted proposal from you. All you could give me was a list of 'I want' and 'I think I feel.' I'm supposed to change the plans you know I've been working toward since I was a little girl, based on a maybe? Well, I can't!"

"You mean you won't," Stephen retorted. He flicked a glance at their audience—Becky—listening from the other side of the green-bean patch. He lowered his voice. "Can't we go somewhere private to talk?"

Josie looked at her sister, who gaped unashamedly back at her. She turned to Stephen and shook her head. Tiredness made her head spin. "As I said before, Stephen, I don't see the point. All we'll end up doing is arguing more, and I simply don't have the time or the energy."

Stephen held out his hands. "But, Josie—"

"No." Josie pushed a strand of hair from her eyes. "I've told you how I feel, and that hasn't changed. I love you, but I won't give up my plans to teach because you can't seem to decide if you love me. Until you know for sure, one way or another . . ." Swirling emotions tangled her insides into knots. "I wish you would just leave me alone."

Stephen's voice was hard. "That's what you really want? For me to leave you alone?"

Josie shook her head once, meeting his eyes. "No, Stephen, it's not what I want, but I think it's what is best. If you care for me at all—even a little—please try to stay away from me. When you come, you give me hope, and then you can't say what I need to hear, and that makes things so, so hard for me. So please don't come around here, trying to change my mind, until you can look me in the eyes and honestly tell me you love me."

Stephen stared at her, something in his face making her look away. "Truthfully, the feelings I have right now are far from loving."

His words delivered such pain, he might have slapped her. Josie ducked her head, blinking against a rush of tears.

He went on in a low, grumbling tone. "All right, then. You win . . . for now. Go off to Winston. Go play teacher. But when you're ready to stop chasing silly dreams and come back to reality, don't be surprised if I'm not sitting around waiting for you. After all, turnabout is fair play."

He whirled away, but Josie stepped quickly forward and grabbed his shirtsleeve. "Is that all this is to you, Stephen? A game of comeuppance?"

"Of course not." He yanked his arm free. "I'm not a child."

Josie shook her head slowly. He wasn't a child, but sometimes he behaved like one. He must have read her thoughts, because his face flushed red. He took a giant backward step.

"Good luck to you, Josie. I hope you'll be very happy with your decision. I hope teaching meets your every need." He'd kept his voice quiet—friendly even—but the undercurrents were there. He was making his position abundantly clear.

Josie kept her voice on the same even track he had taken. "Thank you, Stephen. I'm sure everything will work out for the best."

Stephen stomped off, raising his feet high as he stepped through the green-bean patch and made his way to his waiting horse. Josie watched him go, a lump in her throat that felt like it would choke her. He mounted his horse and spun away without a glance back in her direction.

So that's that. Her heart hurt worse than it ever had in her whole life.

"Josie?" Becky's tone held love and sympathy.

Josie turned to face her sister.

"Do you want to go in and . . . I don't know—rest or something?"

Josie sighed. She swallowed hard, trying to dislodge the lump that clogged her throat. She wished she could crawl into a corner somewhere and bawl for an hour or a day or a week, but there was work to be done. She lifted her chin. "No, I don't. Let's just get the beans picked."

Becky used the hem of her dress to wipe the sweat from her forehead and sighed. "I reckon if you can concentrate on picking green beans after losing your beau, then I don't have any right to complain, either." She went back to plucking beans from their vines.

Josie returned to the task as well, but her trembling fingers lost their ability to grasp the beans. With a strangled sob, she pushed to her feet and raced from the patch. She'd enjoy a lengthy cry in the barn. Then maybe she'd be able to work.

On Josie's last Saturday at home, Pa and Ma hosted a large party in her honor. They invited the entire congregation of the Bruderthaler Mennoniten-Gemeinde, and half of the church members attended. People wandered everywhere in the yard and house, drinking lemonade, eating watermelon and crullers, and enjoying an afternoon of pleasant conversation.

Priscilla Koehn and her parents were in attendance, but to Josie's enormous disappointment, Stephen didn't come. Even though their last conversation had gone very badly, she still had hoped he would come for old time's sake. His mother made shamefaced apologies for him, with the excuse he was needed at the mill. Josie suspected the truth, but she wouldn't let Stephen's stubbornness spoil her day.

She'd fixed her hair in a puff that resembled half a donut strung from ear to ear on the back of her head, donned one of her new "teacher" dresses—the green watch-plaid skirt and ruffled blouse, and pinned the cameo at her throat. Becky claimed the grown-up dress and hairstyle added years to Josie's look of maturity and professionalism, and she felt sophisticated and confident as she moved among the circles of family members and friends in her fine clothes and fancy hairdo.

As the afternoon progressed, a few wispy tendrils of hair worked themselves loose from the hairpins and waved in the breeze. She was pushing at one strand that continually drifted across her face as she tried to carry on a conversation with David.

He laughed at her attempts to keep the hair out of her eyes. "Here, let me help." Josie stood still while he tucked it back into its place. "There. That's got it."

"Thank you, David." Josie shot him a bright smile. "Goodness, my hair just never wants to behave."

"Well, then, your students better not take their cues from their teacher's hair." They both laughed, and David added,

"Actually, it never looks ill-mannered to me. This style is particularly becoming on you." He surveyed the loose puff with exaggerated interest. "How do you do that, anyway?"

Josie's chuckle was short and rueful. "By standing on my head, almost. A braid is sure easier, but I guess now that I'm the teacher, I'll need to look like more than a farm girl."

"Well, the teachers I remember pulled it straight back into a tight little bun, put a pair of glasses on the end of their noses, and looked at all of us like this." He lifted his chin, arched his eyebrows high, and made a prune face.

She burst out laughing. "But I don't wear glasses."

David shrugged and dropped the pose. "Forget it, then. It wouldn't be effective."

Locking her hands behind her back, Josie swayed in place, enjoying their teasing banter. Over the recent weeks in Mountain Lake, David had gradually lost his reserve, and she enjoyed seeing this relaxed side emerge. She wouldn't mind visiting with him longer, but other guests required attention too. With a reluctant sigh, she started to excuse herself, but he spoke first.

"You know, Josie, I'm going to miss you." No hint of teasing colored his tone.

Warmth filled Josie's cheeks. She flicked a glance at his sober face. "I—I'll miss you, too, David." She realized she meant it. "You've become a friend. A good friend."

A smile lifted the corners of his lips, but something akin to disappointment lingered in his eyes. He said, "You'll have to make sure you look me up on the weekends and let me know how your teaching is going. I'll bet I get only good reports, though. You're bound to be a wonderful teacher."

How she appreciated his words of affirmation! "Thank you, David. Thank you very much. And I will be sure to let you know.

I'll see you at church on Sundays, and as always you'll join us for Sunday dinner from time to time."

"That sounds good."

She took a deep breath. "Well, I guess I should—"

"I ought to let you—" he said at the same time.

They both laughed. He motioned with his hand. "Please, ladies first."

"I guess I should see to my other guests."

He offered an elegant bow. "And I ought to let you."

She flashed David a smile of farewell then moved toward two women from church. She couldn't resist sending a glance over her shoulder, and she caught David standing still as a statue, gazing after her. Something in his expression made her pulse hiccup. The look of longing in his eyes lingered in her memory as she moved among the crowd.

avid watched Josie joining a group of older women, who welcomed her with hugs and immediately included her in the conversation. He shook his head, marveling. Josie was so charming and caring, she fit with young or old, male or female.

How many heads would she turn when she arrived in Winston? He couldn't help but feel uncomfortable with that idea. Samantha had confided that Josie and Stephen had suffered a falling out that appeared to be permanent, which left the door open for him . . . but only if no one else came along. How could he keep himself in the forefront?

An idea struck him.

David headed out across the yard to corner Adam, who was visiting with a gray-haired man in striped bib overalls. David interrupted them midsentence. "Adam, how—?" Realizing what he had done, he apologized and stepped back.

The man with Adam lifted a hand in farewell. "I guess I'll go get myself something to drink. See you later, Adam."

"I'm very sorry—"

"No problem." Adam clapped David on the shoulder. "I was ready to move on to another topic anyway. You can only discuss the fertility problems of swine for so long." Both laughed and ambled toward the table that held the watermelon. Adam asked, "What were you going to say?"

"I was wondering how Josie will be getting back and forth from Winston." He was pleased at how casual he'd kept his tone.

Adam picked up a huge knife and whacked off a slice of watermelon, halved it, and handed one piece to David. "We're all taking turns—Pa and Frank and me—and maybe Jake or Arn once in a while," Adam said around a mouthful. "With harvest in full swing, it'll be tough working it all out. But if we alternate, it shouldn't put any one of us out too badly. Why do you ask?"

David leaned over and held the dripping watermelon well in front of him. "Would it help if I volunteered to make the trip each weekend?"

Adam eyebrows shot high, and he spit out two seeds. "Are you serious?"

David took a bite of his own slice of watermelon, trying not to appear too eager. "If it would help, I'd be glad to." He waved the melon in the air. "I'm always done at the mercantile by two on Fridays, so I could go then and have her home by supper time. Then I could run her back on Sunday afternoons. It wouldn't be a problem for me."

Adam chewed the inside of his mouth, his brow puckered in thought. "Well, it sure would free us up. At least on Fridays . . . Sundays we wouldn't be working anyway, so you wouldn't need to go both times."

"Well, suit yourself, but I wouldn't mind." David nibbled at the slice of watermelon, his heart pounding with hope.

Adam said, "I'll talk to Pa about it, if you're sure it wouldn't be an inconvenience for you."

An inconvenience? Four hours every weekend with Josie? His pulse doubled its tempo at the pleasurable thought. He continued his light tone. "It would be no trouble at all. And I'd enjoy the chance to get out a bit. I'm pretty confined to the store most of the time."

"As I say, I'll mention it to Pa, and his will be the final word. But I'm sure he'll appreciate your willingness to help out. We do need to be in the fields this time of year, and any daylight hours are valuable." Adam flung the rind of his melon into a big barrel and wiped his hands on his pants legs. "Thanks, David. And Pa will let you know if it will work out."

David smiled. "Sure thing."

An hour later, as the crowd was thinning, Simon Klaassen caught up with David. "Thanks for offering to take Josie back and forth to her teaching job. I'd be glad to pay you for your trouble."

Time with Josie would be payment enough. "That's certainly not necessary—"

"Well, we'll settle that later. I'll make sure either Arn or Teddy is available to ride along too." Si sent a glance around the yard at the people gathered in small groups, then gave David an apologetic glance. "Not that I don't trust you, David, but it's best not to open the door for idle gossip. We don't want people to get the wrong idea."

David hadn't considered the propriety of the situation. The thought of a chaperone took a bit of his anticipation down a notch, but he'd tolerate the extra company to keep unpleasant speculation at bay. "That sounds fine."

"I'd already asked Jost about renting one of his buggies; he has some comfortable two-bench ones that would work well. Can't spare my wagon for the length of time it'd take you to drive there and back. But if you're sure you don't mind committing so much of your weekend, we'd like to accept your offer."

David sucked in a breath, holding back his shout of elation. He gave a little shrug. "I'm sure, and I appreciate it."

"All right then. It's settled. Thank you, David." Si whacked David lightly on the shoulder and sauntered off.

David jammed his hands into his pockets before he socked the air in jubilation. His chest expanded, joy exploding behind his ribs.

Josie, our friendship will blossom into something more. I just know it. Life is grand!

❧

David drove Jost's finest buggy—a Cabriolet Phaeton usually rented by wedding parties, which he thought had some nice implications—to the Klaassen farm Sunday afternoon. He felt like a prince seated on the tufted leather seat with the carriage's brass lanterns gleaming in the afternoon sunlight. He, Josie, and Teddy would ride in style for the twenty-mile drive into Winston.

As Arn and Si loaded Josie's trunk and woven satchel on the backseat of the buggy, Josie hovered near, clasping and unclasping her hands in excitement. She wore her new garnet dress and the ostrich-feather hat, held in place with her graduation hatpin. Her hair was pinned into the puff that David had admired. It provided a perfect setting for the fashionable little hat. "Leave room for Teddy," she admonished. She shook her head, looking at the narrow gap remaining between her items. "It's a good thing Arn isn't the one going this time. He'd never fit back there."

As soon as Si and Arn stepped back, Teddy clambered into the buggy and wedged himself into the seat with a chuckle. "Just right," he called out, his grin wide. "Let's go!"

David stood on the left side of the buggy, watching Laura hug Josie long and hard, rocking her back and forth. "Take care, *liebchen*," he heard her say.

Josie whispered, "I will, Mama. Don't worry about me." Josie moved from Laura's embrace to Si's, and David looked away, feeling a bit like an eavesdropper as Si murmured last-minute endearments and cautions against Josie's hat.

Becky gave her sister a quick hug accompanied by an impudent grin. "Goodie—with you away, I get my own room. I won't have to sleep with Sarah anymore."

"That's what you think," Josie retorted, pinching her sister cheerfully on the end of her nose. "I'll be back every weekend, and I intend to be in my own room."

"Yeah," Sarah said, sticking her tongue out at Becky. She squeezed Josie tight around the middle. "I'll miss you, Josie."

"I'll miss you, too, imp."

Arn offered a manly handshake, but Josie laughed at him and hugged him anyway, sending color flooding his cheeks.

She stepped back and hunched her shoulders, reminding David of a little turtle trying to shrink into its shell. "Well . . . I said good-bye yesterday to Adam and Sam, Liz and Jake, and Frank and Anna at the party, so I suppose that means I'm ready to go." But she didn't move toward the buggy.

Teddy bounced on the backseat. "So come on and get in. What'cha waiting for?"

Josie, shoulders still high, gave a small chuckle. "I don't know. I've been looking forward to this day for years, but now that the moment of leave-taking is upon me, I—I don't want to go." Another giggle ended in a strangled sob. "I suppose—I suppose dreams up close look different than when they're just . . . dreams." She turned to Laura and burst into tears. "Oh, Mama!"

Laura wrapped Josie in her arms another time. "Now, now . . . It's a big step, honey, leaving home for the first time. You're bound to be a little scared, but you'll be just fine. We're only twenty miles away, and we'll see you again in less than a week, so you aren't leaving forever."

"I know." Josie sniffed against her mother's shoulder. "I feel so silly."

Laura pulled a handkerchief out of her pocket and gave it to her daughter. "I'm going to need it back if you don't stop it," she said with another hug and some chuckles around the little circle.

David was touched more than he could fathom. What must it be like, to feel such bittersweet emotions at leaving one's home? He could only imagine.

Si stepped in and guided Josie gently toward the buggy. "You're not silly, Josie. You're getting butterflies, which is to be expected. But your mother is right. You will be fine. We've watched you grow up, and you've got the gumption to see this through. You've also got all our love and prayers going with you. And to come home to."

Josie dabbed at her eyes. "Thank you, Papa. That's everything I need." She fell against him, wrapping an arm clear around his neck. He squeezed back, then helped her up into her seat.

David climbed in beside her. Si held Josie's hand while looking at David. "Have a safe ride."

"We will, sir." David smiled at Josie. "Are you ready?"

Josie took in a big breath, determination glowing in her brown eyes. "I'm ready." David brought down the reins and the horse started forward.

The family waved and called, "Good-bye, Josie! Good luck! We'll see you soon!" as the buggy pulled out of the yard and into the lane. Josie and Teddy turned completely around, waving and calling back.

When they had rounded the bend, Teddy began a close examination of this fancy new mode of travel. David glanced at Josie and saw unshed tears glittering in her eyes, and she was back to clasping and unclasping her hands in her lap.

David tried to think of a way to distract her from her worries. Finally he asked, "Want to hear something funny?"

She turned her face to him, but no interest lit her face.

"Back there, when you were saying your good-byes, I felt kind of envious."

Josie's eyebrows rose. "Envious? Why?"

David offered a self-conscious shrug. "Because it was so hard for you to leave your family, even for such a short while. It must be wonderful to love them so much when it makes you so miserable to leave."

"Oh, David, I'm so sorry you didn't feel that way when you left home." Her eyes were full of sympathy.

David chuckled. "You're sorry I wasn't miserable?"

Josie made a face. "You know what I mean. And I'm not exactly miserable right now—not really. More just nervous . . . and contemplative. Even though I'll be going back on the weekends, I know it will never be the same. I'll never live at home full time again, and I won't be Mama and Papa's little girl anymore. As exciting as it all is, it's rather scary too."

David nodded. "I know what you mean. But you're ready, Josie. Your whole life, your parents have been preparing you for this day, by teaching you to be independent and to think for yourself." He paused. "And I've got news for you. No matter how grown up you get, to your folks, you'll always be their little girl. I can tell."

Josie smiled and placed a hand on his knee for just a moment. "Thank you, David."

"For what?"

"For making me feel better. You really are a good friend." She gave him a dazzling smile that lit his insides clear to his toes.

"Hey, guys—I saw a doe and two fawns!" Teddy called from behind them. "They must have been born last spring. . . ." and on the boy went in his excitement.

David had a hard time concentrating though. The feel of Josie's hand on his knee, and the sincere appreciation in her eyes, remained in the forefront of his mind as they trundled on toward Josie's new life.

*T*hose feelings of acceptance and appreciation carried David through the week. He worked industriously at the mercantile, cheerfully waited on customers, and efficiently delivered the orders, opened crates, and put away arriving stock. And all week he looked forward to Friday, when he would drive to Winston for Josie.

Jost had promised to have the buggy ready and waiting for David on Friday afternoon. When three o'clock rolled around, all David had to do was wait for Teddy to trot from the schoolhouse to the mercantile, and the two of them would walk to the livery.

Mr. Jost offered a friendly howdy, but David didn't waste time on chitchat. He gave Teddy a boost into the front seat, then climbed in beside him and headed for Winston.

Although well into September, the day held a summer-like feel. Trees were green and full, a cheerful playground for chattering squirrels and raucous blue jays. A grainy scent from cut wheat filled the air, and the marigolds continued to bloom on each side of the road. Teddy's head was lifted to the sky. David flicked a glance upward and caught sight of a circling hawk high up, no doubt looking for his supper.

The horse's hooves landed briskly against the dirt road, sending up tiny puffs of dust. Each clip-clop brought him closer to Winston. Closer to Josie. A perfect day.

David drove directly to the school building rather than the boardinghouse. Josie had told him she'd stay there and correct papers until he arrived, then they would go together to the boardinghouse to collect her bag for the weekend. He pulled up in front of the tall, square brick building and set the brake. Just as he hopped down, Josie emerged from the building and ran down the wide concrete steps.

"David, you're here!" She nearly knocked him off balance with her welcoming hug. Then she whirled on Teddy, capturing him a in hug that lifted him from the ground. "Hey, little brother! It looks like you grew!"

Teddy wriggled loose and gave his sister an impish grin. "Did you make the kids mind?"

She laughed. "You bet I did."

"You must have had a good week. You sure sound—and look—happy," David commented.

"Oh, I had a wonderful week, David! I can't wait to tell you about it, but first I need to collect my things from my desk, and I'd like you to meet the other teachers—oh! and come in and see my classroom. I've already had the children hang some of their pictures on the walls to cheer up the room. Come on!" She caught Teddy's hand and David's arm, tugging them both toward the school building.

Josie was bubbling with excitement as she pointed out the cloakroom, her classroom, and the others in the building. The three teachers were still in their rooms, so she introduced them in turn—Miss English, a bookish-looking woman who appeared to be somewhere in her forties and taught the fourth through sixth grades, Mr. Tompkins, the seventh- through ninth-grade teacher who sported a thick beard that compensated for his thinning scalp, and Mr. Isaac, who taught the oldest students and looked as if he might have swallowed a persimmon.

In comparison, Josie appeared thirteen years old, but she didn't seem to be fazed by it. She chattered constantly as they made their rounds, and as she left the building she called out gaily, "Good-bye, everyone! I'll see you on Monday."

"So, what do you think?" she asked as they headed for the boardinghouse, side by side on the front seat while Teddy draped his arms over the backrest.

David nudged Teddy's hand, winked at him, then joked to Josie, "So you mean you're going to let us talk now?"

Teddy snickered and Josie grinned. "Sure. It's your turn now. What do you think?"

David couldn't take his eyes off her. I *think you're adorable* hovered on the tip of his tongue, but with Teddy hanging over the seat between them, he didn't dare. "I think you've found your niche. You love it, don't you?"

"Oh, I do. I am so glad I came! And I have so much to tell you."

Josie talked nonstop all the way to the boardinghouse, then instructed David and Teddy to wait in the parlor while she put her books away and grabbed her satchel, informing them in a whisper, "Mrs. Porter doesn't allow male visitors in our rooms. Even if one of them is my brother."

Teddy roamed the room, openly curious, while David sat on a camelback sofa that smelled of mothballs, staring at a ticking grandfather clock. He couldn't get over the change in Josie. She'd always been cheerful, but now—why, she glowed. She didn't talk, she bubbled. She didn't walk, she bounded. She didn't merely smile, she beamed. It was as if a cocoon had been split and a butterfly had been released, flitting and winging its way through a bright new world.

A clattering on the stairs caught his attention. Josie, wearing her bright smile of happy abandon, skipped into the room. She put down her satchel and aimed a finger at him. "I'll be right back," she said on her way past. She disappeared through a door at the rear of the parlor, and he could hear her voice coming from somewhere down a hallway.

"Mrs. Porter, I'm leaving for home. I'll be back Sunday afternoon." Another voice answered something David couldn't catch, and then he heard Josie's soft laughter before she added, "Yes, that's true. Well, good-bye now."

Then she was back, still seeming to float, still with shining eyes. "Well, fellows, are you ready? Yes? Then let's go." She ushered Teddy out the door. David trailed on their heels with the satchel.

She clambered aboard without assistance. David swung the satchel into the backseat, and Teddy immediately curled against it, looking like he might be getting ready for a nap. David stepped in beside Josie, who sat on the edge of the front seat, hands on knees and arms straight, holding herself erect. With her chin angled high, she seemed almost to be drinking in the air. David couldn't stop marveling.

The instant the reins touched the horse's broad back and the buggy squeaked into motion, Josie sat back and began talking. She told him how nervous she'd been when first faced with the roomful of giggling youngsters; how she'd broken the piece of chalk while trying to write her name on the board; how she'd played ball with the children at recess and hit a homerun, endearing herself to the third-grade boys; how one little boy named Bradley had run up to her excitedly on the first day.

"He was so cute, David!" she enthused. "He has all this spiky red hair sticking up and freckles all over his face and no teeth in the front—just the cutest little boy—and instead of saying hello he tells me, 'My papa made me a coaus-er wagon for my birfday an' that thing juth goeth like heck. Mebbe you can come thee it thometime an' I'll give you a ride.'" She'd repeated the child's words verbatim in a little-boy contralto, even including his lisp. "Oh, I fell in love on the spot."

"Hmm," David mused, finally getting a word in. "So only a week away from home, and you already have a beau, huh?"

Josie laughed. "You betcha. Bradley's one of my first graders. I must admit, I like the littlest children the best, but they'll never hear it from me. I treat them all equally." And she went on to tell story after story, needing no encouragement from David to continue.

David was enchanted as her happiness spilled over in every word and gesture. Would she be this happy at the end of every week? He hoped the joy wouldn't wear off when teaching was no longer new. Then he had a worrisome new thought. If she was always this happy—if teaching fulfilled her completely—she wouldn't feel the need for anything else . . . like a home and family of her own.

He pushed the niggling worry aside as selfish of him and determined to enjoy riding with her beneath a cloudless sky, listening to her happy chatter and basking in her joy.

They finally rattled up the lane that led to the farm. She had suddenly quieted, straining for a glimpse of her home. He gave her a sidelong glance and asked what he'd wondered about since they left the boardinghouse. "What was true?"

She shot him a mystified look. "What?"

"Back when you were telling your landlady good-bye, I heard you laugh and say it was true. What was true?"

To his amazement, Josie blushed crimson, the color spreading from her collar clear to her hairline. She turned her face forward. "She—um—she said something, and I just agreed."

What could have created such a reaction? Curiosity got the best of him, and he couldn't help but push the issue. "What did she say?"

Josie cleared her throat and suddenly became very interested in a hangnail on her right thumb. "She said—she merely said, 'That's a handsome young man sitting in my parlor.'"

David held his lips against a delighted smile. "And you said, 'That's true'?"

She nodded, still bright pink.

Now it was David's turn to blush, but from pleasure, not discomfort. She had agreed that he was a handsome young man, and he wanted to crow in celebration. But with embarrassment staining her cheeks, he didn't intend to put a damper on her cheerful spirits.

"Well," he said, keeping his tone light, "that was a polite thing for her to say. But actually, I thought your parents had taught you to be honest."

Josie peeked at him out of the corner of her eyes. Slowly her lips curved into a grin, and her eyes snapped with mischief. "She did, and stop your fishing for more compliments."

"Agreed," David answered around his own grin.

Teddy roused, blinked around, then leaped out of the buggy as it rolled to a stop. He dashed across the yard, bellowing, "Ma! Ma! Josie's home!"

The back door flew open and Laura emerged, arms outstretched, followed closely by Sarah and Becky. Josie hopped down and into her mother's waiting embrace.

"Josie, it's so good to have you home!"

"Oh, Mama, it was just wonderful! I have so much to tell you. The children . . ."

The two women had linked arms and were headed for the house with Becky and Sarah trotting along on their heels. David swung Josie's satchel from the back of the buggy and gave it to Teddy. He grabbed it and ran to catch up with his family, the bag banging against his knees as he ran. When the women reached the stoop, Josie turned back and waved at David.

"Thank you for coming for me, David!" And then her attention returned to her mother and siblings as they entered the house together, shutting the door behind them.

David stayed where he was for a few minutes, absorbing the wonder of the day. The joyous hug of greeting, the cheerful chatter, the admission that he was thought to be a handsome young man . . . And the homecoming. What he wouldn't give to be welcomed home as readily and joyfully as Josie had been.

He turned toward the buggy. Before he took two steps, Teddy came pounding across the yard. "Hey, David, Ma says come on in and have some supper with us."

More time in Josie's company? He wouldn't turn down the opportunity. He clamped a hand around the back of Teddy's neck. "That sounds just fine, Teddy. Thanks for the invitation."

The two walked back to the house where David got to sit across from Josie, whose beaming face and more endless chatter filled his senses. He ate Laura's wonderful cooking but tasted not a thing. No one else got a word in—Josie's stories filled every minute of conversation. David had heard them once already, but he didn't mind a repeat performance. He had decided somewhere between Winston and the Klaassens' dinner table that he wouldn't mind listening to Josie for the rest of his life.

fter the first weekend of transporting Josie, David established a routine. He'd retrieve the buggy from the livery at three o'clock Friday afternoons with Teddy in tow, drive to Winston, enjoy a pleasant two hours of private conversation with Josie while Teddy drowsed or read in the back, then stay for the evening meal with the Klaassens before returning the buggy to Jost's. After church Sunday, he'd go out to the farm for *faspa* and a couple of hours of relaxation before driving Josie back to Winston once more.

By the time October arrived, the ride was cool enough for a quilted lap robe, the leaves had changed from green to gold, and Josie and David had developed an easy friendship that made both look forward to their weekly drives.

Casual sharing of the week's activities gradually changed to serious conversations covering a variety of topics, some of them rather heartfelt. David slowly opened up, dropping the air of indifference he carried with most people and giving Josie rare glimpses of what his life had been like before he had come to Mountain Lake and was reunited with Samantha.

In turn, Josie began to share her deepest thoughts and feelings. It was only natural that in time, some of those feelings would involve Stephen. After all, he'd been a big part of Josie's life, and both of them knew it.

David, though, was unprepared for the turn their relationship would take when Josie told him about Stephen's position in her life and heart.

On the third Sunday in October, Josie was commenting on the beautiful colors of the leaves. "I particularly like the maples." She pointed to a stand along the road. "Look at the variety of color. Orange, gold, red . . . It's as if an artist painted them for his own personal pleasure."

"They are beautiful," David agreed.

"I think I'll take the children for a walk to gather leaves, and then we'll make printings with them. Have you ever done that?"

David shook his head. "No, I guess not. How's it done?"

"Oh, it's simple." Josie pulled the lap robe a little more snugly around herself. "You brush a light coat of paint on the back side of a leaf, then press it down on paper. When you lift it up, the imprint of the leaf will remain. You can overlap several colors, and it makes a wonderful collage." She pantomimed her instructions as she spoke.

David shot her a quick grin. "Sounds pretty. Did you come up with that yourself?"

"Oh, no, a teacher I had when I was a child showed us how." She sat for a moment, then laughed to herself, as if remembering something. "You know, it was the day we did leaf prints that I first really noticed Stephen."

David felt like his heart stopped temporarily. He gave the reins a little flick and forced a casual tone. "Is that right?"

"Uh-huh." When Josie turned sideways in the seat, bending her knee to fold it up underneath her, it grazed his thigh beneath the lap robe. "I must have been a second grader then. A toothless, freckled wonder!" She gave a brief snort of laughter that David echoed before she continued. "The whole class gathered up leaves, and then we made these leaf prints. I was so proud of mine. I thought it was the most beautiful work I'd ever done.

"Well, even back then, Priscilla was a spoiled brat and troublemaker! After school, I was waiting outside the building for Liz and Adam and Frank and Daniel, and Priscilla came up and asked to see my picture. I was so proud of it, I mistakenly showed it off to her. And what does she do? She drops it in a mud puddle—on purpose, of course." Josie's arms were waving around, and her face was animated to match the various dynamics of her tale. "Oh, I was so upset. I started bawling and carrying on, and Priscilla acted all sorry and tried to wipe the mud off, but all she did was make it worse."

David hid a smile. If she was this lively in front of her classroom of small students, she'd have no trouble holding their attention. "That sounds like Priscilla, all right."

"Doesn't it, though?" Josie raised her eyebrows and gave a quick nod. "I stood outside, crying my eyes out, and here comes Stephen. He was already a big boy by then—twelve or thirteen. Since he was a friend of my brother Frank, he knew me, too. He came over and asked me what was wrong. I pointed at Priscilla and blubbered out what she'd done to my picture. Well, he took Priscilla's leaf picture away from her, dropped it in the same mud puddle, and stepped on it. Then he gave it back to her and asked her how it felt to have her picture ruined. Oh, you should have heard her screech! She ran home, howling all the way— you could hear her from three blocks' distance!"

David laughed. "I can imagine. She does have a set of lungs."

"I found out later that Stephen got a whipping from his father for spoiling Priscilla's picture." Josie straightened her leg and turned forward again in the seat. "After that, Stephen was my hero. I thought he was bravest, most handsome boy in town." Her voice had lost its animated tone and now sounded melancholy. She paused, her head cocked sideways, lost in thought.

David sneaked a glance at her. Had he ever, in his entire lifetime, impressed anyone the way Stephen had impressed that little seven-year-old Josie? They rode in silence for several minutes before she turned to him with a deep sadness in her brown eyes.

"You know, David, when Stephen started calling on me, I was—" She paused, searching for the right words. "I don't know. Astounded, I guess. I'd had a crush on him ever since that day he got back at Priscilla in my defense. I idolized him, but I figured he only saw me as a little kid. He and Frank called me 'little tagalong' when I trailed after them on the playground. 'Go along, little tagalong,' they'd say when I dogged their steps. But while Frank scowled, Stephen would grin when he said it. I never felt like he was slighting me."

David had held the impression that it was all over between Josie and Stephen, but maybe that was because he wanted that to be the case. During these weeks on the road between Mountain Lake and Winston, she hadn't mentioned the man except in passing. But now David was forced to realize her feelings for Stephen went back a long ways—and they hadn't changed. From the longing in her eyes and her pensive tone, he could see she still cared for him deeply. David's hands tightened on the reins.

She went on in that same hurt tone. "I think I loved him even before he started courting me. I could talk to him so easily, and he always listened."

"Listened, but didn't understand." The words slipped out before he could stop them.

"Don't judge Stephen by his recent behavior, David." Defensiveness had crept into Josie's voice. "You haven't known him as long as I have. I can't understand why he's been so bullheaded about my teaching, because it just isn't like him. The Stephen I fell in love with is kind and considerate and giving. . . ." As her voice trailed off, David's heart sank further, and he tried to swallow the lump in his throat.

He remembered his initial impression of Stephen. He had liked him—genuinely liked him—and had thought they could be friends. But when Stephen had hurt Josie, David had pulled away from him, turning his attentions toward Josie instead. Now he wondered . . . had he gotten to know Stephen better, would he have found him to be the type of person Josie had just described? He remembered, too, Hulda Klaassen's description of Stephen as a fine young man, worth ten of Priscilla. David realized he had been casting stones without the right to do so.

He reached over and touched Josie's arm. When she looked at him he said, "I'm sorry. You're right—I don't know Stephen, and I have no business putting him down."

She gave a sad smile. "I suppose it really doesn't matter, because I'm sure I've lost him." Her brown eyes flooded with sudden tears, and she turned away to dash the moisture away. "He hardly even looks at me anymore, and we certainly don't talk. After all those years of following him around, dreaming of him, loving him . . . it just hurts to have to let go." She pressed her lips together, then burst out with, "If only I could understand."

David's thoughts turned inward. If Stephen could have seen Josie bound out of that school after her first week of teaching, he'd realize Josie was born to this. Maybe the man would then put his own wants aside long enough for her to do what she was meant to do. But I guess when you've waited for years for a little girl to grow into a woman . . .

Realization struck. Why, that had to be why Stephen had been so adamant about Josie staying in Mountain Lake, marrying him immediately. He had been watching Josie grow up, waiting for her to be old enough to become a wife. And then when she was old enough, she wasn't ready for the role. How frustrating that must have been. David could almost sympathize with the man.

Josie sat in silence on the seat beside him, obviously also lost in thought. Should he interrupt her contemplations to tell her about his observations? It might help her understand Stephen, maybe even encourage her to try to reconcile with him.

But did he really want to help her reconcile with Stephen? It pained him to see her sorrow, but wouldn't she eventually give up her childhood fantasy? And then she would see David in a new, deeper light. Right now they were friends—close enough for her to share her greatest hurt. If he continued to be her friend and confidant, surely she would be able to put those old feelings for Stephen aside and lean on a new hero.

David had a fleeting thought that a true friend would do everything possible to ease a burden. . . . What should he do?

While he was still debating the issue, Josie spoke. "David, I'm so glad it's worked out for you to take me back and forth to Winston."

"I've enjoyed it, too, Josie."

She smiled at him, but it didn't quite reach her eyes—she still looked sad. "I appreciate the friendship we've developed. You'd think with all the brothers and sisters I have, I wouldn't need anyone else to talk to, but there are some things I just couldn't say to any of them." She sent a quick glance into the backseat, making sure Teddy still slept. She looked at David again. "They are too close to me. They'd immediately jump to my defense, and while I understand that only means they love me, it isn't always helpful. Sometimes you just need to get everything out and look at it logically instead of trying to fault find."

David considered her comments. While he wanted to be more than a sounding board, he was pleased that Josie felt comfortable enough to tell him things she wouldn't share with someone else. He began carefully, "You mean a lot to me, too.

I want you to be happy." But I *want to be the one to make you happy, not Stephen.*

She sat quietly, biting her lip. He got the impression she was trying to decide whether or not to tell him something. He knew when she had gotten her thoughts straightened out, because she took in a big breath and turned to him, looking at the same time apologetic and determined. He braced himself.

"David, because we are such good friends, I feel I can tell you this without you misinterpreting my true intentions."

David held his breath.

"You've been so helpful, taking me back and forth every week, and I don't want you to think I don't appreciate it. It's a lot of hours of your time that could be spent elsewhere, and I've enjoyed the talks and the opportunity for us to get to know one another. I just wonder if . . ." She broke off, her eyebrows pulling downward.

David, on pins and needles, prodded, "You wonder if . . . ?"

She drew in a deep breath, then blurted out, "It's possible that if Stephen drove me back and forth, he wouldn't feel left out of my life, and maybe . . . maybe we could work things out between us," she finished in a rush.

David's breath came out in a long "Ohhh . . ."

Her face drew together as if she would cry. "I'm sorry, David. I didn't mean to say . . . well, I didn't mean it to sound like I'd rather be with Stephen than you."

David managed a low chuckle, his eyes on the horse's rump. "Hmm. I think you just did."

She turned crimson. "But I didn't mean I didn't want you to—oh! I don't know how to say it. Forget I said anything." Scooting down in the seat, she crossed her arms and turned her face away, looking like a disgruntled first grader.

Despite himself, David had to laugh. "Hey, what would you do if one of your young students behaved this way?" But she obviously didn't see the humor. So he bumped her with his elbow. "All right, Josie my friend."

She didn't budge but grumbled, "What?"

"Are you pouting?"

"No."

"You look like you're pouting."

"Well!" She shot him a scowl. "You're mad at me."

"I'm not mad."

"Yes, you are."

"Would I be laughing if I was mad?"

"I don't know. Maybe."

"Well, I'm not mad. Disappointed, perhaps, but not mad."

She finally looked at him and straightened up in her seat. "Disappointed?"

He shrugged. "I've enjoyed these rides, too. It gets me outside instead of being cooped up in your uncle's store all the time. And I look forward to . . . our conversations." His heart skipped a beat as he dared to add, "I cherish your friendship, Josie. I don't want to lose it."

"Oh, David," she said, leaning toward him, "I wasn't trying to get rid of our friendship. But it has developed and gotten stronger because of these rides, and I thought maybe it might do the same for Stephen and me. I love him so much, and I really miss him. . . ."

David's chest went tight once more. Oh, how he wished she could say such things about him. A friend. She considered him just a friend. He sighed. "Well, Josie, if that's what you want to do, ask him. I just hope he won't disappoint you—again." He peeked at her sideways without moving his head.

She was biting on her lip again. "You're sure you wouldn't mind?"

Oh, he minded all right. But how could he say that without opening himself up to a whole new conflict? No, the best he could hope for was that Stephen's stubbornness would hold out, and he'd be there to pick up the broken pieces of Josie's heart.

He tried a half truth. "It sounds like that would be worth a try, Josie. But would it be okay if I still made the drive occasionally? I think I'd miss it." *And you.*

Josie smiled joyfully, her cheerful spirit restored. "No, I wouldn't mind. Besides, I have to keep my best friend up to date on everything, don't I? When else would we get a chance to talk?"

Best friend . . . Those words caught him right below the breastbone and held with almost a physical pressure. No one had ever called him a best friend. Although it wasn't what he had anticipated when he began making these trips, it felt good. It warmed him.

By now they were both familiar with the road and knew the landmarks, and Winston was waiting just over the next hill. Josie perked up, looking ahead, going into her "teacher mode" as David called it. It tickled him the way her concentration turned inward when they reached this spot in the road. She most thoroughly enjoyed her position.

As he helped her down from the buggy in front of the boardinghouse, she woke Teddy to tell him good-bye, then gave David her usual sisterly hug. After turning toward the door, she suddenly slapped a palm to her forehead and exclaimed, "Oh! Dummy me! I nearly forgot." She came back and said, "Next weekend I won't be coming home. The other teachers and I have meetings with the school board on Saturday, and they'll be doing an evaluation on me, so I have to be here."

David protested, "But next Saturday evening is the party at the schoolhouse to celebrate the end of harvest. You won't be home for that?"

Josie's face scrunched together in disappointment. "I want to be there, but I can't. I have to go to those meetings. Please tell Ma and Pa for me, will you? And I'll see you in two weeks."

David heaved a sigh. "All right. I'll do that." He carried her satchel up the walkway and into the parlor. She took it with a thank-you and held on to it with two hands against her skirt. The landlady, Mrs. Porter, sat on her starched sofa with some knitting, observing them through her round-lensed spectacles.

"Thank you again for the ride," Josie told David primly.

Aware of Mrs. Porter's sharp ears, David responded formally. "Certainly, Josie, I enjoyed it. I'll pass the word along about next weekend, and then I'll see you the following Friday." He leaned forward and gave her a friendly kiss on the cheek that set Mrs. Porter's needles clacking.

"Bye, David, take care." Her customary parting.

He returned to the buggy, swinging himself into the seat and tugging the lap robe tight around his legs. He took a moment to pull on gloves; it would be dark and much cooler by the time they reached Mountain Lake. He looked up at the lace-shrouded window he knew belonged to Josie, and waited for the light to appear. He shook his head sadly. Two weeks. Maybe longer, if Josie asked Stephen to make the trip next time and he agreed.

In David's opinion, the man would be a fool to refuse her. One didn't cast aside a girl as special as Josie. If she and Stephen managed to work out their differences, he wondered how he'd survive it, and then felt guilty for his selfish thoughts. *Get your mind elsewhere, O'Brien!*

"Giddy up now," he said, flicking the reins slightly. He turned the buggy expertly and headed away from the lighted window and from the girl who had won his heart without even trying.

He sighed, his breath hovering in a little cloud around his face. The ride always seemed longer without Josie at his side.

he post-harvest celebration was as well attended as a wedding or funeral, with every farm family plus most of the townspeople showing up to enjoy a full afternoon and evening of food and fellowship. Reverend Goertzen began the activities with a prayer of thankfulness for a bountiful harvest, then everyone dug into the mountains of dishes provided by the womenfolk.

Someone wisely organized games for the children which took them out into the school yard. The schoolhouse doors remained wide open, and the happy laughter and shouts of fun by the crowd of children echoed throughout the building. After weeks of hard field work with little time for relaxation, everyone enjoyed this time of socializing.

David was there too. As Samantha had pointed out, he was the brother of a farmer's wife, and that certainly made him welcome. Everyone knew him from the mercantile, so he didn't lack for conversation. But he sorely felt the absence of one farmer's daughter. As far as he was concerned, the entire community of Mountain Lake couldn't make up for Josie not being there.

He wandered to the food table and selected a ham sandwich. As he lifted it to his mouth, he watched the Koehn family enter the school building. The sight of Stephen brought a tight feeling to his chest. Had Josie written and asked him to drive to Winston to pick her up for her next trip home? Curiosity tangled his stomach into knots, but he certainly wouldn't ask Stephen. Deep down, he was afraid to know.

He turned his attention back to Samantha, who was engrossed in an animated conversation with several other women. They reminded him of a gaggle of geese, heads together, tongues wagging.

Anna and Frank had recently announced they were going to be parents somewhere around Easter the next year, and that seemed to be the topic of discussion. He listened in as advice was handed out to Anna.

"Now don't eat too much cabbage or beans right now. It's bad for your digestion, dear, and it will make the baby colicky" was just one tidbit of helpful information. David struggled to hold his mirth inside, but Sammy was taking it all in, an expression of longing in her eyes. He knew how much she wanted a baby too, and he hoped soon she would be the center of a circle of well-intentioned women, receiving their blessings and experienced advice.

A tap on his shoulder, and there was Stephen Koehn at his side.

"Hello, David. How are you this evening? Enjoying the party?"

"Oh, sure." David held up his half-eaten sandwich. "Plenty to eat. That's about all a bachelor can hope for."

Stephen gave the expected chuckle. He hitched his fingers in his back pockets, rocked on his heels, and he seemed to be carefully avoiding facing David. "So . . . I hear you've been carting Josie back and forth from Winston."

David took the time to swallow a bite before answering, "Yup." He, too, kept his eyes forward rather than on his conversation partner.

"She's not . . . here tonight? She didn't come home?" Questions rather than a statement. So he hadn't heard from her. He sounded wistful.

"No. She hated to miss the harvest party, but she had meetings today—an evaluation or something. She stayed in Winston for the weekend." Still they didn't look at each other.

A pause, then, "How is she?"

David could have said a lot of things, including "missing you," but he intentionally made his voice casual and matter of fact as he responded, "Oh, she's doing great. She really enjoys her time with the children. She's a wonderful, natural teacher. The kids love her as much as she loves them."

Stephen nodded slowly. "Yes, I can believe that. Josie has a kind heart; she'd be good with kids."

Was Stephen thinking along the lines of Josie being good with her own children? David wasn't sure how to respond to Stephen's last statement, so he stood quietly, observing the milling groups and finishing his sandwich.

Finally Stephen sighed. "Well, I reckon I'll get myself something to eat. It looks good."

David experienced a flash of unexpected irritation. Stephen had proposed to Josie, made her feel terrible for going off to teach, and the man couldn't even ask David to deliver a message to her? At the very least, he could have asked David to tell her hello. But David kept the impatience out of his voice, "Yes, go ahead. Enjoy the party."

David shook his head, watching as Stephen took a plate and ambled his way down the row of serving tables. What a stubborn cuss. Josie deserved better than a man who was as self-absorbed as Stephen seemed to be. David was still looking at Stephen when Priscilla crossed his line of vision, hanging on the arm of her current favorite flirtation, Lucas Stoesz.

Self-absorption must run in the Koehn family. Priscilla acted as if she were the only person in the room, fluttering her eyelashes at Lucas and simpering in a way intended to keep his attention. Lucas didn't seem averse to giving it to her, either.

David turned his gaze away from the pair, searching out Sammy once more. He smiled to himself. He had certainly lucked out in the sister department. Samantha was a jewel. And even more so when compared to Stephen's sister. He wiped his palms on his handkerchief and walked over to drop an arm around Samantha's shoulders. She smiled up at him briefly before turning her attention back to Anna and their friends. He let his gaze rove over her head and found himself being watched by a pair of bright blue eyes.

Priscilla clung to Lucas's arm, her head tipped toward him as he whispered something in her ear. But instead of looking at Lucas, her gaze was aimed right at David. He got the impression the smile on her face was intended for him, too. He maintained a deadpan expression. He was not inclined to give her the least bit of encouragement.

As he watched, Lucas removed her hand from his arm and held it around his waist, circling his own arm around her shoulders. Apprehension stirred through David's gut. What was Lucas suggesting? Whatever it was, Priscilla played along. She pretended to resist, pulling back slightly as he began to pull her toward the door. She threw back her head, making sure her eyes caught David's once more before allowing herself to be persuaded by Lucas.

The pair headed out the back door of the schoolhouse, and David shook his head, tightening his hand on Sammy's shoulder. I'm a lucky man, he told himself again with a shake of his head, and he put Priscilla from his mind.

"C'mon, Pris." Lucas tugged Priscilla none too gently across the school yard through the shouting throng of children. "It's too crowded around here. Let's go take a walk, get some air."

Priscilla gave him another dose of her eyelashes, puckering her lips into a practiced moue. When she'd noticed what she hoped was David O'Brien watching her with Lucas, her heart had leapt. A perfect opportunity to make David jealous! She couldn't explain why it was so important to win David's attention. After all, there were certainly other men—like Lucas—who were more than willing to shower her with it. But it was David's interest she wanted.

Lucas's wiry arm around her shoulders guided her down the walkway leading away from the school building. Priscilla laughed and pushed away his arm playfully. "You, sir, are incorrigible!" Without an audience, the game had lost its greater appeal, but it was still exciting to see how she could manipulate Lucas. If she couldn't have David's attention, she'd settle for Lucas. For now. He was certainly better than nothing.

Lucas grinned, allowing her to slip away from him. "I've been called worse," he quipped, and she laughed again. This was the kind of play Priscilla liked best—dangerous and forbidden, but always within her control.

They reached the main street of Mountain Lake, and Priscilla paused, looking back toward the school. Might David be watching for her return? "Where are we going, Lucas?"

Lucas shrugged. "Jost has a couple of new horses in. One's got a star on its nose—real pretty. Wanna go see it?"

Priscilla hesitated only a moment before turning her face to his and flashing her beguiling smile. "Are you sure you only want to look at horses in Jost's barn?"

Lucas laughed, his white teething shining in the moonlight. "What else?" His comment sounded innocent enough, but his eyes indicated he had something else in mind.

Priscilla punched at his chest with her fist. "I'll go with you, Lucas, but you better behave! Or I'll tell my daddy on you!"

Lucas feigned great fear, staggering around with one hand holding his chest and the other flung outward. "Her daddy! Oh, no! I would never want to tangle with her daddy! Oh, Pris, no, don't tell on me to your daddy!"

Laughing, she punched him again. "Lucas, don't make fun of me!"

He caught her hand and gave a tug that set her feet moving toward Jost's Livery and Blacksmith Shop. Priscilla shivered, hunching her shoulders. The late October air was crisp, and she had left her shawl at the schoolhouse. Lucas wrapped an arm around her, resting his hand on the curve of her waist. She peeked at him, considering voicing a protest, but the warmth was welcome, so instead she smiled acquiescence.

They reached the blacksmith's barn in a matter of minutes and stepped into the livery part of the large structure. The gentle snoring and snorting of contented horses greeted them. There was little light, but the air was warmer here and rich with the odors of hay, wood ashes, and horseflesh. Lucas led Priscilla directly to the stall of the new horse with the white star on his nose.

Priscilla reached between the bars of the stall door and cooed, "C'mere, girl, let me pet you."

Lucas laughed. "Silly goose. He's not going to come to you if you call him a girl."

Priscilla pretended to be insulted. "Well, how am I supposed to know what it is?"

Lucas gave her a calculating look. "Do you want me to tell you?" And his hand slipped around her waist.

She stepped sideways, twisting her body slightly to elude his touch. She arched her brows and assumed a tart tone. "No, I do not think that will be necessary."

Lucas laughed at her again. There was a gleam in his eye that Priscilla found slightly disturbing, and she was beginning to question the wisdom of coming here alone with him.

"I could tell you lots of things, Pris." Lucas moved stealthily across the hay-covered ground toward her. "And I guarantee you'd like every one of them."

Priscilla backed up just as quickly as he advanced, but with less grace considering her full skirts, the lack of light, and the uneven ground. "I don't think so, Lucas. And I know my daddy wouldn't like it."

Lucas grinned. "Ah, we're back to your daddy again, are we? Well, let me remind you . . . your daddy ain't here." His tone lost its teasing quality, causing Priscilla's heart to ram against her ribs in fright. "All right, Pris, it's time to stop teasing. A man can take only so much of that before he caves in. You've been asking for this for months, turning those brilliant blue eyes on me and batting your lashes, sending me come-hither smiles. The time has come. So stop teasing and come here."

She backed herself against a stall and could go no farther. She made to dart past him, but Lucas grabbed her by the upper arms, pushing her against the stall door again. Her lips parted in fright as he neared, and he lowered his head and placed his eager mouth over hers. She pushed at his chest, twisting her head and making sharp little sounds of panicky protest. At last she pulled her head free.

"Lucas, stop it!" Her demand exploded breathlessly against his cheek.

But Lucas didn't let go. He slid his hands down her arms until he gripped her wrists tightly, pushing them against her chest and pressing painfully against her breasts. Sandwiched between his hard hands and the unyielding stall door, she had no choice but to stay put, but she moved her head back and forth in frenzied motions.

His breath came heavily against her hair as he murmured, "Stop fighting me, Prissy. You've wanted this as much as me. I've seen it in your eyes. Kiss me back."

"No-o-o," she gasped out, struggling to free herself. But Lucas ignored her protest, pursuing her relentlessly. Her back hurt where it pressed against the wood of the stall gate, and the horse in the stall whickered nervously. Her mind raced, frantically seeking a means of escape. She pulled her left foot back, then swung it forward as hard as she could. The pointed toe of her shoe cracked against his shin.

He gave a grunt of pain, and in the moment of distraction, she shoved outward with her arms, throwing him off balance. Scrambling awkwardly, she darted around him and made for the entrance of the barn as quickly as her skirts would allow.

But Lucas was infinitely more sure-footed. His clumping steps closed the ground behind her. She released one high-pitched squeal as he caught her by an arm and swung her in a small circle to land solidly against his chest. His arms locked around her, pinning her there, and his eyes bore into hers with a hard, angry expression that made her blood run cold.

"Oh, no, Pris." His eyes snapped with temper. "You're not goin' anywhere. It's high time you gave me a little of what your eyes have been promising." He gave her a little shake as she continued to moan and fight against him.

She began to cry as his lips crushed down on hers once more.

A party without Josie was really no party at all. David said his good-byes, receiving a hug and a promise from Samantha to get together soon, and then he slipped on his jacket and left. It was a pleasant night for a walk. The air was cool but not biting, with the fresh promise of snow in the air. The moon provided enough light to see where he was going. Stars twinkled brightly in the clear sky, and a hoot owl called its echoing question from a nearby tree. When the nocturnal bird asked deeply, "Whooo? Whooo?" David smilingly answered, "Just me." The flap of wings cut the air as the bird departed.

His long-legged stride carried him quickly across the boardwalk, his steps echoing hollowly in the quiet evening. He whistled softly to himself, his breath whirling around him in a cloud as he moved briskly toward the boardinghouse and his own private room. His mind ran idly through the various tasks that would require his attention at the store tomorrow. He almost missed the low sound of a moan that came through the gaping door of Jost's Livery and Blacksmith Shop.

He paused a good ten feet from the opening, cocking an ear. Could that have been a horse? It sure hadn't sounded like one. Then it came again—a low, frightened sound that couldn't have been made by an animal. The muffled sounds of a scuffle followed. What on earth?

David crossed quickly to the door and looked in. In the dim light provided by the moonlight slanting through several high windows, he spotted two people. It was obvious even in the shadows what was taking place, and he considered moving on, but then he heard a woman's gasp in a fear-filled voice, "No, Lucas! Let me go!"

Lucas Stoesz—with Priscilla. And she was not a willing participant. Without further consideration he stormed into the stable.

Lucas had his back to the door, so the hand that clamped down on his shoulder caught him by surprise. David pulled him away from Priscilla with one hand and landed a felling blow against his jaw with the other, all before Lucas had a chance to react.

"Hey!" Lucas yelped as his seat hit the floor and he slid backward at least three feet.

Priscilla caught hold of David's arm, but he shook her off. "Get back, girl!" She skittered away.

Lucas bounded up, coming at David with both fists raised. For a moment David questioned taking on the stocky farm boy. Lucas was accustomed to wrestling bales of hay and obstinate calves. Could a skinny storekeeper come out the victor? But what David lacked in girth he made up for in indignation. He deflected Lucas's swings, delivering a punishing blow to the younger man's left eye and then sinking a fist into his midsection. Lucas clutched his stomach and sank to his knees, fighting for breath. Priscilla stood off to the side, shaking hands covering her mouth, tears raining down her pale cheeks.

David, winded, propped his hands on his knees and glowered at Lucas. "You ought to be ashamed of yourself, forcing yourself on a woman. Get yourself up and out of here before I give in to the temptation to beat you senseless."

Lucas pressed the back of a hand to his lip. It came away with blood on it, which he wiped on his pants with a growl.

"I wasn't forcing nothin'. I know you've seen how she prances around. . . . She's been askin' for it."

"Yeah, I've seen," David said, ignoring Priscilla's indignant gasp, "but when a lady says no, that means no."

Lucas snorted. "She's hardly a lady, O'Brien."

David glanced briefly at Priscilla, taking in her shame-faced expression, before retorting sharply in retaliation. "Well, then, what does that make you?"

Lucas's gaze narrowed angrily, but he didn't respond.

David straightened, his chest still heaving as he caught his breath. "Next time you make a pass and the . . . the young woman says no, you'd be wise to listen to it. A gentleman would listen. Now, pick yourself up and get out of here." Lucas sat on his knees, staring at David belligerently. David made as if to come at him again. "Out. Now."

Lucas stood up, dusted the hay from his knees in a deliberately slow gesture, then stalked out, his head high. The minute he cleared the door, Priscilla raced across the barn floor and threw herself, sobbing, against David's chest. He allowed her exactly ten seconds of self-pity before he took her by the upper arms and shook her hard. "You stop that right now, Miss Koehn."

Priscilla ceased her sobbing immediately. She stared at David through tear-filled eyes. "B-but, David, I thought—"

"You thought wrong." His fingers tightened on her upper arms. "I might've blamed Lucas for this, but you are just as much at fault. What were you doing here with him, anyway?"

"Trying to make you—" She bit down on her lip and wrenched free of his grasp. "I came to look at a horse!"

"Yeah, sure." David gave a sarcastic snort. "Girl, you don't have the sense God gave a goose. You knew good and well what Lucas was after, and you came anyway. I saw you leave with him, and you weren't resisting. What did you expect to happen in here?"

Priscilla started to cry again. "Nothing! I didn't expect anything to happen!"

"Then you are dumber than I thought." David's low voice rumbled with barely controlled anger. He shook a finger under her nose. "Let me tell you something you should have figured out long ago, Miss Koehn. When you ask for something, you're likely to get it. And when someone rises to your bait, you've got no right to cry and complain and act put-upon. You and your flirting ways nearly got you into serious trouble tonight. I hope this all serves as a good lesson for you."

She blinked away tears and lifted her chin in defiance. "What gives you the right to—?"

"The fact that I came barreling in here in your defense gives me the right, you spoiled little brat." He balled his hands into fists on his hips. "I'm thinking now I should've just left Lucas to have his way with you. Maybe that would've brought you down a peg or two."

Priscilla covered her face and dissolved into frightened sobbing which only angered David further. Why couldn't the girl see she'd brought this on herself? No, Lucas didn't have the right to force himself on her, but her actions had contributed to the situation. And further, why did it bother David so much that she didn't seem to understand her accountability?

David barked, "Stop crying before I do what your own father should have done years ago and give you a good reason for all those tears." She sobbed harder, and he shook her again, but gentler this time, and said in a softer tone, "Come on, Priscilla, it's over, and he's gone. Now it's time to dry up."

At the kind tone—and the use of her Christian name—Priscilla raised her chin and looked into David's eyes. Her face crumpled once more, and she choked out, "I'm sorry, David." She fell against his chest once more, sobbing brokenheartedly.

David let her cry for a few seconds, then firmly pushed her upright. "Priscilla, listen to me." He waited until she had released one more shuddering sob and wiped her face with her hands. When she finally lifted her face and was looking at him, he said, "You cannot carry on with young men—even me—like you have been doing. Do you understand me?"

She nodded and started to cry once more.

"I'm not sure you really do, Priscilla. I want you to look at me."

She stared into his face, and this time she seemed to realize the gravity of the situation from which she had just been rescued. Her voice breaking over the words, she said, "Oh, David, I'm very sorry. I didn't mean for him to . . . I really didn't know . . . ."

He just shook his head.

She admitted in a whisper, "I was so scared!"

David finally reached out to pat her shoulder. "I know, Priscilla. And I'm glad I came along when I did." He paused a moment. "I'm sure you've learned an important lesson tonight."

"Oh, I have. I'll behave from now on." The gaze she turned on David bordered on adoring. Even in her rather disheveled appearance, with puffy eyes and tear-stained features, her striking natural beauty was fully in evidence. David felt more ill at ease with this subdued, obedient Priscilla than he had the willful, obstinate one. At least he'd known how to handle the untamed Priscilla.

He turned stern. "I certainly hope so, because if I ever have to pull you out of a predicament like that again, I guarantee I'll haul you straight to the woodshed." He pulled his eyebrows down in a scowl.

To his surprise, instead of bristling at his threat, Priscilla gave a meek nod. She wore an expression of contrition and gratitude that made him wonder if she had indeed had a change of heart.

David said gruffly, "You'd better get home and clean yourself up, then head back to the party. Your folks will be wondering where you are."

She nodded, her eyes still on him, but she made no move to leave.

"Go on now, Pris."

She started to move away, then turned back. "Would you mind . . . well, will you walk with me, please?"

It was the first time in his memory he could recall hearing Priscilla Koehn use the word *please*. He hesitated.

"I'm afraid to be by myself in the dark."

He stepped forward and nodded, looking down at her. "All right, Priscilla, I'll take you to your house."

"Then back to the schoolhouse?"

He knew he should deny her request. After all, she was getting her way. Again. But her eyes beseeched him, and for once they held not a hint of coquettishness. Her sincere entreaty tugged at his heart in a way he found disturbing. At last he sighed and caved in. "All right."

"Thank you, David." She tucked her arm into his.

David didn't trust himself to answer. He merely nodded once more, and they made their way out of the barn, arm in arm.

*P*riscilla lay in her bed, staring at the ceiling. The lace curtain rose and fell in the breeze drifting through the open window, sending shadows across the rose-printed paper. She hadn't extinguished her bedside lamp. Never afraid of the dark before, her heart now pounded with fear and anxiety. Her eyes burned with the effort of keeping them open. Each time she allowed her lids to close, she saw again Lucas's leering grin as he forced her against the stall gate.

She rolled to her side, pressing her fist to her mouth and battling the urge to call out for Mama and Daddy. Why hadn't she told her parents what Lucas had done when David returned her to the party? Daddy would have pummeled the fellow into the ground. Her father wouldn't simply have landed a few blows and sent Lucas on the way, as David had. Wouldn't she find some satisfaction in seeing her attacker punished for the dreadful assault?

But deep down, she recognized the situation wasn't entirely Lucas's fault. Shame rose from her middle as she acknowledged David had been right. Her deliberate flirting had given Lucas reason to believe she wanted him to kiss her—and more.

Tears trickled down her cheeks and into a damp place on her pillowcase. She'd so wanted David to notice her and give her attention. Well, she'd gotten what she'd been after. Oh, how he'd paid attention! But instead of feeling victorious, she only felt ashamed. And sad. He'd risen to her defense like a knight in shining armor. Afterward, he'd certainly been angry, but he was also kind. She wasn't sure how she should act around him now. Priscilla Koehn, unable to discern how to behave around a man!

For as long as she could remember, she'd enjoyed using her wiles to garner attention from boys. Boys clustered around her like bees around a honeysuckle vine. She'd welcomed them, encouraged them, teasing and beguiling and enjoying every minute of control. Until the moment she lost control. *Or maybe I lost control long before then.* . . .

Lucas's disparaging comment—"she's hardly a lady, O'Brien"—echoed through her mind. How many others in town held his sentiment? Such an ugly reputation she'd established for herself. Maybe the face she saw in her mirror each morning was not beautiful. She swallowed, rubbing her fist beneath her nose, groaning out her distress at such a thought. Who was she, then, if not "the lovely lady, Miss Priscilla Koehn"?

But David had extracted a promise that she give up her flirtatious ways, and she fully intended to keep the promise. And maybe—just maybe—David would look at her as more than a fickle flirt. Maybe he'd see the lady she truly wanted to become.

❦

"Here you go, David." The postman handed David a fistful of mail through the little barred window of the post office front. "All of Hiram's and Si's, plus one in there for you, too."

David gawked in surprise. "For me?" He began thumbing through the envelopes in his hand. Sure enough, he found one with his name on it. The address—Mr. David O'Brien, Mountain Lake, Minnesota—was spelled out in a neat, slanting script. He recognized the envelope from the stationery set he had given Josie for her graduation. His heart leaped just looking it.

He mumbled, "Thanks," before heading back to the mercantile. He held the envelope, unopened, in front of him, staring at his name as if merely looking at the handwriting would give a clue to the contents. What would she say? *Come for me—don't come for me—come for me—don't come for me.* . . . The words reverberated through his head, alternating with each step. Then realizing he was playing a childish game of chance, he pushed the letter into the middle of the stack and held them stiffly against his side as he walked.

Hiram looked up when the cowbell clanged above the mercantile's door. "Mail all in?"

"Yes." David pulled out the envelope of shell pink, pocketed it, then laid the stack on the tall counter. He kept his voice light as he inquired, "Mr. Klaassen, would it be all right if I took my lunch break now?"

Hiram pulled out his timepiece, snapped the cover, checked the time, and nodded. "Ja, David, go ahead. It's been slow today. Freight will not be in until two. Why don't you just plan to come back then?"

"Thank you, sir." He'd have plenty of time to stop at the café for some lunch, read his letter, and maybe even pen a reply. If one was required. He wasn't sure what was proper; he'd never received a personal letter before.

Minutes later he slid into one of the high-backed benches at Vogt's Café. The café's plump waitress, Maudie, came over to take his order. Unable to even think about what he might want, he requested the daily special.

"Ham and beans with cornbread today, David." Maudie's round face and dark eyes peered at him from beneath heavy eyebrows.

David fingered the envelope in his pocket. "That sounds fine."

"Want some coffee or pie to go with that?"

David didn't answer.

"David?"

"Um—sorry?"

Maudie's lips took on a teasing grin. "Wrong time of year for spring fever, but I'd say by your starry-eyed look your mind's not on food."

David ducked his head and gave a brief laugh.

Maudie repeated, "Want some coffee, or some pie?"

"Coffee would be fine, but no dessert today. Thanks anyway."

"Young folks . . ." Maudie shook her head and chuckled to herself as she headed back to the kitchen.

David folded his fingers around the square of paper in his pocket, wondering if he should read it here. It was still early, so few people were in the café, and, situated within the confines of his high-backed booth, he had some privacy. He removed the envelope from his pocket and laid it on the checked tablecloth. He spent a few moments admiring the neat handwriting, imagining how Josie's hand might have looked as she dipped the pen and set it on paper, forming the letters of his name.

Suddenly an image of Priscilla Koehn's hands placing a pair of suspenders on the counter at the mercantile flashed through his mind. *Where did that come from?* Determinedly, he turned his attention back to the envelope in front of him. He lifted it, and, after checking around to make sure he wasn't observed, he brought it to his nose and sniffed. There was no scent save the faint odor of glue. A little disappointed, he turned it face down on the table and at last slid a thumbnail beneath the flap to open it.

Inside he found two sheets of matching pink paper, folded in half. He began to read:

Sunday, October 21, 1918

My dear David,

He read her chosen greeting several times, his heart beating more rapidly each time.

After spending a fretful hour in thought and prayer, I felt I really must write to you and try to settle my aching conscience.

I feel terrible about the clumsy way I approached the subject of Stephen today. I should realize that you, as my friend, are committed to be as protective of me as my family has been, and would wonder at the sensibility of my asking anything of Stephen again. He has hurt me with his withdrawal, and although I don't wish to be injured again, I am having a hard time letting go. As I told you earlier today, I do love him. I actually can't remember a time when I did not.

Often, as you and I have laughed and talked, I have thought of Stephen. The hours of solitude, of one-on-one communicating, have helped you and me develop a wonderful, caring friendship. That is why I couldn't help but wonder if Stephen and I had time alone together, if we might be able to come to some sort of accommodation between his desires and mine.

That's why I suggested what I did. I know now how ungrateful and selfish it sounded, and I apologize. I certainly didn't want to offend you, or make you feel unappreciated. I really am sorry, David.

Something else has occurred to me during our rides, and I think you might be too much of a gentleman to speak of it. That is, you are spending so much of your free time carting me back and forth, not much is left over for you to pursue other relationships. I am sure that you could think of other people (or another young lady?) with whom you would like to spend time. I wonder if I'm being unfair to you, taking advantage of our friendship and your kind nature by counting on you more than I should, and perhaps these rides are hindering you.

I want you to know that if that is the case, you certainly can tell me. You won't offend me.

David lifted his head from the page as Maudie appeared, holding a crockery bowl of steaming soup and a plate piled high with wedges of cornbread. David tucked the letter under the edge of the table. Maudie set his food down with a curious glance at him but only said simply, "Enjoy your meal," before disappearing back into the kitchen.

David pushed the bowl aside and picked up the letter once more, sliding the first page behind the second. He continued to read:

You deserve some free time, too, David, so even if Stephen refuses to come pick me up after this coming weekend (as I trust you are still planning to come for me this time!), I intend to speak to Father about making other arrangements. Now that harvest is over, he or one of my brothers should be able to make the trip without any problems. (When the snowfall hinders travel, there will no doubt be times when I will just stay here on weekends.) I wouldn't mind a bit if you still made the trip once in a while, but I don't want to be a burden on you and leave you the full responsibility for getting me back and forth. You have certainly performed your duty already!

I just want you to understand, and I hope you will forgive my clumsy way of bringing up the subject earlier today. I do just fine when talking to a roomful of little children, but expressing myself clearly to a grown man is quite another thing. I hope you meant it when you said you weren't angry with me, because I cherish your friendship, David, and I don't want to do anything that would jeopardize it. You mean a great deal to me, and I imagine you always will.

Affectionately yours,

Josie

By the time he finished, he was pinching the bridge of his nose with one hand and creasing the pages of the letter with the other. She'd pretty much told him the same thing on that last ride together, but the words were somehow more real, more poignant, when written on paper and staring back at him, black against the pale pink. Slowly he set the last page down and lifted the first page to reread a section:

> *Often as you and I have laughed and talked, I have thought of Stephen.*

How disconcerting to realize that all the time he thought they were becoming closer, another man was on her mind— that she was thinking about possible ways to restore a relationship with the man she really loved.

David honestly hadn't been angry before, but he battled the emotion now. Josie was making a mighty big assumption that he had other things he wanted to do with his time. Maybe he had waited too long. Maybe he should have come right out and told her what he'd hoped would be the outcome of these rides together.

But reality came crashing through his what-ifs. No, that simply would have ended their rides earlier. If she had known his feelings for her went deeper than friendship, she would never have agreed to these times with her. Not while she still loved Stephen. And, he thought further, not while I am an "unbeliever." Josie was honest and straightforward. She would have come right out and said it wasn't a good idea for them to have these long buggy trips together.

His eyes glanced down the page of even, slanted script.

> *I am sure that you could think of other people (or another young lady?) with whom you would like to spend time. . . .*

Why did Priscilla Koehn's face seem to float above "another young lady"? He'd not viewed her as anything other than a spoiled, shallow, self-centered annoyance. And in light of the latest encounter, naïve to a fault. Oh, she was certainly beautiful, but she lacked all of Josie's sweetness and honesty. Yet with Josie's simple words, Priscilla's faced pressed into his mind and refused to depart.

He leaned his chin on his hand and sat staring out the window. He pictured Priscilla as she had looked after he had chased Lucas from Jost's barn. He remembered clearly her wide, tear-stained eyes and penitent expression as she'd begged him to walk her home. He remembered, too, the feel of her hand tucked into his arm; the gentle swishing sounds her skirts made as they walked together along the planked boardwalk; the sight of her tumbling, glossy curls cascading down her narrow back and shining blue-black in the moonlight. . . .

He sat up abruptly, slapping his hand on the tabletop. Good heavens, what was he doing, sitting here fantasizing about Priscilla Koehn? This letter from Josie must have had a more disheartening effect on him than he realized. He folded the pages and slid them into the envelope, then pushed it deep into his pocket.

According to the letter, Josie expected him to pick her up this Friday, presumably for the last time. Well, he'd set her straight on that one. He had four days to think of the proper way to word what needed saying. In the meantime, his soup was getting cold. He picked up his spoon.

~◦

A pink envelope was in the Koehn family's mail, too. Stephen recognized Josie's handwriting the instant his father placed it in his hand, and he ducked around a corner in the mill and tore the entire top off the envelope. He held the two pages side by side and scanned them briefly before laying them back together for more serious reading. He leaned against the wall as he began, taking time over each word and sentence.

The beginning paragraphs were chatty, newsy things—telling about the boardinghouse and the others who lived there. There was an anecdote about a little girl named Essie who, after a lesson on balance, cut off one of her braids to see if it might make her tip sideways. She mentioned an art project involving paper, paint, and leaves. And his mind carried him backward, remembering the adorable little pigtailed girl he had known many years ago. . . .

And then he got to the real purpose of the letter.

> I have missed you, Stephen. We've been friends for such a very long time and were closer than friends for a while. I think of you often, wondering how your work is going, if you have time to play checkers with the old-timers at the mercantile on Saturdays, and if you ever think of me.
>
> When we talked last, I asked you to leave me alone unless you could tell me you loved me. You've honored that request well, and I've regretted my hasty words. You said something, too, that has plagued me. You said when I was ready to stop "playing teacher," I shouldn't expect you to be sitting and waiting for me. I wonder if you have some regrets, too, about those words. A part of me certainly hopes you do.
>
> I would like to spend some time with you when I come home this next weekend. I realize I'm not being very ladylike, just saying it out like that, but right now I think being honest is more important than being lady-like. I have missed my dearest friend, and I would like to "catch up," so to speak.
>
> If you would like to see me, too, I will be at home Saturday. I can make us a lunch, and we can have a picnic in the barn loft. It would be

warm in there, as well as quiet, so we could talk without interruption. I would like to try to regain our old easy friendship, Stephen. I hope you would like that, too. If you don't come, please know that I will not blame you. I'd rather you be honest than courteous. But I will then know you are no longer interested in pursuing a relationship with me, and I won't bother you again.

Well, I must sign the letter now and get it in the mail before I grade some papers. The third graders wrote their first essays yesterday, and I am eager to read them. I hope to see you on Saturday next. I will be praying that we make the right decisions concerning the future.

Take care, Stephen.

Affectionately yours,

Josie

Slowly Stephen folded the letter in half, second page on the top. She missed him. She thought of him. She wanted to spend some time with him, to talk. . . . He hadn't had a moment with Josie since that day in July in the bean patch, months ago. His heart hammered in his chest, thinking of some time with her again. Yes, he wanted to go on a "loft picnic" with her, wanted to talk easily and openly as they once had before her desire to teach got in the way. But could they? So many words had been spoken in anger, so much time had passed. Could things really be fixed now?

And did he really want to fix things? Josie wouldn't change her stance on needing to hear "I love you" from him—not just the words, but the meaning of those words—before she would marry him. And she obviously enjoyed teaching. Would she give that up for him? The things that had created the problems in the first place were still firmly planted. Was there any point in getting together again, talking, and risking another argument?

He held the letter tightly in his fist, unconsciously crumpling the pink sheets in his agitation. He remembered the advice his brothers had given him. They were quite certain he would never find contentment with Josie unless he "laid down the law" and let her know who was in charge.

Sadie, Mary, and Lillian obviously respected their husbands' positions as head of the household. His brothers were of the opinion that their marriages were the way it was supposed to be—with the man fully "in charge." The idea certainly represented his parents' marriage too. But what did it really mean?

Stephen couldn't help but wonder if being the head of the house actually meant being dominating and bossy. Because that's what his father and brothers were. In addition, the males in his family treated their wives as if they didn't have one brain between them. He could well imagine bright and assertive Josie's reaction to that kind of treatment.

As angry—and as hurt—as he had been by her refusal to accept his proposal, he had mixed feelings concerning what was the proper way according to his brothers and what was actually right. What if he went to one of his brothers right now and showed him the letter with Josie's invitation, what advice would he give? Stephen snorted. No doubt the response would be along the lines of "that woman is trying to dictate to you again" and "don't give in to her."

No, he wouldn't show the letter to his brothers. And his father was out of the question. John Koehn's dictatorial attitude extended beyond Millie to include his male offspring. Stephen didn't want to set himself up for a lengthy lecture. So who to talk to about this?

What about Ma?

Stephen chewed on his lip. A female viewpoint could be helpful. And if he was able to talk to Ma alone, without Pa

around, maybe she could help him understand Josie's determination to hold out for what she wanted.

But there was no point in standing here stewing about it
right now. Saturday was still five days away. He had time to
think about it, talk to Ma, and—as Josie had said—pray about
it as well. If it turned out that he showed up at the Klaassen
farm Saturday, he knew he would be sending a strong message
without uttering a word. He'd have to be very sure of what he
wanted—what God wanted for Josie and for him—because if he
accepted her invitation, there likely would be no turning back.

osie stood inside the schoolhouse, holding the door open a mere inch to look out like a child peering through a knothole. Cold air blew in the opening, carrying biting snowflakes that stung her eye. But still she remained, silent and waiting. What kind of a greeting would David give her? Would he feel awkward and uncomfortable after the letter she'd sent? She certainly felt awkward!

Josie hated conflict. Oh, she wasn't averse to it if the situation merited it; she would stand her ground as required. But she greatly disliked dissension, and that's precisely what she had created when she brought up the subject of Stephen with David. David was as close as family, and of course he would take her side, come to her defense.

She heard the sound of wheels on the road, and then David in the driver's seat came into view. She held her breath and watched as he brought the vehicle to a halt, set the brake, then looked toward the school. She opened the door more fully, and they looked at each other across the expanse. Embarrassment swept over her. What must he think of her, standing there in the cold watching for him?

But then his face broke into a broad smile. "Hi, Josie! Are you ready to go?"

As amiable as ever. Josie's heart lifted, and she beamed a smile back at him. "I sure am!" She pulled her shawl snug around her ears, stooped over to scoop up her books, and ran down the steps.

At the boardinghouse, even though Teddy clambered out to accompany her, David declined her offer to come inside. "I'll wait here for you. If I go in where it's warm, I'll just have to get used to the cold again."

Josie promised to be quick. In only a matter of minutes, she hurried a dawdling Teddy down the wooden steps and followed him into the buggy. Teddy crouched in the narrow floor space between the seats with a book, pulling a wool blanket clear over his head like a makeshift tent.

David handed her the lap robe. "Bundle up tight. It's really nippy today."

Snowflakes danced in the wind, clouds blew past the sun, and bare trees stood out starkly against the pale blue sky. Josie shivered as the buggy pulled out of town. She'd worn her warmest wool dress, a wool coat, heavy shawl, woven scarf, and gloves. Even with the lap robe pulled close, she still shivered.

From beneath the scarf, her voice sounded muffled. "It won't be long, I imagine, before I'll have to just stay in Winston for the weekends. It will be too cold to make this trip."

David glanced at her. "I suppose that would be preferable to getting frostbite—especially your nose." He lifted her scarf between thumb and finger a little higher, covering all of her face except her eyes. He smiled—a sad smile, it seemed.

"Josie, I want to talk to you about . . ."

Another tremor—a different kind of cold—struck Josie, and she shivered again.

David frowned. "You really are cold, aren't you?"

Hugging herself, she nodded. "Y-yes."

His breath hung heavy in the crisp air. "Well, I suppose it is too cold for conversation." He sighed. "You just hunker into that robe, and I'll get you home as quickly as possible. All right?"

"Th-thank you, David." She scooted down on the seat, pulling the lap robe up around her ears. They rode along in companionable silence, the buggy jolting over ruts in the road and the horse's steamy breath creating little clouds of condensation. Although she felt bad for having discouraged conversation—they'd enjoyed such pleasant chats in the past—she appreciated David's willingness to let her keep her attention on staying warm.

⤳

Stephen drew in a breath for fortification, knocked and turned the handle on the door, and entered his father's office. "Pa?"

Pa looked up from the ledger, his bushy eyebrows low. "Yes? What is it?"

"Can I head home a little early today?" He tapped one finger against his jaw. "Tooth." The evening before, he'd suffered a toothache. Although the twinge was mostly gone, he couldn't think of another excuse his father would not question for letting him go before quitting time. And he needed to speak to Ma alone.

Pa waved him off. "You've put in extra hours since harvest ended. Go ahead—have your ma doctor that thing. Clove usually works." His father returned to his bookkeeping.

Relieved at having escaped further discussion, Stephen hustled home and accepted the clove bud Ma offered. He held the strong-tasting spice between his back teeth. Ma made hot tea for them both and brought it to the dining room. Stephen followed, choosing a chair across from her.

Ma clucked in sympathy. "You are quite uncomfortable, Stephen?"

Stephen lowered his head. Yes, he was uncomfortable, but not physically. He reached into his pocket and withdrew the pink sheets with Josie's neat handwriting and slid them across the table. Millie looked at him, puzzlement in her eyes.

He kept his jaw clenched to hold the clove in place. "Would you please read the second page, Ma?"

Ma placed a hesitant hand against her chest, her brows raised high in query. "Me?"

Stephen understood her confusion and guilt smote him. He'd never come to Ma with a problem before. He'd treated her with the same distant affection that Pa employed. He gentled his voice. "I need your advice, Ma. Would you read it, please?"

A smile of wonderment tipped her lips and lit her eyes. She set aside her cup, reached for the letter, and began to read. Stephen fidgeted, eager to hear what she'd say.

Her gaze lifted from the page, her expression hopeful. "Josie appears to want a reconciliation between you two. Is that what you want, Stephen?"

He shrugged. "I'm not sure, Ma. That's what I wanted to talk to you about." He paused, struggling with the choice of words. How could he ask his mother if she thought Josie was too independent to make a good wife? In the end, he talked around what he really wanted to know. "Ma, what do you think is the most important element in a good relationship between a man and woman?"

To his surprise, Ma didn't hesitate. "The most important element in any relationship is respect. If you respect each other, then your treatment of one another will always be what it should be." She seemed to lose herself in thought for a moment.

Stephen couldn't help but think of his father's attitude toward Ma. Did Pa respect Ma? He sure didn't act like it. Instead of questioning Pa's feelings toward Ma, Stephen decided to pursue his mother's feelings. "Do you respect Pa?"

"Of course I do." Ma picked up her cup and took a drink. "If I didn't, I couldn't be a good wife."

Without thinking, Stephen blurted, "Pa isn't a good husband, though, is he?" In an instant he wished he could take the words back.

His mother turned scarlet and set the cup down with a trembling hand. "Your father is a Christian man. He is faithful to me and a good provider. He has brought you children up to honor your parents and be good, God-fearing people. Of course he is a good husband."

Stephen moved to the chair next to his mother. He put a hand on her arm as he asked gently, apologetically, "But does he respect you, Mama?"

She hung her head.

Stephen went on quietly. "You just told me that respect is the most important part of a good relationship. I have to say, it doesn't seem to me that Pa respects you or your feelings much." A lump filled his throat as he recognized the truth of his words.

Millie's hands clasped together tightly on the tabletop, trembling beneath Stephen's touch. "Son . . ." Her voice broke. She lifted her face, and tears shimmered in her eyes. "I don't wish to speak ill of your father. He's my husband. I love him and respect him. But . . ." She swallowed, blinking rapidly, and raised her chin. Determination seemed to spread across her face. "If I speak truth and answer you honestly, I might be able to keep you from making the same mistake we—your parents—have. So listen to me carefully, son."

She looked Stephen full in the face and smiled weakly. "You are right, Stephen. Your father does not respect me or my feelings." Her tone gained strength as she continued. "But that isn't his fault. It was his father's way, and it is what he knows. In his mind, he is treating me the way a man should treat his wife. A man is to lead his wife. How he does it is his interpretation of a biblical concept. Your father believes he is right."

Stephen was amazed at the way she explained the difficult subject. "But is he?" he asked.

Ma gave another sad smile. "For me, it is enough that he thinks so, Stephen."

Stephen removed the clove from his mouth and asked softly, "Is it really, Ma?"

Ma's shoulders slumped. "In our early years, I told myself that if I was a good, obedient wife, then John would love and respect me. We've been together now for thirty-six years, and I've come to understand and accept that, in his way, he loves me. We've brought five children into the world, we've supported each other through good times and bad times and all the monotonous, unemotional times in between. Your father has always seen to my physical needs and has provided me with many extras my friends don't have. That counts for something. So yes." She gave a firm nod, her eyes glittering. "For me it has to be enough."

But then she leaned forward, taking Stephen's hand and squeezing it hard between her soft, warm palms. "But, Stephen, it doesn't have to be enough for you. I see a tenderness in you that your brothers lack. I see a . . . a fairness in you. I think you understand that what your father and I have isn't necessarily the only—or best—way. To lead lovingly, you need only to ask, not command."

Stephen thought back to the countless times he had thought Pa was unreasonably hard and domineering with Ma. At those times distress and sympathy for his mother had welled up. "You're right, Ma. Sometimes I have felt Pa doesn't treat you right."

"Well, then, son, listen to your heart. I know when children are small, they think their parents can do no wrong. But parents aren't perfect. You're a grown man, Stephen, and it is time for you to decide the kind of man you want to be. The kind of home you want to have—yes, to lead. You have a choice to make. You can be like your father—and I'm not saying that everything he does is wrong. He has good qualities, too, that I would be proud for you to follow. But if there are things you feel should be different, your other choice is to find another path to follow."

Ma paused. Her hands had been pressed around Stephen's, but now she released them and picked up the folded pink papers bearing Josie's words. Her gaze remained on the letter as she said, "You seem to wonder whether or not you really do love Josie. Do you want to know how to be sure?"

Stephen waited silently, heart pounding. This probably was the most important question he faced.

"When you want her happiness more than you want your own, then I would say you love her."

Stephen saw the wistfulness in his mother's expression, and his throat constricted with the effort to control his emotions.

Ma waited a moment, staring into her cup. "Loving another means respecting that person enough to let them be the kind of person they need to be." She looked up and searched his face. "If you can't do that for Josie, then you shouldn't meet her tomorrow, Stephen. You would be misleading her, and it would not be right or fair. And I think, Stephen, you want to be right and fair."

Stephen nodded. "Yes, Ma, I do." He meant it.

Ma passed Josie's letter across the table into Stephen's hands. "Then, son, I will encourage you to spend some time in prayer and consider what is in your heart. And I'll be praying, too, that you and Josie will both know what's best." She lifted her cup and Stephen's and turned toward the kitchen.

Stephen rose quickly and reached for the teacups. "I've got them, Ma. I'll put them in the kitchen for you." At her startled expression, he smiled. After everything she did for all of them, he could do a small act of kindness for her. "You sit here for a while. I'll join you again in a minute."

When he returned, he paused behind his mother's chair to clamp a hand on her shoulder and squeeze. Millie looked up to meet his gaze, and in that moment Stephen recognized the sorrow in his mother's eyes. No, he didn't want that for Josie. Not Josie. "Thank you, Ma, for what you have said to me today." He slid back into his chair. "Your wisdom and counsel have already helped me, and you've given me much to think about, pray about."

Her tremulous smile spoke volumes.

Swallowing a lump of regret for the mindless way he'd treated his mother in the past, he rose. "I'm going to search out Scripture about marriage." A grin twitched at his lips. "And about being a husband."

"Don't miss First Corinthians 13, Stephen," she said with a solemn nod. "It tells you just about everything you need to know."

As he passed through the hall, his thoughts turned inward, he almost missed seeing his sister standing in the shadows of their parents' bedroom doorway. Tears clung to her thick eyelashes, and instantly Stephen knew Priscilla had heard every one of their mother's heartfelt words.

osie took extra care with her appearance on Saturday. Normally she would have worn a work dress, but not this time. Not when she might be seeing Stephen. Her heart fluttered in anticipation, but she quelled the eager rush. He might not come.

Her royal blue wool dress wasn't showy by any means, but the crisp lace collar and lace-edged cuffs and sweeping skirt were attractive. She pulled the sides of her long hair upward, catching it in tortoise-shell combs and leaving it cascading down her back in a girlish style that suited her.

She took one last look in the mirror. With some surprise, she found her same familiar, freckled reflection peering back. She felt so much more mature since going away to teach. Why didn't it show?

In the kitchen, she shooed her sisters out from underfoot before frying a chicken and making a batch of baking soda biscuits. Holding her skirts, she went into the cellar to fetch a jar each of dill pickles and pickled beets. The food was simple by necessity; she couldn't prepare a fancy dinner and serve it in a barn. To compensate for the homely meal, she carefully packed two china plates, linen napkins, and two place settings of Ma's finest silverware. A jug of cool water and two mugs completed the essentials.

Hands on hips, she surveyed her preparations. With a sigh, she closed her eyes. *Dear Lord, You know my heart and how I care for Stephen. If we're meant to be together, open the door to reconciliation. Whatever happens today, let it be Your will for us.*

Another glance at the unpretentious offerings brought a smile to her face. The picnic items were not as important as what might be settled between Stephen and her.

At a quarter to twelve, Josie tapped on the boys' door upstairs. Teddy stuck his nose out. "Yeah, what'cha want?"

Josie clasped her hands in front of her. "I hoped I could talk you into helping me with something."

"What?"

"Carrying some food and stuff out to the barn."

Teddy's eyes popped wide. "The barn? What for?"

"Never mind what for," she retorted, her smile softening the words. "Will you help me or not?"

"But it's cold out," Teddy protested, "and I was putting a puzzle together."

Josie stifled a sigh. "Teddy, your puzzle will keep, but I need to have everything in the barn before noon. Will you please help me?"

Teddy narrowed his eyes and lifted his chin. "What'cha up to, anyway?"

"If I tell you, will you help me?"

He shrugged, grinning impishly.

"I'm setting up a picnic out there for Stephen and me."

"In the barn?"

Josie's patience waned. *Brothers!* "Yes, in the barn. Where else can we go to get some privacy around here? Teddy, please—"

Teddy threw up his hands. "Oh, all right. Let's go. But I think you're nutty, eating a lunch out in the barn when there's a perfectly good table and chairs right downstairs in the kitchen."

Josie muttered, "With six other people around it." No, the barn might be crude, but it would be quiet. It would have to be the barn.

By ten after twelve, Josie had swept a spot clean in the loft, spread a checked cloth on the planked floor, and carefully laid out her picnic. A fierce wind whistled and rattled the barn shutters, but the warmth of the animals within the solid log construction of the huge building kept it a comfortable temperature. She found she didn't need her gloves, but she left her shawl around her shoulders. All was prepared. Now it was a matter of waiting. And hoping.

She paced back and forth. Would he come? What would he say? In spite of best intentions, would it turn into a fight again, with each spewing angry words back and forth? Oh, she hoped not. She wanted so badly to find the kind, sweet Stephen she'd looked up to since she was a little girl. She prayed he was still somewhere inside of the demanding, stubborn man she'd seen lately.

The creak of iron hinges alerted her, and she dashed to the edge of the loft, peering down through the hole in the floor where the ladder descended. A man was pushing the door closed against the driving wind. He shut it with a muffled thump, then placed a length of wood through two clamps to keep it shut. His back still to her, he pulled the hat from his head and ran a gloved hand through the thick, dark hair. He hadn't turned around yet, but Josie would have known that figure and the wondrous head of hair anywhere.

He'd come! Her heart hammered in her chest so hard she was sure he'd be able to hear it over the whining wind and snoring cows.

He turned then and lifted his face toward hers in the opening of the loft floor. He stood stock still with the hat against his chest. His cheeks were ruddy from the cold, his hair uncombed. To Josie, he looked wonderful. His eyes met hers, and time stood still as the two admired, thrilled, worried—and wondered who would break the silence first.

Stephen did. "Hello."

One simple word, and her heart went winging. Her breath came in nervous little huffs, and she wasn't sure she could talk. So she let her beaming smile offer a welcome.

Stephen moved across the dirt floor, holding his hat by the crown, his uncertain blue eyes still locked on her hopeful brown ones. His pants must have been new and stiff; they made a swishing sound as he walked, along with the slight thud of his heels against the hard ground.

He reached the ladder and tossed the hat aside, then paused, his hands wrapped around the rails, one boot propped on the lowest rung. He looked upward at Josie. Was he holding his breath, too? A smile dimpled his cheek. "If you want me to come up, you'd better shift aside."

She scrambled a few feet away from the opening and watched until his head emerged, then his shoulders, and then he was sitting on the edge and with his legs dangling below. Josie found her voice and said with no small amount of wonder, "You came."

"Uh-huh." He rubbed one hand up and down tan fabric covering his right leg. A nervous gesture.

Josie sought to put him at ease. "Are you hungry?" She moved to the array of food laid out on the cloth. "I fixed chicken and biscuits, and got out some of Ma's pickled beets and sour pickles you like so well." She looked over her shoulder. He remained seated in the loft opening with the same tentative look on his face. "Stephen?"

In slow motion he pulled his legs up and swung them around, rolled onto one hip, then pushed himself to his feet. He crossed the wide planks and knelt beside her, looking over the china plates, the silverware, the baskets of food, and finally turned his gaze to meet hers. "This is all really nice, Josie. You went to a lot of trouble."

She shrugged. "Not so much." She tried a smile. "I wish it was more, but . . ." Her voice drifted off, and she dropped her gaze to the crusty biscuits.

"I don't deserve having a fuss made over me."

She sent him a startled look, taken aback by his penitence.

"After the way I've treated you, I don't know why you did this for me."

She reached out timidly, touching his sleeve with shaking fingers. Softly, honestly, simply, she said, "Because I love you, Stephen."

The words hung as heavily as if proclaimed on a banner. She hadn't planned to say it. She'd meant to keep things light and casual between them. But he'd been there less than five minutes, and she'd said it.

It would have been easy for Stephen to respond, "I love you, too, Josie." She held her breath, waiting and hoping, but although he didn't drop his gaze, those words were not spoken.

Disappointment washed over her. To hide it, she reached for the basket of biscuits. "Let's eat now. I'm sure you need to get back to work soon."

This time Stephen's hand closed over Josie's. With his other hand he reached out and lifted her chin, turning her face toward his. "I don't have to be back soon. I have lots of time, and I'm really not all that hungry. The eating can wait. Please— can we talk?"

"A-about what?"

He turned to face her, drawing up his knees and wrapping his arms around them. Once he was settled, he said, "Tell me about Winston—and the kids in your class, how the teaching is going."

Her eyebrows rose. "Really?" It seemed unlikely that he was really interested, given his past responses. "You'd rather listen to me talk than eat?"

"For now."

The teasing grin on his square face reminded Josie of sweet times from long ago. Her heart thumped hopefully beneath her wool bodice. She answered in a light tone. "Well, all right, but I have to warn you: once I get started, you might not be able to shut me up. I'm awfully fond of the children in my class, and I'm likely to brag for hours."

His dimple showed. "I can take it. Brag away. I want to hear everything."

She twisted around until she sat with her legs folded to one side, her skirt in a circle around her. She flipped her hair back behind her shoulders and dropped her hands, palms up, in her lap. "All right, Stephen. Let me tell you about . . ."

*S*tephen listened carefully as Josie told him about the first few days of loneliness when she only wanted to be home again, then of forming attachments to the smallest children in her care who were as homesick from their daily separation from their mamas as she was from her much longer one. She told him about planning lessons to keep three different grades busy and learning, and how challenging she found the task. She shared funny stories and touching moments, and while she talked, he found himself absorbed by the sincere, almost passionate expression in her face and voice.

He watched her countenance change from smiling and amused to thoughtful and introspective. He listened, and through her descriptions he was able to see and feel what it was like to be in front of a classroom of wiggly but responsive children. And he found himself thinking, *What a wonderful experience she's having. I wouldn't deny her the memories she's forming for anything in the world.*

And with that thought, something else struck him. For once he was thinking of Josie's happiness rather than his own. What had his mother told him? If he wanted someone else's happiness more than his own, then . . . His heart almost stopped, and he was so stunned by the realization that he didn't hear Josie's question.

"Stephen?"

He shook his head, still in shock from the revelation. "What?"

She gave a brief laugh. "I don't think you've heard a word. Did I put you to sleep?"

He stared, his mouth opened slightly in wonder. He loved her! It had taken her leaving him before he could find the truth, but now he knew. He loved her. He made himself answer calmly. "No, I'm not asleep. I just—" He grinned sheepishly. "What were you saying?"

Josie pretended to bluster. "Honestly! You men. Tell a girl to talk, then drift off somewhere into unknown places and don't even listen. I asked if you were ready to eat yet. The biscuits are getting hard."

Stephen couldn't wipe the grin off his face. He stared at her, awestruck. She looked so different to him now. He'd always thought her pretty, but now she seemed to glow with something even better than beauty. Was it the happiness she'd found in her new position or his love for her creating that glow? He couldn't be sure.

"Stephen?" She shook her head in mock impatience. "What on earth is wrong with you?"

He dropped his arms from his knees and turned slightly. He felt as though he'd awakened from a long nap—drowsy and warm and content. He shook his head. "No, I'm not ready to eat."

She stared at him, her brow furrowed, then gave a quick nod. "Oh." She flipped her palms outward. "Well, then—"

"It's my turn to talk, Josie." He waited until her eyes were focused on his. "There are some things I need to say, but first I have to ask. . . . Have I muffed up things between us for good?"

A soft smile crept across her face. "Would I have asked you here today if I thought that?"

He scooted forward until his knees touched hers. He took one of her hands, sandwiching it loosely between his own. Josie sat in silence with her lower lip caught between her teeth, as if half afraid. Her reaction stung, but what else could Stephen expect after the emotional battering he'd delivered? He must settle things once and for all.

"Josie, I owe you an apology." He leaned forward, bringing his face so close to hers he could count the pale freckles dotting her nose. "I've been bullheaded and obnoxious about your wanting to teach. I should have respected your feelings, but instead I only thought of myself." With as much sincerity as he could muster, he added softly, "I'm sorry. Would you forgive me?"

She stared at him, so silent and unmoving it seemed she'd turned to stone. He leaned back slightly, still holding her hand, and sighed. "I suppose it's pointless to explain why I acted the way I did."

Josie came to life. She tipped her head, strands of soft brown hair spilling forward over her shoulder. "Why, no, I don't think it's pointless, Stephen. I'd like to understand why you got so angry."

Stephen bolted to his feet and stalked four paces away before turning and facing her again. "I know this will be hard for you to understand, because I spoke to you as if I was angry. But I wasn't angry, I was . . . I don't know how to put it." He rammed a hand through his hair. "This is so hard."

Josie rose and crossed to him. "What is it, Stephen? What were you feeling?"

He rested his hand gently against her cheek. The feel of her soft skin beneath his rugged palm soothed him. He took in a great breath and admitted, his tone ragged, "I felt abandoned."

Josie didn't flinch. "Abandoned? By me?"

He caressed her cheek briefly and then lowered his hand. "Yes. Teaching was so important to you, you were willing to say no to my marriage proposal and just take off. I felt like I didn't matter that much to you. It hurt, so I reacted in a spiteful way. It was wrong—"

With a slight frown, she said, "Stephen, it wasn't just my desire to teach that made me decline your marriage proposal. There was another, more important reason."

He nodded. "I know, and I'm not blaming you. I should've waited until I was sure of my feelings before I brought up the idea. But I'm twenty-three years old, and my father still treats me like a child. I wanted to get out from under his roof, and I . . . well, I suppose I jumped the gun."

Josie stepped back a pace. "So you saw me as a means of escape?" She ducked her head.

Stephen moved to her side in an instant and took her hand. "No! No, Josie, I didn't propose to you just to get away from my father. That isn't true. Please, Josie, look at me."

He waited until she tipped her head to meet his gaze. "Josie, you are everything I want as a life's mate. You are intelligent. You have a sweet, caring spirit. You're a strong Christian with sound moral values. And to top it off, you were the cutest little tagalong I'd ever seen." A soft rose graced her cheeks, and he reached out to tap the end of her nose. "I want to see your delightful, adorable face across the breakfast table from me for the rest of my life." With a deep sigh, he dropped his teasing then. "When I got your letter, I was so uncertain. I knew that if I came out here, I'd be walking through a door that only went one way."

Josie drew in a breath and held it, her eyes wide.

"I wasn't sure I should come, because I still wasn't sure how I felt about you, in here." He placed a wide, work-roughened palm against his chest. "I wasn't sure, Josie, because I didn't know what it means to love a woman."

Josie's breath whooshed out, her expression dubious. "How can you not—?"

Stephen silenced her with two fingers gently against her lips. "Just listen to me, please? Withhold your questions till I've said my piece." He resorted to pacing—five steps away, five steps back—then took her hands again.

"Josie, in my house, my father is in charge. When he says jump, you don't question the order, you simply obey. That's the way it's been my whole life, and that rule applied to me, my brothers, and to my mother as well. I've not really known a give-and-take relationship between a man and his wife."

He laughed ruefully. "Well, maybe I have: Ma does the 'give' and Pa gets the 'take.'" Sadness washed over him as he admitted, "I'm not sure my father loves my mother, Josie. I know he has the capacity to love—he certainly showers Priscilla with his affection—but I haven't seen him treat my mother in a loving way."

Josie gave his hand an encouraging squeeze. He drew courage from the sweet pressure of her fingers, and he rubbed his thumbs against her knuckles.

"All three of my brothers are already married, and not a one of them is any less demanding with his wife than Pa is with Ma. Matt, Mitch, Stan . . . Every one of them is the boss—the deliverer of orders that better be obeyed. And their wives respond just like Ma. They do what it takes to please their men." He paused, cringing inside at the picture he was painting of his family. "I suppose it sounds as if I'm making excuses, and I don't want it to sound that way, but the reason I couldn't say for sure that I loved you is because I wasn't sure how a man who loves a woman acts."

Very slowly, Josie nodded. "Of course I've observed the favoritism your father has always shown Priscilla, but I hadn't realized the effect it had on the rest of the family. Do you feel as if you've been abandoned, emotionally, by your father?"

Although Stephen had never given the idea much thought, he realized that deep down he had never felt as though he measured up to Pa's expectations. A new awareness made his scalp tingle. He nodded slowly. "Yes, I think that's a good way to put it. Priscilla's always come before everyone else. Ma, my brothers, me . . ." He gulped. "I suppose when you seemed to make teaching such a priority, I thought I was . . . again . . . less important. When you insisted we wait to get married, it said to me you didn't care about my needs." Spoken out loud, it all seemed so petty. Heat filled his face.

But Josie didn't turn away. She smiled and gave his hands a reassuring squeeze. "Stephen, thank you for telling me about this. I know it wasn't easy for you. And I'm sorry, too—for making you feel you didn't matter to me. You do matter, so much so that it nearly tore me apart, making plans to leave with such hostility between us."

Stephen bowed his head. "I didn't like it either, but I didn't know how to set things right." He looked up. "So I talked to Ma. And she helped me understand some things about her relationship with Pa, and—well, some other things, too." He blew out a noisy breath. "I don't want us to be like my parents, Josie. I want you to be more than someone to make me happy. I want to make you happy, too."

Tears swam in her eyes. "You've made me happy by coming and telling me these things, Stephen. And I'm not upset with you anymore."

"Good." Stephen heaved out a sigh. He felt as though a great weight had been lifted. "Now that I've gotten that off my chest, maybe we can eat." He escorted her to the picnic on the floor, but before sitting, he caught hold of Josie's arms. "Josie? I need to know something."

"What?"

"You'll be finishing the year of teaching at Winston, right?"

Josie nodded. "I've made a commitment, so . . . yes, I will."

He stared at the floor for a moment, nodding. "I figured you would." Then he met her gaze, offering a smile. "I'll take you there myself Sunday, but before you go, there's one more thing you need to hear." Cupping her face in his hands, he lowered his head until he could see his own reflection in her irises. Then he said, clearly and fervently, "Josie, I love you."

She gasped and clapped both hands over her heart. Her lips parted in an expression of surprised exultation. "Ohhh . . ." The word was carried on a wavering breath of wonder. "Y-you do? You're sure?"

He nodded.

Grasping his wrists, she peered into his eyes through a veil of tears. "How do you know?"

"I figured it out when you were talking about teaching." Tears stung behind his nose, and he sniffed. "I could see the joy in your eyes and hear it in your voice. Teaching makes you happy, and suddenly I was glad you'd gone and found that happiness. Your happiness was more important than me getting my way. And that's love, isn't it, Josie?"

The tears spilled over and left silvery trails on her cheeks. "Yes, Stephen, that is love."

Stephen ran his hands through her tumbling curls, coiling the strands around his fingers. "My stubborn pride has been getting in the way of your happiness—and mine!—but from now on, things will be different. If I have to wait fifty years to marry you, I'll wait, because there's no other woman on this earth who could take your place in my heart. And if you'll accept me, I'll do my best to always treat you with the respect you deserve and to do everything in my power to make you the happiest woman who ever lived."

"Oh, Stephen." She swished the moisture from her cheeks with shaking hands. "Those words are all I need to make me the happiest woman who ever lived! Oh, I love you, too!"

Stephen opened his arms wide, and Josie stepped into his embrace, wrapping her arms around his torso beneath his jacket and clinging hard.

She wept against his shirt front. "How can I leave you now?"

Stephen shook his head, chuckling. "You mean now that I've told you I'm glad you want to teach, you don't want to go?"

"It doesn't make any sense at all, but . . . yes!"

Stephen laughed. "If you aren't a bundle of contradictions." He set her away and offered her a handkerchief. She used it to good advantage before smiling at him sheepishly. Stephen brushed her cheek with his knuckles. "Josie, you and I both know you have to go to Winston and finish the year. You've made a commitment, you love what you're doing, and you won't be happy with yourself if you quit midstream. You've had this dream for too long to give up on it now. I don't want to stand in your way any longer, so I'll get you back there myself, you hear?"

"Are you sure that's what you want, Stephen?"

He nodded with certainty. "Yes, I'm sure. I've had a long, lonely time of stewing to think about it. It's for the best. But"— he shook a finger at her, offering a mock scowl—"I will bring you home each weekend from now on. No more of these drives with David O'Brien. And you'll spend your free time with me."

She locked her hands behind her back and smiled. "That's fine with me."

"And when this term is done, we'll sit down and talk about whether or not you should continue for another year. It will be our decision—made as a team. Agreed?"

"Agreed."

"And the next time I ask you to marry me—and I will, soon—I will say 'I love you' first and 'marry me' second, so your answer will not be no. Right?"

"Absolutely."

Silence fell while Josie's brown eyes searched Stephen's face, as if seeking peace and contentment. She must have found what she was looking for, because she burst into a smile rivaling the bright ribbon of sunlight coursing through the loft's square window. She tipped her head. "Stephen, if you're done laying down all these new laws for us, will you kiss me, please?"

Stephen did so, gladly. When done, he said, "Now, woman, stop making demands and let me eat."

Chuckling, they seated themselves on the blanket. And it mattered to neither that the biscuits were as hard as sun-baked bricks.

*W*hat?" David stared at his sister. His hands clamped around the broom's handle so tightly his knuckles turned white. "When?"

Samantha held the tails of her shawl beneath her chin and blinked up at him. "Earlier today."

In a town the size of Mountain Lake, news traveled fast. In fact, he'd once heard Hulda Klaassen brag that she often knew someone's business before the persons concerned knew it themselves. He supposed he shouldn't be surprised to receive word of Stephen and Josie's reconciliation the very day it occurred. But did Samantha have to be so joyful about it? David snorted. "Isn't that just fine and dandy."

Samantha apparently missed his sarcastic tone because she nodded enthusiastically. "As a matter of fact, it is. Josie has said all along she loves Stephen. This change in his attitude is what she's prayed for. Aren't you happy for her?"

David regained control of himself and managed to reply in an even tone. "Well, of course, I want her to be happy. I just— well, I'm just taken by surprise, I suppose." *I wanted a chance to talk to her. I wanted her to know how I felt!*

Samantha smiled. "So am I. I certainly wouldn't have imagined Stephen giving her his blessing to continue teaching after the way he's acted. But his willingness to accept it has put the spring back in Josie's step."

David gave the broom a harder swipe than necessary against the mercantile's porch floor. Samantha jumped back as a cloud of dried leaves danced toward her feet. She stared at him, her eyes wide. "David!" Then she tipped her head, her brows pinched together. "Are you jealous?"

Despite the cold wind against his face, heat flooded his cheeks. "I—I'm . . ."

She touched his arm. "David, she was spoken for long before you came to town."

David bowed his head, not even considering an attempt to deny what Samantha intimated.

"I'm sorry if you thought otherwise." Tenderness glowed in his sister's eyes.

David sighed. "It's okay, Sammy. It was a fool notion anyway. What in the world would a woman like Josie see in a man like me?"

Samantha raised her chin, sparks flying in her eyes. "Now listen here! Nobody is going to insult my brother—not even you." She jerked his sleeve. "There's plenty to see in you, Davey. You're hardworking and kindhearted and one of the best-looking men around."

David made a face, and she glared at him fiercely.

"I won't let you think just because Josie doesn't see you as more than a friend there's something wrong with you. It just means Josie isn't the right one for you." She softened her tone as she added, "Besides Josie's longtime love for Stephen, there's something else you need to realize, David. Although Josie is friendly to everyone, she would not allow herself to consider a non-Christian in a more serious light than friendship."

"I know that," David snapped. "Why do you think I—?" He clamped his jaw shut on any admissions about his reason for church attendance.

Samantha gave him a seeking look which he did his best to ignore. Finally she spoke again. "Davey, I'm sorry if you're hurt, but sometimes when you really care about someone, you have to let them go. This may be one of those cases."

David nodded.

She threw her arms around him in a tight hug. "I need to run my errands and then get home. I'll see you in church tomorrow, won't I?"

He gave her a few halfhearted pats on the shoulder around the broom. "Sure." And at church, maybe he'd take Josie aside for a private chat. Before she committed herself to Stephen, she should at least know how David felt about her.

But when Josie entered the sanctuary of the Mennonite church Sunday morning, David found himself tongue-tied. Her joy was palpable. Her eyes sparkled with an inner joy, and she seemed to float rather than walk across the floor. An inner happiness kept a permanent smile on her lips.

He took his regular spot, and Josie took hers, at the end of the bench on his right. She turned her radiant smile on him. "Good morning, David! Isn't it a beautiful day?"

David had thought it windy, gray, and too cold for comfort, but he refrained from raining on her happiness. He cleared his throat. "You're in high spirits this morning."

Josie giggled—a sound that resembled creek water tripping over stones. "Yes, as a matter of fact, I am. And, David, I owe it to you."

David's eyebrows rose. "Me?"

"Well, yes." She lowered her voice and leaned into the space between them. "Remember that day I was so upset, and you told me everything would work out? You kept my hope alive, and you were right. I kept praying that if Stephen and I were to be together, it would somehow iron itself out. And everything has come together wonderfully. Stephen has professed his love to me and given me his blessing to go on teaching in Winston.

From now on, we're going to discuss together any decisions that affect both of us and work out a compromise. He's made me so happy!"

He couldn't respond because people were pouring in, filling up the aisle, and Josie sat up straight on her bench. In spite of everything Josie had said, David fully intended to catch her after the service for a private chat. But Stephen came up the aisle as soon as the service was over and took her arm. David watched her walk away, smiling up at Stephen with that brilliant glow. She seemed to forget David even existed. He stared after the pair, dejected and forgotten.

Adam and Samantha approached. Samantha tucked herself under David's arm and beamed up at him. "Come with us to Adam's folks'. Mother Klaassen invited us all over for dinner."

"We're having a celebration for Josie and Stephen," Adam added.

David's chest tightened. "I have some leftover chicken and corn muffins in my room that need to be eaten before they spoil."

Adam sent David a speculative look. "Are you sure? Josie will be disappointed."

Josie won't even notice I'm gone if Stephen is there. David held the errant thought inside. "I'm sure. Please give Josie my best, and tell her I'll try to see her soon." Although no one had said so, he knew he wouldn't be driving her to Winston this afternoon.

Adam shrugged. "All right then. I guess we'll talk to you later."

Samantha reached up to hug her brother, whispering in his ear, "Things will work out for you, too, David. Don't be sad."

David returned Samantha's hug a little too firmly. "I'm fine, Sam." He added with forced cheerfulness, "Go enjoy your meal. And eat enough for me, too. Laura's a wonderful cook."

Adam laughed and told David as the three made their way outside, "I'll tell her you said so, and maybe she'll save you a piece of pie."

"Sounds good to me." David jammed his hands into his trouser pockets and headed for the boardinghouse. In his room, he sat on the edge of the bed and nibbled on a dry corn muffin. He glanced around the quiet, unadorned space, absorbed in gloomy thoughts.

This room is no different than my room in Minneapolis—or the ones back in Wisconsin. I'm still alone. I sit alone, I eat alone, I sleep alone. . . . Sammy is here in Mountain Lake, but she has her own family and circle of friends, and I'm always the odd man out. I'm just as lonely as ever.

He put aside the muffin and crossed to the window overlooking the street. The wind waved leafless tree branches and swirled the powdery snow in snakelike patterns along the hard surface of the street. David unbuttoned his shirt and drew it off, tossing it across a chair in the corner. In long johns and pants, he looked outward. Not much to see—no one around. Sunday afternoons were family times. And he didn't fit anywhere.

He pulled the wooden chair next to the window and sat, his stocking feet propped up on the windowsill. He aimed his gaze out the window, unseeing, as self-pitying thoughts continued to roll backward, considering all the ways he'd been dealt a raw deal by life. Fathered by a man who loved liquor more than his children. Mothered by a good woman but who died far too young. Partly raised by a grandmother who went to heaven too soon.

How different his and Samantha's lives would have been if Mama hadn't died in childbirth. If she'd lived, he wouldn't have left home so early, losing his sister in the process. He wouldn't have ended up in Minneapolis, pretending to be someone he wasn't. All those years of loneliness would have been filled if he could have stayed in his childhood home with his parents and sister.

His self-pity changed quickly to recriminations as a stab of guilt pierced through his heart. The choice he'd made his last night at home—the long-ago night when he had sneaked into Sammy's room—overwhelmed him. If he closed his eyes, he could still see the look of complete trust on his sister's face as he promised he'd come back for her. But he'd failed her, believing Pa's lie that she'd run off too. His stupidity and helplessness to forge ahead anyway and find her had cost her years of suffering.

Sammy had forgiven him. But he couldn't forgive himself.

He sat up abruptly, his feet hitting the floor with a resounding thud. His head sank low, his hands clutched his head, his back curled forward as if carrying a burden too heavy to bear. What kind of a person leaves a little girl in a home like that? He knew the answer: a person unworthy of love. Someone like himself. A person who had harbored feelings of hate and resentment for years, who had lied about his own identity for his own selfish ends. A man who was even now misleading the people he supposedly cared about into thinking he was interested in their God by sitting in their church services with them. Yes, he was unworthy of love.

It must be true. Surely if he was worthy of love, he would have it by now. Surely if he was worthy of being loved, Josie would have returned his feelings. He pictured her again as she had looked in church that morning, smiling and happy and glowing. Glowing with love—for someone else.

He hadn't known a heart could actually ache, but his pained him with an intensity he found frightening. He rose slowly, painfully, and stumbled to the bed with its rumpled sheets and leftover muffin crumbs. He dropped across it, burying his head in the pillow. No, he wasn't worthy of Josie's love—he firmly believed that—but he still longed for her presence, her goodness, her gentleness. In his mind, she was the epitome of perfection.

"And too good for you, you fool," he berated himself.

Josie was better off with Stephen, the man she prayed would come to her. It was for the best. She could never be happy with the likes of David O'Brien. David was a grown man, not a child, but he finally gave in to his aching heart and wept.

*D*avid awoke with a dull ache at the back of his head. He groaned and sat up, rubbing itchy eyes. Unfolding his stiff muscles, he stood and padded to the window. The shadows were long now—late afternoon. He must have slept for several hours.

He crossed to the wash basin that sat next to the bed and splashed some water from the pitcher into the washbowl. After scrubbing his face, he lifted his head and encountered his own reflection in the small, square mirror hanging from a nail above the washstand. His face was pale, the freckles standing out like poppies in a field of daisies. He looked just the way he felt—washed out.

Glancing at the small wind-up clock on the bachelor's chest across from the bed, he realized it was nearly time for the evening service at church. Although the idea of listening to a sermon had no appeal, the thought of staying alone in this room the rest of the evening appealed even less. After his soul-wrenching time of loneliness, he needed to be with people. He had time for an all-over wash and a change of clothes, and then he would attend the service.

Evening services were much less formal than morning worship times, David had discovered the few times he'd gone to the second one. There was more singing, less structure, and instead of standing behind the wooden pedestal and delivering a sermon, Reverend Goertzen came down to sit on the organ stool and presented a simple lesson. During the winter months, he had spent Sunday evenings expanding on the character traits of various Bible-era men.

Tonight the minister opened his Bible to the book of Psalms and began to read. "'Why are you in despair, O my soul? And why have you become disturbed within me? . . . O my God, my soul is in despair within me . . . I will say to God my rock, "Why hast Thou forgotten me?"'" He paused, glancing over the congregation. "Do these sound like the words of a happy man?"

David stifled a snort. The words sounded like him.

Reverend Goertzen continued, "These are the words of a man named David."

David? He sat up, intrigued.

"I know we've all heard stories about David," the pastor was saying. "David the shepherd boy, protecting his sheep by killing a lion and a bear with only his hands. David as a boy on the battlefield, winning the battle against the giant Goliath, using only a sling and stones as his weapon."

David listened closely. A child had done such things?

"Even as a youngster, David had a mighty faith in God. And he grew up to do great things for his God." Reverend Goertzen held up a finger, and one eyebrow raised high. "But—he was also human, and he made many mistakes. Those mistakes, and the guilt he experienced as a result of those mistakes, led him to write the words of anguish I just read for you."

David found himself captivated by this namesake in the Bible. Perhaps it was the common name that had caught his attention, perhaps it was the despairing words the man had written, perhaps it was that this man from the Bible was human and made mistakes. Whatever the reason, he leaned forward to hear what would be said next about this other David.

Reverend Goertzen set his Bible on the organ and placed both hands on his knees. "I can't help but acknowledge David as a great man of faith. He firmly believed that God was the power that undergirded his own strength. He knew God's protecting hand kept him from harm. He looked to God before battles, asking for God's wisdom. And the Lord was there." He looked once again out over his audience. David, from his seat in the back of the room, wondered if the preacher was looking for him.

"But David, despite his great faith, also made terrible mistakes. He once murdered a man, so he could take that man's wife. And he engaged in adultery. Many times, he went off on his own selfish excursions, ignoring God's leading. Because, you see, David was human."

David found it interesting that the minister could refer to a man who had performed such atrocities—adultery, murder—as a man of great faith. How could this well-known Bible figure have faith and still do such horrendous things?

"And God, in His great wisdom," Reverend Goertzen said, "recognized David's humanness and therefore could forgive him his transgressions. David was always sorry for his wrongdoings. Oh, he made attempts to hide them from God. Once he even cried out"—he picked up his Bible again—"'Turn Thy gaze away from me, that I might smile again . . .' I believe David knew he had been wrong and was ashamed to have God seeing his weaknesses. But we can't really hide anything from God, can we? He sees our hearts just as clearly as he saw David's, and He is willing to forgive us just as He was willing to forgive David."

David's brows came together in puzzlement. Could this really be true? God could look on a man's evil heart and still be forgiving?

"You see, it's a matter of faith," the minister went on, almost as if he was answering David's questions. "This man of such contradictions, when all was said and done, had faith. He knew deep down that God was bigger, wiser, and more powerful than King David could ever be. God knew what was best, and David knew that, too. It didn't keep him from going his own way, doing some abhorrent things—that was the human part of him coming through. But because David had faith, his heart ultimately was open to God's guidance, and he was still able to receive God's blessings."

Reverend Goertzen smiled at the people gathered in the small church. "Those same blessings can be ours, even with our imperfections and unworthiness. All it takes is faith—the same faith David had—in a wise and loving God. Our fears and feelings of worthlessness can be set aside, knowing that God cares for us and wants to guide us along the pathways He knows are the best."

David glanced up the aisle at Josie, who sat near her mother. Maybe Josie was being guided down the right pathways with Stephen at her side. Should David stand in the way of what was best for her?

The minister said, "Once we believe, as David did, that God is sovereign—the One who is all powerful, all knowing—then we give Him the reins of our life, the control, and we are then ready to receive the precious gifts He wishes to bestow on us. All it takes is the laying down of our selfish notions, and by faith receiving Him into our lives."

He paused, thumbing through his Bible again. He looked up. "Let me read to you some more of David's words: 'For the Lord God is a sun and shield; the Lord gives grace and glory; no good thing does He withhold from those who walk uprightly. . . . How blessed is the man who trusts in Thee!'"

He closed the Book, laid it in his lap, and smiled once more. "Those are not words of despair. Those are words from a man who had done wrong, but who has not lost his faith. May we learn from David's life."

David could hardly wait for the closing hymn to end. Unmindful of the others in the congregation, David shot up the aisle's pine boards to the minister. He clasped Reverend Goertzen's hand and blurted, "I want to learn more about this David."

The reverend drew back momentarily, as if startled, but he quickly recovered his smile. "Why, certainly. Come with me." He led David to a small bookshelf at the back of the church and re-moved a leather-bound Bible from the top shelf. He placed it in David's hands. "You can read about David in First and Second Samuel. That will give his background and tell the events of his life. In Psalms, you will find words that David himself wrote, including those I quoted tonight."

Reverend Goertzen put his hand on David's shoulder. "I be-lieve you will learn from David's humanness and his desire to do what was right. And of course if you have questions or if I can be of help to you in any way, please call on me anytime."

David looked down at the Book in his hands, eager to get back to his room and begin reading. "Thank you. I'll do that." Intent on beginning his journey into David's life, he said a quick good-bye to Samantha and Adam and left the church. He lengthened his usually long strides to get him home quickly. He hoped to find how this man David could still be worthy of God's blessings when the man had failed in so many ways.

⤺⤻

Without the deliveries to Winston filling the weekends, David had extra time on his hands. He spent Friday evenings with Samantha and Adam and Sunday afternoons reading the Bible Reverend Goertzen had provided. After reading about David, he went on to read about other biblical characters, and he found he could relate to many of them. But after he discovered the Gospels, he found he liked reading about Jesus most.

He engaged Adam in many in-depth discussions that seemed to thrill Samantha as much as they intrigued David. He began to understand that sometimes the all-knowing God allowed difficult things to happen in life that could potentially result in good. With that understanding came a blessed acceptance that, although his thoughts and actions were often far from perfect, he could still find forgiveness and happiness.

The hardest thing, though, was coming to accept that Josie was meant to be only his friend. He truly missed those times spent with her and wondered if someone else would ever be able to fill the empty void left by those treks back and forth to Winston with Josie.

The freezing temperatures of November were keeping her holed up in Winston instead of coming home on weekends. He missed her, even merely seeing her in church, and he was sure Stephen must miss her too. Sometimes he even could sympathize with the man instead of envying him.

Fortunately, the store kept him busy. Hiram and Hulda had established a relationship with him that he found touching, ". . . almost like the son we never had," Hulda told him once. He was fond of them, too, and was glad to be included as part of their family. It made him work all the harder, wanting to please these two who put so much trust in him.

The Tuesday before Thanksgiving celebrations, Priscilla Koehn and her mother came into the mercantile to make some dinner purchases for the coming Thursday. While Millie picked through a basket of yams, Priscilla wandered the dress goods section, idly smoothing her hand across bolts of cloth. Hulda was helping Millie, so David wandered over to offer Priscilla assistance.

He hadn't spoken to the girl in weeks, although their paths had crossed many times. Each time, Priscilla had averted her gaze, and David had not tried to get her attention. It seemed odd, not having her look for occasions to spar with him.

He experienced a prickle of unease as he stopped on the other side of the fabric table. "Miss Koehn, can I help you with anything?"

She turned, her wide-eyed expression containing none her coy and flirting manner he had come to expect. Her lips tipped into a small smile before she shook her head. "Oh, no, I really don't need another dress. I was just looking. I enjoy seeing the new fabrics."

She was cordial—very pleasant, with no undertones—and she had said she didn't need a new dress. *This is Priscilla?* "Well, then . . ." he turned to leave her on her own. "I guess I'll just—"

"David, wait a moment, please." Priscilla scuttled around the table and reached out a hand that didn't quite touch him.

He paused, looking into those blue eyes. "Yes?"

She twisted her fingers through the fringe of her shawl. "I—I never really thanked you. You know, for . . ." She turned her face away.

David nodded his understanding. "It's all right, Miss Koehn. I trust he—I hope you have not been bothered anymore?"

Priscilla shook her head, her wide blue eyes still locked on David's. "No, and I haven't given him any reason to."

Despite himself, David had to smile. She looked like a little kid giving a report on her school grades. He felt almost fatherly as he replied, "Well, I'm glad to hear that."

She dropped her gaze then, still fussing with the fringe on her shawl. After a few minutes of awkward silence, she looked up and asked, "So, do you have plans for Thanksgiving?"

"Thanksgiving?" The abrupt conversational turn caught David off guard. He gathered his thoughts. "Why, yes, thank you. I do. The Klaassens have invited me to join them."

Priscilla nodded and smiled. "Oh, that's nice. I would hate for you to be all alone on Thanksgiving. I think Stephen will be having dinner with our family, then go out to spend the afternoon with Josie. He's looking forward to it. He hasn't seen her in three weeks."

"Yes, well . . ."

"Priscilla? I'm finished," Millie called. "Are you ready to go?"

"Yes, Mother." She gave David a last sweetly shy smile. "Have a happy Thanksgiving, David."

"Yes. You too, Priscilla." He watched her go. *She's a beautiful girl, and today was even enjoyable. So what do you think about that, David O'Brien?*

riscilla's thoughts remained in the store with David during the walk home through the brisk air. Actually, her thoughts had been on him for weeks, ever since he'd rescued her in Jost's barn. The way he'd fought Lucas and then turned around and scolded her still confused her. There were many times her father had jumped to her defense even when her behavior had been questionable, but he had never then accused her of bringing it on herself. She couldn't understand David at all.

He intrigued her. He had never succumbed to her teasing and flirting. She supposed she should find that insulting, but for some reason it gave him a strength of character she found attractive. She discovered that, deep down, she didn't really want to be able to lead him around by the nose; if she could, it would demean him. For once she'd found a man who wouldn't put up with her nonsense. But why did she find that appealing?

She helped Mama put the groceries away before shutting herself in her bedroom. Stretching out on her stomach across the bed, she propped her chin on her hands and let her thoughts drift. Closing her eyes, she could picture David clearly—his tall, slender frame, his unruly hair of autumn shades, his pale blue eyes that watched her warily.

His eyes were always wary, except that time in the barn, after Lucas had left, and she was crying. He had looked at her differently then. She remembered his expression—that odd, unreadable look—before he'd begun to scold. He'd first been comforting her, and he had become stern again. Her heart lifted with hope. Could it be possible that he found her just a little bit attractive?

She swung herself off the bed and crossed to the large mirror in the corner. She gazed at her reflection, trying to see herself as David might see her. She'd been blessed with the best of both parents' features—Mother's high cheekbones, heart-shaped face, and perfectly formed nose, and Papa's full lips and eyes of deep, dark blue. Her almost black hair required little attention, thanks to the natural waves passed on by Papa. Her figure was trim—not skinny, but she was without any unnecessary padding. All in all, she was a pleasing package. And she'd always figured out ways to show it off to good advantage.

How many hours had she spent in front of this mirror, practicing pouty looks and secretive smiles and fluttering, flirtatious gazes meant to capture the attention of any available male? Those hours seemed wasteful now, when what really mattered was what David saw.

And she knew what he saw: a spoiled, selfish brat! He'd made that clear enough when he'd said those very words.

It stung once more, reliving the humiliating way he'd berated her. She threw herself back across her bed with enough force to make the springs twang. It was frustrating and mortifying, but who could blame him? She knew he was right, that she was spoiled and manipulative, and she usually acted without conscience. She'd been that way since she was a very little girl; her earliest memories were of being pampered and petted and told how pretty she was. It hadn't taken much practice to learn to manipulate everyone around her, and she'd always enjoyed it.

Until now. Now, impressing David was much more important than getting her own way. She wanted him to see her differently, but first she had to be different.

She certainly felt different. Ever since the frightening experience with Lucas, she'd been less sure of herself. Just as she'd promised David, she had given up flirting and teasing. When balanced against the possible consequences, it had lost its appeal.

She'd tried very hard to be demure and polite in the mercantile today, and she thought David had noticed. She hoped David had noticed. . . .

Rolling onto her back, she threw her arms above her head and stared at the rose-papered ceiling through the veil of the lace canopy. Somehow, she wanted to win David's heart. But how?

A tap on her door interrupted her thoughts, and she sat up. "Come in."

Stephen stuck his head in. "Sorry to disturb you, Prissy, but Ma needs your help with supper."

She set her thoughts aside and stood up. "I'm coming." Stephen was turning to leave when an idea struck. She ran to the door. "Stephen, just a minute, please."

He stopped. Was her use of "please" the reason he stared at her so thoughtfully?

"What is it, Pris?"

"You're going out to the Klaassens' Thanksgiving afternoon, aren't you?"

"Yes . . . why?"

"May I come along? I haven't seen Josie lately either, and I'd love to find out how she's doing with teaching and everything. Do you think it would be all right?" All right, she was gilding the lily as was her habit, but maybe just this once more . . . ?

Confusion clouded her brother's face. "You've never been overly friendly with Josie before. Why now?"

Priscilla sputtered, "I—I'd like to catch up. If she's going to be my sister-in-law, shouldn't we try to be friends?" She could tell Stephen didn't believe her and was ready to say no. Old habits rose to the fore. "I suppose I should ask Papa instead of you."

Stephen rolled his eyes. "I suppose there's no point in arguing with you. All right, Pris. You can go out with me."

Priscilla smiled. "Thank you, Stephen. And I'll stay out of your way, I promise." A trickle of guilt followed her to the kitchen. She shouldn't have fabricated a reason, and she shouldn't have used her father as leverage against Stephen. But this was the last time, she told herself. It was necessary, this time. Once she'd won David over, she'd never do it again.

⌖

David sat in the midst of the sixteen people crowding around the kitchen table. Two high chairs side by side at the foot of the table held Liz's twins, who added more than their share to the lively conversations.

"Mama?" Sarah's voice carried over the din.

Laura leaned forward to locate Sarah sitting at the other end of the table. "Yes, sweetheart?"

"When we're all done, can we go skating on the pond?" Sarah's bright face looked hopeful. David had helped celebrate her ninth birthday a week ago, and his present was her first pair of ice skates. Hiram had given David a nice discount from the mercantile stock. Sarah's eagerness to try them out sent a little shiver of pleasure through him.

The girl continued, "Frank says it's frozen solid. Can we go?"

Laura turned to Frank. "You've been out to the pond, Frank, and it's frozen?"

Frank swallowed his last bite of mince pie and nodded. "Anna and I have been out there twice already."

Arn joked, "You've had Anna on ice skates? How does she keep her balance with her belly sticking out in front?"

Laura laughed with the rest but made an attempt at admonishing her brash son, while Anna threw her napkin at the teenager. "Now you hush! I can still see my feet."

More chuckles, then Laura looked to Si for his approval before turning back to Sarah. "All right, if your older brothers go with you, you may go ice skating. But—" with a gesture she stopped Sarah from jumping up and running off immediately—"first we need to get this mess cleaned up. You can help with that."

Sarah made a face, but at her father's warning look stood up and began clearing dishes. Becky, Josie, Samantha, Liz, and Anna joined in while the men rose and headed off in various directions—some to the barn, others to the parlor. David chose to stay at the table and sip another cup of coffee, content to be in the warm kitchen listening to the women's cheerful chatter along with rumbling snores from well-fed males in the parlor.

In short order, the table was cleared, the few leftovers were stored in the icebox, and the dishes were washed and put away. The minute the last plate was on the shelf, Sarah ran over to her mother. "Now can we go? Please?"

Laura laughingly hugged her daughter. "Yes, little monkey, you may go now. Wait for Frank and Adam. . . ."

Sarah clattered up the stairs with Becky close on her heels before Laura could finish her sentence. Laura looked at David. "Would you wake Frank and tell him Sarah is ready?"

In the end, half the Klaassens plus David went out to the pond. David and Samantha were the only ones without their own skates, but Josie had decided to stay at the house and watch for Stephen, so she lent hers to Samantha. Frank offered David the use of his skates, but David shook his head.

"I've never ice skated, Frank, and I reckon I'd just end up freezing my backside."

Frank smirked and looked David up and down. "Well, maybe you're wise. They say the bigger they are, the harder they fall. You'd probably crack the ice." They all chuckled, including David, and trudged onward through the snow. Sarah prodded them forward with impatient calls.

"The ice will keep, Sarah!" Adam told her, his arm around Samantha to help her through the drifts. He looked down at his wife. "Are you excited? This will be your first time on the ice too."

Samantha sent a dubious look his way. "I don't know, Adam. If I fall, I won't crack the ice, will I?"

Adam and Frank both laughed hard. "You?" Frank smirked. "A little pipsqueak like you wouldn't even make a dent! But now, Anna here . . ." He let his words drop away as he patted Anna's rounded coat front.

Anna rose to the bait, scooping up a handful of snow and trying to push it down in Frank's collar. They tussled briefly, both of them laughing, before Frank came up with a mock apology and gave his wife a kiss.

At the edge of the pond, they found places in the snow to sit and attach the metal skate runners to the bottoms of their boots. When they all were ready, Frank warned everyone, "Now stay along the edges. I'm pretty sure the middle is not solid enough yet to hold us up."

Adam helped a shaky Samantha to her feet, and she bit down on her lower lip as her ankles turned wobbly on her. Adam assured her, "We've all skated out here every winter for years, honey. Just do like Frank says and stay along the edge. We'll be fine." He kept a firm grip on Samantha's hand as they ventured onto the ice.

David, the only one without skates, cleared snow from a spot on the bank and sat down to watch. He chuckled to himself, observing Sarah's unsteady shuffling in between frequent falls. Teddy and Arn weren't all that graceful, but they managed to stay upright. Tomboy Becky proved surprisingly agile, and Frank and Anna glided along together with practiced ease despite Anna's additional bulk. Samantha didn't do badly, either, holding on to Adam's elbow with two hands and sliding her feet one at a time. David smiled at her as she sailed by his perch, and she tried a little wave and almost lost her balance.

Sarah landed hard on her backside for the umpteenth time. "Ouch!" She slammed a small mitten-covered fist on the ice. "Oh, this makes me so mad!"

Arn skated over and offered a hand. "Come on, Sarah, I'll help you."

Sarah pushed him away. "No! I want to skate by myself!"

Arn backed away, palms raised. "All right then, Miss I-Can-Do-It-Myself."

He skated off as Sarah struggled to her feet, her mouth set in a determined line. She kept her eyes on the tips of her toes as she started out again, elbows high and rear poking out behind her. David propped his elbows on his knees and observed her fledgling efforts with amusement.

But suddenly concern gripped him—she was almost to the center of the pond! He leaped up and waved his arms. "Sarah! Come back this way!"

Sarah paused and looked toward David, fear blooming across her face. She stood stock still, looking around, clearly uncertain what to do.

David considered hollering for Adam or Frank, but they'd skated to the other side of the pond, unaware of Sarah's predicament. He'd waste time waiting for them to return. So he headed onto the ice, moving gingerly. "Hang on, Sarah. I'm coming. Just hold still."

Teddy and Arn skated up and halted near David. Arn said, "David, you're heavier'n me. Let me go."

David held up his hand. "No, you go for help. I'll get her, don't worry."

Arn shot away, calling over his shoulder, "I'm going after Frank and Adam. Teddy, you stay here." And he zinged off.

Teddy hunkered down on his heels to watch as David slid one foot and then the other across the ice. Sarah had obediently remained still but reached her arms for David as he approached. It seemed to take years to reach her, his feet slipping precariously. But at last he took hold of Sarah's hand and gave her a reassuring grin.

"There." He pulled her toward him. "Nothing to it."

The pair turned, Sarah's hand clasped tightly within David's, when a strange noise—a roll like thunder—seemed to come from beneath their feet.

"David!" Sarah's scream combined with the frightening sound of cracking ice.

David reacted instinctively, putting his hands around Sarah's waist and giving her a mighty push. Her arms waving wildly, she went sailing across the ice a good twenty feet before losing her balance and landing face first, spread-eagle. She skidded another four feet before twisting to a stop. Teddy skated to her, grabbed her hand, and pulled her, still on her belly and crying, to safety.

*P*riscilla was laughing and chatting with Stephen and Josie as they walked to the pond to see how the skaters were doing. After trailing Stephen into the house, she'd seen the look of surprise on Josie's face, but within a few minutes Josie was her happy, relaxed self and acting as if Priscilla had visited dozens of times. Priscilla discovered she enjoyed visiting with Josie and berated herself for her prior ill-treatment of Stephen's girl. She hoped they'd be able to become real friends.

When the little group topped the hill, Stephen pointed. "What's David doing out there? That's not safe."

Priscilla's mittened hands went to her mouth, and fear shot through her whole body.

"Come on, hurry," Stephen ordered. He grabbed both women's arms, and the trio took off, awkwardly running and slipping down the hill. They were almost there when they saw the ice beneath David's feet open up.

Priscilla's shrill scream echoed over the ice as she watched David scramble for some kind of handhold along the edge of the hole, his face filled with terror. The ice gave another loud crack! . . . and he disappeared.

Priscilla stood, frozen, a few yards from the edge of the pond while activity exploded on the bank. The ones in skates were at the spot where Sarah and Teddy were huddled together, crying. They all tore off their skates while Stephen snatched up a dead tree branch from beside the pond and rushed onto the ice, skidding toward the spot where David had disappeared. Samantha, terror etched on her face, started to follow, but Adam held her back. "Sam! No! Stay here—we'll get him. I promise."

Anna caught hold of Samantha, holding her back with both arms, and Adam and Frank inched their way over the ice. Stephen stretched out on his belly and thrust the branch into the hole. He called over his shoulder, "Careful! Down! Too much weight on the ice!"

Adam and Frank dropped to crawl the last few feet.

Stephen swept the branch back and forth, his face crunched in concentration.

Adam yelled, "Can you find him?"

Stephen's excited shout echoed across the pond. "Yes, I think so! I've grabbed something, and I think it's his coat. But I can't pull him up—help me!"

Priscilla's heart leaped with hope. She found the ability to move, and she bustled to Samantha, pulling her snug in a helpless effort to shield her from the awful sight. Josie and Anna stood in a huddle with Arn, Becky, Teddy, and Sarah.

Sarah cried, "It's my fault! I'm so sorry—it's my fault!" Priscilla wished someone could comfort the distraught child. To her great relief, Josie knelt and put her arms around her little sister.

Frank slid on his belly to one side of the hole with Stephen on the other. They both reached into the water, their bodies shuddering in response to the frigid water and fear. Priscilla trembled from head to toe as she held tight to Samantha, who sobbed within the circle of Priscilla's restraining arms. Priscilla resisted watching the drama out on the pond, but she seemed unable to tear her frantic gaze away.

Then Stephen gave a triumphant yell. "Got 'im! Help me pull, Frank!"

The men pulled together at the fragile edges of the hole, and first David's arms and head, then his shoulders, emerged. He lay face down on the ice, with most of him still dangling through the hole. Drenched and limp, he might have been a large, discarded doll. Priscilla bit down on her lip, withholding a cry of alarm as his body seemed to slide back toward the opening.

"I'm going to lose my grip on him." Desperation tinged Frank's tone. "Adam, help us!"

Samantha pulled away from Priscilla's grasp, her fist pressed to her mouth. She moaned, "Oh, please, please don't let him drown . . . or any of them out there." Priscilla wrapped her arms around the frightened woman once more, finding a small measure of comfort in her attempt to soothe Samantha.

Adam inched forward on his stomach. Minutes dragged like hours until Adam took a grip on the back of David's coat. With three of them tugging, they finally managed to drag David from the water and onto the ice.

Once David was clear of the jagged hole, Samantha squirmed to get away, but Priscilla held tight. "No! We can't have any more weight on the ice. You've got to stay here!"

"But I—"

"The danger isn't over yet," Anna barked, her tone severe. "Don't get in the way, Samantha. Do you hear me? They could all go in!"

Samantha collapsed in Priscilla's arms, wailing, "Oh, God, please let them be safe! Don't let them drown. And please, please, help David—"

Priscilla held tight to David's sister, willing Samantha's words to find their way to heaven and be honored.

Still on their stomachs, Adam, Frank, and Stephen snaked backward, pulling David's unresponsive body with them. Snaps and crackles accompanied the men, giving every moment an increasing sense of urgency.

Finally the rescuers reached the edge, and they struggled to their feet and pulled David to safety while everyone else gathered around. Adam immediately began stripping the water-soaked coat from David's inert frame. Samantha hung over his shoulder. "What are you doing? Why are you taking his clothes off?"

"We've got to try to warm him up, Sammy," Adam said through clenched teeth.

Frank had already yanked off his own coat. He and Stephen wrapped it snugly around David while Adam used his own coat to dry David's face and hair.

Samantha leaned forward to touch her brother's chalky face. "Davey?" The tall man gave no response—not even a flicker of his eyelids. "Davey, please be all right." Her broken plea caught at Priscilla's heart, and she hugged herself as a deep fear chilled her from the inside out.

"We've got to get him back to the house." Adam turned to Arn. "Run on ahead and have Pa go for Dr. Newton. Tell Ma to get a bed ready and some hot water going. Hurry!"

Arn scuttled off through the snow.

"Do you think you can carry him?" Anna asked.

"We have to." Stephen took a firm hold on David's legs, and Adam and Frank each grabbed an arm, with Adam sliding a hand beneath David's neck to support his head. "Ready?" Stephen asked. The others nodded, and he said, "All right—lift!" They struggled to their feet.

"Girls, you're going to have to lead," Adam panted. "Break us a wider path. We can't carry him and get through the snow too."

Josie directed, "Anna, not you in your condition. You follow behind with Sarah and Teddy. The rest of us can do it. Come on, four abreast—and quickly!"

Priscilla hurried to Josie's side, joined by Samantha and Becky. They linked arms and began stamping a wide path in the snow for the men to follow. Priscilla risked a glance over her shoulder and caught sight of David's white face bobbing up and down with each uneven, staggering step. A sob rose in her throat as she looked at his blue lips and motionless form. Surely they were too late. It didn't appear as if there was any life left in him.

A solemn group waited in the parlor for the doctor to come down and give them news. Priscilla sat in the corner, away from the others, chewing her thumbnail in nervous anticipation. With no downstairs bedrooms, David had been placed into Si and Laura Klaassen's bed after an arduous trek up the stairs. Laura and Samantha stripped him of his wet clothing, rubbed him down with towels, and dressed him in some of Si's warm, woolen long johns and a nightshirt. They'd then bundled him under several layers of sheets and quilts.

Samantha tearfully told the rest of the family that all the time they worked with him, David never opened his eyes or made a sound. "But he was breathing, even though it was awfully shallow," Samantha finished.

Adam took his wife's hand. "Then we have hope." And Samantha nodded before slipping into his embrace.

Arn stood staring out the window. He released a sudden huff. "This is all my fault. I knew he was too heavy to go out there, but I didn't stop him."

Sarah, cuddled on her father's lap, argued in a tear-choked voice, "But if I had let you help me skate, I never would've ended up in the middle, and nobody would've had to come after me. It's my fault, Arn, not yours."

Frank added, "I feel to blame. I was off laughing and having fun. I should have stuck close to keep an eye on Sarah. If anyone is to blame, it's me."

Samantha lifted her head from Adam's shoulder and frowned at everyone. "It's nobody's fault. It just happened, and blaming yourselves isn't going to help anything. David wouldn't want us down here faultfinding and feeling sorry for ourselves."

Priscilla blinked in amazement as various family members tried to take responsibility for David's accident. After years of pointing her finger of blame at others, she found their selflessness admirable, and she experienced a prick of conscience at her past self-serving behavior.

Adam hugged Samantha close again, resting his cheek against her tousled hair. "Sammy's right. It's a waste of energy to try to decide who's to blame here. I think we'd be better off using our time to pray for David."

Priscilla jolted, a wave of recognition washing over her. Her heart had risen into her throat the moment she'd seen David fall below the surface of the ice, and it was still lodged there, pumping hard enough to hinder her breathing. But in all the time of worry and fear, not once had she thought about praying. For the first time in her life, she wanted to pray, but she didn't know how. The realization frightened her.

Hiram charged into the parlor and announced, "Dr. Newton is coming down."

Samantha and Adam rushed to the stairway, followed closely by everyone else. Priscilla joined the throng near the center, held in place with the crush of expectant bodies. The small, wiry doctor came down, with Hulda making her plodding progress right behind him. His feet had barely reached the bottom step before Samantha addressed him.

"Dr. Newton, is my brother going to be all right?"

The doctor placed a hand on Samantha's shoulder. His eyes behind the spectacles glowed with compassion. "Samantha, come here. Let's sit down." He held his hand toward the table, but Samantha shook her head.

"I can't sit there right now." She turned her glittering gaze on Adam. "We gathered there just a few hours ago—a lifetime ago—laughing and talking and enjoying Thanksgiving dinner together. . . ." Her voice broke. "I—I can't sit there."

Adam nodded, his arm pulling her tight to his side. "It's all right. Doc, just tell us, please."

Priscilla held her breath, begging for good news. Samantha had lost so much; it hardly seemed fair she might lose her only brother, too.

The doctor sank down in the nearest chair and removed his spectacles. Then he gave Samantha a serious look. "I'm not going to lie to you. David is in a very serious state."

A collective gasp traveled through the little group.

"He was in the water, without oxygen, for quite a while from what I've been able to piece together from everyone here. There's no doubt he took water into his lungs as well. His body temperature is below normal, and he's having a hard time breathing. The lack of oxygen could result in brain damage."

"B-brain damage?" Samantha clutched at Adam, and his hand patted her back. She asked the question quivering on Priscilla's lips: "When will we know?"

"Not until he wakes up." The doctor took in a big breath. "Right now we need to keep him warm, make sure we give him lots of liquids, and as a safeguard I'm going to set up a mist tent and keep steam going for him to inhale. It will help clear his lungs and aid his breathing. I wish there was more, but . . ." He broke off to rub the bridge of his nose. He returned his glasses to his face, looked at Samantha again, and said kindly, "We'll just have to wait and see. If we can see him safely through the next forty-eight hours, then I think there's a good chance for full recovery."

Samantha nodded woodenly. She turned to Adam. "I'll stay here and help care for him."

"Of course, sweetheart. I wouldn't ask you to leave as long as your brother needs you."

Samantha spoke to the doctor. "May I go up to him now?"

"Can we all go?" Josie added. Priscilla strained forward, eager to see David for herself.

Dr. Newton nodded but held out a restraining hand. "Only if you promise not to cause a commotion. You can all take a peek at him—assure yourselves that he's safe now—but then you've got to clear out. And another thing . . ." He placed his hand on Samantha's arm, delaying her passage. "He might seem to be asleep right now, but I'm convinced he can still hear you. No crying or saying anything negative up there!" His gaze swept over everyone assembled in the room. "There may be no scientific basis to it, but I still believe positive thoughts and comments bring about positive change. So remember that when you go into his room."

Samantha promised, "I'll be positive. I have to be. I can't bear the thought that I might lose him."

She hurried upstairs with Adam close behind her. Priscilla moved along with the throng, and when she got a look at David lying still and white beneath the pile of covers—his breath coming in rattling gasps—she forgot Dr. Newton's command to be positive. Tears sprang into her eyes, and a low moan crept from between her lips. She pressed her fist to her mouth to hold back any other sound as Samantha turned and flung herself against Adam's chest, clinging and crying soundlessly.

Adam rubbed his hands up and down across her shaking back. "Shh, now, Sammy. Remember what Doc said?"

"I kn-know, Adam, but he—he looks—"

Don't say it! Priscilla's thoughts commanded.

Adam whispered firmly, "None of that, Sammy. He's alive, and we're going to do everything in our power to keep him that way."

Samantha gained control, taking in a deep shuddering breath that halted her tears. Priscilla determined to be just as brave. She sniffed hard, blinking rapidly to clear her vision, and watched Samantha make her way to the bed. She sat gingerly on the edge of the mattress and stroked David's wild hair. "David, I'm here. And I'm going to stay here until you're all better."

Priscilla thought her heart might break as she listened to Samantha speak to her brother.

"You were so brave, going after Sarah. I'm so proud of you. You were thinking of her then, and she's fine because of it. Now it's time to think of yourself. We're all fighting for you, Davey, so you fight, too. Try really hard to get well. B-because if you d-don't, I—I—" Her shoulder convulsed.

Adam gripped her upper arms and lifted her from the bed. "Come on, Sammy. Let Ma see to David for now, and you rest. You can come in later and spell her, okay?" He bobbed his head at the others, and as a group they shuffled out the door. Priscilla held to the doorknob, waiting until everyone passed.

Adam led Samantha out the door, and Laura Klaassen approached Priscilla. She offered a tender look. "Go on with the others, Priscilla. I'll take good care of David." With a gentle nudge, she urged Priscilla out the door.

Priscilla tipped sideways as the door slipped closed, receiving one final peek of David's colorless face. She feared the image would be imbedded in her memory forever.

ल७

It's cold—so cold! And dark . . . God—oh, God, I can't breathe . . . Sarah? Is she . . . ? Where is she?

"Sarah! Sarah!" His own voice rasped in his ears, and a rustling penetrated David's fuzzy brain. Someone caught his hand and pressed a kiss to its back. "It's all right, David." The soothing voice—his sister's voice—seemed to come from far away. "Sarah's fine. You saved her. Rest now." He could hear the words, but they didn't make sense.

David flailed beneath the covers, yanking his hand free to clutch fitfully at the edge of the quilt. The voice continued to murmur, a hand touched his hair, his cheek, while he thrashed, frantically trying to fight his way through the darkness.

Exhaustion claimed him, and he ended his fight. With a rough expulsion of breath, he collapsed against the bed and submitted to the welcoming blackness once more.

❧

Samantha allowed Hulda and Laura to talk her away from David's bedside occasionally, with the caution that she wouldn't be able to care for him at all if she totally exhausted herself. The three took turns sponging him down with cool water to combat the fever—his body temperature had risen during the first night and then refused to go back down—spooning clear broth and water into his slack mouth, applying soothing glycerin to his chapped lips, filling the kettle to keep a steady stream of steam clouding the room. . . . It was an enormous effort for all three of them, but especially for Samantha for whom the mental and emotional stress was far more draining than the physical.

The critical forty-eight hours had passed three days ago, and David was still with them. Except for the one time he had called out in his sleep, though, he hadn't spoken or opened his eyes at all. His lack of response was especially disheartening to Samantha, who sat beside his bed and whispered encouragement for him to open his eyes until her throat was hoarse.

Dr. Newton checked in twice a day, monitoring David's temperature and listening to his chest. David had contracted pneumonia, Doc determined the second afternoon, and he added application of mustard poultices to the list of necessary duties.

After the sixth day, the doctor took Samantha downstairs and sat her in a rocking chair. He pulled a kitchen stool close and told her she needed to get a day or two of rest at home.

"But I can't leave him!" Samantha exclaimed tearfully.

"Yes, my dear, you can, and you must. Your brother is in very good hands here, and you will not be able to participate in his care if you are sick yourself." He patted her on the shoulder, picked up his hat and coat, and turned to her before stepping out the door. "Doctor's orders," he said with a little smile. But the finger he shook at her delivered a strong message.

Laura stepped into the kitchen and sat on the kitchen stool. She cupped Samantha's cheek with her hand. "*Liebchen*, I heard what Dr. Newton told you. And I agree. I promise you Hulda and I won't leave David for even a minute."

Samantha put her face into her hands as fresh tears welled. How could a body manufacture so many tears? "B-but what if— what if he slips away," she finally gasped out, "and—and I'm not here to say good-bye?"

Laura embraced Samantha and scolded gently, "What kind of thoughts are those? You can't sit by his side waiting for him to die."

Samantha pulled back, sniffing hard. "I can't help it. He looks so—so deathly white. And he's so still."

"He's gaining strength." Laura spoke with certainty. "This is the body's way of healing after the kind of trauma David has faced. And now you must rest too. Please, Samantha. Go home for a little while. Get some sleep in your own bed, see Adam, and then you can come back. Take a little time for yourself. We'll take good care of David. I promise."

Samantha looked into her mother-in-law's face. At last weariness won out, and she dropped her head. "All right, I'll go. But if anything—anything—changes, send Arn or Papa Klaassen for me right away, please?"

"Of course," Laura promised.

"I'm going upstairs once more just—just to tell him where I'm going, that I'll be back. . . ."

"Yes, that's fine, Samantha. I'll have Si take you home."

When Samantha returned to the kitchen, ready to go home after nearly a week away, she was surprised to find Millie and Priscilla Koehn sitting at the table.

*P*riscilla sat primly at Mama's right with her hands crossed on the tabletop and her shoulders set in a determined angle. She'd see David today if she had to fight for the opportunity.

Laura Klaassen placed mugs of steaming coffee on the table as Samantha stepped into the room. Samantha sent a puzzled look at Priscilla and her mother. "What brings you two out in this cold weather?"

Mama sighed, sniffling. "Priscilla brings me out. She said she simply had to see how David was doing and wouldn't take no for an answer. So here we are."

Laura smiled, as relaxed as if Priscilla and Mama visited every day. "It's sweet of you to be concerned. David is still sleeping. He roused once the second night, apparently having a dream, but he drifted back off again. We continue to give him liquids, keep a mustard poultice on his chest, and the steam kettle going. . . . Other than waiting, there's not much more we can do. Isn't that right, Samantha?"

Samantha sat sideways on the kitchen bench, resting an elbow on the table to prop up her chin. Priscilla reached across to pat Samantha's arm. "How are you holding up?" Samantha's brows furrowed, and Priscilla sat still and unwavering beneath the other woman's perusal. Finally Samantha sighed. "As well as can be expected, I suppose. The waiting is just so hard. . . ."

Honest sympathy welled in Priscilla's chest. "You look as if you need a rest."

"Yes, she does," Laura put in, "and Samantha has just agreed to take one. Hulda and I will be watching David so Samantha can go home and get some sleep."

Priscilla sat up straight. "Mrs. Klaassen, may I help, too?" The women stared at her, open-mouthed. Heat flooded Priscilla's face at their obvious shock. She ducked her head, shamed. She deserved such a reaction. "I know what you're all thinking, and I don't blame you. But I—I care for David too, and I want to help. Really, I do."

Her mother leaned close. "It isn't easy, nursing. Are you sure you know what you're asking, Priscilla?"

"Probably not, Mama." Priscilla's straightforward answer earned another round of wide eyes. "But I want to try, anyway." She turned to Samantha. "Please, I can understand why you might not even want me to help; I've been awful to you and to David. But—" Her eyes welled with tears. "But I feel if I don't do something to help him, I might die. I hurt in here." She placed a shaky hand against the bodice of her dress. "I need to help."

Samantha looked at Laura, who looked at Mama, who gawked at Priscilla as if seeing her for the first time. Priscilla waited silently for Samantha to make up her mind.

At last Samantha sighed. "It's all right with me if Mother Klaassen doesn't mind showing you what to do. I must be on my way home before I change my mind."

Mama rose. "I brought our sleigh, so I'll take you home myself, Samantha. Prissy, I'll send Stephen or your father out for you later."

"Thank you, Mama." Priscilla stretched both hands toward Samantha. "Rest well." Samantha nodded, bundled herself in her coat, and followed Mama out the door.

Upstairs, Priscilla listened attentively as Laura explained how to keep the steam billowing, how often to change the poultices, and the best way to prop David's head to keep him from choking when spooning liquids into his uncooperative mouth.

The woman touched Priscilla's arm. "Are you sure you want to do this?"

Although her stomach rolled with apprehension, Priscilla nodded. "I am very sure, Mrs. Klaassen."

"All right, then. I'll be downstairs fixing supper if you need anything."

"Thank you, ma'am." Priscilla removed a cloth from the pan of water next to David's bed and wrung it out, then gently draped the cool cloth across David's forehead. She listened until Mrs. Klaassen's footsteps faded down the stairs then she scurried to the door. Peeking right and left, she ascertained no one was near enough to overhear. On tiptoe, she returned to the bed and sat on its edge, placing her hand lightly on David's chest.

"David?" She watched his face for any reaction. "David, it's me, Priscilla. I know you didn't expect me, but I'm here just the same. I had to come. There are things you have to know. So I want you to listen to me, please."

Leaning forward, she spoke directly into his ear. "I've been a rotten, loathsome person my whole life. You called me spoiled and selfish, and you were right. I've always treated everyone around me badly, and I never cared if I hurt someone. All I cared about was getting my own way. When you came along, and you wouldn't pay any attention to me, it made me mad, and at first all I wanted was to get even with you. But then that changed.

"I went off with Lucas that night just to get your attention. Did you know that? You probably did; you're the only person who ever truly saw through my games. You defended me, then got irritated with me, and I wasn't sure if I should be mad or thankful that you'd come."

Her breath stirred the curls near his ear. She smoothed the hair with her fingers as she continued. "But I've had time to think about it, and, David, I'm thankful for it. I needed someone to wake me up and make me see that the way I was behaving was all wrong."

She sat up straight, tossing her head. "Oh, you've infuriated me with your smugness. But at the same time, I've admired the way you've never given in to me. And maybe you've not given up on me either."

She wasn't sure now if she was talking to David or to herself, but she went on. "I know it sounds funny, but I needed someone to make me be good. And you're the only one who's been able to do that. I hope it's because you cared about me, that you scolded me and told me that I needed to grow up. Because I care about you, David."

Tears clouded her vision, and her throat felt so tight it was hard to speak, but she leaned down again. "David, can you hear me?" Her lips encountered his soft curls. "I'm telling you I love you. I love you! For the first time in my life, I'm thinking about someone other than myself, and it's because of you." She pressed both palms against his chest, feeling the thready beat-beat of his heart. "David, you have to wake up and hear me. You have to know that I love you. I can't go on if you don't know. Even if you don't love me back, I still have to let you know how I feel. David? David!"

She stared at him, waiting for some sort of reaction—a flicker of an eyelid, a twitch of a finger, anything.

Nothing.

Priscilla lifted her face to the ceiling and spoke in a tear-filled voice. "God, are You listening? Do You hear me? I'm praying to You now. I know I've never talked to You before, and I probably shouldn't expect You to listen to me now, but I'm not asking for anything for myself." A choked chuckle escaped. "That sounds very strange coming from me, doesn't it? But it's true." Closing her eyes, she pleaded, "God, heal David. He's such a good person, and his sister loves him so much. What would Samantha do without him? What would I do without him . . . ?"

She paused, lowering her gaze to take in David's relaxed face, white as the pillowcase beneath his head. Her head drooped low as she continued to pray. "God, I know we're not supposed to bargain with You. I have been hearing those sermons all my life. And I hope You won't hold this against me, but I have to offer You something. If You let David live—if You answer this prayer—I'll be Yours from now on. I know I'm not much right now, but I can be good. I really can! And I will be, for You, if You'll please just heal David. It doesn't matter if he never loves me back. I don't want him well for me, I just want him well. Please, God, please . . ."

In time Priscilla opened her eyes. David slept on. She checked the poultice. It was cool. She lifted it and moved quietly across the room to a basket which she then scooped up to take downstairs. She paused by the door, peering back at him, her heart aching with the desire to see him sit up and smile or scold or even tell her to get out of there.

"I'll be right back, David." In a whisper, she added, "I love you."

⁓

Fog everywhere. Thick, white, choking clouds. *Where am I? I can't see. . . . A voice out there somewhere . . . What? What did you say? Oh, you love me. . . . You love me? Who loves me? Who's there? Come where I can see you.*

The man strained beneath the weight of bedclothes. He tried to lift his head. It was so frustrating, the pressing weight.

If he could get out from beneath this heaviness, maybe he could escape the cloying fog.

The voice came again: "Can you hear me?"

Yes, I hear you. . . . But who are you? You are saying you love me. . . . Who? Who?

Suddenly an image of a little girl broke through the clouds, rushing at him. Her hands were held in a gesture of entreaty, her face wore an expression of pain, and he could tell she'd been crying.

Sammy, Sammy, baby, it's all right. I'm here, Sammy. Don't cry. The image faded, sliding backward. . . . *Sammy, where are you going? Wait, Sammy. Wait, come back!*

But she was gone, lost in the swirling mists. Someone else was there now—a man with a leering grin and foul breath. His face loomed, pulled back, then loomed again. He raised a fist and shook it, threatening. . . .

Pa? Is that you? What are you doing here? The man reached out a stubby hand and laughed raucously. "Comin' with me, boy?" *No, Pa, leave me alone! Where did Sammy go? I want to be with Sammy. . . .*

The clouds swallowed the man then changed from white to gray, spinning angrily like a wild, errant whirlwind. He had to get away. He jerked his hands, fighting the grayness that threatened to surround him.

Someone—anyone—help me, please! I don't want to be here all alone. I'm afraid. I know someone is there. Who is it? Sammy, is it you? Reach for me, Sammy. Please, help me out of here.

A voice came as if from a far distance, echoing and resounding, and he couldn't understand the words, only the tone. It was a sad voice, pleading—no, not pleading, it was praying. Praying for him. His heart beat in sudden hope.

Yes, pray for me. Call upon God. He can bring me out of here. God has the strength to push away these clouds and help me find the sun again. *Pray for me. . . . Yes, please, pray for me. . . .*

Slowly, painfully, the gray mists lightened. The swirling clouds slowed to the gentle swaying of wheat tips touched by a sweet spring breeze. Comforting motions, backlit by a yellow brightness. Light dawned—at first, from far away, but drawing closer, closer.. . . Warmth touched him. He felt strength filtering through him as the light beamed around him and the warmth spread from his head to his arms, his chest, his legs. . . .

He struggled, concentrating. It took more effort than anything he'd ever attempted before, but slowly, surely, with great difficulty, he opened his eyes.

A shaft of sunlight from somewhere on David's left hit him square in the face, and he winced. He snapped his eyelids shut again. It was much easier to keep them closed. But where was he? This wasn't his room at the boardinghouse. He braced himself and fought to open his eyes once more. He wished he could raise his hand to shield his eyes from the bright sun, but his arms felt weighted. He didn't have enough strength to lift them.

He squinted, taking in his surroundings, struggling to raise his head slightly from the soft pillow. With effort he turned his head. Unfamiliar wall coverings greeted him—a yellow floral instead of the gray and white stripes of his own room. And furnishings he'd never seen before, part of a bedroom suite with matching etchings and the same maple finish. Where were his own mismatched pieces? His eyes settled on an overstuffed chair in the corner. A woman slumped in it, apparently sleeping. A tangled mass of auburn hair hid her face.

What in the world?

Too tired to make sense of it, he closed his eyes again and let his head slump back against the pillow. As his head fell, the bedsprings creaked gently, and someone yawned noisily. The yawn ended with a startled gasp. Hands curled around his shoulders, and his sister's voice blasted in his ear.

"David, are you awake?"

David forced his heavy eyelids open once more, focusing.

Samantha leaned over his face, her eyes swimming with tears. A smile of hosanna lit her face. "Oh, David, you are awake!" Her hand pressed to his forehead. "You're cool. The fever's gone!"

David, completely disoriented, asked croakily, "Where am I?" He winced. His throat felt parched and sore. He rasped, "What are we doing here?"

But Samantha raced to the open door and called, "Everybody, come quick! David's awake!"

The clattering of footsteps on the stairs multiplied David's confusion while the entire Klaassen family, in various stages of dress, congregated around the bed, smiling and laughing and crying and hugging each other. Samantha remained at the forefront of the joyful throng, leaning across David with a look of wonder on her face. "Oh, David, thank the good Lord, you've come back to us."

"Come back?" David battled to make sense of the commotion. "Where have I been?"

Samantha laughed—a joy-filled laugh that several others echoed. She shook her head. "It doesn't matter now. How do you feel?"

He grimaced. His head felt fuzzy, and his whole body felt weighted down with a pressing weariness. It took great effort to form an answer. "I . . . feel . . . lousy." He hadn't intended to be humorous, but his reply earned another round of laughter.

Laura stepped up, stroking his forehead then taking his hand. "Do you remember what happened, David?"

He shook his head. At least, he thought he shook his head; it was so hard to move. "I'm not sure."

Sarah pushed her way in front of Laura. "You saved my life, David, remember? You pushed me away from the crack in the ice—then you fell in. Remember?"

And then it all came back—the opening beneath his feet, the frantic scrambling to get himself above water, the engulfing darkness and bone-rattling cold of the freezing pond, the terrifying battle to breathe. . . . But beyond that, he couldn't recall a thing—how he got out, how he got to the Klaassens' . . . or why images of Priscilla floated around in the back of his mind.

There was something else, too. Somebody had been talking to him—and praying for him. Somebody who had said she loved him. The effort of putting it all together was too much. He opened his mouth to ask, but nothing came out. Instead, his eyes slid closed, his jaw fell slack, and he drifted off to sleep.

✑◯

When David woke next, instead of a disheveled Samantha hovering near, he found himself being thoroughly perused by Dr. Newton. When the doctor noticed David's open eyes, he smiled broadly. "Well, good day, Mr. O'Brien. I can't tell you what a relief it is to see what's underneath your eyelids."

David yawned. "How long have I been asleep?"

"Eight days." Dr. Newton used a cheery tone. "Are you hungry?"

He did feel empty. He nodded, the motion causing his head to spin.

"Well, we'll get you fixed up in just a minute, but first—" The doctor placed an odd silver cone with a tube attached to it on David's chest, plugging the other end of the tube in his own ear. He listened, scowling, for several seconds, then straightened, a grin splitting his face. "Much better. The poultices and steam seemed to have done their job." He shoved the instrument down into the belly of a black leather bag and shut it with a snap. He perched on the bed, his left leg crossed over the right, and folded his arms across his chest. "So . . . do you have any questions?"

Remembering not to nod, David answered slowly. "Yes, I do. Is Sarah all right?"

"Right as rain. Only a bad scare. Anything else?"

"How'd I get here?"

"Stephen, Frank, and Adam pulled you out. From what I understand, Stephen got hold of you under the ice, and the others helped fish you out. Then they carried you here."

David guessed he owed a few men some thank-yous.

"Any more questions?"

"Yes, one." David was so tired. Talking was torture, but he had to know. "There was somebody here . . . when I was sleeping. Somebody was talking to me, praying for me. . . . Do you know who it was?"

Dr. Newton uncrossed his arms and patted David's shoulder. "Yes, young man, I've got a good guess on that. But I think I'd better let her tell you her name. Now—" He stood up, clapping his hands together. "I'll see if I can't find something for you to eat. It will be a while before you regain your strength, so don't try to get up too soon. Let the ladies baby you a bit longer. I'll be back to see you tomorrow." He pointed an official finger at David's nose. "After your lunch, rest."

"Yes, doctor." He'd have no trouble obeying the order.

The doctor hadn't been gone five minutes before Samantha came in carrying a tray with a bowl of thick vegetable soup, two slices of bread, and a glass of milk. She smiled when she saw he was still awake.

"Hi, Davey. Dr. Newton says you're hungry. I'm sure glad to hear it." She set the tray on the table next to the bed and scolded, "I'm pretty tired of forcing liquids down your throat."

"Sorry to be a bother." His throat felt raw.

Samantha sat on the bed near his hip. "You're not a bother, my dearest brother. And I intend to feed you right now, so open up."

David grinned, his eyelids drooping. "You're bossy."

"Uh-huh, I am. Open up."

David ate some of the soup, half a slice of bread, and drank most of the milk before holding up a hand. "No, Sammy, no more."

She set the spoon aside. "Dr. Newton said your appetite would return slowly, so I won't force any more on you." She sat back, smiling at him.

David held his eyes at half-mast. With his stomach full, he felt stronger and ready to talk a bit. "What are you smiling at?"

"You." Samantha released a happy sigh. "It's just so wonderful to see you awake and to hear your voice. You really scared me."

"I'm sorry. I think I scared me, too."

"Please don't ever try to be a hero again." Samantha's eyes filled with tears. "If something had happened to you—" She covered her face with her hands.

David reached up to the back of her neck. His grasp was weak, but he pulled until Samantha rested her head on his chest. He let his arm lie across her back. "Don't cry now, Sammy. I'm fine. And Sarah's fine. I couldn't let another little girl down. . . ."

Samantha cried harder.

He gave her several weak pats. "All right, the time for tears is over."

"I know," came her muffled voice. "These are relief tears."

David chuckled briefly, which made him cough. Samantha sat up quickly and gave him another drink. When he had calmed, he said, "You women cry for the strangest reasons. . . ."

"Yes, well, you had lots of us crying," Samantha informed him, swishing away the tears with her fingertips. "Me, Josie, Sarah—even Priscilla."

His body jolted with surprise. "Priscilla?"

"Yes." Samantha shook her head, wonder in her gaze. "Priscilla was there when you fell in, and she stayed with me, comforting me. Then she helped take care of you so Mother Laura and Tante Hulda and I could get some rest. She was like a different person; she surprised all of us. I could get to like her, if she would stay this way."

"Priscilla Koehn?"

Samantha nodded. "I think she was as worried about losing you as the rest of us were. You came so very close to slipping away from us, Davey." Her voice wobbled as she battled another bout of tears. "I'm not sure what kept you with us, but I'm thankful for it."

David knew what had kept him from slipping away—the call from the person who claimed to love him. He was convinced of that. But he still wasn't sure who the person was. "Sammy, did you talk to me when I was sleeping?"

Samantha nodded. "Yes. Did you hear me?"

David frowned, trying to remember. Had it been Samantha's voice he'd heard—the one that had called him back? It had been a familiar voice, one he should know, but he didn't think it was Samantha's. "I heard someone, but—" He paused, pressing his memory. "Did anyone else talk to me?"

"Well, yes. Dr. Newton, and Adam and Frank and Josie. Mother Laura and Tante Hulda—all of us talked to you nearly constantly. Priscilla did too when she was here."

Priscilla . . . Could the voice he had heard—the one that prayed for him and told him "I love you"—have been hers? "Where's Priscilla now?"

"Arn took her home yesterday evening. Why?"

"I . . . I should thank her for helping." His mouth stretched in a yawn.

Samantha rose. "Thank-you can wait, big brother. Right now, you need to sleep some more. So I'm going to leave you to it." She kissed his cheek. "Rest well."

David gave a smile in answer and settled back against the pillows once more. Before he drifted off, he thought hazily, *It must have been Priscilla. . . . She loves me, and she prayed for me. . . .* The significance of the realization wouldn't strike him for some time. He slid back into blissful sleep.

or the first few days after David's "reawakening," he spent most of his time in peaceful slumber. He would wake to eat, visit a bit, then sleep again. By the third day, he was ready to sit up in bed with the doctor's blessing, and on the fourth day he even walked with Samantha's protective arm around his waist to the overstuffed chair across the room. They celebrated with cups of hot cocoa, David seated in the chair as proudly as a king on a throne, but with the room reeling around him. He didn't fuss about climbing back in bed.

But by the sixth day, he was restless and making noises about returning to his own room at the boardinghouse and his job at the mercantile. Hiram put that idea to rest in short order.

"Absolutely not!" the little man decreed, his volume belying his diminutive stature. "You will stay right here until you have completely regained your strength. Hulda and I are managing, and your job will keep." He softened, placing a hand on David's shoulder. "You have been through an ordeal, David. We appreciate your dedication to us and the mercantile, but it is more important to take care of yourself right now."

"That is right, David," Hulda added, stepping forward to pat David's hand. "You came dangerously near death, my dear boy, and we must take special care of you now."

Their concern warmed him. He wouldn't worry them by arguing. "All right, Mr. Klaassen and Mrs. Klaassen. I promise to be lazy and demanding for at least another month."

The older couple laughed, with Hiram joking that they couldn't hold his position that long, and bid David a fond goodbye. As they left the room, David pondered their acceptance of him. They viewed him as family, and he felt as close to them as if they were kin. With a jolt, he noted that he'd become an honorary member of the entire Klaassen family. He'd thought Josie was the key, giving him access to belonging, but belonging had been there all along. He simply needed to recognize it. The realization whispered peace around his heart.

Hiram and Hulda weren't the only ones who looked in on David regularly. Frank and Anna, Liz and Jake, Stephen, Reverend Goertzen, and all of the young Klaassen family members stuck their noses in his room to express their joy at his recovery. And of course Samantha visited so often he wondered if she spent any time at her own little home. Adam kidded that he had to visit David to see his own wife.

One person remained pointedly absent, though—Priscilla. He wondered about that during quiet moments when he'd been left alone to nap but didn't feel like napping. If she had helped care for him while he was unconscious—and if she had been the one to plead with the Almighty for his health and proclaim her love for him—then why didn't she come now that he was doing better?

Between visits and between naps, David had time to contemplate not only Priscilla's odd absence, but some other things as well that had pressed on him since he'd regained consciousness. From what he had been able to piece together from the various sources willing to tell their share of the story, it hadn't been an easy feat to get him out of the pond. He'd been in the water for a considerable length of time, eventually developed pneumonia which was often fatal, and had required round-the-clock attention to keep him from dehydrating when he was unable to even sit up for a sip of water on his own volition. By rights, he could have died three different ways. So why hadn't he?

He'd been saved. Certainly all the people caring for him had played a role in his recovery, but he couldn't help but believe there had been something more, some Divine Intervention, as he'd heard the reverend call it, as well. Could there be some purpose he had yet to fulfill—a destiny he was meant to serve? Although the thought seemed egotistical, he couldn't set it aside.

He recalled hearing the sweet voice raised in prayer on his behalf. He was sure that had been a significant one of many prayers that had saved his life. And in one quiet moment two weeks into his recovery, he walked unsteadily to the window, knelt before it and looked out at the beautiful snow-laden landscape. With the golden sun on his face, he spoke his first prayer.

"God, I can't say I understand everything about You yet. But for now, I reckon it's enough that I believe You sent Your Son into this world to be my Savior, just like Reverend Goertzen said. I believe You care. You had Your hand in bringing me back to life, so from now on, my life is Yours. I ask that You forgive my past unbelief, and I trust You to guide my pathways. I know whatever You have planned for me will be what's for the best. Use me in any way You see fit, for You've convinced me I'm a person worth Your love and attention. I surrender my heart to You, God."

A lump of emotion blocked his throat as he gazed outward at the beautiful day. Was it his imagination, or did the sun shine brighter than it had been before?

The morning after placing his life into the keeping of his heavenly Father, David decided it was high time he got some questions answered. When Laura brought in his breakfast, he started, "Mrs. Klaassen, I don't want to be a bother, but—"

Laura's eyebrows rose. "And who has said anything about you being a bother?"

He shrugged sheepishly. "Well, I've been sleeping in your bed, eating your food, taking up your time. . . ."

"And not a one of us have had a single complaint. Now, what do you need?" Laura's no-nonsense attitude put David at ease.

"I hoped someone could get word to Priscilla Koehn that I'd like to see her." He paused, fidgeting under Laura's unwavering gaze. "I've thanked everyone else for their part in caring for me, but Priscilla hasn't been around. I'd like to express my gratitude to her as well."

Laura smiled. "I think that's a lovely idea, David. I'll send a note into town with the school children this morning, and I imagine it won't take her long to arrive." She cocked her head and looked him over. "Before you have a female guest, though, may I make a suggestion?"

Hesitantly, he nodded.

"Now please don't be offended, but you are a mess. Your whiskers have been growing all this time, your hair has gone unwashed, and we've only given you sponge baths. Would a long soak in a tub and a shave feel good?"

David rubbed a hand across the scraggly growth on his chin and scratched his head. "You're right. A bath would be wonderful. But, Mrs. Klaassen . . . ?"

"Yes?"

"You've washed me for the last time. This one's up to me."

Laura laughed. "That, Mr. O'Brien, is exactly what I was thinking."

A knock at the door interrupted the Koehns' breakfast. Stephen rose. "I'll get it."

Teddy Klaassen stood shivering on the doorstep. "A note for Priscilla," he said, thrusting a folded piece of paper into Stephen's hands. The boy's breath came in puffs, and his cheeks glowed red from the cold.

"Come in and get warm," Stephen invited.

Teddy shook his head. "Nah—gotta get to school. See ya!" He took off at a trot.

Stephen handed the note to his sister and slid back into his chair. Fork forgotten in his hand, he watched her face as she read. When she lifted her head, her eyes held a mix of apprehension and elation. She looked from her father to her mother then back down at the note. She waved it slightly. "It's from Laura Klaassen. She—she says David has requested a visit . . . from me."

Pa scowled. "Well, young lady, I didn't complain when you spent most of the day out there nursing him. After all, he was at death's door and needed all the care he could get. But from what I hear, he's doing just fine now. And I'm not sure I can spare the time to take you—"

Intrigued by something in his sister's expression, Stephen put in, "I could run her out there at noon, Pa."

Pa plucked the note from Priscilla's hand and scowled at it. "What does he want?"

Mama sighed. "I'm sure everything will be fine, John."

Pa read the brief note then dropped it on the table. "Well, I don't know . . ."

Priscilla rested her clasped hands on the edge of the table. "I would like to see for myself that he's doing better."

Pa blustered, "But you don't even like the man. You've said so many times."

Priscilla's cheeks flooded with pink. She appeared flustered—unlike his normally self-assured sister. Slowly, she raised her head to meet her father's gaze. She spoke with forthrightness that held everyone at attention.

"Daddy, I know what I've said. I acted like a perfect ninny, and the only reason I said I didn't like David was because he wouldn't put up with my nonsense. But David made me see some things about myself that needed to be changed—and I'm trying to change them. I owe him a big thank-you, and I'd like to tell him so."

Stephen gawked in wonder. This was Priscilla speaking? Their Priscilla?

Several minutes of stunned silence passed before his mother finally cleared her throat. "Well, John, the visit would be supervised by Laura Klaassen. I . . . I think it would be all right, if Stephen is willing to give up his noon break to take her out there."

Pa opened and closed his mouth several times like a banked fish gulping air. At last he seemed to find his bearings. "It seems . . . settled then." His Adam's apple bobbed above his white collar as he swallowed. "But you be home well before dark, young lady, do you hear?"

"Yes, I hear." Priscilla sent a grateful smile around the table. "Thank you, Mama, Daddy. You, too, Stephen." She headed for her bedroom.

Pa hollered, "You haven't finished your breakfast!"

Ma said, "Oh, let her go, John. She's excited."

"About what?"

The look Ma sent her husband said everything. Stephen hid a smile. It was Pa's turn to turn red.

When Priscilla climbed the staircase in the Klaassen farmhouse at half past twelve, she carried David's lunch tray. Samantha had planned to bring it up, but Priscilla begged for the honor. She was trying to figure out how to balance the tray against her hip and turn the doorknob when the door swung open.

There stood David in a pair of brown broadcloth pants, a pale blue chambray shirt, and leather house slippers. He was pale and looked thinner, but his cheeks were clean shaven, his hair was neatly combed, and he smelled of Ivory soap.

Her heart set up a wild kawumping. "David! You're up and around!"

He stepped aside to let her enter. "I've been on my feet for several days, off and on. You would have known that if you hadn't been making yourself so scarce around here."

Priscilla set the dinner tray on the small table beside the chair and began rearranging things that didn't need rearranging. "Yes, well, I thought perhaps I would be in the way."

David's feet scuffed across the floor as he moved toward her. He gently took her arm and turned her to face him. Her pulse galloped, having him so near. The smile in his eyes nearly melted her. "From what I understand, Priscilla, you were very helpful. Thank you."

She swallowed. She couldn't take her eyes from his. "You're welcome." Then she gestured to the plate of food. "Y-you'd better eat, before everything is cold. There's nothing worse than cold dumplings."

"Dumplings." David patted his flat belly and sank into the chair. "They'll have me fattened up in no time."

While David consumed his meal, Priscilla roamed the room and pretended to examine Mrs. Klaassen's few pieces of bric-a-brac. But her gaze flicked in his direction frequently. The very sight of him ignited a joy she found difficult to restrain. Every ounce of her being longed to throw herself into his arms and cry tears of delight at his recovery. But she'd promised to curtail her flirting ways, and he might misconstrue an embrace. So she ambled aimlessly about the small space, hands clasped behind her back, hoping to present a picture of decorum David might find pleasing.

⌒⊙

David watched Priscilla as he ate. Was she acting bashful because she'd murmured words of love in his ear when he lay ill? Or did she prefer to be somewhere else? This shy demeanor was a far cry from the obnoxious girl he'd met several months ago.

When he'd finished, he set the tray aside and sighed. "That Laura is a very good cook. Have you ever made dumplings, Priscilla?"

She angled an uncertain look at him. "Are you making fun of me?"

He blinked. "I don't think so."

She sucked in her lips for a moment, her brows low, before answering. "No, I don't make dumplings. I've not spent much time in a kitchen, I'm afraid. I've never had to."

David nodded slowly.

"But I've been helping Mama lately. She seems to appreciate the company, and I've found it's not as tedious as I always thought. I'm sure I'll learn to make dumplings. Eventually." She drew in a deep breath and folded her arms. "But I'm sure you didn't ask me here to find out about my skills—or lack of skills—as a cook. Why did you send that note, David?"

David couldn't stop a short huff of laughter. "You're nothing if not direct, Priscilla."

Priscilla ducked her head and shrugged. "I suppose I am." She lifted her face. "Does that bother you?"

"No, not particularly. I prefer honesty to mealy mouthed platitudes. How about you?"

"Me?"

"Yes, you. Do you prefer directness or beating around the bush?"

Priscilla examined him for several seconds, as if seeking hidden motives. At last she brought an embroidered stool over from beneath the vanity and seated herself on it, her hands in her lap. "I prefer directness."

"Good." David leaned back in the overstuffed chair and propped his elbows on the armrests. "I would like to ask you a few direct questions, Priscilla."

Priscilla's blue eyes grew wider as she stared at him. The tip of her tongue wet her lips, then disappeared again. "All right."

David looked at her unblinkingly. "Priscilla, when I was unconscious, did you pray for me?"

"Yes, I did."

David's eyebrows shot up at her unfaltering response. Ah! Then she likely was the one. He found the next question a little harder to ask. "Did you also tell me that . . . that you love me?"

Priscilla stiffened. Her fingers wove together as her dark blue gaze fell to her lap and then up again. She looked him full in the face. Her chin lifted proudly. "Yes, I did. And I meant it." When David sat in stunned silence, Priscilla went on evenly, "I do love

you, David. I'm not sure why or how, but I do. When you were sick, I—I thought I might die, too, if I didn't get the chance to tell you how I felt. So I told you I loved you." She paused, her breath heaving in little puffs. "I didn't realize you could hear me."

"Yes, I could hear." David shook his head. "I just wasn't sure who it was. So it was you. . . ."

Priscilla jumped up and paced around the room, her skirts swishing. "I can't understand my feelings at all. You've called me spoiled and selfish and willful and impudent. . . ." She whirled to face him, her expression serious. "And I thank you for it. I needed someone to wake me up, to make me see how wrong I was. I'm glad I have the chance to tell you so. You've helped begin a big change in me."

David stared at her, flabbergasted. Would he have ever imagined her—prim and proper, with those bright eyes wide and truthful and her curling hair framing her perfect, beautiful face—thanking him for his bluntness? What could he say in response?

In time, he found himself. "I need to thank you, too, Priscilla."

She waved her slim hand in dismissal. "You've already thanked me, David, for helping with your care."

He shook his head. "No, not for that—although I am grateful. I owe you a thank you for praying for me. There were lots of people praying for me. But I believe it was your prayers that brought me back."

To his surprise, Priscilla's eyes brimmed and spilled over. She sank onto the stool and covered her face with her hands. One sob rent the silence of the room. David crossed to her, bending down to touch her shoulder. "Why, Priscilla, what did I say? How did I upset—?"

She shook her head, her spiraling curls bouncing over her shoulders. "Y-you didn't upset m-me."

"Then what is it?" Honestly, he'd never understand women and their tears.

She wouldn't uncover her face, so her voice was muffled. "You said—you said my prayers brought you back. Oh, David! That means so much to me. They were my first prayers ever, and if God heard them and answered them, then—." She lowered her hands until her fingertips rested on her lips. Her tear-filled eyes glowed with some inner wonder. "Then that means He really does care. For me . . . and for you too. Don't you see?"

David sank to one knee beside her and ran his hand down the length of her hair, his heart lifting with the joyous recognition of God's unfailing love. "Yes, Prissy, I do see."

Priscilla rushed on, "When I prayed, David, I wasn't asking for anything for me. I was asking for everything for you. It was the first unselfish thing I've ever done. I told God—" Suddenly she seemed shy, and David had to prod her a bit with a smile and a reassuring pat on her shoulder.

Her voice quavered as she continued. "I told Him if He let you live, I would spend the rest of my life doing what He wanted me to do, instead of what I wanted to do. I wasn't sure He'd answer, because I'd never done much for anybody, ever, and I wasn't sure I was even worthy of His attention. But He answered, and you're well, and that means—Oh, David! That means I'm worthy too!"

David was touched by her amazement. "Of course you're worthy, Priscilla. But not because of anything you did or can do. Just because . . . He loves." The truth of his words ignited a new fire of joy. How he wished he hadn't wasted so many years hiding from God's deep love. He leaned in slightly and shared, "I made a similar commitment myself."

"You did?"

"Yes, I did and don't look so surprised. It just occurred to me that perhaps God let me live for a reason. I don't know what the reason is, but He must, and I want to be open to His leading."

They sat staring at one another. David marveled that they had reached out to the heavenly Father at the same time. It gave him a common ground with Priscilla, a common bond. He found it sobering and exciting and frightening all at the same time. Where might this take them?

David's knee complained about being pressed on the hard floor. He rose awkwardly and moved the few steps needed to reach the chair and sit again. From his vantage point, he could look at Priscilla's face.

There was much to admire—not only her physical beauty, which had always been eye catching, but the beauty now shining from the inside as well. It stirred him in a way he wouldn't have thought possible. The expression on her face was serene, confident. . . . She was like a completely new person.

He chuckled. "Can you believe this?"

"What?"

"You—me. Us. Sitting here relaxed and talking, not sparring with each other."

She smiled. "It's nice, isn't it?"

"Yes, it is, Priscilla."

"Do you think it means anything?"

He frowned slightly, puzzled. "Like what?"

"Well, I told you how I feel about you, and I don't want you to feel obligated to me, but I was just wondering if—well, if maybe—you might come to feel the same way about me."

David gave a disbelieving laugh. He rolled his eyes and said, "When I called you direct. . . ."

She plunked her fists on her hips. "I think it's a fair question."

He laughed again. "You would!"

She crossed her arms and set her face in a teasing scowl that was still prettier than most women smiling their best smiles.

David stifled his mirth. "Come here, Priscilla. Please?"

After a moment she sighed, rose, and stood before him, head tilted to the side.

He smiled up at her. "Yes, Miss Priss, I think there's a very good chance of my returning those feelings you divulged while I was lost in sleep."

With a triumphant grin, Priscilla perched on the arm of the chair like a sparrow on a fencepost. "Well, it's about time you admitted it."

He shook his head indulgently. "You are about the sassiest thing I've ever known."

"Well, you needn't worry," she replied, "because I am going to be the most agreeable, most complacent, most unsassy wife in the whole world."

David leaned into the opposite corner of the chair, staring in open-mouthed amazement. "Priscilla Koehn, did you just propose to me?"

"Of course not." Her eyes sparkled with mischief. "That would be presumptuous, to say the least. And it's far too soon for us to consider matrimony. Daddy will insist on a lengthy courtship. But just so you know—when you propose to me, the answer will be yes."

He chuckled, taking her hand and weaving his fingers through hers. "You really are something, Priscilla." One thing about it, with Priscilla as his wife, life would never be dull. He turned his head to gaze out the open window, admiring the crystal blue sky streaked with wisps of white.

His thoughts turned inward. "Well, God, You sure have a way of working things out. I came to Mountain Lake just to be with my sister. But You had much more for me, didn't You? With surrendering of my heart to You, I found a place to call home and someone who loves me . . . someone I can love back. You brought me down some rocky roads to get me to this place, but I know now Your Word is right—all things do work together for good. Thank You."

LAURA KLAASSEN'S VERENIKE (CHEESE POCKETS)

Dough:

1 cup water or milk

1 egg white

1 tsp. salt

2 1/2 cups flour

Cottage cheese filling:

1 egg yolk

salt and pepper to taste

2 tblsp. finely chopped onion, if desired

1 pound dry curd cottage cheese (or farmer's cheese)

Roll out the dough to about 1/8-inch thickness. Cut into 3- or 4-inch squares. Place a heaping teaspoon of the cottage cheese filling in the middle of the square. Bring the opposite corners together. Pinch the edges firmly. Drop the *verenike* into boiling water and cook slowly for about ten minutes. Drain.

Serve with fried ham or sausage. Make a gravy of the meat drippings to pour over the *verenike*.

LAURA KLAASSEN'S CHERRY MOOS

1 quart sour cherries
2 quarts water
2/3 cup sugar
5 tblsp. flour
1 cup sweet cream

Add water to cherries and cook until soft. Add half of sugar to cherries.

Combine remaining sugar with flour and add cream to make a smooth paste. Add paste to cherries and cook until thickened, stirring constantly.

Serve warm or cold, as desired. (Makes 6 to 8 servings.)

Acknowledgments

Mom and Daddy, my first teachers, who taught me to trust in Jesus . . . Thanks to your showing me how to surrender myself to Him, I am never alone and always have a place to call Home.

My husband, Don, who often cooks his own supper and puts up with me sneaking away in the middle of the night to play with my imaginary friends . . . I'm grateful for your support and understanding.

My band of prayer warriors—Connie, Eileen, Margie, Darlene, Sabra, Miralee, Kathy . . . You're always there when I need you. I appreciate you more than you know.

My agent, Tamela, who goes "above and beyond the call of duty" on my behalf . . . Thank you for your consistent encouragement.

Finally, and most important, God . . . You bless me beyond imagining. May any praise or glory be reflected directly back to You.

When A Heart Cries

Dedicated to
Kristian, Kaitlyn, and Kamryn, of course—

You fill my heart
with love and laughter every day!

"Every good and perfect gift is from above,
coming down from the Father of the heavenly lights,
who does not change like shifting shadows."
James 1:17 (NIV)

Contents

Klaassen Family Tree

Simon James Klaassen (1873) m. Laura Doerksen (1877), 1893
  Daniel Simon (1894) m. Rose Willems (1892), 1913
    Christina Rose (1915)
    Katrina Marie (1916)
    Camelia Ann (1921)
  Hannah Joy (1895–1895)
  Franklin Thomas (1896) m. Anna Harms (1900), 1918
    Laura Beth (1920)
    Unnamed baby boy (1922–1922)
    Kate Samantha (1923)
  Elizabeth Laurene (1898) m. Jacob Aaron Stoesz (1897), 1915
    Andrew Jacob and Adam James (A.J.), (1917)
    Amanda Joy (1921)
  Adam Earnest (1899) m. Samantha Olivia O'Brien (1900), 1918
  Josephine Ellen (1900) m. Stephen Koehn (1896), 1918
    Simon Stephen (1920)
  Arnold Hiram (1903)
  Rebecca Arlene (1906)
  Theodore Henry (1909)
  Sarah Louise (1911)
Hiram Klaassen (1872) m. Hulda Schmidt (1872), 1898

O'Brien Family Tree

Burton O'Brien (1870) m. Olivia Ruth Stanton (1873–1900), 1891
  David Burton (1894) m. Priscilla Millicent Koehn (1900), 1918
  Samantha Olivia (1900) m. Adam Earnest Klaassen (1899), 1918

amantha Klaassen gazed in wonder at the tiny bundle in her arms. Jenny Millicent O'Brien was absolutely beautiful. The baby's fine dark hair stood out like a halo around her perfectly shaped head, her dark eyes wide lined by nearly invisible lashes and a tiny button nose tilted impishly. When the newborn's mouth stretched into an adorable yawn, Samantha laughed softly.

She lifted the infant higher to press the soft cheek against her own and breathe in the sweet milky smell that said *baby*. "Oh, Pris . . ." Samantha spoke to her sister-in-law but lilted her voice for the baby's ears, "you must be so proud."

Priscilla shifted herself higher against the pillows in her tall bed. Her tangled hair, black as midnight, spread across her shoulders, and she pushed it aside. "Proud but tired. Whatever doctor attached the label 'labor' to describe giving birth wasn't just joking! It's the hardest work I've ever done. You'll find out one day—mark my words!"

Samantha felt her heart lift. "Oh, I hope so." Samantha gently placed her new niece into Priscilla's waiting arms. She watched as little Jenny immediately nestled against her mother, as if sensing she was back where she belonged. Samantha's chest filled with longing for her own sweet baby to cuddle.

Priscilla smoothed the blanket away from Jenny's face. "Where's Joey? It's too quiet out there."

Samantha smiled, picturing her brother David and Priscilla's firstborn, a son named Joey. At two and a half, the toddler was a never-ending cyclone of activity. Under the best of circumstances, he was a challenge. Now that Priscilla had a new baby to care for, how would she keep up with the little boy? Samantha answered, "David took him to the mercantile for a while so you could get some rest."

"Oh, bless his heart," Priscilla sighed and shook her head. "I know he took Joey with him to help me out, but my poor husband always comes home grumpy after he's had to battle with Joey at the store."

"Well, he'll only have Joey there a short time." Samantha leaned over to stroke Jenny's soft cheek with one finger. "He said Josie would pick him up to spend the afternoon playing with Simon, so maybe it won't be so bad." Only two months separated cousins Simon and Joey, and the two little boys got along famously.

"That's a relief." Priscilla sighed again. "If I could just regain my strength, I could be more helpful around here, but it seems—" The tears that were always just below the surface these days spilled over again. Priscilla hid her face in the crook of her arm. Samantha sat back, feeling so helpless at the depression that had taken hold of Priscilla days after Jenny's birth.

Wanting to provide some sort of assistance, Samantha offered, "Why don't I plan to pick up Joey from the mercantile and take him home with me for a few days? Auntie Sam can spoil him a bit, then bring him home. You could use the rest, and I could use the company. With harvest in full swing, I hardly see Adam during the day. I'd enjoy having someone to keep me occupied." Samantha's husband, Adam, would be gone from dawn to dusk for several more weeks, working with the community members to harvest wheat and corn. Even with the help of gas-powered machinery, it was a long process and required the participation of every area farmer.

Priscilla blinked at Samantha with eyes red rimmed and raw from all the tears that had been shed in the past two weeks. "Oh, Sammy, I appreciate that, really I do. But I don't know what David would say. He seems to think if I'd just get up and get moving, everything would go back to normal, but—" She sniffled.

Samantha sat on the edge of the bed and patted Priscilla's hand. "I'm sure it's just that David is worried about you. This birth was harder on you, and it will take a while to get back to your old perky self. I tell you what: I'll talk with Davey and make sure he knows it was all my idea to take Joey. I'm sure I can make him see the sense of it. Would that be all right?"

Priscilla sent her sister-in-law a grateful look. "Oh, would you, Sam? I'm sure I can get my strength back if I don't have to chase after Joey for a day or so."

"I'll go talk to him right now." Samantha leaned forward to place a kiss on Priscilla's wan cheek. "You rest while Jenny's still sleeping. I'll check in on you tomorrow."

"Thank you." Priscilla's eyes were already closed.

Samantha paused in the doorway for a moment, capturing the scene of mother and child snuggled together beneath a bright patchwork quilt. The sunlight slanting through the lace curtain at the window created a weblike pattern across the foot of the bed. Priscilla and little Jenny were a picture of contentment. Samantha couldn't help the envy that rose inside, and she turned away.

As she drove her wagon to the mercantile, she reflected on all the changes in the family over the past three years. Priscilla and David had Joseph and now Jenny; Priscilla's brother Stephen and his wife, who was Adam's sister, had Simon; Adam's brother Frank and his wife, Anna, had Laura Beth and were expecting another child before Thanksgiving; Adam's sister

Liz and her husband, Jake, already had three little ones running around the house—the twins, Andy and A.J., and now little Amanda; and Adam's oldest brother Daniel and his wife, Rose, had added a third daughter, Camelia, to their family the same year Amanda had been born. Everyone's families were growing . . . except Samantha's and Adam's.

It wasn't fair, Samantha mourned. She and Adam had been married longer than David and Pris, Josie and Stephen, too! When would it be her turn for the congratulations and gifts of tiny gowns and teasing comments about her expanding waistline? Everyone told her to be patient, that her time would come, but Samantha's patience was spent. She wanted her time to be *now*.

When she entered the town's mercantile, which David managed, she was still feeling resentful and swung the door harder than necessary. The cowbell above the door clanged angrily, and she grabbed it to still the sound. Another noise reached her ears from the storeroom at the back—Joey's plaintive cry and David's scolding voice.

"Joey, I don't know how many times I've told you: you can't climb on the shelves! Look at the mess you've made for Papa now." It seemed David's patience was spent as well, but for a far different reason, she thought.

Samantha pulled back the curtain over the storeroom door and peeked in. Startled, her hand clapped her cheek as she gaped at the fiasco. The wooden shelves that had been secured to the wall hung crazily. David stood knee-deep in overshoes and work boots. He held Joey, who was hollering and doing his best to free himself from his father's grasp. Samantha immediately knew what had taken place—and what else would soon take place if someone didn't intervene.

Although Samantha tried not to butt in to her relatives' child rearing, she hated to see Joey punished for what she considered to be normal curiosity. What little boy didn't like to climb? Besides, it seemed like a perfect time to borrow Joey for a few days. "David?"

David turned to the doorway, exasperation creasing his narrow face. "Oh, Sam."

When the wailing Joey spotted his Auntie Sam, he reached his chubby arms for Samantha. She waded through the mess to take him. "Looks like Joey's been busy," Samantha offered with a wry smirk as she lifted him into her arms.

David threw his hands upward. "When isn't he?" David surveyed the disorder. "I declare, Sammy, I can't keep up with that child! He goes from one thing to another, and another, and another. . . . And he leaves messes behind wherever he's been." Her brother blew out his lips in disgust.

Samantha found herself unable to generate even a wee bit of indignation at Joey's mischief making. "At least you'll never lose track of him," she quipped.

David shook his head. "You never lose patience, do you, Sam? It's too bad—" He broke off, but the unspoken words, *it's too bad you don't have any children of your own*, hung in the air between them.

Samantha steered the conversation elsewhere. "I thought Josie was going to pick him up."

"She was—she is—but not till noon. If I last that long." David gave his sister a look that told her he'd had enough.

"Well," Samantha said with forced brightness, "given my penchant for patience, I have a request."

"What's that?" He had started sorting through the jumbled pile of shoes, trying to pair them up again.

"I'd like to take Joey home with me for a few days. Would you like that, Joey?" Samantha noticed David's sharp gaze settle on her, but she ignored his stern expression. "I'm so lonely with

Adam gone all day, I would very much enjoy the company. Plus Priscilla seems to need some extra time to rest, to get back on her feet."

"Did Priscilla put you up to this?"

"No, it was all my idea. But she didn't oppose it, if that's your next question."

"It was." David high stepped through the chaos to his sister and placed a hand on Joey's dark head.

Joey had laid his head on Samantha's shoulder and was sucking his fingers contentedly. Samantha rocked him back and forth. She loved the feel of Joey's hair against her cheek. Samantha looked up at David. "It was my idea, and I think it's a good one. Pris is really washed out from the difficult delivery. Joey is just too much for her right now. And I don't see how you can expect to keep him here and still pay attention to the store. I'm serious about wanting the company." She paused, tipped her head and asked in her best pleading voice, "Please, Davey?"

David lost his stern expression, the lines around his eyes turning into a smile. But to Samantha it looked like a sad smile. "I can't say no to you when you look at me that way, Sammy."

"Good!" Samantha whispered in Joey's ear, "You get to come home with Auntie Sam for a few days, Joey!" Joey continued sucking his fingers, but his dark, fine eyebrows shot up in happy speculation. She looked up at David. "I'll stop by the house and collect a few of his things on my way home. I'll check on Pris too once more."

"Thanks, Samantha." David perched on the edge of a crate and ran a hand through his wavy hair. "It's been rough since Jenny was born. Priscilla just sits and cries and practically ignores Joey. I guess it's small wonder he's been into more mischief than usual. I can't figure out what's wrong with her."

Samantha didn't have much advice to give. She couldn't begin to understand all of the emotions that might accompany childbirth. But she could offer sympathy. "I'm sure Pris is just tired, David." She placed a hand on David's wide shoulder. "Wait and see—a few days of relaxation, and she'll be back to her same sassy self."

"I hope so." David shook his head. "These constant tears and melodramatic sighs are wearing me down."

Samantha left David to his mess. As she held Joey's small hand and walked to the waiting wagon, she told the little boy, "What fun we're going to have, Joey! For a while we'll pretend you're my little boy and forget all about everybody else! Yes?"

Joey blinked up at her innocently and echoed, "Yes."

For the moment, her joy would be in pretending.

*A*dam Klaassen lowered the crossbar on the barn door and ambled toward the house, the warm glow from the windows a beacon of welcome. The aroma of supper—vegetable soup, if his nose was correct—drifted across the yard, and he hurried his steps. Although he'd eaten a hearty noon meal and an afternoon snack as well, he'd never turn down Samantha's well-seasoned soup made from vegetables from their own garden. His heart gave a bit of a leap, as it always did, when coming home to his wife. How he loved her . . .

"I'm home!" he called as he entered the kitchen. Surprised, he saw Samantha in her favorite, scarred rocking chair with their nephew Joey squirming in her arms. When Joey spotted Adam, he wriggled all the harder, and Samantha released him with a sigh.

"Unc'oo Adam!" The little boy galloped barefoot across the floor, his nightshirt flapping. He threw pudgy arms around Adam's legs.

"Hey there, big guy." Adam scooped up the giggling toddler and hoisted him high onto his shoulder. "What brings you here?"

"Joey tum home wif Auntie Sam." Joey grabbed two fistfuls of Adam's hair for support. "We betendin' I Auntie Sam's widd'oo boy."

Adam wasn't sure that was a healthy pastime for Samantha, but he chose not to broach the subject. He carefully dislodged Joey's hands from his hair and set him back down on the floor. Joey kept a two-handed grip on Adam's wrist, suspending

himself happily, while Adam leaned over to receive a kiss from his wife.

"I hope you don't mind if we have Joey for a couple days." Samantha lifted Joey into her lap and set the rocker in motion. "When I visited Priscilla this morning, she looked so worn out, and David was at wit's end, trying to keep track of Joey at the mercantile. I felt sorry for them both and on the spur of the moment offered to help out. I didn't think about checking with you before it was all settled."

Adam pulled over a pressed-back chair from the table and seated himself backward, stacking his arms on the top to prop up his chin. He grinned at Joey, who continued to wiggle in Samantha's embrace. "There was no need to check with me, honey. Besides," he chuckled, "watching him will be your responsibility, since I'll be gone all day." He grinned as he observed Joey's constant wriggling. "Looks like you'll have your hands full."

Samantha leaned forward to give Adam another kiss, and Joey said, "Ooooh! Tisses!"

Adam joined Samantha in a laugh. He reached out to poke Joey's tummy. The boy giggled and pulled up his knees to protect his ticklish belly. Samantha wrapped her arms around him and held him tight. "Shhh now, Joey. It's time for sleep." She began humming a lullaby.

Adam got up, poured himself a cup of coffee, and leaned against the kitchen counter to watch Samantha play mommy. She rocked and sang softly, stroking Joey's dark curls back from his forehead in a rhythmic gesture that appeared to relax him. Joey's fingers went to his mouth as his eyelids dropped. Samantha rocked, her face wearing an expression of bliss.

Adam swallowed hard. "It feels good holding him, doesn't it?" Adam asked quietly.

Samantha nodded. She pressed her lips to Joey's temple, her eyes sliding closed. The beauty of his Samantha cradling a child made Adam's chest ache. Tears pricked his eyes. Yet he couldn't look away. He remained across the room for several minutes with only the squeak of the rocking chair runners against the wood floor and the measured tick-tick, tick-tick of the mantel clock providing homey intrusion.

When Joey's fingers slipped from his mouth, Adam put down his cup and crossed to the chair. He held out his arms. "Let me put him to bed now."

Samantha's grip tightened for a moment, but then she transferred Joey to Adam.

Adam whispered, "Which room do you want him in?"

Samantha's forehead creased. "The nursery."

Adam cringed. He wished she'd stop referring to the small bedroom at the right of their own as the nursery. The room, away from the head of the stairs and with a door connecting it to theirs, would make a perfect nursery. But it contained no cradle and no baby, so using the term only served to hurt her. And him.

She added in a raspy whisper, "I made a pallet on the floor for him."

Adam carried the slumbering little boy upstairs. The child's weight in his arms felt good. Right. He knelt and carefully placed Joey on the folded quilts. Joey snuffled, wrinkling his nose, then rolled onto his tummy and hiked his bottom in the air. A chuckle rose in Adam's throat, but he held it inside as he eased a blanket over the little boy and tucked it in around him. He remained crouched beside the pallet for a few moments, gazing down at Joey's peaceful face, before leaning over to deposit a kiss on the child's round cheek.

He closed the door silently behind him and tiptoed downstairs. As he reached the bottom, Samantha rose from the rocker to meet him. Adam beamed at her. "He rolled over, stuck his little behind in the air, and started snoring."

Wordlessly Samantha stepped into him, wrapping her arms around his middle and burying her face in the hollow of his throat. He closed his arms around her and rested his chin on the top of her head. "When, Adam?" she asked, her voice muffled by his collar.

He knew what she wanted to know. But he had no more answers than she, so he could only say, as he had many times before, "Give it time, Sammy."

She pushed against his chest, freeing herself from his embrace. "Please stop saying that."

He reached for her, but she stepped away from his touch. "Samantha . . ."

On the other side of the table, she planted her feet and sent him a dismissive look of frustration and hurt. "I mean it. I'm tired of hearing it. Everyone keeps telling me, 'Give it time.' I've given it time, Adam! I've given it five years!" As quickly as her temper flared, it sputtered and died. She dropped into a kitchen chair, her head in her hands. "Oh, Adam, when we built this house we had such hopes of also building a family. Four bedrooms upstairs. Three of them unadorned, furnitureless, *childless* rooms."

Adam inched forward and seated himself at the table, placing his hand on her shoulder. She remained in her hunkered-down position. His heart ached with hers. The empty rooms upstairs echoed a hollowness in his own chest. He too longed to fill those rooms with children.

With a sigh, she raised her head. Tears swam in her pale blue eyes. "For the first year, it didn't matter so much. I was so busy being a wife and homemaker, learning to accomplish everything a farmer's wife needs to do. I enjoyed visiting our family and playing with our nieces and nephews and dreaming about the day we'd have our own little one. It wasn't a pressing need then, because we'd only been married a year."

One tear trailed down her cheek. "But then Priscilla and Josie announced the impending arrival of little ones before a full year of their marriages had passed. And it didn't seem fair. We'd been married longer; we deserved to start our family first."

Adam winced, recalling how he'd teased her about getting busy and adding a new member to their family since they were getting left behind. He hadn't meant to be hurtful, but no doubt his comment had stung. As did the rambling size of their house.

When they were first married, they'd lived in the dugout Grandpa Klaassen had built for his own bride. The tiny home carved out of a hill toward the back of the farm was primitive but cozy, and they'd been happy there. But Adam, eager for their own family and wanting space to spread out, had decided to build this big farmhouse. There was never any doubt, as the house plans were drawn and the two-story frame home was erected, that they'd soon fill the house with a whole passel of little Klaassens. But Adam and Samantha's recent fifth wedding anniversary had passed, and it was still just the two of them.

Adam took Samantha's hand and gave it a gentle squeeze. "Don't lose heart, honey." He forced his lips into a smile. "Who knows? You might be expecting right now, and—"

She pushed away from the table. "I'm not expecting. Not now." Her lips pursed into a tight line for several seconds, her chin quivering. "I'm beginning to understand why some women refer to their monthly time as a curse. It's certainly that for me, dashing my dreams month after month, year after year. . . ."

Adam rose and came around the table to embrace her. If only he could remove the pain she carried. He rubbed his palms up and down her back, then gently set her aside. "Go on upstairs, honey. I want to eat a bowl of your soup"—although his appetite had fled—"and then I'll be up."

She flicked a look of hurt betrayal in his direction that cut him to the core. Who did she feel was betraying her—himself or God? He reached out to stroke his thumb across her cheek and gave her a smile meant to convey his understanding.

Samantha simply turned away and trudged up the stairs, her eyes downcast and her shoulders slumped. As Adam watched her joyless ascent, his heart ached for the desire to fulfill her dreams. They were his dreams, too. He wanted the babies Samantha longed for as much as she did.

Clenching his fists, he turned his face heavenward and repeated Samantha's question. "When, Lord?" But he heard no reply.

"Oh, Joey, sweetheart, no no!"

In the less than ten minutes Samantha and Joey had been in the vegetable garden, Joey had managed to pull down three tomato vines and stomp what was left of the carrots. Samantha scooped him up and set him outside the garden fence. "Joey, you stay right here where Auntie Sam can see you," she said with as much enthusiasm as she could muster. "Play with these little soldiers." Joey swept his hand across the painted tin soldiers Samantha had lined up in the dirt. "I hewp!"

"But, sweetheart—"

Joey's lower lip poked out and two tears formed in his blue eyes. He tilted his head. "I hewp?"

Samantha melted. She pulled Joey into her arms and hugged him for as long as the active little boy would allow.

When he wiggled loose, she had to laugh. "All right, little monkey, you come help. But you stay close to Auntie Sam. And don't pick anything unless you ask first, all right?"

"Aw right!"

They spent the better part of an hour with Joey trotting back and forth, depositing dried cucumber vines into a big pile at the corner of the garden and scooping up dirt from the potato mounds with a trowel. By the time Samantha finished her tasks, Joey was filthy and required a bath that took nearly another hour.

Samantha enjoyed Joey's bath much more than Joey did—and Joey had a pretty good time. What joy she found in lathering the little boy's sturdy back, arms, and legs, blowing bubbles through her fist to make him laugh, pouring cups of water through his open hands, then holding out her own hands for Joey to pour water over. Samantha was nearly as wet as Joey by the time he'd finished splashing, but it was worth every minute of the time it took to clean up the water mess and change her clothes.

After a simple lunch, Samantha put Joey down for a nap and laid down with him on the pallet, stroking his back until he finally fell asleep. She stayed beside him, listening to him breathe for a long time after he dropped off.

A knock on the front door brought her quickly tiptoeing downstairs. She peeked through the oval cut glass opening, surprised to find David on the other side. She swung the door wide, and he stepped in, catching her in a quick hug. "Hi, Sammy, where's Joey?"

Samantha placed a finger against her lips. "He's upstairs napping." She closed the door with great care.

David's eyebrows shot up. "You got him to take a nap?" He whispered too. "How'd you do it?"

Samantha grinned. "Laid down beside him and rubbed his back. He went out like a light." She snapped her fingers.

David shook his head. "Sammy, you'll spoil him. You know Pris and I don't have time to coddle him that way." His kind tone softened the reprimand.

Samantha shrugged. "Well, I do. Besides, I did it as much for me as for Joey. We're having a wonderful time." She drew her brows together. "You haven't come to take him home already, have you?"

"No, actually I came to check on you, to see how you were holding up. Joey can be a handful, to put it mildly."

"A delightful handful," Samantha insisted. "He helped me in the garden"—she ignored David's smirk—"and then he had a bath—"

"—which I'm sure he needed—"

"—and some lunch—"

"—which he probably wore—"

"—and now he's napping. So there!"

They laughed and Samantha turned toward the kitchen. "I baked carrot cake yesterday. Come sit and have a piece with me."

"You don't have to ask me twice." David followed her to the round table in the center of the kitchen. He noted matter-of-factly, "Pris never has figured out that it's nice to have sweets around. Any kind of cake is a treat to me."

Samantha laid a large piece of cake on a plate, poured a glass of milk, and carried the treat to the table. He dug in immediately and complimented her with a smiling "mmmm."

Samantha sat opposite him and propped her chin in her hands with a smile. "Now I know where Joey gets his sweet tooth. I had to promise him cake to get him to eat his green beans last night."

"And it worked?"

"Yep. He ate all two of them."

"Two!" David's fork stopped midway to his mouth. "That's all you gave him?"

"Well, it seemed fair—one for each year of age."

David put down the fork and pushed the plate aside. "Sammy, we've got to talk."

Samantha's scalp prickled at his tone. "About what?"

David folded his hands on the tabletop. "I know you love Joey, but it isn't fair to him—or to us—for you to give in to him so easily."

She sputtered, "I don't give in to him. He ate his vegetables, and I got him to take his nap, and—"

"Yes, you did," David said, "but in both instances bribery was involved. Joey is a very strong-willed little boy, and I know how difficult it can be to get his cooperation. Priscilla and I are trying to teach him he has to obey simply because we know what is best for him. If you offer sweets and extra attention to get him to obey, then you undermine what we're trying to do."

Samantha bristled. "Have you considered I have the time and patience to work with Joey? Besides, I'm his aunt, not his parent. I don't want to be the disciplinarian."

David sighed. "Samantha, I think I know why it's so hard for you to say no to Joey or to any of your nieces and nephews. Pa always said no to everything we asked because it took less effort. I know how many times your feelings were crushed by his negative reaction."

Memories—none of them pleasant—flooded through Samantha's mind. She turned her face away.

David continued in a reasonable tone. "You can't compensate for Pa's harshness by being overly indulgent with the children in the family. Of course all the little ones adore their

Auntie Sam. But wouldn't it be better for the children if you exercised control? As they get older, they might begin to take advantage of you."

Samantha refused to answer.

"Sammy, listen to me, please?" David took Samantha's hand and tugged it until she shifted her gaze to meet his. "I'm not saying this to hurt your feelings, sweetheart. But children need structure and discipline so they can learn to discipline themselves. You're going to spoil them if you're always offering sweets or some other reward for appropriate behavior, and we both know there's nothing less attractive than a spoiled child."

Samantha gave a small nod of acknowledgment. David's wife, Priscilla, had been spoiled shamefully by her father. For years she made people miserable with her willful, selfish behavior. Samantha wouldn't want Joey or any of the others to behave in such an unpleasant manner.

David continued, "Someday you will have children of your own, and—"

Samantha shot out of the chair so fast it balanced on two legs for five seconds before crashing against the floor. She fled to the pantry and stood with her back to the kitchen. Pressing her fist to her mouth, she held back sobs of anguished fury.

Strong hands descended on her shoulders and turned her around. David gazed down at her in confusion. "Sam, what's wrong?"

The frustration welling inside erupted, and she thrust her fist against David's chest. "I'm so tired of being told *someday* I'll have children of my own. Doesn't it occur to you that I want someday to be now? I'm tired of being just Auntie Sam! I want to be a mama!" Mingled hurt and fury propelling her, she pulled her fist back for another swing.

David's eyes wide in shock, he caught her wrist and wrestled it downward. "Samantha, stop! What's gotten into you?"

Samantha froze and stared at him, startled by his heartless question. Slowly, realization dawned. He didn't understand. How could he? He had his family—an adorable son and a sweet little daughter. He had *everything*. And he couldn't see how special the gift was. Distress washed through her, and she forced herself to calm down. When she relaxed her fist, David released her. She left the pantry in silence.

She moved to the table and began sweeping nonexistent crumbs into her hand. "I'm sorry, David, I shouldn't have turned on you like that. And I'll try not to be so lenient with Joey, if it will please you." She turned to face him again. "But don't expect me to be as strict as you and Priscilla are. It's not my place as Joey's aunt."

David stood several feet away, examining her face. He seemed afraid to approach her. A hysterical giggle built inside her at his obvious consternation. "All right, I won't strike you again," she promised.

Finally his head bobbed in a slow nod. "All right, Sammy." He paused. "Are you sure you're . . . up . . . to keeping Joey?"

Samantha gave a brief huff of laughter. "Yes, Davey, I am definitely. . . up . . . to keeping Joey." She made it a point to imitate his vocal tone.

"Well, all right," he said, still sounding uncertain. "But Pris misses him. Would you take him into town to see her when he wakes from his nap?"

Samantha nodded. "That would be fine."

He pulled out his timepiece and flipped open the cover. "I've got to get back. I've left Arn alone at the mercantile far too long." He gave Samantha a kiss on the cheek and headed for the door. "Thanks for the cake. I'll see you later."

When he had gone, Samantha crept upstairs to peek in at Joey. The little boy still slept—flat on his back with his arms stretched above his head. She smiled. No matter what David thought, a little indulging wouldn't ruin Joey for life. While she had him, she intended to pamper him silly.

*M*uch to Samantha's disappointment, David and Priscilla chose not to have Joey stay another night with his Auntie Sam. Priscilla claimed she missed him too much, and David stated it was taking unfair advantage of Samantha. Samantha thought they were being unreasonable, but what could she say? They were Joey's parents and had the final word.

She stayed at David and Priscilla's past the supper hour, building block towers with Joey and cuddling little Jenny. The sun was a thin magenta slice of brightness along the horizon when she arrived home.

Adam met her at the back door. "Sam, where've you been? You didn't leave a note or anything. I've been worried sick, wondering what happened to you and Joey."

Normally Samantha would have apologized for worrying her husband, but her pride still stung from the notion that she wasn't capable of handling Joey correctly. Adam's lecture seemed to underscore her lack of responsibility. "In case you hadn't noticed," she shot back, "you've not been getting home before dark, so I assumed I would be back long before you were. If I'd known you would beat me home, I would have left a note, but I didn't know." She whirled away from him. "I am a grown woman, and I don't need to be told what to do!"

She yanked off her bonnet hard enough to dislodge the knot of hair twisted on the back of her head and flung it on the kitchen table. Adam stood gaping in stunned silence as she stomped over to her rocking chair, sat down, and began to rock much faster than necessary.

Adam approached slowly, stopping in front of her. In an even, unruffled voice he said, "Do I dare ask what brought that on?"

Samantha gave him another hard stare that lasted only seconds before she gave a sigh and let her head drop against the back of the rocker. "I'm sorry, Adam." She aimed her gaze toward the ceiling. "You had every right to be concerned when I wasn't here, and I shouldn't have yelled at you."

Adam bent down on one knee and sandwiched her hands between his. "David said you hollered at him today too."

She tilted her face to look at him. Her throat went tight. "When did you see David?"

"He stopped by the Voth farm on his way back to town this afternoon."

Samantha pulled her hand away and covered her face, mortified. "I can't believe he went and tattled on me!"

Adam tugged her hands downward. "Don't be unfair, Sam. He wasn't tattling. He was concerned for you; you weren't acting like yourself."

Hurt and embarrassed, she retorted, "And that's why he kept Joey?"

"I wondered if they would insist you bring Joey back home." He rubbed his thumbs back and forth over Samantha's knuckles, the touch soothing. "He said you were . . . highly emotional."

Samantha gave a little snort.

Adam raised one eyebrow. "I have to admit, just a minute ago you reacted very differently than I would have expected."

Samantha pulled her hands free. "Well! You tied into me the minute I came through the door! Questioned me like I don't have enough sense to take care of myself, and David insinuated that I spoil Joey and undermine their attempts to discipline him. And I'm not supposed to be upset?"

"I'm not convinced, Sammy, that what David said is what's upsetting you right now."

Samantha's pulse tripped hard and fast. She glowered at Adam with narrowed eyes. "Oh? And what is it you think is upsetting me?"

"Those bedrooms upstairs, Samantha. Those empty bedrooms."

~⌒⌒

Adam watched Samantha fight for control. Her chin quivered, her eyes filled, but she didn't cry. She set her jaw tightly and simply stared, wide eyed, at him. Suddenly she bolted out of the chair, pushed past him, and stood before the kitchen window, her arms crossed and shoulders stiff.

Adam let his head hang low for a moment, remaining on one knee in front of the rocking chair. The same one in which Samantha's great-grandmother had rocked baby Samantha to sleep. The rocking chair in which Samantha had planned to rock her own babies to sleep.

He lifted his head to look across the room at his wife. He'd never seen a sadder sight, Samantha with her silent sorrow pulling her down from the inside. Slowly he pushed himself to his feet and walked up behind her, placing his hands on her shoulders and pulling her against his chest. She allowed his comforting embrace, but offered nothing of herself to it—standing stiff and unyielding against him.

In time Adam said gently, "Sammy, it's been more than five years."

He heard her sharp intake of breath. "I know, Adam. I've counted each and every one of those years, months, weeks, days—my heart breaks a little more with each new month that passes childless for me. . . ."

He tightened his hands on her shoulders. "I think it's time we saw a doctor. Maybe there's something—"

"Maybe there's something wrong with me—" she jerked away from him—"that's what you were going to say?"

Adam came after her, wanting to hold her, but she held up her hands as if to ward off a blow.

"No, Sammy. I was going to say maybe there's something a doctor could do to help us."

Samantha's expression softened, and her arms lowered until they hung limply at her sides. "I'm afraid." Her words were almost a whimper.

This time when Adam reached for her, she came willingly, clinging to him like a drowning person clings to his rescuer. Adam admitted, "I'm afraid too. But we have to find out. We can't go on wondering and wishing . . . and letting the desire for children dictate everything we do. We have to find out if there's a problem, and if there is, then find a way to solve it."

Samantha lifted her head from Adam's chest. The fear in her eyes made his pulse race in apprehension. "What if there is a problem, Adam? What if—?"

He placed two fingers against her lips, then pulled her snug against him and whispered in her hair, "We'll cross that bridge if we come to it. Let's try to think positively, yes?"

Samantha nodded. She relaxed against him, and he circled her with his arms, seeking to provide security with his embrace. His entire body ached with the desire to give her all she longed for. If love could make everything right, their child would already be in their arms.

With her face pressed against his dusty plaid shirt, she said, "We'll pray too, Adam. Won't we?"

"Of course we will." Adam planted a kiss on her tousled russet hair. "We'll put it all in God's hands." For the first time since he was a little boy, Adam discovered no sense of peace in handing his problems to his heavenly Father. The realization frightened him even more than what the doctor might discover.

$$\sim\!\!\infty$$

Mountain Lake had only one physician, Dr. Robert Newton. Samantha trusted him completely. He'd delivered several of her nieces and nephews, had been there for simple things like earaches and stomachaches, along with more serious things like David's near-drowning accident and Teddy's broken arm. She had already talked with the doctor once about her desire to conceive a child, so visiting with him a second time was easier than she might have thought. Although she found it difficult to admit her fears, at least she was sharing them with someone she knew.

After a cursory examination, Dr. Newton instructed Samantha to dress and meet him in his small office. She hurried into her clothes and then joined Adam on a narrow bench which faced the doctor's scarred, cluttered desk. Dr. Newton leaned back in his squeaky chair, very much at ease. Samantha perched stiffly beside Adam, very much on edge.

"Samantha, Adam, I wish I could give you the answers you're looking for, but I'm afraid I'm simply not well versed in the medical field of reproduction. I am a family practitioner, not a specialist. Samantha, when you came to me two years ago, I gave you special instructions on how to determine the best time of the month for conception. I assume you followed my directives?"

Samantha gave a little nod. "It means so much to both of us to become parents. Of course I did what you instructed."

Dr. Newton sighed, pushed his spectacles toward his forehead, and rubbed his eyes with the pads of his thumb and first finger. When he'd settled his wire-rimmed glasses back in place, he said, "Then that's as much as I can do for you."

Samantha sent Adam a confused look. Were they just to give up their dreams?

Adam held his hands out to the doctor in query. "Then what do you suggest *we* do?"

The doctor leaned forward, resting his elbows on the desk top and pressing his interlaced fingers against his chin. "I suggest you see a specialist."

Samantha's stomach flip-flopped. "A specialist? But . . . but . . ." How could she speak of such intimate matters to a stranger?

Dr. Newton nodded solemnly. "There's a hospital in Rochester called the Mayo Clinic. It's a wonderful facility. They have specialists in all fields of medicine, including reproductive medicine. I'm sure they would be able to give you the assistance you need."

"Rochester?" Samantha clutched for Adam's hand. "We don't know anyone there!"

Adam laced his fingers through hers. "Dr. Newton, do you believe someone there can help us?"

"They know all there is to know, Adam. If anyone can help you, they can."

"Then we'll go. We'll do whatever is necessary to have the children we want."

Adam's lack of hesitation spurred Samantha's courage. She nodded resolutely. The decision was made.

*T*wo weeks later Samantha and Adam entered the office of Dr. Phillip Zimmerman, Women's Specialist. Samantha couldn't help but think of Dr. Newton's small office back home. Its typically disorganized interior was the opposite of this white, sterile, a-place-for-everything-and-everything-in-its-place room.

And Dr. Newton was small of stature. Dr. Zimmerman stood taller than Adam and twice as big around. Dr. Newton was uncombed and rumpled, but Dr. Zimmerman looked—and smelled—as if he'd just stepped from a barber's shop. Dr. Newton always seemed relaxed and informal; Dr. Zimmerman's approach was brusque and business-like. But from the moment of introduction, Samantha sensed this man held a great deal of knowledge. How she prayed he would have the answers they needed.

"Mr. and Mrs. Klaassen, please sit down." The burly doctor gestured toward two upholstered chairs. He settled his rather impressive frame on a wheeled, wooden chair, crossed right leg over left, and balanced on his knee a slim board that held a writing tablet. He fixed Samantha with a serious gaze and angled graying brows low. "Now—I understand you have been married for five years, four months. Mrs. Klaassen, you are twenty-three years of age?" At Samantha's nod he turned to Adam. "And you are twenty-six, correct, Mr. Klaassen?" Adam, too, nodded. "Mm-hm, certainly of child-bearing age."

Samantha flicked a brief sidelong glance at Adam. He offered an assuring smile.

"Mrs. Klaassen . . ." Dr. Zimmerman began a series of questions that would have been embarrassingly intimidating had they not been stated with such forthrightness. Although Samantha had to swallow a couple times, and her voice quavered hesitantly, she managed to answer everything he asked. In a matter of minutes the doctor had scribbled down a long list of notes that seemed to have meaning for him. He reviewed them, his lower jaw thrust out and his eyes narrowed thoughtfully. Then he looked up, the pen paused above the paper. "Have you conferred with a doctor before?"

Adam cleared his throat and leaned forward. "Samantha went to our town doctor a couple of years ago, then again recently. He recommended we come to you."

The doctor made a checkmark on the paper. "What did he tell you?"

"He told her women can only conceive during certain days of the month, and he explained how to know when those days were."

"And you followed his guidance?"

Samantha squirmed in her chair, and Adam turned a bit pink around the ears. He said, "Yes, sir."

"And you've charted your fertile days for over two years without a pregnancy. . . ." The doctor stroked his chin with his thumb and first finger, staring at his notepad. He then sat forward abruptly and wrote something else. Samantha tried to get a peek at the pad, but she couldn't read a word of his messy-looking handwriting. He leaned back, reaching behind him to slap the pad onto his desk top. He capped his pen, dropped it on the pad of paper, and then offered the first hint of a smile since she and Adam had entered the room. "I will need to do a thorough examination. If you will follow me, I'll take you to an examination room."

Fear swirled through Samantha's stomach, bringing a rush of nausea. She gripped Adam's hand. He rose, tugging her up with him and whispered, "It'll be all right, Sam. Go on now. I'll wait for you here, and I'll be praying."

Samantha took a deep breath to gather courage. With one last look at Adam, she followed Dr. Zimmerman down a long hall filled with many bustling, gray-garbed women and men. They all appeared so filled with purpose! Eyes aimed straight ahead, feet moving briskly, their faces a study in determination. Samantha found herself wishing that just one of them would look at her—really *look* at her—and recognize her misgivings, offer some reassurance.

The doctor opened a door on the right side of the hall and held out a hand, indicating she should enter. Samantha looked around nervously. Directly in the middle of the small, square room sat a table—tall, flat, and covered with a white sheet. A shelf along the back wall held all sorts of unrecognizable metal instruments, toweling, and glass jars filled with everything from white cotton puffs to small wooden sticks.

In one corner a white cotton curtain hung suspended from the ceiling, creating a small cubicle. Dr. Zimmerman crossed to it and pushed it aside, revealing a short bench and two silver hooks on the white-painted wall. The doctor said, "You may undress back here, Mrs. Klaassen. Please remove all of your clothing. Then lie down on the table, and cover yourself with the sheet. In a few minutes, a nurse will check on you. When you are ready, I will begin my examination."

Samantha pressed her hands against her queasy stomach. She licked her lips, battling a fierce desire to escape.

Dr. Zimmerman had headed for the door but glanced back. His expression softened. He crossed to her and placed a hand on her shoulder. "I realize this is all new to you, Mrs. Klaassen, but please trust me when I say we are here to help you." His fingers briefly tightened. "However, I cannot help you unless you cooperate with me. Will you do what I've asked?"

The kind contact, however brief, gave Samantha the courage she needed. But her mouth felt dry, so she simply nodded.

"Good." He turned brisk again. "I will return when you are ready." He left her alone in the small room that smelled of strong disinfectant.

Samantha paused for a moment, realizing the great significance of the next several minutes. Soon her greatest desires or her worst fears would be realized. Her eyes rested on the tall, stark table, and her heart leaped into her throat. *Oh, Lord, please let him give me good news.*

The exam, which the doctor had promised would be thorough, took a little less than an hour. But Samantha felt she aged a year for every minute spent on the table. Tense and expectant, she waited for the doctor to suddenly cry out: "ah, ha!" and give her a miracle cure. But of course he didn't. When he finished, the attending nurse waited while Samantha dressed and then escorted her to the doctor's office.

Adam greeted her with a kiss on the temple. "Dr. Zimmerman told me he'll need time to go over the information before he can make a diagnosis."

Samantha sucked in a nervous breath. "How much time?"

"He wants us to come back tomorrow afternoon at two o'clock. He'll discuss his findings then."

Every muscle in Samantha's body wilted. She leaned into Adam's arms. "The waiting is so hard. . . ."

Adam offered a sympathetic frown. "I know, honey. But tomorrow's not so far away. And while I was waiting for you, I asked a receptionist about good places to stay. He recommended a hotel nearby. Let's go get a room, shall we?"

Despite everything, the prospect of staying in a hotel for the first time in their married lives seemed an adventure. Samantha nodded, and soon she and Adam checked into the Kahler Hotel.

"Well, this is all rather exciting, isn't it?" Adam smiled at her as he dropped their small valise on the dark-green chenille spread that covered the brass bed.

Samantha stared in awe at the heavy velvet draperies and fine, velvet upholstered furnishings. "This room is like a palace." She turned to Adam, feeling guilty. "How can we afford a place like this? And all because I—"

Adam stilled her words with a gentle kiss. "Sweetheart, the expense is nothing compared to our peace of mind. I have every confidence in Dr. Zimmerman. I'm glad we came. Aren't you?"

Samantha closed her eyes for a moment, trying to put aside her anxieties for Adam's sake. "Yes, I'm glad we came. And I trust him too."

Adam kissed her again, a little longer this time. Then he released her to slap a hand on his belly. "I don't know about you, but breakfast was a long time ago, and I'm hungry. What say we find a fine restaurant and dine like kings?"

"Do we have enough money?"

Adam grinned at her. "Thank you for being so frugal, my sweet. That's a sign of a good wife, but I do believe we indeed have the funds for two steak dinners." Samantha sent him an uncertain look. He laughed and said, "Darlin', we have to eat. Will you please believe me when I tell you we won't need to wash dishes to pay for the meal?"

Samantha laughed at herself. This was the first time she and Adam had been away from their home alone since they'd gotten married. Why shouldn't they relax and enjoy a bit of fun as long as they were here? She assumed a bright smile. "All right, let's go. But a walk first, please, to relax. And instead of steak, may I have shrimp? I've heard it's wonderful."

"Shrimp it is!" Then he teased, "But I think you only want to walk to save us the cost of a taxi cab."

How well he knew her! *Oh, Lord, I don't deserve a man like Adam. Thank You for giving him to me anyway.* Adam gallantly held out his elbow, and Samantha took it with an exaggerated flourish.

They walked in proper fashion through Rochester's finest housing district. Arm in arm, relaxed and happy, they enjoyed the sight of tall, Victorian houses with gingerbread millwork, cut-glass windows, and neatly manicured yards. The shrubs on the lawn of one particularly grand house were trimmed to resemble a bear, a swan, and an elephant.

"Oh, Adam, look!" Samantha pointed, as excited as a child. "Isn't that unique? I wonder how they did it."

"Yes, it is something. Someone is certainly talented."

They came upon a green, flower-filled park sporting a marble fountain. In the center of the fountain's pool, a marble cherub stood frozen in a delicate pose with its hand upraised, spewing water from its mouth. Samantha leaned to dip her fingers in the sparkling water, and she noticed a scattering of coins across the bottom of the pool. "It must be a wishing fountain. May I have a penny, please?"

Adam gave it, and Samantha closed her eyes tight. She didn't need to form the wish—God already knew what she longed for the most. Opening her eyes, she sent the copper coin sailing to the fountain's bottom. Then she flashed a smile at Adam, and she sensed in his tender gaze his desire to see her wish come true.

At last they entered a restaurant with an entrance bigger than their parlor at home and containing more stained glass than any church she'd ever seen. A gentleman wearing a black swallow-tail coat escorted them to a linen-draped table. The man had very large ears and walked with his hands clasped at the base of his spine and his head held high. His stiff stance gave him a swaying gait. Adam caught Samantha's gaze and imitated the man's posture, and she covered her mouth to stifle a giggle. The man seated Samantha with somber solicitude, informed them that a waiter would be with them shortly, and walked away in the same dignified way he had come.

Adam leaned across the round, candlelit table and said, "Didn't he look like a penguin?"

Samantha whispered, "No. Penguins don't have ears."

Then followed a lively conversation on whether penguins were truly earless or if they had ears that didn't show. By the time the waiter arrived with the elegant menus requiring two hands to hold them up, both were in a state of hilarity that was impossible to squelch.

After a brief perusal of the choices, Adam formally ordered steak for himself and the promised shrimp for Samantha. But his lips twitched and his eyes danced as he obviously stifled amusement. Samantha bit the insides of her cheeks to keep from laughing at her husband's antics. Their stern-faced waiter didn't seem the type to appreciate levity.

"I shall bring your drinks posthaste, sir," the waiter said with great dignity.

Adam responded, "Yes, posthaste would be just fine."

Samantha dissolved into giggles when the man walked away. She reached across the table to hold Adam's hand and smiled a genuine, down-to-her-toes smile. "Oh, Adam, this is wonderful."

Adam agreed. "Yes, it's just what we needed."

For the next few hours, they did their best to be light-hearted and unburdened, the way young people in love should be. And for those few hours, Samantha even managed to forget the purpose of their excursion.

*E*ven without a rooster's crow or open windows beckoning the first rays of dawn, Adam awoke promptly at his normal time of five-thirty. He rolled over slowly to avoid disturbing Samantha. She had tossed and turned restlessly far into the night.

Gently he lifted the coverlet, slipped out without so much as a *ting* from a bedspring, and padded over to the heavily draped windows. He pulled the green velvet curtain aside enough to see that most of the sky was hidden by the city's expanse. But a space between two four-story buildings allowed him a limited view of the early morning sky. Even in Rochester, the sunrise was beautiful. He decided it was a hopeful sign to see that some things here in the city were like home in Mountain Lake.

Creaking of the bedsprings alerted him, and he looked over his shoulder to see Samantha stretching beneath the covers. She sighed, balling her fists to rub at her eyes. Her gaze met his, and she smiled lazily. "Good morning."

He stifled a chuckle at her sleep-laden voice. "Good morning to you." He crossed to the bed and sat on the edge near her hip, then leaned down to start the day with an affectionate kiss. "It's early yet. Why don't you try to sleep a bit more since we don't have chores to tend to?"

Samantha twisted around a bit beneath the covers, snuggling against the pillows. "I don't know if I can. Once an early riser, always an early riser." And she smiled again contentedly.

"Well, then," Adam suggested, "why not take advantage of our private bath and start your day with a nice soak in the tub?"

Samantha's eyebrows raised, and she looked toward the door that led directly to the attached bathing room. "Mmm, that does sound nice." But she remained in her nestling spot. She held out a hand for Adam to hold, and they sat in quiet contentment for several minutes with Samantha under the covers, Adam perched beside her. Slowly her eyes slipped shut.

Adam said, "So are you getting up or not?" His voice was very soft.

Her eyes still closed, Samantha answered. "Not."

Adam smiled, placed her hand back beneath the sheets and tucked the covers up to her chin. He gave her a kiss on the forehead, then sat for a few minutes, gazing down at her sleeping form. When she began to lightly snore, he chuckled, rose, and disappeared into the bathroom to enjoy his own soak.

Samantha slept peacefully until the hour hand on the little clock on the bedside table pointed to eight. Adam was sitting in one of the velvet-covered chairs beside the windows, looking at a newspaper when she sat bolt upright, eyes wide and hair flying around her face. Adam put down the paper and laughed at her startled expression. "Well, hello again, sleepyhead. Are you awake for good this time?"

Samantha hunched her shoulders sheepishly. "It was perfectly lazy of me, but we are on a little vacation, aren't we?"

"Yes, we are, and being perfectly lazy is part of the plan." He held up his paper. "I've been out and about already, though, and I'm starting to get restless. Why don't you get your bath, and then we'll rustle up some breakfast."

Samantha swung herself out of the warm bed and headed to the bathroom. She called through the open door, "If we eat a late breakfast, we won't need lunch, and we'll save ourselves the expense of three meals out today."

Adam released an amused snort. Would she never let up? "Samantha, will you please stop worrying about money? We're set just fine."

The squeal of spigots being turned and the spatter of water hitting the claw-foot tub sounded through the now-closed door. He had to lean forward in his chair and strain to hear her say, "But, Adam, we'll have the cost of the doctor's exam, too, plus the train fares, and the hotel, and food. . . . I just don't want us to run short."

He chuckled indulgently. "Stop worrying. I've got things under control." But her focus on their finances pleased him. If she was concerned about money, she wasn't worrying about the doctor's verdict.

The water stopped, and the sounds of mild splashing and the occasional squeak of wet skin against slick porcelain carried into the room. Then her voice came again, subdued this time. "Adam?"

"Yes?"

"What do you think he'll say?"

Adam closed his fists around the paper. "I don't want to guess, honey. Let's just wait—and trust."

A long pause, and then her quiet response. "Yes, Adam."

But Adam had a hard time following his own advice. All during the morning as he and Samantha wandered the shops of Rochester, his thoughts ran ahead to the two o'clock appointment with Dr. Zimmerman. What would the doctor say?

Part of him hoped they had found something to explain why Samantha hadn't conceived a child yet. After all, if there was absolutely nothing wrong, then it would only frustrate her further, wondering why they hadn't been blessed with a child. But if there was something wrong, what if it couldn't be fixed? Finally he gave himself a mental kick, determined to put it out of his mind. As he'd told Samantha, the only thing they could do was wait and trust. And pray. A constant prayer hovered at the back of his mind.

✦

Samantha found herself silently praying as she and Adam moved from shop to shop. She would look at a fine piece of lace and comment on it, all the while thinking, *Please, oh please, God!* When she and Adam stopped to eat a late breakfast— what the young man who took their order called a brunch— one word echoed over and over in her mind with every bite, *Please, please, please, please* . . . So much depended on what Dr. Zimmerman would say, it was impossible to think of anything else.

She nearly sagged with relief when one-thirty rolled around and she could give up the pretense of being interested in their surroundings and return to the hospital. A solemn-faced nurse led them into Dr. Zimmerman's office. Samantha tried not to read anything into the woman's expression; she reminded herself that all the staff had looked that way yesterday, and she hadn't been examined yet. She sat in the same chair, crossed her ankles in the same way, rested her hands in her lap—right over left—and waited.

Adam couldn't seem to sit still. He twisted this way and then that way in his chair, propping an ankle over a knee, then putting it down and reversing the process. He placed his arm across the back of Samantha's chair, tapping with one finger against the wooden frame. Softly, between his teeth, he whistled as he tapped his finger and bobbed his foot. Samantha bore it as long as she could, but finally she could not bear it any longer "Adam, please! You're making me nervous!"

He gave a start, then smiled apologetically, dropped his foot, and removed his hand from her chair. "I guess I'm a little anxious."

She shook her head, raising one eyebrow. "A little? I'd hate to see you a lot anxious!"

Their shared chuckle relieved an edge of the tension in the room, but Samantha's pulse immediately sped up when the office door opened and Dr. Zimmerman entered. His gaze fell on her, and for a moment he paused. Then he shut the door and came across the room, hand extended.

Adam half rose with the handshake, then seated himself again as the doctor hitched up his pant legs and sat down across from them. Samantha pinned her gaze on the doctor's face as the big man leaned back in his chair, lacing his fingers and resting the heels of his hands against his stomach. Samantha's heart beat in her throat, and she held her breath, wondering what he was going to say.

Dr. Zimmerman cleared his throat. "Mrs. Klaassen, I have completed a study of your examination, and I believe I know the reason for your barrenness."

In unison, Samantha and Adam leaned forward. Samantha groped for Adam's hand, found it, and clung. Finally, she'd have her answers.

But Dr. Zimmerman surprised her by asking a question. "Are you familiar at all with the female reproductive system?"

Samantha's breath released in a whoosh. She looked at Adam, too startled to reply. Adam lifted one shoulder and stammered out, "Well, we know where babies come from—and how, if that's what you're asking." He sounded as confused as Samantha felt.

"It is." The doctor dropped his hands, then turned sideways in his chair and picked up a black and white drawing which he angled toward Adam and Samantha. As he talked, he pointed to the picture to illustrate his explanation. "In order for a child to be conceived, an egg must travel down from a woman's ovaries through the Fallopian tubes to the uterus, where it is fertilized by the male's sperm.

"Now, I know you have already been told that certain days of the month are considered fertile days, while others are not, so I will not waste time discussing that. However, given the fact that the egg must move through the Fallopian tubes between the ovaries and uterus, I believe I can determine why Mrs. Klaassen has not been able to conceive."

Dread and hope warred within Samantha's heart. She doubled her grip on Adam's hand. Between her palms, his fingers trembled, communicating his own mix of emotions.

"Mrs. Klaassen, it appears you have scar tissue around the uterus. In all likelihood, it also involves the Fallopian tubes." The doctor leaned forward, his eyebrows coming down into a sharp **V**. "Have you ever suffered trauma of the abdomen?"

Samantha stammered, "I—I'm not sure what you mean."

"Have you ever fallen against something very hard, or been struck with something, here?" He placed a hand low on his own belly.

Unpleasant childhood memories surfaced, and Samantha grimaced. She couldn't bring herself to answer the question. She pressed her lips tightly and willed the ugly images filling her mind to disappear.

Adam replied, "When Samantha was a child, she was beaten . . . by her father."

The doctor's thick gray eyebrows came down in a stern scowl, and he looked sharply at Samantha. Something flickered in his eyes—sympathy tangled with fury. "I see." Great meaning underscored the simple reply. He spoke again, this time very gently. "May I ask—was this abuse a one-time situation, or did it occur with regularity?"

Adam turned his hand, twining his fingers through Samantha's. "It occurred regularly."

Dr. Zimmerman heaved a sigh. Scowling he shook his head briefly, and then he shifted his attention to Adam. Samantha sensed he didn't intend to exclude her, but to protect her, and her appreciation for the big man increased in those moments while he explained, in the kindest of tones, his findings.

"Mr. Klaassen, when your wife suffered trauma, there was apparently internal bruising that resulted in scar tissue, a thickening of the tissue of the Fallopian tubes. These tubes are quite narrow, you understand, and anything like this causes a closure of the opening. Because of this closure, the egg cannot come down from the ovaries to reach the uterus. Therefore it cannot be fertilized."

Samantha, listening, experienced a rising sense of dread. A question formed on her lips, but fear of the answer kept her from voicing it. Adam—ever attuned to her—asked it in her stead. "Is there any way to open the Fallopian tubes again, once they've closed?"

The doctor pursed his lips and slowly shook his head—left, right, left. Then he looked at Samantha and said very softly, "I am sorry."

The words registered in Samantha's brain. She wanted to block them out, but she couldn't. Her ears were ringing—high and shrill—that should have cut off the sound of anything else, including those horrible words, "I *am sorry.*" But instead they reverberated again and again until she wanted to scream.

Dr. Zimmerman stretched his hand toward Samantha. "I wish I could offer you more, Mrs, Klaassen. I realize a recognition of the problem solves nothing for you unless there is some resolution. But we are limited; we cannot perform miracles." He placed a big hand over Samantha's knee and gave a light, apologetic squeeze. "I wish I could."

Adam stood. "Thank you for your time, Dr. Zimmerman. At least now we know. I think—" His voice broke, and he cleared his throat twice before continuing. "I think now we can go on. The not knowing is sometimes worse than the knowing."

Samantha hung her head, tears stinging behind her eyelids. *Oh, no, the knowing is far worse. Now I have no hope. No hope at all . . .*

amantha?" Adam touched her shoulder. She gave no indication that she was being spoken to. Adam raised his voice a bit. "Samantha, honey, it's time to leave."

Samantha lifted her head, but with such effort—as if it weighed more than her muscles could support. And when at last her eyes met his, the lack of emotion in their depths stunned him. The blank stare was more frightening than the distress he had expected.

"Come, sweetheart, let's go now," Adam coaxed and took her hand. She rose as if pushing through a full flow of water. Adam's heart beat fearfully for her.

Dr. Zimmerman touched Adam's arm. "Perhaps I should order a sedative for your wife."

Had the situation not been so heartrending, Adam might have laughed. A *sedative*? For a woman who seemed incapable of functioning? Adam shook his head. "No, thank you, Dr. Zimmerman. I'm sure she'll be fine."

Dr. Zimmerman said once more, "I am sorry. I wish there was more . . ."

Adam nodded. "Thank you, doctor." He guided Samantha into the busy hallway, but she seemed oblivious to everything except some inner torment that had closed down her emotions. He told himself not to become overly alarmed. Surely it was shock, and it would wear off soon. In the meantime, he tried to downplay his own crushing disappointment. He must take care of Samantha first.

He kept up a steady stream of conversation in the hopes of restoring some sort of normalcy to the situation. "Well, we might as well go pack up our few things at the hotel and check the train schedules. I'm sure we'll be able to find one running yet today that will get us home. Would you rather walk to the hotel or find a carriage? It might be fun to take a carriage ride; we haven't done that yet. What do you prefer?"

Samantha walked woodenly beside him, putting one foot in front of the other but with no other indication of awareness. He waited, but she didn't reply. He tightened his grip on her arm and went on casually, "Yes, I think a carriage ride is just the thing. Let's stay here by the corner and flag one down."

In short order Adam waved over a carriage driver and told him their destination. He helped Samantha step into the sleigh-like carriage and sat down close beside her on the padded seat, placing an arm around her shoulders. He smiled into her empty eyes. "Now, isn't this nice?" And he tried to swallow the fear that rose within when she seemed to stare right past him.

⌒⌒

On her side of the carriage seat, Samantha felt as if it took every bit of strength she possessed just to breathe. She concentrated very hard—breathe in, release; breathe in, release. . . . Did she feel devastated? No, devastated was an understatement, far from capturing her grief. Sorrow this deep had no description.

The doctor had looked at her, had said in a kind, sincere tone, "I am sorry." With three simple words—words that had always meant healing and comfort in the past—he had destroyed her. A part of her wanted to reach out to Adam, to comfort him and receive his comfort. But to do that would be to acknowledge that the doctor's verdict was final. It would mean accepting this horrible nightmare as reality. And Samantha couldn't do it.

So she remained in her shell, shut off and reeling, waiting for the moment of awakening. *This is a dream*, she told herself while the world went on around her in blissful ignorance, *an awful dream that will soon end. Just wake up, Samantha. Wake up. . . .*

⁓᎒

Somewhere between the clinic and the hotel, Adam made a decision. They wouldn't go straight home. Looking at Samantha's white, emotionless face, he knew she wasn't ready to face the family and answer questions about the unsettling news Dr. Zimmerman had delivered. They would all react with sympathy and no small amount of tears, but an emotional display—however sincere and well-intentioned—wouldn't be what Samantha needed right now. And if he was honest with himself, he needed some time to digest this information before having to talk with everyone at home.

Instead, they would take a trip straight north to Minneapolis and spend a few days with his oldest brother Daniel and his family. Daniel was a lawyer, able to mask his feelings. His wife, Rose, was forthright and steady. There would be no blatant displays of sorrow from either of them, he was certain. They would be able to talk things out sensibly and begin to put it behind them. That was what they needed now—calm, rational conversation.

Adam left Samantha in the hotel room to organize their belongings while he walked to the telegraph office to send a wire to his parents. While dictating the brief message, tears gathered in the back of his throat. Telling the family back home made it all so . . . well, real.

He would never be a daddy. He would never pace the floors at night with a teething baby, warn an inquisitive toddler about the dangers of a hot stove, remind a lost-in-play son to feed the horses, or tease a blushing daughter about her host of beaux. All of his long-held dreams of parenthood were crumbling and being whisked away by the winds of reality.

It's not fair! Oh, dear God, it isn't fair!

"Let's see if we got this right." The thin, bespectacled man behind the desk held Adam's message at arm's length. "TO S. KLAASSEN STOP DOCTOR'S REPORT NOT GOOD STOP THERE CAN BE NO CHILDREN STOP DETAILS LATER STOP GOING TO MINNEAPOLIS FOR FEW DAYS STOP A.K."

The man's monotone recital gave Adam time to regain his composure. "Yes, that's correct, thank you." He dictated a second wire, this one to Daniel and Rose, telling them the unhappy news and alerting them to the impending arrival. He paid the required fees, and from there he headed to the railroad depot to determine train schedules. He purchased tickets for the next train to Minneapolis, which didn't leave until the following morning. It didn't register that they would need to spend one more night in the Rochester hotel until he was two blocks away from the train station. He hoped Sammy hadn't finished packing, or she'd just have to undo it all.

Thinking about Samantha immediately brought thoughts of what had been taken from them with Dr. Zimmerman's examination. Adam felt as if he'd been robbed of something priceless. And how much greater must be Samantha's loss?

Samantha had never known the love of a mother—or a father, for that matter. The lack of parental caring had made her long even more fervently for a child to cuddle and nurture. She'd lost so much already in life. How could anyone expect her to blithely accept the fact that she would never bear children of her own?

It had never occurred to either of them that a family wouldn't be possible. They had planned for children as matter-of-factly as they had planned where to place their furniture or what they would have for the evening meal. In their conversations, it was always *when* we have children, never *if*. Having grown up in a large family, of course Adam had wanted his own boisterous brood someday. How disheartening to realize someday would never come.

Eagerness to be with his wife—to hold her, comfort her, and be comforted by her—welled in his soul, and he increased his pace. When he entered their hotel room, he found her sitting on the edge of the chenille-covered bed, the valise beside her, gaping open but still empty. He couldn't help but compare the empty travel bag to the equally empty expression on his wife's face. The sight of Samantha so obviously heartbroken and withdrawn nearly did him in. He understood completely—her dreams of motherhood were gone! It was too horrible to accept. Yet he realized it must be accepted or it would destroy them both. But how to help her understand that? Ah, that was the problem.

"Well, Sammy, it's a good thing you haven't packed up yet." He crossed the carpet and sat beside her. Although in the past he'd always found it easy to take her in his arms, for some reason his hands remained cupped over his knees. He swallowed. "It looks like we'll be here another night. And instead of going back to Mountain Lake tomorrow, I thought we might make a real vacation out of this little trip and go to Minneapolis instead."

Very slowly Samantha turned her head, but her gaze landed somewhere on the buttons of his shirt rather than meeting his eyes. "Minneapolis? But why?"

Adam forced a cheery tone. "We don't get to see Daniel and Rose much. We've traveled this far, why not go a little farther? I thought it might be nice." He paused, trying to read her closed expression. "Is that all right with you?"

Her head dropped, and a tired sigh passed her lips. "Yes, that's fine, Adam."

Encouraged by her brief response, the first words she'd spoken since they left the doctor's office, Adam's heart fluttered with hope. Maybe she was coming out of her shock enough to talk about Dr. Zimmerman's discovery. How he needed to discuss it. Placing a gentle hand on Samantha's arm, he said, "Sammy, honey, Dr. Zimmerman—"

Samantha leaped up as if fired from a cannon. She swung around, her eyes, steely and snapping, pinning him to his seat. She hissed, "I do not wish to speak of Dr. Zimmerman—not today, not tomorrow, not ever. This day does not exist in my life, Adam, do you hear me?"

He sat still, completely stunned by her vehemence. He had expected sorrow, even anger—but this defiance was a total surprise.

Through clenched teeth she demanded again, "Do you hear me?"

"Yes." Adam finally managed a choked whisper, too afraid to say anything else. Maybe he should have allowed the doctor to prescribe some sort of sedative.

Samantha's shoulders wilted. Gazing toward the open window, she said evenly, "Since we'll be here another night, I believe I'll relax a bit with a bath." She moved toward the bathroom, as stiff as a wind-up toy, entered, and turned to firmly lock the door.

Adam begged, *Please, God, let me be able to reach her. We need each other now. Help her to see that.* With Samantha behind the bathroom door, safely out of sight and hearing, Adam dropped his facade of strength, buried his face in his hands, and wept.

*W*hen Samantha closed the bathroom door and turned the brass lock, she leaned against the solid wood door, her head back, her eyes closed. She knew why Adam wasn't taking her home right away. Humiliation gripped her. She was barren, unable to give Adam what he wanted most—a family. She was only half a woman, her ability to conceive and bear children snatched away from her. None of this was Adam's fault—all hers. Obviously Adam didn't want his parents, his family, to see his heartbreak and her shame. They couldn't go home.

Oh, Adam, I'm sorry. So, so sorry . . .

She pushed away from the door and numbly crossed to the tub, plugged the drain hole, and turned the brass faucets on high. But she didn't undress, just stood staring unseeingly at the spattering stream of water as she replayed the afternoon in her mind. The doctor had said there could be no babies. No babies because of scar tissue. Scar tissue because of trauma. Trauma because her father had been a drunk with a temper who had taken his frustrations out on his children.

Anger—an impassioned, fiery anger that burned white-hot—exploded through Samantha's whole being. Fists pressed to her trembling lips, she moaned out her fury. "Pa, you had no right! No right to do this to me—to Adam. You stole my childhood from me with your senseless, fearful rages, and now you've stolen my chance to regain that lost childhood with a child of my own. You took my dream—no, *our* dream!—away from us! I don't deserve this. And Adam—Adam deserves children, a family. How could you do this to me—to Adam?"

She reached through the cloud of steam to stop the water with a violent twist of the faucets. With shaking hands she tugged at her garments with jerky, disjointed motions. She threw the clothing into a jumbled pile in front of the bathroom door. Her throat ached with the desire to cry, but her eyes remained dry. Crying might give release. And Samantha didn't want release. She wanted to nurse this anger, hold it, savor it. By focusing all of her energy into anger with her father, she could fend off any other emotions.

She submerged herself in the tub until only her head was above the water. Heat surrounded her—hot water and billowing steam. And from deep within, the burning flame of anger at the injustice of it all. The bath water grew tepid as minutes passed, but Samantha's anger did not cool. Sorrow, disappointment, even guilt for Adam's sadness, took a backseat to her fury at the man who had robbed Samantha of her chance for motherhood. It was all that could sustain her now.

❧

The train ride from Rochester to Minneapolis was a silent one. Oh, there were noises around them—the chatter of other passengers, the clacking of wheels against rails, the whistling of wind through a crack in the window. But between Samantha and Adam not a word was spoken. Adam gazed quietly out the window, watching the landscape whiz by, aware of Samantha still and tense on the bench beside him. He longed to reach out, put an arm around her in the old, familiar way. But he felt rebuffed and unsure of Samantha's reaction to any overture of comfort, so he remained separated and aching.

Somewhere behind them a baby fussed, and Samantha shot from the seat. "I need some air." She stalked to the door leading to a small landing outside of the car. Adam didn't offer to join her. If she wanted his company, she would ask. Although her silent presence had been difficult to bear, sitting here alone was even worse. He missed her. He missed how they used to be. But how to regain it?

Nearly half an hour later Samantha returned, her face white and pinched. She slid into the seat as the conductor passed through the car, announcing, "Next stop Minneapolis, folks. Minneapolis is the next stop."

Adam gathered his courage and eased his fingers along Samantha's arm. "Do you suppose Daniel and Rose will be waiting for us?"

Samantha shrank from his touch and shrugged.

Her withdrawal and the aloof, uncaring gesture angered him. He gritted his teeth and turned his attention outward again.

◦──◦

Samantha's chest tightened. She was adding further pain to her husband's sorrow. This wasn't his fault. She shouldn't punish him. But what to say? She didn't want to see anyone and wanted to talk even less. So she sat in grief-filled silence, feeling guilty and small but unable to get herself to change it. She was as lonely here beside him as she'd been on that landing outside, clinging to the railing, shivering against the sharp wind generated by the speed of the train.

The train hissed to a halt at the busy station in Minneapolis. By the time they had gathered up their bags and jostled their way off through the sea of other travelers, Samantha's head was pounding. She yearned to lean into Adam's strength, but the tense set of his jaw kept her at bay.

"Adam! Sam!" A familiar voice rang over the chatter of the crowd. Adam's brother Daniel stood near the long sidewalk beside the big depot, waving a hand. Adam placed his palm on Samantha's back to guide her along, but the moment they reached Daniel, it slipped away. Samantha blinked back tears as Daniel leaned down to give her a brotherly kiss. "How was your trip? Did you enjoy the train ride?"

Samantha gulped and forced her lips into a tight smile. "It was fine."

Adam's mouth looked grim, but before he said anything, Daniel captured him in a one-armed hug. "My car is this way. Let's go." Daniel set a brisk pace, escorting Samantha along beside him with a hand under her arm. Adam trailed behind. Daniel kept up a steady stream of conversation that filled the uncomfortable silence between Adam and Samantha. They reached a black Model T, and Daniel turned to grab the carpet-bag from Adam and tossed it into the vehicle's rumble seat. "Well, here we go!"

"Samantha, we can all crowd into the front seat, I think, and give you a better view of the city. You've never been to Minneapolis before, have you?"

He didn't wait for an answer, just pressed on cheerfully as he twisted the key, pulled the throttle, and set the car in motion. "Rose has all sorts of plans for you while you're here—a shopping trip and lunch in town as well as joining her Junior Leaguers for tea. You won't lack for entertainment, that's certain! And, Adam—" He leaned forward to peer around Samantha—"I hope you'll spend a day at the office with me. Otherwise we won't see much of one another, I'm afraid. I've got several cases I'm juggling right now, and I can't afford to be away for long."

Samantha appreciated Daniel's attempt at normalcy even while she inwardly objected to it. Didn't he realize everything had changed? How could he blithely make plans as if the world still turned on its axis and all was well?

Adam's voice was hesitant as he asked Samantha, "Would you mind if I spent a day with Daniel?"

It would be good for him to get away from all the disappointment, the distance she'd created between them. "Not at all, Adam. I'm sure Rose and I can manage to occupy the time."

Daniel added enthusiastically, "And don't forget the girls—Christie and Katie are all excited about your visit. And wait until you see how Camelia has grown; you won't recognize her! She's walking already, has a mouthful of teeth which she'll cheerfully use on your fingers if you aren't watchful, and she's attempting to talk. I tell you, it's thrilling to see how those little ones take off!"

Daniel's exuberant pride in his children pierced Samantha to the depths of her soul. She pressed three fingers to her mouth, holding back a sob. Through her tears she saw Adam's hands clenched into fists.

Daniel emitted a strangled sound. "Argh. I wish I could bite off my tongue. I'm so sorry. I'm trying so hard not to say the wrong thing, I—"

Adam said, "It's all right, Daniel. You have every right to talk about your girls."

Although her aching throat kept her from speaking, Samantha offered a weak nod. If she had children, she'd never stop talking about them to others. But how long would it be before hearing others brag about their youngsters didn't break her heart beyond repair?

Daniel blew out a noisy breath and shot a quick, sad smile in their direction. "I'm glad you two came. Rose and I . . . we

want to help you get through this. With prayer, and with to-
getherness, we'll make it . . . our family will all put in our oars
to pull you through."

Adam gave a firm nod, and Samantha forced a small acknowledgment of her own. But inwardly she trembled. How
could they work together when she and Adam had lost even
their ability to look one another in the eyes?

"Daniel? Are you asleep?"

Rose's soft voice cut through the fog, rousing Daniel. He
rubbed a hand across his eyes and rolled over to face his wife.
"No, honey, I'm awake. What's wrong?"

"I'm really worried about Sam."

In the dusky shadows, Daniel read the concern in his wife's
face. He folded an arm beneath his head, and with his free hand
he massaged Rose's shoulder. "I know. She's having a rough
time of it, isn't she?"

"She's in agony." Rose's urgent whisper indicated her own
heartache. "But she refuses to talk about it. I don't know how
long she can keep all of those emotions locked up inside. She'll
sit and hold little Cami, and you can feel her anguish. Yet she
won't say a word." She captured Daniel's hand and drew it beneath her chin. "Has Adam said anything?"

Daniel released a brief huff. "Adam has talked incessantly.
Of course, the prospect of no children in his life is daunting.
He's disappointed and heartbroken, but I think he could accept
it. What he can't accept is Samantha's emotional withdrawal.
He is more upset by her reaction to the situation than the situation itself. As he put it, he can live without children, but he
can't live without Sam."

"Do you suppose she blames Adam? Maybe that's why she's been standoffish toward him."

Daniel shook his head. "No, quite honestly, I think she blames herself. After all, it isn't a problem with Adam that's keeping them from having children."

Rose shook her head, her brow furrowing. "Then why treat Adam as if—"

"Because she feels guilty." Daniel gave Rose's hand a squeeze. "Think about it. Facing Adam, knowing what she's taken from him, is painful for her. So she pulls away. And in so doing hurts Adam more than the loss of children could."

Rose conceded, "That makes sense, I suppose. But she doesn't act as if she feels guilty. She acts as if she's angry."

Daniel thought about that for a moment. "Perhaps she's angry with herself."

"Perhaps . . . but I don't think so."

"Then what?"

A heavy sigh from Rose. "I don't know, Daniel. I feel so sorry for both of them. Adam and Samantha both are in deep pain, and I want to help them, but I don't know what to do. They almost make me feel guilty for having the girls."

"Now don't think that way," Daniel chided gently. "It won't help to feel badly about a blessing the Lord has chosen to give us."

"I know, and I do feel blessed, Daniel. But I also feel for Samantha. Now that I have our girls, I can't imagine life without them. I think I can understand, somewhat, what Samantha is facing. I just wish she'd talk about it. It's not healthy to keep all of those feelings inside."

"No, it's not." Daniel agreed, but he cautioned, "You can't make her talk about it until she's ready."

"So what do I do?"

Daniel pulled Rose into his embrace. She rested her head on his shoulder and snuggled, content within the comforting circle of his arms. "I don't know that you can do anything, honey, except be available should she choose to talk. And, of course, we can always pray for them." He paused for a moment, stroking Rose's hair, before saying quietly, "Yesterday Adam and I talked about how Mother always says God never closes a door without opening a window. She believes sometimes God allows unpleasant things to happen, knowing later a reward even better than what we had planned will come.

"Adam wants to believe there is a purpose for this. Of course, we can't know what the purpose is, but it's a matter of faith. If only Samantha would believe it, too."

Rose didn't reply, and Daniel lifted his head to look at her. Her eyes were closed, her face relaxed. Daniel chuckled softly at the irony of her waking him to talk, then falling asleep mid-conversation. Now fully awake, Daniel decided to make good use of the time. He closed his eyes and took his concerns for his brother and sister-in-law to the One who never sleeps.

cross the hall beneath an appliquéd quilt, Adam lay on his back, hands beneath his head, staring at the ceiling. Samantha was on her side facing away from him, hands curled beneath her chin. Adam shifted slightly, looking at the back of Samantha's head. Her hair was in wild disarray—evidence of the tossing and turning she'd done earlier. What would she do if he reached out and smoothed it down?

Probably stiffen up and shift away from me. Ever since Dr. Zimmerman's verdict, she'd been skittish and aloof. Although he ached to cradle her against his side, the way they'd slept before, he brought his arms downward and laced his fingers together across his stomach. His chest hurt. He longed for that closeness he'd had with Samantha. Affection had always come easily between the two of them. He missed it—the smiles, the touching, the sharing of small events and deeper feelings. The contentment. Would they ever get it back? Would the fact they would never have children take all of that away?

If only she'd talk to him, even if it meant screams and tears and accusations. He could take the anger he suspected she was harboring if she would just let it out. Her silent withdrawal tore him apart inside. He moved his head sideways on the pillow, staring at Samantha's still form beside him. Her stony silence was as impenetrable as a brick wall. He would not attempt to break down a brick wall unless well armed. And he was too weary, holding too much pain himself, to wield whatever that might require.

He rolled over, also presenting his back to his wife, and closed his eyes against hot tears of sorrow for his double loss.

❧

The sun was inching its way above the horizon when Adam eased his way out of bed, taking care not to pull the covers off of his wife's sleeping form. He knew she hadn't been sleeping long; he remembered the sound of her crying into her pillow before he had finally drifted off only a few hours ago.

He padded quietly to the window, rubbing the back of his neck and lifting the curtains aside to peer outward. Sunrises had always been a symbol of promise to Adam. He looked back at Samantha, heart lifting with a small measure of hope. Maybe today held a promise of change.

The patter of little feet in the hallway captured his attention, and he crossed to the door. Katrina, still in her nightgown, was headed for the stairs. He smiled at the bobbing, multicolored twists of cloth that held her long hair in pin curls. "Hi, sweetie," he whispered, stepping into the hall.

Katrina's face broke into a huge grin, and she ran to him for a hug. "'Morning, Uncle Adam!"

He silenced her with a whispered, "Shh!" and lifted the six-year-old to settle on his hip as he cracked the door behind them and pointed at Samantha. "Auntie Sam is asleep. Let's not wake her."

Katrina nodded, covering pursed lips with one finger. When Adam closed the door again, she whispered, "Why is Auntie Sam still sleeping? It's time to get up."

Adam chuckled. "Well, just because the sun is rising doesn't mean people have to rise too, you know."

Katrina seemed to think about that for a moment before tipping her head and fixing Adam with a frown. "Is Auntie Sam tired from being sad?"

The child's question took him aback. "What—what makes you think she's sad?"

Katrina's face crinkled in thought. "Well, she isn't laughy like she used to be, and even when she smiles it's only in her mouth. Her eyes don't smile—like this." The little girl gave a beaming, gap-toothed smile that lit her whole face. Adam couldn't help returning it with one of his own. Then she sobered again and asked gravely, "Is she sad 'cause she can't have no babies?"

If Adam was startled before, he was dumbfounded now. "How did you know that, Katrina?"

She shrugged. "Heard Mama and Daddy talkin'. Is that why she's sad?"

Adam answered honestly, "Yes, Katie, it makes her very sad."

"And you too?"

Adam swallowed. "Yes, me too."

Katrina wrapped her arms around Adam's neck and pressed her cheek to his. "I'm sorry, Uncle Adam."

Katrina's sincerity made tears prick at the back of Adam's eyes. He hugged her tightly, reveling in the feel of the sturdy little body in his arms, the tickle of the coiled hair against his cheek, the sleep-tumbled smell of the child. *Oh, Lord, I've wanted this so much for myself!*

Katrina pulled back and took Adam's face in her stubby hands. "Uncle Adam, if Auntie Sam can't have babies, maybe I should come live with you and be your little girl."

Adam melted. "Oh, sweetie, that's awfully nice of you. And Auntie Sam and I would dearly love to have you for a little girl. But don't you think your mama and daddy would miss you?"

Katrina wrinkled her nose. "They'd still have Christie and Cami."

Adam smiled. "But they wouldn't have Katie anymore, and that just wouldn't be the same."

The child sighed, her warm breath caressing Adam's cheek. "You're right. I guess I better stay here." She rested her head against his shoulder briefly before straightening and adding, "But, Uncle Adam?"

"Yes, sweetie?"

"I'm gonna pray to Jesus that you get some little girls even if it don't be from Auntie Sam. Daddy says ever'body needs little girls around to keep life int—int—" She scratched her head, obviously trying to remember something. Then her face brightened and she finished, "Interesting. That's why he and Mama had three of 'em."

Adam pushed back the chuckle. She was so sweet and serious! "I suppose your Daddy is right."

Katrina nodded. "That's why he's a lawyer. He gots a good thinker."

Adam laughed aloud. "I'll remember that." And then it was as if a light turned on inside. Innocent Katrina had given Adam an idea. The desire to discuss it with Samantha nearly overwhelmed him. He set Katrina down, sending her toward the spindled staircase with a light pat on her backside. "Now you'd best catch up with your sisters and go get your breakfast."

Katrina scampered forward a few steps, then stopped, asking over her shoulder, "Aren't'cha comin' too?"

"In a bit," Adam said, his mind racing. "I need to talk to your Auntie Sam first."

"Oh. Well . . . see ya!" Katrina bounced around the corner out of sight.

Adam returned to the bedroom, his heart thumping. Katrina's comments had given him a sunrise-bright promise. He replayed her words in his mind—". . . get some little girls even if they don't come from Auntie Sam . . ." *Heavenly Father, could this be our answer? Oh, please let Samantha agree with me!*

But Samantha slept soundly, and he didn't have the heart to disturb her. He knew how badly she needed this rest. So he quietly dressed and went down to breakfast. Sitting between Katrina and Christina, he found himself caught up in a wonderful daydream of someday sitting between some little girls—or boys—who would call him Papa. He smiled and teased, snitched bits of hotcakes from the girls' plates and made them squeal.

"Uncle Adam, you're so funny," Christina told him, and he felt like the wittiest man in the world.

When the girls finished breakfast and headed to their rooms to dress for school, Adam leaned back in his chair, sipped his coffee, and sent his brother and sister-in-law a little smile.

Daniel observed, "You look like the fox that raided the henhouse."

"Yes." Rose peered at Adam over her china cup. "Not that it isn't wonderful to see you in good spirits, but would you mind letting us in on what has you so cheery this morning?"

"Nope," Adam said with a grin. "Oh, you'll hear about it soon enough. But not until I've talked to Sammy." He set the cup aside, then rested his elbows on the lace-covered tabletop. He grinned at Daniel and Rose above his joined hands. "You know, you've got a very bright little girl."

Rose corrected archly, "We've got three very bright little girls."

Adam conceded with a bow of his head. "Yes, you do. But I'm referring now to your middle daughter."

"Katie?" Rose's eyebrows rose in curiosity. "What does she have to do with your rather perky demeanor this morning?"

"You'll find out," Adam promised, a smile twitching at the edges of his lips, "just as soon as I talk to Samantha."

"Talk to me about what?" came a voice from the doorway.

Adam turned to see Samantha, her disheveled hair and the blue smudges beneath her eyes giving her a tired, old appearance that tore at his heart. How he wanted to remove the haunted expression from her face.

"A-Adam?" Her voice quavered. She took a hesitant step into the kitchen. "What do you want to talk to me about?"

Adam opened his mouth to share his idea, but he felt a wave of apprehension. Should he wait? After all, they'd only just been given the news. Maybe this was too soon. He sent up a quick prayer for guidance, but even before he voiced the "amen," Samantha caught hold of the doorframe and gaped at him, tears flooding her eyes.

"You're sending me away, aren't you?"

*A*dam had leaped out of his chair, and shock widened his eyes as he stared at her across the room. "Sending you away?"

Samantha blinked back her tears and forced herself not to recoil. She wouldn't blame him. And she would be strong, no matter what he told her. "I would understand, if you did. After all, I—"

Adam dashed to her and captured both of her hands, looking directly into her eyes. "I will never send you away."

"But—"

"You're my wife. I married you for richer, for poorer, remember? For better, for worse, in sickness and in health, till death parts us."

His voice rose with conviction, lighting a fire of remorse in the center of her soul. She didn't deserve a man like Adam.

He squeezed her hands and said in a ragged tone, "I love you. Nothing will change that."

She tipped her head, her tangled hair trailing across her shoulders. "Then what is it, Adam, you are wanting to tell me?"

Adam looked over his shoulder at his brother and sister-in-law. "Let's go up to our room. We can talk there."

Samantha allowed Adam to guide her up the stairs and into the guestroom. Relief that he still loved her made her knees weak, but worry about what he might say made her breath come in little spurts. She sank onto the foot of the bed and fixed her gaze on Adam. But instead of talking, he began pacing back and forth across the room, his brow furrowed. His unusual behavior increased her anxiety. "Whatever it is, just say it!"

He slowly turned to face her. Something flickered in his eyes. Uncertainty? Fear? Before she could determine the emotion, he moved over to her and dropped to one knee. Twining his fingers through hers, he drew in a breath. "Sammy, earlier this morning, Katrina—bless her heart!—said something that got me thinking. . . ." He paused.

Samantha wondered if her heart might pound its way from her chest while she waited for him to share his thoughts with her.

Sympathy glowed in Adam's eyes. He gave her hand a gentle squeeze. "Sammy, it tears me apart to say these words out loud, but they must be said."

Samantha's chest began to heave with her short, stuttered breaths. She tried to pull her hands away and rise, but he held tight.

"We cannot have children." Adam's voice, so tender, stabbed as painfully as if he'd plunged a knife into her breast. "We want children. We've dreamed of children. But there will not be any children—not by birth."

Samantha jerked her gaze away from his. "I know, Adam."

"Yes, we know," Adam agreed quietly. He cupped her chin and turned her to face him. "But we haven't accepted it, have we? Instead, we've avoided it. And, sweetheart, we can't avoid it any longer. We really must talk about it."

Samantha ducked her head and clenched her hands so tightly her fingernails dug into her flesh. "Talking about it won't change it. Talking about it only makes me feel bad. And I don't want to feel bad!"

"Neither do I," he countered evenly, "but I don't think pretending this problem doesn't exist will solve anything." His tone took on a pleading quality as he said, "Honey, you and I have always been able to talk things out. No matter what the problem was, we could share it with each other, and it always helped."

She brought her head up sharply. "But before we could always solve the problem by talking it out. This time, there is no solution, Adam!"

"But there is a solution. I've found the solution, thanks to Katrina."

Adam's wide, guileless eyes begged Samantha to listen, but she couldn't imagine how a six-year-old child could possibly solve a problem a highly educated medical doctor couldn't. She blinked once, slowly, and dared to ask, "What is it?"

A smile grew across his face. "Katie and I were talking this morning, and she said she was going to pray that even if you couldn't have any babies, we'd still be able to get some babies."

Samantha shook her head, impatience again rising. "Adam, I don't understand. . . ."

"We could . . . someday, when we're ready . . . adopt a baby."

∽◯

Samantha felt like her insides were being squeezed, and the room seemed to reel around her. Adopt a baby? As if that could possibly be the same! How could he even suggest such a thing? After a week of silence—of avoidance and tension—he had the audacity to suggest taking in someone else's child? She hadn't even had time to come to terms with the fact that she was barren, and he was ready to set aside her long-held dreams of having a baby and just go to some orphanage and pick one out. How could he? "Oh, Adam . . ."

Adam tugged at her hands. "'Oh, Adam,' what?" His head tipped to the side. "We both want a baby, don't we? And if we can't have one, then—"

Samantha jerked her hands free and shot out of the chair, pushing past him to stand before the window. Her stomach ached with an emptiness nothing would ever fill. She wrapped her arms around her middle, wishing . . . oh, *wishing* . . . her arms might be crossed over a pregnant belly.

Adam came up behind her and gripped her shoulders. He spoke against her tousled hair. "Tell me what you're thinking, Sam dearest."

A harsh, dry laugh exploded from her mouth. She shook her head. "Oh, you really don't want to know what I'm thinking." She spun around and glowered at him. "How could you even suggest something like this? As if—as if it doesn't matter that I can't bear children. As if our baby can be replaced by some . . . some little foundling no one else wants!"

Adam stared at her. "I never meant to imply it doesn't matter. Of course it matters! It's horrible and unthinkable and beyond the scope of reason that you can't bear our children. It hurts me as deeply as it hurts you, believe me, Sammy."

"It *can't* hurt you as badly as it hurts me."

"Why not?"

"Because it isn't your fault!" She thumped her own chest. "It's my fault!" Then she clenched her hands before her and shook her head wildly. "No, it's not my fault. It's my father's fault! And because of what he did to me, you're being punished, too!"

Adam pulled Samantha into his arms. Although over the past week she'd yearned for his embrace, now she fought for freedom. Freedom from his kindness, which she didn't deserve. Freedom from the pressing truth of her inability to conceive. Freedom from the pain that held her captive. But Adam's arms, as strong as he'd always claimed his love for her was, held tight, and eventually she collapsed against his chest. Her silent tears soaked his shirt.

"Samantha . . ." Adam's voice drifted softly to her ears, tender yet sad. "You told me long ago that you'd forgiven your father. Forgiving him helped you heal. Please don't open those old wounds again."

Her face pressed to his shirtfront, she groaned. "I can't help it. How can I not revisit the wounds he inflicted now that . . . now that we know how terribly he hurt me?" She gulped out a sob. "It isn't fair that you can't have children because of what my father did to me. Can't you understand?"

He kissed the top of her head. "Sammy, honey, I do understand. But you need to understand something, too. You are not responsible for what your father did to you. I don't blame you, and neither should you."

Samantha shifted her face to the familiar curve of his shoulder, breathing in his unique scent. "I can't help but blame me. Because of my father, you can't have any children."

Adam's hand stroked through her hair, the touch so sweet and loving it made her heart ache anew. "We *can* have children—by adoption. Daniel is a lawyer. He could—"

"No!" She swung her arms outward, knocking his hands from her shoulders. She skittered sideways until she was out of reach.

Adam took two steps toward her, his hands held out in a gesture of entreaty. "Why not? It would be a way to have the family we dreamed of, Sammy. It would give a little one a chance—"

The moan from the very center of her fractured soul escaped, and both hands went to her mouth. How could she make him understand? And then a long-buried memory surfaced. Her body trembled as emotions from years ago collided with the tension of the day. On shaky legs, she returned to the bed and seated herself. With a pleading look for Adam to listen, she began to speak.

"When I was a little girl, I found a baby bird in the yard. It had fallen from its nest. I knew it would starve on its own, so I put it in a little basket and took care of it." Adam's brow was puckered, but he remained silent. Slowly, he approached the bed and sat beside her, his knee brushing against hers. With his brown eyes locked on her face, she continued her story. "For three days I took care of that little bird. I kept it warm, covering it with a piece of flannel Gran gave me. I dug worms for it and gave it drinks by dipping a cloth in water then holding the cloth above and letting drops of water fall into its mouth." A mirthless chuckle found its way out as she recalled, "I even sang lullabies to that stupid little bird."

Adam placed his hand over her knee and squeezed gently.

"On the fourth morning, I went to the basket, and the bird was dead. I was inconsolable. I had grown to love it. I had fed it and played with it and dreamed about the day I would see it grow strong enough to fly. I felt like a part of me had died too. . . ." Samantha put her hand over Adam's, needing contact. "Davey helped me bury it, then I just sat by the tiny grave for hours. I couldn't stop crying. My heart was broken.

"That afternoon, to cheer me up, Gran went to town and bought me a lollipop. It was as big as my pa's hand, with a coil of pink, green, and white stripes. It was a wonderful lollipop, and since Davey and I rarely got candy, it was a very special treat. I thanked Gran, then I took it outside and gave it to my brother. I couldn't eat it. There was no way that a lollipop— even a big, beautiful lollipop like that one—could make up for the loss of my baby bird. I appreciated what Gran was trying to do, but it wasn't enough."

Samantha looked at Adam, his image swimming through a mist of tears. "Don't you see? For me, adopting a baby would be like a lollipop after the promise of a bird in flight. I can't accept it. It would be a distant second best." Hot tears rolled down her cheeks as her heart begged for his forgiveness. "Please don't be angry with me. Please try to understand."

⌒の

Adam lowered his head and squeezed Samantha's hand. "I understand, honey." And he did. All through her life, she'd been forced to accept whatever life threw at her—a drunken, abusive father instead of a caring, nurturing one; a grandmother who was unquestionably loving but was with her for only six short years and could never take the place of a mother; a childhood filled with hard work and mistreatment instead of lightheartedness and caring. Then she became an adult, gradually learned to accept Adam's love, and then dreamed of giving birth to her own child. A child by any other means was to her another lost dream, and it could never be a replacement for that dream.

Adam once again put his arms around his wife and pulled her close, resting his chin on the top of her head. She sat passively within his embrace. Somehow he felt she was asking for understanding for more than her feelings on adoption; she needed understanding for the way she'd reacted since the day they'd visited the Mayo Clinic. Now that she'd shared her feelings with him, he could offer a more complete understanding and support. What a heavy burden of guilt and shame she'd carried so bravely on her own.

"I'm not angry with you, Samantha." He meant it. "I've never been angry, but I have been hurt." When Samantha tried to shift away, he cupped her cheeks and raised her face. "I've been hurt by your withdrawal from me. Sweetheart, I love you, and I've needed you desperately these past few days. We were handed a great disappointment! And by pulling away from me, you've only made things harder on me. And maybe on yourself, I think."

Tears left a silvery trail down her pale cheeks. She gripped his wrists. "I didn't want to hurt you. I love you, too. I'm just so full of pain, I haven't known what to do."

Adam swallowed as he looked into her red-rimmed eyes, so full of sorrow. Caressing her temples with his thumbs, he dared to share the deepest fear he'd carried over the past week. "Sammy, I told Daniel a few days ago that it would be difficult to give up my dream of having a family, but I could do it. What I could not give up is you." He paused, searching her face. "Am I to lose you, Samantha?"

A ragged sob burst from her throat. Her arms flew around his neck, and she buried her face against his shoulder. Her tears flowed, as did his. Despite their anguish, Adam couldn't deny his heart thrilled at holding her, comforting her, joining her in sorrow at what had been taken from them. He rubbed her back and felt her hands paint circles on his shoulders.

Their shared mourning was bringing them together again. *Thank You, Lord. Thank You. . . .*

In time she pulled back to wipe her eyes and finally answer his question. "No, Adam, you aren't losing me. And I'm so sorry I hurt you. I love you so much! I've been miserable thinking of how I've disappointed you. I couldn't face that thought."

Adam looped her tangled hair behind her ears, leaning in to deposit a kiss on her lips. "You didn't cause my disappointment, Sammy. Do you believe me?"

"I'm trying to." Samantha's shoulders slumped, and her voice dropped to a whisper. "I just ache so much inside . . . I feel as if my heart is crying."

Adam drew her against his chest and rocked her gently, but he had no words to comfort her after a confession like that.

t a light tap at the door, Adam reached into his back pocket for a handkerchief which he offered to Samantha. He waited until she had wiped her face before he went to the door and opened it. A plainly dressed young woman waited in the hallway, looking at him through a fringe of unevenly cut bangs. Her hands twisted nervously on the wooden handle of a feather duster.

"I'm sorry t-t-to disturb you, sir, b-b-but I do h-housekeeping f-f-for Mrs. Klaassen, and I'm to clean the upstairs, and I-I-I've done all the rooms but this one. C-c-could I c-c-come in and clean now?"

Adam glanced over his shoulder at Samantha, still on the edge of the bed in her nightwear. "Would you give my wife a few minutes, please?"

"Oh, yes, s-s-sir." The woman waved the feather duster to include Samantha. "I'll j-j-just go on downstairs and d-d-dust the parlor first."

Adam closed the door and returned to Samantha, taking her hands and offering a smile of encouragement. With her red-rimmed eyes, raw nose, and hair in disarray, she looked very young and vulnerable. Adam hoped he was doing the right thing. "Sweetheart," he said as kindly as one would speak to a frightened child, "I told Daniel I would spend some time with him at the office today. But after that visit, I would like to buy some train tickets and get us headed home. Would that be all right with you?"

Samantha looked down at their joined hands for a moment before nodding. "I want to go home, Adam."

He drew her in for a brief hug, then set her away from him and instructed gently, "Get dressed, then ask Rose's house-cleaner to help you pack our things. I'll see if I can't get us home by nightfall, all right?"

Samantha rose and moved to the dressing table in the corner. Adam watched her for a few minutes, wondering if he should leave her alone. When she noticed him, she sent him a quavery smile. "Go on and see Daniel. I'll be fine."

He blew her a kiss before leaving her to dress in privacy. He headed downstairs and found Rose in the butler's pantry, arranging fresh-cut daisies in a china vase. Cami sat nearby in her high chair, messily gumming a biscuit. He planted a kiss on the top of the baby's head—the only clean spot he could see—and told Rose, "I guess I'm going to pop in on Daniel a bit early. Samantha is dressing, and then I'm wondering if your maid could help with some packing."

"Packing?" Rose asked. "Are you planning to leave?"

Adam fingered the curl on the top of Cami's head. "Yes, our time here has been good for both of us, but we need to get back into our normal routine."

Rose placed the last flower in the vase and wiped her hands on a towel. "I suppose there is work to be done, and busy hands are good therapy."

"Thank you for letting us join your family for a while, Rose."

Rose chuckled and came at him, arms outstretched. "You know you're always welcome here, Adam. We were glad to have you."

Adam savored her hug, then stepped back. "Thank you. Would it be all right for the cleaning girl to help Samantha pack?"

"Perfectly all right." Rose used a rag to clean Cami's face. At her protests, Rose raised her voice to be heard over the baby's complaints. "Esther is usually finished by noon, but I'm sure she won't mind spending a few extra minutes to assist Sammy." She lifted the baby from the chair.

Adam headed for the front door, an arm around Rose's shoulders. "Well, then, I'll go say my good-byes to Daniel and stop by the train station before I come back for Sam. Don't hold lunch for me. I'll pick up a sandwich along the way."

"Would you like me to call a carriage?" she asked.

"Nope. It's pretty out. I'll walk." He gave Rose one more hug, tweaked Cami's nose and laughed when she swatted at him and burbled, then headed out the door.

❦

Samantha finished dressing, then opened the door to let the maid know she could come in. The woman, who introduced herself as Esther, nodded her agreement when Samantha asked for assistance in packing. She carried the clothing articles from the wardrobe and set them gingerly on the bed where Samantha folded them and placed them in the travel bag.

When the last items had been fetched, Samantha offered the other woman a small smile. "Thank you for your help."

Esther's gaze flitted in Samantha's direction as she nodded. "Y-you are welcome, ma'am. I'm—I'm glad to help you."

Samantha couldn't help but notice Esther's eyes, which were large and expressive, a deep brown that reminded Samantha of Adam's, and the only attractive feature in an otherwise plain face. Esther's brown hair had been pinned back in a severe bun, but over the course of the morning several lank strands had escaped around her narrow face. Her brown calico dress and tan apron, both of which were well worn and patched, only increased the woman's colorless appearance. The simple clothing, the plain face, the stammering, and the begging eyes all seemed to indicate an unhappiness that tugged at Samantha's heartstrings.

But Samantha tried hard not to look at Esther too much. The pleading brown eyes pulled at her, but the woman's expanded belly—obviously pregnant—created a stab of pain in Samantha's chest. So she remained quiet.

"You—you have s-s—such pretty things," Esther offered shyly as she watched Samantha snap the closure on the carpet bag.

Samantha glanced sideways to see Esther fingering the frayed pocket of her apron. "Thank you," Samantha managed to say, unreasonably piqued by the pregnant belly that seemed to mock her. Then feeling small for being standoffish—it wasn't Esther's fault Samantha would never experience her own pregnancy—added more kindly, "I have lots of time to sew, so it isn't that expensive for me to have several dresses."

Seemingly encouraged by the friendly overture, Esther said, "I—I sew, too—for m-m-my children. But—but with working, I—I d-don't have time to—to sew for m-me."

Samantha's gaze dropped to the woman's stomach, then up to her eyes again. She couldn't determine how old Esther was. The woman gave the appearance of age with her severe hairstyle, plain clothing, and somber face. Her eyes, though, were unlined and held the intensity of youth, although there was a pleading undertone Samantha didn't understand. In all likelihood, Esther was younger than Samantha yet already had children to sew for, as well as another baby on the way. The thought rankled her.

Samantha turned away and swung the valise off the bed. She moved to the door and let the bag drop with a *thump*. Turning to the other woman, she said in a tight voice, "Yes, well, I'm sure you'll have time to sew for yourself when your . . . children . . . are older."

Esther's eyebrows crunched together. Head down and hands twisting in her apron she scurried to the door like a whipped pup. "If—if there's—there's n-nothing else, ma'am?"

Samantha's heart caught in her throat. She'd hurt the Esther's feelings. She must get these racing emotions under control and stop taking her frustrations out on everyone around her. *Lord, help me, please!* By way of apology, she pulled a coin from her little carry purse and offered it to Esther with a smile. "You've done quite enough for me, Esther." She placed the coin in Esther's thin hand. Esther opened her mouth to protest, but Samantha shook her head. "No, this was not one of your usual duties, and I appreciate your help . . . and your company. Please keep it."

A look of uncertainty crossed Esther's face as she stared at her closed fist. Then she raised her eyes and met Samantha's gaze. She gave a small, hesitant nod. "All right, ma'am—and th-th-thank you. Have a—have a g-good trip home."

Samantha closed the door behind Esther and leaned against it, releasing a heavy sigh. Home sounded better all the time.

∽◯

Adam settled into the wingback leather chair facing Daniel's impressive mahogany desk. Pride swelled as he looked across the desk at his brother busily scribbling on a notepad. Dressed impeccably in a three-piece suit, precisely pressed white broadcloth shirt, and deep burgundy ascot, Daniel looked every bit the picture of the successful lawyer. This wood-paneled office was a far cry from the farm in Mountain Lake where they'd both grown up. Daniel looked nothing like a farmer's son.

Daniel placed his pen in its holder and pushed the pad aside. His eyes narrowed thoughtfully as they met Adam's. "Your conversation with Samantha? It did not go very well."

Adam gave a rueful smile. Was it the lawyer's mind that made Daniel make statements rather than ask questions? "What makes you think that?"

"For starters, you're here early." Daniel glanced at the Moderator wall clock which read 10:15 before turning back to Adam. "You're alone, and you're looking rather serious."

Adam shrugged. "You're right. She and I . . . well . . ." He ran a tired hand across his face. Leaning forward, he rested his elbows on his knees and looked up at his brother. "I made a suggestion, but she didn't take to it."

"And the suggestion?"

"That we adopt a baby."

Daniel's chair squeaked as he shifted positions. "Ah."

Adam sat back with a wry grin. "She insisted on finding out what we had been talking about at breakfast, and I tried to break the possibility of adoption to her gently. But to her, it sounded like she'd be giving up her dreams."

"And she's not ready for that." Again, a blunt statement.

Adam fell back in the chair. "No, she's not. Not yet." He sighed. "To be honest, it's possible she never will be."

Daniel rested his forearms on the polished top of his desk. "Well, as you've realized, it is rather soon, Adam. Give her time. Don't give up."

Remembering the sad story about the baby bird, Adam grimaced. "Samantha wasn't raised like we were. She didn't have much—not in any sense. But I think what she missed the most was not having a mother."

Daniel frowned thoughtfully. "She had a grandmother who lived with her, didn't she?"

"Yes," Adam said, "and Gran was a loving influence. But she died when Samantha was so young. And we both know what kind of parental experience she had after that." Thoughts of Burt O'Brien brought a surge of righteous anger through Adam's chest. "Being a mother has always been so important to Samantha. She wanted to give her own child all the love she longed to receive as a child. Her heart is broken, knowing it cannot be."

Daniel leaned forward and rested his elbows on the desk. "I wish I could do something to make things easier for you." He chuckled and shook his head. "My job is helping people solve problems. But there's nothing in the law books that can do anything about this."

Adam gave his brother a small smile. "Actually, Daniel, you've been a lot of help. And my conversation with Sam this morning really did end on a slightly hopeful note. We both finally were able to talk about things that will help us move forward. Having you to talk to also has helped me a great deal. Thank you."

Daniel flipped his hand outward. "What are brothers for?"

Adam grinned briefly, then his brows came down. "Could you do one more thing for me?"

"What's that?"

"Dr. Zimmerman is an expert, and he told us there was no way to fix what's wrong inside of Samantha. But if you hear about any other doctors that might think otherwise—"

"I'll contact you right away, Adam, I promise." Daniel paused, his brow puckering. "But I need you to give me a promise, too."

Curious, Adam said, "To do what?"

Daniel assumed his lawyer's pose—hands crossed formally one over the other on the satiny desk top, shoulders back, face devoid of emotion. "Be realistic. Of course if there is some way for Samantha to bear children, you will want to pursue it. But for her sake—and yours—be very careful before spending time chasing after a dream. Some dreams just aren't meant to be fulfilled. I—" He blew out a breath. "This is tough, trying to separate the lawyer from the brother here." He ran his hand through his hair. "I don't want to see either of you get hurt any more than you have already been. Do you understand?"

Adam's chest expanded with gratefulness for family who cared. "I understand. And I'll be careful."

"Well, then . . ." Daniel cleared his throat.

Adam quickly said, "Samantha and I have spent enough time in Minneapolis. We need to get on home."

"Don't feel as though you have to run—"

"I don't, Daniel. But there's work waiting for me, and it's time for us to settle back in our old routine and . . . well, get on with things."

"Do you think Samantha is ready?"

Adam thought for a moment. "Yes. Our talk this morning helped. She got a few things out in the open, which she needed to do. Our visit here gave both of us time to gather our wits, but now . . . we need to go home."

Adam rose, and Daniel followed suit, reaching across the wide desk to clasp his brother's hand. "Adam, I'm glad you came."

"Thanks again, Daniel, for everything." Emotion caught Adam in its grip. He stepped around the desk to embrace Daniel, unashamed of the tears stinging his eyes. Adam gave his brother a few thumps on the back, and they pulled apart with Daniel keeping a firm grip on Adam's shoulder.

Daniel said, "I'm going to keep my ears open for word of any abandoned babies, Adam. Just in case."

Adam smiled but shook his head slowly. "Thanks, brother, but please . . . Samantha—" He broke off, looking downward. No matter how much he wanted a baby, he wouldn't force Samantha in that in direction. Daniel squeezed Adam's shoulder hard once, then let his hand drop. "All right."

Adam turned toward the door. He paused, a hand on the doorknob, and looked back. "Daniel, don't ever take your children for granted."

"I never have, Adam."

Adam nodded and gave a brief wave.

*B*ack in her own home, Samantha soon busied herself with her fall routine. The familiar tasks offered a sense of normalcy she sorely needed right then. But then some little thing would remind her, and disappointment would once again overwhelm her, causing her to react to situations far differently from what would have been normal before the life-altering trip to Rochester.

She couldn't bear the hard, bitter edge that could emerge without warning. When she'd first arrived in Mountain Lake, hurting and wounded, she'd worn a mask of defiance to protect herself. The love of the Klaassens and their God had helped carve away the barriers of anger. But this new deep pain seemed to bring the old Samantha to the surface. She watched her family and friends—and Adam—step carefully around her, and she hated making them uncomfortable, yet she couldn't seem to control her emotions that could erupt without notice. She prayed often for God to forgive her anger and heal her heart, and she wondered why He didn't hurry and answer.

Adam's sister Josie stopped by in early September with six quart jars of strawberry preserves. She pulled the wooden crate containing the jars out of the wagon and said with a grin, "These aren't a gift. I need to trade you for a bushel of dried apples. I didn't get any done this year, and I'll need them for winter pies. Can we swap?"

Josie's little son, Simon, refused help and climbed down to stand beside his mother. Samantha scooped him up for a hug. "And would you miss having apple pies this winter, Simon?"

The boy nodded, aiming a thumb at his own chest. "I wike pie."

Samantha said, "Then I'd better trade with your mama." She led Simon into the house.

Josie followed, grousing good-naturedly, "Now that we've got that settled, where can I put these down? This box is heavy!"

Samantha pointed Josie to the kitchen sideboard. "Adam can carry it to the cellar later." She leaned down to Simon's level and asked brightly, "Do you like molasses cookies?"

Simon's eyes widened, and he looked up at his mother. "Tan I, Mama?"

Josie smiled. "Just one—" she raised one finger—"or you'll spoil your supper."

Simon trotted behind Samantha to the kitchen table where she fished a golden molasses cookie from a crock jar. Simon scrambled up on a chair and seated himself with his legs sticking out as straight as pokers. Samantha placed a cookie on a plate and set it in front of the little boy.

"What do you say, Simon?" Josie prompted.

Simon looked up at his aunt and asked innocently, "Tan Mama hab one too?"

Samantha and Josie exchanged amused looks, but Samantha felt her heart catch. Oh, to have a little one to look out for her in such a way! To cover her heartbreak, she reached for a second cookie. "Of course Mama can have one, Simon."

But Josie held up a hand and said laughingly, "No, thank you, Sammy! They look wonderful, but I really don't need it."

Samantha shrugged, put the cookie back, and replaced the lid. "Let's go sit and visit a bit then, while Simon has his treat."

"Lean over the table, Simon," Josie instructed from the doorway as the two women headed for the parlor. "We don't want to spread crumbs all over Auntie Sam's nice clean floor."

Samantha cupped a hand along the side of her mouth as she leaned toward Simon and whispered loudly, "Don't worry about a few crumbs, Simon. Auntie Sam can always sweep them up afterward."

Josie frowned but didn't comment. As she settled back in the tapestry settee in front of the parlor's bay window, she gestured toward the backyard. "I noticed the garden is bare. Have you finished all your canning?"

Samantha rocked in her chair. "Yes. I've been working like a dervish since . . . well, since we got back from Rochester." She tried a smile and confessed, "I'm trying to stay too busy to think." Josie smiled and nodded her understanding, and Samantha continued, "I still need to dig the potatoes, then finish turning the ground under."

"Why don't you let Adam do that?" Josie asked.

"Because he's busy with his own work," Samantha said. "Besides, the garden has always been mine. No matter what has . . . has taken place, there's no reason for him to mollycoddle me."

Josie opened her mouth to reply, but just then Simon entered the parlor with a face full of crumbs. Josie jumped up. "Simon! Come quick, let's get back to the kitchen before we spread cookie crumbs everywhere."

Samantha felt her hackles rise. There was no need to get so agitated over a few crumbs! If she had children, she would let them scatter crumbs everywhere in the house. She pushed herself out of the chair. "Let him be, Josie. Crumbs can always be cleaned up. There's no need to holler at him and hurt his feelings."

Josie pulled back. "I didn't holler at him, Sam. But he knows to stay at the table until he's been cleaned up."

"Maybe at your house," Samantha shot back, "but he doesn't have to here." She took hold of Simon's small hand.

"I want him to clean up before leaving the table."

"It isn't that important, Josie."

"It is to me."

"But it's ridiculous! There's no reason to be so particular."

Josie glanced at Simon and said evenly, "Let me clean him up now, Samantha."

Samantha looked down at the little boy standing between his aunt and his mother, looking from one to the other with a wide-eyed look of confusion on his face. She released his hand and sighed. "All right, Josie. Go ahead."

Josie walked Simon back to the kitchen, and Samantha sank down in her rocking chair. She covered her face with her hands, willing herself to calm. Shame washed over her. She tried so hard to curb her anger. Why did she so easily lose control?

When Josie returned to the parlor, Samantha apologized immediately for her behavior.

"It's forgotten, Sam." But when Simon would have gone to his aunt, Josie pulled him into her own lap instead. "I understand you're bound to be a bit . . . high-strung."

Samantha grimaced. *High-strung!* Well, perhaps Josie was right. Even so, defensiveness sharpened her tone. "I don't like feeling this way, Josie."

Josie sat in silence.

Samantha sighed again and rose from the rocker. "I'll go get your apples." She headed outside to the cellar door. But when she'd opened it, instead of going down, she stood at the head of the earthen steps, her head drooping low and her throat stinging. She spun when someone touched her on the shoulder.

Josie stood there, her eyes sad. "Samantha, I'm sorry I was impatient with you just now. I don't suppose any of us really understands what you're going through. We already have what you want, so we look at things differently." She took a step closer and put her hand on Samantha's arm. "But you must try to understand that parenting can't be shut off when we come to your house. You have to respect my position as Simon's mother and allow me to guide him, discipline him, even if you don't agree with me and would do things differently if he were yours."

This time it was Samantha who remained silent.

Josie lifted her arms, her eyes begging for Samantha to allow her to offer comfort. Samantha stood stiffly for a moment, then stepped into Josie's embrace. The two women clung for a long, hard minute. Against Samantha's hair Josie whispered, "I'll try to be more patient."

Samantha said raggedly, "And I'll try to get my emotions under control."

But how? If she only knew how . . . She pulled away and said, "I better get those apples."

∽◦

The winter-readiness duties that had given Samantha much pleasure before had become drudgery instead of delight. The last two weeks of September she dug up the mounds of potatoes and carried the gunny sacks full to the root cellar. Carrots, turnips, and onions were already there, as well as pumpkins, squash, ten-gallon crocks of sauerkraut, and row upon row of canned fruits and vegetables of every variety. All evidence of Samantha's industry.

The first day of October found her carrying a final batch of applesauce to the cellar where she placed the quart jars on the rough pine shelf next to the peaches and strawberry preserves. The poor shelving bowed beneath the weight of their bounty. The task completed, Samantha stood back, hands on hips, and surveyed her handiwork. In the past, it had given her a heady, satisfied feeling to see all the food ready for the long winter months. But now she caught herself muttering dismally, "At least there's something I can do like the other women."

She gave herself a little shake and said loudly to the rows of jars like so many obedient soldiers, "Enough! I have a good life here—a good home, a wonderful husband, and a family who loves me. I have many things to be thankful for, so I must stop being so melancholy!"

Deep down, Samantha indeed knew she was a very blessed woman. Having Adam and all of Adam's family to call her own was much more than she could have ever imagined as a little girl growing up on the wretched, impoverished side of Milwaukee. And her own brother, David, was the epitome of kindness and patience. He called regularly for chats on the newly installed telephone, always maintaining a measure of lightheartedness she knew was difficult for him when he saw her unhappiness. Of course it was impossible to avoid speaking of their children—they all had them! The subject of babies couldn't be ignored—Frank's wife, Anna, was only weeks away from delivery of their third baby, and all were concerned since she had lost the second, a boy, the year before—but when it was mentioned, it was mentioned briefly, ever mindful of Samantha and Adam's heartbreak.

Yes, in many ways she was fortunate, she reminded herself as she turned toward the cellar stairs. She watched her feet as she mounted the uneven steps. The brisk early fall breeze whizzed down, whirling her skirts around her ankles and sending shivers up her spine. She clutched her shawl more snugly around her shoulders as she emerged, then leaned down to lift the heavy wooden door and swing it closed. The tail of her shawl blew over her face, and she pushed it back, reaching for the door again.

"Here, Sammy, let me do that," came a deep voice, and Samantha straightened to find Adam's father, Si, hurrying toward her.

"Oh, thank you, Papa Klaassen," Samantha said as Si swung the door into place and secured the latch. "That door is troublesome in the best of times, but nearly impossible in this wind!"

Si turned up his collar and grinned at Samantha. "On days like these, a cup of hot coffee is a welcome thing."

"It just so happens I put a pot on to brew before I took that applesauce downstairs," she told him with a smile, "and I have a fresh applesauce cake to go with it."

"Sounds fine to me." Si followed Samantha through the back door into the toasty kitchen smelling of coffee, cinnamon, and apples. Si seated himself at the table in the center of the kitchen, and Samantha cut a sizable square from the applesauce cake and handed it to him on a plate before reaching for the coffee pot.

Si said, "*Dank*, my dear," and took up a forkful of the moist cake. "Mm!" He raised an eyebrow in pleasure.

Samantha settled herself across from him with her own cup of coffee. "Adam isn't back yet?" Adam had left early in the morning with Frank to take the first wagonloads of wheat to the railroad. He had been fretting about the lower wheat prices and whether he would receive enough for his wheat to meet their financial obligations. Si swallowed. "Nah, haven't seen the boys yet." He lifted his cup for a sip, then scowled at her over the rim. He shook a finger at her. "Now, none of that stewing, young lady. Adam knows things can be unpredictable in a farmer's life. It's part of relying on nature for your livelihood. We might not get the price we want this year, but that doesn't mean next year won't be better. Worrying won't change the prices, you know."

She nodded and lifted her cup.

Si took another bite of his cake, then said, "*Solang ein Brot im Kasten, brauchen wir nicht zu fasten.*"

Samantha nearly choked on her coffee. "What?"

Si grinned and looked pointedly at the loaves of bread cooling on racks near the stove. "I said, 'As long as bread is in the cupboard, we need not fast.' I'll start to worry when there isn't enough wheat harvested to provide our own loaves of bread, and I can't imagine that happening any time soon." He leaned back, the cake gone, and rested a forearm on the table.

His teasing apparently done, he said seriously, "We got more than a fair price for our wheat during the war, Sam. Any farmer with an ounce of sense—and that certainly includes Adam—put money aside for a rainy day. I know it's hard to take a lower price when you've put your hard work into it, but that's only fair play, when you balance it against the years when we got more."

"That makes sense," Samantha admitted, "and I suppose you're right." She thought about the storehouse of food in the cellar, letting complete satisfaction roll across her for the first time since she'd loaded the shelves. "We aren't going to starve no matter what the wheat may bring this year. But I know Adam's worried about the mortgage on our house. We've got that payment to make at the first of the year, and if he doesn't bring in much with his crop, then—"

"Then we'll work it out together," Simon put in gently. "That's what families do—help each other out." He pointed at her with his coffee cup and added, "And that brings me to the purpose of my visit."

"Oh?"

"Butchering time is just around the corner," Si said. "This year is Frank and Anna's turn to sponsor the butchering, but with Anna . . ." Si paused and scratched his head.

Samantha prompted quietly, "Anna being in a family way—"

"—being in a family way," Si repeated, "she really isn't up to the amount of work it takes. Would it be all right with you if we had the butchering here this year and at Frank's next year? I know it makes a mess of a kitchen, but the other ladies will be here to help."

Her heart twisted. Every other family had to contend with wee ones underfoot or worry about overtaxing an expectant mother. . . . She said, "That would be fine. I don't mind at all, and I'm sure Adam won't mind. There's plenty of room here . . . and no reason why I can't keep up with the work."

Si reached across the table to cup Samantha's cheek with a work-roughened hand. "Thank you, *liebchen*," he said with deep affection. "I'll let the others know about the change." He dropped his hand then, and Samantha busied herself cleaning up the table. Si rose. "I'd better head toward town. I'll see if I can round up your husband and send him home. Keep your chin up and don't fret. Everything will be fine."

Samantha suspected he was speaking of more than the price of wheat, so she said, "I'll be fine, Papa Klaassen. Don't you worry about me."

He grinned then reached out to pull her against his solid chest for a breath-stealing hug. "Take care, Daughter," he said and plopped his hat back on his head before heading out the back door.

Samantha waved as he strode toward the waiting wagon. She closed the door and turned to the empty kitchen. Her long sigh broke into the silence of the room. "I'll take care," she said aloud. "What else can I do?"

ince coming to Mountain Lake in 1917, Samantha had learned that hog butchering—sometimes called *Schwienskjast*, meaning "pig's wedding"—was an all-day occasion of hard work as well as much merriment. Several days prior, Samantha prepared for the arrival of Adam's extended family by baking—extra loaves of bread, countless *zwieback*, a variety of pies, and two large cakes. She also carried up several quart jars of her own canned vegetables to include with the meals. It would take a great deal of food to satisfy the appetites of the twenty-three people converging on Adam and Samantha's farm place. And it would take every able-bodied person a whole day to butcher the hogs that had been raised solely to provide a winter's worth of pork and related items for six families.

The group began arriving well before the sun was up. Frank and Anna and little Laura Beth were the first, then Jake and Liz with their twins and baby Amanda. Jake and Frank immediately joined Adam in the summer kitchen where he was stacking wood beneath three large cauldrons of water that would be used to scald the carcasses. Liz and Anna and the children joined Samantha in the warm house, fragrant with delightful dishes to feed hungry troops.

Anna looked particularly bulky, one shawl around her shoulders and another over her head like an oversized babushka. After hanging the shawls on the hooks by the back door, she came at Samantha belly-first with hands outstretched. "Poor

Samantha," she said, "having all this work dumped on you! But I promise I'll make up for it. Next year it will be at our place no matter what."

Samantha smiled and squeezed Anna's hands. Her sister-in-law had always been a bit on the plump size, and her latest pregnancy only made her rounder. "I don't mind the extra work at all, Anna. And it only makes sense that you take it easy this year. We need to look out for this one." And Samantha dared to place her hand on Anna's extended belly. The mound was hard and warm under her palm, and beneath the layers of clothing she thought she felt a rolling push against her hand. Her eyes widened, and she pulled her hand back.

Anna clutched her belly with two hands and nodded at Samantha's inquiring look. "Yes, that was the baby. This one is going to be fun to keep up with if it's as active after it's born as it's been in here. Sometimes I think it never sleeps. Here, feel it again," and Anna reached for Samantha's hand so she could feel the kick.

"You feel that a lot?"

Anna nodded, heaving a sigh. "Yes, I do. Especially at night when I'm trying to sleep. And sometimes I wish . . ."

Samantha's heart twisted, and she bit down on her lower lip.

Anna clamped her mouth closed and lowered her head for a moment. When she looked up, she wore a bright smile. Rubbing her palms together, she said, "What can I do to help?"

"I want to help, too," Liz said, bouncing Amanda on one arm while the twins and Laura Beth played under her feet.

Samantha stared, transfixed, at the pleasant scene of Liz surrounded by children. But then she gave herself a little shake and turned Anna toward the kitchen table. "Neither of you need to do anything. Just sit and visit. I was able to get everything ready. Everyone will pick up a plate here"—she pointed to the breakfront cupboard, which held stacks of tin plates, silverware, and cotton napkins—"and serve themselves at the stove. Then they can sit wherever they can find a place! Breakfast will be a rather informal affair, and lunch will be catch-as-catch-can between other duties. But I promise we'll all be able to sit together for the evening meal."

Anna's gaze roved across the skillets of scrambled eggs, sausage, and fried potatoes waiting to be spooned onto a plate. "And *zwieback* to go with it all! You must not have gotten any more sleep last night than I did!"

Samantha laughed lightly, looking again at Liz who now crouched to play a finger game with Laura Beth while the twins and Amanda looked on. She said with a wobbly grin, "No, but it was all my own doing—no little person nudging me awake." Being able to tease Anna about her little sleep-stealer somehow lessened the hurt around her own heart. She breathed easier. *I can do this.*

A firm knock sent Samantha to the door. "Come on in," she greeted Si and Laura. Their three youngest—Becky, Teddy, and Sarah—trailed them inside.

Sarah beamed at Samantha. "Hurray! Butchering day!"

Teddy shot his sister a frown. "Since when have you gotten so excited about work?"

Sarah giggled. "I'm not excited about work. I'm excited to have the day off from school!"

Laura clicked her tongue on her teeth and shook her head, and Sarah shrugged sheepishly.

Josie and Stephen with little Simon came in before the door was closed, then Priscilla and David carrying a well-bundled baby Jenny along with Joey. The little boy galloped across the floor and greeted everyone boisterously, earning a mild reprimand from his father.

The kitchen had become crowded, so Samantha instructed, "When you've got your wraps removed and hung, just get a plate and start eating, then as soon as you older kids are done, bundle back up and head out of here to make room for the others!"

Everyone laughed and obeyed.

By seven o'clock the sun was up and Si's brother Hiram and wife Hulda bustled in. Hulda took over scrambling more eggs to feed the last arrivals. Breakfast was nearly finished by the time Arn arrived with his young fiancée, Martha Kornelson. He took some good-natured ribbing about stopping along the way to do a little spooning instead of getting right to work, and poor Martha blushed profusely at their warmhearted speculations.

"Better be careful," Arn warned Stephen, teasing right back, "or you'll find a pig's tail hanging from your backside!"

Arn's comment earned another round of merry laughter as they recalled times past when each of them had unsuspectingly worn a pig's tail. They played the joke on an unsuspecting recipient every year, and it never ceased to be a great source of amusement to all of them—especially the young boys.

Breakfast over, the real work began. Samantha marveled that such a large task could be completed in one day. Butchering had been done every year for as long as any of the Klaassen siblings could remember, so for the most part they pitched in without having to be told what to do.

Young Sarah was delegated to watch her nieces and nephews in one of the large, empty rooms upstairs. She pulled a face. "Why can't I be in on the real work? I'm old enough to help with the butchering."

Laura responded in her gentle way, "You are helping the most by keeping the little ones out from under foot and entertained."

"But Ma—" Sarah ceased her argument when Si gave her a warning glance. She sighed, turning to scoop baby Jenny from Priscilla's arms. "Come on then, everybody. Let's go find something to do." And she herded the crew of toddlers upstairs.

Samantha was glad she had the dishes to wash before going out to the barn. She always tried to stay far away from the pigpens until she was sure the hogs were dead. The high-pitched squeal when the hog was killed tormented her dreams for days afterward. Adam had assured her that it was over quickly, and the hog didn't suffer, but still she stayed away.

"I'll help with the dishes, Samantha," Arn's Martha offered shyly.

Samantha smiled at the girl. "That would be a blessing, Martha. There's quite a pile this morning."

"I don't mind." Martha rolled up her sleeves. "At home, there's ten of us kids, so I'm used to a pile of dishes."

Ten kids! Envy twined through Samantha's middle. She watched the younger woman covertly as they cleaned up together. Martha was tall and thin, with a rather long nose but a sweet mouth and sparkling green eyes. She was so bashful, she didn't say much, but she was certainly not afraid of work. Her thin arms had more strength than one would think possible. In no time at all the kitchen was clean and orderly, and the two women walked out to the barn to see what should be done next.

They passed the yard where two hogs hung side by side from an oak tree. A thick piece of wood inserted through the tendons of their back legs was attached to a rope-and-pulley rigging over a sturdy tree branch, holding the hogs at a height that made it easy for the men to reach them.

Martha blanched and turned her head away. "My, that's ugly."

Samantha confided, "The first time I saw where pork actually came from, I wasn't sure I could ever eat it again."

Martha giggled, covering her mouth with a slender hand. "I'm glad we just buy our meat from the butcher. I don't like seeing it like that."

"Then I guess it's a good thing Arn is planning to be a merchant rather than a farmer. You can continue to buy your meat at the butcher's shop."

Martha nodded in agreement and the women entered the barn. Laura sat in front of a large washtub, cleaning intestines. She looked up and greeted, "You two are a welcome sight. I can use some help here."

Samantha stifled her sigh. It had to be done, but such cleaning was a tedious and onerous task. First they had to be turned inside out and scrubbed thoroughly. Then they were turned back and the excess fat scraped away by pulling the intestines between two knitting needles held against one another. One had to be careful not to scrape away too much fat and poke holes in the intestine wall, thereby making them unusable. They were needed as sausage casings—the small intestines for red-meat sausage and the large intestines for liver sausage.

As Samantha took the clean intestines and began the scraping process, she commented, "I'd just as soon forget about the liver sausage."

Laura chuckled without looking up from the tub. "It's not as tasty as the others, in my opinion, but some would disagree with me." She laughed again, then went on to tell a funny story about her grandfather who had once eaten so much fresh liver sausage that he had ended up spending the night in the outhouse. Samantha, listening, was struck again how fortunate she was to be part of a family that had a history of memories—both humorous and pleasant—to share. She took careful note of the story so she'd be able to share it with her children someday. The thought brought a stab of pain. *Our own family,* she mourned once again.

Teddy carried in another container of entrails and plopped it next to Laura. He turned to Samantha. "Sam, could you come give Josie a hand? She's grinding meat for sausage and having a hard time keeping up."

"Where's Priscilla?" Laura asked. Samantha hid a smile, knowing Priscilla's penchant for avoiding work, especially this kind. She could imagine Priscilla even hiding in the outhouse.

Teddy said, "David's got her taking turns with Liz, stirring the lard cauldron."

One of the least desired tasks, Samantha thought, trying not to smile over Pris's bad luck. Not only was the smell unpleasant, one tended to be coated with a fine film of grease from the smoke by the end of the day. Laura grimaced. "She'll likely be in fine fettle this evening! Oh, well, it must be done by someone." She looked at Samantha and said, "Go ahead and help Josie, Sammy. Martha and I can handle this."

Samantha crossed the yard toward the house and waved to Adam who was scraping the bristles from the scalded hide of a large hog. He waved back with his knife and called out a warning. "Be on the lookout! Arn has three pigs' tails, and he's looking for victims!"

Arn indignantly looked up from cutting the skin from the lard. "Hey, it's not fair alerting people!"

Samantha laughed and called back, "I'll be careful! Maybe one of them will turn up on you, Arn!" She noted the butchering was well under way, everyone industriously working. Adam and Frank scraped bristles; Arn and Jake cut the lard into pieces for boiling; Si and Hiram sawed the carcasses of two hogs, sepa-rating the lean from the fatty meat; David and Stephen readied another hog for slaughter. She asked Teddy, "How many are already done?"

"Four—and it's only a little after nine. We're doing fine."

Samantha entered the house to find Josie on her knees in the back-porch area of the kitchen, cutting the lean meat into chunks small enough to fit through the hand-cranked grinder.

Josie released a relieved sigh when she spotted Samantha. "Oh, thank you for coming. I can't keep up. They're going so fast out there!"

"What do you want me to do?" Samantha sank down by Josie with her skirts in a pouf around her.

"I'll cut while you grind," Josie replied, her hands still busy. "When your arm gets tired, we can switch, all right?"

Samantha had ground enough meat to fill two gallon-sized crocks when they heard a loud burst of laughter from the yard. The two women grinned at each other and rushed to the back stoop to see what was going on. Hulda also left her post in the kitchen where she was mixing seasonings with ground meat. Hands on hips, she said, "What are those silly men up to now?"

David, laughing, was threatening Arn with a sturdy stick. "You rogue, you!" David waved the stick. "You just put that pig's tail right where it belongs—on your own hind end, Arn, my man!"

Arn hooted, "Ha-ha! You do make a skinny pig, David. Not much lard on you!" Everyone laughed. The fattest pigs were the most prized since they delivered larger quantities of all-important lard.

Priscilla called out, still stirring the lard cauldron, "You just hush your insults, Arnold Klaassen! I happen to like my meat— and my man—lean!"

They all roared. The joke gave them a welcome respite from the hard work and a second wind to get back to it. As they headed to their respective jobs, David tucked the pig's tail he had pulled off the seat of his overalls into his pocket and yelled, "You just wait, Arnold ! When you least expect it, I'll get even!"

Hulda closed the door on the antics, chuckling. "Those men, cutting up like boys. And I know a treat they would all like."

Josie grinned. "*Bubbat*?"

Hulda nodded, her expression smug.

Samantha turned eagerly. "Oh, yes, make a batch of *Bubbat*. Josie and I will get your other work done."

Hulda's blue eyes twinkled behind the round spectacles. "But you have all these nice loaves of bread here for our lunch."

Josie said, "They won't be wasted, will they, Sam? Go ahead, Tante Hulda, and make *Bubbat*."

Hulda joked, "But then everyone might sleep the afternoon away!" They all knew that *Bubbat*, a yeast bread seasoned with chunks of sausage, was almost a meal in itself, tasty and very filling.

"Then make it for our evening meal," Josie suggested. "It can be a surprise."

Hulda nodded. "All right." She scooped out a hefty dish of the ground pork. Hulda, with Becky's help, had taken the responsibility of preparing the noon meal. As Samantha intended, it was a catch-as-catch-can affair, with people coming and going as they could leave their tasks. After the little children were fed, Sarah put them all down for naps and then cheerfully relieved Priscilla and Liz of their lard stirring so they could come in and eat.

"Oh, I'm simply a mess!" Priscilla rolled her eyes. "I shouldn't even sit on anything!" She grabbed a tea towel from a small rack. "I'll sit on this so I don't spoil your chair." She bent to drape the towel across the seat of the chair. Liz pointed, burst out laughing, then clapped a hand over her mouth. Samantha,

Josie, and Hulda looked, too, and had to stifle their own laughter. Priscilla's gaze narrowed. "What's so funny?"

Josie and Samantha exchanged amused looks. Samantha said, straight-faced, "Oh, nothing really."

"Well, it must be something or you wouldn't be giggling like a gaggle of geese. And it isn't polite to giggle but not share the joke," Priscilla scolded.

"I'm sorry." Liz's voice quavered with amusement. She tapped her chin with one finger, assuming a thoughtful air. "I'm wondering if David likes his meat—and his woman—lean or fat."

Priscilla's lovely blue eyes widened as she stared at the others. Then she bounced from her chair and turned circles, trying to see her own rear end. Josie and Samantha howled with laughter. "There's one back there, isn't there?" Priscilla pulled the back of her skirt to the side with two hands, craning her neck to see the back of her dress. "Someone's put a pig's tail on me, right?"

"Yes!" Josie managed between giggles.

Priscilla pointed her backside at Josie. "Well, get it off!"

Still chortling, Josie did as she was bid.

Priscilla snatched it from Josie's hand. "Give me that vile thing. I've got a score to settle." They all laughed again as she marched out the door, her head held high.

The afternoon passed much as the morning had, with efficient routine. When the little ones awoke from naps, Teddy took a couple of clean pig bladders, blew them up, and tied them with a string. Under Anna's watchful eye, the children spent a pleasant time kicking the bladder balloons around the yard. While they had their fun, Arn continued to pursue his own—Si, Hiram, and Stephen each had the dubious honor of wearing a pig's tail at some point during the day, but Arn always escaped retaliation. He took great pleasure in taunting the others about his ability to elude them.

By seven o'clock that evening, all six hogs had been butchered. The hams, chops, roasts, and sausage to be kept by Adam and Samantha were already hanging in the smokehouse or soaking in a salt barrel. The others had loaded their wrapped portions in wagon beds to be preserved in their own smokehouses or cellars. The head cheese had been mixed and would be divided up the following day, after it had a chance to jell. The lard was divided and poured into crocks, and the leftover bits of meat from the spareribs, which had been boiled in the lard, were scooped from the bottom of the cauldron. The bits of meat, called cracklings, were very rich, and were saved for special occasions—such as the end of a successful day of butchering.

"Oh, goodie!" Sarah exclaimed as Laura placed the bowlful of cracklings on the makeshift table. Si and Frank had set up sawhorses and planks in the barn so everyone could sit together. "We're going to have a feast!"

The women filled the table's top with bowls and platters containing roast chicken, fresh sausage, boiled potatoes and gravy, canned green beans seasoned with onion, and stewed tomatoes. Hulda's *Bubbat* loaves, two huge applesauce cakes, and several pies completed the meal. Si thanked the Lord for a fruitful day, and everyone ate until their bellies ached.

Priscilla looked rather smug while the others chattered away during the meal. David looked a question at her from time to time, but she just gave a secret smile and refused to comment. Across the table, Anna took a bite of cake and called to Samantha, "Sammy, this applesauce cake is wonderful! It's better than any I've ever had. Could I get your recipe?"

Before Samantha could answer, Arn teased, "Anna, you don't need any applesauce cake. Your tummy's so big now, you can't sit up to the table!"

Anna threw a chicken bone at him, missing him by a mile. She turned back to Samantha. "Could I have the recipe, Sammy?"

Samantha nodded. "Yes, but not today. My hands are worn out from cranking that silly grinder. I don't think I have enough energy left to write it down."

When the serving platters were empty, Arn leaned back, rested his hands on his full midsection. "Martha, are you ready to head back to town?" he asked.

Martha looked around the table uncertainly. "Maybe I should stay and help Samantha clean things up before I go home."

Anna said, "Josie and I are going to stay and help with the cleanup, Martha. You've more than earned your keep—go on home."

"If you're sure . . ." Martha hesitated.

Arn cut in, "Aw, come on, Marty. You'll have plenty of time to clean up after these mess-makers when we're married." He stood and took her by the hand to urge her from her chair. "Come on, let me run you home before your folks wonder what I did with you."

Martha blushed. "All right, Arn. But at least let's carry our own dishes to the kitchen."

"Yes, ma'am." Arn stood at attention with a mock salute.

Martha's mouth dropped open in surprise, and then she started laughing. Arn looked startled, and Martha continued to laugh, a hand over her mouth. She pointed at something behind Arn.

"What is it?" Arn asked, frowning as he turned to see what she was referring to.

Everyone joined Martha in gales of laughter. The children danced around excitedly, and one of Liz's twins, Andy, burst out, "Uncle Arn's a piggy!" The other children took up the cry, repeating in a singsong manner, "Uncle Arn's a piggy. Uncle Arn's a piggy!"

Arn himself had been fooled! He yanked the tail from his backside and looked around in disgust. "All right, David, you said you'd get even. When did you get me?"

David held up his hands, palms outward. "I'd love to take the credit, Arn, but it was not I."

Arn glared. "Well, then, who put it there?"

Priscilla stood, proud as a peacock, and raised her hand, even waving it a little. "I did," she sang out.

David placed an arm around his beaming wife and crowed, "Oh-ho, Arn! The king is dead; long live the queen!" Everyone cheered as Arn made a face, then gallantly bowed before Priscilla, presenting her the pig's tail on his open palms the way one might bestow a crown of jewels. Priscilla took it with a pretty curtsy.

"Well, family," Si announced when the hilarity calmed, "we've put in a productive day, but now it's time for rest. Everyone grab an armload of dishes and head for the house. We'll get Samantha's kitchen in order and all head for home."

With the family all inside, the kitchen was so crowded that Samantha suggested, "Why don't you all leave the cleanup to Adam and me and get on home? You've all got children to get to bed and meat to put away. Adam and I can do this ourselves."

Laura asked, "Are you sure, Sam? We don't mind helping."

Samantha shook her head in mock exasperation. "It will take twice as long with all of you underfoot!" She made shooing motions with her hands. "Please, just run along and let me take care of my own kitchen."

Laura crossed to give Samantha a hug. "If you're certain . . ."

Samantha repeated, "Adam will help me. Please—you may go."

Hugs, thank-yous, good-byes, and more jokes were exchanged as everyone bundled up for their rides home. When Adam finally closed the door on the last of them, he turned and gave his wife a smile, shaking his head. "Alone again."

Samantha nodded. Her mind followed the others who were far from alone, all with little ones bouncing in the wagons from leftover excitement. It had been a day filled with family, and now it was quiet—too quiet. An all-too-familiar wave of envy washed over her. She sighed.

Adam stepped up behind her and gave her shoulder a loving squeeze. "This is nice, isn't it? Just us."

Samantha turned and looked into his deep brown eyes. Tears pricked. Having Adam for her husband, having his family to call her own, was such a blessing. Lord, *please let me see what I have as enough.* She leaned into his embrace, wrapped her arms around his torso, and held tight. He rested his lips on the top of her head and rocked her for several seconds. In his arms— his strong, warm, secure arms—Samantha experienced a sweet whisper of peace. *Thank You, Lord. . . .*

Renewed, Samantha pulled back and smiled. "Come on, my man, let's get this mess cleaned up."

*T*he next morning, Samantha felt Adam nudge her awake. She opened her eyes, squinting into the early-morning darkness. "Yeah, what?" she asked in a sleep-thick voice.

"Good morning." He scooped her close, and she snuggled her head against his shoulder. He smoothed down her hair and gave her a kiss.

She received his kiss willingly, then protested, "I wasn't ready to wake up yet."

Adam chuckled. "I know you're tired. You put in a hard day's work yesterday. I just woke you to tell you I'm going to ride over to Pa's and help him today. He's got some fence down, and it will probably take most of the day. Don't expect me for lunch. Go ahead and sleep till noon if you want to."

Samantha scrunched her face up. "You woke me up to tell me to sleep till noon?"

"Does sound kind of foolish," he admitted. "But if I'd just left a note, I couldn't kiss you." He delivered another kiss on her forehead, then gently pushed her back into her warm cocoon. He tucked the blankets around her and gave her one more kiss before padding to the hallway. "Brrr, it's cold this morning!" she heard him complain.

By the time Adam had washed and dressed for the day, Samantha had drifted to sleep again with only her nose sticking out from beneath the pile of quilts. The next thing she knew, she felt herself startle awake. She brought up a hand to rub her nose. When she saw Adam's face only inches from her own, she groaned. "You woke me up again."

Adam swallowed his chuckle. "I'm sorry. I only meant to give you one more kiss for good measure."

"Well, you've done it. Good-bye, Adam." She rolled over and pulled the quilts high.

⌒⌒

Snug under the covers, Samantha heard Adam's boots as he tiptoed down the stairs. She sighed at the rattle of the stove lids as he stoked the fire, and then pulled her pillow over her head. But it wasn't enough to muffle the squeak and snap of the screen door as he headed outside. Every sound was an intrusion on the possibility of more sleep. Huffing her aggravation, she muttered to the room, "Who can sleep with all this racket?"

She threw back the covers, shivering as the cool air reached her body, and she raced for the water closet. She performed her morning necessities, then headed back to the bedroom with her arms wrapped around herself. She dressed as quickly as she could, brushed her hair into a neat twist, and quickly tidied the bedroom before going down to the warm comfort of the kitchen.

Usually it was late October before she and Adam closed off the parlor, dining room, and unused bedrooms to make it easier to heat the common rooms of the house. As Samantha got the coffee perking, she wondered if they should close things off earlier this year; it seemed colder sooner. Would it be easier to see a closed door, knowing there was nothing—and no one— behind it? She wasn't sure.

She looked around at the spotless kitchen, then wandered through the other rooms on the first floor, needlessly adjusting crocheted antimacassars and swiping a finger across dust-free picture frames. Nothing required her attention. Her thoughts flitted back to the empty rooms upstairs. If only there were children in the house, her day would be full. She returned to the kitchen and poured herself a cup of coffee, seating herself at the kitchen table. It was hard to imagine all the joyful commotion filling the same room just yesterday.

"I need something to do today," she said aloud. It seemed she spoke to empty rooms a lot these days, just for the sound of a human voice. She sipped her coffee, her eyes idly roaming the neat room until they focused on the upturned crockery bowl covering a leftover wedge of applesauce cake. *Yes, that's right, Anna requested the recipe.*

Samantha went over to the backdoor and peered out. The gray morning assured her of a cold walk, but she would have someone to talk to for a good part of the day. The decision made, she quickly wrote her recipe on a square of brown paper, bundled up, and set out at a good pace for Frank and Anna's farmhouse.

The distance would have required only fifteen minutes on horseback, but she chose to walk, stretching out the time. The air was crisp, but when the sun broke through the clouds, it took on a crystal brightness that warmed her from within. Her feet crunched against the hard dirt, startling two gophers into a skittering escape. She laughed aloud as the tiny striped animals ran frantically to their burrow, disappearing into the mound of dirt.

Her eyes squinted against the sun, slanting through leafless branches above her head, and birds peeked down at her as she passed, tipping their heads curiously and their bright eyes shining. Samantha paused once and waved a friendly finger at a pair of brown finches. The birds swooped away into the skies with her laughter following them. Her happy chuckles disturbed a red squirrel, and it scolded from high in the tree.

"What a cheerful world You created, God," she heard herself say, and she realized her heart felt light. By the time she reached the front porch of Frank and Anna's sturdy house, she was whistling between her teeth and had set aside her earlier dismal feelings. She skipped up the two wooden steps and rapped her knuckles against the door. She leaned sideways to peek through the lace-covered window. When no one answered, she frowned and knocked again, harder this time, looking toward the barn for any sign of activity.

After several minutes, the door finally swung inward with little Laura Beth holding onto the brass knob with two hands. She peered at Samantha from between her elbows. The little girl was dressed, but her hair was uncombed, and her red-rimmed eyes told Samantha the child had been crying. Samantha's heart thumped in sudden fear. She crouched down to her niece and greeted gently, "Hi, honey. Where's Mama?"

Laura Beth threw herself at Samantha, pressing a tear-stained cheek against her aunt's dress front. "Mama's to bed. She won't get up. I been really scared."

Samantha took Laura Beth's hand. "Let's go see Mama." The little girl led her eagerly to Frank and Anna's bedroom. When Samantha saw Anna lying in the bed with her white face holding an expression of pain, Sam rushed to the edge of the bed and placed a shaky hand on Anna's cheek.

Anna's eyes fluttered open. "Oh, Sammy . . ." She struggled to smile. "Thank heaven you're here. I've been praying someone would come. . . ."

"Anna, what is it? It isn't time yet . . . ?" Samantha smoothed Anna's hair from her face.

Anna groaned, suddenly wrapping her hands around her extended middle and curling into a ball. She broke out in a sweat, and the muscles in her neck stood taut. Samantha's muscles tightened in response to Anna's discomfort. After what seemed like forever, Anna relaxed, flattening herself in the bed again. "The baby's coming, Sam."

"But it's too early!"

Anna managed a weak laugh. "I don't think the baby knows that. It's coming now."

"Where's Frank?"

"Turning under stubble in the north fields—oooh!"

Samantha stood helplessly by as Anna held her breath through another contraction. How horrible, seeing Anna in such agony and not able to help. Although close by when several of her nieces and nephews had entered the world, Samantha had never been directly involved with the birth process. And she sure didn't want to be this time!

When Anna had fallen back against the bed, Samantha placed a trembling hand on her shoulder. "Anna, I'm going to the barn. I'll saddle a horse and ride for Doctor Newton or Mother Klaassen. You need one of them with you now."

Anna reached up and grasped Samantha's hand. "No, Sammy, please don't leave me! The baby is coming, and there isn't time for you to go after anyone. We'll have to deliver it ourselves."

Samantha's heart leaped into her throat. "But I—I can't, Anna! What if—?" She remembered Frank and Anna's tiny baby boy who had been buried a little over a year ago.

Anna repeated, "We have to, Sammy. There isn't time for anything else! Please! Don't leave me!" And she coiled again as another spasm struck.

Samantha spun and spotted Laura Beth leaning against the doorframe, a finger in her mouth, her brown eyes wide and fearful. Samantha ran to Laura Beth, knelt, and took the child by the shoulders. "Laura Beth, do you know the way to Grandma Klaassen's house?"

The little girl nodded.

Samantha wondered at the wisdom of sending a not-quite-four-year-old child on such an errand, but what other choice did they have? She couldn't leave Anna alone. She hurried back to the bed. "Anna, I'm going out to the barn to saddle a horse. I'll only be gone a few minutes. Will you be all right?"

Anna shook her head and moaned, "No, Sammy, don't leave me now. . . ."

Samantha didn't have time to explain. "I'll be right back," she reassured Anna as confidently as she could. Grabbing a little coat by the door and a scarf, she took Laura Beth by the hand and flew out the back door to the barn where she saddled Rocky, the calmest of the horses. Her fingers were shaking and clumsy, and she prayed as she tightened cinches—*Oh, Lord, please let everything be okay with Anna and the baby! And get little Laura Beth to her grandma safely!* It seemed to take ages before she'd managed to cinch the saddle securely in place, but at last she lifted Laura Beth, now wrapped in coat and scarf, onto the horse's back. Laura Beth clutched the saddle horn with both small hands.

"Now, listen, sweetie—" Urgency underscored her tone— "you ride straight to Grandma's house and tell Grandma your mama needs her. Can you do that?"

Laura Beth looked down at Samantha with wide, serious eyes. She nodded slowly. "Yes, Auntie Sam, I've rode lots of times with Daddy. I can get Grandma." Her face puckered up in worry. "What's wrong with Mama?"

"Mama will be fine, honey." Samantha reached up to pull the scarf tighter around Laura Beth's cherubic face, inwardly praying she was telling the truth. "And after Grandma comes, you'll get to meet your new baby brother or sister."

Laura Beth brightened. "I want a sister."

Samantha said, "That would be nice. But now go get Grandma, Laura Beth. Mama needs Grandma's help, okay?"

The little girl nodded again. Samantha made sure the reins were wrapped around the saddle horn, then led Rocky out of the barn, turning him in the direction of the big farm. "Hang on tight," Samantha instructed, and when Laura Beth had crouched over the horse's neck, Samantha brought her hand down sharply against Rocky's flank. The horse took off at a trot. Samantha watched long enough to make sure Laura Beth would hold her seat, then raced back to the house.

*A*nna was moaning, rolling side to side in the bed. Samantha sat down on the edge of the rumpled quilts and smoothed Anna's damp hair from her face. "Anna, I'm here."

"My water broke. I've made a mess of the bed."

"No matter." Samantha forced her voice to be calm despite her inner quaking. "We can clean up the bed. Where are the sheets?"

Anna pointed weakly to a large chest against the wall, and Samantha fetched a clean set of linens. She helped Anna roll to one side of the bed and pulled the sheets free on the empty half, then shifted Anna to the bare mattress and removed the sheets completely. She remade the bed the same way, moving Anna back and forth gently.

"I'll ruin—the mattress—if there's not something—under me," Anna panted as the pains came fast and hard. With each one, a trickle of wetness seeped from Anna's body.

Samantha dashed to the kitchen, snatched up a pile of newspaper, and came back to place layers of paper on the bed, then covered them with a cotton sheet. As Anna sank back on the pallet of paper, it crinkled beneath her, and Samantha asked, "Is it uncomfortable?"

Anna shook her head with a winced smile. "It's nothing—compared to this." She held her belly with both hands. Her back arched and she clenched her teeth. "Here comes another one!"

Samantha clasped Anna's tummy too, rubbing lightly with her open palms. Beneath her hands, muscles contracted, then relaxed as Anna's body fought to bring forth the child. Samantha ran her hands comfortingly over the hard mound of flesh until she felt the muscles calm. She looked at Anna. Her eyes were closed, her lips parted, and she was breathing shallowly. "Anna, are you all right?"

Weakly, Anna nodded. "It isn't going to be long now. I can tell—the pressure. . . . We need to be ready, Sam."

Samantha's heart pounded against her ribcage. "What do I do?"

"Get some . . . scissors . . . and clean towels. And some string. You'll find everything you need . . . in the kitchen. Put some water on to boil. . . . We'll need to . . . get the baby warm . . . right away." Anna lurched upright and clutched Samantha's dress front with more strength than Samantha would have thought possible. She ordered harshly, "The baby comes first, Sam! Don't be worrying over me—just take care of the baby, you hear?"

Samantha promised fervently, "I will, Anna. I'll take care of the baby."

Anna fell back on the mattress, limp. While she was relaxed, Samantha ran to the kitchen and gathered the things Anna had listed. She set two big pots of water on the stove to boil, then placed clean towels, scissors, and string in a basket. Once the pots were getting warm to the touch, she scooped up the basket and raced back to the bedroom. She rounded the corner, and came up short at the sight. Anna's hands were above her head, wrapped around the iron rails of the headboard so tightly Samantha expected the bars to be bent. Her head was thrown back, her face twisted in a terrible expression. Samantha dropped her bundle and ran to Anna.

"I-i-it's c-c-coming!" Anna cried out.

And when Samantha looked, she gasped. A cap of dark hair! "Oh, Lord in heaven, help me!" Samantha prayed aloud as she positioned herself between Anna's knees, her hands ready to cup the tiny head when it emerged.

Anna panted heavily, giving instructions, "When . . . the head comes . . . you have to . . . clear its mouth. With your fingers." Anna arched again with the next pushing contraction, her hips leaving the mattress. She made a strange grunting sound, and suddenly Samantha was holding the baby's head. It seemed as if the baby would be strangled, and Samantha thought her heart would jump from her chest, it pounded so hard. She prayed constantly—*Let the baby be all right. Let Anna be all right*—as she opened the baby's mouth and scooped with two fingers inside.

With the next push, the shoulders came free, and Samantha cradled the little head in her hands until suddenly the whole body wiggled through, and Samantha was holding a tiny, perfect baby girl with spindly arms and legs that sprawled in every direction. Samantha breathed open-mouthed in short, hard spurts. *Oh, Lord, a girl! It's a girl!* "It's a girl, Anna!" she rejoiced, unable to take her eyes off of the red, wrinkled baby in her hands.

Anna panted and shook. "T-tie the c-cord, Sam. Then we h-have to m-make sure she's b-b-breathing."

Samantha's chest clutched. She placed the unmoving baby on the mattress and brought the basket to the bed. She snipped two pieces of string, tying off the ropelike umbilical cord twice—once close to the baby's round tummy, and again two inches further out.

"C-cut the cord, Sam."

Samantha shakily obeyed. A snip, and the baby girl was on her own. She picked up the infant. The swollen eyes remained closed, the little mouth puckered, as she lay limp in Samantha's hands. Samantha held her by the back of the head and her bottom and willed fearfully, "Breathe, baby. C'mon—breathe!"

Her mind raced—what should she do? She looked to Anna for help, but poor Anna was lying back with her eyes closed, quivering from the shock of the birth. There'd be no help from that direction. Samantha scrambled to recall the ways she'd heard doctors used to make a baby cry—a sharp slap or a dash of cold water? How could she do something so harsh to someone this small and helpless? But somehow she had to scare the baby into taking a breath.

With sudden inspiration, she took a firm grip on the tiny infant, then swooped the little body through the air, ending with a jerk. The baby's tiny arms flew outward, her back arched, and she opened her mouth, sucking in a great gulp of air. With the release of the breath, she began to cry in a pitiful, mewling fashion. Samantha burst out with a half laugh, half sob. "Anna, she's breathing! And listen! She's crying!"

Anna's eyes opened and she smiled weakly. "It's l-like m-m-music." Both women listened to the baby for a moment, then Anna said, "Wr-rap her up, Sam. Keep her w-w-warm." Anna shivered so hard she could hardly talk. "Th-then w-we need t-to d-d-deliver the af-afterbirth."

Samantha wrapped the baby securely in two thick towels, then laid her carefully on the bed beside her mother. The tiny girl continued to cry in soft, hiccupping sounds as Samantha saw to Anna's needs. Afterward, she covered Anna with a heavy blanket. "I'll give the baby a bath, then I'll be back. Is there anything I need to know about that?" But Anna's eyes were closed, and she did not respond.

Samantha picked up the infant once more and carried her to the kitchen. She poured some of the boiling water into a basin, adding cool water until the temperature felt perfect against her inner wrist. She found some gentle hand soap, more dry towels, and placed the baby gently into the water, keeping a hand behind the small head to steady her.

Washing a newborn proved to be even more of a challenge than she'd thought. There were so many little crannies to clean, and the baby was completely uncooperative, coiling up like a morning glory blossom at sunset and complaining through the whole event. Samantha found herself chuckling softly as she pulled out a little arm and washed all the creases, then watched it fold back. "There's no need to take on so," Samantha cooed as she rinsed away the soap with warm water. The baby continued to sob in soft, raspy sounds that lifted her little chest jerkily. Samantha went on in a kind, soothing tone, "You sure know how to let a person know you're disgruntled! I imagine your parents are going to have their hands full with you."

Samantha couldn't stop smiling. How wonderful it felt to be running her hands over the silky newborn skin, listening to the sympathy-inducing cry, trying to calm and reassure the little one. She'd never performed a more satisfying task. When the baby was clean and dry, diapered and dressed in a soft flannel gown that tied closed at the bottom with a ribbon, Samantha held her snugly in the crook of her arm. The little girl had finally stopped fussing and seemed to look back at Samantha with wide, crossed eyes of darkest blue. Joy coursed through Samantha's chest. She touched a downy lock of hair on the baby's slightly misshapen head. "You're a precious thing. You and I are going to be good friends, little one."

With slow steps she returned to the bedroom, reluctant to take the infant back to her mother. But Anna slept, her mouth hanging slack from exhaustion. She roused, though, when Samantha placed the tiny bundle against her side. Anna touched the baby's cheek, and the little girl turned her face, her lips open and seeking. Anna laughed softly. "Hungry already? You're going to be like your daddy, I can tell."

Samantha watched Anna open her gown and place the baby against her breast. At once the infant found what she wanted and began sucking softly, one tiny hand slipping from the blanket to lie curled against Anna's neck. Something welled within Samantha's own breast at the sight, and tears stung her eyes. "I'll leave you two to get acquainted." Samantha gathered up the soiled bedding and headed for the door.

"Sam?"

Samantha half turned, looking toward the bed but not directly at Anna. "Yes?"

"Thank you. I can't tell you how grateful I am that you came, that you were here."

Samantha shifted her gaze until her eyes met Anna's squarely. A smile trembled on the corners of her lips. "I am, too, Anna. I feel like—" She paused, searching for words to describe all of the emotions that boiled inside of her. At last she finished, "I feel as though I've been part of a miracle."

Anna smiled, too—a soft, expression of understanding. "You have been."

Samantha left, closing the door quietly behind her. She placed the pile of sheets in a basket on the service porch and straightened the kitchen. As she put away the last pan, she heard the rattle of a wagon entering the yard, and she ran outside. Adam was driving the team with his mother on the seat beside him holding Laura Beth. The three looked at Samantha expectantly, but she couldn't speak. Not yet. She stood beside the wagon with satisfaction rolling through her.

Adam tipped his head, his brows pulling together. "What exactly has gone on here? You look as if . . . well, as if you just got nominated for president."

"Better than that." She lifted Laura Beth from her grandma's lap. "You got your wish, sweetie. If you go in to Mama, you'll get to meet your new baby sister."

Laura Beth's eyes flew wide. She wiggled free of Samantha's grasp and ran to the house, her little braids flopping.

Laura hovered half off the wagon seat gaping at Samantha and speechless for the first time in Samantha's memory. "You mean—the baby—did you—?"

Samantha laughed. "Yes, I did! And she's a beauty."

Laura fell back on the seat, a hand fluttering near her chest. Then she broke into a wide smile, hopped down, and trotted to the house, her skirts held high.

Adam stared at Samantha, then eased himself down and stepped toward her as if his boots were made of concrete blocks. "I sent Pa after the doctor and Frank. We figured the baby was coming, and he'd want to be here. But you . . .? Already?"

Taking Adam's hand, she said, "Would you like to come inside and meet our new niece?"

Adam nodded, but he didn't move. His voice filled with awe, he said, "Did you really deliver the baby, Sammy?"

Samantha threw back her head with laughter that captured all the joy and relief she was feeling. "Yes, Adam, I delivered her. And it was . . ." More feelings rushed over her and words escaped her. All she could do was smile—a beaming smile of wonder.

"Oh Sam . . ."

Samantha threw herself against her husband, wrapping her arms around him and laughing against his neck. "Adam, I delivered her, and gave her a bath, and talked to her until she stopped crying, but it was so wonderful to hear her cry for the first time! Oh, she's just so tiny and so perfect!"

Adam held her close, running a hand up and down her back, his cheek warm against her hair. After several minutes,

he tugged at a loose strand of hair and whispered, "I'd like to go see this tiny, perfect baby my amazing wife just helped bring into the world."

Samantha laughed again, giving Adam one last squeeze, then caught his hand, and they ran together into the house, laughing some more as their feet pounded the hard-packed earth.

*A*dam curved his arm around his wife's waist and escorted her to the bedroom where his mother perched on the edge of the bed, gazing with delight at the baby nestled in the bend of Anna's arm. Little Laura Beth knelt beside Anna's hip. "Oh, Mama, she's a little dolly!" Laura Beth exclaimed. "I want to play with her."

"No, sweetie, not a dolly," Anna corrected gently. "You can't play with her yet, but it won't be long before she'll be a good playmate for you."

Laura Beth hugged her mother's neck then said matter-of-factly, "I want a cookie."

The grown-ups laughed, and Adam gave Samantha's waist a squeeze. "What about you? Do you need a reward, too? After all, you had quite a morning."

Samantha moved to the bed and placed a hand on Anna's arm. "Anna did all the work. I just happened to be here."

Anna shook her head. "There's no need for modesty, Sam. Delivering a baby is certainly no small feat."

"But it's still easier than having one, I think," Samantha said.

"Perhaps," Anna sighed. "I'm worn out. It all happened so fast!"

Adam considered leaving the woman alone with this "female" discussion, but before he could make a move, a door slammed open and Frank's voice carried through the house, "Anna! Anna, where are you?"

Adam stepped into the kitchen doorway. "She's in the bedroom, Frank, and stop yelling. You'll wake the baby."

His brother's jaw dropped. "The baby!" Adam stepped back as Frank charged into the bedroom. Frank sank onto his knees next to the bed and took Anna's hand. Dr. Newton hurried in on Frank's heels.

Samantha eased past Adam and took Laura Beth with her for the cookie, but Adam couldn't pull himself away from watching the little scene and his brother's reaction. Frank grasped the edge of the blanket and pulled it down, then stared in wonder at his offspring. His work-toughened finger looked huge in comparison to the tiny baby. "What kind of baby is it?" he whispered.

"A girl." Anna seemed to search Frank's face. "Are you disappointed?"

Disappointed? Adam knew Frank had hoped for a son, but how could anyone be disappointed in something so small and perfect?

Frank's gaze went from the baby to Anna, and he stroked her cheek. "Never." He gave her a lingering kiss. At their shared moment of bliss, something rose inside Adam. Could it be jealousy? After all he'd said to Samantha? He gripped his fists and willed the feeling to pass.

Dr. Newton cleared his throat. "Papa, if you'd move out of the way, I'd like to get a look at that baby myself."

Laura chuckled and stood to step away. Frank moved aside but hovered near as the doctor examined the little girl, making her cry again. The cry was more like a kitten's complaint, and Adam discovered tears stinging his eyes. Such a beautiful, heart-melting sound. A sound he'd wasn't likely to hear in his own home. . . .

"Well," the doctor declared, "she's a little small—probably not much more than five pounds. But she seems healthy in every way."

"Thank goodness for that," Anna murmured.

"Now all of you can move along while I check Anna over," the doctor ordered. "Except for you, Mrs. Klaassen."

Frank leaned down for one more kiss and a whispered "I love you" before he caught Adam's elbow and the two left the room. Adam and Frank joined Samantha and Laura Beth in the kitchen. Adam sank into a kitchen chair, and Samantha sank on to his lap. He wrapped his arms around her, and she leaned against him, resting her forehead against his. She was still sitting thus when Dr. Newton entered the kitchen and stopped before her with his hands akimbo. "Well, young woman, what have you got to say for yourself?"

Samantha stood, her eyes wide. "W-what do you mean?"

The doctor pointed a finger at her. "Anna tells me you helped deliver that little one in there. Now, I'll let you get by with that this time, but don't go making a habit of it. You'll put me out of business!"

Samantha laughed in obvious relief and held up her hands in a mock show of surrender. "I promise, Dr. Newton. Once was enough!"

Dr. Newton put a hand on Frank's shoulder. "Congratulations, Frank."

"Thank you, Doc." Frank shook the man's hand and headed right back to the bedroom.

The doctor leaned down and shook Laura Beth's small hand. "Congratulations to you, too, Laura Beth. You're a big sister now."

Laura Beth nodded solemnly, her mouth encircled with cookie crumbs.

"Congratulations to all of you." Dr. Newton's gaze encompassed everyone in the room. "But now I think I'll get back to town. I'm not needed here any longer."

Adam offered to walk him out, and both men stepped out-side, ambling toward the buggy. Before stepping up into the conveyance, the doctor turned to Adam. "I'm wondering how Samantha is doing, Adam."

The two men looked at each other, and the doctor scratched his chin. "I'm wondering how she's doing since her visit to Rochester."

Adam lifted a shoulder, then said, "She is probably doing as well as can be expected. Things that didn't used to bother her, though, can upset her these days."

Dr. Newton nodded, his spectacles reflecting the sun. "It may be worse for a while. Her involvement in that baby girl's birth . . . well, she seems awfully happy right now, but I'm sure when the joy of the moment wears off, this experience will heighten her awareness of what she's lost."

Adam looked back toward the house, remembering his wife's beaming smile as she met him in the yard. He also re-called the mixed emotions rumbling through his own chest when he'd witnessed Frank's joy. Yes, they both might struggle for a while.

"Just be watchful," the doctor advised. "She may need a bit of extra care and attention right now."

Adam turned back to the doctor. "Thanks, Dr. Newton. I'll keep that in mind."

Dr. Newton placed a hand on Adam's shoulder, his brows arched high. "And how are you with all of this?"

Adam appreciated the opportunity to admit he'd lost something too. "It's been tough. I'd always planned on a big family, you know."

"Well, give it time," the doctor advised. "And don't keep all those feelings inside. Talk to each other. It will do you both good."

Adam nodded. "Yes, it took us a while, but we're learning how to talk about this difficult subject."

Adam watched Doc's buggy until it turned on to the road, then he moved back toward the house. How would Samantha feel when the euphoria of the day wore off? He prayed this experience would remain a joyful memory for her.

Samantha seemed far from despondent when Adam found her in Frank and Anna's bedroom. She was circling Laura Beth on her lap with one arm, her other hand clasping Anna's. As Adam entered the room, Sam looked up with a smile that lit her whole face. "Oh, Adam, guess what they've named the baby!" She didn't wait. "Kate Samantha! I have a little namesake now too!"

Adam remembered the pride he'd felt when his sister Liz had announced that one of their twin boys would be Adam James—A.J. for short. He smiled his thanks to Frank and Anna for honoring Samantha in such a way. "Kate Samantha, huh?" Adam said, placing his hands on Sam's shoulders. "She looks a little bit like you, too," he remarked.

Samantha smiled upward. "Really?" And how do you figure that—?"

"Yep." Adam pointed. "Look—her hair is standing on end just like yours does when you get up in the morning."

"Oh, Adam!" She laughed along with everyone else.

"It's a beautiful name, Anna and Frank," Adam said seriously. "And I hope your little Kate Samantha grows up to be as beautiful as this Samantha." He gave his wife a kiss, and Samantha's cheeks turned rosy.

∽◌

On the way home, Adam sent Samantha occasional sidelong glances. So far she was smiling and humming softly as they jounced along on the wagon seat. Maybe this day would signal the turning point, returning Sam back to her cheerful, peaceful self.

Beside him, Samantha shivered.

"Cold?"

She hugged herself. "A little."

"Well, come here." He lifted an arm, and she slid over. They rode in silence for several minutes, Adam holding her close.

Samantha tipped her head up toward him with a wistful expression. "Adam?"

"Yes?"

"After today I don't think I'll ever be the same."

"What do you mean?"

Samantha pursed her lips. "I helped bring a new life into the world. Honestly, when I saw that baby—that perfect little person—slip into my hands, I felt like I was holding a little piece of heaven. I was—I can't describe it. I was so *full*. . . ." She stopped and shook her head. "I don't know how to say it."

Adam tightened his hold around her waist.

She looked at him, longing in her eyes. "Do you think that's how Anna feels now? So full she can't describe it?"

Adam was uncertain how to answer. "Honey, I don't know. I can't begin to imagine how Anna is feeling right now. But I can tell you how I feel." He gave Samantha a smile. "I am so proud of you. What you did today took so much courage and spunk. I remember when Liz had the twins—just being in the house, knowing what was happening, was enough to scare the pants off of me! But you—you actually delivered a baby." He kissed the end of her nose. "You amaze me."

Samantha ducked her head and picked at the fringe on her shawl. "It went so fast, there wasn't time to be afraid. And afterwards, all I could think was—" She lifted her head, and her eyes were bright with tears. "All I could think was how lucky Anna was, in spite of the pain of the delivery. To create a new life . . ." She broke off, biting on her lower lip. Tears spilled down her cheeks.

His heart turned over. "Sammy—"

"I'm not feeling sorry for myself, Adam. Truly I'm not." She drew in a shuddering breath and whisked the tears away with her fingertips. "I'm grateful to have been there. It was a gift—something I will never forget. And I think little Kate Samantha will always be extra special to me because I was there when she was born." She straightened her shoulders. "If we hurry home, I'll have time to sweep out the upstairs bedrooms and the parlor, and close them up for the winter months."

Adam looked at her, startled. "Already? But it's only early October."

Samantha shrugged. "But it's cold. And it won't be getting warmer for a while. There's no point in heating rooms that aren't being used. It's time."

Adam watched as she turned her face forward, looking determined. He knew better than to argue with her. Samantha was closing doors—both literally and figuratively. And maybe, he conceded, it was time.

*I*t turned out Adam had to admit that winter had arrived early this year. He stood at the kitchen window, a cup of hot, black coffee in his hand, watching a flurry of snowflakes whirl past the frosted pane. Though he usually put off such chores until November, he'd already weatherized the henhouse with bales of hay and brought the livestock into the corral close to the barn so they could sleep inside nights.

Samantha's insistence on closing off the unused rooms of the house early proved to be wise. It took a heap of coal in the cellar furnace to warm the large kitchen and their own upstairs bedroom—keeping a flame going to make the other rooms bearable would have been an all-day task.

October had slipped by so quickly, he wondered where it had gone. The annual postharvest celebration had taken place as usual, but for the first time in his memory, he hadn't attended. Samantha had complained of a headache, but he suspected it was more heartache that had kept her home. She didn't say much, but he knew it was still difficult for her to be in places where mothers cradled infants, bragging back and forth about Susie's new tooth or Jimmy's first steps. He understood, and he didn't push her. Two steps forward and one step back was still getting her further along in her emotional healing than he could have hoped for.

In his mind, the idea of adoption still ran strong. A call to Daniel, and a baby no doubt could be theirs, and she would be in the circle of mothers who proudly showed off their offspring.

But whenever he was brave enough to hint at it, she would simply nod and change the subject.

Whenever they were together with any of Adam's siblings or her brother, Samantha was her laughing, smiling self, spending most of her time with the youngest family members. All of the children loved their Auntie Sam! And she loved them back, willingly playing games or telling stories or singing their silly songs with them. She never tired of it and was happiest surrounded by the little ones. Adam had come to memorize those scenes, drawing on them during the hours that would at times follow the visits—when she would sit in her rocker with tears of silent sorrow drying on her cheeks.

He now turned from the window and crossed to the stove. Holding his cooling cup between his palms, he stared at the flicker of fire between cracks in the stove lid and considered the upcoming Thanksgiving holiday. The family would all come together at his parents' home. There would be children underfoot, babies crying, and much chaos. He relished it—he'd grown up with it and eagerly awaited the reunion times when all of his brothers and sisters were under the same roof once more. He knew Samantha would go most willingly, would enjoy her time with them, but what about afterward? Would the memories of the happiness between parents and children once again rub salt into the wound in her heart?

He thought back to the day that little Kate Samantha had been born. Samantha had been over the moon, proud to have played a part in the baby's entrance into the world. The elation had carried her for several days, giving Adam hope that the depression was behind them, that she had finally been willing to accept their circumstances and seek happiness in other areas.

But the reality that the same joy Anna had would not be hers had come crashing down around her. That day had seen the start of new cycles of highs and lows that wore terribly on both hers and Adam's emotions.

It hurt him, seeing her in pain, but when would it end? Couldn't God give them the inner healing they needed? He wiped the back of his hand across his eyes and sloshed another half cup of coffee into his mug. A creaking on the stairs caught his attention, and he turned to see Samantha standing on the lowest riser, her hand draped across the railing. Her robe hung open—mute evidence of her listless state.

He put down his coffee cup and crossed to her. "Honey, it's too cold to come down like this," he scolded gently, pulling the robe closed and tying the belt. "You'll catch your death."

Her gaze dropped to her bare toes curled over the edge of the step. "I'm sorry. I didn't think."

Determined to bring her out of her melancholy, he rubbed noses with her and teased, "Well, that's obvious. You've lived through enough Minnesota winters to know you don't run around barefoot with your robe flapping." He lifted her into his arms, moving over to the rocker that always sat in the corner of the kitchen during the winter months. She sat in his lap, her legs across one arm of the chair, his arm providing support for her back. He captured one of her hands and turned his face to kiss her knuckles.

"Ah," he sighed, setting the chair into motion, "this is cozy. We haven't shared the rocking chair much since we moved out of the dugout. Remember how many evenings we spent like this?"

Samantha gave a small smile in response, nodding slightly.

Adam chuckled. "Lots of times my legs went to sleep, and I had a hard time walking to bed after you got off my lap."

She sat up and looked at him, a spark of interest in her eyes. "Really? You never said anything."

Adam tightened his grasp and admitted, "Because I was afraid if you knew, you'd never sit with me again. But it was worth it." He buried his face in her tousled hair, and she leaned against him, sighing deeply. The wind whistled outside, rattling window panes, but the kitchen was warm and smelled of fragrant coffee.

Suddenly she sat forward again. "Adam, can you stay home with me today?"

He feigned shock. "Why, Mrs. Klaassen, are you propositioning me?"

A small smile quivered on her lips. "Don't be silly." She shook her head at him. "Just because I'm sitting on your lap and asking you to stay at home with me doesn't mean I'm, well, propositioning you."

Adam pretended to be crestfallen. "Oh."

Samantha gave his chest a little push with the heel of her hand. "It gets lonely here, you know, all day by myself. . . ."

Her winsome confession tore at Adam's heart. If only . . . But there was just Samantha and Adam. It would have to be enough. Today, he decided, there was nothing more pressing than proving to her the two of them could be enough. "All right, Sammy." He lifted a strand of her hair and used it to tickle her chin. "I'll stay home with you today. But I'm not going to sit here and hold you all the time. My legs are already asleep!"

"Oh, you!" she exclaimed indignantly, swinging her legs down and lifting her arm over his head in one smooth motion. "Are you saying I'm too heavy?"

He laughed as she stood to her feet. "Go get some socks on," he ordered, aiming a playful swat at her rear, "and put on some chorin' clothes. We'll see to the animals, then we'll fritter the rest of the day away, just us."

She reached the stairs in four skips, but she paused with one foot on the first riser and looked at him over her shoulder. "Thank you, Adam."

He smiled and nodded. "This was an easy request for a yes. Now go."

She turned and ran lightly up the stairs. He gazed after her as she disappeared around the turn. She'd see—they could be happy, just the two of them. He'd prove it to her.

The day turned out to be nothing particularly special—just a together day that was memorable in its simplicity. Samantha accompanied Adam to the barn. While he milked Bessie, she played with the new batch of barn kittens, laughing at their antics. She insisted on leaving a sardine can of milk for them. When the kittens stood in a circle around the can with their tails sticking straight up over their little backs and the biggest of the group with one paw in the milk, she sent Adam a smile that came straight from her heart. And he winked back, his jaw pressed against the cow's flank, content.

They walked hand in hand to the chicken coop, gave the fowl fresh water and feed, and gathered the eggs. A good-natured contest on who could find the most eggs—the hens never laid them in the roosting boxes, but in the oddest places—sent them scrambling and laughing all over the coop. The loser, Adam, paid the winner, Samantha, a kiss of forfeit that was as much a reward as a penalty.

Back inside, they warmed up with steaming coffee, fried eggs still warm from the coop, and ate Samantha's homemade bread, which Adam toasted. After breakfast, Samantha took a soak in the tub, and Adam generously offered to wash her back.

She grinned and teased, "Now who's propositioning whom?" Adam threw back his head and laughed, delighted to see the sparkle in her eyes.

When Samantha was dressed, they opened the parlor, lit a fire in the fireplace, and spent a pleasant hour curled together on the sofa in front of a snapping flame, reading the paper aloud to each other. Adam, in a burst of silliness, intentionally twisted words around to make the more boring news items interesting. Samantha laughed until she held her stomach and finally begged, "Adam, stop! I can't take anymore!"

Adam tugged her over beneath his chin. "All right, I'll be good."

A bit of husband-and-wife spooning followed that took up the better part of another hour. By then the fire had died down, and a chill crept around them. Reluctantly, they scooped out the coals and closed the parlor up again, heading to the kitchen to chop vegetables for a pot of chicken soup.

"Thanks, but I can do this," Samantha said when brown scraps from potatoes Adam peeled littered her once-clean floor.

"Uh-uh." He shook his head, whacking the knife down again. "You asked me to spend the day with you, so with you I will be." He dropped a handful of cubed potatoes into the large pot on the stove, sending splashes of the broth over the edge.

Samantha squealed and jumped back. "Adam, be careful!" Grabbing a rag, she went after the mess.

Adam deliberately exaggerated indignity in his tone. "I'm only trying to help."

"Well, I already had my bath," she retorted, dropping the rag into the sink. He caught her around the middle from behind, and she shrieked as he spun her around and captured her against his chest. "Adam, I need to put the carrots in." But she made no attempt to free herself.

"The carrots can wait." He grinned down at her, lost in the delicate color of her eyes. Samantha tipped her head sideways, releasing an airy sigh. Adam asked, "Happy?"

Samantha nodded slowly, a warm light deepening her eyes to the color of a cardinal's wing. "Very much so."

"Me, too." Adam rocked her side to side—left, right, left again—before adding, "I'm also hungry. Let's go ahead and get those carrots in the pot." Tomatoes, cabbage, onions, garlic, and chicken pieces followed the carrots. Soon the kitchen was aromatic with the scent of the stew. Adam lifted the lid every few minutes, sticking his nose over the pot. "How long till this is done? My stomach is growling."

Samantha laughed. "You and your appetite. It won't be long now."

"How long?" he pressed.

Samantha peeked in the pot, spooned out a carrot slice and bit through it. "Another twenty minutes," she guessed.

"Twenty minutes! Twenty minutes?" Adam held his stomach and stumbled around the kitchen in a dramatic display. "A man could starve in twenty minutes!"

Samantha snatched up a slice of bread. "Then here you go—eat if you must!" She threw the bread across the kitchen, striking him on the forehead in a flurry of crumbs. He grabbed at it and mock-fumbled it for several seconds before he finally triumphantly clutched it above his head. Samantha doubled over in laughter.

"You little *Spitzmaus*!" He thumped the slice down on the table and came after her.

She let out a squeal. "Adam, no!" They played cat-and-mouse around the kitchen table, with Adam rumbling, "I'm gonna get you," and Samantha begging for mercy. At last he lunged, catching her around the waist and swinging her off the floor.

She clutched his neck, laughing in his ear. "I'm sorry, I'm sorry!" she giggled.

"Sure you are, now that I've got you." Adam grinned wickedly into her upturned face.

"So what are you going to do with me now that you've captured me, Adam dear?"

"I think . . . maybe . . . this . . ." And very slowly he lowered his face, watching until her eyes slid closed in readiness for his kiss. But instead he nipped her lightly on the end of her nose.

"Hey!" She struggled to get out of his arms.

Adam caught her again in a hug of happiness. "That was for throwing food at me, my little spitfire." This time when he lowered his head, the kiss was loving and long. The soup was left to simmer for quite some time after the vegetables were done.

❧

After a nice supper in the warm kitchen and tidying up together, Adam ran out to the barn for final chores while Samantha got two more loaves of bread ready to rise overnight and bake in the morning. Later in their room, Adam leaned across Samantha and turned the key on the bedside lamp, plunging the room into darkness. He flopped on to his pillow, his hand roaming in search of hers. She met it, holding tight, and he released a lengthy *ahhhh* of pleasure.

Samantha gazed at the outline of his face in the faint moonlight. Even with shadows across his face, she could see that his expression was relaxed, his lips uptilted. "It was a good day, Adam." She grazed the underside of his arm with her fingertips. "Thank you for it."

"Thank *you* for it," Adam replied, placing their clasped hands on his chest. He tugged a bit, and she rolled sideways, curling against his side. He chuckled. "Being with you sure beats clean-ing barns!"

"I'm not sure I like that comparison, Mr. Adam Klaassen!" They laughed together, then she asked, "Is that what you were planning to get done today? Maybe I shouldn't have asked—"

"I could have done it today," he put in quickly, "But, then, I can do it tomorrow. It wasn't a life-and-death matter that the barn get a shoveling out today."

Samantha scooted a bit closer and nestled against his shoulder. "Well, then, I'm sure glad you agreed."

They lay in quiet contentment for several minutes, warm and drowsy. Just as she was drifting off, Adam nudged her shoulder. "Sam?"

"Hmm?"

"Today . . . all the horsing around we did . . . You enjoyed it, didn't you?"

She took in a deep breath, sweet memories of their day flooding her mind. "Of course I did, Adam. It was a wonderful day—all of it."

"I was just thinking—" His voice held a hesitance that sent a prickle along Samantha's scalp. "If . . . if there were . . . others . . . in the house, we wouldn't have been able to have a day like today. Sometimes it's kind of nice, having you all to myself."

Samantha's heart constricted. She recognized his inten-tion, and tears of gratefulness built behind her eyelids. He was so good to her! Oh, *my sweet Adam, you try so hard to make me believe I can be everything to you when I know how much you too want a family. Your heart hurts too, yet you only worry about me. And I can make things so difficult for you. . . .*

She didn't know how to change what was in her heart, or even if she ever could let go. But she knew what she could do. She could let Adam know how much he meant to her.

She stretched her arm across his chest and hugged him tight. "I like having you to myself, too. You're the best thing that's ever come into my world, outside of God's forgiveness. I love you." She felt his lips against her hair, and she closed her eyes, savoring the secure, loved feeling his touch evoked.

"But, Adam?"

"Yes, Sam?"

"It still makes me sad sometimes."

Adam gathered her close and kissed the top of her head again. "I know, sweetheart. I know. Me too."

She blinked away tears and kissed the underside of his jaw. "But I promise—no crying tonight. I won't spoil our wonderful day with sadness." She could give him that small gift, at least.

He whispered, "Thank you, darlin'."

dam was carrying a stack of dishes to the dry sink in his parents' home, and he paused to bend down attentively to his nephew and niece. A.J. coaxed his little sister. "Tell Uncle Adam, Amanda, tell him what's a turkey say?"

Amanda, just past two years old, stared into Adam's face and puckered up to blow bubbles.

"Ew!" Andy, A.J.'s six-year-old twin, wrinkled his nose. "That's really icky!"

"She knows how to make a turkey sound," A.J. assured Adam. "She's just being stubborn." He scooped Amanda off the floor, holding her tight against his chest. "C'mon, Andy, let's go teach her somethin' else."

The two boys trotted around the corner with Amanda bobbing against her brother's shoulder.

Liz called, "Careful with her on the stairs, boys."

"Yes, Ma!" they chorused.

Pa had gotten up to pour himself another cup of coffee and chuckled. "Liz, it looks like Amanda is going to be as much of a show-off as her mother."

"Now, Pa," Liz retorted, "the only show-off in this family is Arn, and you know it."

Arn's fiancée, Martha, turned from the sink and nodded emphatically. "Oh, he sure is. I know he wouldn't be too shy to tell everyone what a turkey says."

Arn rose from the table, snitching the last two pickled beets from a relish plate on his way, and strutted toward Martha with his thumbs in his armpits, waving his elbows up and down and gobbling merrily. She flapped a hand at him, embarrassed, as he pranced around her in bent-knee fashion, bobbing his head, and emitted a distant imitation of a turkey's call.

From the parlor where the daughters and daughters-in-law had banished her for a much-needed break after all the Thanksgiving preparations, Ma called out, "Pluck that ol' tom, and we'll serve him for supper!"

Everyone roared with laughter. Even Arn dropped his pose to slap his knees and chortle.

"Yep, the family show-off, that's Arn." Adam chuckled. He plopped his load onto the sink and headed for the table to gather more, side-stepping around others helping with the cleanup. The kitchen of his childhood home was filled with Klaassen offspring, big and small. He found it noisy, crowded . . . and wonderful.

Ma charged through the kitchen doorway, waving her arms. "All right, I've sat long enough. You all clear out now so I can organize the mess. When everything is stacked and ready for washing, I'll recruit your help—a few at a time."

Adam and the others were unwilling to abandon Ma to the task, but she turned firm and shooed them out. Adam trailed Samantha and the others to the parlor. Just as he and Samantha sank onto the settee together, a crash sounded from overhead, followed by a frightened wail.

"Uh-oh." Josie looked upward, and she and Liz hurried for the stairs.

Samantha ran after them, holding out a hand. "Oh, please, let me go. You two take a little break from rescuing."

Liz and Josie glanced at her and at each other, then Liz nodded. "All right, go ahead, Sam—and thanks."

Josie walked into the kitchen, but Liz marched across the parlor and plunked herself down next to Adam. "So, baby brother," she demanded in her typically straightforward fashion, "how is it going with our Samantha these days?"

Adam chuckled. "I suppose it would be pointless to tell you to mind your own business?"

"Yes, it would be."

"How 'bout I plead the Fifth Amendment?"

After a punch on his shoulder, Liz prodded gently, "I wouldn't ask if I didn't care."

Adam gave his sister a one-armed hug. "I know, but I don't know what to say. Some days are very good, and some days . . . Well, some days aren't so good. I think she's arrived at a measure of reluctant acceptance, but I'm not sure she'll ever find real peace."

Liz's brown eyes were as soft as velvet as her gaze settled on Adam's face. "I worry about you. Everyone is concerned about Samantha—and I am, too!—but you lost something, too, and you are the one who must bear the brunt of things. How are you doing with all of this?"

Adam chewed the inside of his cheek for several seconds before replying, "It's tough, certainly. Especially on days like this when we're all together. I see all of you with your kids, and I think, I wish that's what Sam and I had. But then I think of Uncle Hiram and Aunt Hulda, how they never had children of their own and managed to be happy about it. I love your kids and all the other little ones running around here, and I think I can find my happiness in being Uncle Adam, if that's how things turn out."

"Can you really?" Liz's question came softly.

His voice was equally soft as he parried, "Do I have a choice?"

Liz glanced around at the hubbub of activity before squeezing his knee. "Adam, I know you'd like to adopt a baby—"

Adam shook his head. "Don't say it, Liz. Samantha and I have discussed it, and she is adamantly opposed to such an idea. I will not force her to my way of thinking."

"But, Adam, surely—"

"Liz, no!" Adam faced his sister squarely. "I understand your concern, and I appreciate it. I know you and everyone else see adoption as the perfect solution to our problem. But Sammy doesn't share the view, and she's the one who must feel comfortable with it." Liz dropped her gaze, and her lips quivered. He gentled his tone. "It wouldn't be fair to bring home a baby that would not be accepted as truly ours, would it?"

Liz raised her head. "Of course not. I'd never wish such a life on a child." She sighed. "I'm sorry I was pushy. I just want you to be able to be a papa. You'd make such a wonderful father."

"I appreciate your vote of confidence, Liz. But I've come to realize there likely won't be any little ones calling me Papa. I can live with that—as long as I've got lots of little ones calling me Uncle Adam and looking up to me."

Small Laura Beth skipped into the parlor and captured Adam's hand. "Uncle Adam, we wanna play hide-an'-seek, but we need a counter. Andy was bein' it, but he keeps cheatin'. Would'ja come count?"

"Do you think you can trust me?"

Laura Beth nodded hard enough to make her curls bounce. "Uh-huh. And you can count to a hunnert!"

Adam winked at Liz. "That's good enough for me." He allowed Laura Beth to tug him toward the stairs. But as he rounded its bend toward the hide-and-seek game, he heard his sister say, "Adam, I hope you're being honest with me—and yourself. I hope being Uncle Adam truly is enough."

⚬

Before the family returned to their respective homes that Thanksgiving evening, Si gathered everyone around the table once more to carry out a Klaassen tradition—the official giving of thanks. Samantha eagerly joined the others, basking the happiness of the family day.

They joined hands, and Si smiled down the two lengths of the table. "Thanksgiving Day is a time for counting blessings. I count each and every member of this family as a special blessing, and I know we all have much to be thankful for. Let's share our reasons for thankfulness with one another." He looked to the other end of the table, at Laura. "Mother, you start."

Laura didn't need encouragement. "I'm thankful all of my children and grandchildren are able and willing to come home for Thanksgiving dinner. It's wonderful to have all of you here again."

Martha, on Laura's left, said, "I'm thankful to be included as a member of this family. I have truly come to love all of you."

Arn squeezed Martha's hand and said, serious for once, "I'm thankful that by this time next year Martha and I will be joined as husband and wife." To Martha's great embarrassment, but also a blush of pleasure, he kissed her right there in front of everyone.

All eyes turned to Teddy, next in line. Bashful but forthright, he surprised everyone by joshing, "I'm thankful Arn's getting married so I'll have a room to myself." His comment earned a round of chuckles before Sarah piped up, "I'm thankful for four days off from school."

Becky, eyebrows raise, directed her comments toward her younger sister. "I'm thankful for the school here in Mountain Lake, and that I'll be graduating next spring. My teachers have given me a wonderful base of knowledge and prepared me well for what lies ahead."

Sarah rolled her eyes, earning a meaningful glance from her father, before young Katrina said, "I'm thankful I'm getting my pern-a-ment teeth in so I can eat corn on the cob next spring."

Samantha, watching and listening to them all, experienced a swell of longing. With several deep breaths, she managed to calm her tumbling emotions.

Daniel smiled down at Katrina. "I'm thankful those teeth are strong and healthy, and that we all share good health and happiness."

On Daniel's left, Rose cuddled little Camelia. "I'm deeply grateful for the three little girls who call me Mama and the man who calls me honey."

Christina looked up at her mother. "I'm thankful for you, Mama." She leaned forward to peer around at Daniel. "And you, too, Papa." Rose placed her arm around Christina and gave her a squeeze.

They'd reached the head of the table and Si, who beamed around at the many faces. "So many thankful hearts around this table! I'm thankful for your positive spirits."

Frank, next, placed an arm around Anna and smiled down at the infant she held. "I think everyone knows what I'm thankful for this year—a new little daughter, who is healthy and strong. And the one who was there to help her be born." The family all looked at Samantha, and she smiled and ducked her head.

Anna nodded. "Our little Kate Samantha is as much a blessing as Laura Beth. And I'm extra thankful for the telephone Frank just had installed in the kitchen so I won't have to send one of my daughters for help if I'm ever in trouble again!" Knowing how forcefully Frank had opposed the ringing box, calling it an intrusion and a nuisance even though everyone else in the community was getting them, Samantha swallowed her smile. Anna's emergency had proved the necessity of such a modern contraption, especially out in their rural setting.

Laura Beth bounced in her seat. "I'm fankful for Auntie Sam helping Mama an' Katie, an' I'm fankful for my baby sister."

Adam nudged Samantha lightly on the shoulder and grinned at her. She smiled in return, then turned her attention to the twins, who were next. Andy and A.J. looked at each other blankly, and simultaneously scratched their heads. They both turned to Liz. Andy said, "I dunno know what to say, Ma."

Liz prompted, "What are you happy about today, son?"

The twins both broke into matching smiles and shouted in unison, "Gran'ma's pun'kin pie!"

Hearty laughter circled the table, and Samantha marveled that such small boys could consume so much pie—they'd each eaten three pieces after a full meal.

Jake shook his head in amusement at the look-alike pair seated between himself and his wife. Turning back to the others at the table, he added, "I'm thankful for the bounty of harvests the past few years, that I'm able to provide for the needs of my family."

Josie's husband, Stephen, went next. "I'm too am thankful for the farmers' bounty since your crops keep my mill in operation. Your successful harvest makes my business successful." He looked over Simon's head to Josie, who wore a soft, secret smile. He looked a question to her, and she gave a small nod. Stephen leaned down to whisper in little Simon's ear. Samantha pulled in a breath to steady herself.

Simon grinned up at his parents, pulled at a corner of his mouth shyly, then announced in his sweet voice, "Me an' Mama an' Papa are glad 'cause I'm gonna be a big bruvver."

After silence for just a few seconds, Laura jumped up and dashed to Josie, hugging her daughter from behind and whispering something in her ear. Daniel, Frank, and Adam rose to reach across the table and shake Stephen's hand. Becky and Martha exclaimed and offered their congratulations. Teddy scooped young Simon out of his chair and tickled him soundly while Sarah laughed. Si proclaimed they would need a bigger table next year. Anna and Rose immediately volunteered to make one, and the laughter that followed their mock offer was deafening.

Every Klaassen family member rejoiced with Josie and Stephen. From Si down to Amanda, they all smiled and cheered and clapped with happiness. Congratulations and questions about when the baby would come and whether Josie wanted a girl this time filled the room.

While the celebration resounded around her, Samantha kept a smile firmly in place as she rose with a final peek over her shoulder to be certain she was unnoticed, and slipped upstairs.

*S*amantha escaped to Adam's old room at the top of the landing. She sat on the faded patchwork quilt covering the feather mattress and bowed forward, hiding her face in her hands. Oh, how she wanted to celebrate. To add her congratulations to those being offered by everyone else in the family. But how could she ever form the words? She was sure it couldn't happen . . . not until her heart had healed.

Why, Lord? Why did they have to share this today, when I'd been enjoying myself and basking in the love of family? Why, once again, did something have to remind me of what I so dearly want?

Footsteps sounded in the hallway, and Samantha looked up, expecting to see Adam. But Laura entered the room. At her mother-in-law's tender expression tears overflowed, and she held her arms out in a silent bid for reassurance. Laura immediately sat beside her and wrapped her arms around Samantha's frame.

The older woman's dress held the aromas of their Thanksgiving meal—homey, comforting scents that spoke of family, of joy, of God. Samantha breathed deeply, seeking those pleasant memories from the many meals eaten around the Klaassen table. "Oh, Mother Klaassen, I'm so ashamed . . ." Samantha turned her face into Laura's shoulder. "I want to be happy. I love Josie, and I am happy for her, but—"

"But you're envious." Laura patted Samantha's back, her voice holding no recrimination, yet the disagreeable word stung.

Samantha pulled free and wiped her eyes. "I know it's truly awful."

"Nonsense, Samantha. It's honest. And no one can fault you for your feelings."

Samantha peered over at Laura. "You don't think it's wrong for me to feel bad for myself when I should feel joy for Josie?"

Her mother-in-law's gentle smile soothed like a balm. "I don't think there are wrong feelings, Sammy—only bad reactions to feelings."

Samantha's brow furrowed. "I don't understand."

Laura took Samantha's hand. "A person can't always control her feelings. Emotions are a part of us, and feelings of joy or sorrow or worry or envy are normal. It's foolish to think we won't have those different feelings from time to time. God gave us emotions, and we shouldn't deny them. But what we do with those feelings . . . ah, that's where we need to have control."

Samantha dropped her gaze to her lap. "So I shouldn't have run out like I did."

Laura tugged at Samantha's hand. "I'm not faulting you, Samantha. And I understand your wish that it would be you and Adam making such an announcement. But running upstairs and hiding won't help anything, *ne leefste*."

Tears again welled in Samantha's eyes at the endearment. How could Laura call her "dearest" when she behaved so . . . well, so selfishly? "But it's very hard! How do I get past these feelings of . . . of inadequacy? Every time I see a baby, or see Adam with one of his nieces or nephews, I feel as though I've let him down."

"Adam doesn't blame you. Nobody blames you, Samantha."

Sometimes Samantha wished at least Adam would. Perhaps it would give her reason for her anger, and thereby ease her guilt. "I know. He's wonderful to me—you all are—but I blame me. I feel so guilty that we can't have children."

Laura cupped Samantha's face in her hands and spoke softly, sweetly. "*En leefste*, I think what hurts Adam even more than the loss of children is your withdrawals from him. He wants your happiness so desperately. And he can't really be happy—or accepting—if you are not."

Samantha did appreciate Laura's honesty—the woman spoke to her the way a mother might to a beloved but mistaken child. The kindly worded reprimand, though, settled into her heart like a stone. She couldn't have children, and she couldn't even mourn that fact without upsetting those she loved.

"Sammy, come with me, please," Laura said, standing and holding out her hand. "I want to show you something."

Puzzled, Samantha followed Laura down the hallway to her mother-in-law's bedroom. Laura knelt beside the bed, reached beneath it and withdrew a large leather album. "Come, sit." Laura seated herself on the edge of the bed and patted the spot next to her.

Samantha joined her, and Laura pushed the album across her lap until the spine pressed against Samantha's hip. When Laura flipped the book open to the first page, a faded photograph lay across Samantha's knees. Laura reached in front of Samantha to tap the picture with her finger. "This is Si and me, on our wedding day." She laughed. "My, I was such a nervous bride! Si and I didn't know each other very well, you see. In those days, very little contact was allowed between unmarried boys and girls, so although we believed we liked each other, we really were almost strangers."

Samantha looked at Laura in surprise. She would have never guessed that the couple who shared such a close and loving relationship had felt like strangers on their wedding day. Laura turned the page, revealing a picture of a chubby baby in a long white gown. "Daniel was born only ten months into our marriage." Laura stroked the picture lovingly, smiling down at the image. "Si was so excited when Daniel was born—his firstborn, and a son at that! He told me over and over how proud he was of me. And he said our family would be perfect if I was to have a daughter next."

Samantha's heart constricted. Why would Laura be doing this? She knew how much Samantha wanted exactly this. . . .

Laura shifted the book slightly and pointed to the photograph on the next page. "Only a little over a year later, Hannah came to us."

Hannah? Samantha's gaze quickly moved from the album to Laura's face. Who was Hannah?

"We had her such a short time—only four brief months before she went back to heaven."

Samantha looked again at the picture. The baby girl seemed tiny and wan even in the black and white photograph. Although the infant was propped in a rocking chair, weakness showed in the slump of her body, her head angled toward her shoulder. She lacked the sparkle in the image of her brother Daniel. Samantha swallowed the lump of sorrow forming in her throat. "What—what happened to her?"

Laura sighed, her gaze locked on the picture. "The poor little mite was weak from the start. She didn't nurse easily, and oh, how she cried and cried. . . . The doctors couldn't tell us much. They called it a failure to thrive. It was very hard—for both of us—when Hannah died."

Samantha examined Laura's profile. Tears glittered in her eyes, her throat convulsed, and her lips pressed into a firm, quivering line. Hannah must have been gone for over twenty-five years, yet Laura still missed her. Samantha took her mother-in-law's hand. "I'm sorry, Mother. I didn't know."

Laura gave Samantha a small smile. "We don't talk about our Hannah much—it hurts yet, you see. At the time a great part of that hurt was remembering Si's joyful proclamation after Daniel's birth how a little girl would make our family perfect. I felt as if I had let him down by bringing a sickly child into the world. It was a very . . . a very difficult time."

Samantha didn't know what to say, so she sat silent, staring down at the picture of the weak baby girl named Hannah whose parting had left a permanent void in Laura's heart. After several minutes, Laura lifted the page and carefully turned the page of Hannah's picture. On the next page was a little boy of perhaps four, holding a rosy-cheeked baby in his lap. Samantha recognized the older child immediately as Daniel, and she pointed. "This must be Frank, then."

"Yes. This is Frank when he was almost six months old. He came along two years after we lost Hannah. He was a roly-poly baby with a headful of dark curls and the biggest, brightest eyes—a beautiful, healthy baby." Laura took in a deep breath. "And, Samantha, I am sorry to tell you that I was so angry he was a boy I refused to name him."

Samantha mouth fell open in amazement. Laura, the perfect, loving mother, would not even give him a name? "I don't believe you!"

"Oh, yes." Laura met Samantha's gaze. "I was furious. I had specifically told the Lord I wanted a baby girl to replace the one I had lost, and here He went and gave me another son. I already had a son. I didn't want another son—I wanted a daughter. Si finally picked Frank's name on his own. We certainly couldn't give him the only name I had selected—Elizabeth Laurene. So Si named him Franklin for a favorite uncle of his. I think it was his way of telling me he wasn't at all disappointed that this baby was a boy. But it took me weeks to accept Frank."

Samantha sat in stunned silence, unable to believe the Laura she knew would behave in such a way.

Laura went on, "Looking back, I know how wrong I was. My feelings were honest. I was terribly disappointed that I hadn't gotten a replacement for the baby daughter I had lost. And that disappointment by itself wasn't wrong. But the way I handled it all certainly was. It was hurtful to Si, and hurtful to Daniel who was thrilled with his baby brother and couldn't understand his mama's angry tears, and it was especially hurtful to Frank who was so small and innocent and only wanted to be loved. Sometimes I think he developed a temper just to demand the attention I refused to give him for the first months of his life."

Samantha looked at Laura, surprised again. "You think a tiny baby could sense it?"

"Babies aren't stupid, Samantha." Laura shook her head, her face crunched in a rueful frown. "Frank cried more than any of his brothers and sisters, and as a small child was much more demanding. He got frustrated easily when things didn't go the way he wanted. I'm sure he sensed my resentment. And of course, none of it was his fault."

Samantha put her arm around Laura's shoulders. "Frank knows you love him, Mother."

Laura patted Samantha's knee. "Yes, I'm sure he knows that by now. But I had to put to rest my feelings of anger and guilt before I could love Frank for himself. I had to learn to put aside my resentment about Hannah's death before I could even realize how much I loved this new gift from God to our family."

Samantha considered what Laura had shared. In a way, it was similar to her own situation. She of course hadn't given birth to a child, but in a way she had lost one—she had lost the dream of bearing her own baby. And that resentment burned inside of her, tempering her reactions to everything around her.

Laura went on to the next page, this one of a curly haired baby with bright eyes and a laughing smile. "By the time

Liz—my little Elizabeth Laurene—arrived, I had come to realize that another baby would never replace Hannah in my heart, and I was ready to love another little boy, if that was how God chose to bless us. Of course, I was thrilled to have a daughter, as was Si.

"But another little girl didn't make up for the loss of Hannah. The emptiness I felt at her leaving me will always be a part of me, but it ceased to overpower the joy I felt at the arrival of each of my other children. One child can never replace another, but you can find a new and different happiness that is just as special in its own way." Laura paused, smiling softly into Samantha's eyes. "Do you understand, Sammy?"

Samantha blinked slowly, absorbing the words. "I think so." But how would Samantha find a replacement for the children she longed to have? She wasn't like Laura, who'd gone on to deliver eight healthy children after losing Hannah. Samantha's happiness and contentment would have to be found in something other than her own children. Perhaps that contentment was waiting downstairs in the forms of the nieces and nephews she loved so much. And Adam, of course. Always there was Adam, who gave her more joy than she could ever have imagined.

Samantha threw her arms around Laura. "Mother, thank you for telling me about Hannah. I'm so sorry you had to lose her, and I know it still hurts to think of her."

Laura squeezed Samantha close. "The pain lessens, Samantha, with the passing of time. Your pain will lessen, too, I promise you."

Samantha rose, squaring her shoulders resolutely. "I think I should go downstairs and tell Josie how happy I am for her."

Laura reached out to clasp Samantha's hand. "That's a very good idea. I'm proud of you."

Samantha proved her mother-in-law's pride by giving Josie a congratulatory hug and the sincerest wishes for a healthy, beautiful baby. "Would you like me to deliver the baby?" she asked to another chorus of family laughter.

B y the first of the new year, 1924, Samantha felt as though she'd recovered her old contentment. Although there were still times her empty arms brought a pinch of sorrow, she'd set aside those previous hours of despondency and gained control over the unpredictable emotional swings. Christmas with the family had been a joyful occasion, and to her great relief no tears had followed. The nightly prayers with Adam, asking God to fill her so abundantly no emptiness could remain, had accomplished their goal. Peace settled once more over her little world.

At Adam's request, she began accompanying him to the barn while he performed the morning chores. She loved the hand-in-hand walk with her husband through sparkling drifts of snow, followed by together time in the warm barn. She fed the horses their buckets of oats while Adam milked the cow, and they exchanged the chitchat of the comfortably married that started their day in the most pleasant way.

On one morning in early January, Samantha carried her tea-towel embroidery to the barn and sat with Adam while he rubbed saddle soap into a leather saddle thrown across a sawhorse. Midway through her stitching—the image of a gray cat busily scrubbing clothes at a washtub—Adam stopped and slapped his forehead. "Oh, Sam, I just remembered something." He reached into his jacket pocket and withdrew an envelope, and he held it out to Samantha. She didn't often get mail and took it eagerly.

"When did this come? Oh, it's from Rose!" she exclaimed without waiting for his answer. Rose's letters were usually full of amusing anecdotes about the girls or interesting news items from the city.

"It came yesterday." Adam sheepishly rubbed a finger under his nose. "I forgot to give it to you."

She shot him a saucy look. "Well, then that means I'll just read it to myself, and you'll *maybe* get to read it later." She laughed at his scowl, then relented. "Will you open it for me please?"

Adam used his pocketknife to slit the envelope and handed it back to Samantha. She unfolded the peach-tinted pages, sank onto a pile of hay, and began to read aloud.

Dearest Adam and Sammy,

Things here are as hectic as usual! Christmas break is over, and the two older girls are back in school, so my days are quieter. But little Cami is managing quite nicely to fill my time. She's decided to be my kitchen helper—at least, her opinion of helping. Actually, she's quite a hindrance. Yesterday she dumped five pounds of flour in the sink, then tried to wash it down. Needless to say, it set up like cement! We had to have a man come out and open up the drain pipes. Oh, I scolded, and Cami howled and cried and said she was sorry, and despite all the trouble she's still my little helper. I simply haven't got the heart to send her away.

Samantha laughed, imagining the scene. Adam laughed, too, then said, "It's so good to see you enjoying Cami's antics." She understood his meaning, and she sent up a prayer of gratitude. He headed for the little tack room at the back of the barn, scaring a barn cat from one of the stalls. It scampered to

Samantha and preened itself against her knee. She absently scratched its ears as she read on to herself.

We had something far less amusing happen, also. I'm sure you'll remember Esther, the young woman who came to the house to clean for us—you met her when you were here last August. She and her husband, Henry, were killed in a tragic automobile accident two weeks ago. It was a used vehicle but a brand-new purchase, their very first ride, and apparently they blew out a tire. Henry lost control of the auto and it rolled. The only blessing is that they were killed instantly and didn't suffer. But they leave behind four children—two girls and two boys, the youngest one only three months old. Since there are no other relatives, the children have been taken to the Foundling Home until homes can be located for them.

Daniel says he is certain the baby and the littlest boy who is not quite two will be adopted quickly. People are always willing to take in infants. But my heart aches for the older two. They are already well past the age of "baby" and will probably spend the rest of their childhood in dreary institutions. It saddens me to think of the four being separated—they've already lost their parents, and now they'll likely lose one another.

You might remember these little ones in your prayers, as we are doing.

Samantha dropped the letter to her lap and stared up at the barn ceiling. Why had Rose thought to write about such an unsettling event? Samantha remembered Esther—a plain-featured young woman with limp brown hair but with the largest, most expressive eyes. She'd seemed to seek approval, and Samantha recalled wondering what the poor woman was lacking in life to give her that little-girl-lost look.

Adam returned to the saddle cleaning, a fresh rag in his hand. "Sammy? Bad news?" he asked, looking at her with concern.

Samantha gave a start. "What?" She gathered her thoughts. "Oh—yes, I'm afraid it is."

"Is it Rose or the girls—?"

"No—no, nothing like that. It's about her cleaning lady, Esther. She was killed." Samantha briefly told Adam about the accident, then said, "They leave four children. Rose says they're at the Foundling Home, and Daniel thinks they'll find homes easily." Her recital wasn't quite accurate, but for some reason it was too difficult to go into more.

"How tragic." Adam shook his head, his expression solemn. "We'll have to remember them in our prayers."

"Yes, Rose asked us to." She gently pushed the cat from its purring coil at her feet and scooped up her embroidery hoop and thread. "I think I'll go get our lunch started. Anything in particular you'd like?"

"No, whatever you fix is fine, honey." Adam crossed the hay-strewn floor to plant a quick peck on her cheek. "Don't let the letter trouble you, Sammy."

Samantha managed a small smile, reaching up to curl one arm around his neck for a hug. "I'll holler when lunch is ready." The cat followed Samantha to the house, quick-stepping it over the cold snow. Although she rarely allowed the barn cats inside, she held the back door open. "Come on in. I'd appreciate the company."

She pressed her palm against the pocket which held Rose's letter. Four children—two girls, two boys. One baby, one toddler, and two past the baby age, but all needful of a mother's loving care . . . Rose had asked them to pray for the children, and Samantha certainly would, but she found herself more than curious. What were their names? How old was the first one? Old enough to be a surrogate parent to the younger ones? How were they getting along at the Foundling Home? She wished she had more information about them.

Pulling out the letter, she scanned it again, going on to read the second page as well. There was no more mention of Esther and Henry's orphaned children. Samantha hugged the letter to her breast. *Poor little ones* . . . Children shouldn't have to suffer such loss. She imagined the two youngest, especially, not knowing where the familiar faces of their parents had disappeared to . . . would they be coming back . . .?

The cat arched its back and leaned against her leg with a low-toned mew. Samantha slipped the letter back into her pocket and scooped the purring creature into her arms. It lifted its head, bumping affectionately against Samantha's chin. Samantha stroked its silken fur, murmuring, "Yes, kitty, I know. Everybody needs a little love now and then . . . I hope those children all find someone to love them." Her heart lurched. She gave the cat a final sweep from head to tail before setting it on the floor. "I've got work to do, kitty." She turned her attention to lunch preparations.

Over the next several days, as she performed her duties, she found herself patting her pocket and encountering the square of paper containing the news of the tragedy. Each time she whispered a prayer for the children whose names she didn't know, that they might find a loving home.

⌒♥

"You did *what*?" Daniel hadn't intended to be brusque, but based on the defensive lift in his wife's chin, he was sure he had failed.

"I simply wrote to Adam and Samantha and told them about Esther's children." She flicked a glance toward the staircase. "And kindly do not holler at me. You'll wake the girls."

Drawing in a breath to chase away the angry words forming on his tongue, he settled for a simple query. "Why?"

Rose raised one brow. "Why do you think?"

Daniel dropped his stern, hands-on-hips pose and lifted his gaze to the ceiling. "Rose, you shouldn't have done that."

"Why not?" Rose flung out her hands and sat forward on the sofa. "On one side you have a wonderful couple who are childless and who would make wonderful parents. On the other you have four children who need parents. What could be more perfect?"

Daniel crossed the carpet and sat beside his wife, resting an arm across the back of the sofa. "Darling, I realize you meant well, but you know how Samantha feels about adoption. She wants her own children, not someone else's. By telling her about these children, you've no doubt roused her sympathies, but at the same time you'll have given her a reason to feel guilty. Don't you see that?"

Rose set her lips in a firm line.

"Besides that," Daniel went on, "a couple from Minneapolis have already petitioned the court to take custody of the baby girl and little Will."

Dismay bloomed across Rose's face. "Just the two youngest ones? What about Henry, Jr., and Lucy?"

Daniel sighed. "I understand completely how you feel, my dear. But taking in *four* children . . . The couple interested in baby Ellen Marie and Will already have three older children of their own. At first all they wanted was the baby, so I'm thankful they changed their minds about William. At least two of them will be able to stay together."

"None of them should be separated, Daniel," Rose insisted.

Daniel agreed, but he also knew the realities of the situation. "Insisting that they be adopted together may not be in the best interests of the children. They could wait for years until a family willing to take in four at once is found, and the longer they wait, the more unlikely it becomes that *any* of them will be adopted."

"But—"

"As difficult and unfair as it seems," Daniel said with a shake of his head, "the best thing to do is let Ellen Marie and Will go with this family—they are a good family and will provide well for the children. And we'll continue to hope and pray that young Henry and Lucy will find suitable homes in the not-too-distant future."

Rose folded her arms over her chest. "I still think Adam and Samantha—"

"We can't always arrange things the way we want." Daniel placed a hand on his wife's knee and squeezed gently. "We have to make the best of the situation. Please—no more mention of this. It's hard enough for me to be involved in the adoption of these children, and if I'm feeling censure from you about the decision it only is more difficult. I'm asking you to support me in this."

Rose stared off to the side for a moment. Then she sighed and leaned against Daniel's shoulder. "If you believe this is for the best, yes—I'll support you. But don't ask me to like it."

Daniel chuckled softly and dropped a quick kiss on her temple. "I suppose that would be asking too much of a match-maker like you."

"Don't tease, Daniel," Rose said, but she didn't move from her nestling spot. "And I still think my matchmaking would be better for those children than anything you lawyers and judges could concoct."

Daniel wrapped his arms around Rose, his cheek against her forehead. Although he wouldn't admit it, in his heart he believed his wife was right.

*T*he telephone hanging in the kitchen jangled merrily early on the morning of January 23. Samantha lifted the ear piece. "Hello!"

"Hello, yourself," came her brother's voice. "Happy birthday, Sam!"

"Thank you, Davey."

"Listen to this." Some odd fumbling noises filled her ear before Joey's childish voice began to sing off-key. "Happy birfday to you . . ." By the time Joey had finished the song, Samantha was holding her cheeks to keep from laughing into the receiver.

"Thank you, sweetheart. That was a wonderful present."

Joey said, "Dere's more present, Auntie Sam. Mama got a cake an'—"

David's voice cut in, "Joey, let Papa talk now."

"'Bye-'bye," Joey said, and then David's voice came through again. "Samantha, we'd like you and Adam to come over this evening for a little birthday celebration. Will that fit into your plans?"

Samantha warmed at his desire to celebrate her arrival into the world. "You don't need to go to any trouble for me, David."

"I missed too many of your birthdays when you were a child." His voice sounded tender with yearning. "Let me indulge you a little bit now, huh?"

Samantha smiled, cradling the earpiece two-handed against her cheek. "All right. We'd love to accept your invitation. Thank you."

"Great! Be here by six o'clock, sharp, for a birthday dinner."

"Yes, sir!" She replaced the earpiece and stood smiling at the instrument for several seconds, anticipating the evening with her brother. Then she ran to the base of the stairs and called, "Adam!"

"Huh?" His voice sounded faint, carrying all the way from the bathroom at the end of hall.

"David just called. He invited us to their place for the evening meal. All right?"

"Fine, but what's the occasion?"

"What's the—?" Samantha stared upward in disbelief. Adam had forgotten her birthday! She stomped up the stairs, one hand banging against the handrail, the other curled into a fist. She barged through the bathroom doorway. "What do you mean, what's the occasion? You know quite well what today is!"

Adam turned from the sink, his freshly shaved face looking completely innocent. "Well, sure, Sam. It's Thursday, the twenty-third day of January, and it's—" His arms snaked out, catching her in a hug that literally took her breath away. "It's your birthday!"

She laughed into his clean-smelling neck, holding on for dear life as he swung her in a circle. "You big tease, I thought you'd forgotten."

"Forget about the birthday of my favorite girl? Absolutely not." He set her back on the floor. "And I have something for you."

"You do?"

"Uh-huh, and you're gonna like it." He tipped up her face and very slowly he lowered his head until their lips touched once, twice, then again.

"Is that all I get?" she asked guilelessly.

Adam gave a brief huff of laughter then offered a mock scowl. "Shame on you. That kiss should be enough for anyone."

He shook a finger under her nose. "Better behave or you might end up getting something besides birthday kisses that isn't nearly as nice."

Samantha smirked. "You'd have to catch me first." She spun and dashed down the hallway to the stairs, laughing at him over her shoulder.

"Just wait till I get my hands on you!"

She reached the bottom of the stairs. "I can wait!"

His laughter followed her into the kitchen, and Samantha giggled as she pulled out a skillet to fry pancakes. Her happy, flushed face reflected back at her from the kitchen window. She looked lighthearted, relaxed, the way a twenty-three-year-old—no, a twenty-four-year-old—wife should look.

Thank You, Lord, for healing. The prayer winged from her contented heart. She blew her reflection a kiss then set to work preparing Adam's breakfast.

⌒ↄ

"Absolutely not, Samantha." Priscilla put her hands on Samantha's shoulders and eased her back down onto the chair at the head of the table. "You are a guest, and it's your birthday. You will not be doing any kitchen duties tonight!"

Samantha gestured weakly to the array of dishes scattered across the lace-covered dining room table. "But—"

David held up a hand to silence her. "No arguments, baby sister." He grinned, arching one sardonic brow. "The boss has spoken."

Priscilla stuck her tongue out at her husband and shook her head.

David laughed at her and went on. "Besides, Pris is right; you shouldn't do kitchen chores on your birthday."

"I certainly won't do any on mine!" Priscilla shot over her shoulder as she began stacking dishes. "I'll get these out of the way for now and wash them later. Go settle yourselves in the parlor. I'll be out in a few minutes."

Samantha looked at Adam who shrugged and bobbed his head toward the parlor. "Shall we?" Samantha rose and Adam escorted her to the sitting room.

Joey scrambled down from his chair and dashed to the stack of wooden blocks he'd left in the corner. The three grown-ups settled into overstuffed furniture to enjoy a little after-dinner discussion. In a few minutes the clanging from the kitchen ceased, and Priscilla joined them, carrying baby Jenny who had been roused from her sleep, thanks to her mother's energetic plate stacking.

Samantha moved to the rocking chair and held out her arms. "Oh, let me hold her." Priscilla deposited the baby into Samantha's waiting arms, then seated herself nearby. "Hi, Jenny," Samantha greeted the bright-eyed infant. Little Jenny cooed at her aunt.

Joey galloped over to peek at his baby sister. "Whooo, Jenny," he prompted, and Jenny beamed at him, imitating, "Oooo." The grown-ups laughed, and Samantha started the rocker in motion. Joey returned to his block tower, and Priscilla reached beside the chair and brought up a snarl of pink yarn and two knitting needles.

"Not that again," David said with a wry smirk.

"You're the one who suggested I learn to knit rather than buy all of Jenny's items, so don't start belly-aching." Priscilla shot him a tart look.

David chuckled and gestured toward his wife. "I made one comment about the high cost of ready-made clothes, and she took it to mean she should never own another store-bought garment."

"Now, David . . ." Priscilla's tone held a mild warning.

Samantha exchanged an amused glance with Adam. No matter how irritated David and Priscilla pretended to be with each other, their sparring was never taken seriously by either party or their audience.

"I think it looks nice," Samantha said. "Is it a blanket?"

David snorted, and Priscilla wrinkled her nose at him. Her expression brightened when she turned to Samantha. "No, it's the start of a sweater." Typical of Priscilla, Samantha could spot no pattern—just pick up the needles and yarn and begin.

"Oh. I didn't realize you knew how to make sweaters."

"She doesn't." David shook his head indulgently. "But I have no doubt that by the time she's finished wrestling with that boulder of yarn, there will be a sweater in its stead. Once Priscilla sets her mind to something, there's no dissuading her."

Priscilla flipped a thick strand of hair over her shoulder. "That's right, so just sit over there and let me knit, Mr. O'Brien."

"Yes, Mrs. O'Brien," David conceded, hands up and palms outward.

The conversation moved from Priscilla's knitting abilities to the wonderful dinner, to mild complaints about full bellies, to various other topics. Eventually the conversational ball bounced back to Christmas, and Adam commented, "I missed having Daniel and Rose home for the holiday."

"That's right . . ." Priscilla held up the slightly off-square of pink yarn and examined it. Her survey complete, she began twisting the long needles once more. "I had forgotten they didn't make it home for Christmas this year. Have you heard from them since?"

Adam nodded. "Yes, Rose writes frequently. We got a letter from her about a week ago."

Samantha felt her chest squeeze as she remembered Rose's most recent communication. She put a kiss on little Jenny's forehead, praying someone might be doing the same for Esther's orphaned baby.

"Everything all right in Minneapolis?" David asked.

Adam glanced at Samantha and said, "Yes, just fine with Daniel and his family. Rose did share some rather unhappy news, though, concerning a woman who helped Rose with cleaning chores." Briefly, he explained to David and Priscilla about the accident and the children who were now orphans.

"That's sad," David said. He blew out a long breath. "Even after all these years, I still miss my mother. Poor kids . . ."

Something deep within Samantha twined around David's solemn words.

Priscilla's needles clacked an off-beat pattern. "So what's to be done about it?"

Samantha swallowed a sigh. "We're praying they'll find loving homes."

Priscilla looked over the top of her knitting. "Oh. I thought maybe you considered doing more."

Samantha lowered her gaze to Jenny's sleeping face. Her heart pounded fiercely in a rush of apprehension she didn't understand. "Such as . . .?"

"Such as giving them a home." Priscilla nonchalantly lifted one shoulder as if she hadn't just suggested Samantha and Adam turn their whole lives upside down by bringing home four unknown children.

"We couldn't do that." Samantha finally forced the words past her tight throat.

"Why not?" The square of knitted yarn bounced on the needles. "It seems to me that if anyone would understand a motherless child's needs, it would be you. After all, you were a motherless child."

David's jaw dropped. "Priscilla! That was extremely . . . well, it was insensitive!"

Joey looked up from his block building, his dark eyes wide and wary.

Priscilla's hands stilled, and she shot her husband a defensive look. "Well, gracious, David, you needn't shout at me. You've scared Joey." A brief glance at Joey confirmed it, and David reached a hand out to the little boy. Joey trotted across the rug and snuggled against his father's broad chest.

Priscilla's chin angled high. "I wasn't trying to hurt anyone's feelings. I was simply stating my opinion."

"Well, perhaps your opinion isn't warranted, Pris." David looked from his wife to his sister, his expression changing from stern to apologetic.

Defiance flared in Samantha's chest. "David could understand the needs of a motherless child, too. Why don't you consider adopting them if you feel so strongly about it?"

Priscilla didn't deliberate for more than a moment before saying, "David and I have Joey and Jenny already. But you and Adam—"

"Priscilla!" David rose from his seat with Joey in his arms. But the sight of the towering, red-faced David wasn't enough to silence the assertive Priscilla.

Her knitting needles clacked furiously. As her hands flew, she said without a hint of an apology in her tone, "I'm sorry if I've offended you, Sammy. That certainly wasn't my intention." David received another scathing look before she turned back to Samantha and continued in a much less abrasive tone. "I know sometimes I don't say things the right way, but all I meant was that if anyone could give an orphaned child the patience and understanding he or she would require, I think it would be you." Then she shrugged and added, "Or David, too, I suppose." To Samantha again, very kindly, "I believe you could empathize with such a child, where others would simply sympathize. There is a difference, you know."

"Yes . . ." Samantha considered Priscilla's final comment. "I suppose there is."

Priscilla held her work at arm's length. A satisfied smile broke across her face. "There! That should be large enough for the back of a sweater for Jenny, don't you think so, Sammy?"

Samantha looked at the twelve-inch square of knitted pink yarn, then down at the baby who slept contentedly in her arms. "It looks big enough. After all, there isn't much to Jenny yet, is there?"

Priscilla laughed, tied off the end of the yarn, and began removing the knitted piece from the needles. "No, there's not much to her now, but she'll grow in a hip and a hurry!" Priscilla dropped the handful of yarn, needles, and knitted square into the bag beside her chair, then boosted herself up. She reached for her daughter. "I'll take her to bed now. Thanks for rocking her, Sam."

Samantha stood and passed the slumbering infant to her mother's arms, one hand stroking the cap of black curls a last time. Her fingers lingered on the baby's soft hair. "Thank you for letting me rock her. I enjoyed it."

Priscilla stood for a moment with Jenny in her arms, her sharp gaze centered on Samantha. Samantha, watching the play of emotions on Priscilla's face, braced herself. Sassy, assertive Priscilla was preparing to offer more unsolicited advice.

"Samantha," Priscilla announced, "you just said you enjoy rocking Jenny, and I know you do. You enjoy every minute you spend with any of your nieces and nephews, and they all love you to pieces. But, at the risk of being accused of insensitivity"—she sneaked a peek at David, who glared silently at his wife—"I have to say . . . they aren't yours."

Samantha bit down on her lower lip.

David, his mouth set in a firm line, put Joey on the floor and headed for his wife. Priscilla increased the volume as he advanced. "They aren't yours, but you love them just the same. I fail to see how that can be any different than a child you would adopt."

David slipped his hand beneath Priscilla's elbow. "Pris . . ."

Priscilla jerked her arm from his grasp, and at the abrupt movement, Jenny stirred and began to howl. Without a moment's hesitation, Priscilla plopped the baby back into Samantha's arms, and she automatically began rocking and crooning to the wailing infant. Priscilla crossed her arms and grinned in satisfaction. "See?" She flipped a palm toward Samantha and cocked a saucy eyebrow at her disgruntled husband. "You put a baby in her arms, and it becomes hers."

David's arm slipped around Priscilla's shoulder, and the two of them gazed down at Samantha while she calmed the fussing baby. With hiccupping noises, little Jenny ceased her wails and nestled into Samantha's shoulder. Samantha tipped her cheek against the baby's soft curls and sighed. Such a delight she'd found in comforting this little one.

Priscilla now turned her attention on Adam. "I think you should go to Minneapolis as soon as possible and bring those children back here before someone walks off with that baby. Someone will, you know. And Samantha should have the pleasure of rocking a baby that nobody will remove from her arms."

As if on cue, Jenny's eyelids slipped closed, and Priscilla picked her up once more and headed for the hallway. Samantha looked after the two and wrapped her now-empty arms across her stomach. When Priscilla turned the corner, disappearing from view, Samantha turned to discover both David and Adam examining her with serious expressions.

She forced a feeble laugh. "David, despite your best efforts, Priscilla is still sassy."

David sighed. "Yes, she is. I'm sorry, Sammy."

Samantha's cheek twitched. Laughter threatened. She swallowed to hold it back. "Don't apologize. Pris just says what she thinks." She shook her head, muttering to herself. "She's also right."

"What do you mean?" Adam asked quickly.

Samantha crossed to Adam, taking his hands. "Adam, you married a real dummy."

He angled his head. "Well, then, what does that make me?"

Samantha raised up on tiptoe and delivered a light kiss on his lips. "That makes you a real sweetheart, for putting up with this dummy." Before Adam could reply, she released his hands and darted away, suggesting over her shoulder, "But sometimes, sweetheart, you might try putting your foot down."

Adam flicked David a dry look. "I imagine that would do me about as much good as it does you."

Samantha grinned. "Ha-ha." She finished up behind the rocking chair and clasped the high back with both hands, giving it a push that set it into motion. "Adam, I have spent the last five years wasting a perfectly good rocking chair sitting in it all by myself. Priscilla is right—if you put a baby in my arms, it does become mine. I don't know why it's taken me so long to come to my senses, but . . ." She lifted her shoulders in a shrug, then held her hands high, smiling sweetly.

Awareness dawned on Adam's face. He moved toward her. "Sam, do you mean . . .?"

"Yes, Adam, I do mean . . . Let's call Daniel right away and start adoption procedures."

Adam paused, his body looking tense. "There are four of them, Sam."

Samantha felt her chin quiver. "I know there are four of them, and I want to bring every one of them home to live with us." Her gaze flitted briefly to David then back to Adam before she finished quietly, "Brothers and sisters should never be separated, Adam."

Adam rocked in place, as if his boots had been nailed to the floor. "Are you sure, Sammy? Are you absolutely, positively, without any doubts sure this is what you—what we should do?"

Samantha skittered around the chair and clasped Adam's hands, needing at this moment to be physically connected with him. "Adam, at Thanksgiving your mother showed me pictures of a sister you never got to meet. Among other things, she told me that losing Hannah left an empty spot in her heart that was never filled, but that it didn't keep her from loving the rest of her children.

"I know I've stubbornly clung to the idea of having our own children, and I suppose a part of me will always regret that I couldn't birth your babies. But you and I have love we need to share with a child, and in Minneapolis there are four children who have lost their mother and father. Surely they need us as much as we need them. So . . . yes, I'm positively, absolutely, without any doubts sure this is what's right." By the time she'd finished, she was smiling through happy tears, and Adam's face was lit with his own beaming smile.

"Oh, Sam!" Adam scooped Samantha right off the floor with his hug.

Squealing, she clung to his neck. "Adam, put me down! You can't just go around picking up expectant mothers!"

Adam roared his laughter and squeezed her hard enough to leave her breathless before lowering her to the floor. Completely forgetting about their audience, they shared a joyous kiss. When they separated, David came over and wrapped his arms around both of them "What a birthday present." His voice shook slightly. "A family. A ready-made family."

Samantha tipped her forehead lightly against Adam's lips. She heard him murmur, his tone awed, "A family, Sam." She smiled to herself. A family! At that moment, it seemed that nothing could go wrong.

Chapter Twenty-One

*A*dam, I wish you'd called two weeks ago with this."

Adam's hand tightened around the telephone earpiece. He had put a call through to Daniel immediately upon their return home from the birthday dinner. He'd expected an enthusiastic response, but his brother's regret-filled tone created a sense of dread. "Why? What's the matter?"

Samantha tugged at his sleeve. "What's wrong?"

Adam held up a hand to her before asking, "Is there a problem, Daniel?"

Daniel's voice crackled through the line. "A local couple, Dr. and Mrs. Vanderhaven, have petitioned the court to adopt the two youngest children. They are a well-established family with three older children. Their hearing is on the docket for tomorrow afternoon, and it looks quite promising that they'll be granted custody."

"So soon?" Adam was unable to hide his dismay.

"What is it, Adam?" Samantha, brow furrowed, fidgeted in place. "What's wrong?"

Adam shifted the mouthpiece to address her. "Another couple has expressed interest in adopting two of the children."

Samantha's eyes flew wide. "They can't separate them! Let me talk to Daniel." She pushed in front of him, grasping the earpiece so they could press their heads together and share it. "This is Sam. Can't you stop the adoption from taking place? Since it would separate—?"

"It's not that simple, Samantha." Daniel's voice held patience but firmness. "The children are wards of the state, and a wealthy family like the Vanderhavens would provide a fine home for the children."

"But not for all of them!" Samantha argued. "Only two of them! And it isn't right that they be separated."

A sigh carried all the way from Minneapolis. "I agree, Sam, but judges try to do what they feel is best. And a home with the Vanderhavens would certainly be preferable to remaining in the Foundling Home."

"I don't see how separating those children can be the best thing, no matter how rich the people are who pull them apart!" Samantha thrust the telephone earpiece back into Adam's hand and stalked a few feet away, facing the wall and hugging herself.

Adam spoke quietly into the telephone "Is there any way you could postpone the hearing? Maybe if the judge knew there was someone willing to take all of the children . . ."

"I can't make any promises," Daniel said, "but I will try. How soon can you and Sam get here?"

"We can pack tonight, and if the train schedules are running right, be there by tomorrow afternoon—evening at the latest. Do you think you could postpone the hearing one day?" On the other end there was silence. Samantha crept close again, her expression beseeching. Adam added, "Daniel, it's just one day. Surely it's not too much to ask."

"Judge Simmons is handling this case, Adam, and although he's much less . . . well, dignified . . . than many I've worked with, he's a stickler for following schedules. . . ."

Samantha put her face to the receiver again and begged. "Daniel, please?"

Daniel's huff of breath carried clearly through the line. "I'll see what I can do. You two get here as fast as you can."

Adam and Samantha shared a successful smile. Adam said, "Thanks, big brother. One more thing—would you be willing to represent Samantha and me at the hearing? Assuming there is a hearing on our behalf."

"I'd be honored." Adam envisioned Daniel's smile as he added, "I'll even give you my family rates."

Adam managed a brief laugh. "Sounds fair. As soon as our travel plans are set, we'll give you a call and—"

"Don't waste time and money calling," Daniel put in. "Just get on a train and get here. Take a cab directly to the office if you arrive before six, to the house otherwise. And, Adam? Just in case I can't stop the proceedings, would you and Sam consider adopting the older two? A girl and a boy? It will be tough to find a home for them at their ages."

"I'd rather wait and see what happens before I commit to anything."

"That sounds fair. I'll keep an eye out for you."

"All right, then. We'll see you soon. Good-bye." Adam placed the earpiece back in the hook and held his arms out to Samantha. She came at once, locking her arms around Adam's torso.

"Can he stop the adoption?"

"He's going to try."

Samantha buried her head against Adam's shirt front. "Oh, Adam, he's just got to! If we can't bring those children home . . ."

"Now, Sammy," Adam chided gently, "think positively."

"I can't help it! After what it's taken to get me to want them, I can't stand the thought of losing them now. And I just believe in my heart that those children need to be together. Here."

Adam rubbed his hands up and down her spine "I agree with you, and so does Daniel. You probably heard he's going to represent us in court, and I have every confidence he'll do whatever he can to sway the judge in our favor."

"Oh, I hope so," she murmured fervently.

Adam caught her shoulders and gently set her aside. "Now, Miss Birthday Girl, march yourself upstairs and pack your bags. Tomorrow we're going after our children."

Samantha nodded, dashed the sheen of tears from her eyes with the back of a hand, and offered her husband a brave smile. "That's right—*our* children." She ran lightly up the stairs.

❧

Adam hurried through the nighttime chores and headed upstairs to their bedroom. He stopped in the doorway, evidence of Samantha's preparations all over the room. The wardrobe yawned open, and a partially packed bag stood open by the bed. But Samantha was nowhere in sight.

"Sam?"

"In here," came her voice from the small room adjoining theirs. The door stood half open, and Adam crossed to it and stepped through. Samantha stood in the middle of the room, her chin in her hand.

"What are you doing?" he asked, certain he already knew.

"Planning." She turned a slow circle, tapping her lips with her forefinger. At last she dropped her arms and faced Adam. "I've got the room all arranged. The cradle here," she said, stepping to the corner farthest from the doors and gesturing with both hands, "since the noise from our room and the hallway will be least disruptive , and—" she moved briskly to the corner beside the door that led to their bedroom—"I'll put a rocker here. If we can afford a small dresser, it should go here." She pointed to another wall. "With a small lamp sitting on top of it. What do you think?"

Adam smiled and shook his head with admiration and love. In the dim light filtering through their bedroom doorway, she looked very young. He remembered Daniel's question about whether or not they would consider adopting only the older two children. Had Daniel asked because he knew that would more than likely be what was offered to them? In case she hadn't heard that part of the conversation, he should tell her what Daniel had said. But the look of innocent belief on Samantha's face—the expression that indicated her baby would soon be sleeping soundly in a cradle in the corner of the room planned as a nursery—stilled the words.

He stepped behind her and wrapped his arms around her waist. "I think not only should our baby have a dresser with a lamp, our baby should also have a rug on the floor and a wooden toy box filled with toys in that corner." He pointed as Samantha's gaze followed the direction of his finger. "And curtains on the window, and a bookshelf full of storybooks and—"

"Adam, Adam, Adam . . ." Samantha chuckled softly. "You're going to spoil the child if you fill this room with all of that."

"Nah, isn't going to happen," Adam insisted.

"I never thought you would be an indulgent parent," Samantha said, tipping her head and smiling up at him.

Adam raised his brows. "And I never thought you'd be so strict."

"Strict? Me?"

"Yes, strict. Denying our baby a rug and toy box full of toys and storybooks—"

"Adam." Samantha placed a finger on his lip, her expression serious. "Can we afford to do what we're doing? I know the crops didn't bring as much last year, and—"

"We're not wealthy people, Sam. Not like the Vanderhavens in Minneapolis. But we have the means to provide for four children."

"Are you sure?"

"I'm sure. Although we got less than in years past for last season's crop, we have sufficient resources to meet our obligations and with savings left over in the bank." His heart swelled in gratitude for the Lord's provision. "The children may not have dozens of toys or matching furniture or bookshelves overflowing with storybooks, but their needs will always be met. And they'll be showered with love."

Standing in the middle of an empty, echoing room, Adam could imagine it all—the dresser with its lamp and doll, the full bookshelf and toy box . . . all of it. And a sweet baby that would lift its arms to Samantha in eagerness to be held. He hoped the baby's first word would be "Mama."

Samantha relaxed against him, sighing contentedly. As if reading his thoughts, she said, "That sounds perfect." Then she straightened. "Adam, what happens when we bring them home? We don't have beds or clothes or anything ready—"

"One step at a time, Sammy." Adam rocked her back and forth. "First we see the judge, then we get the children, then we fill the house with beds and clothes and toys and all the other things that children need."

Samantha smiled and sheepishly said, "All right, Mr. Adam Klaassen, my wise husband."

"Now, how about you and I get some sleep so we'll be ready to head to Minneapolis first thing in the morning and bring home our children?" He pressed his nose to hers, smiling into her eyes.

Adam watched her enter their bedroom, noted the confident angle of her chin, and smiled to himself. He closed his eyes. *Lord, I believe what we're doing in trying to keep those children together is right. If this is a window You've opened for us, I just ask that You help us climb on through it. And if it's not* . . . He stopped, opening his eyes to stare at the doorway where Samantha had disappeared only moments ago. He couldn't bear to complete that final thought. There could be no more broken dreams for his Samantha. *Please, Lord* . . .

*S*amantha sat quietly on the padded bench seat of the passenger car while the landscape whizzed by the frosted window. They had risen early to finish necessary chores and arrange with family to take care of their animals for a few days. Simon took them in to town to catch the eight o'clock train. The gentle rolling motion of the huge locomotive had lulled a tired Adam into slumber. His head hung toward his shoulder, swaying with the train's rhythmic rock. Glancing at him, Samantha was mildly amused. He didn't look at all comfortable.

She turned her gaze to the snow-covered countryside. On another day she would have marveled at the sight of the sun reflecting off glittering snow, turning icy trees into a crystal forest. Another time she no doubt would have gasped in delight at the brilliant red flash of a cardinal contrasting beautifully against the background of pure white. But not today. Not now.

Though her gaze was directed outward, she was lost in thoughts of the last time she and Adam had traveled by train— the trip to Rochester and Dr. Zimmerman, remembering the sorrow of that time. But she pushed it all away because now here she was again, riding the rails on the way to a dream. The same dream, really, but pursued by an alternate means.

What would happen at the end of this ride? She wanted to believe that even as she and Adam made their journey, Daniel was convincing the judge to withhold granting adoption of the two littlest orphans to the wealthy Minneapolis family, the Vanderhavens. She wanted to believe that the judge would see the wisdom of allowing the children to stay together. She wanted to believe that her long-held dream of hearing a child call her Mama would soon come true.

But as much as she wanted to believe—as much as her heart clamored hopefully in her chest—she was afraid.

After all, she and Adam were much younger—and much less financially secure—than the other couple. How could their inexperience hope to compare to a man and wife who were already successfully parenting three children? How could their simple farmhouse and limited acreage, shared with two other families, possibly stand up against the untold wealth of the Vanderhavens? When viewed from a purely intellectual standpoint, the Vanderhavens were by far the more logical choice, she had to admit, even if it meant separating the children.

But, Samantha continued the argument with herself, why only look at it from the intellectual side? When viewed with the heart, she and Adam could offer just as much—maybe even more!—than the Vanderhavens. After all, they were willing to assume responsibility for all four children, which would mean no separation. And certainly they were capable of loving the children just as much as the other couple. There would be no competition with birth children for love and affection. They would have a wonderful country life, fresh air and animals, and . . .

Adam's head bobbed forward and awoke with a jerk. He straightened himself in the seat, and looked around blearily for a moment before he seemed to realize where he was. He lifted his elbows in a stretch, twisting his neck back and forth to remove the kinks. Only when his arms were lowered—one on the back of the seat, one on the armrest—did he look at Samantha and give her a reassuring smile. "Quit worrying."

Oh, how well he knew her. . . . But she feigned surprise. "What makes you think I'm worrying?"

He grinned and reached out one blunt finger to stroke a line across her forehead. "These furrow marks. When you frown like that, it makes you look old."

"I wish I were older." Maybe she'd be better able to compete with the older and more experienced Vanderhavens.

"You can always get older but you can't get younger, so don't go wishing your life away." Adam slipped his arm down around her shoulders and pulled her securely against his side.

"Oh, I'm not." She turned sideways in the seat to face him. When her back came in contact with the cold window, she shifted forward a bit. "I was thinking that when it comes to impressing the judge with our ability to be good parents, a few more years wouldn't exactly hurt us any."

Adam grinned and examined her with raised eyebrows. "Hmm. No gray hairs yet, and I think you still have all your teeth. Oh, well." He tapped the end of her nose. "Just keep frowning like that, sweetie—makes a few wrinkles, and you'll look like a granny in no time."

"Oh, you," she sniffed in mock impatience, settling against his side with her head on his shoulder. Worrying never changed anything, she told herself. And, as Mother Klaassen once told her, worrying says to God He isn't trusted to meet one's needs. Determinedly, Samantha pushed her negative thoughts away. But she offered a fervent prayer. *Lord, please let that judge see more than a young wheat farmer and his wife when he looks at us. Let him see our hearts . . . .*

⌒⌒

When they reached Minneapolis that evening and disembarked, Adam hailed a carriage and gave the driver directions to Daniel and Rose's home. Adam was at once eager and hesitant to talk to Daniel. *Lord, calm my jangled nerves. Samantha's too,* he added with a sidelong glance at his wife.

The driver angled the carriage into the brick-paved driveway leading to Daniel's large stone house, and Samantha's fingers clamped down hard on Adam's. He gave her hand a reassuring pat and helped her down from the carriage. After swinging their bag from behind the seat, he dug fare from his pocket, added a dime for a tip, and handed it to the driver with a polite, "Thank you, sir."

The driver simply nodded and left. Adam and Samantha stood in front of the house, holding hands. Samantha seemed planted in place, so Adam tugged at her hand. "Come on, sweetheart."

She gave him a wide-eyed look. The apprehension in her face matched his stuttering pulse. But he managed to smile. He tugged again, and this time Samantha's feet moved toward the door. His finger against the door buzzer brought instant welcome by Daniel's wife and daughters. Christina, Katrina, and Camelia all clamored to be hugged. Rose called over her shoulder, "Daniel, it's Adam and Sam—they're here!"

Daniel appeared from his small office behind the staircase, a smile creasing his face and his hand extended in greeting. "Adam, Samantha, you look exhausted! Come in, come in! Girls, step back so we can shut the door." Daniel scooped up Cami and reached past the other two girls to swing the door closed.

Rose herded the older two toward the staircase. "You two were on your way to your rooms to get ready for bed. Now go on up."

"Oh, Mama," both girls protested at once, "we want to see Uncle Adam and Auntie Sam! Please? Can't we stay up?"

Daniel compromised with, "Go on up, get into your nighties, and then you may come back down and visit for a bit before bed."

"Remember to put away your clothes and wash your faces," Rose reminded them.

They gave their father one last pleading look which he chose to ignore, then they reluctantly plodded upstairs. Rose took Cami from Daniel's arms. "I'll get this little pun'kin tucked in and then I'll be right back. Adam and Samantha, make your-selves at home." She, too, headed upstairs.

With the girls gone, the house was suddenly silent, and the three remaining adults stood in a small circle, looking at one another. Finally Daniel broke into a smile and gestured toward the parlor. "Well, come on in and sit down. Can I get you some-thing to eat or drink?"

"No, thank you," Samantha replied, following him. "We had some sandwiches on the train, and I'm never very hungry after being bumped around all day."

"I know what you mean," Daniel agreed. He sat in a side chair, and Adam and Samantha settled themselves on the set-tee in the parlor's bay window. "It's good to see you."

Adam leaned forward, resting his elbows on his knees and looking hard at his brother. "It's good to see you, too, Daniel, but the suspense is killing both of us. Did you talk to the judge?"

"I did."

"And—?" Adam prompted. Samantha sat up as well, her eyes wide and apprehensive.

"And he postponed the hearing until tomorrow afternoon."

Samantha collapsed against the seat's tufted back. Adam took her hand. "Then there's a chance."

Daniel took in a deep breath. "There's a chance."

"A good chance?" Samantha pressed.

Daniel linked his fingers. "There's no way of knowing how things will turn out, Sam, but I visited with Judge Simmons per-sonally. I told him about you two, and your home, your farm, the rest of the Klaassen family nearby, and how you were willing to adopt all four children so they could stay together. Of course, he wants to talk to both prospective couples before making a decision, but I got the impression he was keen on keeping the children together."

"Oh, Adam . . ." Samantha clung hard to Adam's hand.

Adam smiled at her, reading the deep message beneath her simple utterance. This was real, they were hearing correctly, and by tomorrow—tomorrow!—their dream could very well come true. He laughed aloud to express his happiness. "See, Sammy? I told you things would work out. Didn't I tell you?"

Daniel cleared his throat. "Listen, you two. I don't want to throw cold water on your excitement, but let's try to not get carried away too soon. As I've said, the Vanderhavens are a very well-known and well-respected family in this town. The judge may not want to separate the children, but there's no guarantee he won't, based on the history of the other family and their ability to provide very well for the children. I will do everything in my power to get a decision in your favor, but I want you to be aware that there are no guarantees at this point. Do you understand?"

Samantha's bright smile faded, and her fingers dug into Adam's hand. Despite her obvious distress, Adam experienced a wave of peace that could only have been given by God. He faced his brother and spoke with conviction.

"Daniel, when we were here last, a doctor told us we would never have children. We were heartsick, but we had to accept it because it was something that couldn't be changed. But this time it's different. This time our dream can come true. Our desire to love and nurture children can be fulfilled, and I refuse to dash cold water on that flame of hope." He glanced at his wife, bolstered by her straight shoulders and the lift of her chin.

Admiration glowed in her eyes as she watched him. He continued. "Samantha and I both believe taking these children—all of them—into our home is the right thing to do for them, particularly with what they already have suffered, and we aren't going to let anyone—including the well-respected Vanderhavens—stand in our way. We have right on our side."

Daniel shook his head, a crooked smile lifting one side of his mouth. "You've certainly inherited the Klaassen determination, little brother."

"Yes, I have." Adam pointed at him. "And so have you. With us in this together—and with God going before us—we can't fail."

*S*amantha stood before the free-standing mirror in the corner of the same guestroom she and Adam had shared during their last visit with Daniel and Rose. She was focused intently on her reflection, having twisted her waist-length russet hair high and tight in a neat figure-eight at the back of her head. Although she had combed the sides back severely, the weight of the coil tugged it all downward, and a few strands struggled out from the pins. She'd fashioned this style for the court appearance, attempting to capture the essence of maturity. But the wispy tendrils of hair spiraling around her ears ruined the effect.

She surveyed her tidy ivory shirtwaist with its neat row of tucks and its simple string tie in a tiny bow at the back and the deeply pleated navy and brown watch-plaid skirt. The toes of her highly polished high-top shoes showed primly beneath the edge of the ankle-length skirt. Although her most mature-looking outfit, she shook her head at the school-girl reflection staring back at her. Young. Painfully young.

She spun on her heel and marched to her satchel, pawing through it until she located the watch pin David and Priscilla had given her for her birthday. She loved the gold filigree in the shape of a bow with its retractable watch hanging pendant-like beneath the bow. At least she possessed one pretty, very adult-looking piece of jewelry. She pinned it carefully just below her left shoulder, then hurried back to the mirror for another look.

Hands on hips, she frowned at her image. It would take more than a watch to make her look as mature as Mrs. Vanderhaven!

Unbidden, another image intruded—the shy, unprepossessing young woman who had helped Samantha pack all those months ago. Her eyes closed as she silently vowed to do everything she could for that woman's children, to keep them together and give them a secure, loving home. *Please, Lord,* she whispered once again.

The door creaked open, and there was Adam in his double-breasted suit of brown tweed, the crisp white cambric shirt she'd ironed once again this morning, and the deep brown and tan striped tie. He looked wonderful. *And so mature,* she noted with satisfaction. Her heart caught at the strength in his wide shoulders, the even, bold features. With his farmer's crow's feet from squinting into the sun, the smile lines from laughing and joking all the time, he looked every year of . . . of twenty-seven, his age. Samantha sighed.

"Are you about ready to go, Sammy?" He reached into his pocket for a handful of change, bouncing it idly in his palm.

"Do you think I should put my hair in a French twist?"

Adam was counting the coins, shifting them around with one finger. "Your hair is fine, honey."

"Adam! You didn't even look at my hair!"

Adam lifted his head, his eyebrows high. "Sorry, Sam, of course—I'd already seen it. I think it looks nice. Really nice."

She flapped a hand at him, then went seeking hairpins. "Oh, it looks nice, all right. It looks just wonderful—for a twenty-four-year-old. I need something more mature."

Adam pocketed the coins and stepped quickly to her side, pulling her hands away from her hairdo. "Samantha, you *are* a twenty-four-year-old woman, and that's surely no crime—at least that I'm aware of."

He tried to coax a smile from her, but she pursed her lips. This was not a time for teasing.

Adam fixed her with a steady look, gripping her shoulders. "You are a beautiful, bright, giving young woman, and I won't let you to pretend to be anything other than what you are for anyone." He brushed her cheek, adding, "Even for a judge."

Her frustrations melted at his support, though she still felt uncertainty. "But, Adam—"

"The Vanderhavens are no doubt older and richer, but that does not make them better," Adam insisted. "Actually, younger might be a lot better—we've got the energy to keep up with all of them, and the other couple will be a lot older when those two little ones get into their teen years. Now, I want you to stop your fretting, fetch your coat, and let's go to the courthouse before Daniel wonders what happened to us."

When she didn't move, Adam said, "Samantha, last night we put those children in the Lord's hands, didn't we?"

The question brought her up short. Heat flooded her cheeks. "Yes, we did."

"And you think He doesn't care about these children even more than we do?" She hadn't thought of that before, and paused to consider. She shook her head. *Of course He does.*

"And so you can trust Him to handle the situation?"

"Yes, Adam, I can. I'll get my coat."

 ⌒◯

Twenty minutes later Adam was escorting Samantha across the marble entry of the Minneapolis Courthouse. Samantha's heels clicked crisply against the smooth cream-colored marble, and she cringed at the intrusion in an otherwise rather formal, whispers-only environment. They paused in the middle of the two-story foyer, its twin-spindled staircases leading to double balconies above. Samantha was counting the doors that lined the balconies over her head when Adam tapped her on the arm.

Daniel was walking toward them from a hallway between the stairs. "Sam, Adam." He held out his hand in a formal manner, then gave Samantha a quick squeeze and kiss on the cheek. His arm around Samantha's shoulders, he began guiding them back down the hallway. "The Vanderhavens are here already, and the hearing will begin in about ten minutes. It will be simple—the judge will have each lawyer introduce the prospective parents and give brief background information. Then the judge may ask each adoptive couple a few questions." He gave Samantha an encouraging smile. "No reason to be nervous about any of it."

She tried for a smile herself, then said, "Easy for you to say, Daniel. But thanks."

Daniel stopped before the rich mahogany doors, released Samantha, and straightened his tie. He grinned at the pair. "Here we go." He turned the brass knob on the right, pushed it open, and motioned them inside.

Samantha stepped over the threshold and froze, awestruck by the beautifully appointed room. Beneath her feet, a highly varnished parquet oak floor shone like a mirror. Richly stained paneled walls boasted gilt-framed oil paintings centered within egg-and-dart trimmed insets. The ceiling repeated the floor's pattern, and a large brass-and-crystal chandelier hung from a brass-plated chain directly from the center of the soaring height. Spindle railings separated the judge's arena from the spectators' gleaming benches, and decorative carvings graced the ends. Although there were no windows in the large square room, evenly spaced electric lights in globes extending from the walls at shoulder height lit the area. Samantha had never seen a more beautiful room, and she felt totally out of place.

A murmur of voices caught her attention. Three people—two men and one woman—sat at a table on the far side of the railing at the front and visited with the judge who sat on a raised platform behind a tall, paneled desk of mahogany. He leaned on its top with his arms crossed, chuckling at something one of the men had just said. His gaze shifted to the doorway, and a smile broke across his face. "Ah, Mr. Klaassen. You're here. Come on in.—You know the procedure."

Samantha flicked a startled glance at Adam, then Daniel. She would have expected stiff formality and perhaps an amount of sternness in a room such as this. The judge's friendly, casual bearing didn't seem to fit any better than she did.

Daniel put his hand under Samantha's arm and propelled her forward, Adam trailing them. They paused at the second table in the front. "Judge Simmons, this is Adam and Samantha Klaassen from Mountain Lake." Daniel said, with a nod at the judge, then at the two.

The judge nodded back, smiling widely enough to show a gold tooth. "Mr. and Mrs. Klaassen," he acknowledged, then gestured to the table on the opposite side of the tall desk. "Lester, introduce everyone at your table, please."

A small, wiry man rose and squared his shoulders. With a confident sweep of his hand, he indicated the well-dressed, early-forties' couple who remained seated. "Mr. and Mrs. Klaassen, may I present Dr. and Mrs. Herbert Vanderhaven of Minneapolis."

"It's a pleasure to meet you," Adam said confidently. Samantha, unable to peel her tongue off the roof of her dry mouth, offered a tentative smile.

"Likewise," Mr. Vanderhaven responded with a slight nod. Mrs. Vanderhaven bobbed her head, then turned her attention back to the judge.

"All right, everyone, sit down, sit down." Judge Simmons reached into his breast pocket and withdrew a pair of wire-rimmed spectacles. He snatched up a file from the corner of his desk and rustled through the contents as he continued, "We all know why we're here this morning. Both the Klaassens and the Vanderhavens"—he acknowledged each couple as their names were pronounced—"are petitioning to adopt the orphaned McIntyre children." He pulled a sheet from the file with a satisfied "ah!" Holding the paper at arm's length, he read as if by rote, "Lucille Elizabeth McIntyre, age six; Henry Rollin McIntyre, Jr., age five; William Everett McIntyre, age twenty-nine months; and Ellen Marie McIntyre, age three and half months."

Samantha listened eagerly to this brief snippet of information, mulling over the names and ages. Adam glanced over at Samantha with a little smile.

The judge dropped the paper on the desk, interlaced his fingers on top of it, and addressed the Vanderhavens' lawyer, "Do I understand that Dr. and Mrs. Vanderhaven are expressing interest in adopting William Everett and Ellen Marie McIntyre?"

Lester nodded briskly as he stood to his feet. "That is correct, Your Honor."

"Fine, fine, but please let's just stay seated, or you'll all be worn out before we're finished in here, Lester," Judge Simmons said.

Samantha's eyes got wide, then she swallowed a grin at the judge's informal manner.

The judge now turned to Daniel. "And the Klaassens are expressing interest in the older two children?"

Samantha sat up straight, her heart pattering. Beside her, Adam also gave a start. They looked at each other and then at Daniel. He started to rise, then apparently thought better of it. "No, sir," he said quickly. "No, Mr. and Mrs. Klaassen are petitioning to adopt all four of the McIntyre children. They wish to keep these children together in the same home. . . ." His voice trailed off.

Judge Simmons turned his attention to Adam and Samantha, looking steadily at them through his round spectacles. "Mm-hmm," he murmured to himself. He examined the paper again for a few minutes.

With the judge focused on the contents of his file, Samantha sneaked a glance at the Vanderhavens. The woman was dressed in an impeccably styled navy blue velvet suit, and the jabot of her white silk blouse lay in a perfect flurry of ruffles across her bodice. Her hair, in a sleek French knot, was set off with a matching navy velvet cloche in the latest fashion. She wore a choker of pearls with an opal and sapphire pendant, matching opal and sapphire clusters dangling from her ears. Her attire undeniably spoke of elegance and wealth, culture and good breeding.

Samantha, with her simple outfit and youthful face, couldn't help remember the children's fable she'd just read to her niece, Laura Beth—about the city mouse and its country cousin coming for a visit. . . .

She gave her head a single shake and turned her attention back to the judge in time to see him lift his head.

He cleared his throat and set the paper aside. "Very well, then. Let's proceed."

*H*ere we go. . . . Adam fidgeted in his seat as Lester rose, swept his hand through his hair, then extended a palm toward the couple seated at his table. "Dr. and Mrs. Vanderhaven, as you well know, are respected members of the community. Dr. Vanderhaven has been in medical practice for almost twenty years, earning a reputation as a fine physician as well as a caring humanitarian. He and Mrs. Vanderhaven both donate extensive time and not a small amount of financial support to various charities."

He went on to describe their lengthy list of philanthropic endeavors, as well as their spacious home in one of the finest neighborhoods in the city. "You will find letters of reference in their file from many community leaders who verify their kindness and generosity, as well as their ability to more than provide financially for the McIntyre children."

The judge sat with one hand propping his chin as the Vanderhavens' lawyer spoke on their behalf. He raised a hand. "May I ask a question?"

"Certainly," Lester replied.

"Dr. and Mrs. Vanderhaven, I reviewed your file earlier today and took note of your—shall we say—impressive financial position. It seems as if you would have the means to support all of the children. I'm wondering, then, your reasons for choosing to adopt only the two youngest."

Samantha groped for Adam's hand, and he clutched it. Was the judge reluctant to separate the children? His question seemed to indicate so.

Lester began, "Well, Your Honor—"

"Excuse me," Judge Simmons interrupted, "I really would prefer to hear from Dr. or Mrs. Vanderhaven."

Dr. Vanderhaven pushed back his chair and stood, looking rather regal in his carefully tailored three-piece suit, tie, and matching three-point pocket square. "Your Honor, my wife and I have three children at home," he began in a deep, cultured voice. "Our oldest, Nathaniel, is fourteen years of age, Rachel is eleven, and Michael is nearly ten. We believe that adopting four additional children would put an undue strain on our financial budget, but even more importantly, this larger intrusion on our family would be difficult for our natural children to accept.

"I think you'll notice in our paperwork that originally we had only planned to adopt the infant. After some consideration and juggling of figures, we decided perhaps we could make room for the next youngest as well. While we realize this may create some temporary unhappiness on the part of the older two siblings, we also believe they will have a better chance of being adopted if there are fewer than four children involved in the undertaking. Assuming the care and upbringing of four children would be a tremendous responsibility for any family, especially ours since we already have three of our own."

"And your reason for selecting the youngest two?" the judge pressed.

Now Mrs. Vanderhaven responded, remaining seated. "That was my decision, Your Honor. As my husband pointed out, although our own children are far from grown, they are well on their way to adulthood. I greatly miss having a baby in the house. And, in all honesty, I feel it will be much easier to bond with an infant than with a child who has strong memories of another mother."

After listening to the Vanderhavens' refined speech and comfortable manner, Adam wondered if he'd have the courage to open his mouth during the proceedings. But he took a deep breath and told himself it wasn't about social standing, this was about four youngsters who needed love and each other far more than money and the right address.

"Thank you, Mrs. Vanderhaven, I appreciate your honesty." Judge Simmons removed his glasses, massaged the bridge of his nose briefly, then turned to Daniel. "Mr. Klaassen, the floor is yours."

"Thank you, sir." Daniel sat in his chair with a comfortable ease that further soothed the edges of Adam's nerves. "Your Honor, Adam and Samantha Klaassen cannot boast of high-paying positions or membership in clubs or organizations. They are a farm couple from Mountain Lake, Minnesota, where the only 'clubhouse' to which they can belong is the community church—and there they are members in good standing."

The judge chuckled and nodded, further relaxing Adam, and Daniel went on. "Adam and Samantha have been married for five and a half years. Adam is a wheat farmer, making his living on land that has been in the Klaassen family for half a century. His income, although certainly not extensive, is adequate to meet the needs of the children, should adoption be granted. They own their home, which was built two years ago by Adam with help from his family. It has four bedrooms, thus ample room for the children. I'm sure one of your questions to the Klaassens will be why a young couple wants to adopt four children."

The judge nodded, and Adam could see Lester and the Vanderhavens turn as one to look at him and Samantha.

"You see, Your Honor, Adam and Samantha both desire a large family. Adam is one of nine children. Samantha was raised almost as a single child, as her only brother was not in the home most of her growing up years. For different reasons, each looked forward to raising many children. But due to injuries sustained as a child, Samantha is unable to bear children. Thus they are interested in adoption—this group of four children in particular. I might add they met Esther, the mother of the McIntyre children, briefly on a previous visit to Minneapolis. Upon hearing of the death of both Esther and Henry McIntyre, they felt immediate and deep sympathy for the children."

Samantha's fingers clamped hard on Adam's, and he gave a reassuring squeeze. "Adopting the children would serve two purposes," Daniel continued in an easy manner. "Not only would it fulfill their desire to have a family, it would also provide a home where the children could stay together. Mrs. Klaassen, especially, feels strongly that this would be best for these children."

The judge aimed his gaze at Samantha. "Mrs. Klaassen, Daniel has indicated you have a strong belief that the children remain together, is that right?"

Samantha's hand began to tremble within Adam's. "Y-yes, sir."

"Is there a particular reason this is important to you?"

Samantha looked to Adam, and he offered an encouraging smile. Samantha took a deep breath and pushed to her feet, her hand still gripped in Adam's. "Your Honor, when I was a little girl, my older brother left home for . . . personal reasons. We were out of contact for eight years. I spent every day of those eight years wondering where he was, how he was, if I'd ever see him again. . . ." She paused, swallowing. "I wouldn't wish such heartache on any child. I realize the baby girl and the littlest boy probably won't remember their older brother and sister if they're separated now, because they're quite young. But the older boy and girl, Lucille and Henry, will certainly always remember they have a little brother and baby sister someplace. My memories from the age of six are very strong. I can't imagine Lucille's would be less."

The judge's head was angled so the lights reflected from his spectacles. Adam wished he could see his eyes and know what he was thinking.

Samantha finished meekly, her voice nearly a whisper, "They've already lost their mother and father. It hardly seems fair that they should lose one another too." She slowly sat down, her heart beating like it would leap out of her chest.

The judge nodded and turned his attention back to his papers. The group maintained a respectful silence as the gray-haired man on the platform withdrew into private thought.

A pendulum clock on the wall counted minutes while the judge rustled through the papers before him, tapped his nose thoughtfully, and made little sounds like "mm-hmm," and "ah-ha." Adam glanced around, inwardly praying for favor. Samantha's face was pale and her fingers gripped his hand so tightly the nails cut into his flesh. Daniel, apparently accustomed to such proceedings, leaned back in his chair, crossed an ankle over the opposite knee, and waited.

At the other table, Lester took a pose similar to Daniel's. Adam saw Dr. Vanderhaven lean and whisper something in his wife's ear, and she turned to look at Samantha, then whispered something back.

At long last the judge stacked the papers together, slapped them into a brown folder, and set them aside. He pulled off his spectacles and cleared his throat. Time seemed to still in spite of the clock's relentless ticktock, ticktock. Adam held his breath, aware that the judge's next words would affect them— all of them, both the Klaassens and the Vanderhavens—for the rest of their lives.

"I don't want you folks to think the decision I'm about to announce is made lightly. I spent a great deal of time last evening looking over the information in this file"—he tapped it with his spectacles—"and today's hearing was mainly to give me a chance to put faces to the names in here." He leaned forward. "I can see for myself that both of you are fine couples, and both have a lot to offer the children in question."

Turning to the Vanderhavens, he said, "Dr. and Mrs. Vanderhaven, I have no doubt you would care very well for the children. You have the means to support them and provide many privileges to which others are not privy. Since you've already raised three children, I'm sure you have the know-how to raise two more."

He turned his attention to Adam and Samantha. "Mr. and Mrs. Klaassen, I appreciate your convictions in wanting the children to remain together. I can see that you sincerely want what's best for those youngsters. Farming is honest work, and you would surely meet the needs of the children in that vocation." Adam tried to follow the judge's choice of verb tenses, but he could make out nothing firm from what he was hearing.

Beside him Samantha trembled so that the little watch pinned at her shoulder quivered. Tossing aside any concerns about court protocol, Adam slipped his arm around her shoulders and held tight.

Judge Simmons sighed. "What I have here are two fine couples both willing to assume responsibility for someone else's children, children who have been tragically orphaned. My first priority is to do what is best for the children, but I also am thinking of you folks, as well." He linked his fingers and leaned his elbows on the desk, looking fully at Samantha and Adam. Adam detected a hint of sympathy in his eyes, and dread settled over him.

"Mr. and Mrs. Klaassen, let me assure you I have the greatest admiration and respect for you. You've come a long distance to indicate a heartfelt concern for the children of a woman you met only briefly. Not many people would have such caring. You are to be commended. But I would be less than honest if I said I had no reservations. For one thing, you are quite young and, although it's certainly no fault of your own, you have no parenting experience."

Adam's pulse pounded in his ears. No, oh, *please, no* . . . Samantha pressed her fist to her lips.

The judge spoke softly, apologetically, yet firmly. "Taking on four children would be, as Dr. Vanderhaven stated earlier, quite an undertaking for even an experienced parent. For two young adults . . . well, I want you to understand I'm not finding fault with you personally. I think you're fine people, and I'm sure in a few more years you'll be ready for the large family you both want. I'm just not sure you're ready for it now. Therefore, I cannot, in good conscience, grant you custody of four children. I could, however, consider allowing you to assume custody of two of the children. If you are willing, I would like to speak to you following the hearing about the possibility of your adopting the older two McIntyre children."

Samantha ducked her head, and Adam offered the judge a weak nod in acknowledgment.

The judge returned his spectacles to his nose. "Dr. and Mrs. Vanderhaven," he said, peering over the top of his eyewear, "I am granting you custody of William Everett and Ellen Marie McIntyre. I will instruct the authorities at the Foundling Home to expect you next Monday morning by nine a.m."

Dr. Vanderhaven rose. "Thank you very much, Your Honor."

Samantha lurched to her feet. "Your Honor?"

Everyone swung startled gazes in her direction. Adam started to rise, but Daniel caught his arm and held him in place. Samantha braced her hands against the wooden tabletop and aimed her tear-stained face at the judge. "Your Honor, I'm not trying to tell you your job. I'm just the wife of a farmer, and I haven't had that much schooling. But, sir, I don't understand how you can make a decision that will hurt those children for the rest of their lives."

The Vanderhavens' lawyer leaped up. "Now, Mrs. Klaassen, we know you're disappointed, but—"

Judge Simmons held up his hand. "Hush, Lester. Let the lady talk."

Samantha's body quivered and her head drooped—from heartfelt conviction or simply nervousness, Adam wasn't sure. But pride in her swelled as she lifted her head and again addressed the man behind the desk. "I never knew my mother. And my father was . . ." She hesitated, and Adam placed a hand over hers. After a grateful smile to him, she continued. "My father was less than loving. My great-grandmother lived with us and did a wonderful job as surrogate mother, but she died when I was six. After that, the only person I really had to depend on was my brother, David. But as I told you earlier, he had to leave home, and I didn't know where he was for a very long time.

"I can't describe how much the loss of my brother affected me. If I'd had a loving parent, perhaps David's leaving wouldn't have been so hard. But he was all I had, and when he was gone, my whole world was turned upside down. Right now, all Lucille, Henry, little William, and baby Ellen Marie have is each other. I'm not trying to take anything away from the Vanderhavens— I'm sure they're good people, and they have valid reasons for not taking all of them. But, Your Honor, taking the little ones away from the older ones is bound to be hurtful. Haven't they already been hurt enough? Even if you don't let us adopt them, at least give them a chance to stay together with another family. Maybe the Vanderhavens will change their minds and take . . ."

She stopped, glancing around at her audience. Adam's gaze followed hers across the faces, noting the various reactions to her impassioned plea. Daniel's eyes reflected admiration; the judge hid whatever he was thinking behind his spectacles; Lester's face wore an expression of disdain; and the Vanderhavens stared straight ahead, seemingly oblivious to her pleas.

"I'm sorry, sir, if I was impertinent." Samantha bit down on her lower lip, lowering her chin.

"You were not impertinent." At the judge's kind tone, Samantha looked at him. "There's no law against a person speaking her mind. But I will tell you I've made a decision based on my own strong feelings of what is best for all concerned."

Samantha nodded and sank into her chair, her shoulders slumped. Adam put an arm around her again, and she leaned into his embrace.

"Dr. and Mrs. Vanderhaven, you are free to leave," Judge Simmons said. The Vanderhavens thanked him in solemn tones before preceding Lester to the double doors. Adam watched them go, his chest aching. When they reached the doors, Mrs. Vanderhaven paused to look back at Samantha. Adam blinked, puzzled—what did the woman's pained expression mean? She'd won. She should look thrilled. Her husband ushered her out the door, and the judge began speaking again. Adam turned his attention forward.

"Mr. and Mrs. Klaassen, would you be willing to consider adopting Lucille and Henry, Jr.?"

The consolation prize? He pushed the cynical thought aside. Any child was a gift, and he would welcome it. "Yes, sir, but we would like a chance to discuss it. Could Daniel—Mr. Klaassen contact you some time tomorrow?"

"That would be fine. I'll look for you tomorrow, Daniel." Then to Samantha and Adam he added, "It was nice meeting both of you. I'm sorry I couldn't grant your request."

Adam held Samantha's arm, and they followed Daniel to the hallway. Outside the courtroom, Daniel expelled his breath and said, "I'm sorry, you two. I wish—"

"It's not your fault, Daniel." Adam put a hand on his brother's shoulder. "You did your best."

Samantha lifted a pale face to Adam. "Adam, what are we going to do?"

Adam pulled her against his side. "We're going to take Lucille and Henry, Jr., home and do our best to make them happy. We can't just leave them, can we?"

Samantha shook her head. "No, we can't just leave them here. I just hope . . ."

"What?" Daniel prompted.

She sighed. "I hope we can be enough to replace what they will lose."

ose picked at the food on her plate. She'd prepared a fine meal, hoping it would be a celebratory supper. But everyone's sad countenance cast a pall over the meal. Christina, Katrina, and Camelia, young as they were, seemed to sense the melancholy mood of the grown-ups and curbed their usual dinnertime chatter. When the girls finished their meal and had been excused, Rose spoke the words that had hovered in her mind since Daniel had taken her aside and shared the outcome of the court visit.

"Adam and Samantha, I am so sorry I sent you that letter."

Adam's head came up, and Samantha's jaw dropped. Samantha asked, "Why would you be sorry?"

Rose confessed, "I knew if I wrote to you, you'd come for those children. And that's precisely what I intended. If only I had talked to Daniel first, I would have known the Vanderhavens had petitioned for the two younger ones, and I could have saved you a lot of heartache. I am so very sorry I dragged you into this mess." Tears stung her eyes.

Adam swiped a napkin across his mouth, shaking his head. "Don't apologize, Rose. And we don't see this situation as a mess. Of course, Samantha and I are disappointed that the judge has chosen to separate the children, but we are going home with a son and daughter. That's a reason for rejoicing."

"Then why are we all sitting here with glum faces?" Rose asked, lifting her shoulders in a shrug.

Samantha grimaced. "I'll tell you why. I feel guilty. The minute I got your letter, my heart told me to come after those children. But my stubborn pride held me back. If I had asked Adam immediately instead of waiting—"

"Sam, I felt the same way about them, but I didn't say anything right away either," Adam said. "So don't feel guilty for not bringing it up sooner. I could have spoken up just as easily as you."

Daniel waved a hand at them all. "I'm not sure even if you had petitioned earlier the outcome would have been any different. After all, the judge felt you were too young and inexperienced to take on four children at once."

So it was back to Rose again. She sighed. "I still feel I should have kept the information to myself."

Samantha rose and began clearing dishes. "I'm not worried about myself right now. What concerns me most is how Lucille and Henry are going to feel when we take them away from their baby brother and sister." She paused, gazing out the window onto the snow-covered side yard.

Adam crossed to Samantha and wrapped his arms around her. "Sammy, somehow we'll help Lucille and Henry understand. It may be hard for them at first, but they're young. In time, with love and patience, they'll adjust."

Samantha looked up. "Will they, Adam? I never did. I missed David every day of every year that he was away from me. I never stopped wishing he was close to me. I know how it feels, and I'm not sure it's something you ever adjust to."

Rose sent Daniel a helpless look. Samantha's anguished tone cut at her heart. No matter what anyone said, she'd played a leading role in this drama, and now she only wanted to make things right. But *how*? She beseeched Daniel with her eyes, however he only shrugged in reply. Her heart sank even further. There was no solution.

Adam said, "We aren't miracle workers, Sammy. All we can do is our best. That's all any parents can do. I don't know how many times I've heard Ma say, you do the best with what you've been given and pray it will be enough."

Rose hurried around the table to her brother- and sister-in-law. "I'm sure Lucy and Henry will be upset that they must leave Will and Ellen Marie behind. But"—she hesitated, wondering if sharing her deepest concern would do more harm than good—"more than that, they no doubt know the Vanderhavens didn't ask for them. They must be feeling very unwanted and insecure right now."

Samantha turned from Adam's embrace. "I'll make sure they know they are very wanted by us. They'll never have to question that." Her voice held conviction.

Adam nodded. "That's right. We may not be able to do anything about the separation from their little brother and sister, but we can make sure they feel secure and loved."

"Well!" Rose clapped her hands together, determined to turn this evening into a happy occasion. "Right now, Samantha, you and I are going upstairs to sort through Christie and Katie's outgrown clothes. I'm sure there are some things in there your Lucy can use."

A smile lifted Samantha's lips. "My Lucy . . ." She closed her eyes for a moment, seeming to savor the words. Then she opened them with a hesitant expression. "But, Rose, shouldn't you hang on to those things for Cami?"

"Nonsense." Rose took hold of Samantha's elbow and aimed her for the stairs. "By the time Cami grows into them, they will be hopelessly out of style. Styles do change, you know! So let's just leave the dishes until later and go have some fun."

Adam let out a huff of laughter. "Go on, Sammy. And maybe by the time you two come back down, the Good Fairy will have visited and taken care of this mess."

"Sounds like you're volunteering my services too, brother," Daniel said, rolling his eyes. "Well, let's get to work," he added, rolling up his sleeves.

Samantha giggled, making Rose smile too. The two women went up to the little room tucked under the eaves where they spent a cheerful half hour digging through the attic trunks. Samantha chose two nightgowns, underclothes, and a pair of black patent slippers with a tiny strap that buttoned across the instep.

"Are you sure you want to part with these dresses?" Samantha held up a sweet frilly frock of dotted Swiss.

"Please, take them." Rose added it to the stack of calico dresses and ruffled pinafores. "These will be perfect for Lucy to wear to school. And as I said, it will be a long time before Cami can wear them anyway." Samantha still looked doubtful, so Rose leaned forward and patted her arm. "If it makes you feel better you can always ship them back when Lucy outgrows them."

"That's true," Samantha mused, smoothing a hand across the row of lace ruffles on the pale pink dotted Swiss dress. "This one will be Lucy's church dress, and I'll put her hair in pin curls like Christie and Katie's."

Rose smiled, delighted to see Samantha making plans for her daughter. She reached the bottom half of the large trunk, and her breath caught. "Oh, Sammy, look. I'd forgotten about this."

Samantha gasped and reached to take the baby gown from Rose's hands. She traced one finger across the embroidered roses dancing across the unbelievably small bodice and tapped each pea-sized pearl button. A tiny white satin bow graced the neckline. Samantha fingered the bow, her expression wistful.

"Oh, Rose, this is so soft and sweet. It says, in the most innocent of ways, *baby.*"

Rose accepted the gown from Samantha's outstretched hands. Memories of her girls as infants, clean and powdered after a bath, flooded her. She impulsively pressed the gown to her face, burying her nose in the little garment. Only the smells of cedar that lined the trunk and mothballs that Rose used to discourage insects hung in the folds of the fabric, but she imagined she caught the scent of baby powder. She lowered the gown to her lap and shifted her gaze to Samantha. Rose could see the tears shimmering in her sister-in-law's eyes.

"Rose . . . will I ever have my own little baby?"

Pain stabbed at Rose's heart. How could she have been so unthinking . . . again? She set the gown aside and captured both of Samantha's hands and squeezed—hard. "You will, Sam. Daniel might not have told you this yet, but once you adopt through the courts, your name stays on record. If you decide later to adopt another child, it is simply a matter of paperwork, because you've already been approved by the court. You know Daniel will keep his ears open for news of any babies who need a family and will contact you at once. Give yourselves time to settle Lucy and Henry into your home, then come back and try again. You'll have a baby someday, Sam. I just know it."

Samantha nodded, her throat convulsing. "I'm sure you're right. . . ."

"Rose? Samantha?" From downstairs, Daniel's voice interrupted. "Would you two come here, please?"

The women brushed away their tears, set the clothes aside, and descended the narrow attic stairs to the landing. Daniel stood at the foot of the stairs looking upward with an unreadable expression on his face. "There's someone here who wants to speak with Samantha."

Samantha looked at Rose, but she just shrugged. Samantha and Adam didn't know anyone else in Minneapolis. Samantha headed down the stairs first, pausing when she reached the bottom. Daniel gestured toward the parlor.

Samantha came up short right inside the parlor's arched doorway. Seated on the settee was none other than Dr. and Mrs. Vanderhaven.

∽◯

Samantha froze in place, uncertain what to say or do. Her gaze found Adam, who sat on the edge of a side chair nearby. His face reflected the bewilderment she felt.

The doctor rose, holding out a hand as if he were host. "Please, Mrs. Klaassen, come in."

Hesitantly Samantha entered, and settled herself in a Queen Anne chair near Adam. He stretched his hand across the small table between the matching chairs, and she clasped it. *Lord, whatever this is, please help us. . . .*

Dr. Vanderhaven sat back down as his wife angled herself to face Samantha. "Mrs. Klaassen, I have spent the entire afternoon thinking of you. What you said in the courtroom earlier today, concerning your own troubled childhood. . . . I must say, your words were quite . . . well, quite upsetting to me."

Samantha glanced uncertainly at Adam before answering. "I didn't intend to upset anyone. I apologize, Mrs. Vanderhaven."

"Don't apologize, please." The older woman twisted a pair of kidskin gloves in her hands. "Your heartfelt speech made me look at things from a quite different perspective than I had before. You see, my husband and I are accustomed to getting whatever it is we want or need. We have been blessed in many ways—perhaps too blessed," she added, glancing briefly at her husband. "It's been too easy for us to lose sight of what others want and need."

Samantha nodded, but she didn't know what to say. Surely the couple hadn't come across town on this snowy night just to say that her words had touched them. She sat silently, holding Adam's hand as if it were a lifeline, waiting for the other woman to continue.

"Herbert and I have been talking, and—" Her shoulders pulled up, and a single sob broke out. Her husband pulled a handkerchief from his pocket and offered it to her, putting an arm around her shoulders and patting her gently. She held the handkerchief to her lips. "I'm sorry, I was determined not to break down like this."

Sympathy rolled through Samantha's breast. "It's all right, Mrs. Vanderhaven."

She shook her head, speaking through her tears. "No, Mrs. Klaassen, it is not all right. What my husband and I have intended to do is most certainly not all right—not for the McIntyre children."

Samantha's heart began thumping. She could feel the pressure of Adam's hand on her own increase.

Dr. Vanderhaven spoke. "Mr. and Mrs. Klaassen, my wife and I have planned for several years to adopt a baby. It had always been our intention that when our own children were of an age to be somewhat self-sufficient, we would open our home and hearts to an unwanted baby. We firmly believed we would be giving a secure home to a child who would otherwise grow up alone and unloved. When we petitioned the courts to adopt the McIntyre baby and toddler, we honestly felt we were doing the right thing. Neither Lorraine nor I believed anyone would be willing to take on four children at once. We truly felt that by separating the children, we were giving the older two a better chance at finding a suitable home. I hope you will believe that."

The man's tone and expression left no doubt in Samantha's mind concerning his sincerity. Not to mention the tears of anguish that continued to roll silently down Mrs. Vanderhaven's pale cheeks.

Adam said, "We understand, Dr. Vanderhaven. Samantha and I hold no ill feelings toward you or your wife." Samantha swallowed and nodded her agreement.

The doctor offered a grateful smile before continuing. "Now that we've had time to see things, as it were, from a different perspective, we have had a change of heart." He paused, taking in a shuddering breath. "We have concluded that we cannot in good conscience separate the children."

Mrs. Vanderhaven added, "It would be cruel to ask them to grow up apart from one another. Even our own children substantiated it for us when we asked their feelings on the matter. As much as I want the baby, I just can't—" She stopped again, her face crumpling. She lifted the handkerchief to cover her mouth.

Dr. Vanderhaven put a bolstering arm around his wife's shaking frame. "We have withdrawn our request for adoption of William and Ellen Marie."

Samantha's heart lifted wildly in her chest. But then just as quickly she remembered the judge's words—he could not grant custody of four children to a young, inexperienced couple. The children would be separated anyway if she and Adam were to go through with the adoption of Lucy and Henry, Jr. Her spirits sank once more and her stomach whirled as if she'd just ridden a tornado. She'd gone from hoping for four children, to fearing they'd be given no children, to being granted two children, and then back again to no children, all in the space of one day.

She pressed her palms to her quivering belly, willing the fearful churning to calm.

Adam spoke softly, as if reading Samantha's thoughts. "Then the children must remain at the Foundling Home until another family is willing to take all four is found."

"No, Mr. Klaassen, you misunderstand." Dr. Vanderhaven looked from Adam to Samantha. He patted his wife once more, waited for her nod of approval, then said, "Lorraine and I visited with Judge Simmons at his home before coming here this evening. We withdrew our petition only on the condition that all four children remain together in your custody. After seeing you in court and hearing your expressions on their behalf, we truly felt, despite your young years, you could best provide the kind of home the children will need. Judge Simmons agreed to a six-month probationary period, after which a simple hearing will take place. If all has gone well, final adoption will be filed." He paused, looking as if he'd overstepped his boundaries. He added hesitantly, "That is, if you are still interested in adopting all four children."

Samantha was out of her chair and halfway across the room before she was aware she had moved. She held both hands out to the other couple. "Oh, Dr. and Mrs. Vanderhaven, yes, yes, we're interested. It's what we prayed for all along!"

Adam was beside Samantha in an instant and placed his arm around her waist. "We don't know how to thank you."

Mrs. Vanderhaven looked up, her eyes still shimmering with tears. "Take good care of those children. Love them. You will, won't you?"

Samantha took the older woman's hand and squeezed it. "I promise you, we will love them as our own."

Mrs. Vanderhaven nodded, drew in a great breath, and rose. She lifted her chin, taking on the regal bearing she'd carried in the courtroom. "Purchasing clothing and furniture for four children will take a substantial amount. I had already secured several items for the two youngest children. I want you to take them." Samantha opened her mouth to protest, but the other woman held up her hand. "I would consider it an honor to contribute toward the children's new beginning with you. Please allow me this small pleasure."

Samantha, in her usual way, looked at Adam, and he smiled his assent. She turned to Mrs. Vanderhaven. "Thank you, ma'am. We appreciate very much your generosity. For everything."

Dr. Vanderhaven stepped forward. "I am sure you will have your hands full on the train handling the children, so we will have the items shipped to your home. Will that meet with your approval?"

"That would be fine," Adam said. "Thank you."

The four of them stood in the center of the room, uncertain of what to do next. Then Samantha impulsively took one step toward Mrs. Vanderhaven and opened her arms. The other woman had moved, too, and they found themselves sharing a brief embrace. In that moment, as Mrs. Vanderhaven clung unashamedly to her, Samantha recognized the amount of love it took for Mrs. Vanderhaven to let go of the baby she truly wanted and entrust the child into Samantha's hands.

As they stepped back, Samantha said, "When Ellen Marie and Will are old enough, I'll show them the things you bought for them and tell them how much they were wanted by another mother."

Mrs. Vanderhaven touched Samantha's cheek and offered a quavering smile.

The doctor said, "The papers must be signed at the courthouse Monday morning, and then you will pick up the children. I'm sure Mr. Klaassen—" he turned to Daniel, standing with Rose near the door, "—will be able to help you through those details."

"Yes, sir," Adam said, his voice full of excitement. "We'll be there."

"Very well then. Good evening." The doctor took his wife's arm and guided her toward the door. The instant the door closed on the couple, Adam swept Samantha off her feet in a rib-crushing hug and swung her around.

"Thank You, Lord!" Samantha rejoiced, holding to Adam's neck. She laughed and cried at once. Her dreams had come true.

*T*he Vanderhavens' amazing visit occurred on Friday evening. Adam and Samantha couldn't pick up the children until Monday morning. The weekend stretched endlessly before them. They made good use of the time—and Daniel's telephone—first, with calls home to tell the family the wonderfully good news. They also began the search for simple furnishings to fill the long-empty bedrooms at their home.

Si and Laura promised to haul Daniel and Frank's old iron bed over for the two boys to share. Laura's voice trembled just a bit over the telephone when she told Adam of her joy at "getting four more grandchildren all in one swoop!" Priscilla told them her parents had a maple bed and dresser Lucy could use. Jake and Liz offered the loan of a cradle, and Becky and Teddy volunteered to round up a supply of used toys from the various children in the family.

Hulda and Hiram too were overjoyed when they heard the news, and immediately they insisted on providing rugs for each of the bedrooms, including the master bedroom. Frank said he'd burn the midnight oil and make toy boxes for the children's belongings. Stephen and Josie thought there was an old bureau in the attic at Stephen's brother's place—if so, they'd bring it over for the boys' room.

So getting the home ready for the children became a group effort. And even though Samantha and Adam were miles from home, they heard that the rooms for their children were taking shape. Their excitement mounted ever higher with each tick of the clock drawing them closer to the moment of meeting—the moment of culminating their dreams of a family of their own.

On Monday morning, Rose prodded, "Samantha, please, you must eat something."

Adam glanced up from his own breakfast. Sure enough, her plate was still untouched. Samantha held her fork, but instead of carrying food to her mouth, she only used it to push the scrambled eggs, bacon, and fried potatoes back and forth.

"I can't eat." Samantha put down her fork with a shaking hand. "I feel as if there are bats flying around in my stomach. There's no room for food."

Katrina gazed, astonished. "You have bats in your tummy, Auntie Sam? How'd they get there?"

Christina rolled her eyes and nudged her sister none too gently. "Auntie Sam just means she's nervous."

Katrina looked to Samantha. "Is that true? You're nervous?"

Samantha nodded, a hand against her belly. "Yes, sweetheart, that's exactly what I mean."

Katrina sighed with relief. "Whew! I'm glad you don't really have bats in your belly. That would be a very bad thing!" She turned to Daniel. "Daddy, would having bats in your belly be as bad as bats in your belfry?"

Daniel sputtered on his coffee.

"Well, 'member you said Mr. Rooney down the street had bats in—"

Rose exclaimed, "Oh, Katie!" while adults burst into laughter.

"What's wrong?" Katrina looked at them in confusion.

"Never mind." Daniel shook his head. "Just finish up so we can get you off to school."

Katrina shrugged, obviously thinking, *Grown-ups!*, and dug into her scrambled eggs. But she'd barely taken two bites before she turned to Samantha again. "Auntie Sam, why are you nervous?"

Samantha brushed Katrina's bangs to the side with one finger. "Today is the day Uncle Adam and I meet the children we are going to adopt."

The little girl wrinkled her nose. "But I thought you *want* to meet them."

Adam tried to explain. "We do want to meet them, Katie, but it's kind of like going to school the first day. It's very exciting to begin something new, but at the same time it makes your tummy feel funny because you don't know just what to expect."

Katrina looked thoughtful. "Yeah, I guess that makes sense," she finally conceded. "But, Uncle Adam, don't worry. You're just meeting four little kids, and when I went to school there was lots more kids than that. I did okay, and you will too."

"Thank you for the words of encouragement, Miss Katie," Adam said, his lips twitching. "I'm sure Auntie Sam and I will be just fine, like you said."

Samantha, still chuckling, picked up her fork and went to work on her own breakfast.

⌒◯

Promptly at nine o'clock Samantha and Adam stood before Judge Simmons in his office—which Daniel called his chambers—and signed the papers that gave them temporary custody of Lucy, Henry, Will, and Ellen Marie McIntyre.

Adam pressed the pen so hard a spurt of ink shot above the first letter in his name. When Samantha took the pen, her hand shook so badly the signature was barely recognizable. But it didn't matter—the signatures, made in front of the judge and a witness, Daniel, were legally binding. They were officially embarking on their voyage as Mother and Father.

"Now, Mr. and Mrs. Klaassen," Judge Simmons told them, slipping his spectacles off and smiling, first at one, then the other, "Daniel will accompany you to the Foundling Home. The nuns were informed that you'd be coming, and they will have the children ready. Just give them this"—he handed Adam a brown envelope—"and then you will be free to take the children. In six months' time, we will meet here a second time. If all has gone well, at that time we will complete the necessary paperwork to make the adoption final."

Samantha pressed two trembling hands against her ribs and beamed at Adam. He returned the smile with one equally brilliant, then turned to Judge Simmons. Adam shook the judge's hand. "Thank you very much, Your Honor."

"Yes, thank you," Samantha seconded, placing her hand on Adam's arm. "We appreciate very much your concern for the children. You have our word that we will do our very best for them."

"Good luck to both of you," the older man said.

Samantha smiled. "We don't need luck, sir. We have God's blessings, and that's better than any amount of luck. We'll see you in six months."

She walked out of the judge's chambers with an eager, confident step. But then when they reached the rock-paved walkway leading to the doors of the Minneapolis Foundling Home, suddenly a wave of something she couldn't identify—panic? nervousness? apprehension?—struck. Samantha slowed down and pulled on Adam's arm.

"Sammy, what is it?" Adam asked.

Samantha clung hard to her husband's sturdy arm. "I don't know, but I—I think I might faint!"

Daniel reached over and began fanning her with the thick envelope the judge had given them. "Calm down, Sam. You're going to be fine. I can't ever remember anyone fainting from becoming a parent."

"Are you sure?" Samantha gasped in puffing breaths.

Daniel gave a short laugh. "Yes, my dear, I'm sure."

"That's good to know," Adam said, panting himself, "because I think—" he blew out a breath, "I think I'm feeling faint too."

Samantha continued to gasp for breath. "Give me a minute to calm myself. I can't meet our children for the first time while I'm so . . ." But she didn't finish as the reality of the moment tumbled over her like a load of bricks. Such an awesome responsibility, the raising of a child. From this day forward, a separate, living soul—four of them, to be specific—would depend on her and Adam to meet all needs from physical to spiritual. She'd wanted it, had longed for and prayed for it, and now here it was, ready for the taking. A gamut of emotions rolled through her—exhilaration and fear, apprehension and anticipation, all at once.

"Sammy, you're not having second thoughts, are you?" Adam peered at her in concern.

"Oh, no, Adam, it isn't that at all!" She looked into his eyes. "You know how much I want to take those children home. They are our dream—yours and mine! It's just . . ."

Adam squeezed her shoulder with a smile of understanding. "It's just that it's right here looking us in the face, and it's all a little overwhelming."

Samantha nodded. "Yes, that's exactly it!"

"The worst part is over, Sammy—the waiting is done," Adam said kindly. "Right through that door are four little children who have been entrusted to us. And I am ready to meet them and let them know how very much we have wanted them. I think you're ready, too."

Samantha pressed her hand to her stomach and took a great breath. "Yes, Adam. I'm ready. Let's go meet our children." He held out his arm in gentlemanly fashion, and she took it like a true lady would. They exchanged one last long look of silent wonder, and then they moved forward.

Daniel held the door open, and the pair entered together, stepping into a square foyer of sterile white. A short, round nun with smiling face and apple cheeks came forward to greet them. "You must be the Klaassens," she said in a voice soft as eiderdown.

"That's correct," Daniel answered for them, offering his hand.

The older woman accepted it, squeezing it briefly as she introduced herself. "I am Sister Mary Catherine, and I have had the privilege of looking after Lucy and Ellen Marie." She dropped Daniel's hand and took the papers that would officially release the children. She glanced through them, tapped lightly on the official seal of the court, then set them aside on a desk.

Turning to Samantha and Adam, she reached out a gentle hand. Samantha clasped it at once. "We are all so very pleased that our little ones will remain as family. So worried little Lucy has been that someone would take her sweet baby sister from her." Her clear green eyes went from Samantha to Adam, then back again. "They are dear children, but very frightened. You will be patient as they learn to know and accept you as their new parents?"

"Oh, yes, we will," Samantha assured the elderly woman. But a part of her hoped it wouldn't take too long—she was so anxious to be mama!

Adam said, "We're looking forward to meeting the children and getting them settled in their new home."

"Ah, of course you are, Mr. Klaassen, of course you are." Sister Mary Catherine gave Samantha's hand one final squeeze. "The children are being readied now for their journey. If you would please wait here"—she gestured to four wooden chairs in a row next to the wall—"I shall bring the children down directly."

"Thank you," Samantha said. So they were forced to wait a little longer as the nun moved silently up the staircase. Daniel and Samantha sat—Samantha on the edge of the seat with her hands pressed, palms together, between her knees—but Adam paced back and forth, his gaze glued to the spot at the top of the stairs where the children would descend.

They waited, listening to the grandfather clock that stood sentinel next to the staircase. Somewhere in the building, school was in session, for addition instructions could be heard over the sounds of chalk scratching against a blackboard. Traffic noises intruded from the street outside, and once a sparrow perched on the windowsill and pecked at its own reflection in the window.

And then came a creaking at the top of the stairs.

Adam immediately stopped, his face aimed upward. Samantha rose slowly, her gaze, like Adam's, focused above. Her breath caught in her throat and held. The staircase was built with a half wall of plaster rather than a railing, so the first view of their children was merely the tops of two heads—one brown, one blond—moving quite slowly in the way small children, place both feet on one riser before stepping to the next. Sister Mary Catherine carried the baby in her arms, and Samantha strained to see, but the littlest one also was hidden by the nun's starched habit and the shielding stairway wall. So they had to wait until the little group reached the bottom and came around the corner.

Samantha's fingertips flew to her lips and tears flooded her eyes at the first full sight of Lucy, Henry, and Will. Lucy was holding the toddler's pudgy hand securely in her own small hand. The little girl had fine brown hair that fell straight to her shoulders with a few wispy bangs softening the severity of the cut. Her eyes, large and velvety brown, were surrounded by long lashes.

Both little Will and his big brother were towheads, Will's baby hair curling into soft ringlets behind his ears. Henry's hair was close-cropped on the sides with the top a bit longer, and one strand flopped across his forehead. A spattering of copper-colored freckles sprinkled his nose. Both boys had hazel eyes. The children stood in a silent line, their solemn, unsmiling faces and unblinking eyes looking back at the strangers in front of them.

Sister Mary Catherine stopped behind the three, and the baby squirmed in the nun's arms. The woman turned the baby against her shoulder and patted her back. "I had to wake the wee one, so she is likely to be a bit cranky," the Sister explained. She turned her attention to the children and said, "Children, I want you to meet Mr. and Mrs. Klaassen. They are the nice couple I told you about, who want to take care of you." The Sister touched the back of Lucy's head. "Lucy, can you say hello?"

Whisper soft, Lucy offered, "Hello."

Samantha moved forward slowly, dropping to her knees in front of Lucy and holding out her hand to touch the little girl's arm. "Hello, Lucy. I'm so glad to meet you. You and Will and Henry. Your baby sister, Ellen, too." She smiled at each in turn.

Lucy pointed at Henry. "He's Buddy."

Samantha asked, "What, honey?"

"He's not Henry, he's Buddy. Our papa is Henry. He's Buddy."

Samantha smiled brightly at Henry—Buddy. "Buddy . . . is that what you like to be called?"

The little boy nodded soberly, his hair bobbing against his forehead.

"Then Buddy it is." She turned and touched a soft blond coil behind Will's ear. "And I'll bet you get called Curly sometimes."

Will rewarded her with a bashful smile before hiding his face in his sister's dress front, but neither Lucy nor Buddy smiled. Both wore narrow-eyed expressions of wariness and fear. Samantha couldn't blame them. She rose as Adam also knelt to greet the three older ones who stood stiff and sober.

Holding out her arms, Samantha asked the nun, "Please, may I hold the baby?"

The nun nodded with a tender smile. And then Samantha's arms were filled with the sweet weight of Ellen Marie—her own baby whom no one would ever take away. She pressed the baby girl's dimpled cheek against her own, breathing in the scents of milk and talcum. She closed her eyes, savoring the wonder of the moment. Ellen Marie fit just right in her arms—a round, warm bundle of perfection—and holding her, Samantha felt complete.

Perhaps in her joy Samantha unwittingly held the child too tightly, and Ellen Marie planted a tiny fist against Samantha's chin and pushed, beginning to protest. Adam reached for her. "Let me hold her, Sam." But the baby gave him the same treatment—flailing arms and unhappy squalls. Reluctantly, he handed her to Sister Mary Catherine. Ellen Marie settled down in the familiar arms of the nun, and the woman offered a sympathetic look over the baby's head.

"Do not be discouraged. The wee one is just confused by all the changes. Be patient." Her gaze dropped to the children who now huddled in a tight group, Lucy's arms around her brothers. "It may take some time, but all will be well. You will see."

Samantha nodded, taking Adam's hand. She vowed to do whatever it took to erase the looks of fearful uncertainty on the children's faces. Soon her arms would be the ones the baby preferred over all others.

She moved away from Adam and leaned forward, propping one hand on her knee, stretching the other, palm up, toward the sober-faced children. "Come, children. Let's go home."

At the word *home*, little Will released his sister's skirts and placed his chubby hand in Samantha's. Her fingers closed around it as she straightened, sending a smile of success to Adam. He returned it with one of his own, then turned to Lucy and Buddy.

"Yes, children. It's time we take you home," he said.

Lucy looked up to Sister Mary Catherine, and the nun gave her a nod of encouragement, her face wreathed with gentle smile lines. Hesitantly Lucy placed her hand in Adam's, and Buddy followed her lead, taking Adam's other hand.

"The children's bags are beside the door," Sister Mary Catherine told Daniel. "The little basket holds sandwiches and fruit and canned milk for your trip."

"Thank you," Adam said, "that's very thoughtful of you."

"It is the least we can do to send these little ones off on a good start," the nun said.

The little entourage headed out the door, Daniel in the lead, the battered cardboard suitcases bumping against his leg. Sister Mary Catherine followed next with Ellen Marie who protested loudly at being covered with a layer of shawls. Samantha followed, carrying Will, and Adam brought up the rear with the small hands of Lucy and Buddy curled in his palms. Daniel tossed the suitcases into the rumble seat, then helped Samantha crawl into the backseat, and Sister Mary Catherine handed a still-complaining Ellen Marie to her. Will and Buddy climbed in beside Samantha, and Adam and Lucy shared the front seat with Daniel.

"God bless you all," the Sister said warmly before Adam closed the door. And they were off to the train station to begin their journey home . . . and the even longer journey toward becoming a family.

The moment they arrived at the train station, Lucy turned stubborn and refused to leave the automobile. Adam finally picked her up and carried her onto the passenger car. Although he asked her repeatedly what was wrong, she refused to answer, only stared at him with her chin quivering and her eyes clearly displaying her distrust.

Little Will kicked his feet, swung his fists, and cried out, "Mama! Mama!" in a high-pitched wail so heartrending it made Adam want to cry too. Buddy obediently huddled in the seat Adam pointed out for him, but tears rolled down his thin cheeks, dripping from his chin.

And Ellen Marie screeched in an ear-splitting fashion until she was hoarse. She fought against being held, but they couldn't put her down anywhere. She wouldn't take a bottle, but she sucked her fist until a purple spot showed on the back of her hand. She cried and cried and cried. She finally fell into an exhausted sleep, her little chest still rising and falling in shuddering breaths. Adam couldn't help questioning if maybe the judge had been right all along. Maybe four children all at once was too much for them.

Aware of glares from irate passengers, Adam did his best to soothe Will. Samantha, her arms busy cradling Ellen Marie, could offer no help. At last a buxom matron with fuzzy apricot hair and several chins apparently took pity on them. Without a word of warning, she scooped up the wailing Will and pressed him against her ample chest. She ordered the two men occupying the seat nearest Adam and Samantha to trade with her, and they did, too startled to argue. She plunked herself down and began moving back and forth against the seat's padded back, patting Will's bottom in rhythm with her rocking.

To Adam's great relief and appreciation, Will, too, fell asleep, his head drooping back against the woman's heavy arm. "Should I take him now?" Adam whispered.

The older woman shook her head. "Nah, I'll hold 'im till he wakes." She grinned and added, "I've rocked more'n my share of li'l 'uns. M' arms'll hold up."

"Thank you, ma'am," Adam said, and he meant it. The whole train car seemed to breathe a sigh of relief. With Will and Ellen Marie sleeping, the atmosphere was quiet at last.

Adam settled back next to Buddy and placed an arm around the boy's narrow shoulders. The blond hank of hair that hung down across Buddy's forehead swayed with the motion of the train. His hands were planted against the seat to hold himself erect as the train pitched and rolled with the rails. The tears had stopped running, but two drops still hung on the little boy's lashes. Adam used a thumb to brush them away.

"Buddy, I'm sorry you're sad," Adam said. "I'd like to help you, if you'd tell me what's troubling you. I hope you aren't afraid of me, son."

Buddy hunkered into his jacket.

Adam gave the boy's shoulder a light pat. "Please, won't you talk to me, Buddy?"

The child clamped his lips closed and leaned away from Adam. Rebuffed, Adam shifted his attention to Lucy, who sat on the other side of Buddy. "Lucy, can you tell me what's bothering your brother?"

Lucy flicked a quick, resentful look in Adam's direction then turned her face to gaze out the window. Buddy leaned into his sister's shoulder as far from Adam as he could go without leaving the seat. Adam waited for several minutes, but neither of the children acknowledged him in any way.

With a sigh, he looked across the small expanse and met Samantha's eyes. He sent her a weak smile, which she returned. When she yawned, his heart twisted in sympathy. *She must be exhausted—she'd been holding the baby for almost two hours now.* He would offer to take the little one, but he didn't want to risk waking her and creating a new disturbance.

So he sat in silence with a tired wife, two sleeping children, two uncommunicative children, and a heart filled with mixed emotions and more questions than he could answer.

∽◌

By the time the train rumbled into the Mountain Lake station, Samantha's arms ached so badly from cradling the baby she was sure they would fall off. Her ears hurt from listening to Ellen Marie's wails and Will's screaming tantrums, both resumed about the same time as they awakened. Her neck and calves ached from bracing herself against the seat and holding her body as still as possible to keep from jostling the baby. But mostly, her heart hurt.

She hadn't been naive enough to expect the children to love her instantly, but she had anticipated some small measure of cooperation. The children were so obviously upset and unhappy, it was impossible not to experience empathy pangs on their behalf as well as disappointment for the negative response. The first few hours of being a mama were far from what she'd hoped for.

Lucy and Buddy had finally fallen asleep with their heads against the windowpanes. While Adam now retrieved the crying

Will from the helpful matron, Samantha wiggled Lucy's knee with her fingers, coaxing, "Lucy . . . it's time to wake up." She tapped Buddy's knee and added, "Wake up now, children, we're home."

Buddy roused first, twisting his shoulders high and wriggling sideways in the seat. He lifted his fists to clear his eyes, then reached out blindly with a foot and clunked his sister on the shin. Drowsily the little girl lifted her head and tried to focus. She scowled for a moment, looking at Samantha blearily, as if trying to figure out who she was.

"Children, we're home now," Samantha repeated gently, smiling at the pair.

Lucy's features smoothed, and she turned to the window. She pressed her palms and her nose to the glass eagerly. Buddy knelt on his seat and did the same. "Hey!" Buddy flung himself away from the glass. "What's this place?"

Thrilled that he was finally showing some interest, Samantha answered brightly, "This is Mountain Lake, Minnesota, Buddy. This is home."

Lucy turned a fierce scowl on Samantha. "This ain't home! I knew you was fibbin'. To get home we never took a train. Only needed a trolley car. Or we could walk."

Fresh tears rolled down Buddy's freckled face. He pointed an accusing finger at Adam, who stood in the aisle with Will clinging to his neck. "That man lied, too. He called me 'son.' An' he ain't my papa. I want my papa! I wanna go home!" Buddy threw himself into Lucy's arms. She glared at both Samantha and Adam over her brother's shoulder.

Ellen Marie began crying again, no doubt upset at her brother and sister's distress. Samantha bounced the baby and sent Adam a baffled look. Hadn't anyone explained to the children their parents were gone, and they would be going to a new home?

Adam dropped down on the seat next to Lucy and Buddy. "Children, did the Sisters at the Foundling Home tell you about your mama and papa?"

Lucy's lower lip thrust out belligerently, and Buddy blinked against tears. Lucy answered in a near-whimper, "They said Mama and Papa went up to heaven."

Adam nodded and reached out an arm to draw the pair against his side. "That's right. Your parents went to heaven. And that means there is nobody at your house to take care of you anymore. When Samantha and I heard about you, we knew we wanted to take care of you. So we talked to a judge at the courthouse, and he said it would be all right for us to be your new mama and daddy." He whisked a quick glance at Samantha before turning back to the children. "The Sisters explained that to you, didn't they?"

Slowly Lucy nodded, her brown eyes wide in her narrow face. "The Sisters said we'd be goin' home, an' *she* said"—she poked an obstinate thumb in Samantha's direction—"you'd be takin' us home. But this ain't home!"

Obviously the children had completely misunderstood what would be taking place. Oh, how Samantha wished she and Adam had asked a few more questions before removing the children from the Foundling Home.

The conductor appeared at the passenger car doorway and asked briskly, "You folks ready to light out? We've already watered the engine, and we're ready to move on."

Adam answered with a tired sigh. "Certainly. We're getting off right now."

"Noooo!" Lucy flung herself face down on the seat. "I wanna go home! I wanna go home!"

Buddy took up the cry as well, kneeling beside his sister and clinging to her as if his life depended on it. Ellen Marie screamed in body-jerking hysteria, and little Will threw back his head and started wailing, "I want Mama! Mama! Mama!"

Samantha looked helplessly at Adam, on the verge of tears herself, and then a sweet voice intruded.

"Would an extra pair of hands be useful right now?"

Samantha spun to find Si and Laura at the end of the aisle, and her shoulders wilted with relief. "Oh, Mother and Papa Klaassen . . . thank heaven you're here!"

Laura came forward and lifted Ellen Marie from Samantha's arms, taking a moment to pat Samantha's cheek lovingly. "Now you get the other little girl and come on outside."

Lucy had curled her fingers around the seat, but Samantha managed to unloose them and lift the still sobbing Lucy and help her walk to the door. Si scooped up Will and the suitcases, Adam lifted Buddy, and they made their way to the boardwalk. Minutes later, the train chugged around the bend.

Si raised his voice to be heard over the children's wails. "I told the rest of the family not to come meet the train. Figured the little ones would be confused and upset and a huge gathering would overwhelm them."

Samantha, looking down at Lucy's belligerent face, heaved a sigh of relief that the entire family hadn't been there to witness their less-than-happy plunge into parenthood. She said, "The children thought we'd be taking them back to their old house, where they lived with their parents."

Laura's face softened in sympathy as she cuddled the still crying Ellen Marie. "The poor little things . . . how difficult this must be for them! And how disappointing for you, too," she added, sending Samantha a sympathetic smile. "This isn't quite the homecoming you'd imagined, is it?"

Adam and Samantha exchanged looks, and Adam stretched his eyes wide. Suddenly it all struck a funny chord inside

Samantha. The emotional roller coaster of the past few days played briefly in her mind—the hopeful rush to Minneapolis to claim the children, the crushing disappointment of the courtroom scene, the victory of the judge's changed verdict, the excitement of meeting the children, then the hugely depressing train ride. To think that they'd hoped and prayed to bring these children home only to have those same children wailing in despair because they'd been brought home! Whether it was tiredness or hysteria or simply a means to cope, Samantha felt her shoulders start to vibrate with soundless chuckles. Then an amused, very unladylike snort erupted.

Adam looked at her in surprise as she burst into full laughter. She took in his shocked expression and laughed all the harder. Si and Laura looked from Adam to Samantha to each other, their eyebrows raised high in silent query while Samantha continued to laugh and the children continued to wail and the stationmaster stuck his head out of the train depot to gawk curiously.

"Sam, what on earth—?"

"I'm sorry!" Samantha managed through giggles. "It's just—it's just we wanted kids so much! And now—now we've got 'em, but they aren't too happy about it!"

Adam's lips twitched, and then he started laughing as well. Si and Laura stood by, indulgent smiles creasing their faces. Then Laura nudged Si and pointed—Lucy had stopped crying and was peering up at Samantha and Adam with her mouth open and her eyes wide. Buddy had calmed, too, clutching Lucy's hand and staring at the two laughter-crazed grown-ups.

With Lucy and Buddy quiet, Will seemed to decide there wasn't any more reason to be upset, so his tears ceased as well. Only little Ellen Marie continued to sob softly in Laura's arms while Adam and Samantha struggled to get their amusement under control.

Adam finally said, "Why don't we head for home before we all turn into snowmen out here?"

"Yes, we'd better," Samantha agreed with one more giggle. "The spring thaw is a ways off yet."

They shared one more round of laughter before Adam looked down at the now-silent children. "Are you ready to go?"

Buddy surprised them by announcing, "I'm hungry."

"Then we'll feed you the minute we get there," Adam promised. He mouthed to the others, "Don't say 'home' for a while till they get adjusted."

"Come on," he raised his voice and motioned to the children. "Ever been on a hayride?" Adam asked Lucy as he lifted her into the back of Si's high-sided wagon bed spread thickly with yellow hay. Lucy simply shook her head silently.

"Then you're in for a treat," Adam told her. "Snuggle down and pull the hay around you—it will keep you warm. Buddy and Will, you, too."

The children buried themselves in the hay while Samantha settled in a corner with Ellen Marie. When everyone was ready, Si gave a chirrup to the horses, and they started for home.

～◦

Samantha saw Lucy reach for Buddy's hand under the cover of the hay, and he gripped it back. He leaned over and whispered loudly, "They act kinda funny, don't they?"

"Uh-huh." Lucy kept her gaze fixed on Samantha while Samantha cuddled Ellen Marie and hummed a lullaby, pretending she didn't notice. "She looks awful fond o' Ellen Marie."

Buddy shivered. "Reckon we'll be all right?"

Lucy nodded hard. "I'll take care o' you an' the little guys. Don't worry."

Buddy leaned against his sister. She pulled her arm out of the hay and placed it around his shoulders. "I'll make sure we're fine." Her narrowed gaze never wavered from Samantha.

Samantha's heart melted as she remembered another girl, older than Lucy but just as frightened and uncertain, who arrived in Mountain Lake. She'd discovered healing in the folds of the Klaassen family's love, and she'd make certain Lucy experienced the same place of belonging no matter what it took.

*A*dam kept his first promise to Buddy. The moment the newly formed family arrived at the farm, he seated the children around the table and fed them a quick supper of bread, cold sausage, and canned peaches while Samantha gave Ellen Marie a bottle. Buddy ate as if he'd never seen food before, but Will turned fractious, rubbing his eyes and whining, too tired to eat. Although Adam suspected Lucy was hungry, she only pushed the food around on her plate with a stubby finger, a scowl on her face.

When Ellen Marie finished her bottle, Adam reached for her, eager to share in the baby's caretaking. "Let me rock her to sleep."

For a moment, Samantha held tight, but then she nodded. "Very well. I'll give the others a spit bath."

Buddy turned up his nose. "Spit bath? Ick!"

Samantha chuckled softly. "I promise . . . there's no spitting involved. I don't know why it's called that."

Adam sank into the rocking chair with the delightful weight of Ellen Marie in his arms and watched Samantha line up the three older children for a wash. He couldn't stop a smile from growing. Mothering seemed to come awfully naturally to her.

Will stood complacently in his diaper and socks, yawning widely as Samantha ran a warm, wet cloth over his pudgy little-boy body. After drying him with a length of toweling, she slipped a nightshirt over his curls, manipulating his droopy, uncooperative arms into the sleeves. He then leaned against her leg with a finger in his mouth while she subjected Buddy to the same treatment. Buddy proved more challenging as he hunched into himself, apparently trying to hide. The moment she finished with him, Buddy thrust himself into the offered nightshirt and sat back down at the table for cookies, while Samantha reached for Lucy.

"Uh-uh." Lucy stepped away from the dripping cloth and folded her arms across her skinny chest. "I can do it myself. You don't gotta wash me."

Samantha glanced at Adam, her expression uncertain. Adam thought back—he'd bathed himself at the age of six, and no doubt Samantha had, too, since she had no one to help her. But in his wife's eyes he recognized the desire to connect with Lucy in some way. His heart ached for both new mother and child as the pair squared off, one reaching and one resisting.

At last Samantha nodded. "All right, Lucy. After you're washed and dressed, come upstairs. I'll read you a story and tuck you in."

"You don't gotta," Lucy repeated, taking the washcloth and moving a safe distance from Samantha.

Samantha maintained a low, kind tone. "I know I don't have to, Lucy, but I would like to. I'll take the boys up now, and you can join us when you're in your nightie, okay?"

Lucy paused, the dripping washcloth clenched in her fist. Indecision marred her brow, but at last she shrugged. "All right." She turned her back before beginning to undress.

Samantha scooped up Will. "Come on, tired boy, let's get you tucked into bed." Will rested his head on her shoulder, and Adam's heart leaped, witnessing the trusting gesture. She turned to Buddy. "Are you finished with your cookie, Buddy?" When he nodded, she added, "Good, let's go upstairs then." Samantha held a hand out to him, and after only a moment's pause, he took it and together they climbed the stairs.

Ellen Marie was sleeping soundly, so Adam decided to give Lucy some privacy. He ascended the stairs and looked into the bedroom where Samantha sat with Buddy and Will on the bed, the pair of blond heads tipped toward a picture book, her animated voice reading the tale. Adam wished for a camera to capture the scene, but he knew the memory was burned into his mind.

He carried the baby to the nursery, but he discovered he wasn't ready to relinquish the warm, soft body to the cradle yet. He stood near it, gently rocking and watching Ellen Marie pucker her little lips in sleep. A shuffle at the door alerted him, and he spotted Lucy in the doorway. Her hair stuck up at her forehead where she'd swished the cloth across her face, and she held her locked hands behind her back. He smiled. She maintained a stoic face.

"Want me to put Ellen Marie to bed?" Lucy asked.

Adam tipped his head, wondering if that had been one of her responsibilities. "Sure, that would be nice, Lucy. She's already asleep, but you come over here—" Adam kept his voice low to avoid disturbing the baby, "and I'll put her in your arms. The cradle is all ready for her."

Lucy quickly came and stood in front of him, her hands outstretched. Adam carefully placed the infant in Lucy's arms and watched the girl's expression soften. He tipped the cradle, and the little girl laid her baby sister down and patted her a few times. Adam and Lucy both tucked the blanket around baby Ellen and stepped back.

"Why don't you go in with Will and Buddy and listen to the story? They're across the hall."

Lucy nodded silently, her eyes on Ellen Marie. She stood for several seconds before finally turning and heading away on bare feet. Adam, curious, decided to follow.

The moment Lucy stepped into the bedroom doorway, Samantha lifted her head and offered a warm smile. "Come on in, Lucy. There's room for one more."

But Lucy remained frozen in place. "I just came to say 'night to Buddy an' Willie."

Samantha caught Adam's eyes. The yearning in her face encouraged him to touch the back of Lucy's head and coax, "Go ahead. I'm sure you'll enjoy the story too."

Lucy jerked away from Adam's touch. "No." She waggled her hand. "'Night, Buddy. 'Night, Willie. Sleep tight, don't let the bedbugs bite."

Will held his chubby arms toward his sister. "Gimme hug, Woosy."

Without a moment's hesitation, Lucy ran to him and scooped him clear off the bed with her exuberant hug. She kissed his apple cheek twice before plunking him down. The little boy scrambled back into his spot close to Samantha, and Lucy spun and raced out the door, taking care to stay as far from Adam as she could.

Adam flicked a quick look at Samantha and the boys, sending his wife an encouraging nod before once again following Lucy. The little girl hovered against the wall as if uncertain what to do next. Adam pointed, "Your room is right here." Lucy scuttled into the open doorway across the hallway from the boys' room without a backward glance and closed the door in Adam's face.

Irritation mingled with concern. He needed to talk to the child, but he decided he needed to pray for patience first. Lucy had lived through an unspeakable loss, had been snatched away by people she'd never seen before—people who had held out the promise of "home." It would take some time for her to settle in.

He returned to the boys' room in time to see Samantha trying to disengage herself from the pair of sleeping boys. He tiptoed forward and shifted Will from her lap. She helped Buddy slide down until his head rested on the pillow. Tenderly, she tucked the covers up to their chins, pausing to bestow a light kiss on each forehead before turning out the lamp. Then, hand in hand, they crept to the doorway. There Samantha paused, looking back with a small smile creasing her face.

She whispered, "Don't they look innocent?"

Adam nodded, his heart lifting. The two lay with their blond heads tipped toward each other. Will's lower lip puckered out in a sleepy pout, and Buddy already snored softly. *Our boys* . . . The thought filled him with joy. Then he looked toward the closed door across the hall, and apprehension churned again through his middle.

Lucy was going to be the difficult one, he knew. Adam had always gotten along well with children. All his nieces and nephews adored him, just as they did Samantha. For the first time, Adam had found himself uncomfortable in a child's presence, and he knew Lucy's aloof behavior was also creating a sense of insecurity on Samantha's part. Somehow, they had to find a way to assure Lucy she was safe here. And loved.

"Let's tuck Lucy in now, shall we?" he said. With Samantha's hand in his, he stepped toward Lucy's door and tapped lightly. "Lucy? May we come in?"

After a long silence, Lucy's flat voice could be heard. "I don't care."

Adam opened the door and ushered Samantha through. Lucy lay in bed, the coverlet pulled clear to her chin. Her huge brown eyes watched warily as Samantha approached and perched on the edge of the bed.

"You're all tucked in," Samantha commented, smoothing a hand across the cover, leaving it rest on the far side of Lucy's stiff form.

Beneath the layer of blankets, Lucy shrugged. Adam inched to the other side of the bed, his gaze locked on the little girl's face. Resentment glittered in her eyes, but did she rely on resentment to hide her fear? He wished he could read below the expression of the child's eyes.

"We're so glad you're here, Lucy," Adam said. "Samantha and I have waited for a little girl like you for a long time. It makes us very, very happy that you've come to be with us."

Lucy lay still and wary, her eyes darting from Adam's to Samantha's face.

Adam went on quietly. "I know everything seems strange to you now. It's a different house, with a different bed and different people. But I hope you'll soon feel comfortable here. Samantha and I want to be a good mama and daddy for you and your brothers and sister."

When Lucy still didn't respond, Adam said, "Well, let's get you tucked in, shall we?"

Lucy's fingers curled over the edge of the cover. "I tucked me in."

Samantha shot Adam a helpless look. Adam forced a chuckle. "Well, now, you are a big girl then, aren't you? But we can say good night, can't we?"

"I don't care."

Samantha leaned over and placed a kiss on Lucy's forehead and stood to step aside. Adam also deposited a kiss on the child's brow, but then he sat on the edge of the bed, praying silently for guidance. "When I was a boy your age," he said quietly, "before I went to sleep, my ma and pa always came to tuck me into bed and listen to my bedtime prayers. It made me feel safe, to have a kiss and a prayer before I fell asleep. I'd like to say a prayer with you now, Lucy. Would that be all right?"

He watched Lucy's expression for any signs of softening. None were seen, but she didn't refuse. Adam placed a hand on Lucy's chest and closed his eyes. "Now I lay me down to sleep . . ." he recited the simple prayer offered by thousands of children nightly. At its completion, he added his own postscript. "Thank You, God, for bringing Lucy, Buddy, Will, and Ellen Marie here safely. Help them to understand how very much they are wanted and loved by us. Give them happy dreams to take them through this night. Amen."

When he opened his eyes, he found Lucy's gaze pinned on him, a puzzled scowl on her face. He smiled and said once more, "Good night, Lucy. *Schlop Die gezunt.*"

"What did you say?"

Adam grinned, pleased to have finally gotten a response. "I said, sleep well."

"Didn't sound like sleep well."

"It's *Plautdietsch*—the language my family speaks besides English," Adam said, "and it's what my mother always said right before she left my room."

Lucy stared at him unblinking. "My mother always said 'Sleep tight, don't let the bedbugs bite.'"

Samantha asked, "Do you want me to say that to you at bedtime?"

"No. You're not my mother." Lucy rolled over, pulling the covers over her ear, effectively closing herself away from them.

Samantha put trembling fingers over her mouth and reached for Adam's hand. He took it, and together they left the room. The moment he closed Lucy's door, Samantha leaned into his chest.

"Oh, Adam."

Adam stroked her hair. "Sammy, be patient. Both of us will need to practice lots and lots of it. Remember, when you came to our family? You wore belligerence like a shield too." She sniffed and lifted her head to look at him with wet eyes. "But love and a whole lot of patience eventually broke through those barriers," he continued. "She'll come around. She's the oldest, so her memories are the strongest. We just need to make sure she knows that we aren't trying to replace her birth parents, but give her a secure, loving, new home."

Samantha looked toward the closed door. "She's so . . . distant."

"Yes, but expecting instant acceptance isn't realistic." He spoke to himself as much as his wife. "Give her time."

Samantha sighed, nodded, and then her eyes flew wide. "Ellen Marie hasn't cried in over an hour."

"I know," Adam said proudly. "Come here." He led Samantha to the nursery. Lifting a silencing finger to his mouth, he opened the door and guided her inside. On her tummy in the borrowed cradle, Ellen Marie slept peacefully. Her lower lip drooped open, her nearly transparent eyelids quivered, and one tiny fist curled sweetly against her cheek.

Samantha's fingertips rested on the edge of the cradle. "Oh, Adam . . . our baby."

Adam laid his hands on her shoulders and squeezed. "She drank the entire bottle, burped like a sailor, then gave me the biggest smile. I changed her, then rocked her, and she fell asleep in my arms."

"When she wakes, it will be my turn," Samantha said.

Although Adam would have cheerfully met the baby's needs, he knew how much Samantha longed to care for the infant. "Fair enough. But right now, let's let her sleep. Come on." They crept from the room on tiptoe.

On the way down the hall, Adam said, "I should tell you that Lucy came in before I put Ellen Marie down, and she wanted to put her sister in the cradle. I saw a tenderness that was very moving, and I saw a very careful little girl with her baby sister. And for just a minute or so, she and I made a connection."

Samantha looked up at Adam, hope in her eyes. "Oh, Adam, that is so good to hear after the day we've had."

Snug in bed, her head nestled in the crook of Adam's arm, Samantha sighed. "Do you feel any different?"

Adam forced heavy eyelids open. "Different how?"

"Well, we're parents now." Samantha quiet voice held a note of wonder. "From now on, we will be responsible for four children. They'll depend on us for everything. It's exciting, but it's scary too."

Adam gave a brief chuckle. "You know, Sam, I had those exact same thoughts as we were walking up to the Foundling Home."

She twisted her head a bit, and he sensed her gazing at him in surprise. "You did?"

"I sure did." How alike they'd become—as one, just as God intended. The thought warmed Adam.

She went on in a subdued tone. "I hope I'll be able to do it right. When Lucy said what she did, about me not being her mother, it made me think about the fact that I never had one. Will I know how to be one?"

"Of course you will." Her question almost made him laugh. Adam shifted, drawing her closer. "All you have to do is remember the way your gran treated you. Imitate her, and you'll make a wonderful mother. And if you need specific advice, my ma has been known to have an answer or two up her sleeve."

Samantha nodded against his shoulder. "Yes, I can do both those things. The loving part will be easy. I already feel the beginning of love stirring in my heart. It's hard not to, when faced with such worried little faces. And I know what else I can do."

Conviction steeled her tone. "I can let them be children. I had to grow up so fast, I never really got the chance to be carefree and unburdened. I'm going to make sure my children have lots of time to play and just have fun."

Adam gave her arm a little squeeze. "Did you hear yourself? You called them 'my children.' You already sound and look and act like a mother."

"I do want to be a good mother," she whispered. "I know you'll be a good daddy. You were so good with Lucy tonight, and with Ellen Marie."

"Wait and see, Sammy. By the time we go back to the judge to make the adoption final, all four children will be calling you Mama and loving you nearly as much as I do."

Samantha rolled sideways and pressed her lips against Adam's neck. "I love you, Adam."

"I love you, too," he replied. He yawned and pushed his pillow under his head. "Good night, little mother."

"Good night, new daddy."

*T*he first few weeks of parenthood were exciting and rewarding, yet an exhausting time for Adam and Samantha. Especially for the "little mother." Although she allowed Adam to give Ellen Marie her evening bath and bottle, Samantha insisted on performing all of the other duties surrounding the baby's care both day and night. After a few days Ellen Marie was adjusting nicely to her new home, and she thrilled her fledgling parents with her sunny disposition and cuddly nature. But even so she awoke twice nightly for bottles, each feeding taking up the better part of an hour. Consequently Samantha got much less sleep than was normal for her.

Additionally, little Will was still in diapers, so washing two dozen flannel squares had to be fit into the daily schedule. Samantha found the best time to tend to laundry was during Will and Ellen Marie's afternoon nap. Adam encouraged her to rest when the little ones were doing so, but Samantha felt it was more difficulty than it was worth to be filling tubs with water and washing soiled clothes with Will under her feet.

To her undisguised delight, Will became her little shadow. She proudly informed her brother, David, that if she took a step backward, she would step on Will—he was always there. The curly haired toddler was the first of the children to begin calling Samantha and Adam "Mama" and "Daddy." The words were music to their ears, and each time the little boy reached for Samantha and uttered that wonderful word—*mama*—Samantha's heart leaped from happiness.

Buddy, in turn, became a true little buddy to Adam. At first Adam brought the youngster along for chores simply to ease a bit of Samantha's care for the children. But before long he took the boy along just for the pleasure of his company. Buddy was a bright, inquisitive little fellow, curious about everything.

His questions were endless. What do worms eat? How come some clouds are fat and some clouds are skinny? Why do horses have manes? Will that little seed really grow into a big ol' wheat stalk? and so on. Adam answered every question with patience, thrilled with the interest Buddy took in all aspects of farming and animal care. He bragged to anyone who would listen about his "little farmin' buddy."

The only cloud in an otherwise sunny sky was Lucy. After a week, Samantha took the little girl into town and enrolled her in school. Samantha had wanted to keep her home until the next term, but Adam felt it would help Lucy realize this home was a permanent one and give her a sense of stability. Lucy's teacher said she was a better-than-average student, but very withdrawn and uncommunicative, preferring to sit alone rather than join the other children. Adam and Samantha could believe that—although she smothered her brothers and baby sister with affection and attention, the only time Lucy talked to her new parents was to let them know she didn't need their help with something or other.

Samantha did everything she could think of to let the little girl know she was loved and wanted. Lucy had all the freedom Samantha's childhood had never included. Samantha made her bed, picked up her toys, laid out a clean dress and apron for her each morning, and combed her fine brown hair into perfect pin curls held away from her forehead with bows to match her dresses. Samantha pampered her, read to her, tried to cuddle her. But Lucy did her best to keep Samantha at arm's length.

Often she would look up from some chore to find Lucy's narrowed, resentful gaze boring a hole in her. Samantha despaired at ever getting through to the child.

Samantha and Adam privately discussed Lucy's aloofness with Si and Laura, hoping their extensive child-rearing experience would help steer a course toward a solution. They advised normalcy—to simply treat Lucy no differently than the others and hope, in time, she would come to accept them as her brothers and sister had.

So Samantha and Adam established routines to create security, including Samantha's favorite—the bedtime routine. She loved the nightly baths when she would make the boys laugh, blowing bubbles through her fist, cuddling together on the bed while she read a Bible story, and saying a prayer with them before tucking them under the covers and delivering a kiss. Both Will and Buddy relished this nighttime ritual as well. Lucy listened to the stories and allowed Samantha and Adam to pray with her and tuck her in, but the child never smiled—only observed everything with the closed, wary expression that had become all too familiar.

As the weeks passed with no improvement in Lucy's demeanor, their concerns grew. The six-month probationary period was closing in more quickly than they could have imagined. What would they do if, when the time came to make the adoption final, Lucy was still so unhappy? Would the judge still grant them permanent custody of the children? The worry became a dark cloud hanging over their heads.

Winter melted away to a beautiful spring. Crocuses and daffodils bloomed, the songbirds returned, and Adam and his Buddy spent every minute they could outside, taking advantage of the warmer days to ready the fields and repair snow-broken fences.

Samantha appreciated the sunshine too. Now she didn't have to lug all that wet laundry to the attic where it freeze-dried—laundry hung outside on the lines captured the sweet, outdoorsy fragrances, and Will played peekaboo with her between the sheets and long johns. Having him make games out of the chores made the work load move along more quickly, and Samantha appreciated each moment with Will's cheerful presence.

Baby Ellen Marie enjoyed being outside as well. One of the items the Vanderhavens had provided was a wicker pram. At first, Samantha had wondered what on earth they would do with the ungainly thing on the farm, but once the weather was warm enough to be outdoors, she was grateful for the gift. Samantha could push the baby to the side yard when she hung laundry, to the backyard when she worked in the garden, and to the front yard when she sat on the porch to catch up on darning or other handwork. Ellen Marie sat happily in the pram, chewing on a rattle and watching from her vantage point.

One rainy afternoon in mid-May, Adam was attempting to talk Buddy into a nap with his brother.

"Aw, Daddy, do I hafta?" Buddy's green eyes pleaded. "I'm not a baby."

Adam ruffled the boy's hair, then crouched down to his level and smiled. "I know you're not a baby, son. That's why I know you'll understand that I need to talk to Mama alone for a little while."

Buddy looked at Samantha, who was cutting potatoes into wedges to plant in the garden, then back at Adam. "You need to talk to Mama? All by yourself?" His head tilted. "What about?" Another question, not surprising.

Adam couldn't help but grin. He shrugged, feigning a nonchalance he didn't feel. "Just grown-up talk. Sometimes grown-ups need to do that. So I'd like you to lie down for a bit with Will, then when you are done, we'll go to Uncle Frank and Aunt Anna's and take a look at the new calf they've got in their barn. Doesn't that sound like a good plan?"

Buddy wrinkled up his face, three freckles disappearing in the creases on his nose. At last he sighed. "Okay, I'll take a nap. But it won't be a real long one, will it?"

Adam laughed. "No, not too long. Now head on upstairs, and try not to shake the mattress too much when you climb in. Will is already asleep."

"Yes, Daddy." Buddy plodded upstairs with a disgusted slump to his shoulders.

Samantha smiled after him, shaking her head. "I think you just used bribery."

Adam slid into a chair across from Samantha, chuckling. "It didn't hurt anything, did it?"

"No." She dropped two more chunks of potato into the bowl. "My brother might not approve of such methods, but I prefer that approach to commanding the children. They obey you because they know you love them." Tears glittered in her eyes for a moment. "You're a good daddy, Adam."

Adam was touched by her words, and to cover the rush of emotion he affected a haughty pose. "Why, thank you, ma'am. I think so, too."

Samantha snorted. "And you're modest to go with it," she said as she threw a potato wedge at him.

He caught it and plopped it into the bowl on her lap. Then he sat, his chin in his hand, observing her as she continued her task. A meal required a lot more potatoes now that they had four children in the house, and they rarely shared a quiet moment alone together during the daytime hours. He enjoyed sitting, feeling the peacefulness in the cozy kitchen while raindrops spattered against the windowpanes, Lucy was off at school, and the other three drowsed upstairs.

In time Samantha raised her gaze from the potatoes. "What did you want to talk to me about?"

Adam sighed and ran a hand through his hair. "As you might guess, Lucy."

Samantha set aside the bowl of potatoes and knife and gave Adam her full attention.

"I'm worried, Sam," Adam admitted. "I'm afraid Lucy is never going to settle in here. Do you realize it's been four months? And she is no closer to accepting us as her new parents than she was the day we pulled into the depot, and she accused you of lying to her."

Samantha bit her lower lip. "I know. But what can I do, Adam?" She quietly confessed, "I don't think Lucy likes me very much."

The same thought had crossed Adam's mind more than once, but he wouldn't hurt Samantha by telling her so. Instead, he caught her hand and squeezed it. "I don't think Lucy likes being here. I think somehow she blames us for taking her away from her mother and father."

"But surely she understands that her parents are dead and can't care for her anymore. And we certainly can't be blamed for that."

"Of course not," Adam said, "but she's just six, remember. I still get the distinct impression she's angry with us. We took her away from Minneapolis and everything that was familiar. Even though the death of her parents is none of our doing, we are responsible for pulling her even further away from the home she knew with them. In her young mind, we've taken her away from her mother and father."

Samantha's eyes grew wide. "Do you really think so?"

Adam shrugged. "I don't know how else to explain her defiant attitude. She's harboring a strong anger, and somehow we have to help her get past that."

"But how? We've done everything your parents suggested. What else can we do?"

Adam shook his head. Feeling the bleakness of the situation nearly overwhelm him. "I don't know, Sam. I just don't know . . ." He reached across the table and took Samantha's hand. "Lucy doesn't like being here, and time is running out. The only thing we can do is continue to pray. I hope she settles in soon. Because I still think it would not be good to separate those children. If we can't adopt all of them and have them happy here, I'm thinking we should not go through with adopting any of them."

Samantha pulled her hand free, staring at him in alarm. "What are you saying?"

"I'm saying we have two months to hope Lucy understands we want her to be part of our family. If we can't do that, then it's possible all of the children should go back to the Foundling Home—maybe another couple can make it work where we have not been able to do so."

Tears flooded his wife's eyes, nearly breaking Adam's heart. She choked out, "What would our—our children think if we sent them back? We can't do that!"

"I don't want to send them back, Sammy, surely you know that." Adam moved around the table and dropped to one knee beside her. "But I'm at a loss! It isn't fair to Lucy to make her stay with us if she isn't happy here. If after half a year she hasn't accepted us, I wonder if she ever will. It just doesn't seem right to me that we adopt the three younger ones unless Lucy lets us know that she wants to be here, too."

"I . . . I agree they need to stay together. I'm not arguing against that, Adam. But . . ." Samantha clung to Adam's hands. "You know it would tear my heart out to let them go now."

Before Adam could reply, the quiet was interrupted by the sound of Ellen Marie waking from her nap. Samantha's hands were mucky with potato starch, so Adam rose. "I'll get her." He mounted the staircase, his heart heavy. When he peeked over the edge of the crib, Ellen Marie broke into a smile of recognition and babbled merrily. She stretched her chubby arms to him, begging to be picked up. And when Adam reached for her, the baby's jabbers suddenly formed, "Da-da-da-da. Dada."

Adam's hands stilled on the baby's ribs. Had he heard correctly? Had the baby really said—?

"Da-da," Ellen Marie said again, following it with a stream of gibberish.

Adam swept the baby from the cradle and down the stairs with the child bouncing in his arms. "Sam! Sam! Listen to this!"

Samantha met him at the base of the stairs looking alarmed. Adam turned the baby to face Samantha, and prodded, "Come on, Ellen Marie. Dada—say Dada."

"Adam, she's not old enough—"

"Yes, she is! She just said it when she looked up at me." He jostled the baby a bit. "You can do it, Ellen Marie. Say Dada for me." And to Adam's delight, the baby obliged her daddy.

"Da-da," she chortled, her face wreathed into a two-chin grin. "Da-da. Da-da."

Samantha squealed in surprise, startling Ellen Marie. Adam danced the baby around the kitchen until she giggled. "What a big girl! Daddy's so proud of you! But now we need to teach you 'Mama.'" He stopped and looked hopefully at the baby. "Can you say, 'Mama,' Ellen Marie? Huh? 'Mama, mama,'" he coached.

But Ellen Marie just gave him a wet grin of appreciation at all the attention, then jabbered senselessly, ending with the clearly recognizable "Da-da."

Buddy and Will appeared at the top of the stairs, Will rubbing his eyes sleepily while Buddy demanded, "Hey, what's goin' on down there?"

"We're celebrating Ellen Marie's first word." Samantha waved the boys down. "Naptime is over. Come join us."

Buddy took Will's hand and the boys hop-skipped down the steps. "Is this her first word?" Buddy gazed at Ellen Marie in wonder. "She's talkin'?"

"Yep." Adam stooped down and settled Ellen Marie on his bent knee. "Show off for your brothers, Ellen Marie. Say 'Dada.'"

Ellen Marie waved her hands wildly. "Da-da!"

Will clapped his hands and Buddy cheered, "Hey! That's great, Ellen Marie!" He beamed at Adam. "She's really smart to know you, huh, Daddy?"

Samantha dropped an arm around Buddy shoulders. "She's a real smarty pants, for sure."

"Boy, her first word." Buddy grinned up at Samantha. "Won't Lucy be surprised!"

Adam was brought back to reality, imagining Lucy's reaction, but he managed to give Buddy a smile. "Oh, I'm sure she will be."

"This calls for a reward of some sort," Samantha said, turning to the boys. "Up to the table for cookies and milk in honor of Ellen Marie's first word."

Buddy boosted Will into his seat before clambering into his own chair, asking over his shoulder, "Then can we go see the baby calf, Daddy?"

Adam chuckled as he put Ellen Marie in her high chair and reached for a bib. "Sure, Buddy. Right after Lucy gets home from school. Maybe she'd like to see the calf, too."

Buddy nodded, his mouth full of Samantha's homemade applesauce cookies. When he was finished with the bite, he observed, "Maybe the little calf will make Lucy smile. I'd like that."

Adam sent a startled glance in Samantha's direction. He hadn't realized Buddy was aware of Lucy's sullenness. But the simple comment made it clear that he and Samantha weren't the only ones who were concerned. They had to find a way to gain Lucy's trust.

Samantha placed a cup of milk in front of Buddy. "I'd like that too, Buddy."

Buddy turned a thoughtful look on Adam. "I'm really glad Ellen Marie knows who you are. An' I hope she gets to keep you."

Adam's nose stung as he battled his emotions. Buddy's innocent comment indicated the little boy still mourned his birth parents and, in his sweet way, he wanted his baby sister to avoid such pain. Adam wished he could promise none of them would ever lose him, but he wouldn't make a promise he might not be able to keep. A lot depended on Lucy and the next two months.

He stood behind Buddy, tipped the little boy's head back, and planted a kiss in his tousled hair. "I love you, Buddy," he said. "Let's go see the calf."

Help us, Lord—we can't send any of them back. Help Lucy. . . .

*S*chool let out the end of May. Lucy was glad to see it over for the summer. Oh, she enjoyed the lessons, especially reading. If they'd let her, she'd read all day long, books were so fun. But being in a roomful of strange children made her nervous. She missed her brothers and her sister, and it bothered her that she wasn't home to take care of them the way she'd promised Buddy she would do. She was ready to spend her days with them again.

But she quickly discovered that Buddy wasn't around much during the day. Their new daddy took him away every morning and often didn't bring him back until suppertime. Her brother returned filthy dirty and tuckered out from chasing the plow around the fields, but he was always happy. Lucy envied him that happiness. It also made her feel something inside she didn't like. Why was he happy and not she?

At least Will and Ellen Marie stayed at the house all day. Ellen Marie was getting to be fun too. She could sit up and scoot herself around the floor and was even trying to talk! Her hair was finally coming in—blonde curls, just like Will's. Sometimes Lucy toyed with the soft ringlets fluffing out behind her baby sister's ears and wished her own hair was curly so she didn't have to sleep on those lumpy rags her new mama insisted on every night. Maybe if her own hair was blonde and curly like Ellen Marie's and Will's, her new mama would like her better.

Because, she was sure, her new mama didn't like her nearly as much as she liked Ellen Marie, Will, and Buddy. Her new mama insisted on doing everything for them herself, as if Lucy would hurt them if she touched them. She was sure her new mama didn't think too much of Lucy at all. And she knew why; she was too old. Lucy had heard the Sisters at the Foundling Home whispering about how hard it would be to find new parents for her. People only wanted babies and little kids. Lucy believed it, too. Lots of people had come and looked at Ellen Marie at the Foundling Home, but not once did somebody come in and say, "I'd like to meet Lucy, please."

The Sisters' worries about Lucy's age made her sure she really hadn't been wanted at all. These people only took her to get her brothers and baby sister. The day they picked them all up at the Foundling Home, she knew they were taking her back home where she had lived with Mama and Papa and the little ones. But they'd brought her here on a long, scary train ride. She'd known right away that it wasn't going to turn out like she'd thought it would.

Ever since, they treated her like she was some itty bitty kid who couldn't do anything. Every time she thought about it, anger welled.

If Lucy got something out to play with, her new mama put it back before Lucy was done with it. If she pulled a dress from her wardrobe, her new mama said, "Let's wear this one today, honey," and picked something else. If Lucy tried to help Will cut up his green beans, her new mama took the fork away and did it herself. If Lucy started pulling weeds in the garden, her new mama told her, "Why don't you go on and play?" It was clear they didn't want a big girl around. All they wanted was babies and little kids.

On a hot June day, Lucy sat on the porch steps and watched her new mama wheel Ellen Marie to the side yard in her pram. Will trotted along behind with a windup tin goose in his hand. Lucy watched while her new mama dragged a big basket of wet laundry to the line and began hanging wash to dry. Lucy squinted. Were her dresses in that basket? Curious, she scuffed over to look.

Sure enough—her favorite pink-and-white checked dress lay crumpled among Will's and Buddy's things. She shook out the wrinkles and reached for the little bag of wooden picks nailed to the post.

Her new mama held one of their new daddy's shirts in her hands, clothespins at the ready. She looked a question at Lucy.

Lucy pointed to the line. "Gonna hang my dresses up there."

Her new mama came over to Lucy, a smile on her face. "Oh, sweetie, that's nice of you to offer, but you don't need to do that. Why don't you go over and play on the swing?"

Lucy pressed her lips into a grim line. Couldn't she even be trusted to hang her own dress? Fury built inside, and she threw the wet dress back into the basket, whirled, and stomped away in the direction of the barn.

"Lucy, dear, what's the matter? Where are you going?" her new mama called, but Lucy pretended not to hear. When she reached the corner of the barn, she looked back at her new mama for a moment. She stood with her forehead all puckered up. She didn't look happy, but Lucy didn't care. Why should she care if she upset her new mama? Her new mama upset Lucy all the time.

She ran around the corner and ducked into the toolshed. There! Let her new mama do everything herself. Lucy didn't want to help that dumb lady anyway.

⌒◯

Samantha sighed, shook her head, and went back to her hanging. But between each shirt and pair of pants, she turned her head to search for Lucy. Some unnamed uncertainty, even fear, held her captive. Should she go after the little girl? But she couldn't leave Ellen Marie and Will unattended while she hunted. Worry continued to plague her, and finally she stepped to the end of the clothesline, cupped her hands by her mouth, and called, "Lucy? Lucy, would you come here, please?"

She waited, but Lucy didn't appear.

Again she called, panic rising. "Lucy! Where are you, Lucy?"

"Good morning, Samantha!"

Samantha whirled around to find Priscilla, with Joey and Jenny in tow, standing in a splash of sunshine in the yard. Focused on Lucy, she hadn't even heard their buggy arrive. "Oh, Pris . . . And Joey and Jenny—hello." How disheartening to be caught in such a state of failure. She doubted either David or Priscilla would ever lose track of one of their children. She leaned down to receive Joey's boisterous hug and kiss. The instant she let him go he dashed across the grass to join Will, and Samantha reached for Jenny to give her a cuddle.

Priscilla headed straight for Ellen Marie's pram. "I told David I had to come out and compare notes with you. Jenny cut her third tooth last night! It's such fun having children the same age!"

"Mm-hmm," Samantha said absently, her gaze aimed at the barn. *Where was that child?*

Priscilla looked over her shoulder and frowned. "Are you looking for something?"

Samantha drew a deep breath. "I think so. Lucy. She took off for the barn a little while ago, and she won't answer when I call. I can't leave the others to look for her."

Priscilla poked a playful finger at Ellen Marie. "Are you worried?"

Samantha smiled ruefully. "I've been worried about Lucy for months."

"Then go after her." Priscilla flicked her fingers, shooing Samantha away. "I'll keep track of the other two for you."

"Are you sure, Pris?" Samantha handed Jenny to Priscilla, impatience to find the errant Lucy tightening her stomach.

"Of course." Priscilla grinned. "You won't be able to relax and visit with me until you've located her, so just go."

"Thanks, Pris." Samantha took a moment to hold Will's face with her hands and instruct, "Be a good boy for Aunt Prissy, Will. Stay here and play nice with Joey, okay?"

Will nodded, pointing at his cousin. "Wiw pway wif Joey."

"That's right, sweetheart. I'll be right back." She planted a kiss on Will's soft curls and took off at a trot for the corner of the barn where she'd last seen Lucy.

∽◦◟

Lucy huddled in the corner of the dark toolshed. Their new daddy had told them to never go in the toolshed; he said there were dangerous things in there that could hurt them. Lucy had never even wanted to go inside. The shed didn't have any windows so it was dark, and it smelled musty. She didn't like being in here with shadows all around her and funny smells making her nose twitch, but her new mama wouldn't find her in here. She didn't want to be found. Yet she didn't want to be alone, either. Tears stung, and she sniffed. The sniffing made her sneeze. Loud. Two times.

After the second sneeze, the hinges on the door squeaked and sunlight spilled across the floor, shining all the way to Lucy's bare toes. Her new mama stood in the doorway. Lucy pulled her feet back and buried her face against her knees, hoping she wouldn't be seen, but her new mama must have seen her.

"Lucy, you know that you are not to be in here. What are you doing?"

Lucy could have said, "I'm hiding," but she decided not to talk. She hunkered in a tighter ball.

For a long time, her new mama stayed across the room. Then Lucy heard footsteps, and a hand touched her head. "Lucy, why did you run off? I was very worried about you."

Lucy knew her new mama wasn't worried about her. People only worried when they really, really cared. With her face against her knees, Lucy said, "Go away an' leave me alone."

The hand on Lucy's head pulled away, but even though she listened for footsteps, none came. Instead, her new mama said in a very soft voice, "I'm not going to leave you alone, Lucy. I don't think that's what you want." Lucy dared to peek. Her new mama knelt in front of her. Her face looked kind. "I remember lots of times when I was a little girl and all alone. What I wanted was someone to come and hold me."

Lucy gulped. How did she know that Lucy did wish for a hug? Her new mama caught hold of her beneath her armpits and pulled. Lucy tried to resist, but she ended up in her new mama's lap anyway. It felt so good to be there she started to cry. She didn't make any sound, but her body shook. Her new mama held her tighter, but Lucy still couldn't stop crying.

Her new mama rocked back and forth, the same way she rocked Ellen Marie or Will. "Honey, I know you're unhappy. Won't you please tell me what I can do to help you smile?"

Lucy remembered why she'd run off. She remembered all the other times she'd wanted to run off. All of the hurts from the past weeks piled on top of her until she couldn't hold it in. She wriggled to free herself. "Let me go home again."

Her new mama's mouth dropped open. "Lucy . . .?"

Lucy pushed hard against her new mama. "Let me go *home*. You don't want me. You don't need me."

"W-what—?"

"You don't need me!" Lucy scuttled backward until she reached the corner once more.

She crouched, holding herself tight, and glaring at her new mama.

"Lucy, how can you say such a thing?"

Lucy let out a huff and spat out, "My mama, she needed me, but not you. You only need *babies*." Her new mama reached for her, but Lucy hunched her shoulders. "I wanna go home."

For a long time, her new mama sat there with her hands outstretched. Finally, she dropped her arms. She looked very, very tired. Very sad. "Sweetheart, you can't go back to your old home. There's no one there to take care of you."

Lucy sat up straight. "I can take care of me. I did it before. I dressed me, an' fed me, an' I even dressed Willie and Ellen Marie. Sometimes I fed 'em. An' Buddy, too. An' I swept, an' made beds, and did lotsa' stuff. I can do it. I can take care of all of us."

Her new mama hung her head. "Oh, Lucy . . ."

"Buddy, he gets to be the new daddy's helper." Lucy tried to sound accusing, but she didn't feel as angry as she had before. Instead, her chest hurt. The way it had hurt when the nuns said Mama and Papa were never coming back. She sniffed hard. "But *you* don't need a helper. You just need the babies, not me."

"Lucy, please come here, darling, before I cry."

Lucy was suspicious. "Why're you gonna cry?"

"Because I've made you sad, and that's the last thing. . . ." Her new mama held her arms open. "Please, Lucy, come here. I want to tell you a story."

Lucy saw tears in her new mama's eyes, and it made her feel funny. And even though she was still a little mad, a story did sound nice—better than being all alone. Hesitantly she scooched across the floor on her bottom. When her hip bumped against her new mama's legs, at once she folded her arms around Lucy, holding her securely, and that felt kind of good, too. She relaxed a little bit.

Her new mama smoothed Lucy's hair away from her damp forehead and smiled. A tender smile. "Lucy, I'm going to tell you a story about a little girl." Lucy stared into her new mama's face. "This little girl's mama died when the girl was born, so she never had a mama at all. But she had someone else—a grandma. She called her grandmother 'Gran,' and Gran took care of the little girl, the girl's brother and their pa, and the girl's house. Gran did all of the cooking and cleaning and— well, all of the things that a mama would do for her family."

She paused for a moment, shifting her arms a bit more snugly around Lucy, and Lucy rested her elbow in her new mama's lap. "When the little girl was six years old—"

"Same as me?" Lucy interrupted.

Her new mama smiled. "Just the same age as you. When she was six years old, her Gran also died. The little girl was very sad and lonely, because she had loved Gran so much and now Gran was gone forever."

"Like Mama and Papa." Lucy could feel her chin quiver, and she put her hand up to hold it still.

"That's right, honey."

Lucy leaned her head against her new mama's shoulder.

"After that, the little girl and her brother and pa were alone. There wasn't a grown-up lady in the house to take care of things, so the little girl had to be the lady. She had to cook and clean and wash clothes. . . . There wasn't time for playing like the other children did because there was always work to be done. All the work was very hard for her, and she promised herself that when she grew up, if she was lucky enough to have little girls of her own, she would let them play all day and never make them do any chores at all. She wanted her own children to have fun instead of having to work, like she had to do."

Lucy leaned fully against her new mama. "What was the little girl's name?"

For a little while, Lucy thought her new mama wasn't going to answer. But then she said, very quietly, "Her name was Samantha."

Lucy sat up to look fully at her new mama. "You?"

She smiled, but somehow she still looked sad. "Uh-huh, I was that little girl." She took hold of Lucy's chin and looked straight in her eyes. "All I ever wanted was to be a mama and let my children do all the things I never got to do. I wanted my children to be able to play and sing and laugh the day away, and never have to fuss with washing dishes or making beds or any kind of work at all. I wanted my children to have fun."

She stroked Lucy's cheek. Her fingers felt soothing to Lucy. "My own childhood wasn't fun, Lucy. I've wanted yours to be different than mine. I've wanted you to be happy and carefree, not overwhelmed with responsibilities. Do you understand?"

Lucy thought about the story. She felt sorry for her new mama, now that she knew how sad she had been as a little girl. Her new mama hadn't wanted Lucy to be "overwhelmed with responsibilities," she'd said. Lucy stared at her new mama. Maybe she really did love Lucy. Maybe she'd been sent off to play because her new mama was saying she loved her.

"Do you . . . do you and the new papa want me to be here too?"

The new mama made a little choking sound, then wrapped both arms so tight around Lucy she thought she couldn't breathe. But it felt good too.

"Oh, Lucy dearest, I can't tell you how much Daddy and I want you. . . ." It sounded like the new mama was crying, and Lucy wriggled free to look at her.

Lucy said, "I want . . . I want you too." Her throat sounded kind of choked up, but she was starting to feel real good inside. "It would be fun . . . for me . . . to be your helper," Lucy said. "I liked bein' Mama's helper. I didn't hafta do everything that Mama did, but I did some things. An' since I helped her, Mama had more time to play with me. I liked that."

"Oh, Lucy, I would like that too."

For the first time Lucy reached to wrap her arms around her new mama. Her new mama hugged her back, and Lucy closed her eyes. She liked being held this way. The hug made her feel like she was loved after all. She held tight for a long time, then she let go to snuggle down into her new mama's lap.

Her new mama stroked Lucy's hair. "Would you hang up the clothes with me, Lucy? With your help, it will get done quickly, and then maybe we can bake some oatmeal cookies."

Lucy scrambled up. "Oh, yes, Mama! Let's do that"

Mama wiped her tears, stood up, and took Lucy's hand. "Let's go then. We've got a lot to do."

Lucy skipped under the sunshine, swinging her mama's hand as they crossed the yard to the clothesline.

*B*uddy laughed boisterously as Adam swung the boy onto his shoulders. "Watch your head!" Adam warned as they pushed through the front door of the farm home. From the kitchen the sounds of cheerful children's voices could be heard. Light spilled through the kitchen doorway, creating a golden shaft of welcome. The welcoming glow and pleasant murmurs of his beloved family drew Adam like a magnet.

Samantha was stirring a pot on the stove, a smile on her heat-flushed face. In the high chair, Ellen Marie banged a tin cup against the tray. Will stood beside her making her squeal by pretending to grab her cup. Lucy circled the table, carefully placing enamel plates in front of each chair.

Adam called out in a playful voice, "What's for supper, Ma?"

Lucy put down the last plate and ran around the table. She threw her arms around Adam's waist, surprising him so much he nearly dropped Buddy on the floor. "Daddy, guess what?" Lucy enthused, her arms holding Adam's middle and her head thrown back. "I helped Mama hang the clothes today, an' then we made oatmeal cookies with pecans. I chopped the pecans, too. Mama says we can have 'em for dessert if we eat all our supper."

Adam swallowed three times, rapidly, before he could say, "Well, then, we'll have to be sure and eat all our supper, right?"

Lucy released him and danced back to the table. "I'm settin' the table, Daddy, see?" The pride in her eyes was unmistakable.

"An' then I'll put out the spoons an' forks. Mama and I figured out things I can do to help." She returned to her task with all seriousness.

Adam put Buddy on the floor, nearly weak with shock. He crossed the kitchen to stand beside Samantha who smiled at him, her eyes shining with everything she wasn't saying. Adam gestured toward Lucy who had shooed Buddy away from the table so she could put out the forks. "She just called me 'Daddy'—and she referred to you as 'Mama,'" he said in a low voice. "She's actually smiling. . . . What happened?"

Samantha shrugged, but the smile on her lips was a bit tremulous. "We had a talk, Lucy and I. And we decided that since you had a helper—namely, Buddy—I should have one, too. Lucy was the obvious choice since she's hardly a baby and quite capable of being a big assistance to me."

Then she laid the spoon down and admitted in a whisper, "Adam, I made such a dreadful mistake! By doing everything for her, I made her feel as if she wasn't needed. She felt unimportant. She didn't think we really wanted her, and that's why she was so angry inside." She sighed. "Oh, Adam, I of all people should have understood her need to be needed. . . . I'll never forget the weeks I spent working for Liz and Jake—filled with some of the hardest work of my life, yet they were the most rewarding because Liz and Jake genuinely appreciated my help. Their appreciation gave me a sense of worthiness and belonging. In my shortsightedness, I was robbing Lucy of feeling needed and worthy."

Adam placed a hand on Samantha's shoulder. "But it's all right now?"

Samantha nodded, her gaze on Lucy. She was tying a bib around Ellen Marie's neck and chattering away to the baby. "I think things are going to be fine now." She looked into Adam's eyes, wonder blooming across her face. "Do you realize all four of them are calling us Mama and Daddy now? They really have become our children."

Joy exploded through Adam. He swung Samantha up in his arms and danced her around the kitchen. The children watched in silence for a moment, then they all joined in the laughter.

"Mama and Daddy are funny, aren't they?" Lucy told her siblings.

As Samantha spooned oatmeal into bowls, the telephone jangled. Lucy sat straight up, her face hopeful. "Can I answer it, Daddy?"

Adam waved a hand toward the telephone on the wall. "Go ahead, daughter. Remember your manners."

"Yes, sir." Lucy dashed to the phone. She tucked her hair behind her ear, lifted the earpiece, and placed it against her ear. Raising up on tiptoe, she spoke into the mouth horn. "Hello, Klaassen residence. This is Lucy." After a moment's pause, a smile of recognition broke across her face. "Hi! Yes, Daddy's right here. Just a minute, please." She turned, holding out the earpiece to Adam. "It's for you, Daddy. It's Uncle Daniel."

"I'll bet it's about the hearing," Adam murmured to Samantha as he pushed away from the table. Samantha stirred milk into Ellen Marie's oatmeal while she listened closely to the one-sided conversation.

"Hello, Daniel . . . Fine, thanks. How's everyone there? . . . Good . . . Yes, we know it's that time. We're ready for it. . . . Friday at ten? Yes, I think that will work with us if we come in on Thursday evening. . . . Are you sure? There are six of us now, you know."

Samantha smiled, hearing the pride in Adam's voice.

"Well, then, we'll see you Thursday. Thanks a lot, brother." Adam replaced the telephone and returned to the table. "The hearing's set for ten o'clock on Friday," he told her quietly.

Samantha filled Ellen Marie's eager mouth with another bite. "We'll all be ready."

Buddy looked up from his breakfast, a milk mustache on his freckled face. "What's a hearing, Daddy?"

"Betcha I know." Lucy sent a wise grin around the table. "It's when you go hear somebody say something you want to hear."

Adam and Samantha chuckled, and Adam tweaked the girl's nose. "You're not far from the truth, Lucy. A hearing is when you talk to a judge, and he makes a decision for you."

"What kind of dish—decision?" Buddy, of the many questions, wanted to know.

Samantha answered. "Lots of different kinds of decisions, Buddy. But this time he will decide—" She paused, looking to Adam for support. At his nod, she continued, "He will decide whether you and your brother and sisters will stay here as our children from now on."

"Forever and ever?" Buddy asked, green eyes wide.

"Forever and ever," Samantha echoed, reaching to smooth his cowlick into place.

Buddy nodded. "I like it here with you, Mama and Daddy."

"I'm sure the judge will ask you if you're happy here, and if you want to be our son." Adam turned to Lucy. "The judge will talk to you, too, Lucy. And we'll want you to tell him the truth. You know, whether or not you want to live here and be our daughter."

Lucy's face puckered. "Daddy, I—" She bit her lower lip.

Over the past several weeks, Lucy had settled into the home, opening up and becoming as affectionate as her younger siblings. Her sudden apprehension made Samantha's heart flutter. Adam said, "What is it, Lucy?"

She looked from Samantha to Adam, her eyes holding the wariness they thought had disappeared for good. "It's just . . . Well . . ."

"Come here, Lucy." Adam held out a hand to the child. She came around the table, leaning between Adam's legs as he put an arm around her. "Tell me what's troubling you."

Within the secure circle of Adam's arms, Lucy apparently discovered her courage. "I like being here with you an' Mama, an' I want to live here." She paused, picking at a button on Adam's shirt. "But I still remember my real mama an' papa. Sometimes . . . I still miss them." She hung her head as if ashamed.

Buddy observed his sister. "Me, too," he said softly, his mouth quivering a little. Samantha caught his hand and gave it a squeeze of understanding.

Adam hugged Lucy, then stretched out one hand to place his fingers on the back of Buddy's neck. "We hope you don't ever forget your first mama and papa. Your memories of them are a very important part of you, and someday, when Will and Ellen Marie are old enough, you'll want to tell them about them. You can go right on loving them, thinking about them. It is just fine with your new mama and me."

"Really?" Lucy stared into Adam's face.

Adam hugged her again. "Really. We can't take the place of the mama and papa you were born to, but we love you, and we believe you are learning to love us, too." He lifted her onto his knee. "You see, Lucy, God made our hearts in a very special way. A heart seems very small, but there's always room to hold love for one more person."

Lucy pulled back and examined Adam seriously. "I do love you an' Mama. I want to be your daughter."

Adam smiled and placed a kiss on Lucy's temple. "I'm very glad to hear that."

Samantha nearly wilted with relief. "Me, too."

"Will our name be Klaassen like yours after the hearing?" Lucy asked.

Adam nodded. "Is that all right with you?"

Lucy tapped her chin with one finger. "Lucy Klaassen. Lucille Elizabeth Klaassen." She grinned. "That sounds pretty good, I guess."

Buddy said, "What about me? What will I be?"

Samantha poked his ribs. "You will be Henry Rollin Klaassen, known affectionately as Buddy. And your brother, William Everett Klaassen. And this little kitten"—she tapped Ellen Marie's nose with a gentle finger—"will be Ellen Marie Klaassen. All of us will be Klaassens."

Buddy shrugged, grinning.

Adam shifted Lucy from his lap with a gentle push. "Well, now, Klaassens, breakfast is getting cold, so let's finish up."

Will, who had continued eating throughout the conversation, looked up brightly and announced, "B'eakfass aw gone!"

Lucy rolled her eyes. "What a piggy." She and Buddy giggled, and Will joined in, waving his empty spoon. Ellen Marie jabbered and joyfully waved hers too.

Adam and Samantha smiled across the table at each other. Laughter and children . . . It was theirs now, too.

llen Marie dozed in Samantha's arms, and Will hummed happily beside her on the seat of the passenger car. The little boy galloped a tin horse across his knees, and in the seats facing her, Lucy and Buddy crowded in beside Adam, sharing a book. Gazing at the contented children, Samantha remembered the train ride she and Adam had taken with the children only six months earlier.

She almost wished some of the passengers who had glared and bellyached about them the last time could be here to see them now. They wouldn't have a thing about which to find fault—the children were clean, healthy, quiet and well-behaved, and happy instead of sullen. Another prayer of gratitude winged from her heart for the little family she and Adam had been given.

Adam finished his book and handed it to Lucy. "Help Buddy find all the letter A's on the first two pages of this book. If you count them all correctly, I'll buy you a licorice when we reach Minneapolis."

"Yay!" the children chorused. Lucy took the book, and the two little heads bent over the page. Will hopped down from his seat and stood between their knees, poking his head in the way. Lucy shifted him back just a bit, and they began counting.

Samantha clicked her tongue on her teeth, shaking her head.

Adam grinned at her. "What's that for?"

"You and your enticements," she said with a chuckle. "David would be appalled."

"No need to tell him," Adam retorted.

Samantha laughed, startling Ellen Marie. She gave the baby some soothing pats then lifted her face to Adam's once more. "What time is it?"

Adam raised one eyebrow. "Five minutes later than the last time you asked. You aren't anxious about anything this time, are you?"

"Don't tease me, Adam. You're just as anxious as I am, and don't even try to deny it. I've seen you checking out the window every few minutes to see where we are, and if Minneapolis might be around the next bend."

Adam shrugged and ran a hand through his hair. He yawned. "Maybe the time would go faster if we napped."

"I'm too excited to sleep, but go ahead if you want to," Samantha said.

Before Adam could slouch in the seat and close his eyes, Lucy patted him on the arm. "Daddy, there are twenty-one A's—see?"

Adam sat up and reached for the book. "Show me," he said, and watched as Lucy recounted each A with Buddy adding his assistance. When they were finished, he said, "Good job! You've earned your licorice."

Lucy's eyes twinkled. "If we find all the B's, will we get another piece?"

Adam laughed, dropping an arm around Lucy and pulling her tight against his side for a brief hug. "Here's a little girl after my own heart—sweet tooth and all!"

"Will we, Daddy?" Buddy screwed his face up in concentration.

Adam laughed a "maybe" and scooped Will up and settled the little boy on his lap. He pointed to the book and said, "Let's count all the letters and see which one is used the most."

The various games kept them occupied until supper. They ate the sandwiches and cookies Samantha had brought along, then the children gave in to the gentle rocking of the train. Will slept contentedly in Adam's arms, while Buddy and Lucy leaned together and napped. Before they knew it, the screeching of brakes announced their arrival in Minneapolis.

Samantha drew in a breath, anticipation speeding her pulse. "We're here." She shared one brief, glowing smile with her husband—*this is it!*—then readied the children for departure. Lucy took Will by the hand; Buddy grabbed the small valise; Adam handled the larger suitcase; and Samantha carried Ellen Marie.

Adam spotted Daniel at the end of the walk, and soon they were rolling along the cobblestone streets, everyone laughing and talking at once. They made one stop at a corner store to purchase the promised licorice—five cents' worth so they could share with their cousins—then headed to Daniel's home.

The evening passed in pleasant conversation between the adults and companionable play between the children. Eventually Samantha tucked Ellen Marie, Will, and Buddy into their pallets on the floor of the guest room before tending to Lucy's pin curls. As she combed the hair into careful coils, securing them with strips of cloth, Lucy fidgeted.

Samantha said, "If you sit still, Lucy, we'll get this done a lot faster."

Lucy sighed. "Mama, why do we do this?"

Samantha paused, surprised. "You don't like your hair in curls?"

Lucy shrugged, toying with the hem of her nightgown. "It isn't a matter to me if my hair's curly or not. But maybe"—she peeked over her shoulder at Samantha—"you like curly hair better than straight hair? I know you like Will's and Ellen Marie's little curls. . . ."

Samantha pulled Lucy snug against her, wrapping her arms across the child's stomach. "I put pin curls in your hair, because it gives me a chance to spend a bit of just-us time with you. But if you don't like them, I can brush your hair out at night and leave it down. It's up to you."

Lucy tipped her head until her temple encountered Samantha's cheek. After a few thoughtful minutes she said decisively, "Gimme curls, Mama."

Samantha looked into Lucy's face. "Are you sure , Lucy?"

Lucy grinned impishly. "Yes. We gotta use all those bows you made to match my dresses."

Samantha laughed and delivered a kiss to Lucy's cheekbone before finishing the job.

In the morning, Samantha combed Lucy's hair into perfect sausage curls, complete with a huge bow of pure white organdy at the crown. She dressed each of the children from Lucy down to Ellen Marie in their Sunday best. Samantha took as much care with her own attire, and Adam wore the suit he'd worn to the first court hearing back in February.

As they stood together in the home's foyer before leaving for the courthouse, Rose gave them the once-over. "May I make a suggestion?"

Adam said, "Of course."

"After your hearing, stop into one of the photography studios on Main Street and have a family portrait taken. It would be the perfect remembrance of this day."

Samantha was delighted. "That's a wonderful idea, Rose. Can you recommend a good one?"

Rose gave them the name of a photographer their family had used, and then Daniel stuck his head in the door. "The motor's running. Let's get moving, all you Klaassens."

Daniel brought the car to a stop at the curb outside the courthouse. "Hop out. I'll go park and be right back."

Adam herded his crew inside, his heart banging against his ribcage. It seemed as though years passed while they waited inside the doors until Daniel joined them.

They made their way to the same room in which they'd met before. Judge Simmons was already behind his desk, and he raised a hand of greeting when Daniel swung the door open and stuck his head in. "Come in, come in!" the judge called in a jovial tone. "Oh, good, you've brought them all. Hello, children."

Will chirped an unconcerned, "Hewo." But Lucy and Buddy, suddenly shy, remained speechless. Adam prompted them forward until they stood in a row in front of Judge Simmons, their heads tipped back to see him behind the tall desk, eyes wide with awe. Adam and Samantha stood directly behind them, Samantha holding baby Ellen Marie.

The judge smiled. "So have you used these past months to get acquainted?"

Buddy fidgeted, and Adam placed his hands on the boy's shoulders. He immediately stilled. "Yes, sir. The children have settled into their new home. We've all adjusted well, I think."

Judge Simmons leaned on his forearms to peer over the edge at the children. "Is that right, children? Have you settled into your new home?"

Lucy looked up at Adam. He winked, nodding for her to go ahead and speak. She straightened and turned to face the judge, shoulders back. "Yes, sir. We like our new home just fine."

The judge nodded, then turned to Buddy. "What about you, young man? Do you like your new home?"

Buddy nodded, blinking rapidly. "I like the farm, an' the animals, an' bein' in the fields with Daddy."

Judge Simmons smiled. "Thank you, Henry."

Will looked around. "Who Henwy?"

The judge turned to Buddy. "Why, isn't your name Henry?" He consulted his notes.

Will shook his head and pointed at his brother with a chubby finger. "He be Buddy."

The judge leaned back in his chair and chuckled. "I stand corrected." He leaned forward again and asked Will, "Are there any other name changes about which I should know?"

Will turned shy and inserted his favorite finger in his mouth. Lucy spoke up. "Yes, sir. Me, Buddy, Will, an' Ellen Marie—" she pointed to each in turn—"we all are gonna change our name to Klaassen like Mama and Daddy."

"Is that what you want?" The judge was very serious now.

Lucy matched his solemnity. "Yes, sir."

"Then we shall do just that." Judge Simmons reached for a pen and a paper. "Before we sign this legal document," he said, his eyes roving from person to person, "I'd like to say a few words." He leaned back in his chair, interlaced his fingers and rested them on the paper.

Adam scooped up Will, perching the little boy on his broad forearm, and slipped his other arm around Samantha's waist. They turned attentive gazes on the judge.

"I look at an adoption much like a marriage. When two people wed, they vow to care for one another in all circumstances, to honor and respect one another. Mr. and Mrs. Klaassen, by assuming responsibility for the McIntyre children, you are making a similar commitment. Parenting is a twenty-four-hour-a-day obligation, every day of every week of every year for the remainder of your lives. When you sign this paper, you are saying you want the responsibility, and you will take it seriously. Do you understand the commitment you are making?"

Samantha replied promptly. "Oh, yes, Your Honor. We understand, and we make that commitment with our whole hearts."

The judge then focused his attention on Lucy and Buddy. "Children, I want to be certain you understand that from now on, Adam and Samantha Klaassen will be your legal guardians. They will be"—he smiled—"your daddy and mama. By accepting them as your parents, you are telling me you will respect and obey them. Can you do that?"

Lucy took Buddy by the hand. "Yes, sir. We won't ever forget our real mama an' papa, but we've got room to love this mama an' daddy, too." She turned a grin on Samantha and Adam, then faced the judge again. "They're good parents, an' we'll be good children."

"Very well, then." Judge Simmons lifted the document and slid it to the edge of the desk. "Shall we make things legal?"

Adam put Will down and picked up the pen. His hand trembled slightly as he realized the finality of this act, and he paused, savoring the moment—the official bond that would meld them together as a family. Then the pen touched the paper, his signature emerged, and he took Ellen Marie in his arms so Samantha could sign.

Buddy tipped this way and that, trying to see what they were doing. "Do we sign it, too?"

The judge sat up straight, apparently taken aback. "Well, son, I suppose you could, if you really wanted to."

Buddy crinkled his nose. "Don't know how yet. But I'm learnin' my A's."

The judge's laughter joined that of Adam and Samantha, and Adam affectionately rubbed his hand over Buddy's head.

Lucy waved her hand at the judge. "Are we all Klaassens now, Mister Judge?"

Judge Simmons swallowed his chuckles to answer Lucy with all due solemnity. "Yes, Miss Lucille Elizabeth Klaassen, you are all officially Klaassens now."

Her eyes wide and guileless, Lucy stated sincerely, "Thank you very much."

Epilogue

Adam tiptoed from room to room, checking one last time on his children. He took a moment to tuck the sheet up beneath Will's chin, pulling the ever-present finger from the boy's mouth at the same time. He removed the truck that Buddy held in the crook of his arm. The child mumbled and rolled onto his side, curling into a ball beneath the covers. In Lucy's room he smoothed the wispy bangs from her face and placed a gentle kiss on her forehead before moving quietly out. He stood for a long time at little Ellen Marie's crib, smiling down at the funny way her lower lip poked out in sleep. He watched the rise and fall of her little chest, listening to her soft breaths.

Satisfied that all were well, he headed downstairs. He paused to touch the frame on the family portrait which had stood prominently on the entry table for the past three months. Although they would certainly take more family portraits in the years ahead, he intended to always leave this one on display as a symbol of God's great gift to him, to Samantha.

He spotted his wife's silhouette through the lace curtain over the oval glass in the front door. She leaned on the porch railing, her face toward the sky. He couldn't help his smile. She was star-gazing again. His mind skipped back in time, to another porch and another star-studded night when he'd stood beside Samantha and peered skyward. He'd barely known her then, but she had turned a wistful gaze upward and made a wish on a star, forever imprinting her image on his heart. How young they had been back then, how full of hopes and dreams . . .

The desire to share the moment with her propelled him forward, and he stepped outside and stood behind. He wrapped his arms around her and pulled her firmly to him. She stacked her arms over his, tipping her head back to nestle next to his chin. She sighed contentedly as they stood in the darkness, enjoying the pleasant night sounds, the earthy scents of burgeoning fall, and the sky full of shimmering brightness. Suddenly, above their heads, one star streaked across the velvet backdrop of sky.

"A falling star!" Adam pointed. "Make a wish, Sammy."

The star burst into tiny pieces and disappeared into the expanse of black velvet and glittering diamonds.

Samantha held her breath, then let it out, and turned within his embrace to wrap her arms around his torso. The smile she offered warmed him from his head to his toes.

Adam tucked a strand of hair behind Samantha's ear. "So what did you wish for, my sweet?"

Her smile turned secretive. "No wishes, Adam."

"No wishes? What does that mean?"

The tenderness in Samantha's eyes brought a lump to Adam's throat as she answered softly. "I have no need for wishes anymore. I have everything my heart could desire right here—a God who loves me, this home, our children sleeping upstairs, and you."

Adam lifted her face upward and bestowed a long kiss on her smiling lips. They held each other, Samantha's face pressed into the curve of Adam's shoulder, Adam's cheek against her hair.

"Adam, remember when we found out I couldn't have children, and I told you it seemed as if my heart was crying?"

How could he forget? It was one of the most heartrending moments of his life. Instead of answering, he tightened his grip around her.

"My heart was crying, Adam. It was begging for the chance to be a mother—to have a child to love. Of course, at the time I only wanted that to be a child we created together."

"Do you still regret not being able to have a baby, Sam?" Adam asked.

She sucked in her lips for a moment, her expression thoughtful. Finally she shook her head. "No. Regret can mean bitterness. I let go of the bitterness long ago. And I've come to realize something. . . . When a heart cries, Someone listens and answers."

Pulling away a bit, she continued. "Oh, I didn't get the answer I thought I was looking for. But God had something better in mind for us. For them. If God had given us a child back then, we never would have brought home Lucy, Buddy, Will, and Ellen Marie. They are the window that was thrown open when the door to motherhood was slammed shut. To think I could have lost them! Adam, I simply can't imagine not having them in our lives. They are every bit ours. And I think they love us as much as if we had conceived each one."

Adam drew in a deep breath, pulling her beneath his chin once more. "Yes, Sammy, you're right. We've been given more than I could have ever imagined. We are blessed, aren't we?"

From her spot, Samantha offered a reply that filled Adam's heart to overflowing. "Oh, yes. We have been blessed fourfold."

APPLESAUCE CAKE

3 cups flour

3 tsp. baking powder

2 tsp. baking soda

½ tsp. salt

2 tsp. ground cinnamon

½ tsp. ground nutmeg

⅛ tsp. ground cloves

4 eggs

2 cups white sugar

1½ cups vegetable oil

2 cups unsweetened applesauce

1 tsp. vanilla extract

Whipped cream, sweetened (optional)

Preheat oven to 350°. Grease and flour a 9- x 13-inch pan. Sift together the flour, baking powder, baking soda, salt, and spices into a large bowl. Make a well in the center and pour the eggs, sugar, oil, applesauce, and vanilla. Mix well and pour into the prepared pan. Bake in the preheated oven for 40–50 minutes or until a toothpick inserted in the center of the cake comes out clean. Serve warm with whipped cream, if desired.

HULDA KLAASSEN'S BUBBAT

4 eggs

2 cups milk, scalded

1 tsp. salt

½ cup water

5 cups flour

1 tbsp. instant yeast

4 cups ground sausage, cooked and drained*

Scald milk and add salt. Set aside and cool until steam no longer rises. Add ½ cup water to milk. Blend flour, salt, and dry yeast. Beat eggs well, add to liquids, and then stir in the flour with a wooden spoon. Stir in sausage or ham. Spread into a greased sheet pan (13- x 18-inch, with 1-inch sides) or use one 9- x 13-inch pan and one loaf pan. Cover with plastic and let rise one hour. Bake at 350° for 45 minutes. Slice and serve. Wonderful with baked apples!

*May substitute cut-up cooked ham for cooked sausage.

Acknowledgments

As always, I want to thank my parents, Ralph and Helen Vogel, for their steadfast support and for being such models of Jesus for me. Their beautiful legacy of faith lives on through my brother and me.

When I originally wrote *When a Heart Cries* and dedicated it to my daughters, they were all still living under my roof. Now they're grown and raising children of their own (where does the time go?). Kristian, Kaitlyn, and Kamryn, I pray daily for you to follow God's will so your children will grow to understand the importance of seeking a relationship with Him. I love all of you—daughters and grandbabies—so very, very much.

My amazing critique partners and prayer warriors are always there for me. You bless me with your friendship, your encouragement, your sisterhood. Thank you!

To Carol Johnson and the staff at Hendrickson, thank you so much for giving the Mountain Lake stories new life. I so enjoyed revisiting these very first, straight-from-my-heart stories. Bless you for your ministry.

Finally, and most importantly, gratitude and deepest honor to God for being ever available to me. When my heart has cried, He has given comfort, peace, and strength. He gifts me beyond my deservings. May any praise or glory be reflected directly back to Him.